THE LINE OF SPLENDOR

A Novel of Nathanael Greene and the
American Revolution

THE LINE OF SPLENDOR

A Novel of Nathanael Greene and the
American Revolution

SALINA B BAKER

Paperback ISBN: 978-0-9987558-6-1
Hardcover ISBN: 978-0-9987558-7-8

Library of Congress Control Number: 9780998755878

Printed in the United States of America

For my husband, John,
who believes in my passion, nurtures it, and shares in it.

"I am determined to defend my rights and maintain my freedom, or sell my life in the attempt."

—General Nathanael Greene, June 1775

Preface

This novel was meticulously and lovingly written to venerate a great and good man who gave everything to his country, the cause of freedom, and the American Revolution—Major General Nathanael Greene. I wrote this so we can hear his voice, that of his beloved wife Caty, and the voices of the people they knew or who influenced their lives. Those voices largely come from hundreds of letters written between Nathanael and others as well as biographies of them and the many people who touched their lives. Some of these letters are part of the conversation while others stand on their own. I have taken the liberty to correct some of the spelling to clarify the words. Nathanael Greene's story is also the recounting of the American Revolution. So, let's journey into the life of this often overlooked hero.

Foreword

Nathanael Greene stands head and shoulders above all the generals who served under George Washington in the American War for Independence. A Rhode Island, Quaker iron founder turned general; Greene quickly became Washington's most dependable and steadfast subordinate. In what may be a letdown to fans of the musical Hamilton (I count myself as one), Greene was Washington's right-hand man. Indeed, Washington relied on and trusted Greene as he did no other general. The Rhode Islander was an accomplished combat commander; perhaps the best quartermaster general of the Continental Army—a thankless job Greene fought against, but in which Washington's importuning prevailed—and a department (theater) commander who never won a battle but prevailed in the campaign. Like Washington, Greene's formal education was decidedly lacking, and like Washington, he possessed a serious interest in military affairs. A self-taught military man, like most of the Continental Army's officers, Greene was an ardent student of history, philosophy, the law, and military science. Mindful of his lack of formal schooling beyond the basics of reading, writing, and arithmetic, Greene overcompensated. His painful awareness about his education led him to fill his letters with lengthy references to ancient history, philosophy, and more.

Because of his correspondence, most of it published, we know much about Greene the general. Sadly, however, we know little about Greene the man, the husband, or father. Most of the letters between Greene and his wife, Catharine Littlefield Greene, have been lost. Caty, as she was called, destroyed her letters to Nathanael, thus what we know of Greene's personal life is through interpretive conjecture drawing from his surviving letters to Caty. Our picture of Nathanael Greene is, therefore, incomplete and historians are forced to speculate, our imaginations limited by the evidence that drives our work. The inner workings of Greene's mind, his friendships, his personal interactions, and more therefore remain but hazy pictures faintly glimpsed. History's constraints, however, are not limitations on the imagination of the novelist.

In *The Line of Splendor: A Novel of Nathanael Greene and the American Revolution*, Salina Baker has given readers an insight into the realm of the possible. Stepping beyond the limitations imposed on historians by their craft and discipline, Salina's portrait of Nathanael Greene is suffused with imagination. Drawing from Greene's correspondence, visits to his Rhode Island home, and the battlefields he served on, Salina Baker has given readers a lively story of Nathanael Greene and his service in the American War for Independence. Salina has read between the evidentiary lines and created conversations and situations that humanize and enliven Nathanael and Caty Greene, their circle of family and friends, and the officers and soldiers who fought in the war.

The Line of Splendor is clearly a work of love. Having met and come to know something of Salina Baker, she has put her heart into this novel. Salina's passion for her subject is evident from the beginning. Join her, as she invites you into *The Line of Splendor: A Novel of Nathanael Greene and the American Revolution*.

Ricardo A. Herrera
18th and 19th century American military history historian, Professor U.S. Army War College, Department of National Security and Strategy; author of *Feeding Washington's Army*

one

The Current of Rebellion

The flames soared in orange tongues so intense that the men could get nowhere near them despite close access to the waters of Pawtuxet River that flowed behind the iron forge in Coventry, Rhode Island. Nathanael Greene, his older brother, Jacob, and the forge workers could only watch as everything, including the iron furnace, succumbed. As owner and operator, Nathanael was entrusted with the operation of the family forge. It was a personal and financial disaster.

The consolation he clung to a few days later, on August 19, 1772, was a letter he received from his friend in Westerly, Sammy Ward, Jr. Nathanael sat on the remains of one of the old shafts and read it. He paused and rubbed his smoke-irritated right eye where a smallpox scar had settled. He had been afflicted after he was inoculated in 1770 when he was twenty-eight. He surveyed the rubble. It reminded him of his desire for Sammy's sister, the fair-haired, blue-eyed, Nancy Ward. Their relationship seemed as hopeless as rebuilding the foundry from the smoking debris.

She had rebuffed his affections, and now, when all seemed glum, he poured his heart out to her little brother in a letter. "I am surrounded with gloomy faces, piles of timber still in flames, heaps of bricks dashed to pieces, baskets of coal reduced to ashes. Everything seems to appear in ruins and confusion. I have seriously considered the connections between me and your sister, the way it began, and the manner it has been carried on. It is your advice to stop the correspondence. To stop the correspondence is to lose her forever, to continue is to overwhelm myself with agreeable distress and pleasant pain."

Jacob Greene sat down beside Nathanael. He heard his brother wheeze. "I am going home," he announced. "There is no need to watch the destruction cool down."

Nathanael's lambent blue eyes slipped to the carnage for a moment and then he said, "I shall send a message to you in Potowomut."

"I know it has been an arduous year, but try not to despair. We, and all the men who depend on the forge for a living, will rebuild because it is a necessity. We will be hammering out anchors for those fishermen in Newport in no time." Jacob nudged him. "We boys managed our childhood in Potowomut under Father's stern hand. We can manage this."

"You know I never liked it here in Coventry," Nathanael said. "It is an isolated, dismal, smoky place. If it was ever tolerable it has now become insupportable."

"It has to be better than driving cows, herding sheep, and the innumerable chores we performed as children. It sounds as if your asthma will keep you awake tonight. Try to get some sleep if you can," Jacob advised. "I should be going. Peggy is expecting me."

Nathanael nodded and rose. He coughed and pressed a hand to his tight chest. His tall shadow followed him across the treeless grassy lawn toward Spell Hall, the drafty two-story house he had built in 1770 when his father insisted he move to Coventry to build and run the forge. The house, far removed from the nearest neighbor, stood on the brow of a hill overlooking the babbling Pawtuxet River.

He laid his letter for the post on the table by the door. The white walls stared as he washed up. He thought of the fine old home where he and his five brothers grew up in Potowomut on the tip of a peninsula that jutted out into Narragansett Bay. His father, Nathanael, Sr. was the sole proprietor of Nathanael Greene and Company. Nathanael's mother, Mary, his father's second wife, passed away in 1753 when he was eleven. His two older brothers, born to Phoebe, were dead like their mother. The Greene brothers toiled the family business: a grist mill, an iron forge, and a farm. They were laborers who had developed the strong bodies of those who sweated for a living.

He dried his face, neck, and hands, boiled a pot of water for tea, and then went into his extensive library where solace awaited. This was where his dreams and choices as a boy and then a man countermanded his stern Quaker upbringing. Knowledge lifted his spirits. The world was wide, but the Quaker world he grew up in was marginalized. It was a world dominated by men and governed by the religion his father had passed to his children and the congregation he had led in East Greenwich. Strict customs regulated his pastimes, even a swim in the creek with his brothers or a visit to a friend's house.

Nathanael pulled John Locke's *An Essay on Human Understanding* from a shelf. Locke's book was one of his favorites. It argued against innate knowledge, asserting that human beings cannot have ideas in their minds of which they are not aware. Therefore, people cannot be said to possess even the most basic principles until they are taught them or think them through for themselves.

This reasoning, among others, resonated in Nathanael's mind. His early education was confined to Bible studies. "The truth can only be found in the Scriptures. Other literary pursuits lead to the raising of doubts," his father had told him and his brothers.

He thumbed through the pages of Locke's essay. Jacob's parting comment brought back memories of the days when he and his brothers had discovered the truths of another world in which there was dancing and discussions on philosophy. Even the beatings Nathanael's father delivered with a horsewhip after a night of sneaking from his room were worth the social evenings spent with lovely young ladies who glided around the dance floor with him and overlooked his limp. On October nights, before a dance, he relished huskings that celebrated the new corn crop.

Jacob's youthful voice spoke in his head, "Father says we cannot quit the field until we have plowed to that rock."

Nathanael's younger brothers, William and Elithu, elbowed him and said, "Watch Jacob," as if they had been part of the hatched plot. Jacob fetched the rock and moved it halfway closer. The brothers pealed with laughter. "There, we shall be out dancing in no time," Jacob declared.

A knock startled Nathanael out of his recollections. He shelved the book and answered the door. "Ah, James, please come in," he said to the man who stood outside.

James removed his hat. "I see the forge is destroyed. Even the mill race is dry."

"Fortune will change that if we can acquire the funds. I expect we will have her up soon. How is the new house in East Greenwich coming along?"

"Well," James said as he followed Nathanael into the library, "Mrs. Varnum is quite pleased with it so far. I came by to talk about the Dudingston case. I heard it was resolved and ruled in your favor."

"You are always the lawyer," Nathanael commented with humor. "Please sit down. Tea?"

"Yes." James ran a finger over the book spines on a shelf. "Are you aspiring to become a lawyer yourself? I see you have Jacob's *Law Dictionary* and Blackstone's *Commentaries*. Have you been to Newport's bookstores again?"

"You know they were recommended to me by Lindley Murray, a law student in New York, so that I had command of techniques of legal practice when cases arose from my father's business."

James' eyes roamed the room. "Aside from your voluminous collection of books, this place is as barren as a desert. I shan't say that it needs a woman's touch as I suppose that is insensitive."

Nathanael passed him a cup. "Have you seen a desert?"

"No, I have not," James acceded with a smile. "Now, about Dudingston?"

"His terror has been set to rest as you know. His Royal Navy ship, *Gaspee,* which was running down our vessels in order to enforce the British crown's taxes, was burned. The good Lieutenant William Dudingston managed to infuriate the Kent County sheriff, Abraham Whipple, and that was the result. After Dudingston treated my cousin roughly and confiscated my ship, *Fortune,* and its cargo of rum and sugar, I sued him for illegal seizure. Sheriff Whipple had been trying to serve him papers for months."

"The *Fortune* was carrying contraband," James said. He removed the tea strainer from his cup.

Nathanael's eyes sparkled. "We have all been avoiding Newport and the reinforcement of the Parliamentary Navigations Acts that taxes ship cargo enforced in that port."

"I heard you were accused of being a party to the *Gaspee* burning led by John Brown."

"I was in Coventry with my brother, Kitt, and my cousin, Griffin, that night. It is all settled, although it was a trying time," Nathanael said. "I was tempted to shoot that rascal Dudingston if I could come at him. There were rumors that those he accused of burning his ship would be transported to London for trial."

"It is not the first time our rowdy Rhode Island men attacked the King's revenue ships," James conceded with a laugh.

"I have been visiting a distant relative of mine in East Greenwich, William Greene. The social evenings give us time to air our frustrations with British taxes and discuss possible solutions for relief."

"I would not mind being a part of those conversations," James said.

"I am going to East Greenwich in a few days. William Greene always welcomes visitors."

"Since their home is very close to mine, I may accept that invitation." James set his teacup aside and rose. "If there is anything I can do to assist with rebuilding the forge, please let me know."

Nathanael raised a small smile.

James understood. The Greene brothers' prideful ways precluded asking for help.

❧

The promise of autumn was in the air when Nathanael rode the eight miles to East Greenwich. He followed the Pawtuxet River for a time until it curved off to the east. A comfortable house on the side of a hill came into view. He spurred his horse, Britain, in a burst of anticipation of his arrival.

"It is good to have you," William Greene said when Nathanael entered the house that smelled of cigar smoke and rose water. "Sammy and his father, Samuel, have arrived from Westerly. Sammy has promised to keep his language tempered, although my niece, Caty, finds it amusing. Young people are lively."

"There you are, Nathanael." The handsome, dark-haired, fifteen-year-old Sammy Ward greeted him with mischievous rollicking laughter. Sammy's mirth was harmonized with ringing laughter. Nathanael saw Sammy's seventeen-year-old cousin, Catharine Littlefield, standing in the parlor door. Her wit was perceptible in her snapping dark eyes. Her flossy black hair was the antithesis of the fair-haired Nancy Ward.

Nathanael's heart strings fluttered for a moment. *She is always cheerful when I am here.* He bowed and said, "Miss Littlefield."

She swept forward. "I hope you did not think Sammy and I were having a laugh at your expense." Her eyes fell on her cousin for a moment. "His merriment pleases me."

"I thought no such thing," Nathanael assured her.

"Shall we repair to the parlor?" William asked. "Whiskey, Madeira, and ale are on offer for your pleasure. Oh, and here is James Varnum. We are happy to have you." As more men arrived for the evening discussions, Caty joined the gentlemen in the parlor. She knew they would immerse themselves in the injustice of British taxation that had been exacerbated by the seizure of the *Fortune*.

"First, we are subjected to the Stamp Act which taxed every piece of paper we used but was thankfully repealed. Then, Parliament enacted the

Townshend Acts. I believe that was two years later in 1767," William said. He lit a cigar and filled his favorite bumper glass to the brim. "Now we suffer the enforcement of the Navigation Act that resulted in the confiscation of Nathanael's ship."

"As long as we are burdened with Britain's need to pay for the war with the French and Indians ten years after their victory, we may need to consider other recourses than those we have followed thus far," Sammy said with the mindfulness of a Rhode Island college student.

"Perhaps," Nathanael offered. He sipped his whiskey. "The question now, I think, is how defiant can we be without provoking more action from Parliament and King George III?"

"We protested heartedly against the Stamp Act, throwing caution to the wind, and we were triumphant," James added. "We defeated The Townshend Acts that imposed duties on British imports."

"They thought we could not live without their china, glass, lead, paint, paper, and tea," Caty's brother, Billy Littlefield, said. Then he shrugged. "We could and thus boycotted those goods."

"Ah, yes, but in response to our protests and boycotts, the British sent two thousand troops to occupy Boston and quell the unrest that has spread across Massachusetts, New York, Connecticut, and our own colony of Rhode Island," Samuel replied.

"This is my point," Nathanael said impatiently. "Tensions between us and the British troops finally boiled over in Boston when British soldiers shot into that angry mob. They killed five Americans in the bloody massacre that occurred two years ago."

"Their lawyers John Adams and Josiah Quincy, Jr. saw to it that their captain and all but three of the soldiers were acquitted," Sammy argued.

William puffed his cigar and then said, "The Townshend Acts were repealed that April, except for the tax on tea and that shall—"

William's voice faded in the background as Nathanael's lambent blue eyes met Caty's dark eyes. Until this moment, he had not noticed that she had matured into a young woman. His conversations over the past year had been dominated by the *Gaspee* affair, and the forge's destruction had occupied his mind further. There were many younger men in the room who had arrived to join the social.

Or have they come to fall under her irresistible spell as she listens and chats with rapt enthusiasm? Nathanael thought. *I wonder if my stature and maturity is more alluring than the nescience of youth. Nancy Ward did not seem to think so.*

ॐ

By January 1773, the sound of massive bell hammers beating iron into anchors and the smell of smoke filled Coventry, Rhode Island, again. The stout, often uneducated iron workers could get on with their livelihoods. Nathanael knew, however, that no matter how prosperous his family, he was still a rough country bumpkin who was destined to stoke the fires of an iron furnace or become a farmer unless he quenched his thirst for knowledge and polished the less-than-shining figure he cut among East Greenwich society.

His thoughts began to reflect his ever-growing irreverence for the anti-intellectual, insincere ideals of his Quaker upbringing. He wrote to Sammy, "I feel the mist of ignorance to surround me, for my own part I was educated a Quaker, and amongst the most superstitious sort, that of its self is a sufficient obstacle to cramp the best of geniuses: much more than mine."

He was also aware that he had done things that had garnered the disapproval of the Quakers, also called the Society of Friends. Suing Dudingston was one of those things and using martial terms when he acted as a lawyer for a man involved in a lawsuit with the town of Coventry. "You go forth to battle armed with solemn instruments."

Nathanael surprised even himself when he was angered over the Rhode Island clergymen's protest of a performance of a play called *The Unhappy Orphan*. Plays were prohibited under the colony's law, and a ruckus followed the play's debut. Yet, he took the side of one of the actors.

His younger cousin, Griffin Greene, came knocking one hot June morning with the knowledge that Nathanael had a rare day off. "You need to get out of this house," Griffin insisted.

Nathanael chuckled. "I was out and for far too long."

Griffin narrowed his eyes and asked, "Benjamin Gardner's wedding?"

"So, you have heard?"

"Everyone heard. The wedding party lasted four days, and you celebrated the occasion on each day."

"You would have accompanied me if you had not been predisposed," Nathanael argued good naturedly.

Griffin glanced at the volume in his cousin's hand. "Put aside the writings of Frederick the Great and get properly dressed. We are going to Plainfield, Connecticut to a public house and a military parade away from disapproving eyes, regardless of our mindfulness to them."

On the twenty mile ride, the cousins talked of family matters and Griffin's impending marriage to a third cousin, Sarah Greene. Nathanael said nothing about Nancy Ward or Caty Littlefield. He realized that he might be falling out of love with one and in love with the other.

Men's voices rose in the public house and talked of Parliament's latest attempt to salvage one of their tea-trading businesses—the East India Company.

"They have cut out American merchants, therefore only the company's agents will make money," grumbled a man smoking a clay pipe.

"Just as matters have seemed to have quieted down, a new matter arises," Nathanael said with a shake of his head.

"The military parade is tomorrow," Griffin reminded. "All matters put aside, we can enjoy that, especially you."

"I can imagine I am witnessing Hannibal sweeping down on Northern Italy to the sound of fife and drum," Nathanael countered.

"That deserves a toast," Griffin proclaimed. He raised his tankard.

Nathanael raised his tankard. "All matters put aside!"

However, all matters were not put aside. The Society of Friends caught wind of the cousins' jaunt and did not find it amusing. They were called to the monthly meeting held at Cranston on September 5. Afterward, the committee announced:

> *Whereas this meeting is informed that Nathanael and Griffin Greene have been at a place   in Connecticut of public resort where they had no proper business, therefore this meeting orders an inquiry into the matter, and to make a report at our next monthly meeting.*

The cousins agreed to silence, which exasperated the Friends. At the meeting held the next day, the report was, "They had given no satisfaction." On September 30, the minutes read:

> *The matter referred to this meeting concerning Nathanael and Griffin Greene as they have not given this meeting any satisfaction for their outgoing and misconduct, therefore this meeting doth put them from under the care of the meeting until they make satisfaction for their misconduct.*

Although he occasionally still went to meeting, the new Tea Act of 1773 began to change things. Those changes pulled Nathanael into the current of rebellion. In Providence, Rhode Island, the Sons of Liberty, radical agitators against the strongarm tactics of the British ministry, burned 300 pounds of tea.

On December 16, 1773, the Boston Sons of Liberty disguised as Indians boarded tea ships in Boston Harbor that waited to unload their cargo. The Sons dumped 342 tea chests into the water. The protest fanned the burning flame of American disenfranchisement and infuriated the British ministry.

ᐱ

Britain's punishment for the Boston Tea Party was swift. In March 1774, Lord North, the Prime Minister of Great Britain, passed the Boston Port Act.

It closed the port until payments were made to the East India Company for the destroyed tea and to the king for the lost taxes. Only food and firewood were permitted into the port.

In May, as part of the British attempt to intimidate the residents of Boston, King George III appointed General Thomas Gage, who commanded the British Army in North America, as the new military governor of Massachusetts. Gage's appointment made it clear to Bostonians that the crown intended to impose martial law.

After debate in Parliament, King George III assumed an active role in deciding punishment for the rebellious colonists. The Boston Port Act was the first of the five Coercive Acts that were intended to quell the colonists and force them into submission. General Gage controlled civil law, where his soldiers quartered, and a change of location to Great Britain in the event of a jury trial. The acts further inflamed Massachusetts. Circular letters from the Massachusetts Committee of Correspondence, which pled for help, reached the other colonies.

Nathanael returned to William Greene's house in East Greenwich and engaged in heated discussions over the turn of events.

"How can we help these poor people in Boston?" William Greene posed to the men and women in his parlor. "Many have no work and are starving."

Caty tried to keep her eyes from drifting to Nathanael's face when she asked, "Is it possible that we can get donations to the disaffected? We have relatives there. Aunt Catharine and I used to take trips to the city to shop."

Her uncle, Samuel Ward, Sr., nodded approvingly. "Perhaps through the Neck. It is a port closure not a confinement. It would require cooperation from many in and outside of Boston."

"The British soldiers in Boston are insolent above measure," Nathanael groused. "Soon, very soon, expect to hear the thirsty drinking in the warm blood of American sons."

"Are you suggesting that they will be uncooperative of our relief efforts?" Samuel asked.

"It is a consideration we cannot overlook," Nathanael replied.

Caty settled her dark eyes on Nathanael's delicate nose and sensuous mouth. He slid a clandestine sideways glance her way and smiled. The smallpox scar on his right eye only endeared him to her. In Caty's opinion, there were too many prying eyes in East Greenwich, too much talk about the boiling crisis in the colonies, and too many men always appearing at her uncle's door with excuses to visit.

It was time to take Nathanael away and immerse him in the world where she lived as a child—Block Island off the Rhode Island coast.

Caty and Nathanael sailed across the calm blue waters of the sound, which would often abruptly become tumultuous as gray, heavy storm clouds foretold of a gathering gale. But their sailing vessel—a double-ender—was well-built and equipped to sail and row. It was in these vessels that as a little girl, Caty and her family took occasional trips to Newport across the thirty-mile sound. It was also where Caty developed a fear of a stormy sea.

On this day, the sun shone like points of diamond light on the small crest of lazy waves. This was the island she wanted to share with Nathanael, where one could stand atop a cliff and see the coast of the mainland. It reflected the freedom her ancestors sought in the 1660s when her great-grandfather, Simon Ray, one of the men who purchased the island, became the patriarch of the settlement. They had come to avoid the dogmas of Massachusetts.

Caty and Nathanael arrived on the island's shore, which was covered in colorful stones. Caty's father greeted them.

"Father, you know Uncle William's relative, Mr. Nathanael Greene," she said in introduction.

"Yes. My sister-in-law, Catharine, who is Caty's aunt and William's wife, has spoken of you," John said and offered his hand. "I am John Littlefield."

"It is my honor to meet you, sir," Nathanael replied and returned the gesture.

"Come, my wife and Caty's brothers and sisters will be pleased to make your acquaintance," John invited.

He led the couple toward the Littlefield home that was near an inland pond protected from the ocean by a high ridge. He pointed to the dirt paths trudged into semblances of roads by oxen- pulled carts.

"Because we have no streets, our homes are laid out aimlessly, and we have no trees to shade them for their growth is stunted by the constant wind," John explained.

Nathanael tried to control his limp. His knee was stiff from riding in the double-ender. The last thing he wanted was John Littlefield's criticism for the shortcoming he could not harness. Caty slid her hand into his.

"There is no judgement here," she whispered. "This is a place where time has little meaning and conventions are discarded. We only answer to one another here."

Nathanael squeezed her hand in response. It was then that he knew she had paid more attention to his words and behavior than he had imagined. His afflictions did nothing to hinder his prowess on the dance floor. The visit was filled with parties Caty organized where she and Nathanael danced until all hours of the night. Caty's love for fun was an intoxicating elixir to the thirty-one-year-old bachelor.

The wind whipped Caty's skirts as she and Nathanael stood on a high hill surrounded by low stone fences. "This is my mother's grave," she said solemnly. Her fingers traced the lettering on the gravestone. "Phebe Ray Littlefield. She died in 1761 when I was six years old."

She stood and looked into Nathanael's lambent eyes. "Your mother died when you were a child as well?"

"Yes, when I was eleven," he said.

"Did you grieve?"

"Yes. I have always felt distant from my stepmother."

"My father sent me to live with Aunt Catharine and Uncle William when I was eight years old so I could have an education because there are no schools or tutors on the island. My mother's two other sisters live in Boston. And now, as you saw, Father is raising a second family with his new wife." She offered her hand. "Come, let us walk and talk of happy things."

Nathanael took her hand then hugged her light agile body to his broad chest and kissed her. "I am happy just being here with you."

They leisurely walked the oxen paths. A woman in a pair of riding breeches passed them. Nathanael raised an eyebrow. "Do all the women here ride horses like that?"

"I learned to ride like that," Caty responded with a merry laugh.

Nathanael chuckled approvingly. "I have no doubt that you are superb."

"Did I tell you that my Aunt Catharine was once a companion to Dr. Benjamin Franklin? It was in the 1750s before she married. He was married and much older than her. He was interested in romance, but my aunt refused his intentions."

"And will you refuse my intentions?"

"What are those intentions?" she teased.

Silence hung between them.

She stopped walking and studied his serene countenance. "Nathanael?"

Her eyes held everything he thought he had imagined—everything that he had once hoped to see in Nancy Ward's eyes. *How am I to reply when I have been spurned before?* he wondered.

He took her delicate face in his hands. The answer rolled off his tongue in a flurry.

"Yes, my dear Mr. Greene," Caty replied. "Yes, I will be your wife."

On July 10, 1774, Sammy was surprised when he received an envelope stuffed with wedding invitations and a note.

> *Please to deliver the enclosed Cards to your sisters. On the 20th this instant I expect to be married to Miss Caty Littlefield at your Uncle Greene's. As a Relative of hers and friend of mine, your company is desired upon the occasion. The company will*

be small consisting of only a few Choice Spirits. As she is not married at her father's house she declined giving any an invitation but a few of her nearest relations and most intimate friends. There will be my brothers & their wives, Mr. Varnum & his wife, Christopher & Griffin Greene and their Wives, and who from Block Island I don't know. Those are all except your family. Believe me to be your sincere friend. Nath Greene

Ten days later, the small wedding ceremony was held in the East Greenwich house on Love Lane on the hill where the green valley stretched out below. Now, Caty was Mrs. Nathanael Greene, and the years of her carefree youth were passed. She moved from dependence on the men in her life to dependence on her husband. It was what elevated her in the eyes of society. She assumed she would settle down into the serene life of a respected, well-off gentleman's wife.

Nathanael and his new bride rode through the peaceful Rhode Island countryside to his house in Coventry. Caty wandered through the small rooms—four on each floor topped with low ceilings. Nathanael's extensive library was on the first floor. She trailed her fingers across the book spines. Her eager and curious mind envisioned reading while she and her new husband sat in front of a cozy fireplace. Through the window she could see the iron forge. The heavy sound of hammers and the whir of the furnace would become familiar.

She walked outside and down to the river that bubbled merrily almost in contrast to the unwieldy noise of the forge. Arms slid around her waist and her earlobe tickled with the playful tongue that teased it. "What are you doing out here, my angel?" Nathanael asked amorously.

Her gaze remained on the clear river. "You were busy with business at the forge, therefore I—"

He whirled her around. "My business is with you, now and forever." His mouth found hers, and as if from a fairy tale, he swept her up in his strong arms and carried her inside.

❧

The situation in Boston had not improved, and the people's desperation for food and assistance grew as British warships blocked the harbor and the port closure continued. Nathanael, James Varnum, and other men of East Greenwich started a fundraiser to raise money for the suffering citizens of Boston. Nathanael donated three pounds, and all the money was used to buy food and livestock.

By September 1774, the spark of colonial rebellion was further fueled by the meeting of the first Continental Congress in Philadelphia where political leaders from the thirteen colonies met to discuss America's future under growing British aggression. Nathanael felt compelled to see what was happening in Boston firsthand.

"Must you go so soon and alone?" Caty asked with a small tremor of fear in her voice.

"If I go alone, I can travel with haste." He kissed her on the tip of her pert nose. "It is only for a few days. Jacob and Peggy will stay with you."

"There is nothing to do here when you are absent. The boredom will stretch out eternally."

"It is not that long, my angel."

She knew she had no choice, so she helped him prepare for the journey. When she saw him off, she feared he would never come home or somehow be jailed in Boston for something that the British might perceive as a crime.

❧

It was a fifty-mile ride to Boston. Nathanael arrived late the following afternoon. The sentries at Boston Neck stopped him. "What is your name, from where do you hail, and what is your business?"

I should have been prepared for this. What am I to tell them? he thought. *I cannot tell them I have come to see the fortifications here on the Neck or watch British soldiers drilling.*

He produced a grin, gave his name and his residence, and then said, "I have come to buy a novel called *Tristram Shandy*. Have you heard of it?"

One of the sentries narrowed his eyes. "Do you not have bookstores in Rhode Island?"

"Maybe he's one of them Quakers," the other sentry said. "Are you one of them Quakers? Are you armed?" he asked Nathanael.

"Quakers do not read novels," the first sentry declared.

The truth was that Nathanael had already read the nine volume novels and had even gone so far as to entertain his brothers by mimicking one of the characters—the little, squat, uncourtly figure of Dr. Slop portrayed as an incompetent quack.

"Let him through," the second sentry ordered. "There is a bookstore in Cornhill opposite William's Court. The name is the London Bookstore. The proprietor is Mr. Henry Knox."

Nathanael spurred his horse, Britain, and passed the checkpoint. He knew where he was going. He had been to Knox's bookstore several times, but this was the first time he had been detained at the Neck. He was actually pleased as it gave him time to observe the fortifications. He rode past Boston Common where British soldiers were drilling. He dismounted and stopped to watch. The grass on the common had been obliterated by their boots. They sweated profusely in their heavy woolen redcoats, but they performed their maneuvers with professional preciseness.

Nathanael moved on before he was found taking notice and arrived at the London Bookstore. Henry Knox, the rotund twenty-four-year-old proprietor greeted him when he walked inside. "Mr. Greene!" Henry exclaimed with a jolly smile. "It is a pleasure to see you again. Have you come to purchase more military manuals?"

"I have come to buy a musket," Nathanael said in a low voice.

"A musket?"

"Your store is a great resort for British officers and Tory ladies as well as many colonials, Mr. Knox. You must know where I can purchase one."

"Let us sit over coffee and discuss the latest literary offerings I have received from London or perhaps our favorite subject, military science," Henry said with a sparkle in his eye. He led Nathanael to a table. "I heard you were recently married, just a month after I married my Lucy." He waved a hand at the barkeep who brought them coffee. Their conversation traversed everything from marriage to military science to muskets. It was a budding friendship that neither man knew would blossom with the growing dissent and would change with events they could not foresee.

❧

To Caty's relief, Nathanael arrived home as the sun rose. She ran out to greet him. Her alleviation spilled out in a rush. "Thank God you have returned home safe! Is that a musket strapped to your saddle?" Her eyes darted to the house. "Your family will be mortified if they see you have a gun."

"Caty, you know the Friends suspended Griffin—and me—over a year ago. I think it makes little difference now if they find I am armed."

"This has something to do with the letter that arrived from Mr. Varnum before you left, does it not? Do you think I have not heard from my Aunt Catharine what the men in her neighborhood are about?"

"What have you heard?" he asked. He dismounted, removed the musket from his saddle, and grasped Britain by the bridle.

"That they are forming a military company in case trouble spreads to Rhode Island," she said.

He led Britain to the stable. Caty followed.

"Then you know that this is happening all over the colonies," Nathanael said. "And, yes, I have agreed to join them. In fact, I spoke to a former British officer in Boston who has agreed to drill and train us."

"But the—"

"That is enough. It is done. Where are Jacob and Peggy?"

"Sleeping I believe. I do not think Peggy likes me. She said she had never met a woman who could not knit."

Nathanael removed Britain's saddle and filled her feed bag. "You will learn in time. I believe there is much that we all will learn in time."

❧

In October 1774, the new militia obtained a charter from the Rhode Island

General Assembly to form the Kentish Guards. Nathanael became a private in the group. They wore red coats with green trim, white waistcoats and breeches, and hats with a black cockade. They also bought cartridge paper and lead to make bullets.

"You should run for lieutenant," Griffin encouraged. "You are a charter member from a prosperous family."

When the votes were counted, Nathanael was denied. One of the guards took Nathanael aside. "Your limp and asthma are an embarrassment to the Guards. It takes away from the company's manly, martial appearance," he said. "We cannot have an officer with these afflictions leading us."

Nathanael poured out his humiliation to James Varnum, the militia's captain. "I was informed that I was a blemish to the company. I confess it is the first stroke of mortification that I ever felt from being considered within private or public life a blemish to those with whom I associate. I confess it is my misfortune to limp a little, but I did not conceive it to be so great. But we are not apt to discover our own defects."

"There is nothing I can do," James said, "I am sorry."

Nathanael resigned. Then, he changed his mind. He drilled faithfully in martial maneuvers that winter. *At the least*, he thought, *we can pass the time as a pretty little society in meetings where we might relax ourselves a few hours from the various occupations of life.*

On the night of April 18, 1775, 800 British soldiers gathered on the shore of Back Bay in Boston, Massachusetts. General Thomas Gage ordered them to Concord, fifteen miles away to capture rebel armaments stored in the town. A messenger brought the observation to Dr. Joseph Warren, a Boston politician and Son of Liberty. Warren feared for the lives of fellow patriots John Hancock and Samuel Adams who were hiding in Lexington away from the long arm of General Gage. He dispatched two other Sons of Liberty, silversmith Paul Revere and tanner William Dawes, to warn the countryside that the British regulars were out.

Just after dawn on April 19, the British entered Lexington. The local militia under Captain John Parker was waiting for them as the vanguard led by Scottish Major John Pitcairn marched on Lexington Green.

"Lay down your arms, you damned rebels, and disperse!" Pitcairn ordered the thirty-eight militiamen.

Parker and his men broke up, but they held on to their muskets. Then a shot rang out. Eight Americans lay dead on the green. Who fired the first shot was not known.

The British marched on to Concord. There, they were met with resistance from the gathering rebel militia and minutemen on a hill near the North Bridge. As the redcoats searched the town for armaments, shots rang out, killing both British soldiers and Americans. On the return sixteen-mile march to Boston, angry militiamen fired at the regulars from behind stone walls and houses in a bloody spree that enraged the British soldiers who endured suffering from an unseen enemy.

Mounted messengers relayed the news of the battles to Providence, Rhode Island, crying out, "War, war boys! There is war!" It filtered through to the smaller towns and villages. That night, Nathanael and Caty heard approaching hoofbeats. The lone rider dismounted and pounded on their front door.

Caty heard the animated conversation between Nathanael and the rider. "Do you have to go?" she asked with trepidation.

"Yes, the Guard is gathering in East Greenwich, and then we are marching to Massachusetts," Nathanael said.

He changed into his uniform and gathered his musket and cartridge box. "I promise I will make arrangements for my family to care for you as soon as possible." He pulled her into his strong arms and kissed her. "I love you with all my being," he breathed.

"Please come home to me safe," she begged and pressed a hand to her belly.

From the threshold, she watched him mount his horse and fade into the night to join the Kentish Guards under the command of James

Varnum. They set out for Massachusetts and got as far as the Massachusetts border. An order from Rhode Island's Loyalist governor, Joseph Wanton, halted their progress.

∼

Nathanael returned home. He assured Caty that the danger was over for the moment. Then he was gone again, this time to Providence to attend an emergency session of the General Assembly on April 22. The lawmakers authorized a Rhode Island army of 1,500 men called the Army of Observation. They would cooperate with similar forces from other New England colonies for the common defense of the provinces. The army needed a general to lead it.

Nathanael was shocked when the assembly called his name. "Private Nathanael Greene, you are a man known to us through your relations to William Greene and Samuel Ward, Sr., as well as your business connections with your brothers and your good reputation. What say you to command this army?"

He regarded the faces anticipating his response. It was an earnest offer. Doubt teased him for a moment, but the call of the cause was louder. He rose and bowed. "Gentlemen, it is my sincere honor, and I shall execute the title with forthright actions."

The Kentish Guards had considered him a blemish incapable of cutting a physically shining figure, but now he was a general. He went home and showed Caty his commission.

She read it aloud, "You are hereby in his Majesty's Name George the Third, by the Grace of God, King of Great Britain authorized empowered and commissioned to have, take, and exercise the office of Brigadier General." She looked into Nathanael's proud eyes and asked, "You are an officer committed to lead a rebellion commissioned by King George III?"

"There is no other authority by which a citizen, Loyalist or Patriot, can obtain a commission. It is people like Thomas Gage and the British ministry who are the enemy," Nathanael explained. "You know I will have to see to my duty. The provincial army has Boston under siege, and my army must join them. The challenge will be daunting to me and my inexperienced army."

After dinner, the two snuggled in the library and sipped glasses of wine. The forge was quiet. The babbling water of the Pawtuxet River sang like a lullaby.

Nathanael held her in his arms and kissed the top of her dark head. "While I am away on military duty, Jacob will run the forge. He and Peggy will move into the house with you. You can stay here in Coventry, or you can move in with the rest of my family at Potowomut. You know my brothers adore you. But if they request anything unworthy of you, maintain your independence until my return, and I will see justice done you."

His last statement shocked her, but she said nothing.

two

I Am Determined to Defend My Rights

By late May, Nathanael was in Roxbury, Massachusetts with his men to join the gathering force of New Englanders. The farmers, shopkeepers, artisans, fishermen, doctors, and lawyers were armed with everything from muskets to axes—white, Negro, Native, illiterate, educated, young and old. Nathanael's troops straggled in by companies, well accoutered with blankets, a knapsack, and a month's pay. His artillery consisted of six 3-pounders and twelve heavy cannon, some forged in Coventry.

There had been no national call to arms—only a plea from Dr. Joseph Warren and the Massachusetts Committee of Safety to help defend their wives and children from the butchering hands of an inhumane soldiery. All had come to challenge the most formidable army in the world. They surrounded the port city of Boston in a semicircle, cutting off communications and supplies by land. General Thomas Gage saw the danger these "rabbles" posed even if the ministry in London did not.

On arrival, Nathanael reported to General Artemas Ward, the senior general of the Massachusetts provincial troops who was presiding over the siege. "It is good to have you, General Greene," Ward acknowledged.

"I would like to assign your men to the right wing of the army under Massachusetts General John Thomas."

"I accept the assignment, but I will need to establish a camp and then return to Rhode Island to recruit more men."

"Certainly," Artemas said. "I warn you that each colony jealously guards the independence of its militia, and I have no authority over them. Each regiment is an army of its own, including yours."

"Understood."

"I do not think you do, but you will in time."

Nathanael located a hill in Roxbury where he laid out his camp on a sixty-acre estate that once belonged to the Loyalist governor Frances Bernard. The position was an excellent post for observation. The grounds included a mansion, a pond, and a hothouse that the Rhode Islanders used as storage. Then, he informed General Thomas that he was leaving for Rhode Island to recruit more troops.

His recruiting efforts failed. His army was supposed to be 1,500 strong. It was closer to 1,000, and the men were undisciplined, untrained, and raucous. When he returned to Rhode Island, he found that the colony's Committee of Safety, which included his brother, Jacob, had devised no mode of supply. Yet, his belief in the patriotic cause did not waver.

From Providence, he penned a letter to his beloved wife explaining why he had left her so soon after they were wed. "It would have been happy for me if I could have lived a private life in peace and plenty. But the injury done my country and the chains of slavery forging for posterity calls me forth to defend our common rights, and repel the bold invaders of the sons of freedom. I am determined to defend my rights and maintain my freedom, or sell my life in the attempt."

❧

The Rhode Island camp was in disarray when Nathanael returned to Roxbury on June 3. Some were even preparing to march home because the supply line for the army's food had broken down. The ill-fed, dirty, poorly trained troops were infected with poor morale, rowdy behavior, drunkenness, and laziness.

They sulked when reprimanded, paid little heed to their officers, and often did not bother to dress properly when on the parade ground.

Nathanael realized they were completely unprepared for military life. His experience supervising his workers at the iron forge and drills with the Kentish Guards proved beneficial. He drilled his troops daily on how to fire their muskets in formation. He insisted they scrub their firelocks, the mechanism in the musket that generated the spark that ignited the gunpowder. He insisted that they shave and clean their clothes.

"No swearing and no card playing," he proclaimed.

Discipline was harsh. The public punishments were thirty-nine lashes or a ride on a wooden rail with guns tied to the offender's feet. It was a strain on Nathanael's temperate nature that as a fledgling general he had not expected. He led by example. He rose early, inspected his troops, attended to the many details required of his rank, and worked late into the night. Exhaustion was a side effect he bore, but his leadership efforts began to materialize. This improved his chances for recruiting, and he returned to Rhode Island to muster more troops and garner more supplies.

To his delight, he found time to visit Caty in Coventry. She was ecstatic to see him when his horse pulled up to Spell Hall. They fell into a clinging embrace as if they would be parted in a moment's notice.

When they entered the house, Nathanael's brother, Jacob, greeted him, "We did not expect you."

"I was able to take some time away. I need to wash away the dust from the road, and then we can talk over supper."

The floorboards creaked under his boot heels as he walked down the long hall to the bedroom he shared with Caty.

"Have you been to Providence shopping?" he asked when he saw a neat rack of new dresses.

"I shall need them," she insisted.

"Of course, but where do you plan to wear them?"

She took his hand and guided it to her belly. "Your child sleeps in me. I will need them to fit my changing figure."

"You are pregnant?"

"You seem disappointed."

"Far from it, my angel. I have been blessed even as impending war lies at my feet."

She cupped his cheeks and kissed his full lips. "*We* have been blessed."

The broad smile she missed brightened his countenance. Nothing could dim his outlook that night, even the knowledge that his sister-in-law, Peggy, had ousted Caty from the kitchen, a sign that his wife's bumbling domestic skills had not improved. As much as he wanted to remain with Caty in the bedroom, they joined the others for dinner.

"Tell us of camp," Jacob encouraged his brother over glasses of ale.

"My task is hard and my fatigue great—applications you cannot conceive of unless you are present. My officers and soldiers are generally well satisfied nay I have not heard one complaint."

Nathanael's luminous eyes brightened. He turned his attention to Caty and said, "I have been accorded the greatest respect, much more than my station or consequence entitles me. But that does not equal the pride I am feeling at this moment."

His tone changed and the contours of his face sharpened. "We have major problems to overcome before we can starve the British out of Boston. If we do that, the citizens will also starve. The British have transports and ships, and we have no American Navy to oppose that. They also have sufficient cannon. Furthermore, Great Britain has sent three major generals to help General Gage quell the rebellion."

It would be last of his complaints while he was with his wife. On June 18, after two blissful days spent with his family, he was interrupted as the waning gibbous moon looked down upon Coventry. A messenger arrived and woke the household. Nathanael opened the brief message.

General Greene the British have assaulted Americans positioned on Breed's and Bunker Hill on the Charlestown peninsula north of Boston. You are ordered to return immediately.

He would be gone in the stifling heat of a June night when Caty was taken with a chill she could not shake.

At daybreak, Nathanael arrived in his camp at Roxbury. From the hill, he saw the village of Charlestown had been burnt to ashes—the battle was over. The American redoubt accidentally built on a hill closer to Boston, Breed's Hill, when it should have been built on Bunker Hill, had been overrun by British soldiers led by General William Howe when the rebels ran out of gunpowder. The results of the battle were appalling. Even Howe was shocked by the victory too dearly bought. Of his 2,300 redcoated troops that stormed the peninsula, over 1,000 had been killed or wounded. The Americans lost 440 killed or wounded including Dr. Joseph Warren, the ablest of the American commanders, whose loss was deeply mourned.

The definition of victory changed, however, for the horde of provincial soldiers surrounding Boston. They had lost many friends, loved ones, allies, and even colonial rivals, but they saw that they were capable of devastating the enemy. Nathanael wrote to Caty and Jacob and described what he knew about the battle. Then he added, "I wish we could sell them another hill at the same price we did Bunker Hill."

On June 14, before the battle at Breed's Hill commenced, the Continental Congress officially adopted the troops near Boston, thus creating the Continental Army. They nominated George Washington, a forty-three-year-old planter from Virginia, as commander-in-chief.

On the afternoon of July 2, the town of Cambridge heard approaching fifes and drums. Everyone dashed out into the pouring rain to witness the arrival of General George Washington and his entourage. The majestic general from Virginia came into view astride his horse like a king, wearing a resplendent buff and blue uniform. George received word of the battle at Breed's Hill as he rode from Philadelphia to Cambridge. He made his quarters in Vassall House on Tory Row, a road lined with large homes owned by people loyal to King George III, known as Tories or Loyalists. Most of the residents had fled to Boston seeking the protection of General Thomas Gage after the recent armed conflicts.

Washington was accompanied by his aides, Joseph Reed, a lawyer, and Thomas Mifflin, a merchant—both men in their thirties and both from Pennsylvania. Also with him were Generals Charles Lee, his second-in-command, and Horatio Gates—both men in their forties and Virginia landowners like Washington. The three generals fought for the British years before in the ill-fated Braddock Expedition during the war with the French and Indians. Now, their allegiance was to the rebel cause.

Once Washington was settled in Vassall House, he performed a review of the New England soldiers and militia stationed in Cambridge, Roxbury, and the encampment on Prospect Hill in Somerville. Under the glare of the hot afternoon sun, his commanding figure cast a long shadow as he walked with deliberation among tattered tents, rotting lean-tos, putrid trenches, and human stench and disease. His immaculate and resplendent buff and blue uniform was a sharp contrast to the colonists' shabby homespun and deerskin clothing. To his surprise, Nathanael's Rhode Islanders had some semblance of discipline and cleanliness.

George invited Nathanael to a personal meeting in Vassall House and received him in his office.

The first thought that ran through Nathanael's mind was, *He is going to notice my limp and judge me blemished just as the Kentish Guards did, or my asthma will flare, and it will bear the same judgement on me.*

George quietly watched Nathanael enter the room. He did notice Nathanael's limp, but George was a shrewd observer of character and that was not where he focused his attention. He summoned a servant to pour glasses of Madeira.

"Please sit down," George said. "I received your letter of introduction, General Greene. I intended on meeting you, nonetheless. The Continental Congress has appointed four major generals and eight brigadier generals from among the provincials here. I would like to congratulate you on the appointment of brigadier general. I was told that you are thirty-two years of age. That makes you the youngest appointee."

Nathanael was as stunned as when the Rhode Island Assembly saw fit to commission him as a provincial brigadier. "I cannot express the extent of my honor that I was selected as a commander in our new Continental Army," he said.

"Someone in Congress saw the value in your service as short as it has been. I, however, found that the promises made by the gentlemen in Congress were not forthcoming. I was led to believe I would find 20,000 battle-tested troops. What I found is not a proper army. There is little gunpowder, cannon, and other supplies to be had. The condition and behavior of officers and soldiers alike are deplorable in many cases, but what concerns me greatly are the regional prejudices and loyalties to individual colonies among the troops," George confided as he sipped Madeira.

"For my own part, I feel the cause and not the place. I would as soon go to Virginia as stay here."

"Do you know that I was taught to believe that the people of New England are a superior race of mortals? Finding you of the same temper, dispositions, passion, and prejudices changes my esteem of you."

"Therefore, you are saying that you carry your own parochial sectionalism," Nathanael observed.

George considered Nathanael for a moment and then said, "I know that many of these men take issue with a Southerner leading them. For now, it is a New England army commanded by a Virginian. Perhaps that will change when Virginia sends companies to join us."

An expression of soft introspection filtered through Nathanael's voice when he said, "I hope we shall be taught to copy your example and to prefer the love of liberty in this time of public danger to the soft pleasures of domestic life with fortitude."

"You are a man like myself—someone willing to sacrifice comfort for the cause of an idea. Tell me, General Greene, do you have a formal education?"

"No. I was absorbed with working my father's farm and iron forge. I am a Quaker. Only Bible study was approved when I was a youngster so my ideas would remain pious. I have educated myself in theories—military, philosophical, and admittedly, many novels."

"I suppose you are no longer a Quaker?"

"My cousin and I were on suspension, but I chose to reject the formal doctrines of the Friends."

George nodded. Religion made no difference on this day when he was spending time getting to know his new general. "I too was required to work on my mother's farm where there were no libraries or schools. Self-education is a difficult but necessary road for all those who thirst for knowledge."

They spoke a little longer of ways to unify the army and of family and home.

"My wife Martha is waiting for me at home," George explained with a gleam in his eye. "We live at Mount Vernon, an expansive plantation on the Potomac River in eastern Virginia. I lived there for some time as a boy."

It was a good day. The first days of a long friendship always were.

Late in the day, as Nathanael was returning to his camp, he ran across an old acquaintance. "Henry Knox!" Nathanael exclaimed. "I had no idea you were in our 'camp of liberty,' so they call it."

The tall, robust bookseller pounded Nathanael on the back with one hand; it was missing two fingers he had lost in a musket accident. "I heard you were here and that you are now a brigadier general in the Continental Army."

"What are you doing here?" Nathanael asked as the two mounted up for the ride to Roxbury.

"I fought at Bunker Hill. General Ward put me in charge of designing and building fortifications around Roxbury."

"That was your device?" Nathanael asked.

"Yes, and I have been training gunners. You know I did some of that when I was a member of the Boston Grenadier Corps, not to mention all the books I have read on the subject."

"Where is your wife?"

"I sent my Lucy to Worcester for safety," Henry frowned. "Her Loyalist family, the Fluckers, disowned her when we wed. I was not up to their social status or way of thinking. They are in Boston."

Uncertain how to respond, Nathanael grinned, changed the subject, and said, "Mrs. Greene is expecting our first child."

"Wonderful news! Have you met His Excellency, General George Washington?"

"I did this day. His Excellency, as you called him, has a great desire to banish every idea of local attachments. In fact, in addition to my three regiments from Rhode Island, he has assigned me four from Massachusetts and has redeployed me from Roxbury to Prospect Hill. I am to report to General Charles Lee."

"The new generals have to reduce order from almost perfect chaos," Henry chuckled. "Washington believes in corporal punishment to rein in unruly troops. The lash has not been spared for those who break the rules. I wholeheartedly approve." Henry lifted his chin and said, "Ah, General Lee is approaching as we speak."

Nathanael turned to see the English-born aristocratic, educated general who fought for the British in the war with the French and Indians and had served in the Polish Army. As was everyone, Nathanael was suitably impressed with Lee's known military knowledge and experience. A Pomeranian sat in the saddle between Charles Lee's thin thighs while a pack of other little dogs gamboled around his horse. A man servant rode serenely behind.

Henry made the introductions.

Charles' little dog barked sharply while the others sniffed the ground.

"Be silent, Spado," Charles cooed and wrinkled his hawkish nose. He turned his attention to Nathanael. "General Greene, I look forward to having you and your men join us." He bowed tall in the saddle and rode on toward Cambridge.

As soon as Lee was out of sight, Nathanael's respectful countenance changed to facetiousness, and he muttered, "His uniform and personal appearance was unkempt. I am not certain if he was demeaning me or if his sentiment was honest. I suppose I shall find out soon enough."

The siege of Boston dragged on through the heat of the summer. The Continental camps remained in deplorable condition. Dysentery broke out. Food was unfit, and the soldiers' filthy clothes hung on them like rags. Nathanael tried to restore order, but he was learning there was more to war than battles and drilling. Supplies, discipline, and the health and morale of the troops were essential.

The opposing armies did little more than observe one another through spyglasses. The British sometimes lobbed shells into the American camp as the lines moved closer to the city. Sniper fire was often exchanged. The Americans, short on gunpowder and ammunition, sometimes chased the unexploded cannonballs. Then, Nathanael's first Rhode Islander was killed. Augustus Mumford, a member of the Kentish Guards, was decapitated during one of the lazy exchanges.

Caty's summer was miserable without Nathanael to comfort her and ease her fears for his safety. Jacob received letters from his brother about the state of war. Although he was in agreement with it, he spent many nights carping about the probable impossibility of it. One hot July night, she and Jacob both received an optimistic letter from Nathanael that George Washington of Virginia had been appointed commander-in-chief of the new Continental Army.

For the third night in a row, Jacob sat in the parlor and interminably went on about conditions at the forge. "I find my hands overflowing without Nathanael here to balance supervision and oversee supplies. I understand his many concerns and happiness at the arrival of a new commander, but it seems he has abandoned all thought of his responsibility to us."

Caty laid her book aside and said with repugnance, "That is untrue. He writes often and pours his sensibilities into each word."

Peggy, Jacob's wife, pressed her lips together and kept her eyes on her mending.

"I know you feel distress over your condition," Jacob pointed out to Caty. "Perhaps if you made an effort to perform more domestic chores, they would keep your mind focused on something other than Nathanael's absence and every ache and pain you perceive as an ill."

"Perhaps, if Peggy would put aside her insistence that she run my household along with her impatience with me, I would shed my resentfulness," Caty snapped. She addressed Peggy. "You have six children, yet you have not offered advice or guidance as to what I am feeling four months into my pregnancy."

Peggy laid aside her mending and said, "You have not asked, and it is not my place to instruct you."

"You know I have not been feeling well. What if something is wrong?"

"You are imagining too much," Peggy retorted.

"Am I? No one has bothered to listen to my complaints," Caty rose from her chair. "You had your husband by your side during your time. You did not fear that he could be killed or taken sick at any moment."

She saw Peggy and Jacob exchange glances. She said, "I think I shall go to Potowomut where the rest of your family can help me through this, and my doctors in East Greenwich will be closer."

"I assured Nathanael that I would do justice to you in his absence," Jacob protested.

"Nathanael told me that I could go to Potowomut if I chose," Caty countered.

Peggy sighed. "Let her go if that is the only way she will find comfort."

Caty left to pack. Jacob agreed to secure transport for her. In Potowomut, Caty's doctors petted her and assured her she was healthy. Everything she was experiencing was a nervous reaction, which was understandable under the circumstances. Soon, she was squabbling with her in-laws, but only the women. Distraught, she wrote to Nathanael who always took her side, but then would chastise her for not forwarding personal items he had sent for weeks before.

❧

As the summer wore on, Caty lost forbearance and returned to Coventry. In August, Colonel James Varnum arrived with a letter for her. "Mr. Varnum, I am so pleased to see you again."

"I am afraid you will not be so pleased when you read the letter Nathanael asked me to give you."

Caty took the letter from James' hand with apprehension.

> *My Sweet Angel, The anxiety that you must feel at the unhappy fate of Mr. Mumford, the tender sympathy for the distress of his poor lady and fears and apprehensions for my safety, under your present debilitated state, must be a weight too great for you to support. Let us put our confidence in God and recommend our souls to his care. Stifle your own grief my sweet creature and offer a small tribute of consolation to the afflicted widow.*

"He is asking me to visit Mr. Mumford's widow to convey condolences?" Caty asked as she looked up from the letter.

"Visiting a dead soldier's family is your duty as a general's wife."

"I have dreaded that duty but will do to it for my husband's sake."

It was followed with another reason for her to fret. Sammy Ward, Jr., now a captain, joined Colonel Benedict Arnold's expedition to Quebec, Canada. Nathanael had tried to convince Sammy to remain in Cambridge, for the journey would be perilous.

What was worse was that Jacob received a letter from Nathanael that he was depressed about the Continental Army's prospects. "Hundreds will perish and I among the rest perhaps."

"There must be a time I can go to Nathanael," Caty told Jacob and Peggy. "He invited me to winter camp after the child arrives. He said that the opposing armies would be settling down. The cannonading has already stopped, and I hear that Mrs. Washington, wife of General George

Washington, is going for a visit."

Peggy looked mortified. "You plan to have the child in an army encampment?"

"Why not? There are good doctors in Cambridge, near Nathanael's camp. Take me to Newport shopping. It will be fun away from the tedium of housework."

࿆

In late November, with a driver at her disposal, Caty packed her new wardrobe and baby clothes in a carriage and began the sixty-mile trip. She was seven months pregnant.

Caty's carriage rumbled through the town of Cambridge, Massachusetts. Crowds of soldiers spilled through the streets and drilled on the Common. Classes at Harvard College were cancelled, and the dormitories were converted to barracks. The carriage pulled up near Hastings House. Standing taller than most men, her heart's desire appeared through the bustling noise. Nathanael's limp seemed more pronounced, and he looked tired, but his lambent blue eyes and subtle handsomeness aroused her emotions.

He boarded her carriage before she had a chance to climb out. "Prospect Hill encampment," Nathanael told the driver and gave instructions. When the carriage moved to the northeast for the one-mile journey, he pulled Caty into his strong arms and kissed her passionately. His hand traveled to her belly. "Your presence here will warm me and my heart as if the coziest of hearths was lit to soothe me. But should you have taken such a trip in your advanced condition?"

"I wrote to you that I was coming. You did not protest."

Nathanael kissed her again and then said, "I did not know what to expect when I saw you carrying the little creature God has given us."

"The little creature is well," Caty assured. Her eyes moved to the carriage window and the multitudes of wagons, horses, and soldiers—many with their wives and children herding livestock or hauling water. "I did not know what to expect when I arrived. How many soldiers does the army have?"

39

"Twenty-eight thousand, but enlistments expire on December 1. General Washington is concerned he will not have an army to attack the British in Boston if the time arrives. British General Thomas Gage was sent back to England for his failure to quash us. General William Howe has taken his place as commander-in-chief of British forces in America. General Washington held a war council on October 18 to determine if attacking Boston was a sensible plan. I was included among the generals with whom he conferred," Nathanael said with pride. "I was surrounded with experienced men. Some are veterans of the war with the French and Indians. General John Sullivan is an experienced militia officer. Charles Lee and Horatio Gates served in the British Army."

Caty gazed out the window again. "Obviously, the council decided not to attack," she said.

"Yes, and I agreed. However, although the plan was impractical, if we could land a thousand troops, I would support an attack."

The carriage rolled up the gentle slope of Prospect Hill and through the encampment. The toughened men from Massachusetts and Rhode Island carried an assortment of muskets, rifles, and fowling pieces. The Rhode Islanders wore broad-brimmed headpieces bent into cocked hats, homespun shirts and breeches, long stockings, buckle shoes, and colorful coats and waistcoats.

They arrived at Nathanael's headquarters, the William Pepperrell House, at the top of the hill. Before he helped his wife, he said, "We are both inoculated for smallpox, but I want you to be aware that an epidemic has broken out in Boston. The British are turning infected people out of the city. I have required that my officers submit to inoculation. My headquarters is a place they can go during the quarantine period."

"Your concern shines in every way," she said lovingly.

Nathanael teased the spray of lose hair around her face and smiled tenderly. "My concern for you is foremost, and my desire has simmered like a waiting flame only capable of igniting at your touch."

Caty's dark eyes snapped as he led her into the bedroom they would share. She unwound his cravat, kissed his neck, and then pulled his shirt over his head. They lay in one another's arms that night and listened to their hearts beat with the after-effects of their love. Nathanael rested his hand on Caty's naked belly. The babe kicked, and toe-shaped mounds appeared on his mother's stomach.

Once settled into Nathanael's headquarters, Caty walked along the top of Prospect Hill with its orchards and commanding view of the Charles and Mystic Rivers and Boston Harbor. The spyglass she held allowed her to see the charred and skeletal ruins of Charlestown and the British Army's encampment on Bunker and Breed's Hills two miles away. The sound of bugles shrilled across the bay. The streets and buildings of Boston were filled with soldiers and people. Some were destroying wooden structures for firewood.

She returned to headquarters and shook off the cold. With Nathanael occupied by a myriad of correspondence and responsibilities, she went to visit the officers who were quarantined. Nursing them seemed like an impossible task in her advanced stage of pregnancy, but she could cheer them up.

"Mrs. Greene," a young lieutenant of a Massachusetts regiment exclaimed when she entered the room he shared with nine other convalescing officers.

Caty went to his bedside. He was well enough to pull up a chair for her. "Hello, Lieutenant White," Caty greeted. "You look better today. May I get you something? Ale, perhaps?"

"A nurse brought some for me, but you could read to me from the book you have in your hand," he said.

Caty smiled brightly. "Of course." She settled in. After a moment, she was surrounded by the other men. Their faces, which revealed various mild stages of smallpox, shined like boys gathered for story time.

three

Liberties of America

In October, the Continental Congress and its president, John Hancock, authorized George Washington to seize the cannon at Fort Ticonderoga located on Lake Champlain 300 miles north. The previous May, Colonel Benedict Arnold of Connecticut with Ethan Allen and the Green Mountain Boys captured the fort from the British. The country between the fort and Boston crossed rolling hills, winding rivers and lakes. On November 16, George issued orders to Henry Knox to take the cannon at Ticonderoga. A few days later, he was on his way to New York City with his younger brother, William, before sailing north on the Hudson River.

While Henry was nearing his destination, Martha Washington arrived in Cambridge with her adult son Jacky and her little entourage of family and servants. She settled into Vassall House with her husband and his large staff of young men in their twenties. Regardless of the fraternity house atmosphere, she was soon taking visitors. Caty was one of those visitors. The two women greeted one another in the paneled parlor across the hall from General Washington's office.

"My dear, you are so lovely," the short, plump forty-three-year-old wife of the commander-in-chief beamed. "When is the child due?"

Caty favored Martha with a vivacious look despite their twenty-three-year age difference. "My lying-in will be in January," she said. She absorbed Martha's effortless and cordial manner.

"Come, Mrs. Greene. I would like you to meet my husband. As wives of generals, I am certain that we will be spending much time together."

"Then you must call me Caty."

"And I am Martha."

They crossed the wide hall and entered George's office. He rose from his desk. His muscular six-foot two frame towered above the two petite women before him. "So you are the lovely wife of our Quaker preacher," George said approvingly. "I am honored to meet you."

Caty issued a small curtsy. "It is my honor, sir. In fact, I shall name my child after you if I am lucky enough to have a boy."

"Perhaps you should confer with General Greene before making such a promise."

Caty smiled. "There is no need."

It soon became evident that the Washingtons' frequent dinner parties held for the high ranking officers and their wives was evolving into a tradition. George let Martha entertain, which gave him a chance to relax and listen to the ladies chatter. The wives agreed to stay for the winter. They jested that their husbands would freeze at night if they were not there to keep them warm when firewood was scarce.

Nathanael insisted he and Caty entertain likewise. "It is a general's duty to reciprocate," he said when Caty protested that she could not cook. "My angel, I shall find someone who can cook. I did not expect you to do so, especially in your advanced state."

Caty relaxed, and soon camp life became a social circle where her convivial nature blossomed.

❧

New Year's Eve 1775 dawned, and the numbers in camp dwindled as their expired enlistments came to an end and soldiers went home. The Continental Congress authorized Washington to recruit new soldiers for one-year enlistments which would expire December 31, 1776. George and his generals discussed the issue.

"I think we should offer bounties," Nathanael said during a meeting at Vassall House.

There was a smattering of agreement among the generals present, including Israel Putnam, Horatio Gates, Charles Lee, William Heath, and Artemas Ward.

"The soldiers are already well-paid," George contested. "Congress will argue that bounties will be the first step to creating a standing professional army. It is not the republican idea of a citizen army they have envisioned."

"Your Excellency, recruiting numbers are disappointing," Nathanael pointed out. "I believe bounties would raise an army of seventy thousand. We have had only a few thousand men sign up for service beyond the New Year, and only a small number of those men are from my own colony. The troops who remain suffer prodigiously for want of wood, and many regiments are obliged to eat their provisions raw."

"The best arms, such as are fit for service, were detained from the soldiers who were going home, but it created much uneasiness in the very teeth of an enemy," William Heath added.

"I have no answer on how to achieve recruiting such a large number of troops," George admitted. "And now, King George III has declared America to be in a rebellious war carried for the purpose of establishing an independent Empire and pledges to send twenty thousand new troops to quash us. He proclaims he has received friendly offers of foreign assistance—German soldiers."

"We have no reason to doubt the King's intentions," Nathanael warned. "We must submit unconditionally, or defend ourselves. The calamities of war are very distressing, but slavery is dreadful. I have no reason to doubt the success of the colonies. We are now driven to the necessity of making a declaration of independence."

What George did not say was that he had already acted to strengthen the solidarity and resolve of his troops. On January 1, 1776, in general orders he announced, "It is the first day of a new army, which in every point of view is entirely continental. The importance of the great cause we are engaged in will be deeply impressed upon every man's mind. Everything dear and valuable to freemen is at stake."

To celebrate this event, he replaced the large red flag previously raised by General Israel Putnam on the heights of Prospect Hill. With the crash of a thirteen-gun salute, he raised a new flag of thirteen red and white stripes with the British colors and the crosses of St. George and St. Andrew represented in the canton.

Caty stood beside Nathanael on that cold January day and watched the ceremony. They were surrounded by soldiers, wives, and mistresses. The baby kicked, and she realized it was time for her to return home to be among her favorite doctors in East Greenwich when the babe arrived.

"I know I am leaving you to the miseries of this camp," Caty lamented to her husband. She stood beside her carriage and waited for the driver to load her trunk. "My heart shall remain here with you."

"Until I receive a letter that all is well with the child's arrival, I will not feel content or settled," Nathanael said.

She stroked his wind chapped cheeks. "I think you have much here to keep your worried mind occupied. Furthermore, I can hear you wheezing, which tells me that your asthma has flared, and you will get little sleep tonight."

"It has been better as of late without the smoke of the campfires to irritate it," Nathanael confessed. He helped Caty into their carriage.

The American soldiers in Canada had endured much worse circumstances; they had suffered a major defeat in Quebec. Colonel Benedict Arnold and his forces were repelled. Arnold was wounded and their commander, General Richard Montgomery, was killed. Nathanael's friend and Caty's cousin, Sammy Ward, Jr., as well as Nathanael's third cousin, Colonel Christopher Greene, were among the men who were captured.

Nathanael continued to enforce strict discipline among his well-armed and bored troops and spent his days with them. He issued orders to the 700 men, "Playing cards brings on a habit of drinking; and the habit of drinking leads to disputes and quarrels, disorder and confusion which disturbs the peace and tranquility of the camp and often proves fatal to individuals."

"General Greene, we have to have something to do during this perpetual siege," one of the Rhode Islanders grumbled.

"Be quiet, Harry," another man said. "The general will make us drill or clean our firelocks just for fun."

"I have my doubts," Harry said. "The general does not look well."

Nathanael said nothing because he knew his men were right. He was fatigued, and his stomach was always upset. It did not help that his asthma kept him awake at night as Caty had feared. Yet, his mind never faltered, and he continued to spend his evenings writing correspondence and letters to the glow of candlelight.

A messenger arrived at his headquarters on one of those nights with a letter. "For you from East Greenwich, General Greene," the young man said.

Nathanael ripped it open and read:

> *My darling, your son has been born healthy and I am well.*
> *I have named him George Washington Greene as I promised*
> *General Washington. I am in good care and anticipate seeing*
> *you so you can hold your son in your arms.*

Over the next several days, his joy turned to concern. One morning, he looked in the mirror and saw that his face and the whites of his eyes had turned yellow.

The plump Lieutenant William Blodget who was with the Rhode Island 11th Continental Regiment came to call on his old acquaintance. "My God, Nathanael, you look as if you are racked with ague."

"I feel worse," Nathanael conceded.

With great effort, he rode to Cambridge to speak with General Washington. When he arrived, a militia guard admitted him into the crowded, noisy Vassall House and led him to Washington's office.

"General Greene, to what do I owe this visit?" George asked, rising from his desk. His aide, Colonel Joseph Reed, who was writing correspondence, looked up from his task. Joseph saw from one glance that Nathanael was afflicted.

"I saw one of the regimental doctors, and he has determined I have jaundice. I am asking for permission to return home to recuperate," Nathanael implored.

"Indeed, you look terrible," George said. "I am not unfeeling, but I cannot afford to have you gone at this time. I am planning a war council to determine if we should attack Boston. General Howe appears to be complacent at this time, settled in for the winter as European customs of war demand, but by spring, he may have reinforcements."

"Yes, Your Excellency," Nathanael weakly conceded. It seemed fatigue would never leave him alone, but this was his duty. He went back to his headquarters on Prospect Hill and tried to rest. The never-ending stream of demands pressed upon him and exhausted his already racked body.

It became more than he could bear, and he wrote to his brother, Jacob. "I am as yellow as saffron, my appetite all gone, and my flesh too. I am so weak that I can scarcely walk across the room. I am grievously mortified at my confinement as this is the critical period of the American war. If Boston falls, I intend to be there if I am able to sit on horseback."

In late January, Henry Knox and his expedition arrived at Framingham, Massachusetts from Fort Ticonderoga with fifty-nine pieces of iron and brass cannon, mortars, and howitzers that collectively weighed nearly sixty tons. Henry went to Cambridge and was surprised with the news that he was now a colonel in the Continental Army in charge of the Artillery Regiment. John Adams and George Washington had seen to it while Henry's expedition was traversing the Hudson River and battling the slopes of the Berkshire Mountains in western Massachusetts. John Adams, a lawyer and politician, was returning to the Continental Congress after a holiday leave at his home in Braintree, Massachusetts. He passed through Framingham on his way to Philadelphia to inspect the cannon.

With Henry back from his successful mission and the artillery desperately needed by the Continental Army, the commander-in-chief was intent on attacking Boston and held a war council. Nathanael was unable to rise from his bed and attend, but he had previously made his feelings known: "An assault on a town garrisoned with regular troops could have horrible consequences. Horrible if it succeeds, and still more horrible if it fails."

General William Heath endorsed Nathanael's sentiment, "Even if we could get past the entrenchments surrounding the city, an attack would transform Boston's narrow streets into a bloody labyrinth of house-to-house fighting."

General Artemas Ward reiterated his long-standing opinion, "An attack must be made with a view of bringing the enemy out of Boston. That will be answered better by possessing Dorchester Heights."

"General Howe has promised to sally forth if we try to occupy Dorchester. We could be facing another Bunker Hill," Washington pointed out.

"I must agree with General Ward," General Horatio Gates interjected. "Our present army has neither the numbers nor the discipline to secure success in an assault on Boston. Our defeat may risk the entire loss of liberties of America forever."

It was agreed to build the fortifications on Dorchester Heights.

Caty received the news that Nathanael was ill weeks after the war council. On February 20, she packed her things, and with baby George set out for Prospect Hill. Undaunted by the sights and smells of an encampment filled with men, she was horrified to find her husband suffering terribly.

"My love, we are here and will stay as long as allowed," she said tenderly as she laid their infant son in Nathanael's weak arms.

He studied the baby's tiny face and then looked up into his wife's lovely countenance. "Just your presence encourages me to find my strength."

Days later, Nathanael was back on the field with his troops. He received orders from Washington to begin planning the defenses on Dorchester Heights with Generals Israel Putnam, Horatio Gates, and John Sullivan.

Caty attended gatherings at camp. At twenty-one, with a limited education and little experience in the ways of the world, she relaxed and indulged in her preference for the company of men or evenings spent playing cards, dancing, and drinking wine. The young aides fell smitten with her charm and beauty, the same qualities that had attracted Nathanael. She listened to their stories with honesty and participated in pleasantries.

When Henry Knox met her at a dinner party held by the Washingtons, he frowned and exchanged glances with his often-gloomy pregnant wife, Lucy. "I do not know what to make of her light-heartedness," Henry whispered. "Her behavior appears superficial."

"The ladies in camp have noticed that General Greene never attends church when Mrs. Greene is here," Lucy added.

Caty's eyes moved to the Knoxes. She felt no fondness for them and their reaction to her. She gave her heart to no one unless they earned it, and the Knoxes had yet to do so.

Along with the gatherings, preparations were made to occupy Dorchester Heights, southeast of Boston. Twin hills comprised the heights of the Dorchester peninsula. The distance from those summits to the nearest British lines at Boston Neck was a mile and a half, within range of 12- or 18-pound cannon. The operation would be as challenging as the military engagement. The plan was to occupy the Heights on a single night before the British knew what was happening as they had done at Bunker Hill.

On the night of March 2, huge guns began thundering from the American works on Cobble Hill, Lechmere's Point in Cambridge, and Prospect Hill. The Greene house shook, and the windows rattled as the British returned fire. Caty was home alone with little George. Nathanael was in Cambridge where he was preparing flat-bottomed bateaux in anticipation of a probable amphibious British assault. If that happened, his division was to land south of Barton's Point and secure Copp's Hill and then join General John Sullivan of New Hampshire to force the works at the Neck.

Caty remained awake all night, watching over her infant son who slept through the commotion. Late in the night, a huge explosion from a shell rocked the house and woke the baby. To Caty's relief, he did not cry. An hour later, she received an anxious message of concern from Martha Washington in Cambridge, who had heard the noise.

The firing continued on the night of March 4. The incessant roar of cannon and mortars continued from both sides while the provincials toiled steadily with picks and shovels, breaking the frozen ground for earth and stone to fill chandeliers and barrels. At sunrise, the British were shocked to see two redoubts atop the hills of Dorchester Heights—one facing east toward Castle Island and the other facing north toward Boston—with two smaller works on their flanks.

British General William Howe exclaimed, "My God, these fellows have done more work in one night than my whole army would do in three months!"

Howe ordered an assault on Dorchester Heights, but a storm drove the transports away from the shore. The following day, he called a staff meeting where it was decided that the army must abandon the city because their warships in the harbor were in range of the cannon on Dorchester Heights.

On March 17, the British fleet weighed anchor and left Boston Harbor, taking with them the British Army and thousands of Loyalist refugees. The fleet fell down to Nantucket Roads and sat rocking on the waves for ten days until they weighed anchor and put to sea. Washington gave his word that they could leave unmolested if they did not burn the city as Howe had threatened.

On March 24, George issued orders of the day: "General Greene will dispose of the regiments in Boston to the best advantage. The wagon-master and companies of Boston are to receive and obey all such orders and directions as Brigadier General Greene shall think proper to give."

Nathanael rode into the city on horseback at the head of his Rhode Island brigade. He sent for Caty two days later.

"My God, Nathanael," Caty said as she surveyed the city that looked nothing like she remembered. "Look at the people. They are casualties of starvation and smallpox. They stare at us with hollow eyes."

Nathanael pointed at the sad parade of civilians who moved along Orange Street with creaking wagons. "It appears that some are coming back into the city," he observed.

"Boston has been decimated," she said. "Windows are shattered. Buildings are pulled down, trees and gardens are destroyed. Boston Common is scarred with trenches. Surely you will curtail our soldiers' looting what little is left."

"I have lectured the troops and told them that if any should be base enough to commit any acts of plunder and attempt to conceal the effects, then their messmates will be considered an accessary to the crime and will be punished accordingly."

"I believe now I better understand your need to discipline the unruly," she said.

"Not everything has to be so morose," Nathanael replied with an impish grin. "Because the baby is with a nurse, we are free to accept dinner invitations extended to us. Mr. John Rowe has invited us to a victory supper. General Washington is holding a celebration at the Bunch of Grapes tavern for his generals."

Caty beamed. "You know that I look forward to them."

George Washington greeted Caty with a bow when she and Nathanael entered the Bunch of Grapes. "Mrs. Greene, I am pleased you could join us."

"General, please, it is Caty."

He led her to a seat beside him at the table. She exchanged kisses on the cheek with Martha before sitting down. Elizabeth Gates, wife of General Horatio Gates, cast Caty a disapproving glare, which Caty ignored.

"The officers look so handsome in their dress uniforms," Caty told Martha.

Nathanael tossed his wife an approving glance as the dinner commenced, the wine flowed, and tongues loosened. Caty listened with rapt attention as General Israel Putnam, a fifty-five-year-old veteran of Bunker Hill, told stories about his adventures over the years. "I was once the only survivor of a shipwreck off Cuba and floated to land on a piece of debris," the short, stocky general said with laughter.

Lieutenant Tench Tilghman, an aide to Washington, placed his elbow on the table and propped his chin in his hand. His adoring eyes never left Caty's countenance.

A pamphlet titled *Common Sense* dominated much of the conversation. Written by Thomas Paine and first published in Philadelphia in January 1776, it was a scathing polemic against the injustice of rule by a king. Paine eloquently argued that Americans have "…every opportunity and every encouragement before us, to form the noblest purest constitution on the face of the earth. We have it in our power to begin the world over again." His message resonated as a Patriot conviction.

During dinner, a message arrived for George. There was more to celebrate. "The British fleet has finally set sail for open sea," was announced to those gathered.

The question still remained in many minds: *Where are they heading?*

George Washington and British General William Howe, as well as members of the Continental Congress, believed that New York City was the key to the continent and the Hudson River was the highway.

New York had to be the answer.

four

This Anxious Time

On April 1, the Continental Army marched south toward New York. On April 4, they arrived in Providence, Rhode Island—Nathanael's home state. He issued orders to his brigade, "Everyone will dress well and be washed with their hair combed and powdered and their arms cleaned in order to salute our commander-in-chief as he passes."

Caty proudly watched her husband ride beside General Washington as the citizens of Providence cheered the troops and their officers. When the army moved through the city, Nathanael broke ranks and guided his horse toward his wife's carriage. "My angel, I have permission to escort you and my son home to Coventry," he said gallantly.

Just one more night, she thought. *Just one more night to hold him in my arms and listen to his gentle wheezing as he sleeps. Then, he will be gone.*

The next morning, Nathanael kissed his wife and baby goodbye. "I will write to you as soon as we arrive in New York," he promised. He turned to Jacob and said, "I depend you will take care of my little family."

"Stay safe if that is possible in the face of the enemy," Jacob urged his younger brother.

"I can make no promises," Nathanael said.

He took a last look at Spell Hall and mounted his horse for New London, Connecticut, where his brigade was boarding troopships bound for Long Island, New York. A winter storm blew in that separated the transports. In good weather, the journey to Long Island would take a day. Nathanael's boat did not arrive until April 17.

George Washington had arrived in New York on April 13. The geography was nothing like he expected. New York Island was a long tongue of land indefensible by an army of Washington's size. Two important rivers bordered the island. The East River, with its flat, sloping shore, led to New England. The Hudson River, bordered by palisades on the opposite shore in New Jersey, was accessible to ocean going vessels from the north. Here, with their overwhelming naval might, William Howe could strike at will and from almost any direction. The enemy could sail down the Hudson and sever New England from the rest of the colonies. No British sails appeared, but there was no doubt that they would come. The rebel army had much to do to prepare for the event.

Discipline and dress among the New England troops had hardly improved, made worse by the number of new, raw recruits. An army of Yankees was now an army that included battalions from New Jersey, Pennsylvania, Maryland, and Delaware. Many felt a superiority to the New Englanders, remarking that they did not come up to the ideas formed of the heroes of Bunker Hill.

When Nathanael arrived, a broader field opened before him with a wider range of duties and a greater weight of responsibility. Washington assigned him command of a string of forts laid out earlier in the year by General Charles Lee at Brooklyn Heights on Long Island with the East River in the rear. His line of fortifications stretched from Wallabout Bay to the north and Gowanus Pass to the south. With Generals John Sullivan and Lord Alexander Stirling, he developed an alarm system. It would signal when the sails of British ships were first sighted on the horizon; it consisted of a series of flags, depending on the number of ships spotted. Washington, who was headquartered at Kennedy House in the city, reinforced Nathanael's Rhode Island regiments with two other regiments that included rowdy Pennsylvania riflemen.

Long Island was rich in farming, and many of the hamlets and villages were owned and inhabited by the Dutch. The majority of the residents were Loyalists. Nathanael's army was an unwelcome intrusion, and citizens destroyed crops and lay the land to waste, thus preventing them from providing aid to the rebels.

It was no surprise to Nathanael that his new command required much more than supervising the construction of trenches and fortifications. He still had his men to care for, and it occupied much of his time. One afternoon, while he was writing a letter to John Adams, Lieutenant William Blodget entered Nathanael's headquarters at Fort Greene.

"My apologies for the interruptions," William said.

"Nathanael looked up from his task. "What is it, Billy?"

"Colonel Olney sent me to tell you that we took delivery of the straw, wood, spears, and the grindstones you asked the quartermaster to provide," William said, stifling a grin.

Nathanael raised an eyebrow. "But…there is something else."

"Colonel Olney said you might want to know that some of the troops are straying to the Holy Ground brothel across the river in the city." William bit his lip to keep from laughing. "Also, we have had complaints from civilians that your men are often spotted swimming nude in a nearby pond."

Nathanael's eyes dropped to the letter on his desk. He ran his ink-stained fingers across his mouth, which did nothing to contain a snicker. Finally he rose and said, "Thank you."

William left the room in a cloud of laughter.

Nathanael had Colonel Jeremiah Olney gather the troops.

"We talked about behaving yourselves around the local inhabitants," Nathanael began as he paced in front of the lines. "You were to stop ruining their meadow grounds foraging for greens, and those complaints have diminished."

The men shifted as Nathanael paused to assuage his somewhat amused, flippant anger. "I realize that many of them are Loyalists, therefore, their complaints may be frivolous. However, complaints have been made by the inhabitants near the mill pond that some of the soldiers come there to swim in open view of the women. And, that they come out of the water and run up naked to the houses with a design to insult and wound the modesty of female decency. 'Tis with concern that I find myself under the disagreeable necessity of expressing my disapprobation of such a beastly conduct. Have the troops come abroad for no other purpose than to render themselves both obnoxious and ridiculous?

"Do not forget to avoid bad habits; that when you give the day's password to sentries, do it softly, as if the enemy is encamped in this neighborhood. Dismissed."

The soldiers dispersed among murmuring, but no one dared laugh within hearing distance of their general. Nathanael returned to his quarters to finish his correspondence to John Adams. He shared his concerns about engaging people in the service and filling the ranks, which was more difficult than talking about it in committees.

He worried about the soldiers' inefficiency of pay. "I could wish the Congress to think seriously of the matter. I am asking that you establish a support for those that get disabled in the army or militia. Is it not inhuman to suffer those that have fought nobly in the cause to be reduced to the necessity of getting support by common Charity?"

This was the first of a long correspondence between two headstrong men, which represented often-clashing interests—the military versus the political wings of the revolution and Nathanael's persistent requests to Congress. The young general was learning the value of caring for his men and his country, even if he did indeed defend his rights and maintain his freedom or sell his life in the attempt.

The boredom and Greene familial control Caty experienced in Coventry and Potowomut before her son was born took a turn for the worse after she came home from Prospect Hill. The strict Quaker households forbid even card playing, and she was constantly reminded of her lack of religious views and female improprieties.

"Your ways are not our ways," Sarah Greene, the wife of Nathanael's cousin Griffin, haughtily reminded Caty when she was in Potowomut.

Caty bit her tongue to avoid more confrontation. She endured the disapproving looks Sarah favored her with that reminded her of the sour countenances of the other women in the Continental Army camp, except Martha Washington, who treated her with respect.

She tearfully wrote to Nathanael. He wrote back with instructions:

> *Invite Sarah to the house in Coventry and make an attempt to mend things. That is all I ask.*

Sarah refused Caty's attempt. Then, her Aunt Catharine in East Greenwich got wind of the gossip and building reputation that her niece was a selfish, irresponsible woman who coquetted with little regard for her husband's wishes.

With no one to turn to, Caty wrote to Nathanael again, "Aunt Catharine is becoming hostile toward me. For what purpose I do not understand. She even went to my father and complained of my behavior."

Nathanael wrote to his younger brother, Christopher, who the family called Kitt, in an effort to encourage reconciliation. His letter went unheeded. Out of frustration, Nathanael wrote to Aunt Catharine. "I appreciate your earlier endeavors to educate Caty, but I see no excuse for exposing her faults to family and friends instead of trying to correct them. I have told Caty that she need not go more than half way to repair your relationship."

It was all Nathanael could do from afar to help his wife. He had his own conflict to resolve. He desired a promotion to major general. With irritation, he wrote John Adams arguing that General Washington should control promotions, not Congress as they had no insight, which could result in sometimes unjust decisions based on a single act of bravery.

John replied that giving Washington that power could be more dangerous.

Exasperated, Nathanael crossed to Manhattan and rode the mile and a half north to Richmond Hill where the Washingtons had set up residence. The beautiful mansion stood on an eminence with a view of the Hudson River; it was large enough to house the members of his Excellency's personal staff and aides.

When Nathanael was seated in his office, George said, "I assume all is well maintaining the fortifications at Brooklyn Heights."

"All is well," Nathanael confirmed.

George considered his youngest brigadier general. Nearly a year had passed since the two met and began forming a working relationship—a less formal one as well. He wanted to believe that he and Nathanael understood one another. He ventured into the territory he knew Nathanael had really come about. "You have been lobbying for a promotion," George said as he accepted a glass of Madeira from a servant.

Nathanael reached for his offered glass.

George sipped his beverage and then said, "Your campaign has been neither subtle nor adulating to those who have been the target."

"I have been exceedingly happy under your command, but this is a matter of my own esteem. As I have no desire of quitting the service, I hope the Congress will take no measures that lay me under the disagreeable necessity of doing it," Nathanael said without humility.

"You are threatening to quit if you do not find satisfaction," George stated. He leaned forward over his desk. "As I told you when we met, I see in you some of the same things I see in myself."

"Some of those things are not what you believe them to be."

George leaned back in his chair. "I see much more than you know, Nathanael. I see you believe there is insult where there is none. All men carry insecurities. Yours perhaps are more warranted than others, but I do not stand judgement over any man who finds the strength to overcome, even if the method requires some refinement."

Nathanael drained his glass, rose, and bowed. As he left the office, George said, "I think you will not be disappointed when Congress announces the names of the new major generals in August. Perhaps you should consider candidates for aides."

❧

When Nathanael returned to his headquarters at Fort Greene on Brooklyn Heights, there was a message for him that read: *Mrs. Greene is at Kennedy House in the city.* Nathanael crossed the East River from the Brooklyn Ferry again and landed at one of the slips along the harbor front. Kennedy House was not only Washington's main headquarters; it was Henry Knox's headquarters, as well.

Lucy Knox was in residence with her husband and their baby daughter when Caty arrived. "We have sent for General Greene," Lucy said as she shifted her babe in her ample arms. "Where is your son?"

"I left him with Nathanael's brother Jacob and his wife at home in Coventry. I thought he would be safer there."

Lucy pressed her lips together. *I cannot imagine leaving little Lucy with relatives,* she thought. *But then again, mine have deserted me completely.*

The ladies heard the front door open and then shut. Henry's booming voice announced that Nathanael was there. Strained from everything she had been through in the past few weeks, Caty ran into the loving protection of her husband's arms. He kissed her on the tip of her pert nose and asked, "Why have you come here now when the British fleet is known to be in Halifax, Nova Scotia and are expected to sail for New York at any time?"

"Are you not happy to see me?" Caty asked.

"My angel, I am always happy to see you, but my need to protect you will divert my attentions during this anxious time."

Already, the stinging gossip about her behavior drained away. "I believe I can change your mind," she inveigled, running a finger over his sensuous bottom lip.

Lucy and Henry excused themselves to allow Mr. and Mrs. Greene to enjoy one another without censure as they would have wished for themselves. Like Nathanael, Henry worried over the safety of his wife and child not only from the threat of a British armada, but also from smallpox that was infecting the Continental Army.

~

Earlier in June, at the behest of General Washington, Henry and Nathanael had traveled to the northern tip of Manhattan to scout the terrain and plan fortifications overlooking the Hudson River. General Israel Putnam wanted to build a fort at King's Bridge to safeguard a possible retreat route. Henry and Nathanael disagreed and thought any defenses would be ineffectual unless a fort was built on Mount Washington. His Excellency agreed.

Troops built Fort Washington on the eastern shore of the Hudson River in New York. Fort Lee was under construction on the palisades on the New Jersey side of the river. The dual forts were to be stationed like sirens meant to entrap unsuspecting sailors who dared to venture down the Hudson. Between the two forts ran a line of sunken obstructions to prevent British ships from passing.

Lucy and Caty often visited Mrs. Washington at Richmond Hill for midday meals at which the other generals' wives renewed their acquaintance with them. They strolled the barricaded streets of Manhattan, where the waterfront was lined with batteries armed with artillery and redoubts.

After a wonderful day in the city, Caty returned to Brooklyn Heights to be with Nathanael at Fort Greene. She took a flat-bottomed ferry equipped with sails and oars that took two hours to cross the tricky currents of the East River. Her anxiety flared during the voyage. Water travel always made her nervous.

On June 27, a dispatch arrived for Caty from Coventry from Jacob Greene:

> *Little George is sick. Peggy and I ask that you return home without delay.*

She burst into Nathanael's office regardless of the many lower ranking officers coming and going with constant requests for their general. "I must return home. Our son is ill. Please find passage for me on the first ship back to Rhode Island."

Nathanael came around his desk and extracted the letter from his wife's hand. "It does not say what ails him."

"All the more reason for my haste."

An officer arrived and said urgently, "General Greene, His Excellency requests your attendance at the hanging of his Life Guard, Sergeant Thomas Hickey, tomorrow in the city."

"Who?" Caty asked.

"The man who plotted with New York Governor William Tyron and Mayor David Matthews to assassinate him," the officer said.

Caty's eyes widen. "Life Guard?"

"Yes, His Excellency has personal guards. You have seen them. They are always near him. Sergeant Hickey was one of many who were arrested for conspiracy, but only Hickey was convicted. It is a shame. He was one of Washington's favorites—" the officer said.

Nathanael interrupted, "Assure His Excellency I shall be there. Dismissed."

The officer saluted and left.

"Nathanael, please. I need to go home," Caty implored.

"It is time you go, anyway. General Washington sent his wife home to Mount Vernon this morning because of the certainty of a British invasion. If that happens, I will not be able to attend you."

Two days later, on June 29, 1776, the first ships of the British Royal Navy arrived under the command of Admiral Lord Richard Howe, General William Howe's older brother. It was William's advanced guard of his invasion force. Henry and Lucy were eating breakfast in Kennedy House when the ships marred the panoramic view of the open blue-green waters of lower New York Harbor.

Henry rose from the table and knocked it askew with one chubby thigh. "I should have insisted you leave when Lady Washington left," he said to Lucy.

She stood next to him and looked across the harbor and asked, "How will we get back home, now?"

"The Boston Post Road is still open. Get packed. The great being who watches the hearts of the children of men knows I value you above every blessing, and for that reason I want you and little Lucy to safety immediately."

❧

Regardless of the alarm, on July 6, 1776, John Hancock sent a letter to General Washington with the complete text of the newly adopted Declaration of Independence. The letter read:

> *That our affairs may take a more favorable turn, the Congress have judged it necessary to dissolve the connection between Great Britain and the American colonies, and to declare them free and independent states.*

The thousands of Loyalists in the city were powerless to stem the tide of elation that began on the Commons after the reading of the Declaration of Independence on July 9. American brigades marched on the parade grounds. Taverns filled with revelers. Patriot families picnicked and rejoiced. A mob marched down Broadway to Bowling Green where the gilded lead statue of King George III atop his colossal horse was perched. The immense crowd threw ropes over the statue's head and pulled it down in a cacophony of celebration. The head came off, and they carried the body through town to the sound of fife and drums.

Admiral Richard Howe's fleet continued to arrive in astounding numbers and strength, the likes of which the Americans had never seen. The *Victory* mounted ninety-eight guns, dwarfing Admiral Howe's flagship, *Eagle*. Their force grew to nearly 32,000 men, which included hired German soldiers called Hessians. They set up camp on Staten Island to await orders.

From his defenses on Brooklyn Heights, Nathanael worried that many of his men were too sick to oppose the vast force across the harbor. He ordered the commissaries to serve more vegetables and fruit and issued another order regarding hygiene. The men were to use soap and use and clean the latrines instead of using the ditches, a practice Nathanael found disgraceful.

General William Heath arrived from the fortification he commanded at King's Bridge fifteen miles north of Brooklyn Heights. "There are thousands of soldiers sick in the city," William said when Nathanael lamented the condition of his men.

Relieved to have someone to voice his concerns to besides writing to John Adams who was a hundred miles away in Philadelphia, Nathanael confessed, "I have endeavored to enforce healthy habits in my troops, yet we still face sickness."

William looked around. "It is not your fault. In almost every farm, stable, shed, and even under the fences and bushes the sick are to be seen."

"My worries extend beyond that. I wish I had been given more time to discipline my men before they face the inevitable British onslaught. I fear my defense will merely be made a mockery of. I have done no battle, only heard the screams of the dying during the destructive days of the siege."

"The scenes of battle are a horrible sight to be sure," William said, reflecting on the massacre the rebel militia he commanded inflicted on the British during their desperate retreat to Boston on April 19, 1775.

"What falls to my lot, I shall endeavor to execute to the best to my ability," Nathanael vowed. "Tell me, does the burden of administrative work fall heavily upon you, William? They pile upon my desk and interfere with other work. I have no aide to help me."

"It is the duty of a general to sign passes, dictate orders, and preside over court-martials, among the many responsibilities."

Nathanael shamefully admitted, "It is impossible for me to attend to the duties of the day. The science or art of war requires a freedom of thought and leisure to reflect upon the various incidents that daily occur. That cannot be had where the whole of one's time is engrossed in clerical employments."

"I believe you should convey your sentiments to His Excellency," William advised. "He sees that you are competent and an earnest leader of men—self-taught, as many of us are. Now, I need to return to my own men before the British decide to attack and I am caught off my duty."

Nathanael took William Heath's advice and penned a complaint to Washington. While he waited for Washington's response, Nathanael rode to The Narrows and spotted thirty-six new ships with troops on board.

ஒ

General Henry Clinton, his subordinate General Charles Cornwallis, and Admiral Peter Parker arrived from South Carolina with a fleet of nine battered warships and thirty-five transports, further filling The Narrows. General Charles Lee prevented Parker's fleet from entering the harbor at Charleston, South Carolina. The battle raged from a militia fortification constructed from palmetto logs on Sullivan's Island off the coast and ended in a British defeat.

The enemy, still encamped on Staten Island, had not made a move except to sail up the Hudson River or shake their sails out in the sun to dry after days of fog that screened the view of British activity. The American's quandary over where the British would strike grew daily. Nathanael worried to the point of posting sentries on night patrol near his headquarters. He executed the late resolve of Congress and ordered cattle removed, mills dismantled, and threshed grain removed to avoid benefiting the enemy if they landed. He wrote to John Adams, "I confess my fears that the strengthening enemy is more than my troops can defend against."

Then, a letter from Caty uplifted his downtrodden spirits. She was pregnant again. It occurred to him that he might die seeing the end of a British bayonet, leaving Caty, his infant son, and the unborn child without husband or father.

On August 14, William Blodget arrived with a dispatch from Congress. Nathanael almost dreaded opening it. His face brightened when he broke the seal and unfolded the letter.

"Billy, I have been promoted to major general," Nathanael burst out. "Do you know what this means? I am entitled to appoint aides." He looked up from the correspondence and said, "I want you to be one of them. It brings a promotion to major."

William bowed deeply. "I am honored and at your service."

Nathanael also chose forty-three-year-old Ezekiel Cornell, known for his dependability to keep discipline, and Major William Livingston. At last, Nathanael would have some assistance with all the mundane duties of his position.

During that hot summer, his men and hundreds of other American soldiers came down with "putrid fever," despite Nathanael's efforts to prevent it. The army was ill-prepared to care for so many sick soldiers. He wrote to Washington, "Great humanity should be exercised towards those indisposed. Kindness on one hand leaves a favorable and lasting impression; neglect and suffering on the other is never forgotten."

On August 17, Major William Livingston came to report to his general there was no evidence of an immediate attack and found him in bed with a raging fever and barely able to sit up. "General, you must see a doctor. Have you told His Excellency that you are ill?"

"Yes."

Livingston and Blodget exchanged skeptical glances. They vigilantly remained with their general all night. Nathanael tossed and turned with fever. It alarmed Livingston, and he sent off a message to Washington:

> *Your Excellency, General Greene has had very bad night of it and cannot be said to be any better this morning than he was yesterday.*

Nathanael resisted his illness like an unwanted suitor. The critical situation of affairs made him more anxious. William Blodget attempted to help him put a better light on his condition by informing Washington:

> *The General desires me to acquaint your Excellency that he finds himself considerably better this morning; and is in hopes in a few days, to be able to go abroad, though still very weak.*

When Nathanael began to fall in and out of consciousness, his aides sent for Dr. John Morgan, the director general of hospitals.

"Dr. Morgan treated your jaundice when you were at Prospect Hill; he knows you. Do you want me to inform your wife?" Livingston prodded as he wiped sweat from Nathanael's brow.

"No, she is with child, and I cannot have her here with the enemy across the harbor and disease lurking in camp. Please write to my brother Kitt in Potowomut."

Dr. Morgan arrived and examined Nathanael, whose usually fair complexion was ruddy. "Your fever is dangerously high, General. How is your appetite?"

"I have none, and my head is throbbing."

"Is your asthma troubling you?" he asked as he untied Nathanael's constricting cravat.

"No."

"I suggest you alert a family member as your condition is dangerous," Morgan said.

"Major Livingston has written to one of my younger brothers."

"I insist that you are removed from Long Island to a healthy air house in Manhattan," Dr. Morgan said. "There is a doctor's house near Broadway."

Nathanael did not have the strength to argue. He was taken to the ferry and endured the long rough crossing of the East River.

On August 20, George Washington came to his bedside. He acknowledged Nathanael's brother, Kitt, with a silent bow. "Nathanael?" George asked, addressing his young general lying motionless and exhausted with his eyes half-closed.

"My brother is falling in and out of delirium, and it is frightening," Kitt said. "He can only sit up for an hour at a time when he is lucid."

Kitt and Nathanael's attending aides noted that Washington addressed Nathanael by his given name. He had to be not only concerned for his general's life, but for the impending crisis that was heightening across the harbor four miles away.

"Nathanael, please speak to me," George implored.

A dry rasping cough gripped Nathanael when he tried to speak. At that crucial moment, George knew that he was suddenly and indefinitely deprived of his trusted commander who was most familiar with the essential Brooklyn Heights defenses and the intricacies of the surrounding terrain. He began to feel a sense of foreboding.

five

I Would Burn the City

Washington was forced to fill Nathanael's command until he recovered. First, he chose General John Sullivan of New Hampshire, but after walking the ground with him, George felt that John was not prepared for what he was taking on. Instead, he assigned General Israel Putnam.

On Thursday morning, August 22, 1776, the British frigates *Phoenix, Rose,* and *Greyhound,* backdropped by the green hills and meadows of Staten Island, weighed anchor and fell down The Narrows accompanied by two bomb ketches, *Carcass* and *Thunder.* British Generals Henry Clinton and Charles Cornwallis with an advance corps of 4,000 of the King's elite troops pushed off in flatboats and proceeded across the three miles of water to the long beach at Gravesend Bay on the southwest tip of Long Island.

Warships pointed their cannon at the beach. By eight in the morning, the whole coast swarmed with boats. By noon, 15,000 troops with forty artillery pieces had landed ready to attack the fortifications on Brooklyn Heights. Another 5,000 Hessians and along with General William Howe landed two days later. The British encamped at Flatbush to discuss strategy and get the lay of the land while Washington sent an additional 5,000 troops to support the 4,000 already stationed at Nathanael's fortifications.

On August 26, at 9:00 p.m., British General James Grant led 5,000 redcoats and Hessians north along The Narrows Road toward the Red Lion Inn with colors flying and field artillery out front. They flanked the Americans' defense in a pincher movement in a bloody rout.

In the house on Manhattan, Nathanael and Kitt heard the guns roaring on Long Island. Kitt brought reports from the field to his anxious brother, "The details are sparse," Nathanael bemoaned. The smoke and thunderous noise that drifted across the harbor told the story.

The following morning at 9:00 a.m., William Howe fired two cannons, announcing his arrival in the village of Bedford north of Jamaica Pass. General Israel Putnam had neglected to station forces at the pass—a ridge that ran across Long Island from Brooklyn to the Sound, thereby affording Howe the opportunity. By nightfall, Howe's army had crushed Washington's forward defense. He ordered his men to halt instead of storming the American fortifications on Brooklyn Heights.

Kitt provided his feverish brother with more tidings from the field. This time, there was more agonizing news.

> *Major Mordecai Gist's Marylanders were flanked and anni-*
> *hilated trying to cover the Patriot retreat near Red Lion Inn.*
> *Generals John Sullivan and Lord Alexander Stirling have*
> *been taken prisoner. There are still American troops trapped*
> *on Long Island.*

Nathanael read with tears streaming down his cheeks.

Early in the morning of August 30, word came that the army was over the river and relatively safe in Manhattan. The forts Nathanael had toiled to make impregnable were lost, but 9,000 troops and their equipage were saved. For the first time in weeks, Kitt heard exultation in his brother's voice.

"It is the best effected retreat I ever read of or heard of considering the difficulties."

I Would Burn the City

❧

Kitt Greene left for home carrying a letter from Nathanael to Jacob and Caty.

> *Gracious God! To be confined at such a time. And the misfortune is doubly great as there was no general officer who had made himself as acquainted with the ground as perfectly as I had. I have not the vanity to think the event would have been otherwise had I been there, yet I think I could have given the commanding general a good deal of necessary information.*

Nathanael did know the ground perfectly. With the loss of the fortifications on Long Island, the defense of New York City was untenable. The Americans could not challenge the might of the Royal Navy. Washington was intent on defending the city. Nathanael thought otherwise.

On September 5, from his sick bed, he wrote unsolicited advice to the commander-in-chief. "The critical situation which the army is in will, I hope, sufficiently apologize for my troubling your Excellency with this letter. The object of consideration is a general retreat or no. To me, it seems the only eligible plan to oppose the enemy successfully and secure ourselves from disgrace. Two-thirds of the property of the city of New York and the suburbs belongs to the Tories. I would burn the city to prevent the enemy from taking possession. I give it my opinion that a general and speedy retreat is absolutely necessary. I would advise to call a general council on that question."

To Nathanael's surprise, George agreed that the city should be burned, but Congress wanted no damage done to New York. On September 7, Washington called a war council. Nathanael was present.

The commander-in-chief reconfigured the army into three divisions. He spread his ragtag force thinly along the fourteen and one-half miles of Manhattan's eastern shore—from the Battery at the southern tip of Manhattan northward to King's Bridge.

"I support a retreat," Nathanael reiterated to the council composed of generals with more seniority. "But dividing the army seems like folly. Our troops are so scattered that one part may be cut off before the others can come to their support."

He could not leave the matter alone. His insistence that the army evacuate all of New York Island bordered on insolence. Nathanael passionately pressed Washington to reconvene the war council and drew up a petition that stated:

> *The Situation of the Army under your Excellency's command is, in our Opinion so critical and dangerous that we apprehend a Board of General Officers should be immediately called for the purpose to consider it.*

Although Nathanael was the only major general to sign the petition, another war council was held at General Alexander McDougall's headquarters. The army's youngest major general proved his acumen, and it was voted to completely evacuate New York. They immediately began to move the whole army up to Harlem Heights. The horses and wagons, loaded with sick and wounded soldiers, tons of supplies, and ammunition and artillery were moved from the city—a colossal undertaking. Colonel Henry Knox and his artillery regiments were to assist General Israel Putnam's 5,000 troops in guarding the city and its neighboring areas.

In the meantime, General William Howe and his brother, Admiral Lord Richard Howe, prepared for the invasion of Manhattan. Howe spread his troops from Hell Gate to Red Hook on Long Island along the shore opposite Manhattan. He did nothing to cross the East River and pursue the Americans.

On the night of September 3, the first British ship, the frigate *Rose*, towing thirty flatboats, started up the East River with a north-flowing tide. The *Rose* reached the mouth of Newton Creek, directly across from a large cove on the New York side known as Kip's Bay. In the following days, transports and flatboats moved up the East River.

William Howe and Henry Clinton did not see eye to eye on the landing. Clinton thought the Harlem River and King's Bridge was the key to victory. He told Howe, "York Island is a bottle and Harlem Heights is the neck. Close it off and Washington and his rebel army will be trapped. Throw the troops onshore at Morrisania, which is across the river from the tongue of York Island. Then move forward directly to King's Bridge."

Forty-three-year-old William Howe often scorned his somewhat younger second-in-command's advice. He had come to resent Henry's constant pestering, although he took Henry's advice to flank the American Army on Long Island.

William grumbled that there was no need to land troops at Morrisania. It would only serve to complicate matters as they tried to cross Hell Gate with its treacherous currents at the confluence of the East River and the Harlem River. He proclaimed, "We are invading York Island tomorrow at Kip's Bay. I shall rally the troops with a bayonet assault, and then we can get on with this ridiculous affair and go home."

As the army retreated north toward Harlem Heights, a Connecticut brigade was positioned below at Kip's Bay. A third of them were sick, only half of those left were fit for duty—many of them were farm boys who had just joined the army. Among those manning the trenches was a teenaged boy named Joseph Plumb Martin and his messmates. At dawn on September 15, four British ships pointed more than eighty cannon at the Connecticut regiments and let loose a fury that was impossible to conceive. It was a roar so terrible and incessant that few even in the British Army and Navy had heard it before. The Americans in the trenches, many of them militiamen, ran for their lives.

At Morris House south of Fort Washington on the summit of Harlem Heights, Washington and his staff heard the harrowing bombardment. They saddled up and galloped south down the post road. They reined up at a cornfield about a mile inland from Kip's Bay. Men were scurrying in every direction.

George plunged his horse in among the men and tried to stop them. "Damn it," he cursed and drew his sword. "I will run through each and every one of you if you do not stop and take the cornfield." When no one obeyed, he threw his hat on the ground and bellowed, "Are these the men with which I am to defend America?"

Nathanael witnessed the scene. He had never seen Washington that angry. He informed the governor of Rhode Island, "We made a miserable and disorderly retreat from New York, owing to the disorderly conduct of the Militia who ran at the appearance of the Enemies advance Guard. Whole Brigades ran away from about fifty men and left his Excellency on the Ground within Eight yards of the Enemy, so vexed at the infamous conduct of the troops that he sought death rather than life."

General William Howe halted his northward advance that day without assaulting Harlem Heights. More than 9,000 thousand additional British troops landed at Kip's Bay and marched south unopposed toward Manhattan.

"I think it is time I get the rest of our men out of the city," General Israel Putnam advised Washington.

≈

By the morning of September 16, Israel Putnam and Henry Knox successfully retreated from Manhattan with little loss of men. However, most of their heavy cannon and part of their stores and provisions were unavoidably left in the city. The whole of the Continental Army regrouped at Harlem Heights. On that hot September day as General William Howe marched into the city, a party of 300 British light infantry marched on the Heights.

Nathanael and his 3,500-man division were posted on the rocky southern slopes of Harlem Heights, but even his pickets out in front could not see the British encampment. It was across a valley called Hollow Way and concealed by the dense growth of trees. Then gunfire signaled a skirmish nearby. Washington summoned Connecticut Colonel Thomas Knowlton to distract from a British encircling movement. Thomas quickly formed a scouting party of 150 rangers. They moved south. An hour later, they hit the advanced British pickets in the woods of the high-lands at Hollow Way.

The British mobilized and charged Knowlton's Rangers, whose men unleashed rounds into the enemy. The enemy returned fire. Smoke and powder instantly choked the early morning air, making it difficult to see what was happening in the gloom of the gray shroud.

The enemy appeared in open view. A bugle horn sounded in the most insulting manner as if someone were concluding a fox hunt. The Rangers fired at the approaching British infantry. If the frontal attack continued, they would soon be overrun. Washington appeared with his aide, Colonel Joseph Reed, followed by Nathanael and Israel with their brigades.

"Perform a counterattack across the Hollow Way," Washington ordered Knowlton. "I want you to move to the left and encircle them. That way, they will be entrapped in Hollow Way. Generals Greene and Putnam will lead the main attack. I have also sent three companies of Virginians on the encircling move."

Suddenly, a skirmish turned into a full-fledged battle with thou-sands of troops engaged. This was Nathanael's first battle. He coughed and wheezed in the smoke-choked air, but the horror of seeing young men die and hearing the screams of the bloodied and mangled wounded drowned out his own discomfort. Among the pleas for mercy, he turned in his saddle and witnessed the tall, elegant looking thirty-one-year-old Colonel Thomas Knowlton take a shot to the head.

The British fell back with the Americans in pursuit, but they were dangerously close to the British main camp. The rebels stopped the advance to avoid a general engagement. The fog and heat of war washed over Nathanael like a tidal wave of fear and understanding.

The loss of New York City was a blow to American hopes. On September 21, the city erupted in flames that some accused the rebels of igniting. The fire began shortly after midnight on the southern tip of the city. Fanned by strong winds which drove the flames northward up the city's west side, heavy smoke choked the air littered with burning flakes of shingles. Terrified women, children, sick, and elderly ran screaming from their homes to the shelter of other homes only to be driven away when those buildings succumbed.

Nathanael watched the conflagration from across the Hudson River in New Jersey. The day after the battle at Harlem Heights, Washington assigned him command of the completed Fort Lee. His detachment comprised three brigades plus militia—nearly 5,000 men. General Hugh Mercer, a fifty-year-old surgeon and Scottish-born general from Fredericksburg, Virginia, who was in the army of Bonnie Prince Charlie in 1745, was already there and appointed second-in-command.

It was a position of great responsibility. Nathanael was still a new general, but Washington's confidence in him and zeal for his countrymen and the cause were evident to every observer. There was a growing sentiment spoken among those in the army that if Washington was killed, Nathanael was the man to take his place.

Lieutenant Tench Tilghman, Washington's aide from Maryland, told a friend, "You have a very just idea of Greene's importance. He is, beyond doubt, a first-rate military genius and one in whose opinions the General places the utmost confidence."

Conditions at Fort Lee were as appalling as any in the Continental Army, and Nathanael's humanitarian and disciplinarian nature demanded he look after his soldiers. He begged John Hancock, the president of the Continental Congress, for medicine for his suffering soldiers and to expand the abysmal army hospital. He pressed the latter and asked for a general hospital large enough to receive all the sick because Dr. John Morgan, the director general, said he had no authority to supply the demands of the regimental sick. Over the next few weeks, Nathanael oversaw the construction of new barracks and found it necessary to glean information from those who were already stationed there.

"How many militiamen are among the garrison?" Nathanael asked Colonel Jonas Whitmore. He had been stationed at the fort since its construction began in July.

"There is no way of telling, sir. They come and go at will being their enlistments are short. However, the men say they can see a great change with respect to the discipline of the troops, which was lax before your arrival."

Nathanael rubbed his forehead. He was saddled with militiamen who ran at the first sight of a red-coated British regular as they had done at Kip's Bay. He thought it prudent not to complain to Colonel Whitmore. Instead, Nathanael aired his frustrations to William Blodget. Billy bore them well and happily.

"The policy of Congress has been the most absurd and ridiculous imaginable, pouring in militiamen who come and go every month. A military force established upon such principles defeats itself."

Nathanael thought of the young men lying dead at Harlem Heights who would never see their families again and then said, "People coming from home with all the tender feelings of domestic life are not sufficiently fortified with natural courage to stand the shocking scenes of war. To march over dead men, to hear without concern the groans of the wounded, I say few men can stand such scenes unless steeled by habit or fortified by military pride."

Soon after, a committee of Congress arrived in camp to make an inquiry into the condition of the army and to resolve to augment regiments. Nathanael immediately wrote home to Rhode Island and the Assembly asking that they send officers and troops from his home state, but he knew there was a material difference in enthusiasm and raising men. His request brought on accusations of partiality. His harshest critic was his former commander at Boston, General Charles Lee, who returned from South Carolina on October 14 and resumed his place as second-in-command of the army.

Nathanael's sleepless watchfulness began when the British brought up a cannonade from Paulus Hook ten miles south. Then General William Howe put his army in motion again. By noon on October 12, an advanced force of 4,000 men led by Henry Clinton landed at Throg's Neck. At the first report of the Throg's Neck landing, Nathanael assumed he and his troops would be called back to New York. He readied three brigades to reinforce the commander-in-chief.

❧

On October 16, General William Heath at King's Bridge sent a messenger to the Morris House on Harlem Heights to advise General Washington that the position of the American Army should shift. Without Nathanael present, George held a war council. Through prisoner exchanges, Generals Alexander Stirling and John Sullivan, who had both surrendered during the battle of Long Island, rejoined the army.

George created seven divisions; he gave General Charles Lee the largest division—the left wing of the army. The next day, 1,000 men under Colonel John Glover from Lee's wing were dispatched to Pelham near the British landing to deter their movement. William Howe was unfazed. He encamped and waited for supplies.

George had already ordered Charles Lee to spend two days familiarizing himself with the area north of King's Bridge. Now, the commander-in-chief wanted a report.

"I advise a complete retreat from Harlem Heights to White Plains to prevent encirclement by the British," Charles informed the council. "I also suggest evacuating Fort Washington. Her value is questionable."

"On what do you base the White Plains recommendation?" Joseph Reed asked.

"There are a series of low hills near our supply depot at White Plains that would provide good terrain for our defenders to repeat their effective performance against British frontal attacks as they did at Harlem Heights."

"This coupled with reports that General Howe's army is advancing slowly with troops from his center and right, moving along the road from New Rochelle, we may want to be expedient," John Sullivan suggested.

"Are we agreed?" George asked his council.

The council of war agreed to withdraw most of the army to White Plains.

During this time, Nathanael realized he had not written to his pregnant wife in weeks. From his headquarters at Fort Lee, he caught her up on all that had happened since the army's withdrawal from Manhattan.

Nathanael confessed that she was much missed in camp. "Colonel Bedford lodges with me and wants you to come. Colonel Biddle is continually urging me to send for you to go to Philadelphia and spend some weeks with his lady. But as you are at home in peace I cannot recommend your coming to this troublesome part of America. Your brother, Billy is captain of my Guard. Major Blodget is quite fat and laughs all day. General Mercer tells me of the wild scenes when he first met General Washington—how he had seen him ride over the fatal field of Monongahela in 1755 untouched by bullets."

Caty wrote back. "I want to come to you. Perhaps a route through New Jersey would pass far enough north of New York City to avoid great risk."

Nathanael's reply was emphatic. "No. I cannot see to your welfare as I am engaged in reinforcing Fort Washington and its outer defenses with a thousand more soldiers."

A week later, on October 28, General Howe personally led his troops and defeated Washington's army in White Plains. Then, William Demont, adjutant to onsite commander of Fort Washington Colonel Robert Magaw, defected to the British. Demont carried with him sketches of the plans for Fort Washington's layout. Fort Washington became an object of greater concern for Nathanael. He expended every exertion to understand the enemies' position and intentions.

General Israel Putnam arrived at Fort Lee in time to witness three British ships pass between the high guns of Forts Washington and Lee. The guns inflicted considerable damage but did nothing to stop their passage. Washington was inclined to abandon Fort Washington. His decision-making vacillated as he continued to ask Nathanael the same questions regarding the fort.

On November 8, George wrote Nathanael:

> *If we cannot prevent vessels passing up the Hudson and the enemy are possessed of the surrounding country, what valuable purpose can it answer to hold a post from which the expected benefit cannot be had?*

An exasperated Nathanael replied, "Upon the whole, I cannot help thinking the garrison is of advantage, and I cannot conceive the garrison to be in any great danger. The men can be brought off at any time. Our giving it up will open a free communication with the country by way of King's Bridge; that must be a great advantage to the enemy and injury to us."

At White Plains, the American troops decamped and wearily marched to the banks of the Hudson River. Washington with 2,000 Continental Army troops crossed on flatboats. From there, they moved south to establish a camp at Hackensack, New Jersey, six miles east of Fort Lee. Letters between George and Nathanael continued in a constant flurry while Nathanael and Hugh Mercer reconnoitered, keeping an eye out for signs of the enemy and arranging for supplies spread along the Hudson in New York to be shipped across the river.

At noon on November 15, 1776, a drummer beating a parley and several mounted British officers approached Fort Washington with a white flag to demand its surrender. Colonel Robert Magaw met the adjutant general of the British Army, Colonel James Patterson, in the open field.

Patterson demanded, "I have a message from General William Howe. Surrender the fort or face death to all those captured if you refuse to surrender. You have two hours to answer."

"You cannot just march to meet us and then make an assumption that we will yield," Robert argued. He signaled the Americans surrounding him. They presented their muskets. "Give me leave to assure His Excellency that actuated by the most glorious cause that mankind ever fought in, I am determined to defend this post to the very last extremity."

Robert returned to the fort to send a message to Nathanael. Nathanael sent a message to Washington. "Enclosed. You have a letter from Colonel Magaw. The contents will require your Excellency's attention. I have directed Colonel Magaw to defend the place until he hears from me. I shall go soon."

Without waiting for an answer, he crossed the Hudson to Fort Washington with Israel Putnam and Hugh Mercer. George rode in from Hackensack. He roused two sleeping mariners to take him across the Hudson to meet with Nathanael at Fort Washington. Partway across, under the gloom of a cold autumn twilight, he encountered the generals returning.

"What is happening?" George demanded as the bargemen lay on their oars.

"We have asked Colonel Magaw to hold out as long as possible, perhaps until tomorrow night when the troops can be evacuated," Nathanael explained.

"Why can they not be evacuated now?" George asked.

"We have confidence that Magaw can make a good defense," Nathanael said.

"There is no immediate danger despite the warning?" George asked.

"None that we can detect," Israel said.

It was 3:00 a.m. by the time the American generals climbed the palisades and made it back to Fort Lee. As sunrise began to chase away the dark early morning, heavy artillery fire commenced with a massive two-hour barrage from British guns on the east side of the Harlem River as the frigate *Pearl* in the Hudson pounded Fort Washington's outer defenses. The assault came from three directions.

Four thousand Hessians came down from the north and over the bridge at King's Bridge led by General von Knyphausen. A force of British troops led by the competent and aggressive General Lord Charles Cornwallis, plus a battalion of Scottish Highlanders struck from the east and crossed the Harlem River in flatboats. The third force of some 3,000 men came up from the south, commanded by Lord Hugh Percy. By 10:00

a.m., 8,000 troops were committed to the assault; nearly four times the number of those defending Fort Washington.

As the attack was orchestrated, the American commanders came over from Fort Lee and looked on helplessly. George, Israel, Hugh, and Nathanael still did not comprehend that a major defeat was imminent. They proceeded all the way to Morris House where they heard the thunderous sound of marching boots and trotting horses.

"Ye Gods, the enemy is advancing!" Israel crowed.

"Leave, George," Nathanael insisted. "I will stay."

"As will I," Hugh volunteered. "If you are captured, General Washington, the revolution could fall."

"No, it is best for all of us to come off together," George ordered.

The American generals made it to the shore and stepped into the waiting skiff just before the British marched through and captured Morris House. They watched from the brow of the palisades as the Hessians assaulted the redoubt at the northern end of Mount Washington. They exchanged fire with a battalion of Maryland riflemen, who stood their ground from behind their redoubt, but their guns got too hot, and they were overwhelmed. Within the lines that surrounded the fort, several hundred Pennsylvania riflemen fired at the oncoming Hessians, but there were too few Americans to hold the lines. When the British opened fire with a field piece, the men scattered and ran for the fort.

The Hessians under Captain Wiederhold marched forward up the hill to the fort and were obliged to creep up the rocks that lay before them surrounded by three earthworks, one above the other. The troops and riflemen from the fort faced them.

"Stand your ground!" Colonel Robert Magaw shouted. "They will force our surrender if you do not."

The Americans volleyed. Some of the Hessians fell as they tried to scale the height while others were shot dead. The 800 Scottish Highlanders kept coming. They climbed the steep hill from the shore so quickly that they captured 170 Americans. Gunfire ceased. Hand-to-hand combat commenced.

At 4:00 p.m. under Hessian Colonel Johann Rall's demands, Colonel Robert Magaw surrendered the fort. The Hessians formed two lines facing one another, and the 2,800 Americans inside the fort were marched out between them. Besides the loss of ninety officers and 2,800 soldiers, the Americans lost thirty-four cannon, two howitzers, ammunition, and enough food to feed the garrison for a fortnight. The British had taken George Washington's hope.

It was not just Washington's hope. It was also Nathanael's hope. He experienced the devastating brunt of his decision to defend the fort. He knew he would be blamed for the disaster. From Fort Lee, he wrote to Henry Knox, who was hauling cannon toward Peekskill where he could cross the Hudson into New Jersey, "I am mad, vexed, sick, and sorry. Never did I need the consoling voice of a friend more than now. Happy should I be to see you. This is a most terrible event: its consequences are justly to be dreaded. Pray, what is said upon the occasion?"

When Henry reached Fort Lee, he tried to console his distraught friend.

"I was afraid that the fort and the redoubt we advised building was not done, or little or nothing done to it," Nathanael said. "Had that been complete, I think the garrison might have defended themselves a long while, or been brought off. I am afraid there is no one who will see that my efforts were rigorous."

"Do you want the truth of what I have heard?" Henry asked.

"Yes," Nathanael said with hesitancy.

"You will not take it well, especially after you were lauded," Henry warned. "I am your friend, and I do not wish to trouble you further."

"Speak plain," Nathanael urged.

Henry grunted as he lowered his girth onto a fallen log. Nathanael sat beside him. Nearby, the picket guards formed under his orders to watch the cliffs on the New Jersey shore where Fort Lee sat.

"There are none who are defending your decision," Henry said. He tied the handkerchief he kept wrapped around his hand with two missing fingers. "They are saying they wonder why you are a general at all. You have neither experience nor judgement from which to draw. Washington's own aide, Colonel Joseph Reed, vituperated that opinion."

Nathanael wheezed and coughed in reply.

"Perhaps I should not continue," Henry said. "I am afraid the distress will only aggravate your asthma."

"No, continue," Nathanael said.

"General Lee in his usual duplicitous manner declared to Washington that he did not understand His Excellency's judgement in listening to your persuasion. He claims other officers have accused you of partiality to your own Rhode Island troops."

"Yet he remains near White Plains, New York at Washington's orders and criticizes me from there?" Nathanael asked.

Henry huffed and stood up. "I think that is enough, my friend. Washington has not brought an inquiry against you so have faith in that. Write to Mrs. Greene. Her words will console you like no other's if she has any feelings for you in her heart and I know she does."

Nathanael struggled to keep his voice strong and steady. "I have not been totally remiss. I have made great effort to stock magazines in New Jersey with ammunition, flour, beef, pork, hay, and grains in case the army is forced to march through that state."

A messenger rode up and bowed in the saddle. "General Greene, General Washington has arrived from his headquarters in Hackensack. He wishes to see you, sir."

Nathanael rose and turned to heed the summons.

"Write to your wife," Henry reminded.

Nathanael nodded and composed his emotions.

&

"It is determined Fort Lee is useless without Fort Washington as now we can do nothing to stop the British from sailing up the Hudson River unmolested," George said as he sipped a glass of claret in Nathanael's headquarters.

Nathanael's attention shifted to Colonel Joseph Reed, George's adjutant general. Reed favored him with a smug look. Furthering dissention, the adjutant had openly agreed with General Lee's verdict that the fall of Fort Washington was General Greene's responsibility.

"I am ordering the evacuation of Fort Lee," George went on. "I am certain our enemies in Manhattan, namely General William Howe, will hear of the movement, so celerity is of the utmost importance."

Nathanael concealed the overwhelming thoughts that ran through his mind. *There are 2,000 men here as well as 3,100 barrels of flour, 300 barrels of port, 300 tons of hay, and 10,000 bushels of grain, and we have no wagons.*

George rose. "Nathanael, I have not lost confidence in you. Only disappointment mars my countenance." The commander-in-chief's face brightened. "Mr. Thomas Paine has arrived. He is a civilian and an English-born political activist and revolutionary. You remember. He is the author of the pamphlet *Common Sense* that is a clarion call for unity against the British court. If you wish to consider him as an aide, he would be delighted to see his duty to you."

Bitterness edged into Nathanael's question. "He would not be ashamed of that duty?"

"As I have said," George replied. He pulled on his gloves. "Keep me informed of your progress in relieving the army of this place."

On November 18, Nathanael wrote to Washington to tell him that he was sending off stores as fast he could get wagons. He also sent three expresses to Newark, New Jersey for boats. Huge stores of powder and ammunition were transported by land. He finished by saying, "Our Bergen Guard were alarmed last night but I believe without much reason. I am, dear Sir, your obedient Servant."

The following night and in the pouring rain, Admiral Richard Howe sent flatboats up the Hudson. William Howe dispatched 4,000 British and Hessians under Lord Charles Cornwallis to take Fort Lee. The morning of November 20 dawned fair and clear. Nathanael was asleep when a messenger arrived.

"Where is General Greene?" the sweating, harried man demanded of the picket sentry.

"The general is in bed."

"I suggest you rouse him now! It has been reported that General Cornwallis has landed at Closter's Ferry six miles above the fort, has climbed through the break in the palisades to the road above, and is marching toward the fort."

"Shit!" the sentry cursed. "I will get General Greene forthwith."

Nathanael was awakened with shouting and banging on his headquarters door. "General Greene!" He rolled out of bed fully dressed sans his blue uniform coat and answered the insistent caller. Outside the door his Life Guard had the sentry restrained.

"Let him in," Nathanael ordered the captain of his Life Guard, Isham Gaines.

Panting, the sentry repeated his story.

"Billy, sound the alarm," Nathanael ordered, pulling on his coat. "I thought the enemy could only attack by way of Haverstraw farther north. But our troops know what to do in case of attack. They are to retreat west, crossing the Hackensack River at New Bridge Landing and the Passaic River at Acquackanonk Bridge. I will ensure they get out."

The rotund aide moved as fast as he could to alarm officers and their soldiers. Nathanael followed surrounded by his Life Guard.

As Cornwallis landed, the garrison at Fort Lee fled, leaving their pots boiling and their meals unfinished in their flight. Everything was left behind—guns, tents, entrenching tools, and provisions. They met Washington, who with a group of aides was on the way to help rescue the division. Washington ordered his army to retreat in haste down the road and over the Hackensack River farther into New Jersey. Charles Lee remained at North Castle Heights with 4,000 men. The race across New Jersey was on. It would not be the last time that the well-educated British General Lord Charles Cornwallis and the self-educated American General Nathanael Greene would race to the death.

six

These Are the Times That Try Men's Souls

Before retreating, Washington had Joseph Reed dictate a letter to Charles Lee asking him to cross the Hudson with his brigade and join forces before it was too late. *I would have you move over by the easiest and best passage.* But it was not an order. It was a request.

The two men who had criticized Nathanael so vehemently had their own agenda in mind. Lee rebuffed Washington's request and then wrote to General William Heath that he planned to assault Cornwallis on his own. Referring to the fall of the forts, Joseph Reed wrote to Lee:

> *General Washington's own judgment seconded by represen-*
> *tations from us would, I believe, have saved the men and*
> *their arms. Oh! General—an indecisive mind is one of the*
> *greatest misfortunes that can befall an army. How often I*
> *have lamented it in this campaign.*

Washington's battered and sick army plodded the muddied roads in cold pouring rain through New Jersey toward Trenton. Men ailing with dysentery dashed out of the column for the woods where they could relieve themselves privately. Coughing and scratching and retching moved up and down the lines. The men were in tatters, many without shoes, their feet wrapped in rags. General Cornwallis' forces followed. Their baggage train and artillery were cumbersome in the muck on the road, and they were moving slowly.

"I know some of our troops have deserted," George said to Nathanael as they rode side by side. "I saw them leaving the lines and running across this Godforsaken flat land. There is something else that worries me greatly. In two weeks, on December 1, enlistments for 2,000 troops will be up, and they will be free to go. Morale is so low, and so many are sick, I know my army will evaporate before my eyes."

Indeed, on Sunday morning, December 1, Nathanael reported to Washington, "Two brigades left us at Brunswick. It made no difference that the enemy is within two hours march and coming on. We have not three thousand men, a very pitiful army to trust the Liberties of America upon."

During that agonizing march and at night in Nathanael's camp, Thomas Paine wrote a new pamphlet, *The Crisis. Number 1. These are the times that try men's souls. The summer soldier and the sunshine patriot will, in this crisis, shrink from the service of their country; but he who stands it now deserves the love and thanks of man and woman.*

Soon after, it was published in Philadelphia, the pamphlet was read to the regiments of the Continental Army, and its message swept across America.

෴

Caty received a letter from Nathanael written from Trenton on the New Jersey side of the Delaware River dated December 4, 1776. The weeks of silence she endured only brought bad news—the fall of the forts along the Hudson River, the treatment of the soldiers who were captured, deserters, expiring enlistments, and other ills the army faced. His concern with the unreliable militia dominated his worries.

The virtue of the Americans is put to trial: if they turn out with spirit, all will go well; but if the militia refuses their aid, the people must submit to the servitude they deserve. But I think it is impossible that Americans can behave so poltroonish. Be of good courage. Don't be disturbed—all things will turn out for the best. I wish you abundant happiness and am affectionately yours.

Six months pregnant and lonely for her husband, Caty settled in with her in-laws in the Greene family home in Potowomut. Peace reigned in the fine home on a terrace that overlooked the stream below and the fields that Nathanael and his brothers plowed as boys.

Caty spent her days playing with their son, George, and her nights reading. Those lazy days were interrupted when a British fleet sailed into Narragansett Bay and dropped anchor off the large, sheltered harbor at Newport, Rhode Island. The troops, mostly Hessians under the command of General Henry Clinton, disembarked on December 7 without the least opposition. When informed that the rebels had quitted the works in and about the town of Newport and were retiring toward Bristol Ferry, Clinton detached General Richard Prescott with grenadiers and light infantry to intercept them.

The citizens along the shore, some of whom were Caty's relatives and acquaintances, were terrified as the British pillaged and quartered in their homes.

During the first week in December, the Continental Army began wearily crossing the Delaware River into Pennsylvania. The arduous task of getting men, horses, cannon, and equipment onto the boats and across the river was performed in an orderly fashion. Nathanael was in Princeton. He sent intelligence reports of the enemy's movements that he received from Lord Alexander Stirling to George. The British arrived on December 8, just as the American soldiers in Princeton retreated and crossed the river into

Morrisville. Henry Knox watched with cannons ready as they searched in vain for boats.

Nathanael established his headquarters at the home of Samuel Merrick near Newtown. His kind hosts acquiesced to his request that they paint a rising sun over the fireplace mantel, a symbol of the birth of the American republic.

On that same day, General Charles Lee finally crossed the Hudson with 4,000 troops and reached Morristown, New Jersey. On December 12, he left his second, General John Sullivan, in command and left the encampment. Charles stopped at a tavern at Basking Ridge. He rose early the following morning. Wearing only his dressing gown and slippers, he sipped a cup of tea and wrote a letter to General Horatio Gates condemning Washington.

While he was engaged in his letter to Gates, one of his officers, Captain James Wilkinson, looked out a window and down the lane that led to the house from the main road. "General, there is a party of British dragoons galloping toward the tavern."

Charles' head came up with a jerk. "What?"

Before he could get to his feet, glass exploded into the room as the dragoons shot out all the windows. Sent by General Cornwallis to ascertain Lee's position, the dragoon commander arrested Lee. It was a blow to America's belief that with his experience and education Charles Lee was the man who could win the war.

Nathanael penned a letter to Caty and told her of his former commander's blunder. In it, he released his frustrations, "Fortune seems to frown upon the cause of freedom. However, I hope this is the dark part of the night which generally is just before day."

With the realization that Cornwallis and his army were nearing Philadelphia on their march toward Trenton, the inhabitants of Trenton and Princeton evacuated. The people of Philadelphia were getting out, too. Families loaded wagons and shops were shuttered. The roads were packed with refugees. John Hancock and the Continental Congress finally took Washington's warnings seriously and fled to Baltimore, Maryland.

On a morning so cold he could barely feel his pen, Nathanael wrote to Hancock, "I am far from thinking the American cause desperate, yet I conceive it to be in a critical situation." He went on to urge Congress to delegate Washington full powers without their giving up civil authority.

> *The state of war is so uncertain. A day, nay, an hour is so important in the crisis of public affairs that it would be folly to wait for relief from the deliberative councils of legislative bodies. There never was a man that might be more safely trusted.*

Congress listened to Nathanael and agreed to give Washington temporary authorization with limited powers. He and Nathanael recognized the principle of civil supremacy over the military. And Washington was learning that he could not do without Nathanael's counsel.

While Nathanael aired his concerns and recommendations to Congress, citing, "the enemy in the heart of the country," the enemy was indeed moving. General William Howe left New York to join Charles Cornwallis at Brunswick. Then Howe set up a line of seven garrisons to hold the southern half of New Jersey from Hackensack to Burlington. The smallest of these was at Trenton, manned by 1,500 Hessians under Colonel Johann Rall, who had demanded the surrender of Fort Washington. Satisfied with his arrangements, Howe, with Cornwallis, returned to New York City.

Washington had no knowledge of Howe's and Cornwallis' departure to New York. He was still under the impression that the enemy might attack if the Delaware River froze and that their objective was to take Philadelphia. There was discussion among Washington and his officers about what the Continental Army should do in this wilderness of uncertainties. Pennsylvania militia regiments conducted hit and run raids across the river at points near Trenton and south at Bristol.

As they waited for reinforcements to fill their ranks, both Nathanael and George believed in the hope that the American Army could take the offensive and strike the enemy. On December 21, Nathanael confided optimistically in a letter to Rhode Island governor Nicholas Cooke, "I hope to give the Enemy a stroke in a few days. Should fortune favor the attack perhaps it may put a stop to General Howe's progress."

Then a letter came from Colonel Joseph Reed in Bristol. He strongly urged that they attack the enemy and that *delay is now equal to a total defeat.*

Reed's words were taken seriously. George, with militia and Continental generals, devised a daring plan to stun the British, capture supplies, and reinvigorate American morale—attack the garrison at Trenton on Christmas night.

On Christmas Eve, Washington called a meeting at Nathanael's headquarters to go over the final details and reinforce the plan. Among them were Major Generals Nathanael Greene and John Sullivan; Brigadiers Lord Alexander Stirling, Hugh Mercer, Adam Stephen, and Arthur St. Clair; and Colonels John Stark, John Glover, and Henry Knox.

"We will attack across the Delaware at three places," Washington said as he and his officers gathered around a map rolled out on the table. He moved his finger down the bank of the Delaware River until it came to a stop at Bristol.

"General John Cadwalader is guarding the Bristol river crossings with a force of 1,000 Pennsylvania militia and 500 Rhode Island troops under Colonel Daniel Hitchcock. They will cross downriver there and advance toward Burlington."

Washington tapped his finger on Trenton Ferry and said, "General Ewing is already here with 700 Pennsylvania militiamen. They will attack directly across the river at Trenton and hold the wooden bridge over Assunpink Creek at the foot of Queen Street, which the enemy might use as an escape route.

"The third and largest force of 2,400 of the Continental Army will march together in one column from McKonkey's Ferry to the landing across the river at Johnson Ferry. Once over, we will head south. Then halfway to Trenton, we will divide into two columns, one led by General Sullivan taking the River Road. The other commanded by General Greene taking the Pennington Road farther inland. I will ride with the latter as will Generals Stirling, Mercer, and Stephen. The brigades of Colonel Glover and General St. Clair will ride with General Sullivan.

"Nathanael, you are to move inland and approach the town from the northwest, away from the river. One of your brigades will advance to the Princeton Road that enters from Trenton from the northeast and block that road and encircle the town."

"I have ordered a detachment of the artillery without cannon to use drag ropes, handspikes, and hammers to seize the Hessian cannon at the start of the battle and turn them against the enemy," Henry Knox said.

Washington addressed Hugh Mercer, "I am assigning Major Mordecai Gist and his Marylanders as part of your brigade as you have lost many to desertion."

George's eyes roamed his commanders' faces. "By marching through the night, we should converge on Trenton no later than five in the morning. The attack is set for six, an hour before daylight. Officers are to wear a piece of white paper in their hats to distinguish them. A profound silence is to be observed. I will hang anyone who quits."

seven

Victory or Death

On Christmas Day, the weather turned ominous. A northeast storm gathered over the countryside. Colonel John Glover and his Massachusetts mariners were in charge of the big, flat-bottomed, high-sided Durham boats normally used to transport pig iron on the Delaware from the Durham Iron Works near Philadelphia. Painted black and pointed at both ends, the boats were forty to sixty feet long with a beam of eight feet. The biggest of them could carry as many as forty men standing up, and fully loaded they drew about two feet. The sweep oars used to navigate the boats were eighteen feet long. A scattering of other types of watercraft waited to assist with crossing the river.

Colonel Henry Knox organized and directed the crossing. Drums rolled in camp, and starting at 2:00 in the afternoon, the army began moving out for the river. Each man carried sixty rounds of ammunition and enough food for three days. The army's password was "Victory." The countersign was "Death."

It was nearly dark and raining when the troops reached McKonkey's Ferry. Henry's deep voice boomed above the wind and rain. The width of the river at the ferry was eight hundred feet, but the water was high that night and the current strong. The river was filled with formidable broken sheets of ice.

The first to cross were the men who would serve in the vanguard and keep a watch for the enemy and anything unusual. Captain William Washington, a distant relative to the commander-in-chief, and Lieutenant James Monroe from Virginia were in charge of Nathanael's divisional vanguard.

"Start loading the field pieces!" Henry shouted. His artillerists urged the horses pulling the caissons and cannon onto the flat ferry boats. As each ferry boat returned from the opposite shore, troops led officers' horses and horses pulling baggage wagons on board while the troops carrying their supplies filed onto the boats. The troops stood packed on board as closely as possible. Glover's men used oars and poles to get the big boats across.

Nathanael rode up to the landing as the brigades under his brigadier generals began boarding. He was in a buoyant mood. He had seen 2,400 of the hardiest troops parading through the low hills. If anyone could win the day, they could. John Sullivan and George Washington were at the ferry. "I am crossing early so I can ensure all goes well with my division," Nathanael told the two.

"Yes," John agreed. "I am crossing early with His Excellency as well."

Henry heard the conversation and bellowed to a company captain, "Attend the generals' horses!"

When Nathanael stepped into the Durham boat, freezing water sloshed over his booted feet. He wrapped his cloak tightly against the biting sleet that froze their faces. John and George stepped in beside him. The crossing was slow. The three generals reached the steep New Jersey shore and watched while the wind and snow stung their eyes.

At 11:00 p.m., the storm struck a full-blown northeaster, slowing the crossing further. Sheets of ice grew thicker as they bounced on the wind-blown waves in the Delaware River. The ice was hindering the sweep oars and scraping against the sides of the boats. Some of the soldiers had trouble maintaining their footing. It was 3:00 a.m., three hours behind schedule, when the last of the troops, horses, and cannon were across.

Nathanael rode up to his brigadiers, Hugh Mercer and Lord Alexander Stirling, to confer with them. "Is all in place?" he asked.

"Yes, all of our brigades are across and formed," Hugh confirmed.

"We were told that Captain Washington and his unit are ahead as ordered," Lord Alexander Stirling added.

"I see General Stephen's Virginians. Where is he?" Nathanael asked.

Alexander lifted his chin to indicate Adam Stephen, a Virginian who liked his drink, was with Washington. It was well-known that the two Virginians despised one another from the days when they had fought together in the war with the French and Indians. Washington's angry voice rose above the wind, "You took it upon yourself to alert the Hessians in an act of revenge for killing one of your men? You, sir, may have ruined all my plans by having put them on their guard."

George calmed himself by turning away from Adam Stephen. He went to confer with Nathanael. "At this late hour, the element of surprise seems gone. Do we send our men back across the river?"

Nathanael knew it was rhetorical question but said, "I do not think that is an option at this stage."

George nodded, but what neither knew was that part of the plan was failing. General Ewing called off his attack on Trenton because of ice in the river. General John Cadwalader and Colonel Joseph Reed succeeded in getting some of their troops over to the other side at Bristol, but the ice was piled higher there, and they were unable to move their cannon across.

The march south from McKonkey's Ferry turned into a march of misery when the storm worsened with cold, driving rain, sleet, snow, and violent hail. The troops trudged on in silence. Francis Adams, a thirty-year-old soldier from Taylorsville, Pennsylvania, and father of four children, had no shoes, and his coat was threadbare. He stumbled and died on the road. His comrades stopped and moved his body to the side.

The entire 2,400 men on the march kept together for five miles until they reached the crossroads at Birmingham where the army stopped to eat cold rations and then divided. John Sullivan's column kept to the right on the River Road while Washington's force, led by Nathanael, veered to the left onto Pennington Road. Henry Knox's artillerists led the way in anticipation of heading the assault. The distance to Trenton was four miles either way. There was little light to see by. A few men carried lanterns, and torches were mounted on some of the cannon so the army would not be seen moving through the forested terrain. Men and horses kept slipping and skidding in the dark.

Washington rode out into the lines. "For God's sake, keep with your officers," he said.

John Sullivan sent a courier to tell Washington that the weather was wetting his men's gunpowder.

"Tell General Sullivan to use the bayonet," he responded. "I am resolved to take Trenton."

But the Continental Army was not alone on their march. As dawn approached, civilians living in the countryside rose to run errands or tend to chores. They eyed Nathanael's marching division with a mixture of reverence and fear.

Washington and his generals' columns reached their position outside Trenton at about the same time—an hour after daylight. Most of the residents had fled the village of about 100 houses. King Street and Queen Street were the primary roads. By Washington's plan of attack, the head of King and Queen Streets was where the assault would begin.

The 1,500 Hessians were quartered in houses and stone barracks. Their commander, Colonel Johann Rall, was staying in a frame house on King Street that belonged to an iron furnace owner. He spent Christmas night playing cards. Harassed by rebel patrols that kept coming over the Delaware, Rall established a ring of outposts outside of town and insisted that each night one company sleep with their muskets ready to be called out at a moment's notice. It seemed to some that they were called out more often than necessary, and they were exhausted.

Just before Nathanael's column reached the outpost on Pennington Road, George ordered a halt. He turned to his major general and said, "Deploy your brigades in three attacking columns."

Nathanael wheeled his horse and spurred her toward his brigadiers riding close behind. "Form," he told them. "Hugh, your men will form on the right. Adam, you and Lord Stirling will form in the center." He instructed Brigadier General Matthias Fermoy's Pennsylvanians to the American left. At 8:00 a.m., they attacked the Pennington Road outpost in a blaze of musket fire. Captain William Washington and Lieutenant James Monroe were in the vanguard leading the artillery.

"What is happening?" Hessian Major Jacob von Braam shouted when he heard the sudden sound of a musket volley. He and his company ran out into the blinding snow.

"Who is attacking us?" Hessians shouted at one another. "It is impossible to see through the snow who is attacking and how many."

"Get into formation," Major von Braam ordered.

"Which formation?" one of the guards asked. "We have no idea how many there are or where they are."

"Wait for them to get closer, then fire!" von Braam shouted.

The Americans kept coming in a surge of musket fire and swirling snow.

Major von Braam saw his men were still unable to get into formation. "Retreat!" he shouted.

The Hessians quickly fell back into town, as they had been trained to do when retreat was the only choice. They shouted in warning, "*Der Fiend! Heraus! Heraus!*"

In town, Hessians rushed out of their houses and barracks into the streets. Drums beat, and officers shouted orders in German. Henry Knox positioned his artillery at the head of King and Queen Streets. General Hugh Mercer and his Marylanders and Virginians moved down a hill on the west side of town and swept into the village through alleys and house lots. Snow and clouds of gunpowder intermingled to form a blinding haze. The Hessians retreated into the side streets and an orchard. The storm of nature and the storm of the town mixed to become a horrible scene. Guns became too wet to fire, so the Americans came at them with fixed bayonets.

When the Hessians rolled out a field gun midway on King Street, James Monroe rushed forward, seized it, and turned it on them. James lit the touchhole. The cannon belched a tongue of fire and black smoke when the ball exploded from the muzzle, killing two Hessians.

Colonel Rall—rousted out of bed—was on horseback and in command in the midst of the battle. He ordered a charge, "All who are my grenadiers, forward!" He held fast to his reins and tightened his thighs to stay in the saddle. Rall's men were falling all around him. Then he was cut down by American fire.

Washington took advantage of the situation. "General Sullivan, General Greene, move to surround them," he ordered. "March on, my brave fellows! After me!"

Rall's men tried to get him up and to safety. The Hessians in the orchard, finding themselves surrounded, lay down their arms and surrendered. Washington was unable to see the surrender, and he ordered artillerist Captain Thomas Forrest to switch from round shot to canister.

"Sir, they have struck," Forrest said.

"Struck?" George asked.

"Yes, sir, their colours are down."

Within forty-five minutes, twenty-one Hessians were killed, ninety were wounded, and 900 taken prisoner. Five hundred managed to escape across Assunpink Creek at the foot of Queen Street. Four Americans were wounded. One of them was Captain William Washington, and the other was Lieutenant James Monroe. The only dead Americans were two who froze to death on the march.

"This is a glorious day for our country!" George exclaimed to his generals.

An exhilarated Nathanael proclaimed, "The passions of our troops were exhibited in a manner I had not expected. It was a battle of extreme savagery!"

Henry ordered the cannon secured. They captured twenty pieces, which they would have to cross the Delaware with, in addition to the Hessians and their horses. Nathanael accompanied George to a church on Queen Street where Colonel Rall lay dying. Through an interpreter, they assured Rall that his men would be fairly treated. The Hessian tried to put on a brave face, but his pain was more than he could bear.

Afterward, George called a brief war council. "Should we press on to Princeton and Brunswick?" he asked, desiring to attack the enemy garrisons about twenty miles north.

"I recommend a pursuit," Nathanael said.

"I, too, recommend this course," Henry agreed.

"It appears that some of the troops have gotten into the Hessians' liquor," Hugh Mercer pointed out, "but I am not certain that is a deterrent."

George considered the advice. Nathanael and Henry were the only general officers of this opinion. He decided against it. The army slowly made its way back to McKonkey's Ferry, where after recrossing with the Hessian prisoners, they stumbled into camp. Half of them were too sick or exhausted to report for duty, but they were uplifted because they had done something glorious at last. Nathanael withstood the strain after thirty hours without any refreshment.

The army rested on the Pennsylvania side of the river for three days. For many, their enlistments were to expire on December 31, and droves of soldiers would go home. Another issue weighed heavily on Nathanael's mind. At home in Rhode Island, Caty was about to give birth to their second child.

He scratched out a letter to her describing the victory at Trenton. "Should we get possession of the Jerseys, perhaps I may get liberty to come and see you. I pity your situation exceedingly; your distress and anxiety must be very great. Put on a good stock of fortitude. By the blessing of God, I hope to meet you again in the pleasure of wedlock. Adieu my love."

∂

General John Cadwalader and his Pennsylvanians along with Rhode Island Colonel Daniel Hitchcock finally crossed the Delaware River at Bristol after their failed attempt on Christmas night. Now, George and Nathanael began to think of driving the enemy out of New Jersey entirely. When it was agreed, George sent out a flurry of letters to commit all of his resources to the enterprise.

On December 29, Washington took a force of 5,000 men back to Trenton. Nathanael's division was ordered to cross at Yardley's Ferry. It was worse than the crossing on Christmas night. The ice was already three inches thick. He watched as his infantry left their guns in the wagons, stepped gingerly upon it, and walked across the Delaware River.

Nathanael, astride his horse and flanked by his aides, Majors William Blodget and William Livingston, began to feel anxious as the men who led the horses pulling the supply wagons got closer to the shore. He ordered them to halt.

Artillery Captain John Neil galloped up, "We are going to have to leave the artillery behind, General Greene."

"And the wagons it appears," Nathanael acknowledged.

It was a miserable night for Nathanael's infantry sleeping on the New Jersey shore without benefit of tents. They built roaring fires that nearly roasted them on one side while they froze on the other. Finally, in the morning, the entire 1,400-man division was across with the same brigades he led on the attack at Trenton, though much diminished. They joined the rest of the army in Trenton.

The ragged troops who had their hearts fixed on home and the comforts of the domestic circle began to leave on New Year's Eve. Washington astride his horse, Nelson, rode among the ranks and issued a plea for them to stay, "My brave fellows, you have done all that I have asked you to do and more than could be reasonably expected. But your country is at stake, your wives, your houses, and all that you hold dear."

"We are in need of relief, Your Excellency," a rifleman from Pennsylvania said. "We have not been paid."

"If you consent to stay one month longer, you will render that service to the cause of liberty and to your country, which you probably can never do under any other circumstances," Washington countered. "If you reenlist, a bounty of ten dollars each will be awarded."

Nathanael was impressed with the commander-in-chief's eloquence. He confided to Henry, "God Almighty their hearts listened to the proposal and they engaged anew; happy for America." He smiled—proud of many who were Rhode Islanders. "This is the greatest evidence of New England virtue I ever saw. Let it be remembered to their eternal honor."

At the last minute, William Howe canceled Charles Cornwallis' journey to England to visit his wife and children, complaining, "Trenton was an unlucky, cursed affair quite beyond comprehension." He dispatched Cornwallis to New Jersey to smash the remnants of the rebel army and retake Trenton. Aggressive and fearless, Cornwallis left New York and pushed fifty miles across New Jersey toward Princeton in one day. He had 8,000 well-fed, well-equipped, and well-trained men. Washington had 4,600 mostly untrained troops, including militia, who had endured a hard year.

On January 2, 1777, with Cornwallis bearing down on them, Washington's army took up defensive positions near Assunpink Creek Bridge. John Cadwalader and the army's quartermaster general, Major Thomas Mifflin, answered George's call for reinforcements. They barely were settled in when drums began to beat to arms. Cornwallis was advancing down the road from Princeton.

George sent an advance party of riflemen under Colonel Edward Hand to scout the British movement and deployed troops in a delaying action. The only way Cornwallis could get to the Continental Army's main body was over the bridge. On the east end, George watched the progress of the conflict. In response to their commander-in-chief's summons, Nathanael and Henry rode up. The three conferred and spoke to some of the troops defending their position.

"Nathanael, lead a regiment of your own choosing to support Hand's riflemen," George ordered.

Leading his column of Rhode Islanders, Nathanael marched to meet the enemy on the high ground north of the Trenton side of the bridge. He encouraged them with shouts of "Push on, boys! Push on!" They skirmished with elements of Cornwallis' army who took possession of the hill. Nathanael ordered a retreat, but they succeeded in delaying the British vanguard's arrival until sunset. His regiment and Edward Hand's riflemen fell back through the streets of Trenton and crossed to their side of the bridge.

Henry Knox's artillery crews trundled cannon in place to defend the bridge as Cornwallis' army attacked. The two sides exchanged heavy cannon fire. The bridge over Assunpink Creek was drenched in British and Hessian blood, and the creek began to run thick with it as the bodies of the dead splashed into the water.

Surrounded by the fog of smoke and confusion, Cornwallis called for his troops to fall back three times. When night fell, aware that his troops were exhausted from marching over muddied ground and the subsequent attack, he held a council. He did not want to continue an assault in the dark.

General William Erskine warned, "If you trust those people tonight, you will see nothing of them in the morning."

Cornwallis declared, "We have got the Old Fox safe now. We'll go over and bag him in the morning."

Indeed, in the American camp the "Old Fox" and his generals were debating their next move. George posed the question, "Should we retreat down the Delaware through New Jersey and cross at Philadelphia?"

Nathanael offered an alternative question. "Shall we remain where we are and try the chances of a battle?"

General Arthur St. Clair said, "Better than either of these, let us take the new road through the woods and get into the enemy's rear by a march upon Princeton, and, if possible, even Brunswick."

It was agreed. The Continental Army built raging fires to mask their intentions, sent their baggage to Burlington, and slipped away under a cloudless sky in the dark. The piercing cold air froze the thawed ground solid and made the march easier.

At Quaker Bridge, Nathanael's small division veered off to the left, and John Sullivan veered off to the right with the main army. At sunrise, under orders from Cornwallis to march from Princeton toward Trenton, Colonel Charles Mawhood swung his troops around when they caught site of Nathanael's division near Stony Creek on the main road to Princeton. Nathanael's division could not see them, but from his position, Washington could. A galloper pulled up with a message from the commander-in-chief:

A force of the enemy is approaching you. Take care of them.
The main body is moving on to Princeton.

Nathanael halted his troops and galloped up to Hugh Mercer. He delivered Washington's message and then said, "Lead your brigade out of the ravine toward the advancing enemy."

Hugh gathered a part of his brigade, cleared the ravine, and clashed with Mawhood's forces. They drew up in the Clarke orchard. The flash of flint lit the orchard as a barrage of musket balls clipped limbs and twigs off the apple trees. Outnumbered, British dragoons fell back. When his horse was hit in the midst of a British bayonet attack, Hugh fought with his sword until he was clubbed to the ground and then bayoneted seven times and left for dead. His men ran. Untested militiamen saw them coming through the orchard, panicked, and ran with them. Colonel John Haslet of Delaware stepped up to rally the brigade and was shot in the head. Captain Neil was killed working his guns.

Nathanael and George calmed the panicked militia and fed more troops into the battle. Muskets blazed in a storm of smoke. Henry Knox's cannon blasted. The British line broke.

George bellowed, "It is a fox chase, boys!" He led an attack on Mawhood's troops, driving them back. Mawhood gave the order to retreat.

In the meantime, John Sullivan reached Princeton. Most of Cornwallis' guard retreated, although some took cover in a building at the university. Captain Alexander Hamilton, a twenty-year-old New York artillery officer, shelled Nassau Hall, which convinced the remaining British soldiers to surrender.

Nathanael wrote to Nicholas Cooke, the governor of Rhode Island, "Divine Providence has given a very favorable turn to affairs, and at an hour when people least expect it." His words would resonate when it came time for his own state to raise more regiments for the army.

Washington's generals gathered at John Van Doren's House in Millstone, New Jersey, and contemplated attacking Brunswick where General Charles Lee was a prisoner. But his exhausted army was in no shape for another forced march of nineteen miles or another battle. The army moved north to Morristown, New Jersey to settle in for the winter of 1777.

Washington established his headquarters at Jacob Arnold's tavern located on Morristown Green in the center of town. Churches and other buildings were utilized as hospitals and barracks. Morristown was between Philadelphia and New York and was protected from the British forces behind the Watchung Mountains. The main body of the army was encamped outside of Morristown in Lowantica Valley along with 300 camp followers.

With little food available, the threat of smallpox, and the loss of thousands of his troops, George was strained with worry. It was exacerbated when his disillusioned adjutant, Joseph Reed, returned to his family and law practice in Philadelphia. But Martha was in camp, and with her arrival other ladies joined their husbands. As it had been in Cambridge, a circle of domesticity and pleasure formed with sleigh rides, dances, and fireside chats and games.

Nathanael and his aides settled into the home of a man named Hoffman, an amiable Loyalist. William Blodget kept the Hoffmans in good spirits with his jolly demeanor.

Nathanael was deprived of his wife's company, and he wrote to her about the sad outcome of the battle near Princeton. "Poor Colonel Hitchcock died of Pleurisy at this place. He was buried with all the honors of War as the last mark of respect we could show him. Poor General Mercer is dead of the wounds he received in the Princeton action. May Heaven bless his spirit with eternal peace. Several more brave officers fell that day. Such instances paints all the horrors of war—beyond description."

His mind was torn between the worries of the Continental Army and his absence as his wife's lying in—the traditional practice involving long bed rest before and after giving birth—approached. Anxious, he wrote to her again. "The great distance there is between us, and the few opportunities I have to hear from you leaves me in a very disagreeable suspense. Eight long months have passed amidst fatigue and toil since I have tasted the pleasures of domestic felicity."

George and his newly appointed aide, Colonel Alexander Hamilton, arrived as Nathanael was finishing his letter. He replaced the quill in its holder, stood, and bowed to greet his visitors.

"Nathanael, I have come to ask you to go to Philadelphia to give a report of the army's state to Congress," George said. "I wish you to discuss with them the state of prisoners of war, particularly General Charles Lee. Conduct your matters on the principles of justice and humanity. I have written to them explaining that you are in my confidence and are intimately acquainted with my ideas, with our strengths and our weakness, with everything respecting the army."

"I am honored to do my duty and with your confidence," Nathanael replied.

"You are an able and good officer. I pressed that you deserve the greatest respect."

Nathanael unconsciously rubbed his tired, smallpox blemished eye.

"Are you feeling unwell?" George asked with paternal concern.

"No, it is just that Caty is…" Nathanael glanced at Alexander, whose acquaintance was blossoming into a friendship that was fed by their mutual intimacy with their general.

"I am aware," George said to ease his general's distress. "I know that you are worried, and her absence only serves to worsen it. Perhaps this journey will distract you from some of your familial disquiet."

I despise big cities, and the idea of Congress dragging out each and every interview is beyond my patience, Nathanael thought. Still, he was unwilling to damage the trust he had finally earned with the commander-in-chief, especially after the fall of the forts along the Hudson River. He said, "I will do my best as you prescribe."

George smiled. "Very good. Alexander will see to your arrangements. When you return, you shall enjoy comfortable quarters in Lord Alexander Stirling's country estate in Basking Ridge, New Jersey. General Stirling has extended the invitation to lodge with his wife, Sarah, and their daughter, Kitty, on my approval. I hear there are gardens, vineyards, a park, and an orchard surrounded by lawns at the estate." He bowed. "Safe travels," he said before sweeping out of the room.

When his arrangements came from Alexander Hamilton, Nathanael and William Blodget rode the seventy-five miles south to Philadelphia. Two days later, they arrived at the State House on Chestnut Street. Nathanael was unaccustomed to the urgent noise. Only the soughing damp wind off the Delaware River calmed the storm of the city. The only human activity he liked less was politics. It was an education he would come to loathe and appreciate.

The next few days were a flurry of long committee meetings. With some relief, John Adams extended an invitation to City Tavern. Over a dinner of bread, mutton, pickled cucumber, and claret, the two had a chance to talk away from the shadow of formal committees.

"Mr. Adams, I believe you are pretty well convinced of the truth of the observation I made to you last summer, which was that you are playing a desperate game."

"What game is that?" John asked acidly.

"Our difficulties are inconceivable if you have not been an eyewitness. You and the Congress insist on using militia, which lacks the good conduct and bravery of veteran soldiers. You promote men based on honor and not ability."

The short, round Adams smirked. "Our late promotions may possibly give disgust, but that cannot be avoided. You, sir, are not aware of our political difficulties unless you sit with us day after difficult day where policy is made."

"I beg to make leave to inquire into the policy of some late resolutions of Congress in respect to General Lee. Why is he denied his request of having some persons appointed to confer with him?"

"Does he deserve this request after his capture at a place of questionable reputation?"

"I feel it is good public policy to treat prisoners humanely," Nathanael said as the waiter filled his glass with claret.

"There has been no dispute over that," John said.

"There is so much deliberation and waste of time in the execution of business before the assembly that my patience is almost exhausted," Nathanael said defiantly.

"One must learn patience, General Greene. I admit it is not my best virtue, either."

Nathanael struggled not to scowl. He went on, "The mild and gentle treatment the Hessian prisoners have received since they have been in our possession has produced a great alteration in their disposition. For these and many other reasons that will readily occur to you, I would wish the resolution concerning retaliation might be suspended for a time, at least especially as General Lee's confinement is not strict."

The two ate in silence for a time until Nathanael said, "I wish you to consider what we have spoken of here." He finished his meal and rose from the table. "If you will excuse me, I believe I will reconnoiter the city to determine how it can be defended if it is unexpectedly attacked by the British."

"General Greene, William Howe is snug in New York City with his lovely blonde mistress, Mrs. Elizabeth Loring. I would not expect a sally directly."

Nathanael's eyes reflected amusement. "So I have heard." He bowed. "Now if you will excuse me. I have much to report to General Washington. I believe the business will be settled agreeable to his wishes. That is General Howe acknowledging General Lee a prisoner of War and holding him subject to exchange whenever we have an equivalent to offer."

eight

My Heart Mourns the Absence of Its Counterpart

Nathanael's hope that George would grant him furlough to go home or that Caty might visit him in New Jersey was not to be. On March 30, 1777, the last day he penned a letter to her from Philadelphia, she was in no condition to travel. He wrote in a tone that lured her into joining him, "The young ladies of Philadelphia appear angelic. A few months separation more will put my virtue to a new trial. If you do not wish to put my resolution to the torture, bless me with your company, providing your health favors my wishes."

Caty could do nothing about his wishes. She had given birth to a daughter she named Martha Washington Greene in the Greene family home in Potowomut. The last months of her pregnancy were difficult, and all the fears she was plagued with when she was expecting little George came back to haunt her. But this time, her complaints were founded, and her in-laws recognized them as valid. They summoned Dr. Joseph Joslyn whose convivial nature matched Caty's, and the two sometimes teased each other.

Even in her distressed state, Caty nudged him as he examined her, "Tell me about your intoxicated duck hunting trip on the bay when you accidentally shot yourself."

Dr. Joslyn grinned and said, "You know how this ends. I managed to keep myself from bleeding to death by stuffing a wad of chewing tobacco in my wound."

Caty giggled.

"Now, you must stay comfortable and calm," Dr. Joslyn ordered sternly. He addressed Nathanael's brother, Kitt, and his wife, Catherine. "I suggest you send Caty's toddler, George, to other family members so she may rest."

"No, I want him with me," Caty protested.

"You told me you are dreading your delivery," the doctor reminded her. "You cannot have him about while you give birth."

Caty's beautiful face paled.

"I know you miss Nathanael, and removing little George will only make the ache worse," Catherine soothed. "But it is for the best. He can go to the house in Coventry to stay with Jacob and Peggy."

Caty cringed. *Peggy is deplorably imperious*, she thought. But she had little choice in the matter.

After the babe arrived on March 14, Caty was weaker than she expected. The family was attentive, a far cry from the many times they had erupted into arguments.

"I will write Nathanael for you," Kitt offered.

"Please tell him I will join him as soon as possible," Caty pleaded as she cradled the babe in her arms. "Bring George home so he can meet his baby sister." She fell into a coughing fit and swallowed the sore lump in her throat.

"Perhaps, we should send for the doctor," Catherine suggested.

"No, it is nothing."

Caty did not receive a response from Nathanael concerning the birth until April. She read the letter with a trembling, feverish hand. What had begun as a cough developed into pneumonia, and she was confined to bed.

Nathanael wrote:

I was most agreeably surprised by a letter from brother Kitt with an account of your being in bed. Thank God for your safe delivery. Some superstitious fears have been hovering around me for some time that something would happen to you. When I shall see the poor little beggar, God only knows. I am happy at you being in Potowomut.

As the spring progressed, the Continental Army and Congress were left to guess General William Howe's intentions for the coming campaign. Would he strike Philadelphia? If so, by what route? What was the reason for his torpidity? Perhaps he awaited the arrival of stores, hay and oats, and camp equipment. Rumors spread that he was waiting for a new contingent of Hessians. Murmurs brewed of a British offensive down the Hudson River from Canada to isolate New England from the rest of the states.

George was glad to have his youngest major general back at his post in Basking Ridge. Rumors had come that Cornwallis learned that Nathanael was away and was planning to launch an attack before his return. Nathanael was happy to return to his responsibility of overseeing the well-being of his troops and their horses, although, as always, his pen was in motion under the warm glow of candlelight.

On April 13, 1777, Nathanael received intelligence that Lord Charles Cornwallis was within seven miles of New Brunswick, New Jersey, the major British camp in New Jersey. A force of 500 Americans under General Benjamin Lincoln, a hefty, loose-jowled, forty-five-year-old man from Hingham, Massachusetts, was posted at nearby Bound Brook on the Raritan River. They were to harass British and German outposts and ambush their foraging and raiding expeditions.

With 4,000 British and Hessians, Cornwallis crossed the Raritan River and drove for Lincoln's outpost to make a multi-pronged surprise attack. Benjamin lost his papers and his guns and suffered seventy-five casualties before Nathanael brought up his division and forced Cornwallis to retreat.

"How did you know we would be put upon?" Benjamin discussed with Nathanael as his wounded survivors were treated, the dead were buried, and those who escaped injury caught their breath. "I expressed my concern over this exposed position to General Washington, noting that many units were not in a position to render the least assistance to this post in case it was attacked."

"Washington recognized that Bound Brook was a difficult place to defend," Nathanael conceded. "You are deservedly acquitted from any blame. I know the militia deserted their posts without giving you the least notice."

The attack was confusing because there had been little military movement in New Jersey except foraging skirmishes. Washington called a council in Jacob's Tavern to consult his generals about launching a counterattack. "If I am to judge from the present appearance of things, the campaign will be opened by General Howe before we shall be in any condition to oppose him," George began. "He appears to have an embarrassment of riches under his command. My intelligence reports he has upward of 25,000 troops, and that may be an underestimate. We are in no position to press an offensive with a mere 7,000 soldiers, a third which are holding Fort Ticonderoga on Lake Champlain in New York."

"I suspect the enemy is to take the field the first of June," Nathanael said. "Their delay is unaccountable already. What has kept them in their quarters I cannot imagine. I have begun issuing orders for collecting troops from our outposts. But I fear without great exertions by the commissary department there will be a want of provisions."

Nathanael had much on his mind aside from wondering why the lethargic General Howe remained in New York City. He worried about Caty and their two children, who were living just a dozen miles away from British-occupied Newport on Narragansett Bay. He wrote a flurry of unanswered letters to entice Caty to join him in Basking Ridge. One such letter touted the sensible, polite, and distinguished merits of Lord Stirling's wife, Sarah, and his daughter, Kitty.

After six weeks of silence since the birth of their daughter, he received a letter from Caty telling him that she was ill. Shocked, he immediately responded.

> *I was almost thunderstruck at the receipt of your letter. How different its contents from my wishes: a lingering disorder of five Weeks and from the present symptoms a confinement of two months longer. Heaven preserve you and bless you with patience and fortitude to support yourself under the cruel misfortune. Oh that I had but wings to fly to your relief. My Heart mourns the Absence of its counterpart.*

Caty read Nathanael's letters from her confinement in Potowomut. As a new mother whose maternal emotions were running high and longing for her little family to unite, she savored each letter. Jacob and Peggy arrived from Coventry with little George to visit their sister-in-law.

Caty's illness interfered with her ability to nurse baby Martha, who she nicknamed Patty. Furthermore, she received two letters, one from Nathanael that clearly signaled his desperation for her arrival, yet it hurt her as well.

> *If you think your health and strength will endure the journey, my heart will leap for joy to meet you. Buy whatever you wish. If you are in want of anything from Boston write to Mrs. Knox. But remember when you write to her you write to a good scholar, therefore mind and spell well. You are defective in this matter, my love; a little attention will soon correct it. People are often laughed at for not spelling well.*

The second letter asked her if she was determined to suckle the baby or not. Her liberty to travel depended on it rather than having to depend on a wet nurse. Little George climbed onto the bed. He wrapped his arms around Caty's neck and proclaimed, "Momma!"

She kissed the toddler and handed the last letter to Jacob.

He glanced at Peggy, lay the letter aside, and said, "I shall write to him to inform him of your difficulties."

"No, Jacob, that is not your place," Caty insisted weakly. Her dark eyes drifted to the sleeping babe in her cradle. "Let me attend to this on my own."

"No, dear, you cannot write him in this state. How would you know how to explain this matter?" Peggy advised.

"Nathanael already believes I am culturally inferior to, well, certain persons. I—"

"That is enough," Jacob scolded. "Has not Catherine or Sarah encouraged you to nurse your newborn?"

"I am not a novice mother," Caty huffed in defiance. "I believe it is time that I attempt the journey to Morristown to be with my husband. I was told the British have abandoned their efforts in New Jersey, therefore my safe passage is likely."

"That seems unwise," Peggy scolded.

"You have no say in the matter. Nathanael has told me to buy whatever I want for me and the children. None of my old clothes fit, and the children are growing so fast they will be naked by the time we arrive."

Jacob left the room to consult with Kitt. "I shall write Nathanael despite Caty's protest," he told his younger brother. Kitt frowned in disapproval, but he offered no argument.

❧

In mid-May 1777, Nathanael and Henry Knox were sent to Peekskill, New York, in the Hudson Highlands to inspect fortifications and devise defenses south of West Point. Henry was now a brigadier general. They noted that the fortifications were insufficient, and the construction of a chain to stop oncoming British ships lay across the river at Fort Montgomery. On their return journey to Morristown, Nathanael fell from his horse on a rocky mountain trail.

Henry reined his horse and dismounted. "Are you hurt?"

"I will survive," Nathanael said with a split lip. He stumbled to his feet.

"You will likely have bruises from that fall," Henry clucked.

"I have hopes that Caty will be the only one who sees them," Nathanael groused.

"Come. Let us stop for a visit with your friend in New Jersey, Mr. Abraham Lott. I hear he is quite the host. His wife serves dinners that abound with riches of food and spirits."

Nathanael dusted his breeches off and mounted his horse. "I may have made Caty angry."

"How did you do that?"

"I compared her bad spelling to that of your wife's educated prose."

"Why would you do such a thing?" Henry asked. "Your spelling is not the best either."

Henry climbed into the saddle and pulled up beside him. "I know you are conscious of your lack of education as you are of many other things."

"I think it is you who should be conscious of what is happening," Nathanael challenged. "Congress sent Silas Deane of Groton, Connecticut, to France last year as the first representative of the United American colonies in Europe. Deane has gone to extremes in promising commissions to French officers. He has promised a commission as major general to command our army's artillery and engineering corps to a Monsieur Philippe du Coudray. Du Coudray is the one who recruited engineers in France and also delivered two hundred French cannons to our forces."

"So I have heard," Henry confirmed. "I received a letter from Lucy, who is in Boston. She wrote that a French general, who styles himself commander-in-chief of the Continental artillery, was in town. He announced that he is going immediately to headquarters to take command—that he is a major-general, and a deal of it. She said she is certain I will never suffer anyone to command me in that department."

"So the French invasion has begun," Nathanael said, "I suppose we will see more come to our shores in search of glory and money."

≈

On May 23, a significant portion of the British garrison moved from Rhode Island to New York. This movement alarmed the Patriots, but it still gave them no indication of Howe's intentions. It did, however, issue a sigh of relief in Nathanael's heart and mind, knowing his wife and children were out of immediate harm's way—for the time being.

After the surprise attack at Bound Brook, George Washington withdrew the garrison, and on May 28, he moved part of his army from Morristown to a new entrenched camp near Middlebrook.

General William Howe had his own ideas. He confided to his generals, "If I could draw Washington out of his encampment in Middlebrook and into a battle on the plains of northern New Jersey and defeat them, the remainder of the march to Philadelphia would be relatively simple. A swift victory there may allow time to support General John Burgoyne's force, which is marching south from Montreal, Canada toward Albany, New York, and prevent Washington from sending troops north."

Howe did just that. After marching his army in two divisions from New Brunswick with colours waving and drums beating, they stopped in Middlebrook, New Jersey, and went into camp.

George was not about to sit idly by. The 11th Regiment of Virginia riflemen, known as "Morgan's Rifles," under the command of forty-one-year-old Colonel Daniel Morgan from Fredrick County, Virginia, arrived in camp. Morgan's regiment consisted of 180 Virginia frontiersmen, whom George augmented with 500 handpicked Continentals, primarily from the mountains of Pennsylvania, Virginia, and Maryland, all armed with Pennsylvania long rifles.

Morgan, a towering man with broad shoulders and muscular arms, was an experienced Indian fighter who called himself, "The Old Wagoner." He served as a civilian teamster during the war with the French and Indians.

"You know my hatred for the British, General," his deep voice boomed. "You were there as a militia commander when I lost my temper and struck my superior officer during General Braddock's march to Fort Duquesne in

1755. I was given a drumhead court martial and sentenced to five hundred lashes. I counted each lash from the drummer as I was whipped, and he was short a lash." Daniel hooted with pride.

George smiled at the recollection. "You stayed conscious during the entire ordeal. I had never seen a man's back so bloodied and the skin hanging in ribbons before that time," he mused.

"Then, sir, you know me and my men can perform our duties—and cheerfully," Daniel said.

While William Howe played cat and mouse with Washington, Nathanael's prophecy played out. At 10:00 p.m. on June 13, a ship from France, the *Victoire*, dropped anchor off North Island, South Carolina. It had strayed fifty miles north off its intended course for Charleston. A wealthy and enthusiastic young nobleman was among those on board. In fact, the young man owned the *Victoire* and had paid for and outfitted her for the voyage. Nineteen-year-old Marquis de Lafayette was one of the many Frenchmen granted a commission in the American Army by Silas Deane.

Unlike his companions, Lafayette had not left his pregnant seventeen-year-old wife, Adrienne, for money. He learned of the American Revolution at a dinner given by the Comte de Broglie on August 8, 1775. Lafayette became intensely interested. He saw in the American struggle the opportunity for avenging France's defeat in the Seven Years' War in which his father had lost his life.

A week later, William Howe suddenly withdrew his army toward New Brunswick, simulating a retreat. The Americans followed. Nathanael's division, Pennsylvania General Anthony Wayne's brigade, and Morgan's riflemen closed in on the rear of the British column. The pursuit continued to New Brunswick. Although their fighting blood was up, the American units had trouble coordinating their movements. As the British continued their withdrawal toward Perth Amboy, the Americans broke off the pursuit, but the move succeeded in drawing the American commander out of his defensive positions at Middlebrook.

On June 26, Howe marched out of Perth Amboy in two columns in an attempt to cut the Americans off from Middlebrook, but the effort was too great for his men. They suffered from the intense June heat clad in woolen redcoats and burdened with heavy gear.

Washington withdrew to Middlebrook, leaving the two armies in the same positions they had occupied three weeks before. Howe pulled back and ferried the entire force across to Staten Island. His army was back in New York, and he fell into another of his lapses of torpidity.

It cleared the way for Caty to travel to New Jersey.

Caty left for Morristown with an aide and her son and infant daughter. She traveled overland through the back country, careful to avoid British occupied New York City. Like the roads and rivers that Martha Washington was forced to travel from Mount Vernon in Virginia to the army's winter cantonment, they were dusty, poorly marked paths that turned into muddy quagmires when it rained. Rivers and streams that lacked bridges, and were occasionally dotted with ferries, were often impassable. Tories roamed the countryside, and inns were unfit for women traveling essentially alone with small children. Yet, the Hudson River provided breathtaking views of palisades, which Caty had never seen.

The journey left her exhausted, but she was not too exhausted to fall into her husband's elated arms when she arrived in the Middlebrook camp. He kissed her with unbridled passion, which lifted Caty out of the low spirits that had haunted her for far too long.

"My beautiful angel," Nathanael breathed. "I have desired the pleasures of domestic felicity—and here you are."

"You look tired," she said. She stroked his cheek and asked, "Have you the energy to greet your children?" She nestled baby Patty in his uncertain strong arms. "She has your eyes," Caty said as Nathanael stared in wonder at his tiny daughter.

Nathanael kissed Patty's forehead and laid her in her mother's arms. He squatted to speak to his eighteen-month-old son. "You have your mother's dark hair and pert little nose," he said.

George clung to his mother's skirts and stuck his forefinger in his mouth.

Nathanael stood up. "I do not want to scare him."

"He is not scared. He will become accustomed to you soon enough."

"Caty, I cannot—," Nathanael began painfully.

She put a finger to his lips. "I understand. You have to do what you must for our country. We are here together. Let us not waste a moment."

"Our quarters at the Lott's are less than private," he admitted.

"Why are we not lodging at Lord Stirling's estate at Basking Ridge?"

"The army's move from Morristown to Middlebrook shifted my headquarters," Nathanael explained. "Do you think I wish to share a room?"

"I wish to be where you are," she demurred.

"And I you. I believe you are the one who looks tired and needs rest," Nathanael said as he removed her trunk from the carriage.

That night as the full moon traveled toward its apex in the sky, Nathanael and Caty tucked their little ones into bed. In the small room, devoid of the other expected guests, Caty unbuttoned Nathanael's waist coat and pulled his shirt over his head. She kissed his broad chest, made strong from the years he worked fields and hammered iron into anchors.

"My heart panted to see you," he murmured while he kissed her neck and laid her back on the bed. Their time together would be short-lived.

nine

Rashness, Passion, and Even Wantonness

T he plan General John Burgoyne penned for Lord Germain, the Secretary of State to the American colonies, and King George III, called for a large force to march southward from Lake Champlain. He would assail Fort Ticonderoga on the southern tip of the lake and then proceed down nearby Lake George to the Hudson River and then to Albany, New York. The strategy would effectively cut off the New England colonies from the rest of America and allow combined forces to hunt down Washington and destroy the Continental Army.

In the winter of 1777, Washington's former adjutant, General Horatio Gates, had command of Fort Ticonderoga. It was the fort from which Henry Knox and his expedition had hauled sixty tons of artillery to Framingham, Massachusetts. Gates spent the spring in Philadelphia trying to convince Congress that he was better suited to command the Northern Army than the aristocratic General Philip Schuyler, whose primary residence was in Albany, New York.

John Adams wrote to his pregnant wife Abigail declaring his exasperation over the generals' leadership contests at Congress:

I am wearied to death with the wrangles between military officers, high and low. They quarrel like cats and dogs. They worry one another like mastiffs, scrambling for rank and pay like apes for nuts.

Adams was wearied by much more than that. Nathanael took up his pen to protest the impropriety of putting French engineer Philippe du Coudray at the head of the Continental Army artillery department.

"May we interrupt?" Caty asked when she and the children arrived at Nathanael's cramped headquarters in the Middlebrook encampment.

Nathanael sighed and stilled his busy quill. His aides, William Blodget and Thomas Paine, rose and bowed. "Mrs. Greene it is a pleasure to have you here," William said.

"The pleasure is mine. Do you know if there are dances planned this week? I have not had a whirl around the dance floor in months."

"If there are, I request your first dance," Thomas said with a gleam in his eye.

"Caty," Nathanael admonished, "this is neither the time nor the place."

"You know how well my husband dances," Caty teased regardless of her husband's scolding. "He is being modest."

"You may find there will be no dances to attend when Congress reads my letter," Nathanael cautioned.

"Oh? Concerning the general who has come from France to replace General Knox?"

"I have asked for confirmation of rumors that du Coudray not only expects the appointment, but also expects his rank to commence from the first of August 1776," Nathanael explained lividly. "If that is the case, du Coudray will out rank me, John Sullivan, and many other major generals. I am tendering my resignation if the report is true. Sullivan and Knox are doing the same."

Nathanael rose and stretched his stiff knee. "General Benedict Arnold is here in camp. There has already been derision between him and Congress concerning his rank. Congress finally promoted him to major general, but they refused to restore his seniority in part due to a quota system. In Arnold's home state of Connecticut, Israel Putnam and Joseph Spencer hold that rank."

Caty glanced at Thomas and William whose faces revealed there was much contempt regarding the subject. "I realize the proposed replacement is abhorrent to General Knox, but he is a brigadier is he not?" she asked.

"Mrs. Greene, this is a matter of seniority and foreign officers coming to America and rivaling those who have earned their place," William interjected. "Surely you can understand that."

"Of course," Caty said, trying to hide her annoyance at the aide's patronizing tone.

Little George stood on his tiptoes and reached for a piece of paper on his father's desk. A cascade of papers floated to the floor. The toddler squatted to pat his chubby hand on top of the disorderly pile.

"No!" Nathanael snapped.

George looked up at his father with dark, wide, frightened eyes. Nathanael looked down at his innocent son. George stood and stretched his arms up and said, "Papa."

With remorse, Nathanael lifted the boy into his arms. "I am doing this for you so you can grow up in a world where you have the freedom to choose. I shall never use that tone with you again no matter my annoyance with other influences."

∂

On Saturday, July 12, 1777, with the army temporarily back in Morristown, New Jersey, Washington received a letter dated July 7 from John Adams and Congress—it was clear and threatening:

Dear Sir,

We at Congress have read generals Greene's, Sullivan's, and Knox's letters of resignation submitted to us due to their

dissatisfaction with French General Philip du Coudray's pro-
posal to replace General Knox as commander of the army's
Artillery corps. Their letters are an attempt to influence our
decisions and an invasion of the liberties of the people and
indicating a want of confidence in the justice of Congress.

You are directed to accept the generals' resignations if they
cannot serve their country under the authority of Congress,
and acknowledge their improper attempts to subvert the will
of the national legislature. With great Sincerity, I wish you an
agreeable success. I am still with great Esteem, sir, your most
obedient Servant.

John Adams

George summoned two of the generals in question to his headquarters
at the Colfax House. General John Sullivan was posted in Princeton, New
Jersey, therefore only Nathanael and Henry were on hand. "I appreciate
your zeal," he told them, "but Mr. Adams is asking for apologies for your
recent threatening letters which are an impropriety."

"I absolutely refuse," Henry huffed. "Conscious of the rectitude of
my intention and of the contents of my letter, I shall make no acknowledg-
ments whatever."

"Nathanael?" George asked.

"Adams will not leave this alone," Nathanael retorted. "He sent a
letter to me personally admonishing my choice to make this a public matter
and said that I was guilty of rashness, passion, and even wantonness in
this proceeding. He admitted that Congress had not approved the contract
between du Coudray and Silas Deane. I will not apologize."

George stifled a look of satisfaction. He had no intention of accepting
resignations from his most valued generals. He said, "I suppose General
Sullivan will agree with you."

Horse hooves pounded toward the Colfax House and alarmed George's Life Guard. They deployed to intercept the rider. George's aides, Colonels Alexander Hamilton and Tench Tilghman, also got to their feet from where they sat attending to correspondence.

The young rider and his horse were drenched in sweat when they pulled up to the house. He leapt from his saddle and shouted, "I am Daniel Forsythe. I need to see General Washington!" He impatiently tried to skirt Lieutenant George Lewis, General Washington's nephew and commander of the guards.

Lieutenant Lewis led Daniel inside and allowed him to present himself to His Excellency. "My name is Sergeant Daniel Forsythe of the 9th Westchester New York militia." His hand shook when he handed the message to the commander-in-chief.

George regarded Nathanael's calm face as if it were the only thing that could prevent him from tearing the message to shreds because he knew the news would be terrible. He unfolded the damp piece of paper. "This is from General Philip Schuyler," he said and then read aloud, "Fort Ticonderoga fell to General John Burgoyne on 7 July. General Arthur St. Clair was forced to evacuate in the middle of the night. Further, there was fighting around Hubbardton in the New Hampshire Grants where we have lost hundreds of militia. Skenesborough, New York, has been lost, but Burgoyne's army has been scattered."

He looked up from the letter and addressed the room, "This is an event of chagrin and surprise not apprehended or in the compass of my reasoning. This stroke is severe. King George III and the Continental Congress believe Fort Ticonderoga is the key to the North American continent. Its downfall will require immediate action against General Burgoyne. His slow-moving force of 8,000 will eventually regroup."

Nathanael was distressed over St. Clair's decision to abandon the fort when the American numbers garrisoned nearby, as well as militia, almost equaled that of Burgoyne's. But now was not the time to erupt in judgment and perceived misconduct.

❧

Nathanael and Caty were forced to part again when the Continental Army decamped and left Morristown, leaving New Jersey wide open if Howe turned his eyes that way. "I will send for you as soon as we establish camp and I have new headquarters," Nathanael assured his wife.

Caty's countenance reflected disappointment, but Nathanael, under pressure from His Excellency to gather and lead his regiments did not notice. "I shall await your letters," she promised.

Most of the army stopped near Pompton, New Jersey, twenty-one miles northeast where heavy rain brought marching to a halt for three days. Although it began to rain again on July 14, the army kept moving. The muddy roads made the march difficult and fatigued the troops and camp followers. Henry Knox's artillery mired in the mud, and the baggage wagons lost wheels, which forced the men to leave them behind.

At last they arrived at The Clove, twenty miles southwest of West Point, New York on the Hudson River where iron chains intended to deter the British fleet stretched across the river near West Point to New Windsor, New York. George set up his headquarters at Suffern's Tavern and waited for Howe to show his hand. Each passing day increased his concern.

He relayed his scanty intelligence to General William Heath in Boston:

> *The British are preparing their transports for the embarkation of their troops from Staten Island, are fixing berths for the light-horse, &c., but their destination could not be developed.*

In late July, he received the news that William Howe loaded more than 266 transports and ships of war with some 18,000 military and civilian forces and necessary horse and supplies. His intentions were as unknown to his officers and troops as Washington's own inner thoughts. However, Howe had an option unavailable to his opponent—complete naval superiority. His older brother, Admiral Lord Richard Howe, was in charge of that superiority. The admiral selected his flagship, *Eagle,* to protect the front of the fleet. It was the largest armada ever assembled in American waters.

Howe's destination was not only an enigma to Washington but also to the Continental Congress. John Adams wrote:

> *We here in Philadelphia are tense with rumors piled one upon another about Howe's destination. They might as well imagine them gone round Cape Horn into the South Seas to land at California and march across the Continent to attack our back settlements.*

George began marching and counter-marching his army as the Americans tried to anticipate where Howe was going. He divided his army into five divisions under Nathanael, Lord Alexander Stirling, John Sullivan, and Adam Stephen. The fifth division belonged to Massachusetts General Benjamin Lincoln, but Lincoln would soon be gone, so command fell to the pugnacious General Anthony Wayne from Pennsylvania. There was also the artillery brigade under Henry Knox and a dragoon brigade.

Of the five divisions, Nathanael's was the largest and best organized. It consisted of half the army's Virginia troops and two brigadier generals: Peter Muhlenberg, a German Pennsylvanian, and George Weedon of Virginia.

In early August, Washington, convinced that Philadelphia was Howe's destination, marched his army toward Pennsylvania. In frustration, Nathanael wrote to his friend from Rhode Island, General James Varnum, "His Excellency is exceedingly impatient; but it is said if Philadelphia is lost all is ruined. It is a great object to be sure but not of that great magnitude that it claims. In the spring we had the enemy about our ears every hour. Now, the Northern Army has got the enemy about their heads, and we have lost ours. We are compelled to wander about the country in search of them."

As anxiety over Howe's intentions for the summer campaign heightened, the fall of Fort Ticonderoga in July was also the downfall of General Philip Schuyler. The Dutch-American aristocratic general from Albany,

New York was in command of the army's Northern Department and ultimately responsible for the fort's defense. On August 4, Congress dismissed Schuyler and sent General Horatio Gates to replace him. Washington was pressed to send additional troops north in support.

In a council meeting, it was decided to send General Benedict Arnold because he was well connected to Schuyler and Gates. General Benjamin Lincoln, who outranked Arnold, was also selected for his expertise in raising militia as well as Daniel Morgan and his riflemen.

Fearing he would be George's choice to march to the aid of the Northern Army, Nathanael stifled a sigh of relief. He would not be long separated from Caty—at least not yet.

After all the complaints and letters Nathanael had delivered about foreign officers, he was introduced to one who did not offend his senses. In the Moland House headquarters in Warwick Township, Pennsylvania, twenty miles north of Philadelphia, Nathanael and his aides were employed in endless paperwork. Washington entered the house accompanied by his aide Colonel Alexander Hamilton and another man.

Everyone rose and bowed to the commander-in-chief.

"Your Excellency," Nathanael said formally in the presence of the unknown visitor.

"Alexander, you will translate," George ordered. His aide nodded as the stranger spoke no English.

"General Nathanael Greene, this is the Marquis de Lafayette. He arrived from France in June. With his companions, he made his way to Philadelphia where Congress has seen fit to bestow a major generalship on him. We met at a dinner held by members of Congress in my honor at City Tavern."

Nathanael bowed, "It is my pleasure to meet you, General Lafayette. May I introduce my aides, Major William Blodget and Mr. Thomas Paine."

Blodget and Paine also bowed and spoke of their pleasure of making Lafayette's acquaintance.

The tall nineteen-year-old nobleman looked pleased and enthusiastically said, "*Mon amour pour la liberté est indiscutable et ma soif de gloire inassouvie. J'ai l'honneur de servir aux côtés du général Washington.*"

"My love for liberty is unquestionable and my thirst for glory unquenched. It is my honor to serve beside General Washington," Alexander translated.

"Congress resolved that his service is accepted, despite their attending to the du Coudray contention. The title is honorary, and his assignment has been left up to me," George said. "I wish you to join us tomorrow, Nathanael, to inspect the troops alongside General Knox and Lord Stirling."

The next day, the soldiers lined up. Their clothes were tattered and shredded. Some soldiers were almost naked; many were barefoot and most had no uniforms. Some wore homespun hunting shirts. Others wore a variety of coats.

George attempted to cover his self-consciousness. "We must feel embarrassed to exhibit ourselves before an officer who has just quitted French troops."

But Nathanael saw them with pride. Many of them were his men from Rhode Island. They were all there for the same reason—to defend the rights of their country against a tyrannical monarchy that attempted to rule them from 3,000 miles across the Atlantic. Many of the soldiers had been with their officers since the first shots were fired at Lexington and Concord, Massachusetts in April 1775.

The marquis' reply to Washington showed no signs of shame in his words, at least as conveyed by Alexander, "It is to learn, and to teach, that I come hither."

Nathanael watched this young man with a keen eye and thought, *I believe the marquis is a most sweet tempered young gentleman.*

֎

Rumors had it that Admiral Lord Richard Howe's fleet, with William's army on board, were sailing up the Delaware toward Philadelphia. Henry Knox worked to construct river fortifications in the event the rumors were true. Then, word came that the fleet had turned away from the Delaware Capes and sailed out to sea.

On August 21, George told his general officers at a council of war, "I believe that the armada is headed back to New York to link up with Burgoyne's advance down Lake Champlain in the face of our Northern Army. I have no idea where to send our army without accurate intelligence."

"We should consider marching north to New York to defeat Burgoyne," Henry stated. "The British general has Indians with him who are attacking our troops. This power ought to be crushed at all hazards immediately or the whole frontier will be deluged in blood."

"Philadelphia must be preserved at all events, but in my opinion, it is an object of far less importance than the Hudson River," Nathanael agreed.

Hearing the consensus lay with Henry and Nathanael, George said, "Very well. We shall have to wait for Congress to approve the mission as my command will supersede that of General Gates'."

Henry sidled up to Nathanael. "Are you up to a trip to Philadelphia?"

"Why?"

"Lucy is recovering from an illness in Boston. I want to shop for gifts for her to cheer her."

"If you obtain George's approval, then I shall be happy to go. I received news from Caty that she was suffering from camp fever over the summer. She is still installed in the Lott house in New Jersey. Perhaps, I need to purchase something to cheer her spirits, as well."

Washington gave his approval, and on the morning of August 24, Nathanael and Henry set out on an exceedingly hot afternoon. They arrived in Bethlehem, Pennsylvania outside of Philadelphia. A rider pulled up to them. "General Washington has sent me to tell you to return to the main army. He is marching through Philadelphia on his way south to Wilmington, Delaware, and he requires your attendance."

"What is your name?" Nathanael asked as he shaded his eyes from the sun to bring the rider's face into focus.

"Captain Harry Fellows of the 1st New York Regiment, sir."

"Has there been news of Howe?" Nathanael asked.

"Yes, sir. Signal guns were sounded from rebel lookouts along the Virginia shore of the Chesapeake. Howe's armada was seen sailing up the river."

Nathanael grinned. "I am in hopes Mr. Howe will give us a little time to collect, and then we do not care how soon he begins the frolic. What say you, Henry?"

"I say we shall lay the blame on Howe for depriving our wives of tender gifts from their husbands," Henry chuckled.

"I am certain that we will have to make up for it," Nathanael quipped. To Captain Fellows, he said, "Tell His Excellency that we are on our way."

❧

That day, the army marched through Philadelphia. The rumbling, noisy, and dusty parade took two hours to pass through the heart of the cheering city. Each soldier wore a green sprig in his hat as an emblem of hope. Nathanael rode at the head of his division with William Blodget and a new aide, Captain Ichabod Burnet, by his side. The army moved on from Philadelphia to Wilmington, where Washington established headquarters at the Forsythe House on Quaker Hill outside of town.

A letter arrived for Washington concerning British General John Burgoyne's campaign in the Mohawk Valley in New York.

August 18, 1777 New Hampshire Grants, Bennington

I do myself the honor to advise your Excellency that Col John Stark and I with 2,000 militiamen from this area have defeated a force of approx. 1,400 troops detached from Gen. John Burgoyne's army to raid Bennington for horses, draft animals, provisions, and other supplies. The commanding officers, Hessian colonels Baum and Breymann, were surprised with the numbers in our force but stood against us regardless. Col Baum was killed and Breymann was driven away. We have gleaned information that this has led Burgoyne's native supporters to largely abandon him and deprive his army of much-needed supplies. I am, Dear Genl, Your Excellency's most Obedient and most Humble Servant.

Col Seth Warner

Alexander Hamilton looked up from his secretary's desk and said, "At last, some relief."

"What relief is that, Alexander?" Nathanael asked as he poured a glass of claret and plopped down in a chair in front of the aide's desk.

George passed the letter to Nathanael. Nathanael read it, handed it back, and asked, "What does this mean for us?"

"It means that we are going to Iron Hill to reconnoiter the British who are disembarking from the Chesapeake Bay at Head of Elk, Maryland, and that you and Lafayette will accompany me."

Thunder rolled long and heavy. Streaks of lightning lit the sky. Nathanael rose and peered through the window. Fat drops hit the glass like pebbles. "This storm may deter us," he said raising his eyes skyward. "But if it deters us, then it will deter the British landing."

On August 25, Nathanael, George, Alexander, and Lafayette arrived at Iron Hill near the Delaware-Maryland border with a large body of cavalry for protection. Nathanael raised his spyglass to one eye and peered through the overgrown woods on the hill. "All I can see are soldiers disembarking from longboats." He passed the spyglass to George.

"This is not helping," George grumbled. He urged his horse forward.

Lafayette shifted uncomfortably. *"Général Washington, vous exposez imprudemment au danger ici."*

George raised the spyglass and ordered, "Translate, Alexander."

"He says that you are recklessly exposing yourself to danger here."

George lowered the glass. "You are right. We cannot discern anything."

Gray thick clouds scudded overhead, and the wind freshened.

"I suggest we find shelter," Alexander advised.

The four men wheeled their horses and rode to the home of a Maryland Loyalist. They took supper there and moved out the next day. It was time to confer with the army about their plans to meet General William Howe's army head on. George ordered Irish-born General William Maxwell's light infantry to guard all the roads.

Ironically, the next day when the British moved into town, William Howe established his headquarters in the same house. His troops set about building shelters and rested to recover from their long sea voyage.

ten

Carnage Growled Across the Countryside

On the morning of September 3, Howe's army began moving. The hours before dawn were lit by the eerie northern lights as the regiments filed off to the northeast. Washington assembled an army of close to 15,000 men and positioned them at Iron Hill where woods offered excellent terrain for ambushes. It was between the enemy and their ultimate destination—Philadelphia. Cooch's Mill carried the main road to Wilmington across Christiana Creek just east of Iron Hill. This was where Washington had deployed General William Maxwell's light infantry and some militia. Nathanael strongly recommended moving the entire army to the position, but Washington disagreed.

A running two-mile fight developed as 400 hundred British grenadiers and Hessian jaegers pushed north toward Cooch's Mill and across Christiana Creek. General William Maxwell's infantry slowed the British advance through a series of small ambushes, but Howe sent reinforcements that forced Maxwell's men to flee.

The news of the British advance, coupled with the defeat at Cooch's Bridge, spread panic throughout Philadelphia. Patriots prepared to move to inland towns. Supplies and materials that might benefit the British were moved to Reading and other places in the backcountry. Congress made arrangements to move to York, Pennsylvania.

Washington began stripping the Delaware River defenses of every available Continental soldier and militiaman to reinforce his main army confronting Howe. He summoned Nathanael to headquarters. "I wish you to scour the countryside for a good defensive position from which to challenge Howe," George ordered. "I have other scouts, but my faith in you is compounded as each day your assertive good judgement graces this army. You will make the greatest exertions to remove our stores in the countryside out of the reach of the enemy."

"I believe the troops are in good health and high spirits. I myself will do whatever we must," Nathanael promised. He turned to leave.

George stopped him and asked, "You *do* know I am going to roll the proverbial dice and risk everything by attacking Howe?"

Nathanael nodded and then attended to his duty. He, William Blodget, and Brigadier General George Weedon rode through the farmlands and fields of southeastern Pennsylvania and northeastern Delaware reconnoitering and planning where stores could be moved away from the enemy's probable line of march.

Families fleeing the no-man's land in between the looming armies wearily traveled the winding back trails to escape the looting that had already begun with the arrival of the British Army. The sound of lowing cattle, crying babies, creaking wheels, and jingling horse tack drifted across the landscape.

Many farmers stood in their wheat and corn fields and watched in silence as a man dressed in a blue and buff uniform wearing gold epaulets that signified a major general trotted the loose, winding main road. Nathanael approached one of those farmers, who stood beside a youngster. "What is your name, sir?" he asked.

The farmer removed his hat and wiped his brow with his forearm. "John Farlow. This is my son, Thomas."

"Why are you and your family not leaving?" Nathanael asked as his eyes drifted to the cloud of dust across the fields.

"We shan't leave. We are Quakers and have no allegiance to either side."

George and William shot Nathanael a sideways glance. This territory was more dangerous than the British Army. "You knew they lived in this area," William whispered to Nathanael. "Do not start a tirade."

Nathanael ignored William and sneered. "Still you remain at home. If the British Army comes to you for sustenance, you will provide it will you not?"

"We are conservative, cautious, and anti-violent," John Farlow returned. "But what would you know about it general—"

"General Nathanael Greene. I was raised a Quaker. For all your dogma and your refusal to fight, you will let this country—your own country—fall down about you?"

"Nathanael, you must not—" William began.

Nathanael shrugged him off and continued, "You are villainous people who serve the enemy."

John took a step toward Nathanael. William responded by aiming his pistol at the farmer. John pointed at the distant line of refugees. "Many of them are not of the Society of Friends. They are the disaffected. It has not been just the King's soldiers who have vilified, plundered, and ravished them."

John Farlow and his son turned their backs on Nathanael and disappeared into the corn that was high enough to harvest.

"You know this is true," William ventured, "that our own soldiers are guilty of lawlessness. You yourself have issued orders demanding that the troops respect private property."

"We have work to do, Billy," Nathanael said. He wheeled his horse.

꙳

At 2:00 a.m. on Tuesday, September 9, in response to Howe's advance northeastward, George ordered his army to march six miles north to Chadd's Ford on the steep, often thickly wooded banks of Brandywine

Creek. His decision to defend Chadd's Ford was because it was on the main road to Philadelphia.

There were numerous fords at one-mile intervals northward along the Brandywine: Brinton's Ford, Wistar's Ford, Jones Ford, and Buffington Ford. These names and other local landmarks were not thoroughly familiar to George and his generals as he did not take the precaution of having someone who knew the countryside at hand. On September 10, the British Army, 13,000 strong, was encamped at Kennett Square six miles west of Chadd's Ford and twenty-six miles from Philadelphia.

Nathanael, William Blodget, and George Weedon had spent two days without sleep. Nathanael wrote to Caty, "The country all resounds with the cries of the people. I am exceedingly fatigued. I was on horseback for upwards of thirty hours and never closed my eyes for near forty. Last night I was in hopes of a good night's rest, but a dusty bed gave me asthma and I had very little sleep the whole night, but little as it was, I feel finely refreshed this morning. A general action must take place in a few days."

The commander-in-chief prepared his defenses. He formed his army into three wings. Downstream, the left was guarded by 1,500 militiamen posted at the one usable ford. Nathanael, with his 2,500-man Virginia division, was posted near the Great Post Road to guard a ferry crossing and be within supporting distance of Chadd's Ford. On his right, General Anthony Wayne's 2,000 Pennsylvanians were to defend Chadd's Ford. Thomas Proctor's Pennsylvania artillery unlimbered northeast of Chadd's Ford. John Sullivan's 1,800 men positioned a mile and a half north of Wayne's right flank and anchored the American right to guard Brinton's Ford. Lord Alexander Stirling's and General Adam Stephen's division formed a second line behind Sullivan's men.

The American right extended beyond Jones Ford, and John Sullivan was told by the locals that there was no usable ford for twelve miles. Elements of both armies were moving into Chester County, Pennsylvania. The camp followers were ordered to stay behind with the baggage train and stay away from the lines. Chester County was mainly rural. Quaker and

Baptist meetinghouses dotted the fertile area that was covered with rolling hills and thick hardwood forests of chestnut, hickory, and oak.

Two Loyalists informed William Howe that twelve miles to the north was a ford that appeared to have escaped the Americans' attention. Although William was fighting in the enemy's country, his knowledge of terrain and road networks was superior to George's. He had taken the time to develop a plan of battle by consulting locals.

George and his staff settled in the Ring House and set up headquarters. His army was a half-naked, sick, and starving force whose troops deserted on a regular basis. Still, with his troop numbers nearly equal to the enemy's, he was confident he could win by defending the important fords along the Brandywine.

Only one of the most powerful men in America could be right.

September 11 dawned cool, gray, and dreary with the Brandywine Valley shrouded in fog. A smoky haze drifting from chimneys, bake ovens, and thousands of campfires added to the surreal ceiling that hovered above the armies. In the pre-dawn hours, William Howe's troops, led by Charles Cornwallis, began to march from Kennett Square seven miles to Brandywine Creek along the Nottingham Road that led to Chadd's Ford. About five miles west of the ford, the road intersected the Great Valley Road that led northward toward West Chester.

Hessian General Wilhelm von Knyphausen's division left at the same time and marched directly eastward toward the Brandywine as a ruse to cover the larger army's flanking movement. Hearing of Knyphausen's advance, Washington sent General William Maxwell's regiment back across the Brandywine to harass the enemy's vanguard. The Hessian general turned Maxwell's flank and his left collapsed. He retreated back across the Brandywine in a thick fog of powder smoke, leaving close to fifty dead men. The British and Hessian infantry received orders not to advance any farther and lay on the heights at Chadd's Ford.

At around 9:30 a.m., word arrived at headquarters from General John Sullivan that they had seen no sign of the enemy. Washington ordered

Alexander Hamilton to send for Colonel Theodorick Bland of the 2nd Continental Light Dragoons and order him to reconnoiter and confirm the movement west of the creek.

At 11:00 a.m., Washington joined Nathanael at his position, which was close enough to the Ring House that aides and messengers could find him.

"All is quiet across the creek," Nathanael said.

"Something is wrong," George lamented. "Why are they having such difficulty ascertaining what is happening? I have heard nothing from Colonel Bland. I think the British are heading for Jones' Ford."

"We cannot know that," Nathanael countered. "The fog, dust, and heat make it difficult for the patrols to spot anything at a distance."

The general's speculation was cut short. The first of many confusing warnings arrived, first from Colonel Moses Hazen at Buffington's Ford:

> *The British are making a flanking movement. A strong British column is to the west headed toward the forks of the Brandywine near Trimble's Ford.*

Another message arrived from John Sullivan's aide Major Lewis Morris:

> *A large body of the enemy, from every account 5,000, with 16 or 18 field pieces, marched along this road just now. This road leads to Trimble's and Jeffrie's ferries on the Brandywine. We are close on the enemy's rear and skirmishing with some of their elements.*

"I think the question is has part of Howe's army marched along the river to fool us, or are we facing the entire army across Chadd's Ford?" Nathanael asserted.

"The force in front of us across the creek cannot be their main army," George deduced. "Their army is divided." He issued orders to his aide, Timothy Pickering. "Tell General Sullivan to take his division across the creek at Brinton's Ford and attack Knyphausen's left flank. General Greene will cross at Chadd's Ford and attack Knyphausen's right and center."

Nathanael quickly obeyed the order. The thrust escalated into skirmishes. George received more conflicting reports. Despite some of his wary officers' belief that Howe was executing a right flanking movement as he had done at Long Island, George determined that it was a feint and recalled the attack until he could determine Howe's intentions.

At 2:00 p.m., as George and his staff were having dinner, a message arrived from Colonel Bland, forwarded by John Sullivan:

> *Colonel Bland has at this moment sent me word that the enemy are in the rear of my right, about two miles, coming down. There are, he says, about two brigades of them. He also saw dust back in the country for above an hour.*

George ordered John Sullivan to pull his infantry out of line and shift his division north to link up with Generals Lord Alexander Stirling and Adam Stephen on Birmingham Hill east of the Brandywine.

What Howe was up to was led by Lord Charles Cornwallis. At 1:00 p.m., the vanguard of Cornwallis' column arrived at Jeffries' Ford on the east branch of the Brandywine. The bridge had been destroyed, so they had to cross in three-foot-deep water.

Just east of Jefferies' Ford, the road to Birmingham intersected with the road coming from Jeffries' Ford at right angles, cutting through a sharp defile. It was the perfect avenue to march troops behind, and Washington had not seen to defend it.

The arrival of the British disrupted a Quaker meeting. They watched as the British poured across the Brandywine. Young Quaker Joseph Townsend pointed and said to his friend, Samuel Brown, "Look. The army is coming out of the woods into the fields belonging to Emmor Jefferies...there, on the west side of the creek above the fording place."

The two gawked until the fields were literally covered with British and Hessian soldiers with their arms and bayonets raised. "Their arms shine as bright as silver under the clear sky," Joseph said.

"What is this?" Samuel asked Joseph. "Are these German troops?"

"Aye. Many of them have beards on their lips."

"I think we should retire," Samuel said. "We may have exceeded the boundaries of prudence."

The boys turned and walked down Birmingham Road.

Cornwallis and Howe rested their troops and then settled on Osborn Hill to the north where they had a superior view of the Americans on Birmingham Hill. Once Cornwallis' advancing columns reached the farm fields at the bottom of Osborn Hill, commands rang out to form battle lines on both sides of Birmingham Road. Charles' left wing was composed of 3,000 Hessians and jaegers and light infantry. Royal Highlanders would attack Adam Stephen's division. His right wing made up of Brigade of Guards, British and Hessian grenadiers, and an element of light infantry would strike Lord Stirling's and John Sullivan's divisions.

It was 4:00 p.m. As Cornwallis' front lines began to move, the Americans opened fire with 3- and 4-pound solid cannon shot. Many of the British were killed, but the regiments kept marching. Finally, the Americans switched to grapeshot and canister rounds. The Royal Artillery responded with 6- and 12-pounders. Heavy smoke hung in the air and over the farm fields.

Artillery rounds arced through the muggy air before dropping among the Continentals, shearing off tree branches and sending splinters of both iron and wood flying in every direction. Hot chunks of iron dismembered some and crushed and killed others. Grapeshot ripped through the American ranks of Alexander Stirling's and Adam Stephen's divisions. John Sullivan's Marylanders fled and poured down the southern slope of Birmingham Hill.

It was nearly 5:00 p.m. when Nathanael and Washington heard the sound of cannon and musketry from the north drift over the fields and woods—at first in bursts, then faster and faster, swelling into a continuous roar.

"I am moving forward with Henry Knox, Lafayette, and our staff to ascertain what is happening to the right flank and General Sullivan on Birmingham Hill," George told Nathanael. "I want you to leave this position and march northeast to reinforce that sector."

With a guide, George pushed forward. They arrived at the Brinton House just as the remnants of Sullivan's three-division command were fleeing southeast in disorder with the British and Hessians advancing on the survivors through the little town of Dilworth to the south and east of Birmingham Hill on Wilmington Road. Washington and Lafayette rode hard to rally the troops. During one of the rearguard actions, Lafayette was wounded in the leg.

At Chadd's Ford, some of Hessian General Knyphausen's troops were crossing Brandywine Creek while the sounds of disorder and carnage growled across the countryside. For a moment, Nathanael worried that Anthony Wayne's brigade, with William Maxwell's light corps and Proctor's artillery unit, were alone to defend against the enemy's crossing, but he could not let it distract him.

After briefly planning his attack, Nathanael leapt into the saddle and with brigadier general George Weedon pressed forward by the nearest road and left a trail of dust as his men marched nearly four miles in forty-five minutes, bearing the weight of packs, ammunition, and muskets. By way of another road, he was joined by his brigadier general, Peter Muhlenberg. When Nathanael came to the rescue, John Sullivan was making an attempt to realign his disordered troops. Henry Knox's guns near the Brinton House were raking fire on the advancing enemy.

Charles Pinckney of South Carolina, who was attached to Washington's staff, carried orders from Washington at the suggestion of John Sullivan. The directive to Nathanael was that he was to halt on the northern end of the battlefield to reform Colonel Alexander Spottswood's and Edward Stevens' fleeing regiments in a ploughed field. Nathanael's division moved to both sides of Wilmington Road in an L-shaped line, a mile south of Dilworth. From the north, musketry rattled, and voices drifted on the slight breeze stirred by the setting sun. From the south, General Francis Nash from North Carolina and his brigade reinforced his line. "Our troops look horribly confused," Nathanael lamented to George Weedon as remnants of John Sullivan's broken division joined Nathanael's formed division. "Open ranks for them and then close as soon as they pass."

They were about to face troops under the command of Cornwallis— General James Agnew's 4th Brigade, British Battalion of Grenadiers and Regiments of Foot, which included Captain Johann Ewald's Hessian jaegers; they had attached themselves to the grenadiers. Agnew and Ewald crossed Wilmington Road and marched up the slope in their front. The exhausted British and Hessians were surprised by Nathanael's expansive front. The British Battalion of Grenadiers paused to remove their cloth foraging caps in favor of their impressive fur bearskin caps that made them appear a foot taller. They advanced on Nathanael's right. Agnew's 4th Brigade moved to the left.

General Weedon's men held their fire until Agnew's flanking line was directly in front. When they opened fire, his four Virginia regiments caught part of Agnew's regiments in an open field. They returned fire. The British Regiments of Foot advanced. Weedon's men opened a sustained fire while Knox's cannon crews did the same from the knoll near the Brinton House. The British officer corps was decimated in the firing.

"Keep up the firing!" George Weedon ordered the Americans.

General James Agnew issued the same order to his British and Hessians.

While Anthony Wayne and William Maxwell fought off General Wilhelm von Knyphausen's division and the Queens Rangers that had crossed the Brandywine at Chadd's Ford to the south of Birmingham Hill, Nathanael's division volleyed with Cornwallis' troops until dark. With ammunition almost spent, firing ceased on both sides. The onset of darkness, British fatigue, and a firm American line brought an end to the Battle of Brandywine. The Americans fell back to Chester, Pennsylvania, after suffering nearly 1,200 causalities.

The disastrous decisions Nathanael made in November of 1776 seemed very far away. This time, he had saved an army, and he was entitled to say so. But when Washington failed to mention his division's performance in his report about the battle to Congress, Nathanael sulked.

&

George heaved a sigh when Nathanael came to him about the perceived slight. "There was not even a mention of General Weedon's brigade," Nathanael grumbled.

George bit his tongue and thought, *There are so many more pressing matters of importance, and Nathanael should know this, but his petulant energy only needs redirection at this moment.* He said, "Do you plan to offer a resignation as you did over the du Coudray affair?"

Nathanael's normally lambent eyes dimmed.

"You, sir, are considered my favorite officer," George said as a balm to Nathanael's wounded pride. "Weedon's brigade, like myself, are Virginians; should I applaud them for their achievement under your command, I shall be charged with partiality. Jealousy will be excited, and the service injured."

"It is more than that," Nathanael charged. "Do you believe that I have not heard the same slanderous accusations that you have? Dr. Benjamin Rush and his juntos have a cynical view of our relationship. He complains that you are little more than a cipher for me, Henry Knox, and Alexander Hamilton—particularly me. Rush calls me a sycophant to you, speculative and without enterprise."

Alexander Hamilton, who was carefully replying to the piles of correspondence heaped upon George's desk, kept to his quill and said nothing, as Nathanael had not acknowledged he was there.

George remained silent. He had heard the rumors that there were those who believed the army needed a new commander-in-chief.

&

Caty, still lodging at Abraham Lott's house in Basking Ridge, New Jersey, had recovered from camp fever and waited anxiously to hear from her husband. He had gone south at the beginning of the summer and had not returned to her arms. She hoped to join him in Philadelphia. Then dreadful news arrived.

The Continental lines along the Brandywine Creek had been flanked by General Howe's forces, and the Americans were routed. Nathanael had helped to avert complete disaster, but the tide of defeat was too strong to turn back. Philadelphia now lay exposed, and she was at a loss where she should go. The thought of returning to Coventry and facing a dismal existence was too much to bear.

She received an enthusiastic letter from Nathanael despite the defeat and the gloomy letter Washington was forced to write to the president of the Continental Congress, John Hancock.

My Dear Angel,

There must have been a terrible carnage among General Howe's troops and those of ours who fell behind his lines. He sent a letter to His Excellency asking that the Number of wounded Officers and Men of our Army, to whom every possible Attention has been paid, required our immediate Care and that Any Surgeons we may chuse to send shall be permitted to attend them.

Many reinforcements are coming in and Mr. Howe will find that another victory purchased at the price of so much blood might inevitably ruin him. O my sweet angel how I wish— how I long to return to our soft embrace. The endearing prospect is my greatest comfort amidst all the fatigues of the campaign.

Pray how does all my good friends do at Mr. Lott's—I suppose you have all long faces and fearful apprehensions. Tell them to cheer up and fear not, all things will go well.

She thought of the irony of his final words as laughter resonated from somewhere, and then Betsey Lott entered the sunny room where Caty sat.

All the sunshine in the world could not brighten Caty's spirits or warm her empty fretful heart.

Betsey fussed over a lovely rare myrtle and then set her watering cup aside. "I know all seems bleak," Betsey fawned. "We have arranged for another party and dance to clear away this perpetual gloom."

Caty looked up at her hostess with wet eyes. "Nathanael promised he would soon return to me if kind fortune carries him through showers of leaden deaths unhurt. But it seems as if Philadelphia may be lost and the army is moving again."

"It is not horrid to keep up your spirits if only for the sake of your husband who wishes it for you," Betsey encouraged.

Caty wiped her tears with her fingertips and sniffed. "Another party would be lovely. I so look forward to a night of carefree frolic."

eleven

An Impressive Fight

After the defeat at Brandywine, General George Washington was intent on accomplishing two tasks. First, he wanted to protect Philadelphia from British forces, and second, he needed to replenish the rapidly dwindling supplies and ammunition stored in Reading, Pennsylvania. On September 13, the commander-in-chief withdrew across the Schuylkill River, marched his exhausted, ragged, and shoeless army through Philadelphia, and headed northwest.

A few days later, William Howe moved his army after tending to his wounded troops. Howe's next move had to be for Philadelphia, but by what means and route was a cloud that hung over the American Army like the gathering rain clouds that darkened the sky as mid-September arrived. Washington's troops marched for two weeks before they took up a defensive position near the town of White Horse Tavern, twenty miles west of Philadelphia, to guard the fords of the Schuylkill. British troops led by Lord Cornwallis followed their march. The Continental Congress fled Philadelphia for Lancaster.

The location at White Horse Tavern caused grumbling among the officers. Naturally, Nathanael did not hesitate to make his dissatisfaction known. "This low, muddy ground is an unsatisfactory position for deployment," Nathanael told Henry, whose men were wrestling the Continental Army's artillery into place.

"I have warned George that the soggy valley behind us will force us to abandon our artillery during a retreat," Henry huffed. "If we are engaged to bring the pieces around quickly, it well may be a terrible stroke to us."

The two stood carping until Colonel Timothy Pickering, Washington's adjutant from Massachusetts, hurried by with a scowl on his face and his head tilted toward his companions. They stopped abruptly to bow to the two generals in their presence.

Henry elbowed Nathanael and whispered, "Let us discover what Pickering's pinched face is about." He suppressed his vague amusement and asked, "Colonel Pickering, what is all the haste?"

The sharp sound of distant musket fire distracted them. The camp came alive with drums beating, soldiers dashing to arms, and junior officers shouting orders. "The enemy is approaching," Pickering snapped.

Before Henry or Nathanael could react, George was there, his cloak billowing behind him and surrounded by his aides.

"Surely we are not going to have the troops fight in this position?" Nathanael asked.

Pickering interrupted and said to Washington, "General Wayne has formed an advance guard, but the order of battle is not completed."

"Are we going to meet the enemy on this ground or are we going to the high ground?" Nathanael insisted. "If it is the latter, then we need to march immediately."

"I am in agreement, Nathanael," George said. "I think we had better move out and fall back to higher ground. Draw up the troops to the new position. Colonel Pickering, ensure the orders are disseminated immediately."

The threatening skies let lose the deluge it had been promising for days. Both armies were soaked in the torrential downpour that ruined their ammunition and wet their gunpowder. Men without tents had no shelter and nowhere to protect their provisions. The scrambling American Army redirected their attention to slogging eleven miles to a new position at Yellow Springs and onto Warwick Furnace. Henry needed time to clean his cannon and find new gunpowder.

Washington marched his army back and forth across the Schuylkill River. He sent a cavalry unit under the command of Captain Harry Lee and Colonel Alexander Hamilton to gather provisions for his starving army and to burn flour mills on the Schuylkill to prevent Howe from feeding his own army.

❧

On the afternoon of September 20, Washington left General Anthony Wayne's Pennsylvania Division at Chester, Pennsylvania, to screen the British movements west of the Schuylkill. Wayne attempted to conceal his little force near Paoli Tavern. On the night of September 21, his sleeping men were surprised by five regiments of redcoats led by General Charles Grey, who launched a bayonet attack. Wayne's sentries got off warning shots, but the British were into the American camp before the troops could form and butchered them.

The American Army could not afford any distraction from the enemy's movements. Not even the horrible news of the massacre at Paoli, which tarnished Anthony Wayne's reputation. He demanded a formal court-martial to clear his name. It would have to wait. Washington settled his army on the north side of the Schuylkill River at Pennypacker Mills with the intention of blocking Howe's army from entering the city.

During the night of September 25, George moved his weary army to the west side of Perkiomen Creek. The following day, Howe, with the knowledge that Washington was convinced the British were after his supply depot in Reading, turned his army in the opposite direction and slipped across the Schuylkill at a ford on the Continental Army's left.

At 10:00 a.m. on September 26, Lord Cornwallis at the head of both English and Hessian grenadier battalions with a part of the artillery, marched in triumph into Philadelphia with the bands playing martial music. Three thousand British troops passed civilians waving in the streets. Nine thousand remained encamped outside the city at Germantown.

After an exhausting summer and the grueling battle at Brandywine Creek, the capital had fallen anyway. Already the most populous city in the colonies, the city was now swelled in size by the British Army. Howe was faced with a way to feed and provide for them all.

At a war council on September 28, George told his sixteen gathered generals, "If our river defenses can be maintained, General Howe's situation will not be the most agreeable; for if his supplies can be stopped by water, it may easily be done by land. The acquisition of Philadelphia may, instead of his good fortune, prove his ruin."

"George, Congress has all but given you complete power over the army now that they have fled Philadelphia," John Sullivan said. "What is the delay in making this decision? Do you believe that we can predict something you cannot?"

"The bulk of Howe's army is encamped outside of Germantown," Nathanael reminded the council impatiently.

"According to our spies, the British general seems to have done nothing to fortify Philadelphia or Germantown," Lord Alexander Stirling noted.

"Then let us put to the point," George stated. "Is it prudent to make a general, vigorous, and immediate attack upon the Enemy?"

The drudging war council was interrupted by whooping and musket fire. Everyone in the room got to their feet. George's Life Guard came to attention and covered the windows and doors in a defensive stance.

"Let me pass," an excited post rider insisted. "I have brought important news from the north for General Washington!"

Colonel Tench Tilghman, one of George's aides, stepped forward and accepted the message. "Ensure this man has refreshment," Tench ordered the guard before passing the missive to his commander-in-chief, who indicated that he wished Tench to read it to the room.

"General Horatio Gates' army has inflicted heavy casualties on British General John Burgoyne's army at a place called Freeman's Farm near Saratoga, New York!" Tench exclaimed.

George quietly watched his cheering generals and staff. He leaned in toward Nathanael and said, "Howe has made the main army look foolish and Gates' victory, although impressive, is inconclusive, but to be heralded."

"I suggest a thirteen-gun celebratory salute and an extra gill of rum for each man to show our optimism," Nathanael said.

"I concur," Henry chuckled.

"Then we shall lighten our hearts before we turn our attention to Mr. Howe and his obvious invitation to his door," George agreed.

"And what does that invitation look like?" Lord Stirling asked with doubt.

"We march to Germantown, and then we shall know," George said. His fighting blood was aroused by the news of the Northern Army's victory. "And here is the plan."

❧

On the night of October 3, Washington coordinated an attack on Germantown similar to the strategy he used at Trenton—converging columns moving down on the enemy by different routes to strike at dawn. John Sullivan and Washington commanded the center. Nathanael was in command of Adam Stephen and his divisions on the left flank. General William Smallwood and 2,000 Marylanders were to envelop the British right and rear. Anthony Wayne's division would be to the right of Nathanael to turn the British left. Alexander Stirling's division would be the reserves that moved behind Sullivan.

Before the troops were put on the march, the commander-in-chief issued a rousing speech: "Our dearest rights, our dearest friends, and our own honor, and glory and even shame, urge us to fight. And my fellow soldiers when an opportunity presents, be firm, be brave; shew yourselves men and victory is yours!"

The army moved out from the camp at Pennypacker Mills north down Germantown Road, Limekiln Road, and Shippack Road, respectively. The distance across the whole American front from Wayne's division to Smallwood's was seven miles.

Nathanael's former aide, Thomas Paine, had rejoined him in camp and requested to go on the march.

"I am happy to have you back," Nathanael assured Thomas, "but I would feel better if I knew you were safe in camp. My division has the longest route to march—nineteen miles where the other divisions have fifteen miles to cover. Our target is to turn the British right flank, which is supposed to be heavily reinforced."

Nathanael spurred his horse to catch up to his marching divisions. Already, they had made a wrong turn. Messengers who were trying to maintain communication among the various commanders were losing their way in the dark. He ordered a halt when they encountered unexpected resistance from a small enemy picket guard that fled when they realized they were horribly outnumbered. Major William Blodget and other aides disseminated the order down the lines.

Generals Peter Muhlenberg and Adam Stephen rode up. "We are going to have to turn around and retrace our steps," Nathanael told them.

Adam looked confused. "How can you discern we have strayed off and by how far?"

Nathanael heaved a sigh and tossed Adam a suspicious look. "We have reconnoitered this route—perhaps four miles. Move out!"

The sun began to rise. A gray fog blanketed everything. The Americans still had not arrived at their objective, although Washington and Sullivan managed to stay close to schedule. They had no way of knowing that Nathanael's troops had gotten lost and were desperately trying to make up time. Anthony Wayne struck the British advance guard. His brigade drove through the enemy pickets and swarmed into the camp of the 40th Regiment and the 2nd Light Infantry. The British recognized them and chanted, "Have at the bloodhounds! Paoli! Paoli!"

After a hot exchange of fire, the British light infantry fell back toward Germantown with the Americans at their heels. Despite the officers' efforts to stop them, Wayne's men ruthlessly bayonetted the British who tried to surrender and some of the wounded.

To the south at his headquarters in Logan's House, William Howe, surrounded by his aides and his Life Guards, was aroused by the sound of musket fire and rode out to the fight. "For shame, Light Infantry. I never saw you retreat before. Form! Form! It is only a scouting party!" he shouted.

There was a blast of grapeshot from the enemy.

"General, withdraw, this moment!" his aide, Captain Friedrich von Muenchhausen, insisted.

William rode off at full speed with the rest of the British main body as the regiments under the direct command of Lord Cornwallis put pressure on the American right. John Sullivan's division rushed forward. Musket smoke thickened the fog until men could see no more than thirty yards. Sullivan's men kept coming and encountered British pickets. Among the American infantry, seventeen-year-old Joseph Plumb Martin and his messmates were under orders to fire when they could see the buttons on the enemy's clothes. They managed to drive the British from their camp with intrepidity. The retreating British barricaded themselves in a nearby mansion owned by Benjamin Chew.

As Washington and Henry with the rear troops under Lord Stirling approached the house, Alexander Hamilton advised, "I think we should keep marching to meet up with the lead columns and ignore the barricaded troops."

"No, it is against conventional military wisdom to bypass a fortification and leave enemy troops in a position to attack from behind," Henry argued.

"I concur with Henry," George said.

Satisfied, Henry ordered the field guns to target the house. The artillerists riddled the stone walls with grapeshot for an hour as riflemen pelted it with musket balls. The British fired from windows. Some of the gunners were hit. American troops began chanting, "Set it on fire!"

In desperation, Knox's aide, Major Du Plessis, and Colonel John Laurens volunteered to try. They crept up to the mansion and crawled to a window. A British soldier from inside screamed at them and pointed a pistol in their direction. The two aides raced back toward their troops under cover of American musket fire. Laurens was hit in the shoulder and he fell, dazed.

Nathanael's division finally reached Church Lane and was coming up on John Sullivan's left. His thrust drove deep into the enemy's lines—so deep that some of the Pennsylvanians were momentarily in the British rear and were unable to rejoin Nathanael.

The fog thickened and mingled with cannon smoke. Soon, visibility was reduced to just twenty yards, and confusion entered the scene. Nathanael's brigade under Adam Stephen veered off course and began following Meetinghouse Road. An intoxicated General Stephen became confused by cannon fire coming from the direction of the Chew House and believed the British were attacking the rear. He ordered his men to march in the direction of the booming guns and collided with Anthony Wayne's brigade. In the heavy mist, they mistook them for hostile troops and fired.

Balls whizzed through the soupy air. Anthony's aide took a ball to the head. Blood and brains spattered Anthony's face and shoulders. "My God! Our own men are firing on us!"

John Sullivan's, Nathanael Greene's, and William Smallwood's divisions fell apart under heavy pressure from the British. Their troops suddenly broke and ran. Washington was riding exultantly forward to press home a general attack when he was surprised to see two completely different comportments emerging from the fog on Shippack Road—wild-eyed panicked fugitives and those afraid but composed. Young Joseph Plumb Martin was among the men who were not running.

Cornwallis had twelve regiments in action, and Nathanael took the brunt of the British counterattack. He was forced to retreat. By 10:00 a.m., the fight was over, and 1,000 Americans were dead or wounded. The exhausted, filthy, tired, and hungry men marched twenty-four miles back to their camp at Pennypacker's Mill. Nathanael, with his aides and Colonel Timothy Pickering, rode among the trudging army with the screams of the wounded echoing in their heads and the labored scenes of trying to get them off the field stinging their eyes.

Nathanael's blue and buff uniform was grimy and ripped. His saddle was badly worn, and he had lost a boot spur. During the chaos, he lost a brass pistol Henry Knox had given him with the initials H.K. carved in the barrel. A curl of his hair had been shot off by a musket ball. It was a moment in the heat of their retreat which allowed for a well-timed jest between him and his aide Captain Ichabod Burnet, who had his queue shot off at the same moment.

Nathanael told Ichabod, "You had better jump down if you have time and pick up your queue."

Ichabod responded, "And your curl, too, General."

They stopped to water their horses. Timothy leaned over in the saddle and said to Nathanael, "You do know I was against storming the Chew House."

Nathanael patted his horse's neck in response.

"General Greene, before I came to the army, I entertained an exalted opinion of General Washington's military talents, but I have since seen nothing to enhance it."

Nathanael considered the statement with the knowledge that Timothy was a Harvard-educated lawyer and thought it was perhaps best to avoid voicing his opinion. Instead he said, "Despite the fog and confusion, we put up an impressive fight."

General Anthony Wayne echoed this sentiment in a letter to his wife, Polly:

> *Upon the whole it was a Glorious day—Our men are in the Spirits with bravery and exhilaration—and I am confident we shall give them a total defeat the next Action; which is at no great distance.*

❧

Three days after the battle at Germantown, express news arrived that General Horatio Gates had defeated British General John Burgoyne at the Battle of Bemis Heights in the Mohawk Valley in upstate New York near Saratoga. Washington's defeats at Brandywine and Germantown left a dark stain on what Nathanael had seen as an impressive fight.

Members of the Continental Congress were not only grumbling about Washington's losses, they were also criticizing the commander-in-chief for his failures. John Adams and Dr. Benjamin Rush, both members of Congress, complained that Washington had not planned his campaigns with the vigor that Gates had mastered.

Adams wrote to his wife Abigail in Massachusetts, *I was greatly surprised when I heard the enemy was in Philadelphia without any engagement on our part.*

The criticism spilled over to Nathanael. Rarely one to keep his opinions to himself, he proclaimed that Gates was not the knighted "Hero of Saratoga" Congress claimed, and that honor went to Generals Benedict Arnold and Benjamin Lincoln, the principal instruments in completing the work.

Arnold, one of Washington's best battlefield commanders, had vehemently argued with Gates over tactics. Gates relieved Arnold of command. He offered to give him a pass back to Philadelphia to rid himself of the aggressive general's insistence that they attack the enemy instead of waiting behind the Northern Army's lines for the enemy to come to them. Arnold took the initiative to lead a charge from the American left on a redoubt, which killed and scattered hundreds of Hessians under Burgoyne's command. He was shot in the thigh during the assault and trapped under his dead horse.

Benjamin Lincoln rallied the spirited militia that had enhanced Gates' victory by harassing the British supply line. Lincoln's men were part of the American right that saw no action; nevertheless, Lincoln was shot in the ankle when he and his men attempted to fortify a ford across the Hudson River in their rear.

Nathanael fumed further at the foundation of all Gates' successes—planned under the aristocratic New York General Philip Schuyler's direction. In his opinion, Congress had given Schuyler's command over to Gates just in time to reap the laurels and rewards. *Gates was a mere child of fortune,* Nathanael thought.

❧

The formal capitulation of Burgoyne's army took place on October 17. At the main army's encampment at White Marsh, Pennsylvania, Henry Knox's cannon discharged in the army's artillery park followed by a *feu-de-joie* in celebration of the surrender at Saratoga. Shouts of "Huzzah! Huzzah!" rose from the thousands of soldiers and Patriots cheering the greatest rebel victory.

Over the noise of the festivities, a disgruntled Nathanael privately aired his opinions to a composed but frustrated Washington. "If the southern militia had lent the same aide to your army that the northern militia did to General Gates, Howe never could have got possession of the Rome of America," Nathanael began. "We have had two severe and general actions. Our force has been too small to cover the country and secure the city. The unfriendly inhabitants have rendered the task still more difficult."

George's slave and companion, Billy Lee, poured the generals glasses of rum while the man he served continued to listen patiently.

"I wrote General Alexander McDougall who commanded one of my brigades at Germantown," Nathanael went on as he paced the small office in the Morris House headquarters. "Our own quartermaster general for the army, General Thomas Mifflin, and his creatures have been endeavoring to wound my reputation. There has been some insinuation to my prejudice respecting the Germantown battle."

"These juntos' assessments cannot be answered with any degree of effectiveness. You know this, Nathanael," George said.

Nathanael considered his glass of rum. He downed it in one long gulp and then said, "I needed to hear what McDougall thought of my performance, George. I trust his word. I wanted to know if I showed a want of activity in carrying the troops into action, a want of judgement in the disposition, or a want of spirit in the action or retreat, and if he thought I was blamable in any instances, to be so good as to point them out."

"And did he?" George asked.

"He said he did not see the least indication of my want of activity or spirit in carrying on the troops that day but the contrary."

"Then you must let this go," George advised. "We control the area to the west and north of Philadelphia. The area south of the city had already been pillaged by Howe's overland march to get into the city. We have to turn our attention to maintain our control of Fort Mifflin and Fort Mercer on the Delaware River that are preventing supplies from reaching Philadelphia. With the control of the rivers, we have a reasonable hope of starving out the British Army."

Billy refilled Nathanael's glass. It was difficult for Nathanael to admit he was complaining, and there was no doubt the subject would arise again as Gates, Conway, and Mifflin would raise their aggressive voices. By the expression on George's face, the commander-in-chief knew it too.

"I have called in the troops from the north under Gates," George said. He could see that his friend had calmed down and come to his senses. "With a superior force of continentals at our back and Howe cut off from his supplies, the war might be won this year."

"There are Rhode Island regiments in Peekskill, New York, who have been patrolling the Hudson River to prevent British forces from pushing down the river. I believe it is time to order them to Fort Mercer," Nathanael recommended. "My young friend Sammy Ward, Jr. from East Greenwich is among them."

"And your cousin, Colonel Christopher Greene, commands the garrison at Fort Mercer," George confirmed. "Therefore, there is a satisfying counterpart to this."

George finished his rum with gratification. This was why he allowed Nathanael to gripe. Because no matter the situation, the general from Rhode Island would not back down nor disappoint.

Nathanael returned to his headquarters in White Marsh. Under dim candle-light, he penned a letter to Caty describing the battle at Germantown. He rubbed his eyes and coughed. The room was dusty, and he supposed the night ahead would be a restless one.

A few days later, a man arrived at headquarters. "Someone is here to see you, Nathanael," William Blodget announced. "He introduced himself to me as Colonel Richard Cary and says he knows Mrs. Greene."

"Send him in," Nathanael said. He put his never ceasing correspondence aside.

Colonel Cary entered and bowed. "General Greene."

"Did I summon you?" Nathanael asked, irritated.

"Colonel Marius Dobbs told me to report to you under the circumstances that Fort Mercer was to be manned," Cary replied.

"You are from Rhode Island?"

"No, sir. New Jersey. I am acquainted with your wife."

Nathanael narrowed his eyes. "How do you know my wife?"

"She has been my dancing partner at the socials held at Mr. Abraham Lott's house. She is a very talented young woman and quite vivacious," Cary said amiably.

William afforded a glance at Nathanael, but his general's face was completely composed, which worried William further.

"Does she look well?" Nathanael asked the colonel tightly. "Is she contented?"

Lines formed on Colonel Cary's face. "She looks well, but does not confide her inner feelings to me. I meant no disrespect General Greene. I thought you would be pleased to hear news of Mrs. Greene."

"Thank you, Colonel. Major Blodget will see to your assignments."

After Blodget and Cary left his office, Nathanael left his office and walked through the smoky army camp. The bright waning gibbous moon watched him walk slowly past laughing, ragged soldiers who despite their lack of food or pay or a victory of their own to celebrate, remained with the Continental Army. Many sat hunched over fires, writing on scraps of paper. Nathanael supposed those who could read and write were penning news to their wives and families. He wondered if their wives were dancing while they fought and watched comrades fall screaming and pleading in bloody battles.

Henry, covered in powder smoke, ambled toward Nathanael. "What are you doing out here, my friend?"

"Trying to sort out what is important and what is not," Nathanael replied.

Henry waved a chubby hand. "Ah, yes. Introspection is not always easy or achievable."

"Caty is still in Basking Ridge, and I have had news of her."

"I have a feeling I know what this about," Henry said. "Lucy wrote me a very terse letter. She was angry that I sent her to Boston and would not allow her to stay in Basking Ridge where all the gaiety is held. Do not be too hard on Caty." He pounded Nathanael on the shoulder. "I need to wash up. Good night."

Nathanael watched Henry disappear among the flickering fires. He returned to his headquarters and started a letter to Caty. "I am happy to hear that you are so agreeably employed. I wish the campaign was over that I might come and partake of your diversions. But we must first give Mr. Howe a stinging and then for a joyous winter of pleasant tales. In the neighborhood of my quarters there are several sweet pretty Quaker girls. If the spirit should move and love invite who can be accountable for consequences? I know this will not alarm you because you have such a high opinion of my virtue. It is very well you have. You remember the prayer of that saint—Tempt me not above what I am able to bear. But I promise you to be as honest as ever I can."

A week later, with threats of infidelity and with Quaker women no less swimming in Caty's head, Nathanael's horse reared and threw him ten feet. His head narrowly missed a stone wall. When he managed to get to his feet and attempted to brush the dust from his breeches, he realized his wrist was sprained.

twelve
The Forts

By the last week in October, General William Howe achieved about everything he had set out to accomplish. He had beaten Washington's army and taken control of Philadelphia. He personally revived the entertainment that the Continental Congress had suppressed. His beloved mistress, Mrs. Elizabeth Loring, was by his side again, and the two, along with William's staff, were nestled in Penn Mansion.

But news of Burgoyne's defeat, so catastrophic that it might tempt France to enter the war on the American side, laid doubt on his hard-won battles. He possessed the rebel capital, but it did him little good since he had no way to get his brother's fleet of ships and all the provisions and supplies they contained to the city's waterfront.

The rebels were blocking the Delaware River. On the west side of the river, on a tiny island of mud, was the dilapidated Fort Mifflin, which would require an amphibious assault. On the east side was Fort Mercer, which was accessible by land. The two forts were placed so their guns guarded a two-tiered line of *cheveaux-de-frise*, made of heavy spars ballasted on the river bottom and blocking the channel between Fort Mifflin and the Jersey shore.

On the evening of October 22, Hessian Colonel von Donop attacked Fort Mercer. Donop was mortally wounded, and the Germans were repulsed. To make matters worse, two British warships that squeezed through a narrow gap in the *cheveaux-de-frise* were attacked by rebel galleys. The huge, sixty-four gun *Augusta* burst into flames that rattled the windows of houses more than thirty miles away. A towering cloud of thick smoke rose like a pillar and spread from the top like a mushroom the likes of which no one had ever seen.

"This is a calamitous culmination of events," William lamented as he listened to reports and watched the acrid smoke drift through the air. "Send for Lord Cornwallis," he instructed his aide, Captain Friedrich von Muenchhausen. "I want him aware of what I am about to do."

Thirty minutes later, Charles Cornwallis lumbered into Penn Mansion with his aides in tow. Although William was nine years his senior, Charles' lazy eye, double chin, and large girth made him appear older. The two generals retired to the library to speak behind closed doors.

"I know you will be leaving for England on the *Brilliant* in a few weeks. I do not look forward to your departure," William said.

Charles filled a glass with claret. Like William's aides and Elizabeth Loring, Charles read William's demeanor like a book. He was no fool, nor was he blind. He knew what William was about to say would devastate so many while others would cheer the decision, citing that was what William deserved.

"I left Burgoyne to suffer with no support from me, his commanding officer," William blurted out. "I won Brandywine, Germantown, and Philadelphia, the latter in which you marched without a shot from the enemy. But the conquest of Philadelphia seems to be of no avail. Lord Germain is going to blame me for Burgoyne's defeat. I am resigning as commander-in-chief of British forces in America."

William shared the brief resignation letter he had written to Secretary of State to the Colonies, Lord George Germain. "From the little attention, my Lord, given to my recommendations since the commencement of my command, I am led to hope that I may be relieved from this very painful service wherein I have not the good fortune to enjoy the necessary confidence and support of my superiors. My lack of success balances on this."

"I am sorry, William," Charles said after he read it. "You deserve the gratitude of your country as you have served with fidelity, assiduity, and with great ability."

"Thank you, my friend. I did everything I could, and now I will be forced to face the humiliation of losing my command in the face of the inquiries of Parliament despite that Richard and I have royal blood coursing through our veins."

"Ah, yes. Your mother, Charlotte, was the acknowledged illegitimate half-sister of King George I," Charles said.

"Nevertheless, Henry Clinton will be pleased to hear of my resignation," William said. "He and I never got by, and I am certain the command will go to him."

❧

Nathanael watched the assault on Fort Mercer on Red Bank from the Pennsylvania shore. His concern lay with the Rhode Islanders who were defending it. The defenders performed gallantly. Nathanael proudly told Chaplain Ebenezer David, "There never was a nobler defense in America." Then, he wrote a letter of congratulations to the defenders.

Connecticut teenager Joseph Plumb Martin unknowingly echoed Nathanael's sentiment that brave Rhode Island Yankees fought as brilliant an action as was fought during the war, considering the numbers engaged, Bunker Hill notwithstanding. But Joseph soon found himself fighting for his own life and the life of his comrades under the command of Colonel Samuel Smith and a handful of Maryland Continentals who had arrived at Fort Mifflin the month before to make improvements. Living conditions in the fort were deplorable. The men were short on supplies and equipment—shoes, clothing, and blankets. The soldiers were so sickly that Smith was constantly detaching them and asking for replacements.

Washington ordered Joseph's 8th Connecticut Regiment to deploy to Fort Mifflin. They crossed a narrow strip of water called Province Channel to the muddy little island where the fort stood, made of nothing stouter than earth and wood. The Connecticut men immediately experienced the struggle that was taking place within the fort. Nearly 500 American soldiers had almost nowhere to hide from their assault. Nathanael had no orders to ride to the rescue. All he could do was observe whether the American flag was still flying over the fort.

On the morning of November 15, William and Richard Howe mounted their last attempt to take Fort Mifflin. For five days, the British batteries on the Pennsylvania shore had pounded the fortress. Now, two more warships moved into position on the east side of Mud Island. The fort was in the crossfire of British cannon that fired mercilessly.

Cannonballs tore the fort to shreds. Some of the Americans' meager clothing caught on fire or was ripped from their bodies—pulverized by the solid shot balls. Joseph Plumb Martin watched in horror as his comrades were split like fish to be broiled. The fort was completely ploughed as a field; the buildings of every kind were hanging in broken fragments, and the guns all dismounted. He had never seen such complete destruction.

Those who survived escaped, and Fort Mifflin fell. With the fall of Fort Mifflin, Fort Mercer lay exposed. It was also evident that General Howe was acutely concerned about the river blockade. He sent a column of 5,000 men under Cornwallis.

On November 20, Rhode Islanders Colonel Christopher Greene and General James Varnum stripped as much as they could from Fort Mercer and then set it ablaze. The Delaware was now a British River. The chances of taking Philadelphia back from the British fell with the forts.

Nathanael learned of the fort's loss while marching through Burlington in response to Cornwallis' incursion into New Jersey. He thought through his mission carefully as it seemed to be arguable at that point and wrote to George, "General Varnum has retreated to Mount Holly. I propose to see him and General Huntington early in the morning. If it is practicable to make an attack upon the enemy it shall be done, but I am afraid the enemy will put it out of my power as they can so easily make us take such a circuitous march. I cannot promise anything until I learn more of the designs of the enemy, their strength and the position they are in."

George could not accept that answer. He replied, "An attack would be a most desirable judgement, and I am inclined to have you attack Cornwallis."

Nathanael wanted to give his commander-in-chief a victory that would quiet the juntos in Congress and generals who wanted to see them both removed. But he tempered his enthusiasm when he discovered Cornwallis' numbers compared to his 3,000 soldiers and a shrinking force of 800 militiamen. Nathanael wrote a well thought out reply, part of which said:

> *Your Excellency observes, in your last letter, you must leave the Propriety of attacking the Enemy to me. Would you advise me to fight them with very unequal Numbers? Your Excellency has the choice of but two things, to fight the Enemy without the least Prospect of Success, upon the common Principles of War, or remain inactive, & be subject to the Censure of an ignorant & impatient populace.*

Nathanael kept Washington informed of the difficulties he was facing gathering troops and waiting for the young dashing and gallant Virginia cavalryman Captain Harry Lee, whose services were needed to scout out the enemy. Gathering a substantial force was taking too long despite Nathanael's exertions, and he prudently called off the attack.

At the end of November, the Continental Army moved to Upper Dublin Township. Washington made his headquarters at the Emlen House while his army of 10,000 men was entrenched throughout the township and in various villages. Many were unfit for duty due to nakedness and illness. The Congress, which presided in York, refused to provide the necessary items and insisted the army seize what it needed from Loyalist citizens. Many had already been plundered by the British and Hessian troops, and to the commander-in-chief's disapproval, by some of his own men. George had more respect for civil rights than did the Congressional pundits.

Washington held a war council on November 28 regarding winter camp and renewed assaults on the British. His generals agreed that the cantonment should be as close to the British in Philadelphia as possible, but the final decision still hung in the balance.

Much to George's and Nathanael's relief, brigades began arriving from Horatio Gates' Northern Army. On December 1, Colonel Daniel Morgan's Rifles marched into camp. Three days later, Generals John Paterson and Samuel Parsons of Connecticut and John Glover, Ebenezer Learned, and Enoch Poor of Massachusetts arrived from Albany with their brigades. The Marquis de Lafayette, recovered from the leg wound he sustained during the Battle of Brandywine, proudly returned from his first command—a victory over a superior Hessian force in Gloucester, New Jersey.

George summoned his generals to a council. Some twenty generals attended.

"I wish to recall your attention to the matter recommended to your consideration the advisability of a winter's campaign and practicability of an attack upon Philadelphia," George said to those gathered.

They advised against a winter campaign and cited the many problems facing the Continental Army. Those included resignations, lack of provisions and clothing, disease and illness, unreliable militia, and the strength of the British Army in and around Philadelphia.

Henry got right to the point, but Nathanael responded in his typical verbose manner that concluded with, "We must not flatter ourselves from the heat of our zeal that men can do more than they can. It is impossible for our men verging on nakedness to undertake winter combat. An attack upon the city of Philadelphia appears to me like forming a crisis for American liberty, which if unsuccessful, I fear will prove her grave."

The same day, George received a letter from an infuriated General Lord Alexander Stirling who had delivered his view of the proposed winter campaign from Reading, Pennsylvania, where he was recovering from a fall from his horse. Stirling explained, "I spent the last evening in the company of Colonel James Wilkerson, General Horatio Gates' adjutant. Wilkinson, being in his cups, took the liberty of quoting a passage from a letter Brigadier General Thomas Conway wrote to General Gates regarding His Excellency: *'Heaven has been determined to save your country or a weak general and bad counselors would have ruined it.'*"

Concerns piled on George's desk from the state of his army, intelligence in Philadelphia, gloomy letters from Congress and quartermasters, and now news of a plot to overthrow him. There were some in Congress who believed that Washington was failing as commander-in-chief due to his many losses and that the victorious Gates was the answer to all their problems.

Three generals rose as detractors among the handwringing and second-guessing: Thomas Mifflin, Thomas Conway, and Horatio Gates, who sat on the congressional Board of War. Foremost of these was Thomas Mifflin, who was neglecting his quartermaster duties to the Continental Army and sulking at home in disgust.

George shared Stirling's letter with Nathanael and Henry.

"Let your pen rest," George warned Nathanael when he detected the familiar irreverent air he had come to recognize in his general. "I ask you to let this lie for now."

Nathanael regarded George's young aides, Colonels Alexander Hamilton and John Laurens. He sensed that they had been told the same thing. He sighed. "Then, let us decide where the army will sleep."

"I have somewhere in mind," George said, "but it shall require our army's movement."

Many of George's officers grumbled over his selected location for winter quarters.

"Valley Forge?" asked General Johann De Kalb, a bulky German-born officer who had crossed the Atlantic with the Marquis de Lafayette. "It is a wooded wilderness, certainly one of the poorest districts in

Pennsylvania—the soil thin, uncultivated, almost uninhabited, without forage and without provisions."

James Varnum echoed De Kalb's sentiment. The tall, young Marquis de Lafayette scowled. Lafayette was one of the few foreign generals who laid all his hopes and dreams on the concept of American liberty, pure and simple. Washington represented not only that liberty, but also was a father figure to the Marquis.

"I was born a few miles from Valley Forge," Anthony Wayne offered. "I believe it is our best available compromise."

"My men are barefooted on the ice and frozen ground, however I will carry out your decision, George," Nathanael said although he was suffering his own discomfort—another eye infection.

I support you, George," Henry assured.

"We have been disappointed by our clothier general, James Meade, who has failed to procure the proper apparel," George said in disgust. "Shoes can be produced in this country. Meade has quit his post, complaining of poor health."

"Our army will barely survive even if placed in the warmest houses in the winter," John Sullivan added.

"It is worse than that," George said. "General Mifflin has quit as the army's quartermaster general." Everyone in the room knew Thomas Mifflin's stance on George and suspected that was his motive for quitting.

Late in the evening of December 12, in a blinding snowstorm, Washington and his hungry, tired, and barely clothed army marched over the Schuylkill River at Swedes Ford and down to Gulph Mills, Pennsylvania. The soldiers' tents did not arrive for two days. Food was scarce.

Six days later, the army celebrated the new nation's first Thanksgiving and first official holiday. The Continental Congress proclaimed that on December 18, the nation would stop and give thanks to God for blessing the nation and the troops in their quest for independence and peace. The victory at Saratoga prompted this celebration. Aside from those who were a part of that victory, the men at Gulph Mills felt scarcely a glimmer of gratitude. They were acutely conscious of their own military disappointments.

George addressed his officers and soldiers in his general orders. "I thank you for the fortitude and patience with which you have sustained the fatigues of the campaign. I admit that in some instances we unfortunately failed. Yet on the whole, Heaven has smiled on our arms and crowned them with signal success. There is good reason to hope that the end goal of our warfare, independence, liberty, and peace are within reach."

On December 19 at 10:00 a.m., Washington and his Continental Army marched out of Gulph Mills, past Hanging Rock, down Gulph Road, and fifteen miles north to Valley Forge. By the night of December 19, the bedraggled, freezing Continentals had completed their trek to Valley Forge.

thirteen

Valley Forge

The army awoke to Valley Forge's landscape and sparse offerings. Thick woods filled with giant ancient oaks surrounded the elongated plateau on which the army was camped. Here and there were patches of farmland, long since harvested of their wheat, rye, or corn. There were a few fieldstone houses clustered near Isaac Potts' iron forge. A steep-sided hill called Mount Joy loomed over the plateau. Behind it, on the other side of Valley Creek, lay Mount Misery. The mountains, the creek, and the nearby Schuylkill River to the east were ready-made defenses. The slopes could be fortified with redoubts that would guarantee reasonable security against an enemy assault.

Washington established his headquarters at the Potts House and then issued detail plans to build log huts. They were to be fourteen feet long, sixteen feet wide, and six and one-half feet high. The fireplaces were to be made of wood covered with eighteen inches of clay and were to be in the rear of the huts. Twelve men were assigned to each hut. Officers' huts would have fewer tenants. The goal was a compact community with each hut facing a brigade street.

Moving into dark huts with leaky roofs did little to alleviate the misery of life in Valley Forge. After a week of eating primarily firecake, a tasteless mixture of flour and water cooked on heated rocks, Private Joseph Plumb Martin complained, "To go into the wild woods and build habitations in such a weak, starved, and naked condition is appalling in the highest degree."

Nathanael agreed. He wrote to General Alexander McDougall in the Hudson Highlands, "Our horses are dying by the dozens every day for the want of forage and the men getting sickly in their huts for the want of acids and soap to clean themselves."

Herds of skeletal horses nuzzled the muddy snow in vain. The smell of rotting horse carcasses, unwashed soldiers, and human excrement was nauseating—but the worst was the smell of hundreds of dead and dying soldiers.

There was no solution but to forage the countryside. Under Nathanael's direction, Joseph Plumb Martin and his Connecticut regiment went on expeditions to commandeer provisions. The farmers, although sympathetic to the American cause, were unwilling to part with crops and livestock in exchange for Continental currency that could soon prove worthless. The foraging parties often returned with empty wagons. Someone as sinister as starvation arrived in camp in late January—the Irish born Brigadier General Thomas Conway.

Nathanael rode to the Potts House after returning to camp from a week of foraging. When he arrived, Lieutenant George Lewis of Washington's Life Guard acknowledged, "My uncle is inside." He lowered his voice and said, "General Conway is here."

Nathanael nodded, gathered his temper, and entered.

"General Greene," Washington said.

Conway rose, surprised.

Nathanael's reverence failed. To Conway, he said, "So, you have the impudence to come here after everything you have done to further your rank, advocated that General Horatio Gates replace Washington, and deluded yourself into believing you are the right choice for inspector general to the Continental Army?" Nathanael crossed his arms over his chest. "You mocked the commander-in-chief as an amateur soldier."

"I do not pretend, sir, to be a consummate general, but an old sailor knows more about ships than an admiral who has never been to sea," Thomas said in his own defense. "From what I have heard, you too have criticized General Washington at times."

"Only at his request for advice. I am not attempting to usurp his command."

"I shall not be talked to in that manner," Thomas protested.

"Or you will do what?" Nathanael pressed.

Alexander Hamilton and John Laurens listened in silence. They knew Conway, Gates, and Mifflin intended to dispose of General Greene along with Washington. Nathanael's well-honed sensitivity to criticism from which his anger spewed and cut Conway to pieces amused the two aides, and they struggled to avoid cracking a smile.

"Do you know, General Greene, that the congressional delegate from Massachusetts, James Lovell despises you? He refers to you and General Henry Knox as Washington's privy counsellors, and he speaks for many disgusted patriots." Conway's sneer blossomed. "In fact, according to Mifflin, the ear of the commander-in-chief is exclusively possessed by you. It is just a matter of time before the army will be divided into Greenites and Mifflinians."

Nathanael handsome face turned red, and his full lips formed into a thin line. "Neither you nor Mifflin have principles or virtues."

George rose and summoned Nathanael aside. In a low voice, he warned, "Let me tend to this in my own manner. My aides and some of my officers have been using the pen to combat this mockery by writing to Congress. You know very well that Thomas Mifflin, in support of John and Samuel Adams, and Dr. Benjamin Rush are the juntos in this ridiculous affair."

"And what about Conway's insistence that he should be the Marquis de Lafayette's second-in-command on that farcical military campaign to Canada?" Nathanael growled.

"The Marquis has gone to air his demands to the Board of War concerning that matter, and they have conceded to allow General Alexander McDougall to be his second. They have agreed to provide him with money and provisions and with General John Stark's assistance. Although, I have no idea how they will get the scrappy New Hampshire general to acquiesce," George said.

A moment passed. The light in Nathanael's lambent eyes returned. "There may be a cabal of disaffected officers who want to displace you, but it may be just vain men praising one another at your expense," Nathanael said.

George smiled. The practicality his most trusted general possessed had emerged. Still, Nathanael could not let it drop. "I think Conway a very dangerous man in this army. He has but small talents, great ambition, and without any uncommon spirit or enterprise. He is puffed off to the public as one of the greatest generals of the age—"

"Nathanael—" George interrupted.

"Are you admonishing me?"

"I am not admonishing you. I am merely vexed and I am trying to steady a boat upon a heaving sea of conflict and self-interest that hurts our army," George responded. "I know that you are aware that General Mifflin has resigned as quartermaster general of this army."

"I am aware."

"His resignation is favorable. He has been doing a disgraceful job of running his department. Congress will turn their eyes toward a new candidate. Now," George said with a grin, "let us remind ourselves that there are pleasant things to look forward to. The arrival of our wives."

Despite George's council, Nathanael could not stomach the cabal, and he unleashed a barrage of letters condemning Conway as the greatest novice of war in disciplining a regiment that he had ever witnessed.

~

On the morning of February 7, a snowstorm hit Pennsylvania. It fell for two days and filled the valley so that no wagons could move, which stopped the sparse food deliveries. Men and camp followers went without meat, then they went without bread, then they went without food for days at a time. Soldiers who were literally naked refused to use the latrines and did their necessary business right outside their tents and huts. Even men with clothes risked becoming ill because they were obliged to fetch wood and water on their backs half a mile in the snow. Washington could no longer let the crisis continue. He gathered his general officers, who relayed their troops' frustrations.

"Some of my men came to me yesterday and told of their sufferings in as respectful terms as if they had been humble petitioners for special favors," General Anthony Wayne said. "They added that it would be impossible to continue in camp any longer without support."

"Yes, this is happening all over camp," George confirmed. He addressed Nathanael, "It is of the utmost consequence that the horses, cattle, sheep, and fodder be taken from their civilian owners to supply the present emergencies of the American Army. You will take this responsibility. You will concentrate your efforts in the area between the Schuylkill and the Brandywine Rivers."

Nathanael exchanged knowing glances with George. Neither man approved of pressing upon the civilian population to fill the army's needs, but if they did not do so, the army would cease to exist.

There was a commotion outside the Potts House's door. Lieutenant George Lewis announced, "Lady Washington is arriving."

George exhaled a long sigh of relief. "At last—my heart is here, and she is safe."

On February 11, Nathanael and his foragers moved out. He established headquarters at Springfield Meetinghouse. His specific instructions from Washington were to forage the country naked and to prevent the people's complaint of want of forage. He was instructed to take all their cattle, sheep, and horses fit for the use of the army and issue them certificates in Continental dollars. Nathanael knew that stripping the countryside of forage for civilian horses and livestock would create a different set of problems—the animals left behind would starve.

He contacted Colonel Clement Biddle, a Quaker from Pennsylvania, who had joined the army in late 1776 at Fort Lee. Biddle was engaged in forming supply magazines at Valley Forge. He told Biddle that the Springfield Meetinghouse was in the midst of a damned nest of Tories and moved his position to Providence Meetinghouse.

As always, his pen was busy, whether darkness shrouded the snowy landscape of Pennsylvania or the sun shone bright upon it to warm his cold bones. Nathanael kept Washington constantly informed; he told him that Biddle was having difficulty finding wagons and that the inhabitants were concealing them. "The inhabitants cry out and are besetting me from all quarters, but like the Pharaoh, I harden my heart," he told Washington.

He sent orders to Anthony Wayne, who he trusted completely: "You are to consult and fix upon a plan with Colonel Biddle. You are also to cross over into New Jersey, collect stock, and burn the hay in reach of the enemy."

Anthony replied cheerfully, "I will see to my duty." He did just that.

In addition, Washington sent Captain "Light-Horse" Harry Lee to Wilmington, New Jersey. General William Howe in Philadelphia got wind of the operation. The laborious foraging effort was further slowed when he sent Major John Graves Simcoe and his Queen's Ranger, and others, to interfere. Anthony, Harry, and hundreds of state militia were faced with not only procuring provisions, but also skirmishing with the enemy. Still, the determination of the able officers brought temporary relief to the starving men and women of Valley Forge.

Eleven days after the foraging party set out, Nathanael returned to camp. He lamented the sights of suffering. As snow fell lightly to the ground outside his officer's hut, he wrote to Henry in Boston, "We are still in danger of starving. Hundreds of our horses have already starved to death. The committee of Congress has seen all these things with their own eyes."

As if eyes had seen his words, he was startled when there was a knock at his hut door. Major Blodget rose and answered it.

"General Washington is asking for General Greene's presence at his headquarters," Colonel John Laurens, one of Washington's young aides, announced.

Nathanael shrugged into his coat and put on his hat. He left the hut, swung into the saddle, and, with two guards, rode through muddy brigade streets to the Potts House near the banks of the ice-choked Schuylkill River. George and the committee were already gathered when Nathanael arrived.

"Quartermaster general?" Nathanael asked, stunned when the committee set forth their proposal.

"Are you taking notes, Alexander?" George asked.

"Yes, sir," Alexander Hamilton said. He glanced at the members of Congress. He recognized two who were Nathanael's close acquaintances—General Washington's former adjutant, Pennsylvania politician Joseph Reed, and Gouverneur Morris of New York—as well as Chairman Frances Dana from Massachusetts.

George addressed Nathanael. "You provided that we had stores strategically placed when we retreated across New Jersey in 1776, and now you have delivered fresh food. I need a quartermaster more than I need a good field general right now."

"I do not want this, George," Nathanael said.

"I admit there is too much confusion in the department, money is depreciated, and resources are exhausted," Frances Dana said, "but this is all the more reason we need a dependable man."

"No one has ever heard of a quartermaster in history," Nathanael protested as his eyes moved to Joseph Reed. "I am being removed from the line of splendor."

Joseph heard the distress in Nathanael's voice, but he knew that they were pressing the right man for the position, therefore he remained silent.

"This is not about you immortalizing yourself in the golden pages of history on the battlefield instead of being confined to a series of drudgery to pave the way for it. It is about you being the army's greatest hope for relief," George admonished.

"General Greene, I hear you have a background in business and are capable of solving problems others often cannot," Francis Dana coaxed. "You will be responsible for purchasing, transporting, and distributing an array of supplies—everything from tents to canteens to nails to saddles. The commissary general is responsible for food, and the clothier general is in charge of procuring clothing, but you will be ultimately responsible for the entire department. It will be a challenging job."

"It will be much more than a simple challenge. Let us begin with the difficulty of trading Continental currency for purchases when the British Army is paying in coin," Nathanael said. "It only compounds the strain of army politics—the prejudices some people hold for General Washington and myself—and will make the privations of winter camp worse."

His argument was in vain. Anxiety brought on his asthma, and his eye pained him to the point he was near blindness. In distress, he wrote to Henry in Boston, "The Committee of Congress has been urging me for several days to accept of the Quartermaster General appointment. His Excellency also presses it upon me exceedingly. I hate the place but hardly know what to do."

He had a little time to consider taking the position. His wife would soon return to his tired and empty arms.

Caty arrived in camp without the impressive entourage with which Martha Washington had arrived. She emerged from her carriage with a single escort. Although the trip in freezing weather had been exhausting, Caty looked radiant.

His limp forgotten, Nathanael ran to greet her like a lovesick schoolboy and wrapped his arms around Caty's small waist.

"Where are the children?" he asked with concern.

"I have left them with Jacob and Peggy in Coventry," she explained. "I felt the environment there would be healthier for them."

"Oh…I see," Nathanael stammered with disappointment.

Martha swept forward to greet her friend. "My dear, it is so good to see you well and here with us. General Stirling's wife, Lady Sarah, and her daughter, Kitty, are here. General Knox is in Boston attending to business and visiting his family. His wife, Lucy, will join us after he returns to camp."

Caty squeezed Martha's hands and let them drop. She lifted her skirts and issued a slight curtsy. "General Washington. I am so pleased to see you again."

"Mrs. Greene, the pleasure is mine. Your very presence lights up this dismal camp," he said with a bow.

"Yes, it is dismal," she admitted looking around, "I suppose I shall come to know it well very soon."

"Come, my angel," Nathanael urged. "Let us get you settled into my hut."

Caty looked chagrined. "Hut?" She observed the tiny log huts behind the Potts House where many of Washington's Life Guard lived. "Are you living in one of these structures?" she asked Martha.

"No, but the Potts House leaves much to be desired," Martha tittered and crinkled her nose. "It is like living in a cramped bachelors' hall what with all of his aides lodging there. I suppose, as always, when we are in winter camp, we must make the best of it."

Caty did her best to settle into Nathanael's hut, which also housed his aides. The smoky dwelling had a fireplace on each end and some furniture—a table and four chairs in the front room and six narrow straw mattresses in frames with a tiny chest of drawers in the back room. Straw covered the dirt floor, and pegs lined the walls where the men hung their hats, coats, and scabbards that contained their swords.

It was a situation Caty found intolerable. "I am certain Major Blodget and the other men lodging here will see the necessity of finding other quarters. Some are from our neighborhood at home in Coventry and have known us for a long time. They will be willing to accommodate my wishes," she told Nathanael as she shook out the gowns she brought with her and hung them beside the men's belongings.

"I know not where to send them," Nathanael protested.

"Are you willing to forfeit your connubial pleasure for your aides?"

Nathanael grinned. "You know that I am not, my angel."

"For now, we are alone." She slid a finger under his chin and kissed his sensuous lips and then looked into his blue eyes. "Your eye is infected again?" she asked, alarmed.

Nathanael responded to her touch as if he were a young boy seduced by his first woman. The last thing he wanted to do was talk about his eye.

Caty untied her bodice. The throbbing in her loins urged her to undress Nathanael in quick movements. She stripped off his coat and unbuttoned his waistcoat. He jerked it off his shoulders and pulled his shirt over his head. He pressed his hips against hers and was met with a layer of skirts.

"Caty," Nathanael breathed as he took her by the shoulders and laid her on his narrow bed. He pushed up her skirts, but she resisted.

"Not like this, my darling."

"General Greene, are you in there?" a voice asked from the other side of the hut's front door.

Nathanael looked up, irritated.

She smiled up at him. "Tell him to go away or more suitable, tell him to stand guard."

"What?"

"Tell him."

"He will hear us."

"Then we will be discreet."

Nathanael sighed loudly and slipped on his coat lest he answer the door with the announcement of his physical stimulation.

Caty heard the door creak open and a muffled discussion.

When Nathanael returned to her, she was lying naked in the narrow bed.

He smiled, pushed a lock of her dark hair away from her face, and breathed, "You vixen."

She wrapped her arms around his neck and her legs around his back.

❧

Two days later, on February 24, Nathanael was summoned to the Potts House.

"Where are you going?" Caty asked as he dressed.

"George has requested my presence. We are riding out to meet Baron von Steuben from Prussia who Congress has seen fit to send to us. Washington received a gracious letter from him five weeks ago when he was in Portsmouth, New Hampshire."

Caty detected a breath of Nathanael's impatience. He had already explained the cabal that was brewing among the new members of the Board of War and that he was as much a target of their schemes as Washington and Knox.

"We suspect Congress has sent Steuben to pacify France's desires regarding our war for independence and its success because he is sponsored by Benjamin Franklin and other diplomats in France. Conway has to distrust the introduction of an apocryphal man to the army. He sees himself as the army's greatest hope as its inspector general, a role that would give him authority to train troops as he saw fit, which in a manner would overrule his Excellency's authority."

He slid his sword into its scabbard and then kissed her on the tip of her pert nose. "I have assigned an escort for you while you are in camp. His name is Lieutenant Carson Kavanagh from Virginia. He was recently assigned to my Life Guard."

"Oh? Where is he and how do I request his attendance?" she asked.

"Send a message by way of whoever is standing guard duty outside."

Nathanael put on his hat. "One last thing, my darling, expect to have supper at General Washington's quarters this evening. I love you."

Nathanael arrived on horseback at the Pott's House. William Blodget trailed behind on his own mount. When they entered the house, Billy Lee was dressing George's reddish hair in a neat queue.

George checked his appearance in a small hand mirror and asked, "Is everyone ready?"

"Yes, sir, we are," Colonel John Laurens confirmed.

A stable boy brought around George's horse, Blueskin, a half-gray Arabian that was the complement to the horse he preferred in battle—a less-skittish chestnut named Nelson.

"Have you heard from Lafayette?" Nathanael asked George as they rode to the outskirts of camp.

"I have. He wrote me from Albany. He was appalled at what he saw when he arrived. There were too few troops. Those who were there were poorly equipped," George explained. "There is widespread derision over the plan to prosecute the invasion during the winter months. What is more, he suspects the British and Canadians are expecting it."

Nathanael remained silent. He knew Horatio Gates had planned the invasion of Canada without Washington's knowledge. Washington got wind of the plan only when Lafayette approached him carrying his "commission" from Gates.

The party followed the partially frozen Schuylkill River until a stocky man appeared astride his horse with a dog obediently following and two young men also mounted.

Alexander Hamilton rode forward. He bowed in his saddle and addressed the older man of the three. "Are you Baron von Steuben?"

The man consulted one of the teenage boys with him.

The teenager said to the older man, "*Il veut savoir si vous êtes le Baron von Steuben?*"

The older man smiled broadly and returned the bow.

"Yes, he is," the youth said. "My name is Pierre Du Ponceau. I am the Baron's translator and personal secretary." He indicated the man beside him. "This is Captain Louis de Ponthiere, the Baron's aide-de-camp."

"*Voici Son Excellence, le commandant en chef, le general George Washington,*" Alexander said. "*Et voici le general Nathanael Greene et son assistant le major William Blodget.*"

"*Votre Excellence, j'ai l'honneur de vous rencontrer enfin,*" Steuben said.

"He is honored to meet you," Alexander translated, and then

introduced Du Ponceau and Ponthiere.

Nathanael and George returned the sentiment and bowed in the saddle.

Although Nathanael could not understand Steuben, he noted that John Laurens and Alexander Hamilton looked as if they were infatuated with the older Prussian's smiling face and air of quiet intellect that exhibited not one sign of superiority. George spurred his horse and urged him toward camp. Nathanael fell in beside George. The aides followed in silence. George paused for a moment to allow the Baron to catch up, and the three continued on riding side by side in reticence.

Friedrich Wilhelm August Heinrich Ferdinand von Steuben's first sight of Valley Forge, the smell of dense smoke, and the constant activity of men performing duties was invigorating to an old soldier who had been away from army life too long. Fifteen years had passed since the Prussian Army had finished with him and spat him out.

Martha looked dismayed. "How are we to have a civilized supper in this tiny living room?"

"Relax, my dear. The table is prepared, and those who cannot sit there may be seated around the room. Construction on the dining cabin will begin as soon as your kitchen is completed. Then all will be satisfactory. Now, come meet our guest of honor, Baron von Steuben," George said.

Caty was already in an animated conversation with the Baron and his young aides when Martha and George approached. John Laurens and Alexander Hamilton stood among them in rapt attention along with Nathanael, who took pride in his beautiful wife. Neither Nathanael nor the Washingtons spoke French, but it rolled off Caty's tongue with ease. The barrel chested Baron with close-set eyes looked smitten.

"You must tell us more of your adventures in the Prussian Army," Caty said in French. "What an honor for you to have served under Frederick the Great as a lieutenant general in the Prussian Army."

Anthony Wayne and Lord Alexander Stirling and his wife, Lady Sarah, filed into the crowded little house. The ladies, officers, and most of the aides seated themselves around the table. Thanks to the grand forage, they were served heaping dishes of potatoes, beef steak, bread, and hickory nuts.

"What is that magnificent eight-pointed star on the left breast of your coat?" Lord Stirling asked the Baron as he dished potatoes on to his plate.

Friedrich smiled broadly, and his double chin quivered when he spoke, "This is the star of the Order of Fidelity, a chivalric order founded fifty years ago. My patroness, Princess Friederike of Baden-Durlach, presented it to me. My induction into the order came with the title of Freiherr."

"Hence, your title of Baron," Caty interjected in French.

fourteen

This Intricate Business

Two weeks later, George sipped Madeira and listened with no comment to the dinner conversation in Nathanael's and Caty's hut. He had given Baron von Steuben unlimited access to the camp, allowing him to poke and prod and give his professional opinion of the army. Steuben leaped into the role with gusto.

But George was still vexed with Nathanael. "If you will excuse me, I am in need of some fresh air," George declared, "Nathanael, please accompany me."

Nathanael exchanged glances with Caty, who knowing what this was about, had kept the conversation over dinner lively and engaging so the slight would not be noticed.

Delicate snowflakes drifted in the air as the two generals strolled, trailed by a small contingent of Life Guard. "We—I—am waiting for your answer in regard to the quartermaster general position you have been offered. Have you given it thought?" George asked.

"I have. I want to negotiate terms and have prepared a list of stipulations to Congress—most of which I know you have no control over."

"Have you addressed Congress with this list?"

"Not yet. I want you to know what I want and why before I do so," Nathanael replied.

George raised an eyebrow. "Do you care to enlighten me?"

"I have asked that I retain my rank as major general and that I will not lose my field command when campaign season opens. I have also asked that Congress name Charles Petit and John Cox as my top deputies. I need men I can place full confidence in to conduct this intricate business. Charles is a lawyer and an accountant and will be in charge of the department's books. John is a merchant who will supervise the purchases and monitor the stores and supplies."

"I hear there is a new rate of pay with this position," George said.

"Yes, and aside from my wages, we each receive one percent commission for every one hundred dollars of government money spent on the supplies we procure. That was the arrangement Mifflin had with Congress."

"Have you discussed this with Caty?"

"Yes." Nathanael stopped walking. "If my demands are met, I will accept the position and do my best. I do this for my wife and for my family. More importantly, I do this for you and our army. Did you know my children are with my brother Jacob in Rhode Island? They are literally growing up without me. But many of us suffer a similar desolation."

George nodded solemnly. He had not been home to Mount Vernon in Virginia since the spring of 1775. He could only picture his new step-grandchildren through his wife's eyes.

On Monday March 2, 1778, Congress, taking into consideration the arrangement proposed by the committee, resolved that Major General Nathanael Greene be appointed Quartermaster General of the Continental Army.

꙰

On the night of March 11, the hills and valleys surrounding Valley Forge were cast in silver light. Nathanael penned a long overdue letter to his brother Jacob. The company his father had left to Nathanael and his brothers was not prosperous enough to support the growing families of six brothers. With British warships blocking Narragansett Bay at New-port, there was little demand for the anchors that the Greene men and their workers pounded out in the family iron forge.

In a plaintive tone, Nathanael wrote, "We are almost ready to think that our armies are despised. Every sentiment of humanity, private virtue, and public spirit has left the states. I have spent but a short hour at home since the commencement of the War. I am wearing out my constitution and the prime of my life. It is true I shall leave the consolation of exerting my small abilities in support of the Liberties of my Country, but that is but poor food to subsist a family upon in old Age."

Caty slid her arms around his broad shoulders and rested her chin on one. His eyes moved to her face. *I do not think she has ever looked this beautiful,* he thought. The mournful words cried out as her dark eyes slid across the page.

"Speak to me," she whispered.

He wiped away a single tear that had crept into the corner of the eye marred with the smallpox scar. "How can our countrymen not care about liberty?" he asked profoundly. "How can they not see their stake in it or the need to act in earnest to help us achieve it?" He laid his head on her arm.

She slid a finger under his chin and forced him to look at her with his bewitching blue eyes. "You will do what is right no matter the gloomy prospects nor the blind eyes." She kissed his cheek and continued, "You have never let us down—not your brothers, not me or the children, not your men, your friends, nor General Washington."

Nathanael said nothing. He had heard rumors that officers in camp, like French general Marquis de Lafayette and Washington's young aides, were smitten with Caty and that she had done nothing to thwart their enthusiasm. Even the man he requested to fill the commissary general position, Jeremiah Wadsworth, a married sea captain and merchant from Connecticut, brazenly showed his affection for Caty's charms. If Caty felt something in return, she was carefully guarding it.

❧

March 19 dawned bright over the encampment, sunlight reflected on the dazzling snow. Drums beat to attention as the regimental commanders gathered for the early morning review and received orders of the day. It was drill day on the Grand Parade. Baron von Steuben organized a model company built around Washington's own guards and an additional 100 picked men, which he drilled personally as an example for the rest of the army. To back up the Baron, Washington selected fourteen inspectors—one from each infantry brigade.

Steuben's claim that he was a lieutenant general in the Prussian Army was false, but he knew the details of the Prussian system of marching, forming the line, wheeling, firing, and thrusting and parrying with the bayonet.

Nathanael and George stood aloof and out of sight of the troops to avoid distracting them. In the background, cannon fired from the artillery park and the new redoubts on Mount Misery. "I believe he will have our troops looking like a military force in no time," George commented.

Steuben's voice rose to a deep pitch as he walked the line of volunteers. "*Steh gerade!*" he commanded. Some of the soldiers straightened their backs as they were told, but others wanted to know why they should do that. It was a lesson the Baron himself was learning. Americans did not blindly follow commands as the Prussians, Austrians, or French did.

His seventeen-year-old aide, Pierre, looked harried. He had no grasp on military terminology and was having difficulty translating Steuben's orders from German or French to English. The Baron resorted to pantomime as he taught the rest of the first day's lesson: how a soldier came to attention, how he went to parade rest, how he dressed to the left and right with precise motions of his head, and how to turn at the command, "right about face."

As the snow melted and the grasses began to spike their bladed heads and the smell of wildflowers transformed Valley Forge, the Continental Army was also transformed by a former down and out Prussian soldier and courtier and a self-educated former Quaker with a limp and asthma.

❧

Caty's carriage rolled to a stop and let her off. She hoisted her skirt above the slush of melting snow as she picked her way toward Washington's headquarters. The dreadful sound of the lash snapped in her ears. Another soldier had been caught trying to desert and was enduring the punishment. She wondered if being drummed out of camp for stealing was worse—the humiliation of soldiers astride their horses backward, without saddles, their coats turned inside out, and their hands tied behind their backs.

"Mrs. Greene, please wait," a voice beckoned.

She turned to see the handsome, debonair thirty-two-year-old General Anthony Wayne walking briskly toward her. She waited for him.

Anthony bowed. "Have you no escort?"

She glanced over her shoulder at Lieutenant Kavanagh. "Nathanael assigned one of his guards to attend me. General Wayne, please, it is Caty. And may I call you Anthony?"

"Of course," he said. "Where are you going?"

"Lady Washington's kitchen and dining cabin are done. She wishes for Lady Stirling and me to see them, have a cup of tea, and spend a few hours knitting stockings for the soldiers."

"May I accompany you to your destination?" he asked.

Caty's face softened when she smiled and nodded.

"I hear you and Nathanael are moving two miles away to the comfortable quarters of Moore Hall owned by Mr. William Moore as a benefit extended to the quartermaster general."

"Yes, after Nathanael returns from Morristown where he has gone to tend to his quartermaster general subordinates, partnerships, and business affairs." As they continued walking she asked, "When does your wife plan to come to camp, Anthony?"

"Polly never comes to camp. She endured hardships in Nova Scotia when I brought her there as a new bride on an adventure. Ever since then, she refuses to leave the security of our home in Waynesborough, Pennsylvania, and I seldom return."

"I am sorry to hear of your loneliness."

"I am rarely lonely," Anthony said with an impish grin.

Caty returned the grin.

"I hope you shall find me a suitable guest at Moore Hall when you begin to entertain there."

"I would have it no other way," she assured him elegantly. "I have not heard your stories about your command at Brandywine, Germantown, or even Paoli."

"Mrs. Greene! Lady Washington sent me to find you," Delphi, Martha's personal servant called out. The couple turned. She was running toward them. "She says you is late!"

"Oh, my. I must hasten," Caty told Anthony. "Martha is my dearest friend here, and I do not wish to distress her."

Anthony bowed deeply. "I think I will confirm that my brigade colonels are following instructions for training their men. Good day."

Caty joined Delphi, and they continued on. When they arrived at the Potts House, the generals' wives and daughters were standing outside with arms full of yarn, knitting needles, and boxes of tea.

Alexander Hamilton and John Laurens tumbled out of the house and startled them. "General Charles Lee is arriving from Philadelphia. General Washington wants us to greet him, although if I had my druthers, Lee would be ignored," Alexander said and then announced, "Lady Washington, the general wishes to speak to you about arrangements for a dinner to recognize General Lee's release from captivity."

Caty recalled that General Lee was Nathanael's commander in 1775, and that after the Continental Army crossed the Hudson River on their long retreat from New York, Lee was captured by British dragoons while at the White Horse Tavern in Basking Ridge, New Jersey. Martha remembered as well. She exchanged glances with Caty before she answered her husband's summons.

❧

Martha's new dining cabin, where she hosted the dinner for General Lee, was alive with conversation and the aroma of pea greens, parsnips, mushrooms, boiled beef hocks, fresh shad from the Schuylkill River, and bread, along with an abundance of ale and rum.

Nathanael arrived late. When he entered, the conversation ceased, and all eyes fell on him. Washington stood to defuse Nathanael's embarrassment and spoke congenially, "General Greene, thank you for joining us. Please take the vacant seat beside Colonel Tilghman."

Nathanael bowed and sat down. He noticed Kitty Stirling was present and noted her piercing stare. Kitty's daggered stare was not intended for him. She was glowering at Caty, to whom Alexander Hamilton was surreptitiously tossing approving glances.

Nathanael looked away and settled his attention on the slovenly General Charles Lee. He thought, *If I can take the time to wash and change my shirt, Lee could have taken the time to wash as well.* "General Lee," he said in acknowledgement.

"Charles, will you get on with the description of your captivity if you are going to tell it?" Anthony said impatiently. He tried not to roll his eyes in disgust when Charles' two little black Pomeranians began to yap from where they sat on the floor beside Charles' chair. "And perhaps put those dogs outside," Anthony suggested.

"If you love me, you must love my dogs," Charles declared. "Sit, Spado," he commanded one of the Pomeranians. Spado obeyed and took a piece of bread from Charles' hand. Charles made little kissing sounds. "Mimmo, here you are my sweet." Mimmo snapped a piece of bread from Charles' other hand.

Friedrich von Steuben regarded his obedient dog, Azor, lying quietly beside the hearth.

"Yes, as I was saying," Charles continued. "After I was sent to New York, Congress demanded that I be accorded the status of a prisoner of war with respect normally shown senior officers. General Washington supported that position. General Howe relented, and I found myself comfortably accommodated in a two room apartment with my precious little Spado, instead of aboard the cramped HMS *Centurion* in New York harbor."

Lord Stirling passed a serving plate of shad to Charles. "Anyway," Charles went on after he helped himself, "an exchange with the British was arranged after months of wrangling, and I expect to be exchanged for British General Richard Prescott. You know, Nathanael, the general who was holding your home state of Rhode Island until he was captured."

"Yes, Charles," Nathanael conceded. He glanced at Caty. His wife's face was the perfect picture of poise and patience. He breathed a mental sigh of relief. He felt uneasy and had confided to her as they dressed for dinner that he thought no great good would come of Lee's return. "Lee is a fine officer and scholar, but I am afraid the radical Whigs and those who plotted against Washington and me in recent months will try to debauch and poison his mind with prejudices."

Charles continued, "Officially, I am still a prisoner of war. Until the exchange is finalized, I cannot return to duty, but as long as I do nothing contrary to the interest of his Majesty or his government, I am a free man. I expect that to change as General Washington and General Howe seal the terms of my release."

"I assure you we are glad to have you back, Charles," George said.

"Yes, well, judging from all the new faces around the table, my return may be just what this army needs." He poured a glass of rum and cut a piece of beef for himself and smaller pieces for his dogs. "Baron von Steuben, your training tactics will be an interesting study while I am in York with Congress. I think they will be more than what this army really needs. Anyway, from York I will be returning to Prato Rio, my property in the Shenandoah Valley, until I can rejoin the army."

Friedrich did not understand Charles. He looked to Pierre to translate Charles' English to German. Pierre did so with hesitancy, but the Baron deserved to know that General Lee was questioning his European style of training. It seemed like hypocrisy. Charles Lee had served in both the British Army and the Polish Army of King Stanislaus II.

❧

Henry Knox and his aide-de-camp, Captain Solomon Cartwright, arrived in camp on April 7 just as Charles Lee was leaving. To their delight, they found a new and improved Continental Army. The ranks were still too thin, but the officers and men had shared at least one full campaign. By late spring, all the regiments had a core of veterans. The Patriots learned to make do with less of everything and found ways to get more of out what they had. Steuben's hard drilling and dedication was paying off in the form of disciplined brigades.

Nathanael and his quartermaster and commissary business partners grasped departmental reins, and soon the formal channels of the logistics system began to function better at all levels. Deliveries to the army became more regular, and food, clothing, forage, camp implements, and munitions were no longer scarce. Substantial shipments of French supplies landed in New England and arrived in camp.

On April 21, under the urging of Congress, Washington convened a war council to plot out a military campaign for the spring. Alexander, poised with quill in hand, waited for the commander-in-chief to speak. "I see three alternatives for a new campaign. The first is the most ambitious—to attack and destroy the British Army in Philadelphia and in what particular manner? The second is to transfer the war north by a move against New York. The third is to remain at Valley Forge until General Howe makes a move."

Twelve senior officers responded to George's memorandum with considerable care. They realized that much of the public had grown war weary and was hungry for better news from the front. Military success, the generals told their commander-in-chief, was critical to maintaining support for the cause and discouraging Loyalism. Not all the generals were decisive for one or another of the choices, leveraging their preferences against British actions, availability of supplies, political developments, and other conditions.

Generals Anthony Wayne and Alexander Stirling favored attacking Philadelphia. Generals Henry Knox, Enoch Poor, William Maxwell, and Nathanael favored an attempt to take New York. The third option appealed to the Marquis de Lafayette and Baron von Steuben.

Two weeks later, on May 5, the news that France had officially recognized the independence of the United States and that the French and Spanish governments had entered into an alliance with the new nation reached Valley Forge. Washington ordered a celebration to honor the events. Caty rode to the parade ground in a carriage with Martha followed by Lady Sarah Stirling and her daughter Kitty. The order of procession immensely satisfied Caty.

Steuben choreographed the review. The boom of cannon signaled the end of an open-air church service and the beginning of the review. Afterward, Steuben's troops performed their maneuvers in perfect cadence to the music of fife, bugle, and drum. Henry's men set off a thunderous explosion of thirteen cannon, and the soldiers responded with a *feu de joie*—a perfectly coordinated, rolling musket fire, which billowed smoke as the onlookers applauded.

John Laurens could hardly contain his excitement. He leaned over and whispered to Washington, "Triumph beams on every countenance!"

Washington nodded and then stood to make an announcement. "My fellows, Congress has confirmed Baron von Steuben's appointment as inspector general with the rank of major general."

Cheers of "Huzzah!" followed. A joyful Baron and his aides stood and bowed.

To add to the joy, Lucy Knox and her toddler, Lucy, arrived in camp accompanied by her escort, General Benedict Arnold and his retinue. Henry tenderly greeted his wife and pulled her into his beefy arms. She was as rotund as her husband, but their physical similitude only enhanced their gentle yet assertive complementary personalities.

Nathanael whispered to Caty, "They appear to be a perfect married couple."

"As are we," Caty twitted.

Nathanael slid an arm around her small waist. "What would I do without the comfort of your constant reassurances?" he said.

Lucy extracted herself from Henry's arms and received Caty and

Martha with hand clasping and cheek kissing. Martha crouched to tickle little Lucy under her chin. "Hello, my dear. You are so pretty," she chortled while the toddler giggled and clung to her mother's skirt.

Benedict, cane in hand, struggled to disembark from the coach. He brushed aside the offer of his aide, Richard Varick, to assist him. Benedict's limp from the wound in his left femur suffered at the Battle of Saratoga elicited sympathy mixed with adoration. As a result of the wound, one of Benedict's legs was shorter, which precluded him from assuming a field command.

George greeted him as he emerged from the coach. "Benedict, it is so good to see you." He summoned Alexander, who passed the items in his hand to his general. George offered them to Benedict. "I wish you to have these finely adorned epaulettes and sword knot as a gesture of my affection."

"Thank you for your esteemed gifts," Benedict replied. "I am flattered with the compliment."

Colonel Tench Tilghman stepped forward and said, "General Arnold, for your convenience, there is a vacant hut available. Can you walk a few hundred rods?"

"Yes, yes," Benedict grumbled. He acknowledged Nathanael as he passed. "General Greene. I wish to dine with you soon."

Nathanael's eyes moved to Caty before he said, "My wife and I will be honored to host a dinner for you tonight at Moore Hall."

"I hope we shall be discussing what Henry Clinton is up to in Philadelphia," Benedict said. He removed his hat and wiped his brow. *I hope the journey to the hut is not too long*, he thought.

"We are all wondering exactly what Clinton is up to in Philadelphia," George said. "I have given General Lafayette a substantial force to probe the British defenses near Philadelphia so that we may answer that question better."

On May 11, General Sir Henry Clinton arrived in Philadelphia to take command of all British forces in America from the departing General Sir William Howe. The affable, well-liked Howe, who was one of the British

Army's best, would go home to defend his performance in America to Parliament and the ministry.

As Clinton was about to take over, rumors that the British would leave Philadelphia ran rampant. With the French declaration of war, Britain would have to devote fewer military resources to defeating the rebellion. The British government ordered a withdrawal from Philadelphia and the reallocation of a significant part of the army to the Caribbean.

Nathanael was in Morristown, New Jersey tending to the business of supplies when a courier arrived with a message from His Excellency.

> *Every piece of intelligence from Philadelphia makes me think it more and more probable that the Enemy are preparing to evacuate it. There are some reasons that induce suspicion they many intend for New York. In any case it is absolutely necessary we should be ready for an instant movement of the army. I have therefore to request you will strain every nerve to prepare without delay the necessary provisions.*

He returned to Valley Forge with a sense of urgency.

In late May, with the intentions of the British Army unclear, the officers' wives went home. The women would be dearly missed by all those who benefited from their feminine influences. Nathanael held Caty close to his broad chest and closed his eyes. Her protruding pregnant belly touched his muscled abdomen. The babe was due in four months. He feared he would miss the birth of his third child just as he had the first two.

"I will write to you every little bit of news that comes my way," Nathanael promised as Caty gazed up into his eyes and swallowed her tears. He saw the distress in her eyes, but in her condition he did not know what to say or how to ask after it. He said, "I have arranged for your first night lodging at the home of a friend. Promise me you will rest before continuing your journey. And kiss the children for me."

Caty nodded and climbed into her carriage.

By June 4, his yearning for her got the best of him and he wrote from Moore Hall, "I am here in the usual style, writing, scolding, eating, and drinking. But there is no Mrs. Greene to retire and spend an agreeable hour with. Pray write me a full history of family matters. Kiss the sweet little children over and over again for their absent papa. You must make yourself as happy as possible. Write me if you are in want of anything."

In mid-June, Sir Henry Clinton readied his troops in Philadelphia for an overland march. He sent regiments to defend his eastern footholds in response to Washington's initial offensive deployments and sought intelligence on regional road networks. The British began to move horses, wagons, and provisions to Cooper's Ferry, which provided an entrance into New Jersey from Philadelphia. The baggage train consisted of some 5,000 horses and 1,500 wagons, which at times stretched out twelve miles on the march.

Clinton divided his 11,000-man army into three groups, each of them large enough to hold off a sizable enemy attack force until assisted by one of the other groups. Hessian General Wilhelm von Knyphausen led the column while General Charles Cornwallis commanded the rear guard, which left Clinton in the middle. The army also included 1,070 noncombatants, 700 Loyalist battalions, and 700 women and children. General Alexander Leslie led the vanguard.

On June 18, the army crossed the Delaware River at Cooper's Ferry and marched to Haddonfield, New Jersey. With the army in New Jersey, the last transports commanded by Admiral Richard Howe, with some of Clinton's troops and Loyalists on board, dropped down the river.

The day before, Nathanael had reported to Washington's headquarters for a war council. Five other major generals were present, including Charles Lee—the prisoner exchange complete, which allowed him to return to duty with the Continental Army. Nine brigadier generals joined the council.

Nathanael sat beside Henry, who offered a subtle nod and whispered, "You are of fine fortune, my friend. As quartermaster, you are a staff officer with no say in command strategy and tactics, yet His Excellency specifically requested your presence."

George rose and the council came to order. He said, "I believe that Clinton will try to reach New York via New Jersey. Intelligence reports have come in that they do not have a sufficient number of transports to move the army and will have to march overland."

"It is my opinion that Clinton will go against Maryland. Until his intentions are clear, I advise staying here at Valley Forge," Charles said. His little dog Spado yapped as if in agreement.

"Shut that thing up," Anthony Wayne grumbled.

"I disagree that Maryland is his intention," Nathanael said. "I think Clinton *will* head to New York. I do, however, agree that we should remain here for a time."

Murmuring and head nodding filled the room. George let it go on for a few minutes while he sorted out his own thoughts. He said, "I want strong outposts established along probable enemy routes of march. General Maxwell, you will march to Mount Holly, an important road junction north of Haddonfield, New Jersey. Every possible expedient should be used to disturb and retard the British progress. I will provide you with a dragoon outfit. You are to link up with General Philemon Dickinson, New Jersey's senior militia commander, who can also protect local populations and occupy large swathes of territory."

William Maxwell, the brilliant light troop commander, drank deeply of his glass of whiskey. *Maxwell will be impossible to understand with his thick Irish brogue if he is drunk,* Nathanael thought.

With word of the full British withdrawal on June 18, Washington put his officers on notice that the army was going to move. He called for another war council in an attempt to glean decisive advice on operations.

"Do we try to land a partial blow to Clinton, or do we bring on a general engagement?" George asked.

After a short deliberation, Henry said, "The general sentiment of the council is that it would be the most criminal degree to hazard a general action."

"I disagree," Anthony retorted. "I think we should move quickly, carrying only essentials, and take the first favorable opportunity to strike the enemy with advantage."

The Marquis de Lafayette said, "It is my wish to see this happen as well."

Nathanael knew that the army would march regardless of the conclusions of the council. When that happened, he would be responsible to keep provisions and supplies with different units of the army at all times during the march. The enormous task included procuring wagons, teams, drivers, and artificers to repair bridges, mend broken wagons, harnesses, guns, and anything needing repair. Campsites needed water, wood, drainage, and defense. Before the army could settle in, latrines would have to be dug, wood and straw gathered, and alarm posts established. He was responsible for orchestrating all of it through his deputies and others who he pressed upon to do the duty.

fifteen
Monmouth Court House

On Friday, June 19, General Benedict Arnold rode in a carriage to Philadelphia as the new military governor to preserve tranquility and order in the British vitiated city. On that same day, Washington's army of 13,000 soldiers broke camp and marched from Valley Forge. They were better disciplined and better fed than the army that had settled in Valley Forge in December of 1777. The camp followers moved with the baggage train in the rear, which was guarded by a detachment of Virginia and Pennsylvania riflemen. The rebel army was uncertain exactly which way Clinton would march to New York. Still, the chase was on.

As the British marched, Generals Philemon Dickinson and William Maxwell harassed Clinton's rear guard. The extensive woodlands and many small rivers and creeks, which frequently cut through defiles, afforded excellent protection for lurking Patriot snipers. Clinton was well aware of this, and he told Wilhelm von Knyphausen, whose 2nd Division was protecting most of the monstrous baggage train, "It remains to be seen to what extent the Patriot advanced forces can slow us."

"If the events that took place at Brandywine and Germantown are any indication, I shall assume they are not up to it," Knyphausen mused.

However, Hessian Captain Johann Ewald complained to his general, "They hang on our rear without let up. Furthermore, some of my men have dropped dead from heat exhaustion, and the mosquitos are relentless." Both American and British troops were victims of the intense heat. Torrential rains brought little relief and made the already poor, sandy roads more difficult.

When the Continental Army entered Hopewell on June 23, they encamped. George made his headquarters at the Hunt House. Under a darkening rainy sky, he immediately detached the husky colonel from Virginia, Daniel Morgan, to take some 600 light infantry to reinforce Dickinson and Maxwell.

In a letter to Caty, Nathanael explained the army's situation and wrote, "I have not received a single line from you since you left camp. I am afraid your letters are stopped and opened by some imprudent scoundrel. I hope you got home safe. Colonel Cox is at Philadelphia and Mr. Petit at Congress, and I am left all alone with business enough for ten men. They profess a great friendship for you. Pray write me the first opportunity of everything and particularly about the children and yourself: my love to all friends."

On June 24, the commander-in-chief convened eleven of his officers which included Nathanael, Charles Lee, Lord Stirling, Lafayette, Steuben, Henry Knox, Anthony Wayne, William Woodford, and Charles Scott. "The question herein lies, do we hazard a general action or do we annoy the enemy? What precise line of conduct will it be best for us to pursue?" George asked.

"Why risk the patriot regulars in pointless action against the best-trained professional troops Europe has to offer when prudence would accomplish results equally important?" Charles Lee argued.

"I disagree," Nathanael countered. "I suggest we send a detachment of two brigades to support an assault by light troops on the British rear and flanks. The rest of the army would be in supporting distance."

"Nonsense," Charles sneered.

The taste of disrespect played on the end of Nathanael's tongue. He swallowed it to avoid publicly breeching protocol and Charles' rank as second-in-command of the army.

"What is the general consensus?" George asked the council.

Lord Stirling, Woodford, and Scott agreed with Lee. The majority recommendation that a general engagement would not be advisable was passed. Alexander Hamilton, who was recording the meeting, placed his quill in its holder in disgust and said, "This entire proceeding would have done honor to the most honorable society of midwives and to them only."

Alexander was not the only one who harbored loathing for the verdict. "I do not agree with the war council's consensus," Anthony declared. "I will not sign the council's document stating general approval of this. We must hit the enemy as hard as possible short of bringing on a general engagement."

"It would be disgraceful for the leaders and humiliating for the troops to allow the enemy to cross the Jerseys with impunity," Lafayette said.

"If we suffer the enemy to pass through the Jerseys without attempting anything upon them, I think we shall ever regret it. People expect something from us, and our strength demands it," Nathanael added with the knowledge that wars were not won by battles alone. Public opinion and civilian lawmakers greatly weighed on the success of the war in America.

Anthony, Lafayette, and Nathanael prevailed in their opinions. Over the strong objections from Charles Lee, George agreed that the army would attack Clinton's huge baggage train and rear guard. George offered the command of 1,500 troops led by Brigadier General Charles Scott to Lafayette who accepted with zeal.

"I think we should raise the number to 2,500 or at least 2,000," Nathanael said, although he had agreed with the original number. When the meeting was over, Alexander conferred with Nathanael. The two went to see Washington privately.

"I know what you have come about," George said. "You wish me to fight."

Nathanael and Alexander exchanged glances. "Yes," Nathanael conceded.

"I suppose you will not leave this alone until I do," George said without spite. Silence stretched out until he finally said, "Then, I shall do so and send forth Anthony Wayne with 1,000 select troops."

When Anthony's division expanded the vanguard, Charles Lee insisted that he was entitled to the command.

On the late morning of June 27, the main body of the Continental Army arrived at Manalapan Bridge ten miles from Monmouth. The British and American armies were in dangerously close proximity. Clinton's troops occupied Monmouth Court House and its immediate environs. They were strongly posed with excellent security.

In addition to the advanced brigades totaling nearly 4,000 troops, artillery companies with a combined twelve guns were distributed across the brigades under the overall command of Charles Lee. This was the force Lee would take into battle.

"I want you to hit the British tomorrow morning," George told Lee. "Any attack by you, the vanguard, however, will require the support of the main army. This is to be done at all events."

At 6:00 a.m. on June 28, the advanced guard began moving out toward the rear of Clinton's army. Even as they deployed, there was already a serious miscue. Colonel Daniel Morgan and his men were at Richmond Mills. Daniel received a message at 1:45 a.m. telling him to expect to move the next morning. Morgan took it as meaning June 29, but by the time the confusion was cleared up, he received a message from Nathanael:

> *You are too distant for the main army to support you. You are to avoid a serious action unless you are tempted by some very evident advantage.*

Nathanael remained with George and the main army. With Lee assigned to command the vanguard, George placed Nathanael in charge of the army's right wing. By 11:00 a.m., the temperature was climbing toward 100 degrees. The bulk of Washington's force was nearing Tennent's Meeting House some three miles from Monmouth Court House and only just approaching supporting distance of Lee's vanguard.

Cannon boomed in the distance near a defile called the East Morass and blue smoke drifted slowly through the humid air.

What they could not discern was that Clinton's 1st Division had moved out only to turn around and march for the Patriot vanguard. Aware that Washington had not arrived, Clinton launched the flower of his army—Cornwallis' rear guard and the bulk of his 1st Division—in two columns. Clinton initiated a three-pronged attack to crush the Continental vanguard. A regiment of Royal Scottish Highlanders pursued General Charles Scott's men as they retreated west with General William Maxwell's troops. Their exhausted men had been out all morning.

Nathanael, George, and their entourage approached Tennent's Meeting House at 12:30 p.m. Overwhelmed with information, they encountered Alexander Hamilton returning from a forward reconnaissance. Alexander addressed his commander-in-chief, "Sir, I advise against sending the army forward as a single body. Rather, I propose splitting the troops into two columns with the largest proceeding directly across the West Morass bridge toward Freehold to support General Lee. At the same time, a smaller column could move toward Craig's Mill to protect our right."

Henry Knox rode up as Alexander was explaining his vision. "I am in strong agreement with Colonel Hamilton," he offered.

To Nathanael's delight, George took Alexander's advice. "Nathanael, prepare to march to counteract any attempt to turn our right. File off by the new church two miles from Englishtown and fall into the Monmouth road a small distance in the rear of the court house. The rest of the column will move directly on toward the court house."

"Henry, you will provide Nathanael with whatever artillery he requires," George said.

Before Nathanael or Henry could respond, a militiaman rode up with sweat trickling down his cheeks. "General Washington! General Lee is retreating!"

"How did you come upon this information?" the commander-in-chief asked.

The militiaman pointed and said, "That young fifer coming up the road."

When the bedraggled boy approached, George asked, "Are you part of the army, son?"

"Aye, sir. General Lee has withdrawn. My regiment was one of the first units to pull out."

There was a moment of astonished silence as regiments appeared trudging the road toward Washington. Charles Lee with several other officers rode toward them. Charles was caught off balance when George demanded in a fury, "What was the meaning of the retreat? I desire to know, sir, what is the reason whence arises the disorder and confusion?"

Charles was rendered speechless. *I thought my conduct would draw Washington's congratulations and applause as I have saved the vanguard from utter destruction*, he thought then stammered, "Sir, sir," until George repeated himself.

Charles pulled himself together and explained, "The retrograde was the only real choice open. Intelligence was faulty. Officers, especially Generals Scott and Maxwell pulled back without my orders, and, consequently, I chose not to beard the British under such conditions."

"All this may be very true, sir, but you ought not to have undertaken it unless you intended to go through with it," George snapped.

Nathanael saw no point in continuing to witness the debacle and Lee's excuses. He knew his commander-in-chief would soon bring everything into order and regularity. He wheeled his horse to gather men from the Virginia brigade under General William Woodford as well as French artillery Colonel Chevalier du Plessis and gun crews for a total of four 3-pound cannon, drivers, a few staff officers, and militia vedettes.

As Nathanael's detachment marched, Lord Alexander Stirling took a position on Perrine's Hill that became the American far left. Washington returned Lee to battle and pulled two of Anthony Wayne's battalions out of the retreating column and directed them to a wooded patch to secure the route to the West Morass bridge. They were on the American left and hoped to impede the enemy's approach. But they were soon fighting for their lives against a mob of British grenadiers who stormed the Hedgerow and crossed the bridge.

Clinton ordered General James Pattison of the Royal Artillery to open fire on the Continental line. Pattison happily obliged with 6-pounders, 12-pounders, and 5.5 inch howitzers. Henry Knox answered the British cannons from a grassy rise near Perrine's Hill. Knox's cannon rippled down the Continental artillery line and fired at the Royal artillery near the Hedgerow. The great cannonade was under way.

It was 1:30 p.m.

Clinton's men had already suffered severe casualties, and the heat had sapped them of their strength. He ordered his light troops and two grenadier battalions, who he feared were too far away from the main body, to retire to the Hedgerow until more troops came to their support. Most of his artillery was there. He put units under Generals Charles Grey and William Erskine in motion that included the 1st Battalion of Light Infantry and the Queen's Rangers.

At 2:45 p.m., a local, Colonel David Rhea of the 2nd New Jersey, rode up to Nathanael. "Sir, General Washington has sent me to you. I advised him of the defensive strengths of Perrine's Hill and then a good position on the right at Combs Hill to set up artillery with a field of fire across the terrain. He has agreed and sent me to guide you to that place."

"Thank you, Colonel Rhea. Tell the general I am on my way," Nathanael said. He ordered the march, and by 3:45 p.m., his French artillerist, with a clear view of the British near the Hedgerow, had the cannon in place. Nathanael's four guns roared and pounded the Hedgerow. With marshy ground at the foot of Combs Hill, an attack by Clinton would have been suicide. His artillery quieted and Clinton repositioned his units. His intention was to call off the attack that, in the heat and humidity of the day, had dropped horses and men on both sides of the line. With nothing to shoot at, the guns on Combs Hill fell silent.

Most of the American Army slept where they dropped. Nathanael and William Woodford rested and remained on Combs Hill that night. When the sun rose at 5:41 a.m. on Monday, June 29, its bright rays revealed that the British Army was gone. Clinton had ensured his baggage train escaped, which was his main objective.

On the evening of July 1, the Continental Army began their long march toward White Plains, New York, where they could keep an eye on Clinton's army that had passed through Sandy Hook, New Jersey, and then embarked by transports to New York.

The Americans stopped at New Brunswick, New Jersey to celebrate the second anniversary of the Declaration of Independence. There was a parade, cannon fire, and extra rations of rum. Nathanael was occupied with trying to find horses to replace those that had been killed or died from the heat during the battle. The celebration of the nation's independence was not the only business that needed attended to in New Brunswick.

Four days earlier, before the army moved out of Monmouth, George, calm but frustrated, had come to Nathanael. "I received a letter from Charles Lee regarding our confrontation on the battlefield in which he resorted to name calling and accusations, which I found highly improper. Then, he sent another seeking an apology for my pointed words after his vanguard's retreat. He stated that he held me in the greatest respect, but in this case, he pronounced that I was guilty of an act of cruel injustice toward him."

"And your answer?" Nathanael asked.

"I offered a forum where he could air his complaints. He replied in insolent terms that he wished for a court martial to clear his name and restore his honor. I complied and had him arrested. Lord Stirling will preside over the military court which shall begin on our arrival at Brunswick."

"I am having a difficult time countenancing General Lee's actions," Nathanael responded—an outlook he shared with many, especially George's aides, Alexander Hamilton and John Laurens. "His experience led us to believe in his merits. I grieve that he is an unfortunate man whose vanity and folly has brought him to disgrace."

"You can do nothing to help him," George said. "I know that your determination to judge fairly wishes to influence your views. The road to White Plains will be a long one."

Nathanael reverted to his inglorious duties as quartermaster general on the march. The job required hours of writing and attending to an unending stream of paperwork. Instead of attending George Washington's war councils, he spent eye-straining nights recording accounts. The job, which Nathanael hated, was in some ways perfect for him—a well-organized businessman who knew the intricacies of logistics and supply, and a field officer who knew what was required to keep troops provisioned. But quartermaster general was a thankless position that was only intensified by Washington's failure to acknowledge Nathanael's herculean efforts to keep all organized because he needed to hear those words of thanks.

When the army moved out of New Brunswick, Nathanael took Major William Blodget and members of his quartermaster department to scout out campsites near the Hudson River. The brutally hot weather dragged on Nathanael's ability to withstand the search, and he fell into silence. The silence concerned Washington, but the commander-in-chief used the word "neglect" in his message to Nathanael asking about his progress and demanding his attention.

"I suppose we had better speed our search," Nathanael advised William.

"You cannot take this message as an affront to your capabilities," William said. "Perhaps, you are needed. General Washington is sometimes blunt and hasty in his expression of his irritation and requests."

Nathanael said nothing. The wound was already a painful strike at his ego. He swallowed the rant that he wanted to spew and continued his search for a proper camp near White Plains.

On July 21, 1778, when the Continental Army was settled into camp, Nathanael, his temper somewhat abated, went to speak to George. He spoke with veneration to George's Life Guard standing outside of the commander-in-chief's headquarters at Wright's Mill, "Tell His Excellency that General Greene wishes to speak with him alone."

"Come in. I have been waiting for your return. Please sit down," George said to Nathanael when he entered the room. He motioned to a seat at the dining table piled with correspondence that needed attention.

Nathanael sat down. His nerves were taut, and his asthma threatened to wipe away his words. He poured a glass of wine and indulged in it. Finally, he said, "Your Excellency has made me very unhappy. I can submit patiently to deserved censure; but it wounds my feelings exceedingly to meet with a rebuke for doing what I conceived to be a proper part of my duty and in the order of things."

"Nathanael, I believe you—" George began.

"Please let me finish. If I had neglected my duty in pursuit of pleasure, or if I had been wanting in respect to Your Excellency, I would have put my hand upon my mouth and had been silent upon the occasion. But as I am not conscious of being chargeable with either the one or the other, I cannot help thinking I have been treated with a degree of severity I am in no respect deserving of."

Nathanael drained his glass of wine. He did not need liquid courage to continue, he only needed a moment to catch his breath. "I have not asked for furlough in three years. I have never suffered my pleasures to interfere with my duty. I have never been troublesome to Your Excellency to publish anything to my advantage, particularly in the action at Brandywine. As I came into the Quartermaster department with reluctance, I shall leave it with the want of your approbation."

George struggled to maintain his emotions. This heartfelt plea from his most trusted and capable general tugged at his heart and only reinforced the value he placed not only on Nathanael's service but on his friendship. "I can and do assure you, that I have ever been happy in your friendship and have no scruples in declaring that I think myself indebted to your abilities, honor, and candor."

"I am very sensible of my deficiencies, but this is not so justly chargeable that I was in neglect," Nathanael repeated in his defense.

"When I complained of neglect, I was four or five days without seeing a single person in your department and at a time when I wished you in two capacities, having business of the utmost with Admiral d'Estaing. Let me beseech you not to harbor any distrust of my friendship or assume that I meant to wound your feelings."

George poured another glass of wine for the two of them and leaned forward over the table. "Rest assured that I shall write to Congress informing them of your judicious exertions in transforming the quartermaster department from a confused and destitute state to a department with great facility."

Consoled, Nathanael shared news in regard to General John Sullivan's position in Rhode Island where Washington had sent him in early 1778. The state was in alarm because the British in Newport launched an expedition to break up state troops, plundering as they went.

"I received word from General Varnum, who has just returned from Rhode Island. He says there are 1,500 state troops including artillery regiments. He thinks there cannot be less than 3,000 troops from New England under General Sullivan that can be depended on."

Of this, George was unaware, and he let his general continue.

"I should write to Caty. She is with child living across the bay from Newport. She has written me to ask why Continental troops have not marched to Rhode Island to drive out the enemy."

George rose and said, "By all means, please attend to Caty's concerns. Rhode Island's dilemma has not escaped my attention. We shall speak further of this, but for now, until plans are established with Admiral d'Estaing, remain silent on the matter."

Nathanael also rose and ambled toward the door.

As George watched, he thought, *His limp seems pronounced today.* He said, "You know that I could not give you the laurels you sought at Brandywine and Monmouth because you were in command of Virginia regiments, and those laurels would make it seem as if I was favoring my own state."

Nathanael nodded.

"And please give my regards to Mrs. Greene. She is a lovely, lively lady who deserves a man as admirable as you."

sixteen

I Charge You to Be Victorious

After leaving Valley Forge, Caty fetched her children from Potowomut and returned with them to Coventry. Through letters, Nathanael kept her abreast of the army's activities—letters often filled with his obvious loneliness. Living in Coventry made her feel isolated from her friends in East Greenwich.

Nathanael's brother Jacob advised, "I suppose you should retire to Potowomut where family can look after you and the children."

"I cannot impose on your family another day," Caty said unconvincingly.

Jacob heard the hesitation in her voice and responded, "You perhaps mean that you cannot tolerate another day living with my Quaker family."

"I did not say that," Caty huffed. "I have written Nathanael asking for his advice. He suggested I travel to Westerly and move into the farmhouse he owns there."

Jacob's wife Peggy, who was mending a pair of breeches, deigned to state her opinion.

"You should take care of the roving bands of British rogues lest you should be robbed on your travels, and with my niece and nephew at that," Jacob warned.

"Then perhaps you should accompany us there. My carriage has been mended, although the blacksmith had the audacity to shame me in affairs when I reminded him that I wished to venture out. He said that my proper place is in the home. He thought I should be spinning instead of riding about."

Caty bundled little George, baby Patty, and a nurse into her carriage and traveled twenty-eight miles south to Westerly on the coast near Connecticut.

"Are you certain you will be fine on your own here?" Jacob asked as he unloaded her baggage. "What if something is amiss with your pregnancy and you need a physician?"

She lifted fifteen-month-old Patty and settled the toddler on her hip. "You know I have family here and a woman to come and help me with chores. Dr. Peter Turner, who treated me at Valley Forge, is also nearby."

"Very well," Jacob said. "As long as you are cared for."

"Thank you for your kindness and seeing to my safe journey," she said.

"As his older brother, Nathanael expects this of me. I do so with great pleasure. I am to borrow a horse from the Ward family for my return journey." Jacob fought the urge to kiss her cheek and instead kissed Patty's chubby cheeks. He kneeled and said to little George, "Watch after your mother and be a good boy."

Caty spent the next week wondering when Nathanael would reply to her letter regarding the British presence in Newport and the Continental Army's response to drive them out. "Why does he not respond? Perhaps, he does not wish to see us, or his interest in his family has waned," she mumbled to her children as they played near her feet where she sat on the farmhouse portico under a hot, sunny sky.

The brightness overhead did nothing to lighten the darkness she dwelled on. However, the galloping hooves of a post rider's horse did. She abruptly stood and waited for the rider, who pulled up into the yard and passed a bundle of letters to her. She squealed with delight. A letter from her husband had arrived. She broke the seal and unfolded it.

I received your letter of the 8th instant. You must rest assured that there must be something very uncommon to prevent my coming home. You cannot have a greater desire to see me than I have to see you and the children. I long to hear the little rogues prattle.

It has ever been my study and ever shall be to render you as happy as possible. But I have been obliged in many instances to sacrifice the present pleasures to our future hopes. This I am sure has done violence to your feelings but I trust the motives were so laudable that I shall meet with no difficulty in obtaining your forgiveness hereafter. Although I have been absent from you, I have not been inconstant in love, unfaithful to my vows, or unjust to your bed.

A tear rolled down Caty's cheek. His words were everything she needed and wanted. She caressed her heavy belly. He had not promised to come home, but he had not set their love adrift.

Washington set his hopes on attacking New York when French Admiral d'Estaing sailed toward New York Harbor, but the ships could not pass over the shallow bar at Sandy Hook.

Nathanael relayed his opinion to him about what should be done, "I am optimistic that the fleet could run up to Newport in three days' time to support Sullivan," he told George.

Admiral d'Estaing had the same strategical idea. He sent a message to Washington proposing a joint effort against Newport that would provide a much better base of operations for the French fleet. Washington sent Alexander Hamilton to d'Estaing with a message that he agreed to the plan. Then, George sent Colonel John Laurens to deliver the word to John Sullivan that Newport was chosen as the allied target and that Sullivan should raise as large a force as possible.

Nathanael begged George to send him, but his request was denied. "You are needed to procure supplies and speed lines of communication for the mission."

"I believe I ought to be in Rhode Island defending my home state," Nathanael countered. Then he tried to reconcile his perceived slights in a long letter to a congressman in Rhode Island.

He extended a hand of introspective generosity to John Sullivan. On July 28, he wrote, "You are the most happy man in the World. What a child of fortune. The expedition going on against Newport, cannot, I think fail of success. You are the first general that has ever had the opportunity of cooperation with the French forces belonging to the United States. I wish most ardently to be with you. Your friends are anxious; your enemies are watching. I charge you to be victorious."

As Nathanael finished his letter, George's tall shadow draped his office doorway. Nathanael rose and bowed. "Please sit," George bid, but Nathanael remained standing. "I have come to tell you that I have written to Congress to inform them that I judge it advisable to send you to Rhode Island. Your field experience is invaluable. Your intimate knowledge with the whole of that country, and your extensive interest and influence upon it, are to be considered. You may leave today."

Nathanael smiled, and his lambent blue eyes sparkled.

George returned a rare smile to his general. He bowed to Nathanael's staring assistant quartermaster general deputy, Charles Petit, and swept out of the room.

"I am going home, Charles!" Nathanael exclaimed. "I am going home! I must write Caty."

Nathanael rode 170 miles from White Plains to Coventry in three days. As he rode, the French fleet arrived off the coast of Caty's childhood home, Block Island, and then sailed for Newport harbor to coordinate an attack with American land forces. The British garrison led by General Robert Pigot fled in confusion as French ships shelled the town.

Nathanael was exhausted and elated when he dismounted in Coventry near the smoky Greene brothers' iron forge. Caty, having received his letter, was there waiting with the children. Separated since May, they fell into each other's arms. Nathanael covered Caty's beautiful face with kisses despite the watchful eyes of his older brother, sister-in-law, and their brood of children.

He held Caty at arms' length and caressed the round mound beneath her dress. The babe kicked in response. Nathanael's eyes shifted to the two small children he barely knew. He squatted, smiled, and waited for them to come to him. Patty stuck a thumb in her mouth, but George went to his father and fitted himself between Nathanael's knees. "Papa?" he asked.

Joy engulfed Nathanael, and he swept George up into his arms. "My heart has ached to hear those words," he assured his son. *You shall never endure the beatings I endured when I was a youth after a night of dancing,* he thought.

Patty, not wanting to be left out, let go of her mother's skirt and reached for Nathanael. He swept her up into his other arm and kissed her little face. He saw a vestige of his own face in the toddler.

Jacob came forward and extended a hand. "We are elated to have you home until war calls you back," he said.

"I have a few days and shall make the most of it," Nathanael said.

He bowed to Peggy. She blushed as if she had never seen him before. Her brother-in-law *was* much changed. He was now a weary soldier who had witnessed the shocking scenes of war, dressed in Continental blue and buff with the gold epaulets on each shoulder due a major general.

That night, after the family ate dinner, he and Caty tucked their sleeping children into bed. In their own bed, Caty relished the feeling of his sensual lips savoring the sweet taste of her neck and shoulders. Her hands caressed his muscular chest strengthened from all the years he pounded iron into anchors. When she wrapped her arms around his back, Nathanael blew out the bedside candle.

The next morning, Caty and Nathanael took the children to visit Nathanael's family in Potowomut. His younger brothers, William, Elithu, Kitt, and Perry, and their families streamed outside when the carriage pulled up to the house on the Hunt's River where Nathanael had grown up. Then, they went on to East Greenwich to see Caty's Aunt Catharine and Uncle William Greene, who was now governor of Rhode Island.

Catharine struggled to be cordial to her niece, whose winter forays to the army cantonments and whispered behavior of dancing, drinking, and flirting garnered her disapproval. Despite the tension between the women, Nathanael and William spent two days talking about the war.

As the British set a path of destruction and scuttled their own ships in response to the arrival of the French fleet, explosions rocked the countryside and echoed along Narragansett Bay. Nathanael was called to Providence. He took the horse that pulled their carriage, kissed his anxious wife and babies goodbye, and left them in East Greenwich. In Providence, he attended to quartermaster duties for the army in White Plains and then marched his troops to the American camp in Tiverton. Two thousand Continental troops under nineteen-year-old Marquis de Lafayette and American militiamen streamed into camp.

Nathanael and Lafayette met with General John Sullivan. "I have met with Admiral d'Estaing. He has 4,000 marines aboard his ships," John told the two generals as they sat down to discuss the mission. "We have agreed upon an assault on General Robert Pigot and his British garrison Monday, the tenth of August. We are to cross the strait separating Tiverton from Aquidneck Island, north of Newport. At the same time, the French marines will disembark from their ships and land on the island to the west of Newport. Nathanael, I want you to command my right wing. General Lafayette you shall command the left wing. My troops will hold the center." John poured a tankard of rum and then offered it to the other men in the room, which they accepted.

"It seems half of New England has arrived in support of this operation," John went on. "John Hancock, our former president of the Continental Congress, has arrived here commanding a Massachusetts militia unit with Colonel Paul Revere among them. General John Glover is here with his fishermen from Marblehead, Massachusetts, to ferry our troops down the Sakonnet River. I need time to train the disarranged chaos of American militiamen who have come to camp as we are now 10,000 strong." John drank of his rum and then asked, "Your Rhode Island fellows are also here, Nathanael. Have you seen them?"

Before Nathanael could respond, John's office door swung open. General James Varnum entered the room. Nathanael got to his feet and pumped James' hand. James flashed a perfectly white smile. "It is good to see you," James declared. "I could not let this battle escape my contributions. Your cousin Christopher is here with his unit of free blacks from this state. Sammy Ward, Jr. is with them. They shall want to see you. It seems our Kentish Guards have been reunited, and you shall command them."

"I have orders to serve as quartermaster as well," Nathanael said. "I will be as busy as a bee in a tar barrel, to speak in the sailors' style. If you will excuse me, I must tend to those duties. The men will want more rum. I believe my brothers can provide a satisfactory quantity."

John Sullivan nodded in approval. Rum was his vice and, unknown to him, it would someday literally be his downfall.

On August 9, Sullivan realized the British had abandoned their defenses on Aquidneck Island. He deployed 2,000 troops to secure those works. The move insulted Admiral d'Estaing, but the British soldiers saw hope on the horizon. At 1:00 p.m., British sails appeared. Admiral Lord Richard Howe had arrived with thirty-five ships to rescue the trapped garrison. By 5:00 p.m., Howe's armada dropped anchor between Point Judith and Beavertail Light.

Unhappy with the shift in the weather, d'Estaing weighed anchor and sailed straight for the British fleet. Howe's ships slipped their collars and sailed out to sea with the French pursuing them. John Sullivan sent a message to d'Estaing asking him to stay, but he was met with only a promise to return.

Despite this, Sullivan decided to press on with his attack on Newport. With help from General John Glover's mariners, he ferried all of his troops and provisions across the East Passage to the town of Portsmouth. The rum

Nathanael had ordered arrived and the barrels were ferried across as well; each man received a daily ration of a gill, or four ounces.

A violent summer storm rolled in. Cold rains and lashing winds ruined equipment, and troops left exposed in the open field died with their horses. Some found a sort of shelter under the stone walls that took the place of fences. The tempest battered the British and French fleets out at sea. Nathanael spent two days in a farmhouse that he had taken as his quarters. But the storm raging outside could not compete with his worry for his pregnant wife.

Feeling ill and lonely, Caty had written to him a few days earlier begging him to return the carriage horse so she could leave East Greenwich for Coventry. On August 16, after the storm abated, Nathanael replied to her. "I am sorry to hear that you are getting unwell. I am afraid it is the effect of anxiety and fearful apprehension. I feel your distress. My bosom beats with compassion and kind concern for your welfare, and the more so at this time as your situation is critical. Those dear little rogues have begun to command a large share of my affection and attention. I have sent Vester accordingly with the horse. Remember me kindly to all friends at home."

As the Americans moved within two miles of Newport and dug in for a siege against 7,000 British entrenched behind a line of forts, all eyes turned toward the sea. Both sides of the conflict could see the ocean, and Nathanael could see it from the roof of his quarters. He kept a watchful eye on the horizon. Cannon and mortar dueled for days, mostly without causing damage to either line but driving some of the enemy from their outworks.

At last, at dusk on August 19, the *Senegal,* a frigate taken from the British, was seen on the horizon sailing toward land. It brought a letter from d'Estaing for John Sullivan. The letter told of how the fleet was damaged by the tempest and would have to go into Boston to refit. Sullivan was furious. He had an army of 10,000 men who needed the promised support of the French.

"This movement has raised every voice against the French nation, revives all those ancient prejudices against the faith and sincerity of that people and inclines them most heartily to curse the new alliance," John coarsely told Nathanael.

"I share your anger, John. But the devil has gotten into the fleet. If they will cooperate with us, then the garrison will be all ours in a few days," Nathanael reasoned.

"As commander-in-chief of this expedition, I have expressed my confidence in the volunteers, state troops, and militia who have gathered in my support, but I cannot express my confidence in d'Estaing."

"You have increased the day's rum rations from a gill to a gill and a half," Nathanael observed in a serious tone, "enough to ensure the troops have that liquid, which is necessary to exhilarate the spirits no matter the damage that has been done by the storm."

As the sails of the French fleet appeared the following morning and dropped anchor off Brenton Reef on the southern tip of Newport Island, the damage they suffered was evident. The eighty-gun flagship, *Languedoc,* that had bombarded the enemy from her anchorage in Narragansett Bay, now bore scars. A British seventy-four-gun ship had poured a broadside of cannon balls into her hull. Winds brought down the mighty masts now replaced with inferior jury-masts.

With the ships in sight but d'Estaing refusing to come closer, John went to Nathanael and Lafayette. "I want you to go aboard the *Languedoc* and ask the French for more time. I will procure a skiff to carry you there," he said.

Nathanael knew the skipper of the skiff. John Brown had been a ringleader in the burning of the *Gaspee* affair in 1772.

"Come aboard, generals," Brown invited when Nathanael and Lafayette appeared.

As the two boarded the skiff, Nathanael smiled and said to Lafayette, "If we fail in our negotiations, we will at least get a good dinner."

"*Oui*, general, the French set a fine table," Lafayette agreed.

The small skiff bounced on the waves of the Sakonnet Passage as it neared the *Languedoc*. Nathanael's stomach reeled with every cresting wave. He fought the urge to hang his head over the side of the boat and empty his stomach. He could sense Lafayette's eyes upon him. *I will look undignified if I vomit*, he thought, swallowing against his nausea.

When they boarded the *Languedoc*, the rolling and pitching ship intensified his misery. Admiral d'Estaing's face appeared careworn as he greeted the two American generals. "Please join me and my officers for a war council," the admiral said in French.

Lafayette translated for Nathanael, who pleaded with the council, "If you will remain here for a few more days, we can still obtain our joint objective, but we must operate together."

"Admiral, we have 10,000 men camped near Newport," Lafayette said in support of Nathanael's plea.

The admiral listened politely to Nathanael's and Lafayette's entreaties before he said, "My captains and I have already discussed this, and it has been agreed that our safety depends on making our way to Boston. Nevertheless, we shall give you a chance to appeal, Général Greene, in a memorandum. We will provide you with a place for which you may prepare. Then, we shall have a meal together."

Nathanael thanked d'Estaing and retired to a desk. He spent a miserable afternoon penning his petition as the ship heaved and rolled on the swelling waves. The thought of enjoying that French meal made his stomach roil. Despite his seasickness, he managed to write a lengthy petition that began:

> *The expedition of Rhode Island was undertaken upon no other consideration than that of the French fleet and troops acting in concert with the American troops.*

Promising every assistance to repair the fleet there in Rhode Island, he went on to say:

> *The Garrison is important, the reduction almost certain. The influence it would have upon the British politics will be considerable. I think it highly worth running some risk to accomplish.*

Not being acquainted with d'Estaing's orders, Nathanael was careful not to censure an act which those orders might render absolutely necessary. That afternoon, he presented his petition to the French council, and then, mercifully, he and Lafayette boarded the skiff and returned to camp.

Fearful that their tattered fleet would be forced to face Admiral Howe's return, or a fresh armada from New York, the French answered Nathanael's petition by weighing anchor and sailing away. An apoplectic John Sullivan called a war council of his highest ranking officers during which a formal protest was drafted. The council found d'Estaing's decision:

> *As derogatory to the Honor of France; contrary to the Intentions of his Most Christian Majesty & the Interest of his Nation & destructive in the highest Degree to the Welfare of the United States of America & highly injurious to the Alliance formed between the two Nations.*

They gave nine reasons for the protest using further inflammatory language—accusing the French of unsupported reason, unfavorable impressions, and falsehoods.

John Sullivan and his officers signed the protest, including James Varnum, John Glover, John Hancock, and Nathanael, who clung to the same hope with which he had drawn up his own petition.

Only Lafayette refused to sign. "I find this deeply wounding, and I wish you to alter this," he fumed.

Lafayette wrote a letter to d'Estaing condemning the protest. Nathanael, ever sensitive to slights and criticism, took Lafayette's distress to heart. He personally told the Marquis, "I am conscious of what you feel and the expressions of your complaints."

Lafayette's heart swelled. "Your sensibilities make me very happy. I protest only to do justice to my countryman as we struggle to form an alliance."

Nevertheless, Colonel John Laurens was dispatched in a fleet boat to carry the protest to the admiral. As a commander of the King's squadron, the admiral's reply was couched in silence. The French ships slipped away. Without support of the French ships' cannon or reinforcements, the American militia companies left in droves. Disgusted Newport civilians proclaimed, "The Monsieurs have made a most miserable figure and are cursed by all ranks of people."

But John Sullivan was not finished as he watched his hopes of victory vanish. In his general orders of August 24, he told his discouraged troops, "I hope the abandonment will prove America able to procure by its own arms that which our allies refuse to assist in obtaining."

Lafayette's anger turned to indignation. He wrote another letter to d'Estaing saying that the greater part of the defenders in Rhode Island were forgetting their general obligation owed to France. *They allow faded prejudices to revive and speak as though they had been abandoned, almost betrayed.* Then he wrote a letter to the man he saw as his father figure, George Washington.

Washington, wishing to redeem the potentially international incident and his young French general's honor, wrote to Nathanael:

> *I depend much upon your temper and influence to conciliate*
> *that animosity, which I plainly perceive by a letter from the*
> *Marquis that subsists between the American officers and the*
> *French officers in our service.*

Washington implored Nathanael to keep the incident from being made public and confidently stated that Nathanael knew his meaning better than he could express it himself.

Nathanael and Lafayette calmed d'Estaing's indignation. The admiral even offered to march his 4,000 marines from Boston to Newport, but the gesture was a waste. The American Army needed sea firepower, especially now that troops had dwindled from 9,000 to 5,000 men.

On August 23, John had gone to Nathanael's headquarters in a Quaker's house for advice. "There are one of three measures to pursue…" John started. He wanted a drink but felt it inappropriate to press upon the household. He went on, "…to continue the siege by regular approaches, attempt the garrison by storm, or affect an immediate retreat and secure our stores."

Nathanael summoned the woman servant who attended the house. "Rum for General Sullivan, please." John gave Nathanael a grateful look.

"My opinion is that it would be folly to continue the siege as we are close to New York and reinforcements for General Pigot could be sent at any time," Nathanael said. "A retreat is justified. However, our forces are all collected and in pretty good health, but I think we have too few to attempt an open storm on the enemy's lines."

John listened patiently while Nathanael outlined a stratagem, "We could possess ourselves of the British redoubts south of Newport near Easton Beach. Send 300 handpicked men and have them rowed some distance south of the redoubts. That way, the detachment is between them and our main army."

John drained his tankard of rum and said, "This sounds complicated if not risky." He rose, bowed, and said, "I shall consider this course of advice."

That night, Nathanael, poured out his disappointment in a letter to General William Heath in Boston, who had sent his good wishes for a successful expedition of Newport. "Our hopes have all vanished since the French fleet has left us."

On August 28, 1778, instead of taking Nathanael's advice, John wisely decided to withdraw to the northern part of Aquidneck Island under cover of darkness. At dawn the next morning, a Welsh fusilier, Lieutenant Frederick Mackenzie, saw that the American Army's tents had disappeared from their encampment. He reported the find to General Robert Pigot, who launched a three-pronged attack on the retreating rebels led by both British and Hessian commanders.

From his quarters in the Quaker's house, while Nathanael ate breakfast, he heard the sharp sound of musketry signaling the advance. The servant woman warned, "The British will have you, General."

Nathanael calmly replied, "I will have my breakfast first."

He rode off to assume command of the 1,500 men holding the right wing. Sammy Ward, Jr. was temporarily in charge of the black Rhode Island regiment that also consisted of some Native Americans and whites who guarded a nearby redoubt. Christopher Greene had the army's left wing. Twice, General Friedrich von Lossberg's Hessians attacked Nathanael's position near Turkey Hill. Sammy's troops beat back the Hessians with bayonets and hand-to-hand fighting. Nathanael advanced with two more continental regiments and a Massachusetts militia regiment while John advanced with a regiment of light troops. Lossberg and his Hessians withdrew.

The Americas cheered. They retained all the professionalism General Friedrich von Steuben had instilled in them at Valley Forge. Like Monmouth, they stood up to the British regulars in a toe-to-toe fight that resulted in a draw.

Hearing that Admiral Howe had returned with transports and reinforcements, the American Army began a slow retreat toward their camp at Tiverton. With mooing cattle, oars slicing the water, and men's voices, the rebels noisily dispersed north by way of the Kickemuit and Tauton Rivers. Fleets of flat-bottom boats came out from Bristol. Nathanael crossed from Bristol to Warwick Island then west toward Coventry.

Caty saw and smelled drifting sulfuric smoke and heard the thunder of cannon and musketry from the front door of the house in Coventry. She imagined each shot had taken her husband from her. Every anxious moment increased her ill state. The news that the French Navy had sailed away, leaving the patriots unsupported, caused further dismay.

While his brother was fighting to liberate his home state, Jacob did little to ease Caty's despair. "The Americans are doomed without the support of the French Navy," he told Caty as he kept an eye to the near eastern horizon.

Caty was gripped with fear when the letter dated August 29 arrived from Nathanael's quarters near the Tiverton camp.

We have beaten the enemy off the ground where they advanced on us. A pretty smart engagement ensued between our light troops and their advance party. We retreated back here last night with the intention of holding this part of the island. I write upon my horse and have not slept any for two nights, therefore you will please excuse my not writing very legible as I write upon the field.

A week later, Nathanael galloped up to the house in Coventry. Caty was appalled at his haggard, exhausted countenance. He dismounted and pulled her into his arms. She heard him wheezing. "Were you plagued with asthma the entire time you were at battle?"

Jingling tack, marching boots, and men's voices rose from behind. She turned to see Nathanael's troops streaming into the barren yard. Little faces appeared in the house windows, then Jacob and Peggy dashed outside.

"I must establish my headquarters here until we receive further orders from General Washington," Nathanael explained. "My aides and troops, who behaved with great gallantry, deserve rest. General Lafayette has gone to Boston. He and John Hancock are to attend to Admiral d'Estaing's needs."

Caty looked crestfallen. Nathanael could not bear to see her distressed. That night, with the sounds of the army settling into their tents on the lawn and footsteps tramping the wooden floors inside the house, they lay in bed wrapped in one another's arms. The babe pressed its tiny feet against its mother's stomach. Nathanael hesitated to touch it, but Caty guided his hand to caress the little foot-shaped outline.

"Washington has written to me regarding blankets, shoes, hose, shirts, and uniforms that I am to send to General Heath in Boston, which I have answered," Nathanael said as the tiny feet disappeared beneath his hand.

"Thus your quartermaster duties have not paused. Please, stay with me until this child is born. I cannot bear another miserable confinement without you."

Nathanael propped his head in his hand and smiled. "In my reply, I asked about returning to the main camp in New York. I told him that your lying in is eminent and that I wish to gratify you and soothe your fears. He has granted my request."

Caty relaxed a little.

"However," Nathanael said, "there is more. Washington still expects me to use my influence to ease the incident. I received a message that a mob has attacked a group of French officers. I must ride to Boston." He kissed the end of her pert nose. "I will be back in a few days. The troops will be gone by then, I promise."

~

On his arrival in Boston on September 16, Nathanael learned that due to the efforts of John Hancock and the Marquis de Lafayette, Admiral d'Estaing and his officers were on exceedingly good footing with the gentlemen of the town. Hancock was a master at impressing and entertaining the French officers.

On September 24, Nathanael was impressed with Hancock's extravagant home on Beacon Hill, where a lavish dinner of codfish cakes, baked pork, baked beans, brown bread, boiled potatoes, bowls of fruit, and foremost, a variety of wines, beer, and liquors was to be served.

"I have gone so far as to represent everything with favorable colors to the Court of France in order to wipe away any prejudices," Lafayette confided in Nathanael as they drank Madeira and waited in the crowded house for dinner to commence.

General William Heath approached. He bowed. "Generals." They returned the bow. "Nathanael, you are just the man I wanted to see," William said. "I have received part of the clothing shipment you arranged for. Per your advice, I have assigned a small team of brigade guards." He lowered his voice, "I have heard that His Excellency thinks that Sir Henry

Clinton and his army will leave New York and attack Boston. Perhaps, we should have some Continental troops sent here."

Lafayette bowed, "Excuse me. I believe I shall be more useful entertaining the admiral." He disappeared among the crowd.

"I doubt that attack will occur. Boston is not the only object of their attention in New England," Nathanael replied to William, "I rather think that the growing extravagance of the people here and the increased demands for hay, corn, and oats are more of an immediate threat. I have meetings scheduled with the council of Massachusetts to impress the need for price control."

William's voice was devoid of malice when he said, "Otherwise, you will see your profits diminished as is due your one percent commission you share with your two deputies, Mr. Petit and Mr. Cox, on all department orders."

"The emoluments expected to the quartermaster's department, I freely confess, are flattering to my fortune," Nathanael said indignantly, "but not less humiliating to my military pride."

Thunder rumbled, and the diners glanced at the darkening windows. A messenger knocked at the door of the Hancock house and was admitted by a servant.

"I have a message for General Greene from Mr. Jacob Greene," the man announced.

Nathanael accepted the damp message. His face paled. It read, *Mrs. Greene gave birth yesterday, and she and the child are not well.* With few apologies for his expeditious exit, Nathanael mounted his horse and galloped through a storm that seemed to follow him. He arrived in Coventry at 9:00 p.m., soaked to the skin and worried sick. Caty lay in bed with a tiny bundle in her arms. He kneeled beside his wife and stroked her wan cheeks.

"The babe is a girl," Caty whispered.

Nathanael focused on the fragile, sickly baby. He thought of the days Caty spent at Valley Forge in his arms where this little soul was conceived and the distress his wife had endured during her pregnancy. *What was my role in the fate of this tiny creature?* he wondered.

"I want to name her Cornelia Lott, after the daughter of my hosts when I was in New Jersey," Caty said. "You will stay with us will you not? Little George and Patty need your attention, too."

"Of course, as long as I can," he promised.

❧

Nathanael basked in the warmth of his home and family, sheltered from the demands of the quartermaster job he hated until the war insisted he return to make sure that the soldiers had enough blankets, tents, and tools. He heeded the call because the army was also his family to whom he had to fulfill his responsibilities.

He packed up the new hat Jacob gave him, a bolt of blue cloth for a new uniform, and his favorite poetry book by Horace. As he rode away, he had no idea that he would never return to Spell Hall as his home in Coventry.

seventeen

Upon the Whole We Had a Pretty Little Frisk

Nathanael reported to Washington in Fredericksburg, New York, where the main army was encamped. The war in the North was at a standstill. The main British Army was in New York City, and the war ground to a stalemate in that theater as small skirmishes occurred but no large engagements. The Continental Army waited for them to make a move. The value of the Continental dollar plunged and threatened to bring the Revolutionary War to a halt.

Sir Henry Clinton may have been docile in New York City, but he was not in Georgia as the British ministry turned their sights on the Southern colonies. The news that he sent Major General Augustine Prévost with provincial forces and Hessians to seize the port city of Savannah arrived near the end of September 1778. The populace in Georgia, whose allegiance to the King was already divided by ethnicity, occupation, and religion became further split. As Presbyterian Scottish-Irish immigrants moved south, the back country became Patriot territory.

Already in a melancholy mood after hearing accusations that some of his quartermaster department's agents were corrupt, Nathanael knew that no department was exposed to so much malignant criticism because self-interest clashed with public expenditures. Henry Marchant, a Rhode Island judge and member of the Continental Congress, wrote to Nathanael in October with friendly "hints" regarding the department. Nathanael felt the need to defend the management of his responsibilities and the one percent customary commission he and his agents earned. *Who will defend us if I do not?*

Still, he dutifully worked fifteen hours or more a day maintaining the order levels of supply warranted by the army, the issuance of said supplies, and handling agents. When a message arrived from George Washington, he set aside his quill and answered the summons.

He and his deputy, Charles Petit, walked to Washington's headquarters at the John Kane House through a landscape of majestic maples, delicate quaking aspens, sycamores, red oaks, and hickories in a vibrant symphony of crimson, orange, and spun yellow gold staking claim amongst the deep emerald evergreens. The crisp fall air told him what he already knew. It was time to find winter quarters for the army.

"You summoned me, sir?" Nathanael asked as he and Charles entered George's office.

George was pleased to see that Nathanael's bright eyes and his open countenance that invited admiration from so many men was devoid of drudgery. "I see you look forward to winter camp just as I do," George said. "Our wives' arrival with their soft complexions, gentle words, and frivolous costumes cheer our bleak camp and almost blur the rugged pains of war are to be anticipated."

Nathanael smiled. "It is, although I am not certain Caty will be up to it after just giving birth."

"She has much fortitude just as my Martha and the ladies of the other generals do who share with their husbands the privations of war. Your wife's infectious good cheer eased the early days of the wretched circumstances of the camp at Valley Forge."

"I shall relay that to her. She will be most flattered," Nathanael said.

He and Charles, with Majors William Blodget and John Clark, scouted central New Jersey for a suitable winter camp. Late in November of 1778, Nathanael led his Continental Army troops to Middlebrook where, during the first week of December, he issued orders concerning the construction of winter quarters, making the most of hard lessons learned earlier at Valley Forge. He established headquarters at nearby Van Veghten House.

With the gossamer threads of domestic tranquility clinging to him, he longed to see his wife and children again. He struggled with his urge to demand her presence. Her letters were a mix of reluctance and desire, some of which he understood, some of which did not occur to him—that her fear of another pregnancy might play a part.

On November 13, he wrote to her with enticing sympathy. "General Washington has renewed his charge to have you at camp very soon. Your last letter contained expressions of doubts and fears about the matter. To be candid with you, I don't believe half a kingdom would hire you to stay away. But at the same time, I as candidly confess, I most earnestly wish it, as it will greatly contribute to my happiness to have you with me. Bring George with you if the weather is not too cold."

Caty needed no further coaxing. She left her two little girls with Jacob and Peggy and departed for the Middlebrook encampment situated near the village of Bound Brook along the banks of the Raritan River and under cover of a mountain range. The four-day journey was an exhausting ordeal. The weather turned cold and wet. Worried about robberies and river crossings, she was delighted to find an old friend, General Israel Putnam, stationed near Peekskill. Putnam escorted her and regaled her with his usual humorous stories of his many adventures.

Nathanael was there waiting for her when her carriage pulled up to headquarters, now located at Beverwyck, a stately brick home on a large agricultural estate. Little George bounced out of the coach. Nathanael swept his nearly three-year-old son into his arms and exclaimed, "You are a fine, hearty fellow—full of merriment!"

George giggled and said, "Papa."

Accompanied by a servant and a nurse for George, Caty gingerly stepped from the carriage. Nathanael took her hand and tenderly kissed her lips. "You look pale, my angel," he whispered.

She smiled reassuringly as he led her inside. "Do not fret, my darling. I will look as radiant as a general's wife should. I have brought along new dresses, hats, shoes, and a new wardrobe for our son."

Charles Petit, John Cox, and Jeremiah Wadsworth rose from their seats where they were engaged in paperwork that covered the tabletop. Caty was not so worn out that Jeremiah's appeal did not demand her attention as it had when they met at Valley Forge. *I must remember to guard against our mutual attraction*, she reminded herself.

She was thrilled to find old acquaintances in camp like Baron von Steuben with his aides and his dog Azor by his side. Anthony Wayne was present and unaccompanied by his wife as always. Alexander Hamilton was among General Washington's military family. Lord Alexander Stirling's wife, Lady Sarah Stirling, and their daughter, Kitty, were there from Basking Ridge, which drew Caty's jealousy. She resented Nathanael's boasting about their cultural pursuits.

When Henry Knox lumbered across her path in the smoky, busy camp toward a cupola-topped hall, Caty was ecstatic. "Where is Lucy?" she asked as she and little George fell in beside the artillery general.

"She and our little daughter are lodging two miles outside of camp," Henry said. "She is seven months with child. I must say she will be thrilled to see you again, Mrs. Greene."

"Please call me Caty. What is this building ahead of us?" she asked, noting the heavy field pieces guarding the entrance to a square shaped campus.

"Why, it is my first war college," Henry boasted.

Horse's hooves clattered toward the two. It was Nathanael. "I am afraid your college will have to wait," he said to Henry. "Congress has called me, you, and George to Philadelphia to confer with them regarding military strategy, the devalued Continental dollar, and ordnance department.

None of the soldiers are getting paid. Samuel Adams and Henry Laurens are refusing our requests for half-pay for disabled veterans and officers. I am struggling with getting produce to my agents. It is those politicians who call on us who are strangling the army's effectiveness."

Nathanael dismounted and squatted before his son. "Your birthday is in a few weeks. Would you like to go to Philadelphia with your papa?"

George grinned and nodded.

"You hate big cities," Henry chuckled. "When are we expected?"

Nathanael stood up. "The meetings are to commence on New Year's Day."

"I had better get packed," Caty said gleefully.

"Lucy is going to be unhappy with being left behind, but she is awaiting the arrival of relatives from Boston, Elizabeth and Sarah Winslow," Henry said.

Nathanael frowned. "Sarah Winslow? In my opinion, she is a hussy."

"I am certain Miss Winslow will take umbrage at that remark," Caty said with smirk. "Come, George, we are going with papa on an adventure!"

Nathanael packed his family into their carriage, and with his assistant quartermaster, John Cox, traveled on horseback to John's stately home in Trenton. Before they could continue the journey to Philadelphia, a snow-storm blew in. Instead of enjoying the cozy fireside and the company of friends, Nathanael worried over how the horses in camp were weathering the storm. Finally, on New Years' Eve 1778, he mounted up and crossed the frozen Delaware and went on to Philadelphia alone.

When the meetings commenced, Nathanael was antecedently in a foul mood. Congress' agenda would cripple his already difficult job. They banned the use of wheat as fodder and insisted that all supplies were sent via land instead of by river, which Nathanael preferred because it was faster and cheaper.

He groused to Samuel Huntington, the new president of Congress, "The scarcity of provisions and forage is not a little alarming. Whether the scarcity is real or artificial I cannot pretend to say; but I believe the people's dislike to the currency is one great obstacle to our purchases."

"I have no solution that will satisfy you or General Washington," Huntington said. "We have printed money because there is no other way to pay for things. We anticipated levying a national tax, but the states, unwilling to diminish their own power, refused our right to tax."

Huntington's answer only exacerbated the problem. During a break between endless committee meetings, Nathanael complained to George regarding the politician's deliberations, "They are always beginning but never finishing business."

George agreed. "I have seen nothing since I came here to change my opinion of men or measures; but abundant reason to be convinced that our affairs are in a more distressed, ruinous, and deplorable condition than they have been since the commencement of the war. An insatiable appetite for riches seems to have gotten the better of every other consideration."

"And the extravagant parties held here in the capital. Last night we dined at one table where there were 160 dishes, and several others not far behind," Nathanael said with disgust. "Our winter at Valley Forge is not so far in the past that I cannot recall the faces of starving, naked soldiers."

"They are absorbing attention to the exclusion of the problems of the nation," George boomed without thought for who would overhear.

The parties were a nightly affair that Nathanael, Henry, and George were obliged to attend. The obligation was a little easier to endure when Caty arrived from Trenton and Martha Washington stopped in Philadelphia on her way to the Middlebrook camp. Caty's enthusiasm for dancing, socializing, drinking wine, and wearing new party dresses was somewhat contagious, even for her offended husband and his commander-in-chief.

Philadelphia scandals were as important as socializing. Gossip abounded that the State of Pennsylvania had accused the military governor, General Benedict Arnold, of war profiteering and overstepping his authority. Politician Joseph Reed and his Supreme Executive Council were behind the accusations. Nathanael knew Joseph Reed and the two often communicated. Not only were they friends, but Reed was brother-in-law to one of Nathanael's deputies, Charles Petit.

"I refused to believe these charges," Nathanael told Charles one night after the Arnolds made an appearance at one of the socials. "I am skeptical of attacks against Continental generals, as we have all suffered in some way. I hope he is vindicated from the aspersions of enemies."

The two or three days they were to spend in Philadelphia had stretched out into six weeks. The generals left Philadelphia on February 2, 1779, feeling glum.

❧

When they returned to camp, Nathanael put aside his disdain for extravagance and did his duty as a major general was expected—he and Caty hosted a dance in their living room on February 18, 1779, to celebrate the first anniversary of the Franco-American alliance.

Beforehand, a banquet for 400 guests was held at Henry's academy building. Dignitaries such as Benjamin Franklin and Henry Laurens, the former president of the Continental Congress, arrived. Fiddlers played spirited music. At 4:00 p.m., thirteen cannons sounded, signaling the start of the festivities. After toasts and a dinner, fireworks lit the clear winter sky, and then a ball commenced at Beverwyck where the Greenes were quartered.

George approached the very pregnant Lucy Knox, the presiding hostess of the celebration. He bowed and offered his hand. "May I have this dance?"

Lucy waddled through a minuet. Afterward, musicians struck up a lively tune. Lucy sat with a groan beside Martha. To all the guests' astonishment, George took Caty by the hand and escorted her to the dance floor. The white feathers in Caty's dark shining hair fluttered, and her elegant blue gown rustled seductively.

"She looks lovely and trim so soon after giving birth," Martha confided in Lucy, unconcerned with her husband's obvious infatuation with her younger friend. "See how the golden locket around her neck sparkles in the candlelight?"

"I hear it contains General Greene's picture and was a gift from his aides for her twenty-fourth birthday celebrated just yesterday," Lucy said as George and Caty whirled around the dance floor.

"Yes, and look at the pride on General Greene's face. He looks as if he is smitten all over again," Martha said.

Nathanael was in conversation with Anthony Wayne, but his eyes often shifted to his wife. *How gracefully she holds her fan,* Nathanael thought. Caty's ringing laugh rose above the music, and he heard George tease, "It was not my intention to keep you from your Quaker preacher, however, I believe I can outlast you on the dance floor."

George lost the wager. The two danced most of the evening. Nathanael relayed the event to Jeremiah Wadsworth, "We had a little dance at my quarters a few evenings past. His Excellency and Mrs. Greene danced upwards of three hours without sitting down. Upon the whole, we had a pretty little frisk."

Shortly after, Caty went to a tea frolic in Trenton given by Betsey Petit. There were a number of ladies from Philadelphia and some members of Congress in attendance. She felt the sting of disapproving eyes upon her as she drank wine, discussed the days' events, and exchanged witty remarks. Ladies she did not know gathered near to examine General Nathanael Greene's beautiful, confident wife. Caty merely smiled and continued her conversations. It was then that she realized the impact of her station. She *was* a general's wife, and not just any general's wife. Nathanael was second only to that of George Washington, and all the critical stares in the world could not change that.

During this time, Nathanael wrote letters to his assistants who he had charged with various aspects of the quartermaster department, including Ephraim Bowen, Jr., a deputy quartermaster, and Colonel Clement Biddle, who Nathanael had promoted to commissary general in charge of forage.

A letter dated January 27, 1779, reminded Mr. Bowen of his expected obligations and tasks:

> *I wrote you the 5ᵗʰ of this instant, to charter, in the State of Rhode Island, and in and about Bedford, in the State of Massachusetts, vessels enough to import 1000 casks of rice*

from South Carolina. I wrote to Mr. Benjamin Andrews to charter a sufficient number to import 4000 in the State of Massachusetts Bay; his unfortunate death I am afraid will disconcert the business. I hope you have not failed to complete what was requested of you.

The sluggish Congress that had respectfully listened to Nathanael and George consumed time in debates and committees and failed to produce new recruits to replace men whose enlistments had expired. Although bounties were offered, neither the states nor men were enticed in great numbers. A draft was frowned upon. It was not until January 23, 1779, that Congress allowed Washington to open the enlistment rolls and the infantry training that General Friedrich von Steuben had so carefully executed and written in his Blue Book manual at Valley Forge.

In March, George wrote to the Marquis de Lafayette, temporarily in France, that the American troops were in huts but in a more agreeable and fertile country than they had been in Valley Forge. They were better clad and healthier than they had been since the formation of the army.

Nathanael, however, was concerned about Caty. Disapproval marred his handsome face, something Caty had seen before, when he asked to speak to her. "I am worried about you, my angel," he began as he sat down with her before a warm hearth on a sunny but cold late March day. "I am not trying to deter your pleasures, but I think you have become too fond of wine. Too much wine can lead to coarseness in women and hamper the development of those softer qualities that mark a polished lady. Overindulgence in pleasure can dull wits and ruin health."

"Are you comparing me to the Stirling ladies again?" Caty asked indignantly.

"I am only saying that cultural pursuits might be more appropriate."

"I am aware that your high standing in the army commands respect in every quarter and that your stature as a person is equivalent to your military rank. Are you saying I do not measure up?" Caty huffed.

Nathanael sighed. "I am not saying that. I am only concerned about your health and happiness."

Caty rose abruptly. Nathanael rose as well.

"Do not huff off," he warned. But he saw that look in her dark eyes—the little girl who had been born on Block Island off the coast of Rhode Island where conformity and dogma were amorphous, and shame and guilt were not the most important qualities.

Nathanael endured another frustrating visit to Philadelphia. He felt he was being criticized for his department's commissions, which Congress compounded by refusing to provide more money and more support. In truth, some of his agents were untrustworthy, but the blame fell on him.

He wrote Washington: "I have desired Congress to give me leave to resign as I apprehended a loss of reputation if I continued in the business."

George replied with veneration:

> *I advise you to make your own judgements. I will recommend you as commander of the American army in the South if you so desire. However, you know I cannot make such an appointment, and I do not believe that you are endearing yourself to Congress.*

The fact was, suffering from an ankle wound he received at the battle of Saratoga, Massachusetts General Benjamin Lincoln commanded the Southern theatre and needed no replacement.

Nathanael remained as quartermaster general out of compassion to His Excellency and the army. He focused his energies on business enterprises with Colonel Jeremiah Wadsworth and Barnabas Dean, who hailed from a prominent merchant family. Much of it was privateering, a business Nathanael and his brothers had embarked on in Rhode Island years before. It was not unusual for American officers to concentrate on military and personal financial affairs.

To protect himself from accusations that he was using his position as quartermaster to make money, he told Jeremiah, "It is my wish that no mortal should be acquainted with the persons forming the company except us three. I think it is prudent to appear as little in trade as possible. For however just and upright our conduct may be, the world will have suspicions to our disadvantage."

"Then, perhaps we should communicate in code," Jeremiah suggested with a sly grin. "2030 Company would be amusing."

Nathanael laughed. "Where did you conjure that name from?"

"Would your brothers, from whom you also want to keep this a secret, recognize such an outlandish name?"

"I suppose not."

"Good. If we do not embark on this venture, we will find our commissions paid in worthless Continental currency," Jeremiah contended.

"As you know, Congress formed yet another committee to study the problems and needs of our quartermaster department while at the same time declaring that they have full confidence in me," Nathanael said.

"Aye, how much longer can we continue this folly? Now I hear they are taxing the profits of the citizens of New Jersey who sell goods to the army."

"I will not allow them to put a bad light on my deputies, Charles Petit and John Cox," Nathanael railed. "I have already endured their interminable questions regarding accounts, as if my virtue is not enough for their satisfaction, and they are undermining my authority. Yet I am a victim of my own advice. I recommended to General Washington that the 1779 campaign include wiping out the primary food source for the Indians of the Six Nations in New York. They have terrorized our frontier towns, and it cannot continue, therefore when their corn is about half-grown, General Sullivan will lead the expedition against them. At the least, I hope this expedition will force the Six Nations to sue for peace with us."

"Therefore, you will be chained to the very drudgery you dread," Jeremiah said.

"I have already felt those chains in every letter I have written asking for money, pack saddles, forage, and tools to outfit the expedition. And now, Washington has requested that some of the army break camp and move to the New Windsor camp on the Hudson River. Word has it that General Henry Clinton has sailed up the Hudson and landed a few miles south of West Point. His Excellency wishes to hold a council of war about a new offensive campaign."

"So, he has not turned you away from his councils. Is that not good news?"

I wonder if indeed it is, Nathanael thought.

&

Caty defiantly refused to go home to Coventry where her little daughters remained with Nathanael's family. Instead, she accompanied her husband part of the way on his journey. The relentless summer sun followed them as she rode with him and his aides while he scouted ahead of the army for transportation and supplies.

"Why are you sulking?" she asked him as they neared the New Jersey border.

"Congress left me off the list of officers in command," he complained.

"I know how much that means to you. Perhaps, you can do something to remedy it. Surely General Washington does not agree or he would not require your presence at his war council."

"I do not know what to do. The war council is scheduled for July 2 at West Point, and with General Clinton looming, it is no place for you and our son. Washington is intent on attacking New York if possible as if he cannot reconcile our loss of the city in 1776. I think it is time for you to return to Coventry. I have arranged travel plans for you and little George." He looked over his shoulder at his trailing aides. "Ichabod will take you back to Middlebrook and then take you home."

"I suppose I have little say in the matter, so I shall do as you ask. However, promise me that you will not suffer in silence over your lost field command," Caty said. She decided to avoid mentioning a vague uneasiness that would, if true, worry him more.

The sun dimmed and then brightened as thin wispy clouds raced across it. Nathanael looked up. His mood seemed reflected in the dappled display. *What could I possibly say that would bring attention to my colleagues and serve to allow me to retain my battlefield service?* He sighed and said, "Let us find lodging nearby for tonight." He tossed her a playful smile. "We have wine."

It hurt Caty's heart to know that he had avoided her question and that he no longer felt like a warrior riding into battle.

The following morning, Nathanael continued on toward West Point. Caty returned to Middlebrook. The idea of leaving Middlebrook for Coventry propelled her to the Wallace House where Martha and George were quartered. To her relief, the general was buried in preparations to move the army.

Martha led Caty into her cozy private parlor. Her servant, Delphi, served the ladies tea. "Nathanael wishes you to go home," Martha said before Caty spoke. "I know the ache of saying goodbye not knowing when you will see your husband again."

Tears wet Caty's cheeks. She sniffed and drank her tea to calm herself. "I…I suspect I am pregnant. If that is the case, I will not be able to see him at winter camp this year."

"When did that deter your travel?" Martha asked kindly. "You came to camp very pregnant to care for Nathanael when he had jaundice during the time the army was besieging Boston in 1775."

"I had no other children then," Caty said.

"Are your little girls not reason enough that you should return to Coventry?"

"Yes, of course, but my last two pregnancies were difficult and," Caty burst into uncontrolled tears, "I will be confined. And I long to take my children from that place and—"

Martha got up and pulled Caty into her arms. *I do not know how to console her,* she thought. *My home in Mount Vernon is filled with my grand-children, nieces, nephews, and family and friends I cherish.*

"I should not be crying," Caty admitted in shame. "You have lost three children, and here I am sobbing like a foolish girl."

Martha patted Caty on the back. "You brave the hardships and dangers of camp life like the rest of the wives to be near the man you love so that his children are not complete strangers. You knit and sew to help clothe the soldiers. You soothe their wounds and anxieties with your presence." She smiled. "And assuredly you enjoy the social life like we all do."

Caty nodded. She wiped at the tears wetting her cheeks.

"Stay for another cup of tea, and I will help you prepare to go home. I cannot have you traveling when you are upset and lonely. My thoughts are always with you, my dear friend."

Accompanied by Nathanael's aide, Ichabod Burnet, Caty's trip home was exhausting. When she arrived, Nathanael's brothers were arguing over financial affairs. Eternally pessimistic, Jacob and Peggy Greene glowered and complained. But what cut Caty to the quick was her visit to East Greenwich. She took George, Martha, and baby Cornelia to visit Aunt Catharine.

"You are pregnant again?" Catharine criticized in front of a gathering of women who were cordial to Caty before the war started. "I suppose endless dancing and drinking has not deterred your activities."

Mortified, Caty gathered the children and returned to Coventry. She spent her days caring for her children. At night, she drank wine and longed for the smallest hint at an invitation from her husband to join him in camp. Her misery was compounded when she received a letter from Nathanael explaining who he was sharing his quarters with, including her older brother, Billy Littlefield, and that the merry, rotund William Blodget had left his service as an aide and joined the Continental Navy.

Gloom stretched through the days. Cornelia developed a fever. George suffered a lump in his breast. Patty failed to show improvement from the deformities of rickets despite a physician's care. Caty tended Cornelia and read Nathanael's letters.

On July 15, 1779, General Anthony Wayne led 1,200 handpicked light infantry in a midnight bayonet charge to retake the small but important garrison at Stony Point, New York. One of two American forts that guarded the important Hudson River crossing at King's Ferry, Stony Point had fallen to the British in May 1779. This good news was offset by the bad news that a joint siege attempt between American General Benjamin Lincoln and French Admiral d'Estaing to take Savannah back from the British failed.

She received another letter from Nathanael in August that exuded depression and sadness in his every word.

> *At West Point I was surrounded with old friends: Henry Knox, Alexander McDougall, Anthony Wayne, Baron von Steuben, Lord Stirling, and others who you know. I asked those generals about their opinion on my right to step up and take command if I so desired.*

Caty pictured some of those men in her mind. The good-natured, rotund Henry Knox. The handsome Anthony Wayne. The jolly Baron von Steuben and his dog, Azor. The well-respected Scots-born Alexander McDougall and Lord Alexander Stirling whose wife's and daughter's polished accomplishments often vexed her. She did not want to read on, but she had to hear his agony.

> *There were those that felt I had a right to a position in the line, those I believe did not feel me a threat to their command. But others such as Anthony Wayne disagreed and said it would be a great injustice for me to step in on the eve of a battle. Lord Stirling was emphatic about his opinion. He said that his feelings would be so much hurt at such an incident that he would be ashamed ever to command the division again. Washington has agreed that as long as I am quartermaster, I have no right to a field command. He said that I have executed my duty with ability and fidelity.*

"His vanity hangs on those last words," Caty said to herself. "Yet I have learned something that I did not truly understand. He does not see that he saved the army from starving at Valley Forge. He does not truly comprehend how valued his service is despite Congress' committees, rules, and accusations. It is because he has lost his value as a warrior. The sting of the Kentish Guards' judgement about his limp that precluded his election as an officer still burns even after these five years."

October inched in. With it came the good news that the British Army had evacuated Newport as the British ministry moved its eyes to the war in the South. John Sullivan achieved a somewhat hollow victory by subduing the tribes of the Six Nations only to push many of the natives to side with the British. Caty was unable to enjoy the crisp fall weather that brought bright blue skies. One morning, she awoke with abdominal pain and desperately groped for her washbowl. She was horrified when she saw that she had vomited blood.

Her bedroom door creaked open, and Peggy poked her head into the room. "Caty?"

Caty tried to hide the washbowl. "I am fine," she assured her sister-in-law, "I just need privacy."

The door creaked shut. Her thoughts flew to her husband. He had chided her for drinking wine and dancing. No matter his stern admonishments and the anticipation that he would do so again, she needed him. *What if something is wrong with the child I carry? Or perhaps it is just a happenchance that can be overlooked.*

Three days later, feeling hysterical, she went to Peggy and admitted her condition. The last thing on Earth she wished to do was to ask Peggy for help. "I will have Jacob fetch Dr. Peter Turner from East Greenwich," Peggy said in a gentle manner that surprised Caty, who only nodded.

"You seem perfectly healthy, and I detect no problems with the baby," Dr. Turner assured her upon examination. But Caty was not satisfied. She wrote to Nathanael for advice. He blamed her wine consumption and then immediately regretted his harsh judgements he had written to her:

If I do bar you from the pleasures you so much admire, will you think it unkind? Will you think me more tyrant than husband? Will it lessen your affection? Will it not mortify me to have your affection diminished? Indeed it will. Do I not love you most dearly? Inexpressibly so. I knew your health was in danger. I am going to Washington's headquarters this afternoon to consult Dr. Shippen on your case.

The advice to take salt water several times a day was ignored. She was certain her pregnancy was viable, and she began to feel better. The rest of the year passed with little expectation that she would receive an invitation to join Nathanael in the army's new cantonment for the winter.

Anxious as her pregnancy progressed, she knew that Nathanael was busy. He was responsible for setting up winter quarters for 12,000 men as if he were constructing a defensible village in the event the British sallied out of New York, sailed up the Hudson, and attacked. George and Nathanael agreed on that strategy, unaware of Sir Henry Clinton's intentions.

Despite threatening movements and a few raids on Connecticut, Clinton chose not to tangle with the Continental Army in the north during the waning months of 1779. His sights were set on Georgia and the Carolinas—particularly on the important seaport of Charleston, South Carolina. It had slipped through his fingers during a battle at Sullivan's Island in 1776. Clinton set sail from New York in December 1779, taking the aggressive General Charles Cornwallis with him and leaving General Wilhelm von Knyphausen in command with some 10,000 men.

eighteen
Intolerable Conduct

Another dreary winter blanketed the land with snow and ice as the Continental Army marched out of West Point, New York on December 2, 1779, for winter camp in Morristown, New Jersey and nearby Jockey Hollow. The army had encamped there after their victories at Trenton and Princeton during the winter of 1776–77, and it had proved to be the best of all possible refuges. As the troops marched southward, the winter was already proving to be different.

"Can we possibly endure another winter freezing from lack of blankets and coats?" Private Michael Brown complained to his messmate and fellow from Connecticut, Private Elijah Stratford.

Elijah blinked snow from his stinging eyes and trudged on in silence with the rest of his regiment through a leafless landscape of oak and elm dotted with green pines and the sound of freezing water chunking over rocks and barren shorelines.

Joseph Plumb Martin, who had endured many hard winters and bloody battles, gathered his fellows around when they arrived at Jockey Hollow. "Let us clear snow in these woods. We can pitch our tents in a circle and share a fire in the center."

This they did under an iron gray sky as quartermasters marked out the ground in preparation for the troops to build huts to specifications as they had at Valley Forge. Thick clouds hung ominously as Joseph and his mates went about their duty. A blizzard struck on January 2, 1780, and for four days it dumped snow on top of snow, which had already piled up, burying huts and tents. All movement in the countryside halted, threatening to starve a frozen army. Food and equipment that Nathanael had stored could not be hauled into camp because teams were unable to draw sleds or wagons through the snow.

A young aide shouted outside Dr. James Thacher's hut. He was awakened by the calls for assistance, "Some of the officers have been buried under their marquee tent! Help us rescue them." Dr. Thacher roused his comrades and quickly ordered them to scramble to save the officers.

Nathanael appeared through the violent storm to render help that his mortified aides could not let him perform alone. Nathanael's strong arms and chest were just the tools the men needed to accomplish the rescue. It was what he could do when his ability to dig the army out of destruction was hindered by subversion he could not control.

On January 7, 1780, the blizzard finally abated. Desperate soldiers ate their own shoes and bark off sticks. They took matters into their own hands and waded through snow drifts to plunder homes in Morristown. Nathanael, who was quartered in a tavern owned by Jacob Arnold, summoned the local militia commander, Colonel Benoni Hathaway.

"General Washington has issued a circular letter to the county magistrates apologizing for the troops' behavior and explaining that they are on the brink of perishing," Nathanael said unceremoniously. "However, he has let them know that we have no recourse, and he will not deter them."

"It is not just the army who has suffered," Colonel Hathaway pointed out.

Nathanael went on, "This army is upon the point of disbanding for want of provisions. We have not a sufficiency to serve more than one regiment in the magazine. The terrible storm, the depth of the snow, and the drifts in the road prevent the little stock coming forward from the distant magazines. I therefore request that you call upon the militia officers and people of your battalion to turn out their teams and break the roads between this and Hackettstown. Do not let this information get to the enemy."

"Consider it done, sir," Colonel Hathaway said. He bowed and turned to leave, then stopped and said, "Oh, speaking of the enemy, I have heard that waters around New York City have frozen. The severity of the frost exceeds anything of the kind that has ever been experienced in this country before."

As the roads were cleared and the people of New Jersey answered the army's call for wheat flour for bread and cattle for fresh beef, Caty and her son, George, rode into camp in her carriage accompanied by a driver. Nathanael was certain that Caty would not come to camp with her lying in so close, yet there she stood before him shivering in the cold and safe. He settled them into his quarters. Jacob Arnold sent him a note telling him that he must find other quarters. The quartering of officers was a touchy subject with the residents of Morristown, unlike the winter of 1777 when the army's officers had quartered in the same homes and taverns.

George sent along a note to Nathanael expressing his distress over the situation:

> *I regret that the inhabitants should be unwilling to give shelter to men who have made and are making every sacrifice in the service of their country.*

As quartermaster, Nathanael, too, felt powerless when he found that the New Jersey laws on quartering soldiers in civilian homes was not to the army's advantage. With his next child due in three weeks, he was not about to yield and allow Jacob Arnold to oust him from his cramped quarters.

"You may depend upon it that the officers of the army will not lodge in the open fields for fear of putting the inhabitants to a little inconvenience. Some people in this neighborhood are polite and obliging, others are the reverse. It was and is my wish to live upon good terms with the people of the house and I have endeavored to accommodate my family so as to render it as little inconvenient as possible," Nathanael railed at the tavern owner.

"It is known that you tried to resign your commission as quartermaster general," Jacob said in a bitter attempt to defend himself. "The occurrence executed on December 12 was prompted by the recent resignation of your commissary general, Colonel Jeremiah Wadsworth. I also know that Congress had no reply."

Unable to keep his insecurity in check and aware that Washington himself was blaming everyone, both innocent and guilty, for the catastrophe the army was in, Nathanael snapped back. "You receive us with coldness, and provide for us with reluctance. The army is in great distress for want of provision and forage. A thick cloud hangs over our heads at this hour threatening us with destruction. We are fighting and sacrificing for your liberty!"

The argument did nothing to provide some officers with proper quarters such as General Benedict Arnold, who was in camp to attend his court-martial regarding charges of corruption brought against him by the State of Pennsylvania and politician Joseph Reed. Nathanael's obligation to his fellow general had to be attended to with dignity.

The early purple winter sunset had already darkened the windows in the Greene's small quarters in the tavern. Caty lit another candle and placed it near Nathanael's small writing desk. His quill scratched hurriedly across paper. "What was the outcome of General Arnold's court-martial?" she asked.

"I was not involved in the affair. Henry Knox performed judicial duties in this case. Benedict defended himself, furiously as always, but was found guilty on two charges: using government wagons for his personal use and issuing a pass to a ship he later invested in, although his Excellency pronounced the charges imprudent and peculiarly reprehensible. Benedict was given a reprimand and he returned to Philadelphia."

"Who are you writing?" Caty asked.

"Samuel Huntington, president of the Continental Congress, asking why my December 12 request to resign has been ignored."

"Have you not heard a single word?"

Nathanael's quill stilled. "Why are you asking so many questions, my angel? Have you been to the doctor?" Concerned passed over his face as he noted the tired glow on her countenance.

She stepped back when he sprung from his chair; the quill forgotten. "It has begun," she said.

He nearly tripped over his feet in excitement and passion. "What am I to do? Are you ill? You have been ill in the past, but you did not mention it this time."

She laughed. "Do not panic. I know your absence during our children's birth and my past weaknesses leave you apprehensive. It is still early. A nurse and midwife are on the way. Dr. Thacher will arrive when needed if at all."

"Should I relay the news to Martha or Lucy? They are here in camp with their husbands and are your closest friends. Surely, they will want to know."

Caty removed her cloak and led Nathanael's hands to the ties on the front of her bodice. "Help me into my sleeping gown and into bed. I have asked little George's nurse to take him to Martha's quarters. I suggest that you do the same and ask General Washington for whatever Madeira he has on hand."

"You are banishing me?" Nathanael accused while his sweating, trembling fingers did little to untie the string that held Caty's bodice. "I will not leave."

She kissed his lips and relieved him of the burden of trying to steady his hands enough to be of any use. "Stay until the midwife and nurse arrive. They will decide when women's work begins."

Nathanael looked at her nervously.

"It will not be like that old woman who attended me in Coventry, the one who came with Peggy," she assured him. "Dr. Thacher recommended this midwife."

"You do not know that for certain," he protested.

A contraction rolled across her belly and passed. "If you do not help me get settled, I will have to soothe *you* during the birth," she teased.

Nathanael got his wife settled, and then left for Washington's quarters.

"How long does this take?" Nathanael asked Henry and Lucy, who came to help Martha and George in keeping Nathanael calm.

Snow ticked against the window glass as if counting down the minutes.

Lucy's and Martha's knitting needles clicked in the quiet room. "It has only been a few hours, Nathanael," Martha said soothingly.

Lucy exchanged sorrowful, grateful glances with Henry. Nathanael had fathered more children than Henry, and, unlike the Knoxes who had lost one of three, none of the Greene babies had died. It was unthinkable to deny their friends the joy of bringing a baby into the world, especially when Lucy suspected she was in that condition again.

"What is the date?" Nathanael asked. He refilled his glass with Madeira, then drank half of it.

"You are constantly writing letters," George said, trying to add a modicum of normalcy to a circumstance he had not participated in beyond dogs and livestock. "Do you not date them?"

"Can you just answer my question?" Nathanael snapped back. He ran his fingers through his hair, messing his neat queue.

"January 31," Lucy said gently.

"Where is my son?" Nathanael demanded. "Does he know what is—?"

A knock at the door caused everyone in the room to jump. George's slave and companion, Billy Lee, opened it. Snow drifted into the room on a wave of cold air. A disheveled nurse was standing at the door with a shawl around her shoulders. "Tell General Greene his child has been born."

Congress' neglect, tedious paperwork, the contrary behavior of the citizens of Morristown, and the winter storms could do nothing to quell the Greene's happiness. Nathanael held his newborn baby, a boy they named Nathanael Ray Greene. He stared into the baby's blue eyes, searching for a part of his own essence.

Baby Nathanael's arrival brought tenderness and cheer to camp. Martha, Lucy, and other officers' wives arrived with arms full of clothing and blankets. Lucy held the babe in her ample arms and rocked him. Tears wet her cheeks; tears of joy for this little soul who had survived and tears for her little Julia who died at four months old in the Pluckemin cantonment in 1779.

"I need to write letters to my family and friends," Nathanael happily announced to the gushing and cooing women gathered in the small bedroom. It was the one thing he could do that made sense and over which he had control. As he left the room, he encountered one of his quartermaster deputies, Colonel John Cox, coming to pay his respects.

"Is Mrs. Greene well?" John asked.

"Yes, just very tired since only two days have passed. Can you help me order dresses from Philadelphia for her? I want her to feel pretty when she is up and about. It means so much to her."

"Yes, of course. I know a place from where my wife orders her dresses."

"Good, good. Please come by when you can so we can go over the details of the purchases. I am so happy to have a fine son, even if my purse is not growing with my family," Nathanael quipped. "I am off to write to one of my business partners. He is unmarried. I know not how he can go through life without ever tasting some of the sweetest pleasures that falls to the lot of mortals."

John smiled to himself as his general walked away. He had six daughters living in Trenton with his wife. They were the endearments of his life.

Nathanael wrote letters to his brothers with news of the birth. He was surprised to receive a letter from his quartermaster deputy and friend, Colonel Charles Petit. The news of the baby's birth was announced at a dance Charles attended in Philadelphia. Packages of fruit accompanied Charles' letter with a note that said, "My respects to Mrs. Greene. I rejoice that she has recovered so much health."

Good wishes arrived from other friends and acquaintances, many draped with personal concerns or complaints for loss of property with no reimbursement from Congress. Officers in camp in Morristown held dance assemblies that left Nathanael tired and foggy. After sending yet another letter to Congress asking why his resignation was ignored, all the merriment in the world could not ease the toil, desperation, and disrespect that he was obliged to countenance. Letters arrived with news and demands for reimbursements on everything from ships to horses to forage. Nathanael had no means to address them all.

Charles Petit wrote to him again to inform him that a Committee of Congress had been formed to reply to Nathanael's letters of resignation. He went on to say:

> *Malaise has overtaken the quartermaster department due to lack of money. Congress' solution to use drafts on the loan department is inadequate. Be aware, Nathanael, the committee Congress has formed is composed of three gentlemen, one of whom is General Philip Schuyler of New York. But the general refuses to be involved in the reorganization of the supply departments. Therefore, we have no sufficient means to pay the civilian wagoners who haul our supplies. Our new commissary general, Ephraim Blaine, is touring New England to initiate a state supply system.*

Frustrated, Nathanael reached out to Colonel Jeremiah Wadsworth, who after resigning his post as commissary general, was living in Hartford, Connecticut. "The troops have completed their huts in Jockey Hollow. Yet, as they find warmth in front of their hearths, they are still badly clad and unpaid. A bounty of $100 has been offered to those who enlisted previous to January 23, 1779. Where we shall get the money, I do not know. The business of my department is growing more and more desperate every day. Congress' conduct is intolerable."

Jeremiah replied on March 10, 1780:

> *Where will all this mean, wicked, damnable conduct of Congress end? Are they determined to neglect everybody and*

*affront all their officers? They wish to have you do something
from resentment that will disgrace you. This I know you will
not do. You will never be wrecked on the rock you taught me
to avoid. I am glad Petit sees them as they are. Believe me to
be with great sincerity your friend.*

George had remained a silent spectator to Nathanael's pessimistic
outlook and battle with Congress. Still, after writing his letters, it was to
his aloof general that Nathanael went to with his frustrations and plans.
Billy Lee was shaving George's face when Nathanael entered Widow Ford's
house where George and his staff were quartered.

"General Greene," Billy exclaimed. "The general is dressing."

"Allow him to enter, Billy," George said calmly.

Nathanael crossed the room and sat behind George's desk. The top
was littered in letters, some wrapped in red tape, others lying open. Quill
stands, ink stands, fresh sheets of paper, ledgers, books, and cold candles
added to the clutter. "Your desk looks like mine. Where are Hamilton and
your other aides?"

"They have gone for breakfast," George said when Billy rinsed the
razor in the bowl he had propped under his chin.

"Did you receive the copy of the last resignation letter I sent to
Congress dated the 16th of February?" Nathanael asked.

"Yes." George wiped his face with a towel and dismissed Billy. "The
embarrassments and evils you have stated as crowding and accumulating in
your department are truly alarming. However, how far the condition of our
finances may put it in the power of Congress to remove or lessen them, I
cannot pretend to say."

George rose and tied his cravat around his neck and said, "Colonel
Reed and Colonel Petit have both urged you to meet with Congress in
order to discuss the department's problems and the upcoming campaign,
as have I. You have asked me for general orders regarding the coming campaign, which I cannot give."

"I will set out for Philadelphia in the morning but can plainly see little is to be expected from it unless it is dismissing myself from the department, which I most devoutly wish," Nathanael replied with sarcasm. "I cannot bear their accusations of misappropriation and their neglect any longer."

Nathanael's chest tightened and he tried not to cough, but it insisted attention and then quieted. He said, "I am very certain there is party business going on with this reorganization Congress wants to implement for my department. Thomas Mifflin and his connection to the juntos, who tried to oust us in 1777, leave no doubt of this being a revival of the old scheme. Like General Schuyler said, I think this reorganization plan is designed to embarrass you, George."

"It certainly does seem symptoms indicate that disposition," George said seriously.

The office door swung open. Alexander Hamilton, Tench Tilghman, and James McHenry loudly entered the room.

"Give us a few minutes of privacy," George instructed his aides. Nathanael rubbed his upper lip in thought while he waited for the aides to leave. "I sincerely wish that your embarrassments were fewer, but I am convinced that you will exert yourself to the utmost. Should any intelligence come to my knowledge that will enable me to give you more particular or perfect information, you may be assured that I shall immediately communicate them to you," George said.

Billy returned with his general's waistcoat and sash.

"I purpose to take Colonel Clement Biddle with me to Philadelphia that a clear, full, and particular representation may be made of every branch of the quartermaster's department and the whole be brought to a speedy issue," Nathanael said firmly. "I am also bringing Caty with me. She has procured a nurse for our sons."

"The soothing effect of your lady by your side can only help," George said with a brief smile. "One last thing. Thousands of troops under General Henry Clinton's command are besieging Charleston, South Carolina. There has been a second embarkation of British troops from New York. I am transferring the Maryland and Delaware lines to the Southern Department to aide General Benjamin Lincoln and his 5,000 troops holding the city. If we lose Charleston, it will be a disastrous affair for those in the South and the Continental Army in general."

Nathanael nodded. What was happening in the South with Savannah, Georgia under British control and now the Americans fighting to hold onto the rich and important city of Charleston was out of control. One of George's aides, Colonel John Laurens, had gone to his home state of South Carolina to help defend it. Congress' failure to send help and provisions to General Lincoln and his Southern Army was another example of their lack of military understanding. Nathanael tried to leave the room without limping or coughing, but both seemed like harbingers he could never rid himself of, like the quartermaster department.

❧

As Caty and Nathanael strolled the busy streets of Philadelphia, carriages rumbled by, and livestock and dogs wandered beside pedestrians. On Market Street, the sound of vendors hawking their wares and the aroma of beef, mutton, and chicken cooking drifted on the air. The crowds of people were divided between Loyalists and Patriots, yet the city had an incognizant gaiety as if the war were removed.

The liveliness blurred Caty's vision. She had received a letter from her father John that her older brother, Simon, was ill but was withholding the news because of Nathanael's extreme distress.

"When do your meetings with Congress convene?" she asked in hope that there would be a quick resolution to the miscommunication and accusations that her husband was bearing.

"Tomorrow. Tonight, however, we have been invited to General Benedict Arnold's home as his wife Peggy's guests." Nathanael stopped walking. Caty did as well. His lambent blue eyes held the look of his horrible burden. She wanted to pull him into her arms and keep him safely comforted until the war was over. By the look on his handsome face, she knew he wished the same thing.

After a week of meetings, it became clear that Congress had no intention of changing their policies nor authorizing the money Nathanael believed he needed to support the coming summer campaign. Nathanael, Charles Petit, and Clement Biddle, quartermaster in charge of forage, were subjected to long hours of presentations to Congress and even more long hours of verbal attacks.

The president of Congress, Samuel Huntington, declared to Nathanael, "Before any new arrangements of the quartermaster general department can be completed with regard to a state quota system, we think it inexpedient for you to resign. However, Congress desires as soon as possible to be furnished with a list particularly stated of all the debts due from your department."

Nathanael abruptly rose from his chair. General Schuyler stopped him with a hand to his arm. "Sit down. Let me address Congress on this matter."

Nathanael nodded and did as Philip asked. His eyes drifted to Joseph Reed, one of his few allies in Congress, who had advised him to resign, saying, "I believe you will be blamed no matter what happens."

Philip rose and addressed the committee members and Congress, "Gentlemen, please keep in mind that General Greene is the first of all the subordinate generals in point of military knowledge and ability. If in case of an accident happening to General Washington, he would be the properest person to command the army and General Washington concurs."

Nathanael's fury had already built to a tempest. Despite the well-given advice, he announced, "I am tired of meetings and tired of waiting for Congress to pass a resolution declaring its confidence in the quartermaster's integrity. My presence here is no longer necessary, therefore, I will issue my final resignation and leave Philadelphia immediately."

The men in the crowded room murmured and grumbled among themselves.

Charles leaned forward and said to Nathanael, "I think you should not resign until a successor is found to launch the new system. Perhaps temper your rhetoric."

"You are one of the accused here," Nathanael replied while the committee members conferred. "Even your brother-in-law, Joseph Reed, cannot stop these accusations."

"No, Nathanael. I shall continue to keep accounts for the department," Charles said.

Samuel Huntington brought the session to attention, "We have agreed that in keeping with your views, General Greene, we offer a resolution that you should be dismissed. Not only as quartermaster general, but from the service of the army as a whole."

Nathanael stormed out of the room.

Joseph Reed went after him. "Nathanael, I suggested you resign, but to alienate Congress completely is a mistake."

"I think upon the whole your advice is prudent. What to do or how to act, I am at a loss." Nathanael subconsciously rubbed his eye. "I feel myself so soured and hurt at the ungenerous, as well as illiberal, treatment of Congress and the different boards that it will be impossible for me to do business with them with proper temper." He turned and limped toward the State House exit.

"Nathanael, wait," Joseph called after him.

"I belong on the battlefield," Nathanael said. "I will, however, agree to stay until a replacement can be found." He pulled open the doors and stepped out into the streets of Philadelphia to find the comfort he left at their rented apartment—Caty. On April 10, with Caty by his side, he left the city and returned to Morristown.

Snow blanketed the ground in Morristown when the Greenes returned accompanied by Colonel Biddle. What Caty had kept from Nathanael faced her when they sifted through the seemingly endless correspondence cluttering his desk.

Her dark eyes blurred with tears as she read a letter addressed to her from Jacob Greene. "Jacob has written that my brother Simon died at home on Block Island. There is no explanation, only that he had a fever."

Nathanael pulled her into his strong arms. She sobbed into his chest. "Simon was only twenty-nine."

"Do you want me to make arrangements for your departure to attend his burial? Our little Patty is there visiting your father. Perhaps it is a time for you to gather our daughters to your bosom."

"No, you and our sons are here. Jacob writes that Patty is well and that Cornelia, who is with your family in Potowomut, is very well and is charming. But I sense a hint of distain in Jacob's words about Patty, as if her deformity from rickets is less than pleasing."

Nathanael slid a finger beneath her chin. "Look at me. You tell me what you wish me to do, my angel, and I shall do it."

Banging on the office door startled Caty and Nathanael. "General Greene, His Excellency wishes to see you!"

"Tench, is that you?" Nathanael asked.

"Yes."

"Enter."

Tench Tilghman, one of Washington's aides, swept inside. A late spring snow wetted his cocked hat and weighed down his cloak. "His Excellency has received news of Congress' ultimatum to you. He wants to see you immediately."

"I will look in on little George and baby Nat," Caty assured him. "You must tend to your business."

Nathanael left instructions for his deputies present in Morristown to leave the unanswered letters on his desk as they were. His secret personal business with Colonel Jeremiah Wadsworth and Barnabas Dean could not be discovered as it would be misconstrued as using his department funds for his personal gain instead of using his own commissions. He followed Tench across the barren Morristown green. The smell of smoke drifting from taverns, homes, and churches infiltrated the cold crisp air.

"You look utterly exhausted," George said, noting the dark circles under Nathanael's eyes when he entered headquarters. The truth was that Nathanael *was* exhausted, but he said nothing. He was, however, surprised to see that the Marquis de Lafayette was there, just returned from France. "Marquis," Nathanael acknowledged with a bow.

"Nathanael, I am very happy to see you," Lafayette said with a dimpled smile.

"I trust your journey was satisfying. How are your wife and children?" Nathanael asked.

Joy transformed Lafayette's young face. "Adrienne gave birth to our son, Georges Washington Lafayette, in December 1779. I hear you, too, have a new son."

"Lafayette has brought good news from France," George interjected. "King Louis XVI has resolved to send six ships of the line and 6,000 regular infantry troops at the onset of spring. The news and Lafayette's return have sparked many celebrations between Boston and this camp. I have asked him to write to officials to urge them to provide more troops and provisions to the Continental Army. This may be our chance to attack New York."

"We would feel most unhappy and distressed if I was to tell the French that are coming over full of ardour and sanguine hopes that our little army has no provisions to feed the few soldiers who are left," Lafayette said.

Nathanael glanced at Alexander Hamilton and Tench Tilghman. The aides appeared busy tending to ledgers and letters, but he knew they were already privy to the joyous information. He helped himself to the wine on George's desk and sat down without comment.

"You appear no more optimistic than General Knox's aide, Major Shaw, who declared that it is abominable that we should have to send to France for soldiers when there are so many American sons idle," Lafayette said to Nathanael, "but I hope we shall all make the most of it." He rose and bowed. "I should leave you to your business."

When Lafayette was gone, George said to Nathanael, "I have received your letters from Philadelphia and have also received news that Congress has threatened to dismiss you from the service. I have warned them that it is a fatal mistake and that it should be avoided at all costs."

"Nothing was accomplished. I wrote to Colonel Wadsworth to tell him that our soldiery is neither fed nor paid and are getting sour amazingly fast. Such a temper never appeared in our army before. God knows how it will end. But I need not tell you that," Nathanael said.

"I fear it will end in mutiny. I see them coming and going, looking for what they will not find—their pay which they have gone for months without," George conceded.

"This new system Congress is touting leaves us as destitute of food and provisions as we were months ago. Even if the soldiers were paid, they can buy nothing when a pair of shoes cost twenty-five Continental dollars."

"Yet, Congress has requested your proposals for settling the accounts of the department in such a way as to meet the difficulties arising from the new method of supply."

A month later, on May 25, 1780, the Connecticut brigade paraded and signaled with their drums, shouldered their arms, and went off threatening to seize what they could from the locals. The teenager, Private Joseph Plumb Martin, and his fellow messmates were exasperated beyond endurance and could stand it no longer. Their officers managed to subdue them, and the troops returned to the parade ground with grumbling instead of music.

The soldiers at Morristown had to endure it or desert. As General Baron von Steuben resumed regimental infantry parades, the long winter at Morristown came to a close. The war, which had been slumbering for most of the winter in the north, was taking a turn for the worse.

nineteen

I Will Not Apologize Nor Relinquish

News arrived in camp that the American garrison in Charleston, South Carolina, fell to the British. Washington had warned General Benjamin Lincoln to get out of the city, which was surrounded by unfinished defensive works that the hefty general from Massachusetts did not have the resources to repair. But the civilians of the town begged Lincoln to stay. The loss of the Southern Army, consisting of 3,000 Continentals and 2,000 militiamen, was the most devastating defeat of the war. With the fall of Charleston, the men politically in control of the low country, the Rice Kings, were cowed.

With a victory to his credit and leaving his aggressive general Lord Charles Cornwallis in the South, General Henry Clinton sailed back to New York City where he had left General von Knyphausen in command with 8,000 troops. Spies brought word to Knyphausen that there were mutinies in the Continental camp. Despite being over sixty years old and blind in one eye, Knyphausen was an active officer who served as lieutenant general in the army of Frederick the Great. Buoyed with the news of Washington's army's discontent and believing he could either lure them out of their mountain stronghold in Morristown or attack in their rear, he decided a victory was in his grasp in New Jersey. Clinton disapproved of the move, but if Washington was lured into a battle, he would be free to sail up the Hudson and take the American fortress at West Point.

A body of 5,000 British and Hessians troops crossed Staten Island, New York on a bridge of boats and on the morning of June 6 arrived at Elizabethtown, New Jersey. With Knyphausen looming and the 1780 campaign underway, the officers' wives in camp went home. Martha Washington and Lucy Knox with her newborn son had already departed. Nathanael bought Caty a secondhand carriage from the Kennedys, a Tory family. He drove it into Morristown after stopping for repairs.

Caty clapped her hands and giggled. "Oh, the darling thing!"

Nathanael frowned. "I wish you to get the carriage painted anew with the Greene family arms upon it. I do not choose you to ride in it with the present arms upon it; especially as they are Tory arms."

"It has room for all my baggage and our little boys. I will have it painted as soon as I arrive home."

"I want you to send me new shirts. Mine are in a shattered condition," Nathanael said. He packed up his little family in the carriage and kissed them all. Then he watched as Caty's carriage rolled out of Morristown northward toward Rhode Island.

Nathanael was ecstatic on June 8 after his meeting with George. At last, he would be delivered from the drudgery of endless paperwork and would do what he did best—command an assault against the Hessian general. Nathanael and George agreed that Knyphausen's movement was probably a feint to distract the American Army and sweep around Hobart Gap in an attempt to capture them. Nathanael, with 1,000 regulars and 1,500 militiamen, was deployed to a position in the Watchung Mountains overlooking Springfield to watch Knyphausen's motions.

Small bodies of Continentals patrolled and watched the roads. Knyphausen's army was harassed by musket fire that met them from behind fences and along the road as they marched the five miles from Elizabethtown to Connecticut Farms. In revenge, the British and Hessians set fire to the helpless village of Connecticut Farms. The wife of a local clergyman, Hannah Caldwell, was shot as she sat in the midst of her children with an infant in her arms.

Under the command of General von Steuben, General William Maxwell, who had faced off with Knyphausen across Chadd's Ford at Brandywine, arrived with his New Jersey brigade and some militia to thwart Knyphausen's movements. The young cavalryman Major "Light-Horse" Harry Lee and his legion received orders to do the same. The Americans gained ground and then lost it, but the New Jersey militia began arriving in great numbers. Washington was there, too, on the high ground at Short Hills just beyond the burning village. Nathanael moved his headquarters to Springfield.

It began to rain. Unhappy with his position, Knyphausen was anxious to get back in reach of his shipping across to Staten Island. His men struggled to retreat in the face of blinding lightning and rolling thunder—fearful that the Americans would attack them in the dark.

Meanwhile, Washington called a war council. He posed the question, "The enemy outnumbers us by half. What should we do?"

"When I compare their strength and ours, I am in favor of a retreat," Nathanael offered. "If Knyphausen, as is probable, is making a feigned movement in this direction, and really aiming at the heights of the Hudson River, our retreat will be merely a change of position."

"I think a night attack is favorable," General von Steuben added.

William Maxwell and the scrappy New Hampshire General John Stark agreed.

Acknowledging the majority, George said, "The time, therefore, is set to midnight."

But Knyphausen had managed his retreat to Elizabethtown without molestation hours before the Patriots could catch up. The two sides were now in a stalemate. Washington became more and more anxious over

Clinton's unknown intentions and was certain that he would venture into the Highlands. On June 21, he resolved to move his main army cautiously northward.

"I am leaving you with the brigades of Maxwell, Stark, Harry Lee's cavalry legion, and the militia to cover the country and the public stores," George told Nathanael. "The dispositions for this purpose are left entirely at your discretion."

"And if Clinton's movements to the north are a feint?" Nathanael asked.

"With you here and in command, I feel that I can turn my back without fear and the rear of the army will not be exposed," George assured him.

Satisfaction washed over Nathanael. His commander-in-chief had not lost confidence in his field abilities after all the months of shuffling paperwork and warring with Congress. "I will order the troops to be in readiness to move at a moment's warning if it is necessary."

The main army prepared to move to Pompton, New Jersey—a position close enough to West Point that Washington could respond to a threat. Thousands of men loaded wagons with provisions and supplies and marched out of their mountain stronghold in Morristown while Nathanael remained in Springfield, New Jersey, a quaint little town on the Rahway River.

Late in the afternoon, an intelligence report arrived at Nathanael's headquarters. He immediately wrote Washington that the spy he only identified as "Mr. P" had just arrived from Elizabethtown. "General Clinton and the whole British Army will be in motion this evening. Their intention may be to cut you off at the Clove, the entrance to the Hudson Highlands."

At 5:00 a.m. on June 23, Nathanael was awakened by drums beating and warning shots. He scrambled out of bed and pulled on his clothes. New Jersey militia colonel, Elias Dayton, banged on his bedroom door. Nathanael threw open the door while he buttoned his waistcoat.

"The enemy is advancing from Elizabethtown and said to be about 5,000 infantry, with a large body of cavalry and fifteen or twenty pieces of artillery," Dayton warned. "Their march is compact and rapid and they move in two columns—one on the main road leading to Springfield and the other on the Vauxhall Road."

"Have Major Lee with his horse and pickets oppose the right column. Your regiment will oppose the left."

"Yes, sir."

Nathanael did not bother to put on his coat. The June sun would soon make the day stifling. Badly outnumbered, Nathanael mounted up and hurriedly deployed his troops. He immediately sought out Rhode Island Colonel Israel Angell and New Jersey Colonel Israel Shreve. "I want both of you to take your regiments, pieces of artillery and defend the bridge over the Rahway."

The colonels took the order. Nathanael spurred his horse and began shouting orders to Maxwell, Stark, and all the other commanding officers. Then, he saw the enemy marching straight at them. The bridge defense crumbled when Knyphausen's troops began fording the river. Angell and Shreve were forced to retreat.

The enemy was held in check for thirty minutes by American cannon and musketry, but they bypassed the Patriots' small force and advanced into the village. Nathanael shaded his eyes and saw gray smoke drift into the windless air and tongues of orange flames that blackened into choking smoke.

Dr. James Thacher, the Continentals' surgeon, galloped up, and, with his general, watched mortified while the church and two dozen houses and stores burned to the ground. Then, Knyphausen ordered a retreat back to Elizabethtown.

"Why are they retreating?" Dr. Thacher asked Nathanael.

"I do not know, but it is precipitate," Nathanael answered. He tapped his upper lip with his left index finger, then turned to his aide, Major Ichabod Burnet, and said, "Has General Stark set his brigade in motion to pursue the enemy?"

"Yes, sir," Ichabod said.

Nathanael wheeled his horse and galloped through the field to avail himself of troop losses and dispositions. They trickled in as commanders or aides arrived to communicate to their major general.

At 7:00 a.m., General Stark returned. "The enemy has totally evacuated the point at Elizabethtown. They returned to Staten Island and pulled up their bridge of boats," he said.

"Thank you," Nathanael acknowledged.

He returned to his headquarters and dutifully wrote to George. "I was in high hopes the enemy would attempt to gain the heights but discovered no disposition in attacking us. I am at a loss to determine the purpose of the enemy's exposition. I lament that our forces were too small to save the town from ruin."

Sir Henry Clinton never did move to take the Hudson Highlands. He was secretly engaged with the commander of West Point, American General Benedict Arnold.

Caty was home in Coventry with three of her four children. News arrived of the fall of Charleston and outcome of the conflict in Springfield. She also heard that Congress had selected General Horatio Gates, one of their favorites, to replace the captured General Benjamin Lincoln as commander-in-chief of what was left of the decimated Southern Army in South Carolina.

In July, Caty returned to Block Island for the first time since the war began to visit her brother Simon's grave and fetch three-year-old Patty. The blonde, pretty, bow-legged little girl ran to her mother with a bright smile. "Momma!" she exclaimed as she raised her arms to be picked up.

Caty lifted Patty onto her hip and kissed her chubby cheeks. Caty's father, John Littlefield, walked up the windy hillside where her mother was buried in May 1761, leaving behind five children. Caty wondered if her children would remember her if she died. What saddened her most was that she knew, aside from little George, they would not remember their father if he died.

Her father wrapped an arm around her trim waist and pulled her in close as they looked over the vista of stone fences, paths, ponds, and the sea. Years had passed, and the miles she had traveled to be with her husband and the birth of four children were evident on her face, yet he still saw her unspoiled beauty and vigor.

Caty arrived at the docks in Newport to see the sails of the promised French fleet crowding the harbor. She was pleasantly surprised by the man who greeted her when she stepped off the double-ender sailing vessel that had always been used to ferry her family from the island to Newport.

"General Lafayette," she coquettishly tittered.

The young general bent to kiss her hand. "Mrs. Greene, I am very pleased to see you again. I received word that you were returning from Block Island and could not let the opportunity pass."

"Oh?" she asked as she took Patty's hand and pulled her close to shield her from the bustling activity on the wet damaged wharf—sailors, soldiers, merchants, tradesmen, and laborers. Rigging rustled. Young boys running errands darted through the crowds. Seagulls sailed on the blue skies in anticipation of fishing vessels returning to port.

"General Rochambeau and his officers have asked that I escort you to their headquarters. They are using Newport as the base for their expeditionary fleet and army," Lafayette said. "They wish to meet the wife of the esteemed General Greene."

Caty smiled, but the utter destruction the British left behind became evident. The wharfs were missing planking. Hundreds of houses had been torn down for firewood, gardens and orchards were destroyed, stores abandoned.

"We are trying to make order of this destruction," Lafayette assured her. "General William Heath from Massachusetts is also here. He and General Rochambeau have established a rapport. Ah, here we are," he said. He pointed to a home that was still standing, despite destruction to its exterior.

The distinguished Comte de Rochambeau bowed as Lafayette introduced Caty. "Madam, please flatter us by staying for dinner," the fifty-five-year-old general said in French. "I am told that you speak our language as most of us do not speak English."

That night at dinner, Caty's charms enchanted every officer seated around the table as they told stories about their difficult voyage across the

Atlantic. Only the Chevalier de Chastellux regarded her with quiet candor. The English-speaking writer and historian was a member of the French Academy. Many vivacious women had crossed his path, but Caty, with her dark flashing eyes, dark hair, and trim waistline was stunning.

"Madam, I am interested to know if we will meet your husband," the Chevalier asked. "We have been, shall I say, encouraged, by the young Marquis de Lafayette, that an attack on British-occupied New York is desirous and General Washington's wish. Does your husband concur?"

Caty sipped her wine before she answered. "General Greene has told me very little of the coming campaign or his thoughts on the subject of New York. I am certain, however, that he will look forward to making your acquaintance and alliance."

࿊

On July 15, 1780, while the French were entertaining his wife, Nathanael learned at Camp Preakness in New Jersey that Congress finally adopted its new system for the Quartermaster Department. Despite their threats, they renewed efforts to convince him to continue under the new arrangement. With the states now responsible for supplies, the principal men on whom he depended removed, and salaries decreased, he believed it was a physical impossibility to conduct business.

Therefore, he submitted his resignation and wrote a letter to Washington outlining his grievances and seeking his commander-in-chief's approval of his intention to quit. But the wording and tone of Nathanael's resignation letter dated July 26 so infuriated members of Congress that they again threatened to remove him from the army.

How many times do I have to tell them that I disapprove of the proposed new system? Nathanael wondered.

Enraged and with a pen as sharp as a sword, he wrote, "I voluntarily relinquished every kind of emolument for conducting the business, save my family expenses. I do not choose to attempt an experiment of so dangerous a nature. My rank is high in the line of the army; and the sacrifices I have made on this account, together with the fatigue and anxiety I have undergone, far overbalance all the emoluments I have derived from the appointment. Administration seems to think it far less important to the public interest to have this department well-filled and properly arranged." He went on to say that he hoped others would avail themselves of leaving an employment that was not only unprofitable but rendered dishonorable.

Upon receipt of Nathanael's letter, George called for a meeting in an attempt to soothe his distressed major general. "You have angered Samuel Huntington and other members of Congress with your coarse language. Henry Laurens wondered what could have tempted you to treat Congress with sneer and sarcasm. Other members believe that your letter lessened them not only in the opinion of Congress, but of the public."

"I am sensible my conduct has been viewed by many in a very improper light. I will not apologize nor relinquish," Nathanael said firmly.

"I am not asking you to do either. I have written to Congress warning them that to oust you from this army is a terrible mistake. They have chosen Colonel Timothy Pickering as your successor. I ask that you stay on until he learns the new system."

Nathanael heaved a sigh. *I feel as if I am so bruised I can barely move,* he thought.

George sensed Nathanael's hesitancy. "You conducted the various and important duties of it with capacity and diligence entirely to my satisfaction and with the strictest integrity," he said.

"I will do this at your request, but there must be a limit to how long."

George relaxed with relief. "I will impart this to Congress."

"No, I will do it," Nathanael assured him. He was hardly of a mind to let Congress find yet another fault in his character as if he were hiding behind George.

George tested Nathanael's quiet resolve. "This leaves the matter of attacking New York."

"We scarcely have the force to reduce the garrison under General Clinton at New York," Nathanael argued. "And we have not money enough to forward the public dispatches necessary to direct the preparations. But if this is your intention, then I am at your disposal."

George smiled and poured glasses of rum. "Let us have a drink and indulge in a moment of relaxation, my dear general."

"That is the most pleasing subject I have discussed in a long time."

"Then shall we discuss that tomorrow, August 7, is your thirty-eighth birthday?" George said, raising his glass.

Nathanael raised his own glass and chuckled. "I thought no one cared to remember the date."

≈

Nathanael's quartermaster general skills were at Washington's disposal until such time that Colonel Timothy Pickering would take over. Nothing had improved in the department; therefore he was forced to take cattle, hay, grain, and horses from New York and New Jersey farmers, a practice he despised. He sent a detachment of soldiers on a foraging mission commanded by Sergeant Thomas Duncan of New Jersey.

While Nathanael was on horseback directing his foraging efforts in Three Pigeons, Major Ichabod Burnet galloped up. He bowed in the saddle and said, "Sir, we have reports of plundering from the quarter where you have sent Sergeant Duncan's men. They have rampaged through civilian homes and farms with violence and have fired at two local citizens. I know you do not condone such behavior."

Nathanael wheeled his horse, and with Major Burnet, sought the assistance of Major Harry Lee. "Harry, I need you to saddle up with some of your men. We are going to track down scoundrels."

The wealthy graduate of the College of New Jersey grinned. "It will be my pleasure, sir," he said.

Sergeant Duncan was leading his men in another attack on a private home when he heard pounding horses' hooves. *Shit*, Duncan thought when he saw General Greene. He tried to run, but Harry Lee's dragoons ran him down in a field of unharvested wheat and surrounded him.

Nathanael came up, looked down at Duncan and said, "I will not countenance plundering as if you are a Hessian, Sergeant Duncan. You and those two men who fled are under arrest. Major Lee, please see to the arrest." He spurred his mount and rode back to his headquarters near Tappan, New York

Later, on a hot August afternoon, Nathanael stood stoically by and watched the noose strangle a man—a man who he had put to death.

"General Greene?" his new aide Major Lewis Morris from Rhode Island asked, noting the introspective look in his general's blue eyes.

Nathanael regarded him and then went back to his headquarters. Under the light of a single candle, he wrote to Caty, "There is so much wickedness and villainy in the World and so little regard paid to truth and justice that I am almost sick of life."

∽

Caty was also almost sick of life. Nathanael sent letters saying nothing had been determined for the coming campaign and not a word that encouraged her desire to join him in camp. His letters served to ignite her jealousy over Lord Alexander Stirling's wife and daughter, Lady Sarah Stirling and Kitty. She imagined that Nathanael was spending long evenings with the two women who she knew he admired.

She tried not to cry while she wrote a letter to ask if he saw something more attractive in them than in her. "Please, my darling, tell me the truth of it," she begged from where she was lodging with all four children in Newport.

With all the pressures he endured, the last thing Nathanael could countenance was his wife's jealousy. If he had a hand in the making, he had to soothe her doubts, and she could hear it in his every word.

Let me ask you soberly whether you estimate yourself below either of these ladies. You will answer me no, if you speak as you think. I declare upon my sacred honor I think they possess far less accomplishments than you, and as much as I respect them as friends, I should never be with them in a more intimate connection. I will venture to say there is no mortal more happy in

*a wife than myself. Although our felicity is not perfect we have
a good foundation for solid and lasting happiness.*

She tucked the letter away, knowing that he had spoken from his heart. Her eyes settled on her children playing in the living room. "Come, babies, it is time for bed," she gently coaxed.

"Where is Papa?" George asked as she tucked him in bed. "Is he ever coming to see us?"

She stroked the top of his head. "I do not know when he will see us again. He is busy with the war."

Patty's eyes widened. "Will he get killed?"

Caty struggled not to let her face reveal her constant fear that Nathanael would be killed or maimed. "Close your eyes, my love, and try to remember what he looks like. I do that every night as I drift into my dreams."

She snuggled Cornelia and Nat in under the covers and quietly shut the bedroom door. The living room window facing Newport harbor was open. Ships rocked at their anchors with timbers and riggings creaking. Voices rose in the streets. Carriages and horses stirred dust as they rolled by. Newport was still suffering from the shambles the British had left it in. With the currency depreciated and resources ruined, the people struggled to subsist off much less.

Caty looked up at the thousands of twinkling stars overhead on that cloudless night and then shut the window. She sat at the desk and placed quill, ink, and paper before her. She poured out her love for Nathanael in a poem, knowing that wherever he was, he was probably hungry and poorly clad and perhaps even melancholy over the things that had happened with Congress. At least now he was free of the drudgery and frustrations of the duties of the quartermaster general,

"I nearly forgot that you asked that I send new shirts," Caty said to herself. Laughter bubbled up and rolled off her tongue. She began to write: "You know I am an abysmal seamstress, but I shall try my best because you have done your best for our country, our cause, and our family despite all the obstacles that have stood in our way."

The Line of Splendor

❧

On July 25, 1780, General Horatio Gates rode into camp on North Carolina's Deep River with some Maryland and Delaware troops. The army was the remnants of what was left of the Southern Army and militia after the fall of Charleston on May 12, 1780.

After taking Charleston, Sir Henry Clinton departed South Carolina to return to New York and left Lord Charles Cornwallis in command with Colonel Lord Francis Rawdon, a young Irishman who served under Clinton and Cornwallis in the past. A blood feud of partisan warfare ignited. That summer, confrontations erupted between Loyalists and Patriots led and won by American militia leaders from the South. Then the tide turned.

Cornwallis established a supply depot and garrison at Camden as part of their effort to secure control of the South Carolina backcountry. In July, Gates marched his sickly army into South Carolina, intent on liberating the state from British control. As Gates neared Camden, word of his movement reached Cornwallis, and the British general deployed to take the field. The armies approached one another north of Camden early on the morning of August 16, 1780. The Americans were taken by surprise.

After a brief skirmish, Gates formed his men for battle. He made a critical error in his deployment. Under the custom of 18th century European warfare, the most experienced units were placed on the right of the line. Gates, like Washington, had fought for the British in the war with the French and Indians. He positioned the veterans from the Maryland and Delaware line on the right and positioned inexperienced Virginia militia on his left. He should have recognized that his opponent would do the same despite the warnings from his adjutant, Colonel Otho Holland Williams of Maryland.

When he arrived on the field, Cornwallis formed his veteran Regiments of Foot on his right to face the Virginians. The British advanced and presented bayonets. The Virginians immediately turned and ran. Their flight prompted the North Carolina militia in the center of Gates' line to do the same, and the American position quickly collapsed.

The Continental regulars from Maryland and Delaware withstood the onslaught. Gates' second-in-command, fifty-nine-year-old General Baron Johann De Kalb, maintained a firm stand and ordered a bayonet charge that drove the enemy back in confusion. Cornwallis concentrated his efforts on De Kalb's troops. They were outnumbered, and after several terrific charges on the Maryland and Delaware troops, they were driven back. De Kalb made every effort to rally his men. During the hottest part of the struggle, he was wounded eleven times and fell.

Gates and the rest of the army retreated. He shamefully fled and rode 170 miles in three days, leaving behind 1,000 captured men along with his army and their baggage train and artillery. The defeat cleared South Carolina of organized American resistance and opened the way for Cornwallis to invade North Carolina.

Gates, who had claimed himself the "Hero of Saratoga" while withholding deserved laurels from the fearless General Benedict Arnold, was done with the war in the South. Lord Charles Cornwallis was far from finished.

On September 5, the letter announcing Gates' disgrace reached Nathanael. Washington was hosting a dinner and war council for his officers and aides at the Zabriskie House near Hackensack, New Jersey. The letter was read aloud to the sound of chuckles and guffawing. The sobering news of the defeat and that Baron De Kalb fell and died on August 19 could not dampen the astounding news of General Gates' mode of retreat.

"Was there ever an instance of a general running away as Gates has done from his whole army? And was there ever so precipitous a flight?" Alexander Hamilton asked sarcastically. "One hundred and eighty miles in three days and a half. It does admirable credit to the activity of a man at his time of life."

Nathanael swallowed his urge to laugh at Alexander's quip. "General Gates' late misfortune will sink his consequence and military character. Whether he has been to blame or not, I cannot pretend to judge, and shall leave those who were nearer at hand to fix the common opinion."

The Marquis de Lafayette grinned, and his cheeks dimpled.

Henry Knox's chubby cheeks shook with unchecked humor. He got control of himself and said in earnest, "I think we should forget about a siege of New York until spring and send a joint American-French expedition to liberate Charleston."

George frowned. He was still myopically focused on attacking Clinton in New York and said, "In reaction to this news, I have scheduled a summit with General Rochambeau and Admiral Ternay in Hartford, Connecticut, to discuss strategy." He told Henry, "I want you to accompany me and General Lafayette. Alexander will make the trip with us."

He directed his attention to Nathanael and said, "If our entertainment is quite done, in my absence the command of the army devolves upon you. I leave the conduct of it to your discretion. I do, however, wish you to march the army closer to Tappan, New York to help fortify General Arnold and West Point if the British make a move up the Hudson River."

Nathanael avoided looking at Henry lest he break out in laughter with his friend. He said, "I am honored, George."

"We shall all follow you as our new supreme commander," General Alexander McDougall declared with gusto. He raised a glass.

Shouts of "Huzzah! Huzzah!" circled the dining table.

For once, Nathanael felt not only appreciated but also venerated.

twenty

The Law and Usage of Nations

Washington, Knox, Lafayette, and Hamilton left for Hartfield, Connecticut on September 17, 1780. The Continental Army arrived in Tappan on September 21, after a long three-day march illuminated at night by a waning gibbous moon and under cloudy, wet skies during the day. The army settled in. Nathanael received the poem and shirts from Caty and wrote back, "I will venture to say there is no mortal person more happy in a wife than myself. I am now in temporary command of the army. This makes me a great man for a few days."

The following night, Nathanael settled in to read before he went to bed. The hour was late, and he mysteriously heard ominous firing on the Hudson River. He rose and walked outside. It was dark and little could be seen. Unable to sleep, he wrote to Washington. "There has been some firing on the east side of the North River at the shipping which lay near Tellard's Point, but I have no account of what effect it had other than to make the shipping move a little farther from the shore."

On September 25 at 11:00 p.m. as Nathanael finished a letter to Congress informing them of intelligence he had received about the enemy's movements, an exhausted and harried messenger arrived in camp with an urgent message. "From Colonel Hamilton, sir," the rider announced and left.

Major Lewis Morris shuffled into Nathanael's office with disarrayed hair and sleep in his eyes. "What is the alarm?" he asked.

Lewis listened as Nathanael's eyes widened in disbelief and read the missive aloud:

> *There has just been unfolded at this place a scene of the blackest treason. Arnold has fled to the enemy. Andre, the British Adjutant-general, is in our possession, as a spy. His capture unraveled the mystery. West Point was to have been made the sacrifice. All the dispositions have been made for that purpose, and 'tis possible, though not probable, to-night may see the execution. I came here in pursuit of Arnold but too late. I advise you putting the army under marching orders and detaching a brigade immediately this way.*

"General Arnold has defected?" Lewis asked, stunned.

Hearing the commotion, Ichabod Burnet appeared at the door in a rumpled night shirt.

Nathanael ran his hands through his hair. "I just wrote to General Arnold telling him that we are starving here for want of provisions. I told him that our troops do not get one day's meat in four and that this cannot hold long in my worry about what is to become of us. I have given Arnold a report on the army's shortcomings that he will take to the British."

"Perhaps you should immediately report this to Mr. Huntington at Congress in Philadelphia," Lewis suggested. "Perhaps there is more to be discovered in Arnold's papers and in the family to whom he has wed."

"Get dressed, both of you," Nathanael ordered. "Alert the officers here in camp and sound the night alarm. Be ready to muster the troops in a few hours. I want two regiments of the Pennsylvania line to set out immediately for West Point, and the rest will be held in reserve. Lewis, I will prepare an explanation which you will read to the troops."

As Lewis left, another messenger arrived with a letter from Washington for Nathanael addressed from the house opposite West Point, the Robinson House.

> *I concluded to send to camp tomorrow Major Andre of the British army, and Mr. Joshua H. Smith, who has had a great hand in carrying on the business between him and Arnold. They will be under an escort of horse, and I wish you to have separate houses in camp ready for their reception. I intend to return tomorrow. You may keep these matters secret.*

Outside on the dark parade ground under a waning crescent moon, Nathanael could hear Major Morris reading his account of the affair to the soldiers. "Treason of the blackest dye was yesterday discovered. General Arnold who commanded at West Point, lost to every sentiment of honor, of private and public obligation, was about to deliver up that important post in the hands of the enemy…"

Nathanael's mind wandered, and according to the information he had received from Washington, he pictured what the scene may have been like as the discovery was made. His assumptions were not far off from what had actually transpired.

≈

When Washington assigned Benedict Arnold command of the left wing of the army, Benedict declared he was unable to ride a horse into battle and begged for command of West Point. However, Benedict was disgruntled with the fact that Congress refused to properly compensate the army's officers, and his attempts to petition Congress fell on deaf ears. Therefore, he was already involved in a nefarious plot to sell General Henry Clinton the plans to West Point in exchange for 10,000 pounds and a major generalship in the British Army. Benedict's contact was the twenty-nine-year-old adjutant to the British Army, Major John Andre. Charming and well-liked, Andre was Clinton's favorite.

On September 25, Washington and his staff stopped at West Point on their return from Hartford, Connecticut, after meeting with the Comte de Rochambeau and his officers to discuss combined operations. When they arrived at the fort atop a precipitous plateau of rock, there was no welcoming party, only a few sentries, and most unusual—no Benedict Arnold. However, George made as if to perform an inspection.

"General," Lafayette said. "You know Mrs. Arnold is waiting breakfast for us."

"Ah," George responded with a laugh. "I know you young men are all in love with Mrs. Arnold and wish to get where she is as soon as possible. You may go and take your breakfast with her, and please tell her not to wait for me. I must ride down and examine the redoubts on this side of the river, and I will be there in a short time."

Despite George's offer, his general officers felt obliged to accompany him on his tour. They were appalled at the redoubt conditions and surrounding defensive positions. At 10:30 a.m., George and his hungry staff arrived at the Robinson House where Arnold was headquartered. They were greeted by a single figure, Major David Franks, Arnold's aide.

"Do you wish to have breakfast?" Major Franks asked.

"Yes, we would appreciate that," George replied.

"I must tell you that Mrs. Arnold is indisposed and in her bedroom, and Colonel Richard Varick, the general's chief aide, is indisposed with a fever."

"Do not worry them," George appeased, "we shall have a leisurely breakfast."

Benedict descended the stairs. He bowed. "I apologize for my absence. Mrs. Arnold required my attention." He indicated the dining table and said, "Please sit down."

Alexander was wary of Arnold's sudden appearance because several aides had ridden ahead to inform him of their impending arrival, and Arnold should have been prepared. During the meal, a messenger arrived. "For General Arnold," the man said, saluted, and left.

Benedict tore open the letter from Colonel John Jameson, commander of the advanced American posts, along what was called the Neutral Ground where roving bands of Loyalists, called Cowboys, and Patriots, called Skinners, terrorized travelers and one another. He quickly read it and then ascended the stairs two at a time and burst into Peggy's bedroom.

"Andre has been apprehended. They have found the pass I gave him and the information about West Point on his person. Our plot has been found out, although General Washington does not know of it yet. I am obliged to leave you and my country forever," he confessed.

"What do you want me to do?" Peggy asked, horrified.

"I do not know, but I have to leave in order to save my life," he bawled.

"Benedict," Peggy implored as the door slammed behind him.

A package arrived containing the documents Benedict had given Andre, and a letter from Andre to General Washington was spread out before the commander-in-chief. Within minutes, he knew the full extent of Arnold's treachery and that he had fled downriver in a small boat to board the HMS *Vulture*. Alexander went after him.

George called Henry and Lafayette into the room. "General Arnold has plotted to surrender West Point to the British. He has not only betrayed me, he has betrayed his country." His countenance contorted with sadness, anger, and shock. He asked, "Whom can we trust now?"

Then, he received a message from Benedict begging for mercy for his wife, Peggy.

> *I am induced to ask your protection for Mrs. Arnold from every Insult and Injury that the mistaken vengeance of my Country may expose her to. It ought to fall only on me. She is as good, and as Innocent as an Angel, and is incapable of doing wrong.*

It was a lie. Clinging to her six-month-old baby boy with her hair and clothing in disarray and proclaiming that they had come to kill her child, Peggy Arnold convinced Washington, Hamilton, Knox, and Lafayette that she was also a victim of her husband's treachery. Alexander was so convinced that he wrote to his fiancé, Elizabeth Schuyler, and explained:

> *All the sweetness of beauty, all the loveliness of innocence, all the tenderness of a wife, and all the fondness of a mother showed themselves in her appearance and conduct.*

❧

What Nathanael could not picture were the events that led to Major John Andre's capture. Clinton had warned Andre not to change out of his uniform nor accept documents when he met with Benedict Arnold on September 22, using the prearranged alias, John Anderson. Andre did both. Furthermore, his transportation back to New York City, the HMS *Vulture*, retired upriver when an American militia regiment began firing cannon at the ship. This was the firing Nathanael heard on the night of September 23. Forced to ride through the Neutral Ground, he encountered three New York militiamen, one by the name of John Paulding, who was wearing a Hessian coat. The men surrounded Andre.

"I am a British officer. You had better let me pass," Andre insisted, offering his pass from Arnold. "Your stopping me will detain General Arnold's business."

"If you're about General Arnold's business, then why did you say you was a British officer?" Paulding insisted.

"Strip off his outer clothes and search him for money," one of the militiamen declared. "And take off his boots!"

"Well, look here," another militiaman announced as he waved documents above his head. "He has papers in his stockings. He is a spy!"

They marched Andre twelve miles to the headquarters of Colonel John Jameson. In a letter to His Excellency, Andre portrayed himself as a youthful victim of Arnold's scheme and ended with an appeal. "I am branded with nothing dishonorable, as no motive could be mine but the service of my King, and as I was involuntarily an impostor."

He was transferred to army headquarters in Tappan, New York, where his charms lured a coterie of adoring American officers. But they were not all adoring. Washington assigned Nathanael to preside over the tribunal at the Dutch Church along with thirteen generals, two of whom were Henry Knox and Baron von Steuben.

ॐ

When Nathanael arrived at the church, he noted the gathered generals who sat at a long table near the pulpit. The prisoner was seated off to the side—his fate would be decided today. *This will be a painful business,* Nathanael thought. As he took his seat, Steuben leaned over and said to his aide, William North, "It is not possible to save Andre."

Nathanael brought the court to order. "The prisoner will address the court."

John Andre rose and bowed, then took his seat.

"Read the names of the members," Nathanael told the court clerk, "and let the prisoner say if he has anything to object to any of them."

The court clerk did so.

Andre replied, "Nothing."

"You will be asked various questions," Nathanael continued, "but we wish you to be perfectly at liberty to answer them or not as you choose. Take your own time for recollection and weigh well what you say."

Andre told his story and provided a written account of it.

"Did you consider yourself under the protection of the flag?" Henry asked, referring to a flag of truce.

"Certainly not," Andre answered. "If I had, I might have returned under it."

Nathanael asked, "You say you proceeded to Smith's house?"

"I said a house, but not whose house," Andre replied with indignation.

"True," Nathanael conceded. "Nor do we have any right to ask this of you after the terms we have allowed. Have you any remarks to make upon the statements you have presented?"

"None, I leave them to operate with the Board."

"Remove the prisoner," Nathanael instructed the guard.

The tribunal council rose and conferred in solemnness. When they were done, Nathanael said, "You have heard the prisoner's statements and the documents that have been laid before you by order of the commander-in-chief. What is your opinion?"

The tribunal came to a unanimous vote. Andre had come ashore as a common spy, and agreeable to the law and usage of nations, he must suffer death. Execution was set for October 1. Henry Clinton won a one-day reprieve by requesting a meeting with Washington, asking to give up Andre. Clinton sent General Robinson as his representative, and Washington sent Nathanael.

Nathanael informed Robinson, "If we give up Andre, we expect you to give up Arnold."

The deal was a failure. Andre wrote to Washington pleading with him to let him die as an officer in front of a firing squad and that he should be allowed to wear his uniform. Washington complied with the uniform request but stood firm that he was to hang as a spy.

October 2 dawned cold and windy. Andre was paraded to the gallows to the mournful sound of the dead march played on fife and drum. He stepped into the hind end of a wagon and onto his coffin. While the executioner bound his hands, he saw Nathanael standing among the spectators and said, "I pray you to bear witness that I died like a brave man."

The wagon was suddenly pulled out, and Major John Andre's body violently swung back and forth until he was dead.

Arnold's treason left the command of the important fortress at West Point vacant. This information was certainly known to Clinton. Nathanael wanted the command. On October 5, he approached George at the DeWint House with his request, "A new disposition of the army is going to be made and an officer to the command of West Point. I take the liberty to indicate my inclinations for the appointment. I hope there is nothing indelicate or improper in the application."

George considered Nathanael's open countenance. He knew that Nathanael had lobbied for command of the Southern Army after he had expressed his intention to resign as quartermaster general. "There is neither a definite disposition of the army at this time nor of West Point's situation during winter cantonment. I advise, however, that we detach several brigades to man the post," George counseled. "If under this information you should incline to take the immediate command, it would be quite agreeable to me that you should do so."

"Whatever you wish. My first object is the freedom and happiness of my country."

What George did not say was that he needed a good general in the South. Congress' previous choices had failed: Robert Howe at Savannah, Benjamin Lincoln at Charleston, and Horatio Gates at Camden. George feared who Congress would send next to a part of the country that was rife with disease, warring Patriots and Loyalists, swamps, unnavigable rivers, uncooperative militia, and a serious lack of provisioning while Lord Charles Cornwallis was unstoppable in the Carolinas.

Nathanael accepted his instructions, and on October 7 he marched with four brigades up the west bank of the Hudson River. On his arrival, he wrote to Caty to inform her of his appointment and that he wished her to begin preparations for the journey south to meet him. "If you think you can be happy in this dreary situation with me, I shall be happy to receive you to my arms, as soon as you can render it convenient to come."

The garrison at West Point was in disrepair, the gun carriages for cannon were in bad order and lacked provisions of every kind—food, wood, and lime the most needed. Nathanael put his quartermaster skills to work and carried out his plan for collections. Flour was direly needed for the garrison to subsist. Always concerned about what his soldiers ate, he ordered an immediate supply of roots and vegetables. He recruited the help of his friend, General Alexander McDougall, in command of one of his brigades. When George wrote a letter asking that he provide estimates of the cost of the war, Nathanael gladly responded to the best of his ability.

A letter arrived from George that did not leave him entirely surprised. His former quartermaster deputy, Clement Biddle, had alluded to the likelihood that it would come. The talk about who would replace General Gates in the South was spreading like wildfire. Alexander McDougall, Henry Knox, and the Marquis de Lafayette thought of no one but Nathanael.

The South Carolina delegate to the Continental Congress, John Mathews, specifically wrote to Washington to tell him that he was authorized by the delegates of the three Southern states to state their wish that Major General Greene be appointed to the Southern command.

George's letter to Nathanael contained confirmation of those rumors.

> *As Congress have been pleased to leave the officer who shall command on this occasion to my choice, it is my wish to appoint you; and from the pressing situation of affairs in that quarter, of which you are not unapprised, that you should arrive there as soon as circumstance will possibly admit. I suppose General Heath, if not already at West Point, is on his way from Rhode Island.*

Nathanael confided the contents of the letter to his aide, Major Lewis Morris. "Are you accepting this post?" Lewis asked, knowing that if his general did, he would follow him south.

"Yes, I am. So pack your baggage, Lewis. I am going to ask for time to settle my personal and business affairs, which have been at loose ends for five years. When I marched from Tappan, I wrote to Mrs. Greene to come to camp, and I expect her every hour."

Alone in his room, Nathanael accepted His Excellency's appointment. None of Nathanael's insecurities showed their face, neither his fear of criticism nor his irreverence. *I know I am worthy of this appointment*, he told himself as he dipped quill into ink. "Your Excellency's letter of the 14th appointing me to command of the Southern Army was delivered to me last evening. I beg your Excellency to be persuaded that I am fully sensible of the honor you do me and will endeavor to manifest my gratitude by a conduct that will not disgrace the appointment. General Heath arrived last evening and will take command this morning."

George denied Nathanael's request for time to settle his affairs. "Your presence with your command as soon as possible is indispensable."

Nathanael knew Caty would be miserable, and to make it worse, the duration of his distant command was uncertain.

Caty was dismayed over the news that Benedict Arnold had defected to the British. She remembered meeting his beautiful young wife on one of her trips to Philadelphia with Nathanael. But with Arnold's treason also came good news. Nathanael had been given command of West Point and he had invited her to come.

"Jacob! Peggy! The children and I are going to West Point, New York for winter cantonment," Caty exclaimed as she ran into the library waving the letter in front of her.

Peggy looked up from her knitting but said nothing.

Jacob laid his book aside and rose. Relief washed over him, and he said to Caty, "I know you have been fearful that my brother would be sent to the southward as the rumors have it. It would be nothing but disgrace and disappointment as has attended every commander of that station."

"I must prepare for the journey," Caty declared, unmindful of Jacob's dour words. "Nathanael is sending his aide, Mr. Hubbard, to accompany me."

"I suppose that means you will spend every last penny of your savings on clothes as you always do when preparing for winter camp," Peggy clucked.

Jacob shot his wife a reproachful glance. "I will have your carriage repaired," Jacob offered Caty. "You and your children should be with him when you can."

"No, I will do it as I need it to go to Providence. Nathanael told me to have the Kennedy family's Tory coat of arms painted over so that I may have safer passage through the Patriot friendly territories on the route to West Point."

Caty left Coventry filled with glee and hope. She left her carriage at the wheelwright and then went shopping for clothes for her and the children. Afterward, she went to visit General James Varnum and his wife, Patty. He had resigned his commission in the Continental Army in March 1779 to serve as a delegate to the Continental Congress.

"Caty, it is so good to see you," James exclaimed and welcomed her into the house he was renting in Providence. "I heard the news that Nathanael has West Point."

Her dark eyes flashed as she followed him into the library. "I am thrilled," she said as she sat. As James served her a glass of wine, her voice took on a serious tone. "Have you heard the rumors that Nathanael will be sent to the South? Surely, as a representative to Congress, you must know something."

"I can tell you nothing for certain. I believe Congress may pass that decision on to His Excellency this time."

Caty frowned and considered her wine glass. "You *would* tell me would you not?"

James smiled and said tenderly, "My dear lady, how could I keep something so important from a most lovely friend? Will you stay for a day or two? Or at least for dinner. My wife is very talented at preparing eel, a delicacy for the mouth."

A knock sounded at the door. James excused himself. Caty drank her wine and listened to James thank the man on the stoop. He returned to the library. "This is for you," he said, handing a letter to her. "The messenger said that your brother-in-law, Jacob, suspected that you might be here and to deliver this to your hand."

Caty's stomach lurched. She wanted to tear the letter to shreds even before breaking the wax seal which she recognized as Nathanael's. She drained her glass of wine and brazenly poured another while James looked on. Her fingers trembled as she opened the letter. There was no date or place of origin in the upper right-hand corner of the letter.

My Dear Angel,

What I have been dreading has come to pass. His Excellency General George Washington by order of Congress has appointed me to command of the Southern Army. Gen. Gates being recalled to undergo an examination as to his conduct. This is so foreign from my wishes that I am distressed exceedingly: especially as I have just received your letter of the 2nd of this month where you describe your distress and sufferings in such a feeling manner as melts my soul into the deepest distress. I had been pleasing myself with the agreeable prospects of spending the winter here with you. How unfriendly is war to domestic happiness. I wish it was possible for me to stay until your arrival; but from the pressing manner which the General urges my setting out I am afraid you will come too late to see me. God bless you my love and support your spirits. With my truest love and sincerest affection. I am yours.

NGreene

Her tears wet the letter. *How am I—how are we—to endure this? I will have no chance to feel his arms around me or his lips on my own before he leaves. The children and I do not have the strength to endure a trip to the southward even if we were invited,* she thought.

She looked up at James. "I am sorry, but I must go. What I have dreaded has come to pass as Nathanael conveyed in his letter."

"If there is anything I can do—" James began, suspecting that Nathanael's letter announced his appointment to the Southern Army.

Caty tried to smile, but it would not form on her lips or in her heart. "Thank you," she said quietly. She left his house with as much dignity as she could muster.

❧

At Coventry, Caty received more correspondence from Nathanael as his last days before leaving for Philadelphia and then North Carolina approached. He heard falsely that she was on her way so he hurried to Fishkill, New York, north of West Point, where the route he had suggested to Caty and Mr. Hubbard would take them. He poured out his agony when she did not appear:

> *I have just returned from Fishkill where I went this afternoon in hopes of meeting you. But alas I was obliged to return with bitter disappointment. O, Caty how much I suffer and how much more will you?*

Lacking cash, he enclosed stock certificates and told her that if she was discontented with Coventry that she and the children could move to the farm he owned in Westerly, Rhode Island, but that she should consult her own feelings in her choice of a home. The farm, the stocks, and a piece of land in New Jersey were all the assets he owned. Everything else was invested in his secret partnership with Jeremiah Wadsworth and Barnabas Dean and some investments with Colonel Charles Petit and the Batsto furnace, hardly soluble funds that he could pass on to Caty.

He sent one last letter. She stared at it, wondering how she could bear to hear his pain and distraction:

> *I wanted to see you so much before I set out. God grant you patience and fortitude to bear the disappointment. If Heaven preserves until we meet, our felicity will repay all the painful moments of a long separation. I am forever and ever yours most sincerely and affectionately.*

"Now, I will never be able to answer little George's question, 'When is Papa coming home?'" she whispered to the page.

She fell into silence and would not answer her husband's woeful letters. And then her despondency changed to resentment. She put quill to paper and penned him a brief letter, "I cannot be responsible for the consequences of such a long separation. But I will come to camp if you send for me no matter the difficulties."

twenty-one
The Greatest Degree of Anxiety

Nathanael left West Point and arrived at the camp in Preakness, New Jersey, where he was to receive his final orders. They were waiting for him—George Washington, Henry Knox, Alexander Hamilton, Baron von Steuben, Anthony Wayne, and others.

Henry pounded Nathanael on the shoulder with one chubby hand. "Congratulations on your appointment. We have all agreed that you are the man for the job."

"I will endeavor to be that man at all costs," Nathanael jested, knowing that his friend's sentiments were of the utmost sincerity.

"Shall we sit down to dinner?" Alexander coaxed. "I am starving, and we have many toasts to accomplish tonight."

"I am of that opinion," Steuben said as he dished potatoes and beef-steak on his plate.

"In that regard," George said, "I am recommending that you accompany Nathanael to the South if he will have you, my dear Baron. Your talents, knowledge of the service, zeal, and activity will make you useful in all respects, particularly in the formation of raw troops who will principally compose the Southern Army. You will receive a high command."

Grateful to have access to bread again, Nathanael took a large slice. "It will be my pleasure to have General Steuben, and if Congress approves, I will give my orders to them when I arrive in Philadelphia."

"Very good," George said. "I have also put Major Harry Lee's corps under marching orders, and as soon as he is ready, shall detach him to join you."

"I heard you wrote to John Mathews, a congressional delegate from South Carolina, to let him know Nathanael is coming," Henry said to George as he poured ale into his tankard.

George glanced at Nathanael's relaxed countenance, which did not betray his thoughts. Yet, he was cognizant that his general was not ignorant of the troubles in the South. Not only the army, but also the civil strife. George said, "I did indeed. I told him that I was giving him a general. The caveat was my question to him. What can a general do without men, without arms, without clothing, without stores, without provisions?"

"A former quartermaster general!" Alexander shouted. "Let us raise a glass to our general who has the experience."

"Hear! Hear! To our general!" they exclaimed amid the sound of glasses brought together over the table.

"I wager he will not be running away like Granny Gates did," Anthony proclaimed.

Henry took Nathanael aside and said, "My dear friend, I am happy for you. Everyone agrees that there is not a general here who is more qualified for this assignment than you. I shall miss you, and I hope that we will meet again with laurels upon our heads and victory in our hands."

"I hope for that, too, Henry," Nathanael said in a voice laced with sanguinity and sorrow. "I know not what I am facing in the southern countryside, not truly. Although, we know that it is considered the unhealthiest place in all of America."

For a moment, Henry looked aggrieved and thought, *His health is often a delicate matter. I hope this is not a portent.*

The night went on in comradery, the kind that Nathanael would leave far behind as his hopes of seeing his wife vanished. What he did not say that night was that the feeling that he was going to his doom to fight a hopeless war in the South would not leave him alone. With Savannah and Charleston firmly in British hands and the downfall of the rebel Rice Kings' control of the Carolinas, nothing seemed more dismal except facing the duties of quartermaster general again. But this time, Nathanael would have his own command, something he greatly desired.

General Baron Friedrich von Steuben's dog, Azor, thumped his tail and barked when Nathanael entered the Baron's quarters in the Preakness camp. Nathanael bent to pet the loveable Italian Greyhound. "Good boy, Azor," he said brightly.

"Ah, Nathanael, you are here!" Steuben bellowed with jolly candor. "I am ready for our long journey."

Nathanael smiled and said, "As am I. I have wagons for our baggage and provisions. Are you bringing along Billy North and Benjamin Walker?" he asked, referring to Steuben's aides.

"Yes, of course, and Pierre Du Ponceau."

"I have received news from my friend, General George Weedon, who is in Fredericksburg, Virginia," Nathanael said as he sat down to wait for Steuben to confirm he was ready to travel.

"What is that?" Steuben asked. He dumped silverware, books, and a neat array of clothing into his traveling trunk.

"He told me that good news was scarce and thought I should know. On October 7, American militiamen from over the mountains of Virginia, Georgia, North Carolina, and South Carolina defeated a Loyalist regiment led by Scottish Major Patrick Ferguson at Kings Mountain, South Carolina. It vexed Cornwallis heartily."

"Very good! Have you received word from Major Harry Lee?" Steuben inquired while he finished the last of his packing.

Azor laid his head on Nathanael's lap. The general petted him absently and said, "Yes, he is in New Jersey with the Marquis de Lafayette preparing for an attack on Staten Island. He wrote to me asking whether we go and when."

Steuben nodded, and his double chin quivered. "Well, that is the last of it," he declared, buckling his baggage and latching his trunk. "Azor, come."

Azor did as his master bid. Steuben tossed his baggage in one of the wagons. He and Nathanael mounted up and were joined by their waiting aides and a small contingent of dragoons as Life Guard for their trip south. On October 27, the little entourage arrived in Philadelphia.

On that day, Nathanael sat in his room in a boarding house and wrote the Board of War and the members of Congress a letter that he enclosed with the letter from Washington announcing his choice for the Southern command. A cool breeze soughed through the open window. He stared out of it for a moment and thought about Caty and his children, who with each turn of the wagon wheels and stride of his horse he left further and further behind. He rubbed his irritated right eye and refocused on his letter.

"I am unacquainted with the intentions of Congress with respect to the plan and extent of the war they mean to prosecute in the Southern Department. I am uninformed on how the soldiers are to be paid, fed, and clothed." He went on in that vein and then concluded, "I only have to suggest to Congress my earnest wish of being with my command as soon as possible, and the necessity of making the proper arrangements before I go."

His letter was presented before Congress on October 30, and that day they passed a series of resolutions approving Nathanael's appointment and approving Steuben's assignment to the Southern Army. On the approval of a committee of five, Samuel Huntington, the president of Congress, transferred the same authority to Nathanael that had been given to General Horatio Gates.

"We are extending to you all the instructions and resolutions framed for the Southern Army under your predecessor," Samuel read. "You are authorized to raise an army from Delaware to Georgia inclusively, you may employ the army according to your own judgement though subject to the control of the commander-in-chief, and you will earnestly recommend the states within your department to provide provisions as needed for their troops, but you do not have the authority to force this. You must be aware the Southern states are poor and there is the least probability to procure an article from them."

Steuben leaned over and whispered, "Does this not resemble the frustrations you encountered as quartermaster general? The weight of convincing states that they must equip their soldiers and horses?"

Nathanael suppressed a frown as Samuel Huntington's voice faded into the background. "Is there any other choice? We have been handed a shadow of a Continental Southern Army decimated by Gates and on them is our chief reliance. Militia cannot be trusted to stay for the duration of their agreement."

With the congressional meetings nearly over, the work of securing supplies began, and it was a frustrating effort that reaped very little success. To everyone he turned, Nathanael was met with excuses. He wanted to raise a flying army of 800 horse and 1,000 infantry to augment partisan bands in the South. Shipments of saddles, bridles, and sabers were impossible to procure. To make his point of the importance of Major Harry Lee's cavalry corps, he begged that Lee receive a promotion to Lieutenant Colonel, which was granted.

Henry promised a company of artillery. Nathanael wrote to him and asked for four field pieces and two light howitzers as complete as possible. Whether Nathanael would ever see the artillery was as vague as the other disappointments.

He finally approached Samuel Huntington with his humble request for clothing. "I cannot take unclad men into the field," Nathanael stressed. "They will only serve to fill the hospitals and sacrifice valuable lives. It is doing violence to humanity and can be attended with nothing but disgrace."

"We have no clothes to give you," Samuel replied tersely. "It is ludicrous to trust the Southern states to supply them. I suggest you recruit merchants to do so."

Nathanael rubbed his tense forehead and said nothing. An argument with Huntington was a waste of time. He fetched Steuben, and the two went to City Tavern to meet with local tailors. Over glasses of Madeira and dinner, Nathanael said frankly, "I need 5,000 suits of clothing so that my soldiers may have dignity and usefulness."

Emery Lawson, an overweight, well-established Philadelphia merchant, chuckled and stuffed a slice of beef tongue in his mouth. With scorn he asked as he chewed, "How do you propose to pay for this?"

Steuben glanced at Nathanael as if to say, "I would love to stuff something in his mouth."

Nathanael sighed to keep his tongue in check. He said, "I propose you take bills on France in payment."

Emery laughed, which only encouraged the other merchants seated around the table to bow out of the deal. "We have already exceeded what we can do," was the consensus.

"Thank you, gentlemen, for your consideration," Steuben said with sarcasm and rose from the table. He left City Tavern. Azor lay on the walk waiting quietly for his master's return. The dog got to his feet and licked Steuben's hand.

Nathanael joined them, and the two men walked toward Chestnut Street and the State House among crowds of people and carriages and wagons rumbling through the dusty streets. "I have not asked for arms yet, and I suppose it will go no better," Nathanael said. "I have an appointment with the Board of War, and also Joseph Reed, to ask for the necessary accoutrements."

"What leads you to believe that the president of the Pennsylvania Assembly will be helpful?"

Nathanael coughed and exhaled a gasp before he said, "We are friends, and he has control of the arms of the state. I would expect him to make an effort if the Board of War will not."

Steuben tossed his general a sympathetic glance.

Joseph Reed was no more able to provide arms than the Board of War. "If you would be kind enough to lend us for the service of the Southern Army 4,000 or 5,000 stand of arms, I will engage they will be replaced out of the Continental magazine," Nathanael asked in a private meeting with Joseph. "If you cannot spare this number, let me have all you can spare."

"I know you are frustrated," Joseph said in empathy, "but we can only furnish half that number at best."

Nathanael went to his boarding house that night and lay in his bed that was as dusty as the streets of Philadelphia—a city he hated more each time he went. He gave up on sleep and limped to his desk. His coat, waistcoat, stockings, and boots were piled on the chair. He threw them on the floor and sat down.

With weariness he had not felt since the recent days he was quartermaster general for the army, he penned a letter to Washington. "I intend to try to put subscriptions in Maryland and Virginia for the purpose of supplying clothing. Whether it will produce any good only time will determine. At any rate, I shall have the satisfaction of having done all in my power; and if there is not public spirit enough in the people to defend their liberty, they will deserve to be slaves."

With that, Nathanael embarked to put himself at the head of his little army.

❧

Nathanael, Steuben, and their aides left Philadelphia on November 3, 1780. They were given $180,000 in nearly worthless Continental currency for traveling expenses. They joked that they would not make it as far as Virginia, although Nathanael asked that Congress forward them more money.

"Why you believe they will send it is beyond me," Major Lewis Morris quipped to Nathanael. "But I suppose there is no harm in asking."

Nathanael laughed and said, "We should talk about something less discouraging. The Latin classics might take our mind off what we lack. Perhaps Seneca or Plutarch."

"I noticed you were carrying a volume of Horace's poems, General Greene," Pierre du Ponceau pointed out.

"I must have something to read at night to calm my mind. I also have Ovid's *Metamorphoses*."

Steuben was more interested in talking military strategy that he learned from Frederick the Great of Prussia and the War of the Austrian Succession in which he fought. "I see a similarity between the two of you," he told Nathanael. "A leader should be the first servant of the state. Your concerns about the public parallel his."

Their little entourage rumbled south to Head of Elk, Maryland, where General William Howe had landed his army in August 1777 after an agonizing month-long sea voyage to sweep Washington's army aside at Brandywine Creek in his quest for Philadelphia. Nathanael was determined to have the state of Maryland fulfill its quota to equip its five Continental regiments to the southward. He met with General Mordecai Gist who he first met on Long Island in 1776, commanding a regiment of fearless Marylanders.

"You know I was at the battle at Camden," Mordecai explained. "Lord Cornwallis' cavalry colonel, Banastre Tarleton, pursued my Marylanders for miles after the battle. I managed to escape. I can tell you that it is idle to expect service from the Southern Army unless they receive supplies from the northward to put them in a condition to act."

"It is not just clothing I need," Nathanael said, exasperated. "I need artisans and money for use in the intelligence division."

"Have you written to Governor Rodney of Delaware?" Mordecai asked. "They too have regiments to the south."

"Yes. I have sent him a requisition and told him that the only way to keep the middle states, including Delaware, safe is by giving timely support to the Southern Army."

"And the Legislature of Maryland?"

"They promise they will assist, but they have said that I must place little dependence on them." Nathanael thought for a moment and then said, "Will you take responsibility to supervise the raising of supplies and men from these states? We must move on to Richmond."

Mordecai extended a hand and said, "I shall be honored."

The entourage was on the road again the next day. On November 12, they stopped at Mount Vernon. Martha's son Jack Custis, his wife, Nelly, and their three little girls came to visit from their home at Abingdon Plantation, as well as Lund Washington, George Washington's cousin. Their children were the same age as Nathanael's three oldest children. Seeing them happy and lively hurt his heart and served as a reminder that he had no idea how long it would be before he would see his little ones again—if ever.

Lund gave the guests a tour of the plantation and spacious house that George spent years renovating and improving. The piazza overlooked the dark ribbon of the Potomac River that ran half a mile wide, twisting and turning as it flowed south toward the Chesapeake Bay. Nathanael heard the soft voices of enslaved people floating on the spreading dusk.

Martha took Nathanael aside after the dinner guests, full of food and spirits, began drifting off to bed. She asked Nathanael about Caty.

"She is unhappy with my new command," he admitted.

"I am sorry to hear that," Martha sympathized. "We shall miss her at camp this year. I am leaving for the New Windsor cantonment in a week."

"I am certain she will miss the gaiety of camp life, but I have not had time to write to her."

"I suggest you make time," Martha clucked. "There is nothing worse than a woman wondering what has become of her husband in these times of uncertainty and war."

"Mount Vernon is one of the most beautiful places I have ever seen," Nathanael said in earnest. "I do not wonder why His Excellency languishes so often to return to the pleasures of domestic tranquility."

"This may not be my place to say, but you look tired," Martha observed.

"I am, but we need to get an early start in the morning."

"Men, too, need comfort and looking out after."

Nathanael raised a weak smile. "I cannot afford that. I have a little ragged army to find and spirit up no matter how I feel."

"Of course. I shan't fuss over you like a mother a moment longer."

Nathanael took her hand and raised it to his lips. He bowed and then said, "Good night." As weary as he was, he had letters to write before he could lay his head on his pillow.

⮧

The southern autumn had descended on the land, leaving a biting sunset when, on November 16, Nathanael's wagon train creaked into Richmond, Virginia. He received an immediate confirmation of his worst fears. The want of money and public credit had business at a standstill. The militia had recently been called out due to the appearance of General Alexander Leslie with 1,900 British troops on an expedition from New York to join Cornwallis at Winnsboro, South Carolina.

Nathanael and Steuben met with the governor of Virginia, Thomas Jefferson. The tall freckled redhead bowed as the three made introductions. "Please, gentleman, come into my office and make yourself comfortable." They settled in armchairs near the hearth. "Madeira?" Thomas offered.

Nathanael considered refusing the drink. He needed to get to the subject, and drinking would only delay and cloud what he had come to discuss. But refusing was discourteous so he accepted. "Virginia was asked to furnish a large part of our needed supplies for the Southern Army, which will benefit your own troops in the field."

Thomas put a hand to his chin. "Yes, I received the requisition you provided. It is quite a list: flour, beef, rum, hay, live cattle and 5,000 pounds in coin. Not to mention the artisans you have requested, be them black or white men."

Steuben refilled his glass from the bottle on the table, "Are we to expect the requisition to be filled immediately?"

Thomas considered the question for a moment and then said, "I have full powers of impressment, but I have been trying for three weeks to collect one hundred wagons. Eighteen is all I could procure. Outfitting the state militia takes precedence."

"Mr. Jefferson, it affords me great satisfaction to see the spirit with which the militia has turned out lately in all quarters, but if you depend on them as principal to your defense when they can come and go at a whim, you will hazard your liberties," Nathanael warned.

"They are our defense," Thomas contended. "We have no equipped army here."

"Obviously you cannot withstand a protracted campaign if the enemy chooses to try. The army that awaits me in North Carolina is the only army that will remain for the duration and protect this state. Without it, the public will eventually lose their liberties. Is that not what concerns you the most?" Nathanael challenged.

It was a waste. The quartermaster department in Virginia was completely deranged, and not a man willing to enlist could be trained and equipped to march south with Nathanael.

"I am leaving you here," he told Steuben as they walked past St. John's Church where in early 1775 Patrick Henry had famously declared: *Give me liberty or give me death*. Nathanael went on. "I need you with me, but it is more important to organize recruits and supplies. I must write more letters appealing for supplies."

"I will do my best," Steuben promised, "but I have seen the state of things here just as you have, and it will be difficult." He glanced down at Azor, trotting obediently beside him and chuckled deeply, "His patience sometimes reminds me that I must be patient, which is not one of my virtues."

"Keep me abreast of activities, and I shall do the same. I admit I dread what I will find when I get to Hillsboro."

On that last night, Nathanael had dinner with his aides, Majors Lewis Morris and Ichabod Burnet. Then, as always, he went to his room and strained under the light of a single candle with ink and quill. He wrote to Caty. "My dear Angel. I am now in the capital of Virginia; and I should feel myself tolerably easy notwithstanding the difficulties which I have had to contend with, was it not for the distress and anxiety which you are in; the very contemplation of which hangs heavy upon my spirits; and renders my journey melancholy and dull."

His melancholy spilled over into a letter he wrote to Washington that same night. "It has been my opinion for a long time that personal influence must supply the defects of civil constitution, but I have never been so fully convinced of it as on this journey. I cannot contemplate my own situation without the greatest degree of anxiety. The ruin of my family is what hangs most heavy upon my mind. My fortune is small; and misfortune or disgrace to me must be ruin to them. I beg your Excellency to forward the enclosed letter to Mrs. Greene."

twenty-two
The Southern Army

Nathanael left Richmond on November 21 with new aides—Major William Pierce, Captain Nathaniel Pendleton, and a thirty-two-year-old artillery officer currently without command, Colonel Edward Carrington. Carrington had served since 1775 and was at Monmouth and the disastrous battle at Camden. On the ride to Petersburg, Virginia, Edward filled Nathanael's ear with the details of Camden, and they shared stories of their mutual friend and comrade, General Henry Knox.

They followed the Great Wagon Road that led immigrants from Pennsylvania down as far as Georgia. Nathanael and his companions crossed the Dan River and entered North Carolina with its red clay roads and vast stretches of pine and oak where pine needles blanketed the ground and autumn leaves crunched under wagon wheels and horses' hooves. The weather was dry, warm, and sunny. As idyllic as it seemed, Nathanael and his staff were aware of what raged unseen in the wilds of the area and those that extended far into the Southern backcountry.

Partisan warfare stalked the woods frequently, finding its way to the gentrified plantations and towns. They were overwhelmingly poor

Scotch-Irish who settled in the backcountry of the Carolinas—often squatters and wanderers, loyal, ruthless, and belligerent—men and women fighting a regional civil war. Many were Patriots, and they had vendettas to settle against the Tories, also called Loyalists, like those who fought at Kings Mountain three months earlier. On this day, there was no sound of weaponry, war whoops, or the pounding of driven horses, neither British nor American. Only the occasional curious civilian watched the little caravan of Continentals pass through.

"It appears we will not have a winter respite from the enemy's ambitions," Lewis Morris said as they splashed through another of the seemingly endless rivers and streams that flowed like veins and arteries through the region.

"I assume we have much more to face than we have knowledge of," Nathanael replied. His eyes roamed the dense, hostile countryside occasionally cut with farmland. "Since we have very few wagons in which to haul provisions, I intend to have all the rivers examined on our arrival at Hillsboro in order to see if I cannot ease the heavy business by water."

He pressed one gloved hand to his mouth in thought and then said to Edward Carrington, "You spent much of the fall arranging and transporting supplies for General Gates' army from your supply depot at Taylor's Ferry on the main branch of the Roanoke River. Do you agree that your best use at this time is to extend your survey to the Roanoke River fords upstream to include the Dan River all the way up to Saura Town and the mountains?"

"I do agree, sir."

"When we reach Hillsboro, find some men to engage in the task," Nathanael said. *This was what I had hoped for*, he thought. *Able, talented people who know the terrain and the bitterness of war here. Some with more experience willing to be a part of our army.*

At Hillsboro, they were surprised to find that Horatio Gates' army was not there. Nathanael wrote to General Steuben, "All the troops have marched from hence to Salisbury and some say to Charlotte."

On December 1, they reached Salisbury, ninety miles west. Virginia militia General Edward Stevens was there with his men—survivors of the battle at Camden. The Polish engineer, Colonel Thaddeus Kosciuszko, who Nathanael knew from his time at West Point where the colonel strengthened the fortifications, was also there, although he had not arrived in time to fight with Gates at Camden. To these men, Nathanael gave orders to map the Yadkin and Catawba Rivers, identifying all the critical crossing points, and to collect or construct boats that could be moved by wagons from one river line to another as a bridging train.

To Edward Stevens he said, "I want you to appoint an intelligent officer to explore carefully the depth of the water, the current, and the rocks and every other obstruction that would impede the business of transportation and whether the transportation cannot be performed by bateaux."

"Are we to send the reports to Charlotte, sir?" Thaddeus asked.

"If that is where the army is, that is where I shall be," Nathanael confirmed.

On December 2, Nathanael found his army at Charlotte, a frontier hamlet with two streets, twenty houses, and a courthouse. Nathanael and his aides immediately went to army headquarters in the courthouse. On that cold late autumn day, Horatio Gates and his staff received them with caution like children expecting to be reprimanded. Nathanael and Horatio had not always seen eye to eye, and now the humiliation of Camden—the reason for the change of command—hung between the two.

"Nathanael," Horatio acknowledged with a slight bow and defeat in his voice. He pushed his spectacles up on his nose.

Nathanael returned the bow and removed his riding gloves. For a moment, he realized that all eyes were upon him, and he was at a loss for words. He was exhausted, but Gates looked like a beaten man. "Horatio, I am pleased to see you," he said with respectful sympathy.

"Dinner has been prepared. Shall we all sit down?" Horatio invited.

Major Ichabod Burnet surveyed the faces around the table. These officers were not an army of strangers or amateurs. They were familiar and gutsy, and the war had inflicted suffering on some of them long before Camden.

General Daniel Morgan greeted Nathanael with a big hand to Nathanael's shoulder. "I have not seen you since Monmouth," he declared heartily.

"I thought you had retired," Nathanael said.

"General Gates needed me here. I have command of a flying army with Colonel William Washington's dragoons, four brigades of Virginia riflemen, and three brigades of light infantry from Maryland, Virginia, and Delaware. I believe you know some of my men. We were recently out on a foraging and reconnaissance patrol down in South Carolina where them Tory and Whig militias are feuding."

He chuckled, filled his tankard with ale, and tilted his head. "Colonel Washington, here, is third cousin to our very own commander-in-chief. I released his dragoons to raid nearby Rugeley's Mills, a known gathering spot for Tory raiders. Tell General Greene what you did, William."

William Washington's young face heated up when all eyes shifted to him.

"I remember you, Colonel," Nathanael confirmed. "You were at the battle at Harlem Heights and an artillery captain when you led the vanguard for my division at Trenton, New Jersey."

"Go on, William," Daniel encouraged with a nudge of his elbow.

"The fort was strongly built and surrounded by abatis and ditch," William explained. "Colonel Henry Rugeley was inside with 100 Loyalist militia. I found that to take the fort we needed artillery, something I did not have. I conceived and executed shaping a giant pine tree cut into a log-shaped imitation of a field piece. We brought it up in full view of Rugeley's forces. Rugeley surrendered the post."

"A Quaker gun!" Major Lewis Morris proclaimed. "Is that not ironic considering General Greene was once a Quaker? Raise a glass!"

The room did so and exclaimed, "Huzzah!"

The tall, elegant colonel from Maryland, Otho Holland Williams, raised his glass more half-heartedly than the others in the room. He had served as Gates' adjutant at Camden, but his sufferings went further than that. Ironically, he was stationed at Fort Washington when the New York fort fell to the British in November 1776 after Nathanael had assured General Washington it was defensible. Otho was among the men taken prisoner. He suffered two years on a fetid prison ship, rocking on the waves of New York Harbor. It consumed his health, but not his mind.

Daniel Morgan had a story he often shared—a tale Otho imagined that Daniel told his friends, and wife, and daughters hundreds of times and one he had heard when they were in the same rifle companies at the onset of the war. "General Morgan, tell us about the punishment you received during the war with the French and Indians," Otho encouraged, clinging to the genial mood.

"Back then I called myself the Old Wagoner," Daniel said. His guffaw accentuated the scar on his lip caused by a musket ball. "It was 1755, and I was hauling provisions for the British Army. I struck a British officer and was sentenced to 500 lashes, but the drummer who issued the punishment only gave me 499—I counted. I still bear the scars. 'Course that is before I married my Abigail."

Nathanael found solace in these men who had faced defeat and destruction. He was aware that there were hundreds of difficulties and duties that lay ahead. He had yet to see the troops who he understood were naked and starving and the militia still clinging to the hope for succor and success.

Horatio's expression changed little that evening. When it was time for the others to retire, he took Nathanael aside so the two generals could discuss their plans. Enmities of the past faded as they walked unescorted through the shadowed landscape under a waxing crescent moon that hung low on the western horizon.

"I received word that my only child, Robert, died on October 22," Horatio said quietly without looking at Nathanael. "He was twenty-two and often found too much solace in the bottle."

The grief in Horatio's voice cut Nathanael to the quick. *Perhaps I and this brokenhearted fellow major general have something personal in common,* Nathanael thought, *regret that we are spending the years of war away from home, hearth, and children.*

Horatio sensed Nathanael's sympathy and emotionally reached for it to soothe his aching heart, not only for Robert, but for the atrocity of deserting his army who had faced down Cornwallis and his ruthless cavalryman, the young Colonel Banastre Tarleton. Tarleton's nickname, "Bloody Ban," echoed through the South as if it were a synonym for Lucifer.

"You are aware that this is my planned winter headquarters?" Horatio asked. "I have already proceeded to order the construction of huts."

The construction of huts for the soldiery was Washington's proposal during the harsh winter at Valley Forge. But the circumstances were different in Charlotte. Nathanael did not approve of the decision. "It will be impossible to bring the army into proper order and discipline so long as they depend on the demoralizing process of daily collections for their food—the only process they have for sustenance."

"Perhaps you should withhold judgement until you view the troops in the morning," Horatio cautioned. A shadow of a smile passed his lips. "I wish to offer you the benefit of what I did right and the knowledge that I may not admit what I did wrong. I suppose it no longer matters, not even to those who committed those wrongs with me."

When the sun rose the following morning, Nathanael stood in its weak late autumn rays and witnessed the shivering, naked, and hungry men stand at attention despite their neglect. Horatio's aide-de-camp appeared to announce the change of command, written in Horatio's own words:

The honorable major General Greene, who arrived yesterday afternoon in Charlotte, being appointed by His Excellency General Washington, with the approbation of the honorable Congress, to the command of the Southern Army, all orders for the future issue from him, and all reports to be made to him. General Gates returns his sincere and grateful thanks to the Southern Army for their perseverance and fortitude and suffering they have undergone during his command.

At that moment, the months Nathanael spent as a private with the Kentish Guards in Rhode Island when he was a thirty-two-year-old iron forge owner, and the Guards' scorn for his unmilitary limp that had deprived him of the rank of officer, seemed like another life. Major Ichabod Burnet stepped up to issue Nathanael's statement to the troops.

General Greene returns his thanks to the honorable major general Gates, for the polite manner in which he has introduced him to his command in the orders of yesterday, and for his good wishes for the success of the Southern Army.

The hundreds of problems and decisions he was faced with lay at his feet. His army numbered 2,300, with only 1,500 present and fit for duty. Of these, 950 were Continentals. The rest were militia. Less than 800 of his whole force was properly equipped and clothed. He realized that he had to think differently in this place where feuding was ruthless and American civilian law was damaged. Great bodies of militia roamed and ruled the countryside, the same type of men Nathanael strongly criticized in the North saying they were more interested in pillage and plunder or cringing in battle.

General Charles Cornwallis' trained and equipped principal force of 4,000 was at Winnsboro, South Carolina, seventy miles south of Charlotte and strongly fortified with a string of redoubts that arched across the low country. Underestimating Cornwallis, who had once left a path of destruction in the North and was now subjugating the South, was a bad course.

It was clear that Nathanael would have to rely on partisans. He wrote to native South Carolinian and former Continental Army colonel, militia General Francis Marion. Marion was the bane of Loyalists and the British Army in the Carolinas. Chased by cavalry Colonel Banastre Tarleton and then aggravating him by disappearing into the swamps, Marion had followed orders from Gates to harass the British. Marion's requests to Gates for ammunition, clothing, and a surgeon, among other needs, were ignored.

Nathanael wrote, "I have not the honor of your acquaintance, but am no stranger to your character and merit. Your services in the lower part of South Carolina in aiding the forces and preventing the enemy from extending their limits have been very important, and it is my earnest desire that you continue where you are until further advice from me."

He had one immediate request of Marion, which was to provide needed intelligence regarding the enemy's operations. "Spies are the eyes of an army and without them a general is always groping in the dark." Then, as a show of respect, he replied to Gates' unanswered letters.

The wind huffed through the poorly plumbed walls of the courthouse and intruded on his thoughts. Exhaustion burned his eyes, and he rubbed them without thinking. He began a letter to Washington to report on the state of the enemy, the rebel militia, and American officers. "The inhabitants of this country live too remote from one another to be animated into great exertions; and the people appear notwithstanding their danger, very intent upon their own private affairs." He stressed the wretched condition of the troops, specifically those of the Virginia line.

It ignited his fury with Thomas Jefferson, and his pen spewed anger. "Your troops may literally be said to be naked, and I shall be obliged to send a considerable number of them away into some secure place and warm quarters until they can be furnished with clothing. There must be either pride or principle to make a soldier. No man will think himself bound to fight the battles of a state that leaves him to perish for want of covering."

Letters cluttered his desk with complaints of jealousies over rank that he was forced to smooth with patience. Steuben complained that officers in Virginia were asking for furlough as if the war were on another planet. Georgia and South Carolina had no government, and North Carolina's was meeting in secret.

Nathanael rose from the desk and paced his small headquarters to stretch his stiff knee and calm his temper. Lewis and Ichabod kept to their assigned correspondence, copies, and enclosures the general had dictated with care. They knew where his frustration lay. Diplomacy was his weakness. His strength lay in rebuilding his broken little army. His many abilities would soon be tested by friend and foe alike in the complex landscape of the Southern campaign.

⁊

Caty had not heard from Nathanael since he was in Philadelphia. With the long silence came the probability that she would not be with him this winter. The dismal prospect drove her back to Newport where the courtly French officers were an enticing distraction. She left the children with her in-laws in Potowomut, and with a servant, lodged at General Rochambeau's headquarters. Despite the Newport ladies' often chilly social barrier, Baron Charles Viomenil and his brother hosted a dance in their honor.

Caty swept into the glittering affair unescorted with feathers in her hair and an exquisite gown. The chief commissary for the Newport garrison, Colonel Claude Blanchard, excused himself from his conversation with Captain von Closen and attended her entrance.

He bowed deeply and then regarded her with sultry blue eyes. "Madam Greene," he said in French. "We are so pleased to have you here tonight."

"*Merci,* Colonel Blanchard," Caty simpered.

To Claude Blanchard's slight dismay, his short blond companion arrived and with the bluntness of a suitor announced in French, "Mrs. Greene, I am Baron von Closen of the Royal Deux-Ponts. I am enchanted to finally meet you."

French rolled off Caty's tongue like a second language when she asked, "Oh? You are acquainted with me somehow?"

"I recall you were here last summer when we first arrived. It is difficult to forget such charms." Captain Closen glanced at the nearby guests, leaned in toward Caty, and lowered his voice. "There are many lovely ladies here, but they lack the gentle art of conversation and flirtation."

Caty thought, *I wonder if I should feign a modicum of offense?* The thought drained from her mind when Colonel Blanchard offered his arm. "May I escort you to the dining room, Mrs. Greene?"

"Please, it is Caty," she tittered and tossed a backward glance at Baron von Closen, who followed them like an adoring puppy.

The dinner table was set with glowing tapered candles that cast a soft yellow light over the diners who imbibed great quantities of wine and Madeira, oysters, ham, cheeses, bread, and butter. Caty knew many of the local women seated around the table. They looked at her as if she were frolicking with no regard to her husband's high military rank or her children's welfare.

"They are jealous," Colonel Blanchard ventured to assure Caty when she poured another glass of analgesic wine.

Caty's eyes flashed, and her beautiful face lit up. "You misunderstand me, Colonel. I care not. I am more concerned that I was wearing this same dress the last time I was in this illustrious company."

Colonel Blanchard, Baron von Closen, and General Comte Rochambeau seated across the table laughed. This was what they expected out of Nathanael Greene's candid, alluring wife who never tired of listening to their inner thoughts and triumphs. When dinner was over, the "illustrious" ladies retired to another room while the gentlemen lingered over drinks and a smoke after dinner. Caty refused to join the ladies.

With the pageantry of the French left behind, Caty returned to her desolate life in Coventry where she daydreamed of witty conversation and costumes with red lapels, iron gray coats, elegant long waistcoats trimmed in regiment colors and panaches of colorful feathers. When she awoke, the reality of what her life had become hurt her heart and numbed her senses.

She sat in the grass in the barren yard that overlooked the bubbling Pawtuxet River, and with her little girls, Patty and Cornelia, fashioned dolls made of swaths of material dressed as shabbily as their makers. Nat practiced walking while his big brother, George, steadied him so he would not fall and skin a knee.

Horse bridle jingled. Caty got to her feet. She took Nat by the hand and went around the back of the house where the ribbon of the dusty road passed. Two men approached, sitting regally in their saddles.

Surprised, Caty asked, "Colonel Blanchard. Captain Closen. To what do I owe this visit?"

"You asked that we visit if we were in your neighborhood," Claude Blanchard reminded as he dismounted.

"We were not exactly in your neighborhood," Baron von Closen admitted, as he looked around. "You do not appear to have neighbors."

"There are two ladies who live nearby. My brother-in-law and his family live here, but they are away. Will you stay for dinner?" Caty asked. She gathered her straggling children who had come to stare at the strangers. "My cupboard is a little bare, but I am sure we can find something."

The Frenchmen were not prepared for the destitution they saw as Caty hastily made bread from a mixture of meal and water and then toasted it on the fire. She made no excuses for her domestic situation over dinner. Blanchard and Closen withheld comment. To see a major general's wife and his children subsisting on so little was deplorable, and they could do nothing to change it.

Soon after, Caty received a letter from George Washington in New Windsor, New York, that reminded her that she had not been forgotten.

> *If you will entrust your letters to my care, they shall have the same attention paid to them as my own, and forwarded with equal dispatch to the General. Mrs. Washington, here at headquarters, joins me in most cordial wishes for your every felicity and regrets the want of your company. Remember us to my namesake. I suppose he can handle a musket.*

Two weeks later, Nathanael's letter dashed her last dream of felicity.

> *You have no conception of the circumstances of the country, or manners of the people here. The roads are almost impassable and the trip fraught with hazard. Indeed, you are much better off at home.*

❧

Two important posts were filled. Nathanael appointed Colonel Edward Carrington his quartermaster general. For commissary general, he chose Colonel William Davie, who, like Edward, was without command.

"General Morgan speaks highly of you," Nathanael told William. "Your character leads me to believe you are the most suitable person for this post."

Highly educated and energetic, twenty-four-year-old William was flattered that General Greene, one-time quartermaster general of the Continental Army, would respect his abilities in the service. Still, he protested, "I know something about the management of troops but nothing about money or accounts, therefore I am unfit for such an appointment."

Nathanael thought of his own protests when he was appointed quartermaster general. "No one has ever heard of a quartermaster in history," he had bemoaned. He replied to William, "There is not a single dollar in the military chest or any prospect of obtaining any. You must accept the appointment and supply the army in the same manner you have supplied your own troops."

With the knowledge that he had no choice but to succumb to his general's pleas, William said, "If we are to forage daily, we cannot stay here. The countryside has been laid to waste by rebel horse and men as well as the enemy."

"I have seen the demoralizing efforts of daily food collections by starving soldiers who cannot find sustenance. The result is negligent officers with loose and disorderly troops that often leads to returning home without permission," Nathanael said.

Whatever his decision, he had to be done now. For two days, he lay awake in the quiet hours of the night. Without benefit of a war council, he came to a conclusion that defied all the laws of warfare. A weaker general should never divide his troops when confronted by a stronger opponent capable of smashing the whole. With an army one quarter the size of the enemy's, he ignored the doctrine. To meet Cornwallis in front with an army so inferior in numbers, equipment, and discipline was impossible.

On the morning of December 16, he announced to his officers and aides, "I am going to divide the army. I want to reorganize the current flying army that consists of infantry and horse, and I want General Morgan to command it."

Daniel was elated and said, "I am honored and will do my best."

"We know this is against conventional military strategy," Colonel Otho Holland Williams reminded. "Why would you do this?"

"It makes the most of our inferior force, for it compels our adversary to divide his, and holds him in doubt as to his own line of conduct," Nathanael explained. "Cornwallis cannot leave General Morgan behind him to come at me, or his posts at Ninety-Six and west will be exposed. And he cannot chase Morgan far while I am here with the whole country open before me.

"The main army will stay with me. We are going to move to a camp at Cheraw on the Pee Dee River in South Carolina, seventy-five miles southeast of here. Our engineer, Colonel Thaddeus Kosciuszko, has found that place suitable to support us. Daniel, you will march your army 100 miles west, deep into the upper South Carolina back country beyond the Catawba River. The further object of this detachment is to give protection to that part of the country, spirit up the people, and to annoy the enemy in that quarter."

Daniel was a product of rugged backcountry men and women aware of the brutal war between Loyalist and Patriot militia hunting one another like lions. Acting with prudence and discretion was his priority, but he needed support from the militia under South Carolina General Thomas Sumter and North Carolina General William Davidson. Davidson and Nathanael had previously met. They were both in the Battle of Brandywine opposing Cornwallis in Pennsylvania.

❧

On December 20, after four days of rain, Nathanael took 1,100 men and marched the muddy roads to Cheraw while Daniel with the same light forces he commanded under General Gates—Maryland Continentals, 250 Virginia militiamen, and a body of horse under Colonel William Washington—forded the Catawba River. They tramped over hills and through swamps, crossed the Broad River, and on Christmas Day established a camp on the north bank of the Pacolet River at Grindal's Shoals.

Toward evening, Daniel greeted sixty new volunteers—South Carolina militia under tall, raw-boned Colonel Andrew Pickens, a Presbyterian and man who spoke little. The next week, Daniel's force was further augmented by General Davidson with 120 of his militia. Daniel, in an effort to keep his light forces superior, asked Nathanael's quartermaster, Edward Carrington, for 100 packsaddles to use instead of wagons to carry his provisions and equipment. Meanwhile, Daniel concentrated on collecting supplies and intelligence on the movements of the enemy. He would find out soon enough that the enemy was on to him.

Hicks Creek flowed into the Pee Dee River at Cheraw and into marshy tidewater. Woodpeckers, mockingbirds, and wrens chirped from the branches of towering longleaf pines and white cedar trees. Rattlesnakes, alligators, and insects abounded where the thick woods were soaked in stagnant pools of water that bred mosquitoes even in winter. After six days of marching through the desolate landscape and being forced to forage for food, Nathanael's army arrived at their camp of repose.

Colonel Otho Holland Williams searched for a dry place to pitch the marquee tent he was to share with Nathanael. "Are you certain this is the place of contentment you were aiming for?" he asked.

With arms and shoulders as strong as the days he worked the huge bell hammers in the iron forge, Nathanael helped Otho pull the tent out of a wagon and chuckled, "Our prospects with regard to provisions are mended, but this is no Egypt."

Otho grunted as the tent flipped over the side of the wagon. "I suppose that means there is no milk and honey here."

Nathanael wrangled the unwieldy tent and said, "I suppose there is none. And I suppose this is an importune time and indecently informal, but I want to retain you as my adjutant general."

A smile played on Otho's lips.

"Is that a yes?" Nathanael asked lightheartedly.

Majors Lewis Morris and Ichabod Burnet arrived to assist putting up the tent that would also house them. Otho's aide, Major Elias Brown, rode up and dismounted. "Colonel, there is a report that Thomas Chapman of your Maryland line has deserted again."

Otho exchanged glances with Nathanael, which told him everything he needed to know. "Go after him," he said. "General Greene will see to it that he is punished."

"Yes, sir," Brown acknowledged. He wheeled his horse and rode off.

"You will punish him, Otho," Nathanael said. He reached into the wagon to retrieve the tent poles. "You know in what manner and why."

I suppose hanging a man to improve discipline is the only course, and if I am setting the example for this army, then so be it, Otho thought.

Then, Nathanael surprised him by saying, "Once we get this tent up and everything settled, I want you and the other officers to enjoy dinner with me. I…we need to have a corporate moment in this little band, otherwise I think we will not understand each other."

Enlisted men from the Maryland line drifted in and took the burden of erecting the tent from their officers' hands. When the waxing crescent moon showed its face at 3:00 a.m., Nathanael was still awake. The soft rush of the Pee Dee River whispered beyond his tent. Its waters originated in the Appalachian Mountains in North Carolina where it was known as the Yadkin River and emptied into the Atlantic Ocean. Nathanael squinted under the flame of single candle to avoid disturbing his tentmates' sleep. His pen scratched out orders to Colonel Edward Carrington to ensure among other things that he return from Virginia with nails, axes, and camp kettles—items without which the army would be distressed. He wrote to Steuben regarding other collections for the army and a report to Washington. Letters arrived from Francis Marion and Benjamin Ford, the former referring to intelligence gathering and the latter reporting on hospitals.

The person he desired to communicate with the most was Caty. He had not heard from her since October when he was in Philadelphia and she was in Providence. Her distress and anxiety mentioned in that letter on hearing about his command to the Southern Army weighed on his spirits and crippled his happiness. He had no idea where she was or what she was thinking.

He bent to write another letter hoping he would receive a reply. "I am posted in the wilderness on a great river, endeavoring to reform the army and improve its discipline. The weather is mild and the climate moderate, so much so that we all live in marquees without the least inconvenience. Colonel Williams lives with me, and we have many agreeable moments in recapitulating the pleasures and diversion of Morristown. Good God how happy we were and how little we seemed to know it. I beg you will let me hear from you by all opportunities and give me an account of your health and the children's, those being the most interesting matters to my happiness."

In the morning, fog ghosted close to the ground and through the encampment. Nathanael, Lewis, and Ichabod emerged from the tent to see Otho. He stood among the Maryland and Delaware men with muskets at the ready. Nathanael and his aides followed their line of sight. The deserter, Thomas Chapman, his face red with fear, stood with his hands bound. Major Elias Brown brought a sheet of paper to Nathanael.

Nathanael accepted it. His eyes shifted to Otho and then to the defiant prisoner. By deserting, Chapman had signed his own death warrant. He had underestimated the new general of the Southern Army.

"General Greene?" Major Brown asked as he offered a quill pen to him.

Nathanael read the document. "January 4, 1781. The said Thomas Chapman shot to Death in the Fifth Year of the Independence of the United States." He signed it. The sharp sound of musketry and smoke drifted through the Pine Barrens.

☙

Nathanael worried about Daniel Morgan's detachment camped somewhere in the South Carolina backcountry. He wrote Daniel telling him that he was impatient to hear from him, not knowing where he was or in what condition he was in. He stressed the importance that he should be informed as minutely as possible of his strength, situation, provisions, and means of transportation, all which he begged an account of.

To his relief, he received a letter from Daniel dated December 29 from his camp at Pacolet Creek, South Carolina. He relayed that dragoon Colonel William Washington had caught up with plundering Tories at nearby Hammond's Store before pressing on to Fort Williams and capturing the outpost.

Daniel reported that his food shortage was acute because of trouble with General Thomas Sumter. Sumter's nickname was the "Gamecock," earned from his vigorous speech at a cockfighting game that he frequented as a young man. Nathanael blinked his right eye to chase away the fogginess. He went outside and read the letter in the sunshine.

"News?" Otho asked as he arrived carrying his shaving kit from washing up at the riverbank.

"Yes, it is from Daniel. General Thomas Sumter is refusing to cooperate with him," Nathanael confirmed. "I instructed Daniel to call on Sumter's supporters as Sumter is recovering from a wound he received at an engagement at Blackstock's Plantation in a victory over Colonel Banastre Tarleton. I told him to contact Colonel William Hill, one of Sumter's followers. Hill refused to take directions from Daniel or any other Continental officer. This was Sumter's orders. Daniel has referred the matter to me."

"Perhaps it is time to pay General Sumter a visit," Otho suggested. He coughed, and for a moment his face paled, which reminded Nathanael of his delicate health.

"Would you consider attending?"

"Not me," Otho chuckled. "I am in no mood for a berating. I am aware that Sumter considers the area west of the Catawba River his territory. Write to him but go easy."

"I think I will talk to Governor Rutledge first," Nathanael said. "He bestowed Sumter with unlimited command in this place."

The exiled governor of South Carolina, John Rutledge, looked up from his correspondence when Nathanael entered his tent. "Our government has fallen, and the most I can do now is supply our state militia," John mumbled to himself as he laid his letter to his state delegates aside. "How can I help you General?"

Nathanael explained the situation Daniel was facing and Thomas Sumter's refusal to cooperate. "I want you to write to him today. I realize he is still recovering from his wound, but he can issue orders to his men from his bed. He seemed conciliatory enough when we met him at the home of John Price where he is convalescing."

"I will, but I would not expect much. I cannot rescind the commission I gave him after Charleston fell. Furthermore, Sumter argued that we should attack Cornwallis at Winnsboro, and he is going to say we should have taken that advice."

"I do not care what he argued, just do it," Nathanael ordered. "I have received word that British General Alexander Leslie has sailed up the Santee River with 1,500 reinforcements for Cornwallis, and their numbers will swell to 9,000, including the outposts they hold. We have less than 2,000, and half of those men are with Daniel. I am sending this news to him. He will also need to know what I am doing to encourage Sumter."

As John suggested, Thomas Sumter took umbrage to being berated for his decision not to accept Daniel Morgan's command. Infuriated, Nathanael began a letter on January 8, 1781, to the stubborn general. His intent was encouragement, but his anger built as he wrote, and his pedantic habit flowed from his pen in a diatribe about the capabilities of militia operations.

"I am impatient to hear of your perfect recovery of seeing you again at the head of the militia. General Morgan has gone over to the west side of the Catawba. If he does not meet with any misfortune until you are ready to join him, I should be happy as your knowledge of the country and the people will afford him great security against a surprise. Partisan strokes in war are like a garnish of a table, they give splendor to the Army and reputation to the officers, but they afford no substantial national security."

Then he went on to lecture Sumter about the order of command and William Hill's refusal to aide Morgan; he accused him of inconsideration for the public good.

The rough forty-six-year-old general who lived in the High Hills of Santee near Camden was not deterred. Sumter replied:

> *I confess I have been under some embarrassment respecting Gen Morgan's command, & the orders he has given. As I have been concerned but little in either trust, & believe I have been guilty of no impropriety, and shall always make a point to correspond, & act upon such principles with Gen Morgan, as is most likely to tend to the public good and therefore will not stand upon punctilios, to the prejudice of the service.*

"Did Sumter respond to your letter?" John Rutledge asked Nathanael. The two sat down with Otho on a log, waiting for one of the Marylanders, James McCurdy, to make a breakfast of fried meal and boiled beef.

"Yes, and I believe I will put the matter aside until he is recovered," Nathanael said. He swatted a mosquito buzzing near his face. "I wrote to Daniel, but I have not received a response to my warning that General Leslie is on the march."

His face flushed from bending over the fire, McCurdy offered Nathanael his breakfast on a pewter plate. Nathanael accepted it and ate with a battered and bent fork. "But Daniel's movements are out of my senses," he said like a worried father.

"He is going to write him again," Otho said to John while McCurdy served their breakfasts.

Nathanael's sensitivity to perceived criticisms raised its ugly head. "Are you accusing me of an overindulgence of the pen?" he asked in a doubtful tone.

"You have no idea how happy we are that you are here," Otho said. "Nothing you do would cause me to air a criticism."

Horse hooves pounded the wet ground. The men around the fire rose. "I am looking for General Greene," the rider announced with an express pouch in his hand.

Lewis Morris reached for it and said, "I will accept it for the general."

The rider asked no questions, relinquished the pouch, and wheeled his horse.

Nathanael took the letter from his aide. "It is from General Francis Marion. He and his brigade are settled into winter camp, but he has received intelligence on Cornwallis. The British general ordered Banastre Tarleton and his legion to rid the countryside of Daniel and his troops."

Nathanael wasted no time and scratched out a warning to Daniel. "Colonel Tarleton is said to be on his way to pay you a visit. I doubt not, but he will have a decent reception and a proper dismission." He called on a lieutenant from the Virginia militia with instructions to carry the message to Daniel.

As the lieutenant prepared for his long journey across the Catawba and Pee Dee Rivers, a noise akin to a cattle stampede rose through the pines and across the pools of stagnant water. The noise grew closer, and the first of a legion of 300 light dragoons and infantry emerged elegantly clad in short green jackets, white breeches, black boots, and leather caps topped with a flamboyant plume of horsehair. At their head was twenty-five-year-old Colonel "Light-Horse" Harry Lee.

Harry ordered his cavalry to dismount and his infantry to attention in the presence of Nathanael. His captains, Allen McLane of Delaware, Henry Peyton of Virginia, and Michael Rudolph of Maryland, bowed to set the example.

Harry removed his riding gloves. "General Greene, it was a trying journey from New Jersey, but we are here in one piece. Unlike the north, this is a strange place with low mountains and trees we have never seen."

Most of the men in camp were familiar with Harry Lee, whose given name was Henry, from the years they had fought the war in north. Harry's reputation spread after he led a successful raid on Paulus Hook, New

Jersey, where the British had an assumed impregnable fort that overlooked the Hudson and Hackensack Rivers. Fought on the night of August 19, 1779, the battle had earned him a congressional gold medal and a useless court-martial proceeding initiated by jealous officers.

The colonel, who often had his fellow Virginian General George Washington's ear, was introduced to those who only knew of his exploits. A round of rum and toasting ignited laughter and conversation by the fire as Harry's men settled in with their provisions.

"Your men look finely outfitted," John Rutledge remarked.

"It was not to the credit of the states we passed through, asking for more men and supplies. They refused to outfit their own troops, so I equipped them with my money. Saddles, carbines, and pistols are not so rare a commodity as the states would have me believe," Harry said with a sideways grin.

Nathanael did not show his annoyance. His struggle with obtaining supplies from those same states—Delaware, Maryland, Pennsylvania, and Virginia—had been just as fruitless. With his mind on the urgency of Morgan's situation and Cornwallis' movements, Nathanael said, "Do not get too comfortable, Harry. I want you to rendezvous with militia General Francis Marion at his winter encampment at Snow Island eighty miles south of here along the Pee Dee. He has asked for reinforcements from the regular army so he can stem the growing British and Loyalist retreat in the region above Georgetown."

Harry drank his rum, refilled his tankard, and then said, "Ah, yes. Marion's reputation filtered north. Cornwallis' bulldog Banastre Tarleton was reputed to have chased Marion and his men for twenty-six miles and over seven hours before they vanished into a swamp."

Otho chuckled. "If that is all you know about Francis Marion, then you shall be surprised. Your College of New Jersey education will find its first true challenge in the mind of Marion and his partisan fighters."

"And if General Marion rejects my arrival?" Harry asked.

Otho exchanged glances with Nathanael. Harry caught the exchange, but what fascinated him was what he saw in Nathanael's serene, fair countenance. He saw what lay behind Nathanael's blue eyes and why this ragtag remnant of a decimated army seemed sanguine.

There was hope for the Southern Army at last.

twenty-three

Boys, Get Up! Benny is Coming!

Nathanael and Charles Cornwallis had met in the field before. Not face to face, but as adversaries aware of one another's presence. The troops under their command clashed in the final hours of the battles at Brandywine and Monmouth. It was Cornwallis who had scaled the New Jersey palisades from the Hudson River and overran Nathanael's men at Fort Lee days after he participated in bringing Fort Washington to its knees.

Their disparate backgrounds could not have been more glaring. Nathanael was born to a Quaker preacher, farmer, and businessman in Potowomut, Rhode Island, on August 7, 1742. Charles was born to privilege and position in London on New Years' Eve 1738. What they had in common made them the perfect adversaries: fearlessness and determination. Both had a talent for gathering daily intelligence and acquiring knowledge of the nature of the country around them.

They were second-in-command to the highest ranking generals in the war, George Washington and Sir Henry Clinton. Cornwallis and Clinton had never gotten along. Sensitive to criticism like Nathanael, Clinton submitted his resignation numerous times, always perceiving slights actual and imagined.

Domestically, Cornwallis sympathized with his commander. They had lost their wives. The loss almost ruined both men, and Charles resigned from the army. But now he was back and confident. Clinton was a distant, combative commander stationed in New York and under the impression that Cornwallis was trying to shift the war's seat of power to the South.

Cornwallis, awaiting reinforcements and education about Nathanael's movements and the country through which Morgan was moving, wrote to Banastre Tarleton on January 2, 1781: *If Morgan is anywhere within your reach, I wish you to push him to the utmost.* He ensured that Tarleton had his own flying army with horse, foot, and artillery consisting of 1,200 men.

On January 14, 1781, American reconnaissance parties verified Nathanael's report that an enemy force under Banastre Tarleton was sweeping northward across the Enoree and Tiger Rivers toward Morgan's encampment. He would have to cross the Pacolet where Daniel had guards posted at all the fords.

Tarleton received a message from Cornwallis: *We have left the camp in Winnsboro although General Leslie is not with us.*

Banastre replied: *I am going to purposely force General Morgan to retreat towards the Broad River. If you would proceed up the eastern bank without delay.*

Daniel learned that Tarleton was thirty miles away and gaining. His anxiety increasing, Daniel wrote Nathanael on January 15, told of Tarleton's approach, and reminded him that provisions were scarce. Then, he took his men and retreated north toward the swollen Broad River. A local man led them about five miles from the river's flooded ford along the muddy Green River Road to a place called the Cowpens, an open woods with a few undulating hills for the purpose of collecting cattle once a year for various care. Daniel would make his stand there.

The following night, Daniel walked the pastures in contemplation. Many of the men with him fought at King's Mountain. Most of them were excellent riflemen and could be counted on if forced to perform in open battle against Tarleton's regulars. His mind settled on the force of capable partisan fighters, and an idea blossomed. He went back to his tent and sketched his idea then called his officers.

"Here is what we are going to do," Daniel said to the men bent over the sketch. He tapped a line with one big index finger and said to Colonel John Eager Howard of Maryland, "Your Continentals and seasoned Virginia and Georgia militia will form a line at the crest of southern highest elevation."

Daniel turned his attention to Colonel Andrew Pickens in command of a brigade of South Carolina militia. "You will form a second line 150 yards down the slope. A small body of skirmishers with rifles who joined us recently will line up in front of you," he said.

Daniels tapped his finger on a location behind the line where John was to deploy and turned to William Washington. "Your cavalry and the state militia horsemen will remain in reserve in the rear ready to exploit any breaks in the lines."

"Permission to immediately ready my men? The horses and equipment will need preparation," William said. Daniel nodded and William left to confer with his commanders.

Later that night, the husky general from Virginia moved from campfire to campfire and explained his plan. Smoke hung in the night air like ghosts and laughter rang when Daniel joked, "I can crack my whip over Ban's head, but I need your help."

"We can do that, sir," Thomas Young, a teenage South Carolina militiaman, enthused. His mates around the fire nodded in consent. "That's what we are here for."

With a twinkle in his eye Daniel said. "All I expect from you are three good volleys, and then you can run from the field."

❧

In the wee hours of the morning of January 17, the moon was in its waning gibbous phase. It rose around midnight, and it would be visible until noon if one cared to observe it. At the Cowpens, what the moon could see from its perch in the sky would be of much interest. William deployed a ten-man vedette from his 3rd Light Dragoons to spy on and follow the enemy until dark. They made contact with Tarleton's vanguard, and just before daylight they reported to Daniel that Tarleton had advanced within five miles of his camp and was closing in.

"Boys, get up! Benny is coming!" Daniel bellowed. The men scrambled to form battle lines. "Just hold up your heads, boys; three fires and you are free. Then, when you return to your homes, how the old folks will bless you and the girls will kiss you for your gallant conduct."

At daybreak, after a slow march following the route the Americans had taken the previous night, Banastre Tarleton formed a line of more than 500 infantrymen. Disencumbered of everything but their arms and with drums beating, they began a steady advance up the pasture with fifty horsemen on each flank. The British came on shouting, "Huzzah! Huzzah!"

Thomas Young, riding with William Washington's cavalry, said to his colonel, "Sir, it is the most beautiful line I ever saw. Men resplendent in their red jackets with fixed bayonets standing in perfect order with horsemen on each flank."

"I see the military beauty," William admitted. He also saw something else. It was his duty to stop those horsemen at all costs.

Daniel shouted, "They give us the British halloo, boys. Give them the Indian halloo, by God!"

The front line of Morgan's men under Colonel Andrew Pickens fired two volleys then fell back to give Colonel John Eager Howard's men an open line of fire. Before the British hit Howard's seasoned Continentals, their lines had been thinned; still they had enough men to begin flanking the right side of the American line.

"Wheel to the right and close off that flank!" John ordered.

But the men in the center saw troops wheeling away from the action and believed that the order had been given to retreat. Daniel rode up to the line and encountered John first. He asked, "What is happening here?"

John pointed to Andrew's militia line and said, "The men are not beaten who retreated in that order."

"I see that now," Daniel agreed and then he rode to the top of the next hill and yelled, "Face about, boys! Give them one good fire, and the victory is ours."

The British mistook the action for a retreat and came running. Andrew's men withdrew to clear the field for John's line of Continentals. John's Marylanders gave the British an unexpected and deadly fire.

Banastre shouted to his 71st Highlanders, "Come up on the left and flank their right."

William stood up in his stirrups, leaned forward, and watched this transpire from behind John's third line. When part of Tarleton's light infantry troops spread out in pursuit of Andrew Pickens' men, the chubby courageous cavalry colonel shouted orders to his 3rd Light Dragoons, "Draw your swords and spur your mounts! Charge boys!"

Through the haze of sulfuric smoke, part of the American dragoons were upon the British 17th Light Dragoons like a whirlwind with horses snorting, spurs and bridles jingling, and metal clanging. It was so sudden and violent the dragoons could not stand it and fled. The Americans overtook the British artillery drivers posted on the British right flank, and the 3rd Dragoons shot down the artillery horses with their pistols. They retired back to the rise behind Colonel John Eager Howard's line.

John took his men to the rear so they could halt and rally. "Form boys!" Taking the order, they volleyed with the advancing line of British light infantry and the 7th Fusiliers.

Banastre watched this development from the reserve and shouted orders to his 71st Highlanders. "Pass the 7th Fusiliers before they give their fire, and do not entangle their right flank with the left of the other battalion."

The Highlanders, led by their skirling bagpipes, charged and their infantry swung in on John's line, opening a new break on his flank. William sent his companies of mounted militia under McCall and Jolly. They struck the British with swords aloft and broke the 17th Dragoons wide open, then wheeled about and struck again.

"Bayonets!" John shouted. "Charge."

William's cavalry trumpets ruptured the confusion of the battle. His dragoons and mounted militia rolled forward, circled, and came up on the rear of the British line shouting, "Go boys! Hit the line!" and, "Tarleton's Quarter!" —a rally cry that referred to a battle eight months prior at Waxhaws, North Carolina, where Banastre Tarleton and his 17th Light Dragoons had slaughtered Virginia Continental forces though they had begged for quarter.

Banastre looked at his aide in disbelief. "What is happening?" he blurted out. "We were controlling the ground and now these backcountry rebels are sweeping the line?" He wheeled his horse and galloped toward his reserve dragoons. When he reached them, he saw that they had fallen into disorder, and panic extended along the whole line. He tried in desperation to rally them. "Cavalry form 400 yards to the right of the enemy to check them. Infantry form to protect the guns," he commanded.

All attempts to restore order, recollection, or courage proved futile. Two hundred dragoons forsook their leader and left the field of battle. Fourteen officers and forty horsemen were, however, not unmindful of their own reputation and their commanding officer's situation.

With Banastre's usual fearlessness, he led this small body of horse to make a stand against William's cavalry. William was watching three trailing British officers on the far side of the field. He clapped spurs to his mount and demanded, "Where is now the boasting Tarleton?"

Banastre and two officers charged him. The three advanced abreast, and one of them aimed a blow at William, the effect of which was prevented by a cavalry sergeant. A servant boy rode up and discharged his pistol to disable the other British officer.

Horses' hooves punished the ground, and their riders, William and Banastre, clashed in the center. Banastre grunted and made a lunge with his sword which William parried and hacked at his opponent's fingers. Banastre wheeled about and fired his pistol, wounding William's horse.

Banastre realized at this point that the battle was lost. "Dragoons, move off!" he ordered and raced from the field. William gathered his dragoons riding the field and securing prisoners and pursued. Thirty minutes later, he stopped to ask a terrified local woman if Tarleton had passed by. She pointed down the wrong road. It did not take long for him to realize he was hoodwinked.

It was 8:00 a.m., and the last shots of the battle of Cowpens had been fired. On the field, John Eager Howard dismounted to receive swords from the 71st Highlander officers. Scottish Captain Duncanson desperately clawed at him. "What are you doing?" John demanded.

"We had orders to give no quarter, and we do not expect any, and as my men are coming up, I am afraid you would use them ill."

Another Scotsman was far angrier at the defeat and declared, "I was an officer before Tarleton was born. The best troops in the service were put under that boy to be sacrificed."

One hundred of Tarleton's force were killed, 300 wounded, and 700 captured. The Americans had twelve killed and sixty wounded. They took thirty-five wagons full of baggage and supplies, 100 horses, 800 stands of arms, and two brass cannon.

Daniel demonstrated his elation over the victory by picking up a nine-year-old drummer boy and kissing him on both cheeks. The Americans had entirely broken up Tarleton's Legion, the flower of Cornwallis' army. That evening, he proudly wrote to Nathanael about his victory at the Cowpens and then began a slow retreat south toward Salisbury, North Carolina, so he could be closer to the main army. He assumed Cornwallis would come after him. He could not rejoin Nathanael, for Cornwallis' position at Winnsboro was such that the British could intercept any movement eastward.

He crossed the Broad River and then sent a detachment with prisoners toward Island Ford on the Catawba, instructing his men to meet his own force at Sherrald's Ford on the main stream. He made camp there on January 23 and wrote to Nathanael that he would stay there as long as possible for he was receiving intelligence of the enemies' approach every half hour, and he did not know how long he could wait for Nathanael's orders.

❧

"What do you mean we lost 1,000 men?" Charles Cornwallis fumed. His distorted face emphasized his lazy eye, a result of a sports injury he received when he was attending Eton College in England.

"I am only the messenger, sir," the meek young captain, a survivor of Tarleton's cavalry, said. "Colonel Tarleton has explained it all in his report."

"Where is he?" Charles demanded.

"He is ranging near the Broad and is on his way, sir."

Charles heaved a sigh. He opened the report and read it. The sound of a marching army distracted him. He wadded up the report in disgust before he asked the captain, "What is that noise?"

"General Leslie, sir."

"At least that is something. Dismissed, captain."

Thudding boots and clopping horses' hooves quieted a little only to be replaced with the noise of 1,500 new voices in camp. Alexander Leslie entered Charles' tent unceremoniously with an aide in tow.

Alexander bowed to Charles and then removed his riding gloves. "This place is an abomination," he proclaimed. "We have been marching through mucky swamp for days. Even in the winter, the insects are everywhere. And that damned rebel, Francis Marion, sent patrols that harassed us to no end."

"What are you complaining about? You commanded the British troops during the siege of Charleston, so you know very well what the weather is about here and about those 'damned' rebels." Charles handed Alexander the wadded up report and said, "Read this."

Alexander read it and handed the message back to Charles. "What is your plan now?"

"We leave in the morning to catch Morgan, and then, ultimately, to fight and defeat the main block of the Southern Army under Greene," Charles replied.

"Therefore, my men and horses get no rest," Alexander retorted.

Charles poured a glass of rum and then offered the bottle to Alexander. "I have held council with my officers here, and that is the plan."

Alexander accepted the bottle. For a moment, he considered drinking from it. If he was to face another swift miserable march, rum would make it tolerable. He looked at his brigadier, General Charles O'Hara, nodded, and decided it was a good course.

The following day, Colonel Banastre Tarleton trotted into camp with all eyes upon him. Cornwallis demonstrated his fury by leaning on his sword and snapping the blade. He unleashed his agitation in a letter to one of his favorites, twenty-five-year-old Lord Francis Rawdon: *The late affair has almost broken my heart.*

British officers and Loyalists across the South grieved with Cornwallis.

ॐ

From his camp near Cheraw, South Carolina, on the Pee Dee River, Nathanael received a message from Daniel delivered by his aide, Major Edward Giles.

> *The Troops I had the Honor to command have been so fortunate as to obtain a complete Victory over a Detachment from the British Army command by Lt. Colonel Tarleton.*

"This is delightful news," Nathanael pronounced when he shared it with Otho Holland Williams and General Isaac Huger of South Carolina. "I am warning you that this brilliant victory cannot mask the huge difficulties our army still faces. Do not imagine that Lord Cornwallis is ruined." In the next days, Nathanael wrote those same sentiments to Congress in Philadelphia and his old friend General James Varnum, who was now a congressman.

Despite the dire warning, Nathanael celebrated with his troops. He ordered a *feu de joie*. Otho led the men in a toast of cherry bounce, "They are the finest fellows on earth and we love them, if possible, more than ever!"

Huzzahs echoed through the camp. For one night, the troops and their general drained tension from their minds and hearts as they congratulated one another, and the cherry bounce did its intended operation. It was a temporary bandage to Nathanael's spirit. He worried that the politicians who controlled money and supplies might be inclined to relax after hearing about Cowpens. In the days and weeks to come, he wrote those sentiments to those he believed needed caution.

Two days later, Nathanael received Daniel's letter that he was awaiting him at Sherrald's Ford. Upon reading the letter, Nathanael went to Isaac Huger and confided, "I must unite this army with all haste after which we can give battle if the militia turn out in sufficient numbers."

"What do you purpose?" Isaac asked.

"I want you to prepare at once to lead the command posted here in Cheraw to rejoin the detached light forces in Salisbury, North Carolina. March up the eastern banks of the Yadkin River. Give word to Harry Lee that he is to leave his operations with Francis Marion to the south and join you. I will set out to rendezvous with Daniel to personally be on hand to direct the retreat if needed."

On January 19, the British marched in a northwesterly direction, figuring Daniel Morgan would stay near the Broad River. When he found that was not the case, an infuriated Cornwallis arrived at Ramsour's Mills only to learn that his prey had passed two days earlier and crossed the Catawba River.

"What are we to do?" General Charles O'Hara challenged his commander.

"Our situation is most critical. I see infinite danger in proceeding, but certain ruin in retreating. I am therefore determined to go on." He thought for a moment. "The baggage train is slowing us down. We must lighten the load."

Anguished soldiers watched as their tents, the wagons and their contents, and food that could not be carried in their knapsacks went up in flames. Only ammunition, medical supplies, hospital stores, and salt were spared. The unkindest cut was the rum. Casks were stove in, and the liquor was poured on the ground. Two hundred and fifty Hessian and British troops deserted immediately. Charles O'Hara wrote to a duke:

*In this situation, without baggage, necessaries, or Provisions
of any sort for Officer or Soldier, in the most barren inhospi-
table unhealthy part of North America, opposed to the most
savage, inveterate perfidious cruel enemy, with zeal and with
Bayonets only, it was resolved to follow Greene's Army to the
end of the World.*

∂

On January 28, 1781, a contingent of six horsemen splashed through the
watery wilderness of central North Carolina. Dressed in a blue coat with
buff facings and gold epaulets, Nathanael rode among them escorted by
Majors Lewis Morris, Ichabod Burnet, and a sergeant's guard of three dragoons. It was reckless to leave the protection of his main army, but he
wanted to confer with his officers about what to do next.

Before he left to rendezvous with Daniel at his camp on the Catawba
River, Nathanael directed militia General Edward Stevens to march all the
prisoners taken at Cowpens to Virginia. He instructed his quartermaster,
Colonel Edward Carrington, to assemble boats on the Dan River, along the
border between North Carolina and Virginia, for use in the event of a retreat.

The Rhode Islander was amazed at the weather, and he wrote to Caty,
"The birds are singing, and the frogs are peeping in the same manner they
are in April to the Northward; and vegetation is as in great forwardness as
in the beginning of May."

As lovely as the picture was, he went on to discourage her longing
to join him in the South by reiterating descriptions of Tories and Whigs
persecuting each other with savage fury. With the drifting smell of smoke
from fires that destroyed their homes following them, the sight of displaced
families trudging the dusty roads, sometimes with only the clothes on their
backs, was more than he could bear.

Satisfied that he had done his best efforts to organize his army, he and
his escort rode over a hundred miles in two days. During the journey, an astounding message arrived from Daniel. Cornwallis had burned all his baggage

and was pressing the rain swollen Catawba. Once the river fell, Cornwallis would be able to cross the fords. Daniel wrote that he would not be able to oppose the enemy's stronger force. Nathanael arrived at Daniel's camp on January 31 exhausted, hungry, and splattered with mud. He found Daniel in bad shape, suffering from hemorrhoids and stiff with rheumatism.

"Are you able to continue?" Nathanael asked with grave concern.

"Nothing in my power shall be left undone," Daniel grunted although he was in bed with sciatica. "General William Davidson arrived with 800 North Carolina militia and is down at Beattie's Ford, but the Virginia militia's time has expired, and they are going home."

"I sent their general, Edward Stevens, to take your prisoners to Virginia," Nathanael said. "I am astonished and mortified that they would desert the army at their hour of need."

Daniel winced, shifted in his bed, and said, "Then, I suggest you send an appeal to him. I am certain he will be just as mortified."

"Any plans I had for striking the fort at Ninety-Six to draw Cornwallis' attention are now ruined," Nathanael said. His countenance revealed none of the stress Daniel expected.

The Old Wagoner chuckled and then said, "Your satisfaction over the situation with Cornwallis and his baggage shines on your face. I am much glad to see this part of you instead of the man who is constantly strained to his limit."

Nathanael exhaled a laugh. "I believe he has made a great blunder, and he is ours. So, one glimpse of gratification and you believe I am not strained?" He looked around the tent. "Like Cornwallis, do we have no rum?"

"No, there has been none since before we crossed the Broad River."

"Then you must get up without it." Nathanael's blue eyes reflected a memory. "I once told Alexander Hamilton that I call no war councils, and I communicate my intentions to very few. Today is not that day. We are to hold a war council at Beattie's Ford. Is Colonel John Eager Howard here?"

"No, I sent him to Salisbury as requested with the rest of the Continentals."

"Then it will be you and I, General Davidson, and William Washington."

"Very well," Daniel said. He grunted as he rose from his bed. "I will send Captain Joseph Graham to inform them."

An hour later, under a light rain, the four officers met and sat on logs. Mosquitos buzzed. They were the scourge of the South no matter the time of year. Nathanael slapped at one on his cheek and said, "I had hoped the victory at Cowpens would have inspired local militia to turn out because a confrontation with Cornwallis is nearing. I found it deplorable when I rode through this countryside that was not the case."

"They may never come," William Davidson warned. "They fear leaving their families to the mercy of the Tories."

"I say we retreat into the mountains," Daniel declared.

"We will not," Nathanael said.

"Then, I shall not be answerable for what happens if you try to retreat through North Carolina," Daniel grumbled.

"No you will not," Nathanael said. "I shall take the measure upon myself. What is pressing us at this moment is how to stop Cornwallis' crossing of the Catawba and a subsequent onslaught. The east bank of the river obviously cannot be held. General Davidson, you have a reputation for quick escapes."

Nathanael paused. He scratched out a plan on the wet riverbank with a stick and continued to instruct William Davidson, "I want you to conduct a delaying action at Cowan's Ford to give General Morgan, Colonel Washington, and their Continentals time to head for Salisbury and the Yadkin River where they will link up with the main army marching north under General Huger. I think it probable that Cornwallis may throw cavalry across the river at night."

"I will have patrols best acquainted with this country pass up and down the river all night," Davidson assured.

Nathanael nodded his approval. "I am going to stay behind in hope of recruiting new militia forces and assist General Davidson's retreat, if needed. Once united at Salisbury, we will turn north for Virginia where we have stores and hope for reinforcements."

Clopping on the west bank of the river drew the four officers' attention. "We have visitors," William Washington observed with a smirk. "It appears a detachment of British cavalry have come to stare at us. Their green coats and black boots are as sodden with mud and rain as we are."

With no hope of crossing the river in its flooded state, the British cavalrymen spurred their horses and rode up and down the bank in frustration. Through their spyglasses they could see the Patriots sitting on the log out of musket range.

Their angry voices floated across the river. "We can see you, Washington! And we recognize Morgan," one shouted. "You are all a bunch of rabble and scoundrels."

Another reined his horse and aimed his carbine at the distant Americans. "If that is General Greene with you, I say now he is dead!" He fired the short rifle and only managed to engulf himself in powder smoke.

"Are we clear on our plans?" Nathanael asked, undeterred by the threats and gunshots.

"We are clear," Daniel said.

છ

Rain ticked against Nathanael's canvas tent. He was weary beyond words, still he battled on as he always did. With Morgan's army gone and Davidson's men guarding the fords down river, he wrote orders to his scattered forces that all stores were to be sent beyond Salisbury to Guilford Courthouse. General Isaac Huger was to impress all horses and wagons needed to get the stores out of reach of the British and move toward North Carolina. He added one last pedantic thought, "It is necessary we should take every possible precaution to guard against misfortune."

He left the candle burning, wrapped his damp blanket around his shoulders, and laid his head down. In the quietness of the night, he pictured Caty's beautiful face and snapping dark eyes and heard her ringing laughter. He had shamed her for drinking too much wine and for dancing until all hours of the night. Now, all he wanted to do was sit in front of a fire and drink that wine with her, tell her jokes, and watch her eyes light up with amusement. He wanted to play games with his children and have them crawl into his lap before he tucked them into bed. He coughed until sleep quieted his mind and heart.

It seemed that he had just drifted off when he was jerked awake by the sound of musket fire to the south. He threw off his blanket and limped outside. The sun was still below the horizon, but there was no mistaking the noise. Cornwallis was crossing the Catawba River.

At 1:00 a.m., Cornwallis assembled his men for an attack. Nathanael had no way of knowing, standing there in the rain with his sleepy but alert aides beside him, that Cornwallis had ordered a division under Colonel James Webster to make a feint at Beattie's Ford while Cornwallis with the Brigade of Guards and guides personally led the rest in smashing across the breast high waters of the Catawba at Cowan's Ford.

For the first half of the way, they had only the darkness and the swift current to contend against. But as the head of the column reached the middle of the stream, the light from fires on the other shore shined on them. An American sentinel shot at the British, which alerted the pickets. Musket balls peppered the river. Men began to fall. Horses reared and lost their footing.

"Onward, men," General Alexander Leslie encouraged before he realized that he, his horse, and some of his brigade were drifting downstream with the current.

General Charles O'Hara's horse rolled over on him in midstream. Both emerged shaken but able to go on. With luck, the civilian guides fled under the pickets' gunfire, leaving the British to struggle straight across the river instead of to the regular landing where militia General William Davidson was posted with 300 North Carolina men. Charles Cornwallis was not immune to the picket assault. His horse was shot, but he made it to the shore before it died.

Just as the head of the British column stepped on the opposite bank, the militia was upon them and managed to kill or wound fifty men. The Americans were between their watch fires and the British, making them a sure target, and they gave way. General Davidson sprang to his horse to conduct their retreat. He was shot and died instantly from a musket ball to his chest. His confused and frightened militiamen dispersed. Of the 800 with him the day before, only 300 managed to escape under arms, and they clogged the road to Salisbury.

Lewis got about his senses and tried not to panic. "General Greene, you need to leave now before Lord Cornwallis sends a detachment after you. He knows you are here!"

"Yes," Nathanael agreed. "I want you and Ichabod to ride as hard as you can for Salisbury. I need to make a stop first."

Shaken from the morning's events but not deterred, Ichabod asked, "What for?"

"Do you remember that militia recruiting flyer we left at the crossroads at Torrence's Tavern?"

"Yes, the one you personally wrote."

"I asked those who would join to meet me at David Carr's farm sixteen miles east of the Catawba on the road to Salisbury," Nathanael said.

"You cannot go alone," Lewis protested.

"The guard will go with me," Nathanael assured him. "I want you both up the road toward Salisbury to alert those you can that Cornwallis has crossed the river."

With his aides on the way to Salisbury, Nathanael and his small guard of dragoons galloped toward Carr's farm. Behind him, 300 of General Davidson's fleeing militia drew up at Torrence's Tavern. Behind them, Banastre Tarleton's legion gave chase. The attack on the tavern diffused such a terror among civilians and militia that they fled into the countryside.

Banastre arrived at the tavern the next day. He rifled through the bloody clothes of dozens of militiamen killed at the hands of his legion. "What do we have here?" Banastre said to himself as he extracted a recruiting poster from one of the dead men. He unfolded the paper and read the somewhat threatening and enticing words Nathanael had written.

Let me conjure you, my countrymen, to fly to arms and repair to Head Quarters without loss of time and bring with you ten days provision. You have everything that is dear and valuable at stake; if you will not face the approaching danger your Country is inevitably lost. On the contrary, if you repair to arms and confine yourselves to the duties of the field Lord Cornwallis must certainly be ruined. The Continental Army is marching with all possible dispatch from Peedee to this place. But without your aide their arrival will be of no consequence.

Banastre looked to one of his captains and said with a laugh, "We have discovered General Greene's solicitude for assembling militia. I believe we may have cleared the way for the King's troops to pass through this hostile part of North Carolina without a shot from the militia."

"And now we know where General Greene has gotten off to."

"We have no orders to pursue him," Banastre scoffed. "However, finding and capturing him would be a prize that would garner the highest laurels of praise."

Banastre called in his cavalry, and they returned to Lord Cornwallis' lines with intelligence on Nathanael's whereabouts. Cornwallis read the poster. "Any effort to apprehend Greene will be futile," he grumbled. "He is six miles away and it is pouring rain. We will have to slog through muddy roads, and surely he is not alone."

"If you will let me, sir, I will take my legion—"

"No, Banastre, you will stay with the main army. We know where Greene's army is going, and once we are certain all our forces are across the Catawba, we will deploy."

"Have I lost your confidence, my Lord?" Banastre asked.

"You have forfeited no part of my esteem as an officer by the unfortunate event at Cowpens," Cornwallis said. He regarded the young fierce cavalry colonel for a moment and then said, "I have heard the grumblings that I put a boy in charge of a legion when a man should have done the job. Your disposition was unexceptionable. The total misbehavior of the troops could alone have deprived you of the glory which was so justly your due."

Nathanael sat in the small kitchen at Carr's farm and wrote to Baron von Steuben, commanding the Continental forces in Virginia. With contempt for men who were available but would not serve he bemoaned, "O that we had in the fields, as Henry V said, some few of the many thousands who are idle at home."

His frustrations aired for the moment, he opened his book of poetry by Horace to calm his racing mind. Rain pounded the windows in a staccato, and little rivers ran down the dark windows. Like a mother's heartbeat, the rain drowsed him, and he laid his head on the table.

A hand on his shoulder shook him awake. "General Greene, a message has arrived."

Nathanael raised his exhausted head and saw the man rousing him was one of his dragoon guards, Captain Frederick Hughes. "I am listening," he responded in a weary voice.

"General Cornwallis has succeeded in getting his entire army across the Catawba River. News has arrived of Colonel Banastre Tarleton. His legion murdered many of the militiamen who you are awaiting a response from at Torrence's Tavern. They will never come now. We must leave in haste, sir."

Nathanael glanced at the pendulum clock on the wall. It was after midnight. Rain still beat the window and wind rustled the panes. He pocketed his pistol and sheathed his sword before leaving his respects for his host. His rested and fed horse was with the dragoons' horses in the barn.

The four mounted up and galloped the muddy road toward Salisbury. When the sun peeked over the horizon, the dragoons dispersed to watch for enemy scouts who may have pursued their general. Nathanael stopped for breakfast at Steele's Tavern. An acquaintance, Dr. William Read, who had treated Daniel Morgan at Sherrald's Ford, saw him enter dripping wet and shivering.

"What, alone, General?" Dr. William Read asked.

"Yes, tired, hungry, alone, and penniless," Nathanael lamented.

"Sit with me," William offered.

"Thank you," Nathanael said. He pulled out a chair and wiped the rainwater from his face with one hand.

The tavern owner, Elizabeth Steele, overheard them. She knew by the drooping epaulets on his broad shoulders and his torn blue coat with the soiled buff facings that General Nathanael Greene had just entered her establishment. She stole away then crept back into the room and approached the table. Two bags of silver coins were in her hands. She offered them to Nathanael. "Take these, for you need them, and I can do without them."

Nathanael stared at Mrs. Steele. In this place where Tories and Patriots fought one another sometimes within families, where the militia was difficult, and civil and public matters had decayed, a smiling, sympathetic woman was offering all the coin she possessed. Nathanael wiped a tear that had trailed down his chapped cheek. He stood and bowed. "I am forever in your debt, madam," he said gallantly. "Our army is desperate, but you know that."

"I will bring you some breakfast," Elizabeth said and disappeared into the kitchen.

Nathanael set the bags of coin on the table. A painting hanging over the fireplace caught his attention. It was King George III. Nathanael took it down, and with a piece of charcoal he scrawled on the back, "George, hide thy face and mourn." He hanged the painting backward.

Nathanael reached Salisbury on the Yadkin River with Cornwallis' army on his heels. Starving British and Hessian soldiers left a path of plunder and destruction across the countryside. The detail that had marked Nathanael's service as a quartermaster served him well in the field. He ordered his quartermaster, Colonel Edward Carrington, to have boats ready to bring not only all his troops and stores over the river but countless frightened civilians as well. On February 3, Nathanael's army began crossing the Yadkin River.

The ailing Daniel Morgan spent most of the day employing them. With the river rising, William's cavalry and their horses were able to swim across the river. The boats transported infantry, baggage, and the Continental stores. By that evening, all were across.

When Cornwallis' vanguard led by General Charles O'Hara arrived, a small number of Patriot riflemen volleyed and then disappeared across the river. Lord Cornwallis was incensed. He was left staring across the river at another American camp he could not reach.

"General O'Hara, order an artillery bombardment," Cornwallis commanded with as much composure as he could muster.

"The rebels are encamped behind a ridge, my Lord," O'Hara pointed out.

Cornwallis glared, which emphasized both his lazy eye and his demand. O'Hara ordered the bombardment, and a thunderous fire commenced. Balls lobbed harmlessly across the Yadkin to the amusement of Patriots.

"That will do nothing but anger the farmer who owns this land," Elias Poole, a teenaged militiaman from North Carolina, declared to his fellow, Martin Cunningham, as they huddled by a small fire and puffed clay pipes from which smoke drifted in the misty air.

"Perhaps his lordship can swim the river," Martin snickered.

"Look," Elias exclaimed and pointed, "they are aiming at the roof of General Greene's headquarters! See the shingles and boards flying?"

Martin stood up. The house was indeed the general's headquarters. Inside, Nathanael kept writing dispatches.

Dr. William Read, who rode to camp with Nathanael from Steele's Tavern, looked up at the roof nervously. "Does this not alarm you, General?"

"I have heard it before. What flows from my pen is more important."

"And what is flowing from your pen?"

"There are 1,700 muskets stored here for the militia. All the guns are in miserable condition. Where are the men for whom the guns are kept?" he asked rhetorically. "We cannot stay in this place. Cornwallis will eventually ford the Yadkin as he did the Catawba. General Morgan is in bad condition. General Huger is not yet here with the main army. I am writing to tell him to join us at Guilford Courthouse sixty miles northeast of this place where we might yet be able to make a stand."

"In that case, perhaps I should check on General Morgan's condition," Dr. Read offered. "Last I saw of him, he was very sick—rheumatic from head to feet. I advised him to retire to some place of safety and warm quarters. He told me that he did not know where that was."

"I suggest you find it and tend to him."

Another cannon ball whistled and struck the house. Dr. Read cringed and dashed outside. Major Ichabod Burnet arrived wet and tired from his ride to Salisbury. "You summoned me, General Greene?"

"I am coordinating militia operations between General Sumter, Pickens, and Marion against the enemy in South Carolina and messages to militia commanders near here to gather stores from points of collection at Salisbury. They are to be shipped across the Dan River at the border of Virginia and North Carolina."

Nathanael handed Ichabod the letter and said, "You are to deliver this to Colonel Harry Lee who has been to the southward with General Marion. Colonel Washington's cavalry is reduced to sixty men, and I want Lee's legion with me." A vague smirk crossed his lips. "Tell him if he does not come immediately, he will lose the opportunity of acquiring wreaths of laurels."

☙

On February 1, 1781, a distressing letter arrived from Isaac Huger. Nathanael had tasked his engineer Colonel Thaddeus Kosciuszko to begin construction of boats for use on the Yadkin/Pee Dee River in North Carolina. Isaac wrote that Kosciuszko was missing. Nathanael replied:

> *I hope Col. Kosciuszko has not fallen into the enemies hands,*
> *which I much apprehend, if he set out to join me.*

Cornwallis was determined to catch his prey. He arrived in Salisbury where he paused for three days although he was aware of Nathanael's spies and the time lost in pursuit of the Americans. His starving army had discovered and devoured a small herd of cattle found near the Yadkin Ford. Flour was the fruit of a foraging party dispatched earlier that day. On February 4, he received intelligence that Daniel Morgan was at the Trading Ford upriver on the Yadkin and had not crossed.

Cornwallis sent Charles O'Hara to determine if that was the case, only to find the information was false. "We are plagued with this type of unreliable information," Cornwallis complained to his officers when O'Hara returned. He sent for Banastre Tarleton.

"You summoned me your Lordship?" Banastre asked Cornwallis.

"I did. I want you to take your cavalry supported by the 23rd Regiment and reconnoiter north to scout the Yadkin's upper fords as I am anxious to get my army across," Cornwallis ordered.

The thought that the other officers present may be judging him for his loss at Cowpens never entered Banastre's vain mind when he swept out of headquarters. Cornwallis had forgiven him, and that was enough. He did his duty and reported back that he found no obstacles to impede the course of the main army to the upper fords and no probability of opposition in the crossing of the Yadkin at Shallow Ford.

On February 8, Cornwallis and his army crossed, having marched forty miles from Salisbury in forty-eight hours through the muck of red clay roads. Their crossing did not go unnoticed. A militia party witnessed it at the first cockcrowing when not a human being was to be seen.

twenty-four

The Retreat to the Dan

Nathanael veered away from the army again with just a contingent of light infantry. His spies detected Lord Cornwallis' movements, but Nathanael was watching his adversary from a position in the forks of Abbott's Creek. He wrote to General Washington about his decision to change his army's place of junction from Salisbury to Guilford Courthouse. "Heavy rains, deep creeks, bad roads, poor horses and broken harnesses, as well as delays for want of provisions prevented it."

While Cornwallis camped at Lindseys Plantation three miles from the Yadkin River, Nathanael and his infantry guards moved on to Guilford Courthouse. The small community was the seat of Guilford County, North Carolina. The simple courthouse was part of a tiny cluster of buildings, including the homes of a population of fewer than two hundred, which surrounded a jail and a coppersmith shop. It was also a hotbed of Patriot activity and a settlement of Quakers—the same denomination in which Nathanael had been born and left for good in 1777. Isaac Huger was there, as were Daniel Morgan and Otho Williams encamped in the woods. Nathanael was relieved to be reunited with his army.

"Otho, it is always good to see your cheerful face," Nathanael said as the colonel handed him a flask of rum.

"There is someone else whose face you will be happy to see," Isaac said to Nathanael. "He is a bit exhausted, so come with me."

Nathanael followed Isaac through the smoky camp. With each step men stood and murmured, "General Greene," with enthusiasm and bowed to their commander. Nathanael was shocked at their condition. Indeed, all the men under Daniel were worn out from weeks of marching through muddy roads in a steady retreat from Cornwallis' army. Isaac's men's shoes were worn through from marching more than a hundred miles from their camp at Cheraw on the Pee Dee River.

Isaac approached a wedge tent and poked his head inside then stepped back. Colonel Thaddeus Kosciuszko emerged. His boots were broken and his clothes were dirty, but he acknowledged his general with verve by clapping his hands to Nathanael's broad shoulders.

"What happened to you?" Nathanael asked his tall Polish engineer who Isaac had reported missing days before.

"The countryside is quite treacherous, as you know. My little group encountered men who were armed but not in uniform. When they approached us, they would not say one way or another," Thaddeus said. "We were nearly drowned by rains. If there had not been some hospitable inhabitants along our journey from Rocky River, we surely would have starved or fallen ill."

"Where are the bateaux you were responsible for building?" Nathanael asked.

"Where you requested I build them at the Dan River on the lower fords," Thaddeus replied. "I have scouted the fords, and the boats are not left unattended. There is a small guard there to ensure my efforts are not spirited away."

"Good," Nathanael said. A smile lit up his lambent blue eyes.

"There is also news of Colonel Harry Lee and his legion," Isaac informed Nathanael. "They are in the vicinity and approaching camp from their location at Bell's Mill. Daniel has asked to see you on your arrival. His condition is worse."

"Daniel?" Nathanael asked as he ducked into the Old Wagoner's tent.

"Please to beg if I do not rise," Daniel said from where he lay on a damp blanket on the ground. "I am in terrible pain and discomfort."

Nathanael squatted beside him and asked, "What do you want me to do?"

"There is nothing you can do but let me go home. I feel myself quite unable to encounter the hardships and fatigues which must necessarily follow."

"I need you. We may be making a stand against Cornwallis here. I am going to take an account of this army and then decide what is prudent. I require your active service if we are to meet Cornwallis at this place."

Daniel chuckled despite the sciatica that was burning his legs. "You are always the general first, and I respect that. But I must ask, why do you want to challenge him here?"

"I must contemplate my options. I am going to send expresses out in all directions with urgent appeals to the officers of the militia to join us here. While waiting for them to respond, I shall make a study of this ground," Nathanael explained.

Nathanael was again bitterly disappointed. The militia could not be prevailed on to come out. Those already present at Guilford Courthouse were edgy, mostly remnants from Andrew Pickens' division at Cowpens. Baron von Steuben could not collect and send recruits from Virginia because the traitorous General Benedict Arnold was unleashing hell on Virginia and demanding that Governor Thomas Jefferson move Richmond's tobacco stores and military arms to his ships. If Jefferson did so, he would leave Richmond unharmed. Jefferson lividly refused, declaring that he would not have a turncoat do anything to Richmond's supplies. Arnold was enraged.

British troops started a rampage across the city, ransacking its valuables and supplies, burning government buildings as well as private homes. Arnold led his forces outside of Richmond and began another spree of violence and then marched to Portsmouth for winter quarters. Nathanael wondered, *What is there from preventing Arnold from linking up with Cornwallis and crushing my army between them? To stand and fight Cornwallis at Guilford Courthouse is probably madness.*

He worried about how the Whigs and Tories would react if he abandoned North Carolina and stepped closer to Virginia, where he had a chance to resupply regardless of the turmoil in that state. He employed every ounce of solitary rational thinking to come to a conclusion that would benefit North Carolina, its inhabitants, government, and the American cause. Some good news followed. General Thomas Sumter had recovered from the wound he received at Blackstock's and was ready to take the field. Nathanael wrote flattering letters to the defiant militia general and urged Sumter to rouse the people of South Carolina for military operations in Cornwallis' rear.

While South Carolina Governor John Rutledge—the only authority Sumter acknowledged—tried to patch up the rift between General Francis Marion and Sumter over command in South Carolina, Nathanael enticed Marion to cross the Santee River. Andrew Pickens, now a general for his performance at Cowpens, agreed to assist Marion. The approbations worked, and Sumter and Marion united to attack smaller British outposts in South Carolina.

Although Nathanael did his best thinking under pressure, he was relieved to see an officer ride into Guilford Courthouse with wagons creaking behind him. Many of the troops in camp got to their bare feet and swamped the wagons. Nathanael left his tent to greet his returning quartermaster, Colonel Edward Carrington. "Edward, at last you have arrived. What have you brought us?" he asked.

"Six hundred shirts and three hundred pairs of shoes as well as nails, axes, and camp kettles—items you requested in January," Edward said with the look of a young warrior who had just brought home the spoils of war to his king. "The boats you had me procure are at your disposal on the fords of the Dan River if you should need them, but I lost sight of Colonel Kosciuszko."

"He is here safe." Nathanael frowned. "And of Colonel William Davie? Have you a word?"

"Davie is to follow. Per your request, he went to Halifax and was appointed by the Board of War as Commissary General for the state of North Carolina for your troops and North Carolina's militia."

Nathanael breathed a mental sigh of relief. "Then someone has been listening to my pleas."

"Yes, sir, they have," Edward replied.

"At least now I will be allayed of my burden of acting as a quartermaster again, although there is not a dollar in the military chest," Nathanael said. A commotion rose from the men crowding the supply wagons. The conversation between Nathanael and Edward drifted toward the noise. The Continentals and militia stopped rummaging through the supplies and were staring.

"Give me them shoes," a grizzled North Carolina militiaman of the 2nd Battalion of Volunteers shouted at a young boy in his regiment. He grabbed the heels, and the two began a tug of war.

"They ain't gonna fit you, old man," the boy said as he tightened his grip on the vamps.

"I'll whip you, boy, if you do not let go," the man threatened.

"Your feet are big as hell," the boy spat.

Their colonel, Francis Locke, approached. "Joshua, Ishmael, stop this!" he ordered.

Joshua released the shoes. Ishmael whapped the boy upside the head with one of the heels.

"Who is in charge of doling out these supplies?" Colonel Locke insisted. "Is it you, Carrington? Because if it is, you are standing around doing nothing, and you need to get over here."

Nathanael and Edward exchanged amused glances. Edward strode to the wagons and ordered, "Everyone move away."

The ragged, barefoot soldiers were reluctant to take the order, but they did.

Edward turned his attention to Ishmael. "Show me that those shoes fit you and you can keep them, old man."

Ishmael regarded Nathanael's reproachful countenance and said, "I did not mean to cause trouble, General Greene." His eyes drifted to his fellow soldiers. "You earned our respect. We know your judgment is sound and your energy abounds and influences us, too. We know that you ain't never gonna back down to the enemy unlike that Gates fellow, running off like he seen a ghost and—"

"That is quite enough, Ishmael," Colonel Locke warned.

Satisfied that Edward and Francis had the issuance of the commissary items under control, Nathanael returned to his tent. He was followed by the painful admission that the clothing delivery would not dress all the men in his shoeless and naked little army. Cornwallis had burned his baggage. *Are his troops as barefoot and threadbare as my army? It is possible but not probable,* he thought. Nathanael paused at the flap of his marquee tent and looked at the surrounding terrain. It was time to make a decision—stand and fight Cornwallis or retreat.

As always, he was conscious of political ramifications and his reputation—of rumors and slanders whispered in Philadelphia. The idea that some of his old enemies in Congress such as Thomas Mifflin and John Adams might accuse him of torpidity or cowardice was more than he could stomach. It compelled him to break his own rule for the second time since taking command of the Southern Army. He called a war council.

Isaac, Otho, and Daniel gathered on logs in their camp in the woods under a cool cloudy sky. Chickadees and sparrows chirped in pine and hickory trees unaware of the human anxiety below. Nathanael sat down and laid it out for his council of war, "We have 1,426 infantry, many of whom are badly armed and distressed for the want of clothing, plus 600 militiamen. Cornwallis is less than twenty miles away with 3,000, mostly regulars, all of them clothed, shod, and armed with the best musketry." He paused, coughed, and tried not to rub his irritated right eye. He continued, "The question being put is whether we ought to risk an action with the enemy or not."

Isaac spoke up, "I think we should avoid a general action at all events and that the army ought to retreat immediately."

"I am in agreement," Daniel said.

Otho nodded approval and asked Nathanael, "What are you contemplating?"

"If we can put the wide Dan River between our troops and Cornwallis', then we can buy time to recruit men and supplies from Virginia. But retreating is nearly as risky as fighting. The Dan is some seventy miles to the north in Virginia, and that is a long march for our weary men. The roads are hard red clay, but our horses' hooves and wagon wheels will transform them into mucky mire."

Isaac looked undaunted. "The enemy will suffer the same roads if we are pursued."

As former adjutant general to the Southern Army under General Gates, Otho's mind raced to the loss of their baggage and equipment when Cornwallis defeated them at Camden. "We must send off our heavy baggage," he warned.

"I have asked Colonel Carrington to arrange to have it sent to safety in anticipation of a retreat," Nathanael said.

"If we get caught before crossing the river?" Daniel asked as he shifted uncomfortably.

"We stand ten chances to one of getting defeated, and if defeated, all the Southern states must fall," Nathanael said grimly. It was not a chance he or his officers were willing to take. Through the intelligence of his spies and his own evaluation at Abbott's Creek, Nathanael knew that the retreat he contemplated was not concealed from Cornwallis' spies.

If Nathanael had sent spies to ascertain Cornwallis' conversations with his generals, he would have learned what he already suspected. There was discord between Sir Henry Clinton in New York and Lord Cornwallis.

"Reports have arrived that Greene is moving stores into Virginia in preparation to cross the Dan River," Cornwallis told his officers. "My intelligence tells me he intends on crossing at the upper fords. We cannot allow this without a pursuit."

"Do you believe that Sir Clinton will approve of this fruitless chase? I do not believe he wants us to relinquish South Carolina," General O'Hara challenged. "We are being drawn further and further from our supply depots near Camden."

"What Clinton approves of is not of concern at this moment. He is not here to contend with the challenges of the effects of the defeat at Cowpens and losing our baggage, albeit under my hand," Cornwallis retorted. "Every step we take, we are pursued and foiled, yet we cannot fathom retreating. I will do everything to force Greene to fight."

"Then we must make every effort to get between Greene and the Dan River. If he makes it across, the Carolinas are not safe. He will return rested and in force," Colonel James Webster interjected.

Cornwallis nodded grimly at the advice of his thirty-eight-year-old longtime colonel, a trusted relationship that went back as far as 1766.

"And perhaps we should make an effort to replenish the rum," O'Hara suggested. "I am certain the army would be of utmost appreciation. Do you agree Alexander?"

"To the utmost," General Alexander Leslie said.

Charles ignored O'Hara and Leslie and went on, "I suppose I need to write to Lord North about what we are facing here."

"Do you not mean Clinton?" Alexander corrected.

"Clinton's focus is still on the importance of New York, like that damned fool Washington. The two of them can dance around each other for all I care. Furthermore," Cornwallis said, "Clinton attributes my rapid movement through the South to naked ambition and an attempt to supplant him as commander-in-chief. Because I have allowed no distinction in the treatment of the officers and men and have shared this army's privations, which includes no use of a tent, Clinton wrote mockingly that I have been reduced to behaving like a barbaric Tartar."

O'Hara frowned and thought, *if Cornwallis is behaving like a barbarian then what does that say about my own behavior?* He said, "The violence of the passions of these people in the South are beyond every curb of religion and humanity. To make things worse, we are slowed by prisoners of war and camp followers."

"I agree," Cornwallis conceded with a flick of his hand. "Efforts to recruit Loyalist provincial forces are failed in the Carolinas. The people here are unbounded, and every hour exhibit dreadful, wanton mischiefs, murders, and unheard of violence of every kind. We are unable to distinguish friend from foe because neither side is wearing a uniform."

O'Hara rubbed his chin and asked, "You are married, are you not?"

Charles raised an eyebrow. "You know very well my wife, Jemima, died in April 1779, leaving my two children, Mary and Charles, motherless. Her death effectually destroyed all my hopes of happiness in this world. Why would you ask me such a painful question?"

"Because I want you to think of Nathanael Greene as your wife," O'Hara said. "What is he doing and how is he going to do it?"

Cornwallis contemplated O'Hara for a moment and without hesitation said, "We know his army is fatigued and that militia recruiting is not going as he had hoped. I believe that Greene will avoid an action on this ground. Of this I am certain. It being my business to force him to fight, I will make great expedition to get between him and the fords of the Dan."

Nathanael told the war council that the first move in the retreat to the Dan was to detach 700 of his best men, form a light corps, and march them closer to Cornwallis to protect his own flanks. "The light corps is to detract Cornwallis and angle off toward the shallow crossing at Dix's Ferry to distract the British from the real point of crossing at Boyd's Ferry where boats await us. Daniel, I want you to lead these men."

"I cannot lead the detachment," Daniel grieved. "I am so sore from my rheumatism and piles that I cannot mount a horse. I desire for leave to retire until sufficiently recovered to return to duty."

Nathanael put an index finger to his lips in contemplation. He needed Daniel at this crucial juncture, and if he refused, he would seem unsympathetic. But he and his men were all suffering in their own ways. There were the constant sleepless nights when Nathanael's asthma was so bad he could not close his eyes. His ever-present companion—responsibility—lurked when sleep tried to send consolation. At last he said to Daniel, "I trust you to operate independently at a great distance from me and close to the enemy. I cannot lose you."

Otho and Isaac said nothing. This significant moment was between the generals who held their utmost respect.

Daniel's rugged thinning countenance reflected his pain and the embarrassment of admitting in front of Otho and Isaac that one of his ailments was hemorrhoids. "This is the first time I have ever experienced this disorder. From the idea I had of it, I sincerely prayed that I might never know what it was."

"No," Nathanael said with a dwindling empathy he did not mean in his heart. "I will not grant you a furlough. Cornwallis is upon us. Tarleton is upon us. Our retreat will begin tomorrow after I make final arrangements for our disposition, which I will announce in my orders of the day."

The war council broke up. Nathanael watched Daniel make his arduous way back to his tent. Major Lewis Morris, Nathanael's aide who was at the council recording the proceedings, said, "General Greene, I think you should let General Morgan go home. Can we look at him and feel confident that he is at his best at this crucial hour?"

Nathanael stubbornly held on to his conviction. "Great generals are scarce. There are few Morgans to be found."

Otho's handsome countenance blemished with disapproval that shamed Nathanael into rethinking his opinion.

On that day, Nathanael paused to write to Washington encamped at New Windsor, New York. Never had the separation between North and South loomed so large. He explained Cornwallis' pursuit, General Davidson's death, that his army was reunited, the disposition of the militia, and the composition of his light corps. "We have no provisions but what we receive from our daily collections. Under these circumstances, I called a council who unanimously advised to avoid an action and to retire beyond the Dan River immediately. I have enclosed a copy of the proceedings. General Morgan is so unwell that he has left the Army."

February 10 dawned cold and rainy. In his orders of the day, Nathanael announced who was assigned to the new light corps. Two-hundred forty cavalrymen from Colonel William Washington's 1st and 3rd regiments were detached under Colonel Harry Lee's command along with his own cavalry. Its infantry was composed of 120 infantry from Lee's Legion and Continentals from Maryland, Delaware, and Virginia that totaled 280 men under Colonel John Eager Howard and sixty Virginia riflemen.

"This detachment," Nathanael said, "will fall under Colonel Williams' command. General Morgan has been granted leave to go home."

After short preparations, Daniel was helped into a carriage. There was silence while the Old Wagoner and his small entourage disappeared through the woods as the trees enveloped them in their arms. Nathanael separated his army again. Nathanael and Isaac marched off to the northeast toward Boyd's and Irwin's Ferries on the lower fords of the Dan River. Otho led his screening force northwest toward the British to distract the enemy and shield the main army's retreat.

The race to the Dan River was on.

Otho's light corps was to keep between Lord Charles Cornwallis' much larger force and Nathanael to protect the main American Army from being detected and attacked and to avoid heavy combat. Otho inclined to his left and came out on an intermediate road with the main army to his right and Cornwallis to his left. With Cornwallis camped only twenty-five miles away near Salem, there was immediate contact between Otho's detachment and elements of Cornwallis' advance guard led by Charles O'Hara. It was an extremely demanding assignment that required speed, constant alertness, and rapid response.

On Sunday, February 11, with the British less than eight miles to his back, Otho detached Harry and several dragoons with orders to meet the advancing enemy while the main army crossed over the Haw River. Nathanael received an almost breathless letter from Otho:

Accident informed the Enemy were within six or eight miles of my quarters. I detached Col Harry Lee with a Troop of Dragoons & put the rest of the Light Troops in motion to Cross the Haw River at a bridge. Col Lee met the Enemy's advance, stood a Charge and Captured 3 or 4 men whom I send to you. They say Lord Cornwallis & the whole British Army proceeded by Col Tarleton's Legion is close in our rear.

With Cornwallis pressing them hard, Otho's and Harry's legion dared not sleep without sentinels. The exhausted men slept fitfully without tents that would deter them if they were required to respond to an immediate threat from the enemy. The heat of campfires was the only protection against rain and sometimes snow. But they ate well with their breakfast of bacon and cornmeal— the only meal of the day—better than the main army riding with Nathanael on the retreat.

For the main army, the bounty gained from the land was less than plentiful. Days elapsed without the foraging party getting anything. Three men huddled against the frost at night sharing one blanket. Still, the miserable, shoeless troops continued their painful march toward the Dan River and the deep water crossing at Boyd's Ferry.

On February 13, a local farmer came into Otho's camp while the troops were eating breakfast. "I am looking for Colonel Williams," the farmer, Isaac Wright, said.

Otho stood. "I am Colonel Williams."

Harry approached to hear what the newcomer had to say.

"I was burning brushwood in my field, and I saw General Cornwallis' army. I think they are about four miles away. I thought you should know."

"Harry, verify this intelligence," Otho ordered his cavalryman. "Mr. Wright, you will cooperate with Colonel Lee."

"Aye," Wright acquiesced. He mounted a mangy horse and then led Harry's gathered dragoons out of camp toward the place he had seen the enemy. Wright's old horse had difficulty keeping up with the dragoons' fit horses.

Harry's quick eyes took in the surroundings. "I see nothing," he said. "Mr. Wright, I thank you for your observation, but…" Musket fire blasted Harry's words away. A contingent of the enemy came hurtling at his dragoons. There was no time to act when Captain David Miller killed Harry's bugler, James Gillies. Blind with rage, Harry and his dragoons were upon the enemy, their broadswords drawn and slashing, and slaughtered the contingent.

Amid all this carnage, Cornwallis marched by and onward, but not toward Otho. He had gained intelligence from an American prisoner, and the game was up. Otho put every effort to maneuver himself and his troops between Cornwallis and Nathanael. He tried to calculate the time and distance required for the main army to reach the safety of Virginia. Otho's fatigued men prayed that Cornwallis would rest his troops at night, but the British general was obsessed with stopping Greene.

It was on this day that Nathanael received another letter from Otho.

My Dear General, at Sun Down the Enemy were only 22 miles from you and may be in motion now or will be most probably by 3 O'Clock in the morning. Their intelligence is good. They moved with great rapidity. Rely on it, my Dear Sir, it is possible for you to be overtaken before you can cross the Dan even if you had 20 Boats. I shall use every precaution but cannot help being uneasy.

Nathanael replied:

It is very evident the enemy intends to push us in crossing the river. The night before last, as soon as I got your letter, I sent off the rest of the baggage and stores, with orders to cross as fast as they got to the river. I will endeavor to avoid Cornwallis. You have the flower of the army; don't expose the men too much, lest our situation should grow more critical.

There was more to lament. All but eighty North Carolina militiamen deserted along the march. Otho was experiencing the same problem, but his situation was dire. When the light corps saw fires burning nearby, they cautiously approached. Otho reined his stumbling, winded mount. His uniform coat was ripped and wet, and he had lost a spur and his hat.

Locals greeted him. "General Greene was here two nights ago," a woman said. "We promised him we would keep the fires burning in case you passed this way and needed a respite."

Otho bowed in the saddle and thanked the woman. The corps settled in to catch their breath, but with Cornwallis pressing, they did not have time to cook a meal. Harry joined them. He was as filthy as the rest of the detachment, something the vain, young, educated man abhorred. John Eager Howard arrived. John's boots had fallen apart, and he was as barefoot as his men.

"I do not know how long we can hold off the enemy," Otho said to his gathered officers.

Harry's eyes moved to the infantry, some of whom belonged to his Legion, and his heart rended for the brave and wearied troops. "At this juncture," he said, "I think we will be forced to turn and fight. I believe that our dauntless corps are convinced that the crisis has now arrived when self-sacrifice alone will give the main army a chance to escape."

"I need advice from Nathanael," Otho pointed out. "I can only see what is happening with the main army through his eyes." By midnight, the light corps was in motion again. Otho's wish was granted when a mounted, mud-spattered messenger arrived at 4:00 a.m. with a letter from Nathanael.

Follow our route, as a division of our force may encourage the enemy to push us further than they will dare to do if we are together. I have not slept four hours since you left me, so great has been my solicitude to prepare for the worst. I have great reason to believe that one of Tarleton's officers was in our camp night before last.

The frantic pace of Nathanael's march and the vigor of Otho's troops paid off. With General Charles O'Hara's vanguard pressing, Nathanael reached the swollen Dan River and Irwin's Ferry on February 14. Colonel Benjamin Ford instructed wagoners to begin the crossing in the small boats that waited on the banks of the river. It was slow at first, but once the wagons and horses were across, ferrying the 1,000 troops went quicker. At 2:00 p.m., Nathanael reported that the greater part of the wagons was over the Dan, and the troops were crossing.

Otho nearly broke down when he received another letter from his general that was written at 5:30 p.m.

> *All our troops are over, and the stage is clear. The infantry will cross here, the horse below. Major Hardman has posted his party in readiness on this side, and the infantry and artillery are posted on the other. I am ready to receive and give you a hearty welcome.*

Otho went to Harry and John with the message. The word swept through the 700-man force. Their cheers of relief echoed through the countryside. O'Hara's vanguard could hear the sounds of their celebration, and he knew what that meant.

"We have fourteen miles to cover to the Dan," Otho cautioned his officers and men.

"I will stay behind as the rear guard," Harry volunteered. "Someone has to watch the enemy and deter them." He called to his dragoons, and they wheeled their horses.

Otho and most of the screening force arrived at the Dan that evening to the chants of "Huzzah!" and hats sailing through the air. Nathanael went to greet him. Notwithstanding his poor health, Otho's feat demonstrated perseverance against all odds, not so different from the challenges Nathanael had to face with his own delicate health.

Around 9:00 p.m. under a waning gibbous moon, Harry and his

cavalry reached the banks of the river. The infantry crossed first and sent the boats back for the cavalry with their horses swimming beside them. Harry and quartermaster Colonel Edward Carrington reached the Virginia side last. Harry wrote: *Thus ended, on that night of the 14th of February, this long, arduous, and eventful retreat.*

⌒

On February 15, Cornwallis' footsore troops marched up to the banks of the Dan River where they saw the campfires of the American Army burning brightly on the other side. Nathanael had taken every boat in the Roanoke Valley across the river, and there was nothing Cornwallis could do but stare.

Charles could literally hear the enemy laughing at him from the other side of the river. He stomped his foot and said to Alexander Leslie and Charles O'Hara, "I will not take the bait. My force being ill-suited to enter so powerful a province as Virginia, and North Carolina being in the utmost confusion after giving the troops a halt of one day, I shall proceed by easy marches to Hillsboro."

"Greene has drawn us 240 miles away from our base of communication and supply at Camden, South Carolina," O'Hara said with disgust. "The hardships we have suffered are extreme. We need food. And we know that the King's Friends are fickle."

"We must raise their spirits in this state," Alexander declared with the jeers of the American soldiers ringing in his ears. "We have shown the superiority of our arms, and perhaps now their militia corps will join us."

"Let us retire but leave watch fires so they know of our presence," Cornwallis ordered his weary generals. He contemplated his vacillating Loyalist support. "I suppose a proclamation is in order. I shall erect the King's Standard and invite all loyal subjects to repair to it and to take an active part in assisting me to restore order and constitutional government."

While the British rested without tents or baggage and were forced to kill some of their draft horses for meat, Nathanael wrote to Washington, "Our Army is encamped at Halifax Courthouse in Virginia in order to tempt the Enemy to cross the Dan River. The most pleasing prospect presents itself of a strong reinforcement from the Militia of this State."

In contrast to Cornwallis, Nathanael and his troops were living relatively well. His men bathed their bloody feet in the river and built blazing fires by which to sleep in peace. They enjoyed abundant supplies of food in the rich and friendly county of Halifax where the people received them with the affection of brethren. But Nathanael's thoughts were on reentering North Carolina, and he had no time for exultation.

His quill scratched out a letter to Virginia Governor Thomas Jefferson. "We are on the Dan River almost fatigued to death, having had a retreat to conduct for upward of 200 miles, maneuvering constantly in the face of the enemy, to give time for the militia to turn out to get off our stores."

To Steuben in Virginia he reported, "We have been astonishingly successful in our late, great, and fatiguing retreat and have never lost in one instance anything in the least value."

When news reached the New Windsor encampment where George Washington's main army was encamped, he lauded Nathanael's strategy:

> *You may be assured that your retreat before Cornwallis is highly applauded by all ranks, and reflects much honor on your military abilities.*

As much as Nathanael's sensitivity to criticism needed to hear these words, he thought, *None of you have an idea of what the war here in the South entails.* Still, he was not ready to risk a battle.

"Otho, take two companies of Marylanders and go back across the Dan into North Carolina. Harry, your legion will also deploy. I have sent a message to Andrew Pickens that the two of you are to link up," Nathanael ordered. "You are to harass and annoy Cornwallis and screen our army. The militia is building in numbers. If we can get up with the enemy, I have no doubt of giving them a good account."

Nathanael resupplied, rested, and hoped for reinforcements. He intended to bring the entire army back into North Carolina and pursue the enemy. On February 23, Nathanael did just that. He knew that he and Cornwallis were destined to meet again and very soon.

Throughout late February and early March 1781, the two armies shadowed each other. During this time, Nathanael never took off his clothes, changed his shirt, or bathed. He was too aware that as he dogged Cornwallis' troops, they might attack him at any moment. He kept to himself, rising early, moving among the troops, and attending to strategy and logistics.

The troops knew of his vigilance. One morning in their camp on the Haw River, he had an encounter that he took as a compliment. He was passing by the tent of a snoring colonel from Virginia. Nathanael poked him and said, "Good heavens, Colonel, how can you sleep with the enemy so near?"

The colonel jerked awake and replied, "Why, General, I knew that you were awake."

Nathanael's army now consisted of 1,600 men. They moved to Boyd's Mill on the Reedy Fork River. Here, only three miles from Cornwallis' camp at Hillsboro, fatigue took its toll, and Nathanael was forced to remain in one place for several days. Major Lewis Morris arrived one morning from his assignment to deliver and fetch messages from the detachments. He had a new message from Harry.

"I cannot read it," Nathanael lamented, "I have a violent inflammation in my eyes."

"Have you called for our surgeon?" Lewis asked with alarm. His general's blue eyes were red and cloudy.

"Yes, I have called for him, and he has bled me, but the inflammation is still troublesome and painful. I have called for him again. Will you please go determine his delay?"

"Yes, sir." Lewis turned to do as he was bid.

"Wait. What is the message?" Nathanael asked.

"Colonel Lee writes that in pursuit of Colonel Banastre Tarleton's cavalry, a bloody encounter with Loyalist militia led by a John Pyles ensued.

General Pickens' men attacked them. The militia was marching to join Cornwallis. According to Colonel Lee's intelligence, Cornwallis' attempt to rally Loyalists in North Carolina has been succeeding under pronouncements that he drove us out of the state."

Americans killing Americans had long mortified Nathanael, but this time he kept it to himself. His mind whirled with plans to keep Cornwallis guessing while moving his army and then falling back to an established base. Otho, Harry, and Andrew were again screening the army and enduring skirmishes, raids, and ambushes that never ceased. It was a game of marches, countermarches, and maneuvers that were meant to baffle Cornwallis' skillful and enterprising mind.

Nathanael received a message from Otho explaining that he had to delay his march to wait for a delivery of cattle, as his men were out of provisions. Otho also warned him that Cornwallis' army had picked the countryside clean of forage and recommended a marching route.

That valuable information from his adjutant general led Nathanael to decide to move his army to camp on Troublesome Creek on the road to a familiar place—Guilford Courthouse. He summoned Ichabod and Lewis. "Take down my general orders of the day which you will both disseminate in the morning," he instructed. He dictated his plans but excluded the planned forays to confuse the enemy lest the orders reached British or Loyalist ears.

Nathanael heard the sweet sound of horse tack jingling, boots and shoes pounding the ground, drums beating, and men's voices floating on the cool breeze. He was nearly drawn to tears that would exacerbate his healing eye infection. Surrounded by his aides, officer, and soldiers, Nathanael went forward to greet the steady stream of arriving militia. General John Butler, with General Thomas Eaton, had two brigades of North Carolina militia that numbered 1,000 men.

"I wrote to you to complain of your militia deserting me as we retreated to the Dan River," Nathanael said to General Butler. "What changed your mind?"

"We misunderstood your strategy and assumed the enemy had pushed you out of North Carolina. We will never make that mistake again," John said with sincere approval.

In the next two days, several hundred Virginia militiamen came in under General Robert Lawson. Steuben sent 400 Continentals newly recruited from Maryland. Nathanael recalled Otho's invincible light forces. Nathanael reorganized his army and dissolved the light troops in favor of regular infantry in preparation for the inevitable battle ahead.

On March 12, the commander-in-chief of the Southern Army issued the general orders himself and with the veiled warning, "We have 2,000 new militia reinforcements, but militiamen soon get tired out with difficulties and go and come in such irregular bodies that I can make no calculations on the strength of this army. However, let us offer Cornwallis the battle he is so eagerly seeking."

Cornwallis was forced out of Hillsboro and fell back to Bell's Mill on the Deep River at a torrid pace with Colonel James Webster and Banastre Tarleton in the vanguard. With Otho, Harry, and Andrew buzzing around him like hornets, his foraging parties were harassed, and his outposts were not secure. If the British Army remained there, they would starve. Sometimes they had turnips, or if they came upon a cornfield, they used their canteens to grind the corn for bread. British and Hessians plundered both Tory and Patriot inhabitants at an alarming rate, and the camp followers were worse. The Tory militia whose turnout seemed to be promising went home. Desertions increased even among the prestigious Brigade of Guards.

Charles suffered with his soldiers. He was exasperated and issued orders, "It is with great concern that I hear every day reports of soldiers being taken by the enemy in consequence of their straggling out of camp in search of whiskey."

The army shivered under another rainy North Carolina winter day that prevented them from keeping their fires lit. Cornwallis was dictating a letter to his aide, Major Alexander Ross, for Clinton in New York. Colonel James Webster sat down among his other gathered general officers. "Your thoughts, your Lordship?" he inquired.

Charles glanced at Banastre Tarleton, Charles O'Hara, and Alexander Leslie before he said, "Our nearest point to resupply is 175 miles away in Wilmington. You know the hardships we suffer. Even our Hessians who are well disciplined and paid to fight are absconding. We must give courage to the Tories and swell our ranks with devoted patrons. Without a decided victory, we cannot hold this state." He rose and made eye contact with each officer. "The time is now to do battle with Nathanael Greene and his Southern Army."

At dawn on March 15, 1781, Charles Cornwallis marched toward Guilford Courthouse where Nathanael was waiting for him.

twenty-five

The Americans Fought Like Demons

At daybreak on March 14, the rebels enjoyed breakfast and then moved out of camp at Speedwell Iron Works and marched the road to Guilford Courthouse. Nathanael knew this land well, for he had studied it when his army had rendezvoused after the battle at Cowpens. The choice of position was wholly his decision. When the army arrived, there was still enough light to perform a second survey of the grounds. It lay in the middle of irregular cultivated fields interspersed with small clearings. The courthouse stood on a hill in one of the clearings. A gentle declivity formed an undulating slope nearly half a mile in length. Newly planted cornfields and swamps lay on both sides of the slope.

The American Army consisted of 4,243 foot and 160 horse. Fifteen hundred were Continentals, the rest militia. Nathanael immediately put his order of battle in place. It was a model of Daniel Morgan's at Cowpens.

The enemy would have to march up New Garden Road, a narrow road that led to Salisbury, but it led to a wide clearing where Nathanael deployed the first of three defensive lines. He positioned 1,000 North Carolina militia led by General John Butler on the edge of the woods behind a rail fence. They would have a good view of the British as they marched out of the woods and through muddy fields and across a small stream. Twelve hundred Virginia militiamen formed the second line. Virginia militia General Edward Stevens assigned forty riflemen to stand behind his Virginia regiment with orders to shoot down any of his men who might run as they did at Camden. Fourteen hundred experienced Continentals from Virginia, Maryland, and Delaware drew up on a brow of the gently rising hill near the courthouse and formed the third line. They were in overall command of Isaac and Otho respectively, which included colonels and captains to lead each regiment.

Otho's two regiments differed significantly. The 1st Maryland was one of the best and most experienced units in the Continental Army, led by Colonel John Gunby with John Eager Howard as his second. The 2nd Maryland was filled with new recruits raised by the state and was short of officers. Two days prior, Nathanael became exasperated with rifts between the recently arrived officers and those who had been there for months. The final straw was an argument between Captain Patrick Sims and the younger veteran Colonel Benjamin Ford.

"We are about to do battle, and the smoke and the sight of Cornwallis, his cavalry, and Brigade of Guards will terrify your men," Benjamin warned officers from the 2nd Maryland regiment as they bent over a fire and cooked their meager foraged rations of turnips and a few bobwhite quail. "You will want to consider that."

"My company can stand up to any oncoming redcoat, and we are not afraid of their gleaming bayonets because we have been trained to withstand them," Patrick argued. He spit in the fire and then eyed Benjamin defiantly. Laughter sprinkled the air.

Benjamin lunged at Patrick. "I am not going to stand for that!" he shouted.

Patrick scrambled away from Benjamin's reach.

The men were shadowed by their commander's broad shoulders and chest. They got to their feet. "Enough," Nathanael ordered. Irritation stained his blue eyes and creased his forehead. "This is no time for squabbling and jealousies. Captain Sims, relay to your fellow novice officers that you are not needed here and to pack your baggage and go home." He turned on his heel.

Otho heard the entire confrontation, but he made no comment as he and Nathanael resumed conferring over troop placement.

The army also had four 6-pound cannon and 100 artillerymen under Captain Anthony Singleton. Nathanael posted Singleton and two pieces on the road between the militia regiments and the other two cannon between the Virginia and Maryland fronts. William Washington's cavalry were to protect the right flank while Harry Lee's horsemen were to position themselves on the left. To the rear was the Reedy Fork Road, which would serve as the line of retreat. As at Cowpens, each line would deliver two or three well-executed volleys and then retire to the second line.

Harry's cavalry with a unit of Virginia riflemen moved as the eyes and ears for Nathanael and his officers. With the order of battle understood, the men settled down. On that cold, clear night under the illumination of a waning crescent moon, they set up camp. Each man was issued a gill of rum. They lit campfires and prepared themselves for the ordeal that would begin at daybreak.

Major Richard Harrison's quill scratched on paper. "Mrs. Harrison is pregnant and her lying in is due today," he said to himself. He reread the words he had written:

> *Our general is a great and good man, his army is numerous and apparently confident of victory. This is the very day that I hope will be given me a creature capable of enjoying what his father hopes to deserve and earn—the sweets of Liberty and Grace.*

Nathanael's aides came to him later that night. With a solemn countenance, Ichabod swept off his hat. The other aides shifted uncomfortably but looked Nathanael in the eye. Nathanael waited for them to speak. Lewis cleared his throat. "Do not," he entreated, "expose your person needlessly. Put our lives at every hazard, but be careful of your own. If we fall, our loss will not be felt; but your death will not only be fatal to the army, but in all probability greatly retard, if not destroy, every hope of securing the independence of the South."

Silence stretched out. Nathanael was certain his voice would sound unsteady if he spoke. "I cannot express what this means to me," he finally said with grateful calmness. *This*, he thought, *must be what Caty fears every day, and I have not written a line to her in a month.*

Early on the morning of March 15, a scout from Harry's legion reported he heard the wheels of the British supply train in motion. At 4:00 a.m., Nathanael ordered Harry to take his legion and some riflemen and verify if the British were indeed coming their way. Harry was surprised when he saw the American scouting party gallop in the opposite direction with Banastre Tarleton at their heels.

"In position and wheel toward the enemy!" Harry shouted. The two legions smashed into one another, firing pistols while cavalrymen were dismounted. The main army was having breakfast and a gill of rum. They heard the shots. Harry fell back and returned to report to his general—Cornwallis was on the march. The Southern Army formed battle lines.

The morning sun had burned away the chill of the night, and now it beamed overhead. At noon, Nathanael gathered his aides and mounted his horse. He knew that many of the American militiamen would flee at the first sight of the British and Hessian disciplined formations. Nathanael rode among the first line of the inexperienced North Carolina men. He wiped perspiration from his forehead. He held his right glove in one hand and rubbed his forefinger on his upper lip, a habit he had developed when he was working out momentous decisions. If ever he was to find the words to encourage his men in the field, the time was now.

"Our position is strong," Nathanael began in a clear and firm voice as he rode back and forth down the line. "We are here to defend our liberty and our honor. Three rounds, my boys, and then you may fall back."

His efforts to replicate Daniel Morgan's order of battle varied in several ways. The battlefield at Guilford Courthouse was much larger, and the wooded terrain deterred his three lines from seeing or supporting one another. Nathanael could not see the entire field, which would hinder his ability to react quickly to changing situations.

The sound of fifes, the wailing pipes of the Scottish Highlanders, and the snappy beat of snare drums filtered through the woods. The first British and Hessian troops stepped out into the muddy field and charged the Americans. Muskets thundered, and acrid gun smoke choked the air.

Banastre Tarleton's cavalry arrived on the main road with instructions not to charge without positive orders. They were followed by a second wave of infantry with Cornwallis leading the 71st Regiment of Highlanders and the German Regiment of Bose under the command of Alexander Leslie on the right. Cornwallis' army of 1,900 troops with their swords and bayonets were an intimidating sight as they flashed in the sun.

For a moment, Nathanael, sitting astride his horse thought, *I hope they will not be permitted to cross the open field unbroken*, but it was only a moment's aspiration.

An ineffective artillery volley ensued between the two sides, then the British moved forward. The North Carolina line fired too early when the British were more than 100 yards away. Their center collapsed. The terror-stricken men had done what they were asked to do—fire a volley and then retire, but they panicked and dropped their weapons, cartridge boxes, knapsacks, and anything that hindered their progress through the woods.

Cornwallis pressed Colonel James Webster's 33rd foot and Jaegers forward from the left. "Come on, my brave fusiliers!" he called. Through clouds of gray smoke, the Virginia militia fired and gave fight, some of it hand-to-hand. A powerful, murderous volley thundered that threw back Webster's men, dropping both British and Americans in a blur of blood, smoke, and a cacophony of screaming. Men tripped over the bodies of their own comrades as they tried to maneuver through the woods to face another assault of British infantry. A musket ball smashed Virginia militia General Edward Stevens' thigh, and he was carried from the field. Colonel Webster suffered a mortal wound. His femur and left kneecap were destroyed. Cornwallis was in the thick of the action. His mount was shot out from under him, forcing him to commandeer a dragoon's horse.

There was a brief pause as Colonel Webster's men retreated to reform. Then hell on earth erupted. Charles O'Hara's reserves of grenadiers and the 2nd Brigade of Guards united with Alexander Leslie's troops. They crossed a ravine and emerged from the woods haunted with gray gun smoke and attacked Nathanael's third line, the Maryland and Delaware Continentals.

Many of the 2nd Marylanders fled, but the 1st Marylanders stood their ground. O'Hara was hit in the thigh and his horse was shot out from under him. He turned his command over to the younger forty-year-old Colonel James Stewart. Supported by the grenadiers, Stewart headed straight for the fleeing 2nd Marylanders and made a successful attack on two 6-pounders they had taken from the Delaware regiment. Stewart turned on the 1st Maryland, and the two sides volleyed at the same time. Their colonel, John Gunby, lost his mount and was pinned under it. His deputy commander, Colonel John Eager Howard, took over for him.

A bugle sounded, and William Washington's cavalry swooped down from their right on open ground and, with the Marylanders, retook the cannon. William and his dragoons thundered through the 2nd Guards and slaughtered several of them. The guards were stunned. The dragoons wheeled their horses and rode through them again, cutting down the advancing British.

Colonel Howard regrouped his Marylanders and ordered, "The whole is in our power. Bayonets! Charge!" They let out a whoop and clashed with the guards in a bloody melee of hand-to-hand combat. Colonel James Stewart charged Maryland Captain John Smith.

"Come on, you bloody rebel," James inveigled as he thrust his sword at the captain. John parried. James' sword passed under John's arm, and the hilt bruised his chest.

"Your aggression is less than impressive!" John shouted above the din.

"I shall show you aggression," James countered. He stepped on the body of a dead man and slipped. John raised his sword and sliced the back of his opponent's head. Horrible pain skewed James' countenance, and he collapsed. Satisfied, John's attempt to continue the combat was halted by a shot to the back of his own head. He fell, presumed dead, but John would live another day to tell the tale.

Charles O'Hara's nephew, a lieutenant of the artillery, was killed by a musket ball to the forehead. "My God—" O'Hara began. He looked surprised for a moment, and then collapsed from a second gunshot wound to the chest. His aides urged him off the field.

The shattered British troops tried to reform among their dead and dying. Nathanael pressed forward into the midst of the battle. There was nothing between him and the enemy but woods. Lewis saw the danger and warned, "You are riding into the enemy, General Greene!"

Nathanael calmly nodded, turned his horse, and rode back to his position. It was a difficult moment. He had heard nothing from Harry and feared he was dead.

Cornwallis had to win. Nathanael only had to avoid a serious defeat to preserve his army while making Cornwallis pay. His army had succeeded in crippling the enemy. At 3:30 p.m., two hours after the battle began, he saw that having broken the 2nd Maryland Regiment, the enemy had turned his left flank, got into the rear of the Virginia brigade, and appeared to be gaining his right. The movement would encircle the Continentals. He rode through the discord of the battle, wielding his sword, and ordered a retreat.

Captain Anthony Singleton was unable to remove the four artillery pieces from the field because all the horses used to draw them were dead on the field. This did not prevent the Americans from an orderly retreat nor did the defeat damage their morale.

Cornwallis' victory cost him more than 500 men; twenty-five percent of his army was either dead or wounded. Three hundred Continentals were killed or wounded, 109 militia and 284 Virginians were missing.

Nathanael's troops retreated in good order to the Reedy Fork River and crossed at the ford about three miles from the field of action. They halted and waited to collect most of their stragglers. Then, he led his bedraggled men on a weary march to his old encampment near the ironworks at Troublesome Creek.

He knew Cornwallis would attempt a pursuit, and if successful, Nathanael had no plan but to turn and fight. A dizzy spell accosted him, and he gripped the pommel on his saddle. *This cannot happen now as it has happened before, and I could not control it*, he thought. *Stay calm. Breathe.* Ichabod and Lewis, who were riding beside their general and feeling unwell themselves, noticed that he was lagging behind. Concerned, they turned their horses.

Otho saw this as well and rode up to Nathanael's side. "Nathanael?" Otho asked, appalled at his pale face. When he received no response, Lewis and Ichabod made the same attempt to speak to him.

I can hear them, Nathanael thought, *but I cannot conjure an answer.* The world went dark, and he slipped from his saddle. Otho immediately sent word through the ranks to halt while Lewis and Ichabod dismounted in a panic. Nathanael's quartermaster and commissary, Edward Carrington and William Davie, jumped from their saddles and came running.

Otho kneeled and patted Nathanael's ashen cheeks and put an ear to his chest.

"Is he dead?" Ichabod asked Otho in horror.

"No, he is breathing."

"Sit him up," Lewis declared.

"Where is Dr. Read?" Edward shouted.

Dr. Read's response was immediate. If Colonel Williams had halted the entire army, he knew something was wrong. He squatted and took Nathanael's pulse and listened for a heartbeat. "Help me sit him up," he said, reiterating Lewis' suggestion.

Relief soughed among the attending men when Nathanael's eyes fluttered open. He coughed. The surrounding anxious faces confused him for a moment and then he realized he was no longer on his horse. Hands reached to help him to his feet, but he pushed them away and rose on his own.

"I am fine," he assured them in a wheezing voice—the telltale sign that he was about to have an asthma attack. Sore from his fall, he climbed into the saddle and waved his little army forward. Nothing on earth short of death would stop him from doing his duty.

The day had been clear, but the night brought a relentless, heavy rain as if heaven itself were weeping over the pain that mortal men inflicted on one another. American and British dead, dying, and wounded lay promiscuously on the great expanse of the battlefield in helpless agony. The cold wind carried the wailing of human anguish. Patriot militia Captain Arthur Forbis lay on the battlefield at Guilford Courthouse for a day under a cold March rain with bullet wounds in his side and leg and a bayonet thrust from a vengeful Loyalist until his wife, Elizabeth, found him. Before morning, nearly fifty died from exposure. The British Army remained near the field. Quartermaster Charles Stedman and Charles O'Hara commiserated during those two days, which were so horrible that even the camp followers left.

"I can hardly endure the cries of the wounded," Stedman lamented with his head draped in a blanket that did nothing to stop the incessant rain that soaked him to the bone. "There are few houses near the field of battle to receive them. I know not what to do to ease their pain."

"We are helpless, and it is impracticable to remove or administer the smallest comfort to the wounded," O'Hara admitted, painting the bleak picture further. He groaned and pressed a hand to his own wounded bloodied chest. "But it has been our lot to suffer. We have been naked and for days living upon carrion or three ounces of Indian corn that has totally destroyed this army."

The battle at Guilford Courthouse was an ordeal that Cornwallis would not soon forget. He admitted, "I never saw such fighting since God made me. The Americans fought like demons."

During that rainy dark first night, Nathanael wrote to the Quakers living in the settlement of New Garden asking for their help in tending his wounded, citing his own Quaker background.

> *I was born and educated in the professions and principles of your Society; and am perfectly acquainted with your religious sentiments and general good conduct as citizens. I am also sensible from the misconduct of a few of your own, that you are generally considered as enemies to this independence of America. I entertain other sentiments but I respect you as a people, and shall always be ready to protect you from every violence and oppression.*

The tally of missing trickled in. Two hundred ninety-four Virginians had gone home. General Isaac Huger was slightly wounded. But Nathanael's hungry and half-naked troops were in the highest spirits and eager for another battle.

On March 18, Nathanael took up his quill and wrote to politician Joseph Reed in Philadelphia. "The battle was long, obstinate, and bloody. We were obliged to give up the ground, and lost our Artillery. But the enemy has been so soundly beaten, that they dare not move towards us since the action. They have gained no advantage; on the contrary, they are little short of being ruined."

He had neglected to write to his beloved Caty during those days of tremendous stress. He received a letter from her before the battle. She told of her time in Newport and the respectful attention paid her by members of the French command and gossip of a lady who was smitten with Colonel Williams. The letter contained something much more valuable—a miniature heart locket in which her picture was enclosed.

Caty had enough to worry about with little Nat suffering from illness. She rocked the fourteen-month-old toddler to sleep while she hummed a tune that her subconscious remembered from the long ago days when she was sick and her mother, Phoebe, did the same. A month passed, and she had not heard from Nathanael although she had written to him. She had no idea if he was dead or alive. She clung to his babies, the only corporeal connection she had to him.

The bedroom door creaked open. "Caty?"

She looked up. Her sister-in-law, Peggy, was standing in the doorway with a letter in her hand. "I will look after Nat," Peggy said with unaccustomed kindness in her voice.

With restraint, Caty let her sleeping son slip from her arms. She accepted the letter from Peggy. Tears stung her dark eyes. *He is still alive*, repeated in her mind as if the letter would crumble in her hands. She went to the shelter of the library where Nathanael's extensive collection of books still lined the walls. She carefully opened the letter. His elegant handwriting flowed across the pages.

We have had a very severe action with Lord Cornwallis, in which we were obliged to give up the ground. Many fell, but none of your particular friends. I had not the honor of being wounded. The evening after the action I received your letter which was some consolation after the misfortune of the day. I see by your last letter that you are determined to come to the southward. Nothing but blood and slaughter prevail here, and the operations are in a country little short of wilderness.

Our fatigue is excessive. I have not had my clothes off for upwards of six weeks; but I am in generally pretty good health. I should be extremely happy if the war had an honorable close, and I on a farm with my little family about me. I beg my kind love to my brothers and all their families, to Mother Greene, and all other inquiring friends.

Caty swallowed her unshed tears. Nathanael was in a place she could not picture in her mind. A place so horrible that he had forbidden her to come. He missed not only her and the children, he missed his entire family and the love and support family provided. *I suppose his aides and soldiers are his family,* she thought as she folded the letter.

Jacob intruded on her thoughts. "What news?" he inquired. He sat in front of the fireplace and filled his pipe with tobacco.

"If you are smoking, then you are worried," Caty said. "Nathanael asks about you. He wants to know why he has not heard from you or your cousin Griffin although he has sent you several letters. He also asks after the company business."

Jacob lit his pipe. Smoked curled from it in a sinuous ribbon. "I cannot speak for Griffin, but I have sent my brother letters. I suppose they have been lost."

"You act as if it does not matter that your brother is 1,000 miles away where we cannot even conceive of what is happening."

"Caty, you misunderstand," Jacob said gently.

"How? How do I misunderstand?" The tears that burned the back of her eyes trailed down her beautiful face.

"Perhaps you would be better off at the farm in Westerly where you can have the peace to care for yourself and your children without our children running through the house prevailing on your lonesome thoughts."

"Our children are cousins. Why would you deny them that pleasure and comfort?"

Jacob set his pipe aside. His eyes moved to Peggy's quiet entrance into the library then back to his sister-in-law. "Please understand, Caty. My worries over my brother's well-being are as painful as yours are to you. But I must tend to the business he enquires about so that he may keep his head where it belongs with his campaign. I must keep the iron forge running and our merchant ship, the *Flora*, safe and prosperous."

Caty squeezed her eyes shut and pressed a hand to her mouth. She drew in a breath and opened her eyes. "Nat is sick. I cannot—" Her argument was in vain. Her little boy was not gravely ill. He would soon be chasing his cousins through the house on chubby legs and chiming the ringing laughter he inherited from his mother. Jacob's argument held the weight it was intended. Nathanael's business interests had to be looked after by someone who was knowledgeable and, for now, she was not that person.

❧

Caty was distraught that Nathanael again refused her request to join him in the South. Her heart ached and her despondency mounted to the point that she responded to his letter with unbridled intensity. "I would be willing to change headquarters every night or ride upon a horse among your destitute army to be with you, for I am destitute without you. I cannot say how your denial will affect our marital happiness."

On a lonely, windy night that shivered the eaves of the farmhouse in Westerly, Caty answered a knock on her door. Colonel Jeremiah Wadsworth was standing there with his arms full of provisions.

"Colonel Wadsworth!" Caty exclaimed, taken aback.

She was aware that as a friend and business partner, Nathanael had asked him to bring her much-needed provisions at a time when he would be unable to care for his family, but he had come when her emotions were vulnerable. The attraction she carried for Jeremiah was overwhelming, something she had fought since she first met him at Valley Forge. And here he was, standing there like a knight in shining armor.

"Are you going to invite me in?" Jeremiah asked.

"Of course. How rude of me."

"The private warehouses Nathanael and I own are still stocked. I have flour, salt, and more in the wagon. Where do you want them?" he asked as he stepped through the open door.

A girlish blush bloomed on Caty's cheeks. His blue eyes were fixed on her face, and she felt silly. He had not traveled the twenty miles from New London, Connecticut, as a suitor, but as dutiful friend. "Please bring them into the kitchen and put them in the pantry. The children are asleep. I do not want you to wake them."

"Look what I have brought," Jeremiah exclaimed after he had stocked Caty's pantry. "A dozen bottles of wine. I know how much you enjoy a glass or two. Shall we indulge?"

Wind whistled and shook the windowpanes as if it were a banshee warning of impending danger. She had no idea how long she would be forced to endure Nathanael's absence or a sense of the number of times Colonel Wadsworth might appear at her door with more provisions—and wine.

They moved into the living room.

"Please tell me of the health of your wife and children," Caty said as she accepted a glass from Jeremiah's outstretched hand.

He seated himself and said, "They are well. May sends greetings."

Caty shot him a doubtful look. She knew very well that May, who was twenty years her senior, was not tolerant of Caty's convivial nature that attracted a bevy of men, including her own husband. "General Greene is asking after your business ventures together. Perhaps you should write to him and ease his mind," she said. "I received a letter from Colonel Otho Williams. You remember him. He is in the South under my husband's command. Colonel Williams asked after me and flattered me by saying that he misses an intimacy with my cheerful spirits, which used to render society in the Northern Army so charming."

"He speaks true." A grin spread across Jeremiah's face. "Caty, you are babbling, and that is not like you." He leaned forward. "I know you abound with worry and longing."

She gulped her wine and poured another glass. "It is just that the news that the traitorous General Benedict Arnold is sweeping through Virginia like a barbarian has extremely affected me. I worry for Nathanael's safety that is enhanced by my widowed state far from my friends."

The bottle was empty when Jeremiah reached for it. He supposed it was a sign that he should go home. Seeing Caty in such distress did not blur the pictures of her in his mind: dancing and laughing and the sound of French rolling off her tongue and mirth in her dark eyes. Those pictures surely burned in his friend's memory as he battled a partisan war and the British Army in the South.

He rose. "I must go. Next time, I will send Mr. Wiles, one of my assistants, with your provisions."

Caty set her glass aside and saw him to the door.

Jeremiah stalled in the doorway. "If you need me, send a message, and I will come immediately. I cannot let Nathanael's family starve." He bowed. "I shall write to him as you have asked. He should be informed of the little profit our company is making."

She nodded. The darkness enveloped him and left the sound of squeaking wagon wheels ringing in her ears. That night, for the first time, she cried herself to sleep.

While Nathanael was looking for another battle with Charles Cornwallis, the British general was struggling with his difficulties. He could not meet Nathanael in the field without exposing his army to destruction and he could not retreat. Cornwallis had a seven-day head start on his march to Wilmington, North Carolina, on the coast, slowed by muddy roads and his dying wounded. On March 24, Nathanael broke his camp on Troublesome Creek to pursue Cornwallis.

Earlier in the day, Harry came to voice his opinion on the move. "I am agreed in opinion with you that Lord Cornwallis does not wish to fight us, but you may depend upon it, he will not refuse to fight if we push him."

Nathanael produced a rare smirk. "It is my intention to attack the enemy the moment we can get up with them."

"We are short on bread and ammunition."

"Do you wish to stay at this place and let Cornwallis march away?" Nathanael challenged. Without waiting for an answer he said, "We leave in the morning."

Harry did not argue the point further. He knew that although General Greene held no councils, he had probably consulted his adjutant, Otho. The muddy, rutted roads that slowed Cornwallis also slowed Nathanael's army as did shortages of bullets and food. He rested his army at South Buffalo Creek so they could make cartridges. The vanguard almost caught up with

Cornwallis at Ramsey's Mill. Nathanael found that he was forced to admit to Washington that he was at a loss at what was best to be done. The Virginia militia went home, and he could not attack the enemy without them.

He gave it a few days' thought and then wrote in the same letter, "I am determined to carry the war immediately into South Carolina. Of the British posts there, Georgetown, Camden, and Ninety-Six are the most important; Camden being the strongest. All things considered, I think the movement is warranted by the soundest reasons, both political and military."

There was some discussion among Nathanael's officers about the wisdom of turning his back on the enemy, leaving his flanks and rear exposed. Only Harry was excited about the idea and proclaimed, "I am decidedly of the opinion with you that nothing is left but to imitate the example of Scipio Africanus. I believe a general acts wisely when he takes the course most dreaded by his adversary."

The doubtful discussion left Nathanael unfazed. "We cannot conduct a siege on Wilmington with no naval power and few supplies. We will leave Cornwallis the choice to either follow us into South Carolina, giving up North Carolina, or stay where he is, losing his outposts."

"I have written to Abner Nash, the governor of North Carolina, to request that he send bacon, cattle, cheese, and a wagonload of chickens, turkeys, fresh butter, and turnips," William Davie said to the officers seated in Nathanael's tent.

"I have also asked for a cask of claret wine and a cask of rum. We must not be deprived of that important liquid," Nathanael said enthusiastically, which brought a round of happy agreement.

Before leaving, Nathanael wrote of his plan to Steuben in Virginia, who aside from the Marquis de Lafayette's recently deployed force of 1,200 troops, was waiting in vain for reinforcements to face down Benedict Arnold terrorizing the state.

On the morning of April 6, 1781, Nathanael turned his army southward toward Camden, South Carolina. Frustrated with a lack of available support from George Washington and the uncooperative militia general,

Thomas Sumter, Nathanael's army marched without the protection of Harry Lee's dragoons who he sent to link up with Francis Marion in South Carolina. Their first target would be Fort Watson. Other militiamen had gone west to patrol under Andrew Pickens at Ninety-Six and Augusta. Governor Nash failed to provide any of the provisions except the rum, but William Davie ensured the men were provided with provisions a day in advance.

Nathanael led his valiant troops by easy marches through the spring landscape with fast-running rivers and blooming foliage where there was time for the army to care for themselves and take some comfort. The signs of spring irritated his asthma. There were abuses in plundering the inhabitants and pressing for much needed horses that caused Nathanael to tighten the reins of discipline. Yet, they faced their new prospect together as soldiers.

Nathanael spent every moment of his spare time writing orders. He sent their camp followers away, fearing they would bog down the wagons. His letters to Thomas Sumter bordered on the edge of plaintiveness, asking that he cooperate in the planned assault on Camden by sending horses and some light infantry. "My greatest dependence is on you for supplies of corn and meal. Unless you can furnish me with them it will be impossible for me to keep my position."

The Southern Army marched through country that was extremely difficult to operate—cut by deep creeks and impassable morasses, heavy timber, and thick underbrush. On April 20, they pulled up to the stockade walls of Camden where Lord Francis Rawdon had 900 Loyalist and British troops garrisoned. Aware that it was too strong to attack, Nathanael pulled his army back to Hobkirk's Hill, a sandy ridge two miles north of Camden over which ran the Salisbury Road.

twenty-six

We Have a Bloody Field but Little Glory

Charles Cornwallis suffered under criticism from Henry Clinton who ridiculed his decision to fly to the coast where Cornwallis resupplied. He ordered Cornwallis to secure the South and recover North Carolina. Cornwallis ignored Clinton. He huffed to Charles O'Hara, "Greene's actions are as insulting and irritating as if he had stormed our camp and decimated it with cannon, cavalry, and bayonets."

"Our camp is less than desirable," O'Hara contended. He looked up as rain began to pepper his tent. He shifted uncomfortably and pressed a hand to his healing chest wound. "The inhabitants of this place come into our camp with congratulations for defeating Greene, but none stay when they see the melancholy conditions."

"Perhaps it is time to move on to Virginia. I have written to General William Phillips telling him of our grievous situation. Greene took advantage of my being obliged to come to Wilmington and has marched to South Carolina."

A smirk played across O'Hara's thin lips. "General Phillips and Arnold have created such mayhem in Virginia that the local state defenses have collapsed and fled. Their forces notwithstanding, those stationed at our outposts in Charleston and Savannah bring our army to nearly 8,000 strong in the South. Greene will never challenge our numbers. Lord Rawdon, who you have left to South Carolina, will see to it that Greene is stopped."

Like Cornwallis, the tall, homely twenty-six-year-old Colonel Lord Francis Rawdon was born an English aristocrat. Oxford educated, he served under Clinton for much of the war until he was sent to South Carolina after the fall of Charleston in May 1780. Now, with Cornwallis' withdrawal from North Carolina toward Virginia, the defense of South Carolina was transferred to his aggressive shoulders. Nathanael's army of 1,500 did nothing to deter his decision to attack the American general. Rawdon had received intelligence that General Greene was on his way.

For the past two months, partisan warfare had gone on with unceasing spirit, steadily tearing the British fabric. The communication lines between the British outposts, some running along the Santee River, others along the Congaree or Edisto Rivers, were slowly being destroyed. Thomas Sumter had attempted to destroy Fort Granby in the face of Lord Rawdon's whole force on the opposite bank. Now, Harry Lee and Francis Marion were assaulting Fort Watson on the Santee River.

Nathanael was harassed with letters from Harry, demanding cannon, proclaiming that he had a difficult time taking orders from Marion; that Marion was feeling neglected and that his general should write a letter to Marion to soothe his complaints. Nathanael denied Harry's request for a single cannon, which elicited an unreasonable letter from Harry demanding infantry to support the field piece. Harry and Francis were successful without the desired cannon. Fort Watson fell on April 23 after one of Francis' officers, Major Hezekiah Maham, proposed building a wooden tower from which riflemen could fire down into the fort. Unaware of the victory, Nathanael took the time the next day not only to praise Francis, but also to send him the cannon escorted by quartermaster Edward Carrington.

It was good news that offset Thomas Sumter's fabricated reply to Nathanael regarding horse, infantry, and supplies, "You may rely upon my unremitted endeavors to promote and facilitate your designs." The brightest news they received that day by way of intelligence was that Lord Cornwallis left Wilmington, North Carolina, headed for Virginia.

≈

Thomas never arrived with the "promised" facilitations. On April 24, Nathanael issued orders of the day that called for absent soldiers to be reported and punished. Every part of the army was to be in readiness to stand arms at a moment's notice.

In the early morning hours of April 25, 1781, a skittish drummer deserted from the Maryland line. He carried word to Lord Francis Rawdon. "There is a bedraggled boy here at the gates, your Lordship," a British sentry announced.

Francis listened to the apprehensive boy. "Sir, General Sumter has not yet come up with General Greene." The boy's eyes shifted to the dour looking sentry.

"Go on," Francis encouraged.

"Our army is weakened by detachments and lack of food. General Greene has no artillery with him. It is in the rear along with the baggage train. He desires that you venture out from behind your defenses because he believes his army is stronger than yours, but I think his army is vulnerable to a surprise attack."

"Is that so?" Francis asked. He addressed the sentry, "Take this boy and arm him along with every man in the garrison, including musicians and drummers. We have had the pleasure of some few hundred militia reinforcements. I believe we can meet Greene's challenge. Call for my adjutant to issue my orders of the day, which I shall draw up forthwith. We will attack immediately before Greene has a chance of being reinforced by Marion, Lee, or Sumter."

≈

Nathanael's troops were camped on Hobkirk's Hill in order of battle in a wide line across the hill. Otho had overall command of the Maryland troops to the left of the road, and Isaac ranked command over the Virginia

Continentals to the right. Otho's two regiments were the 1st Maryland, commanded by Colonel John Gunby and the 2nd Maryland commanded by Colonel Benjamin Ford. Gunby's deputy was the brilliant Colonel John Eager Howard, who had commanded the regiment at Cowpens and taken up the command at Guilford Courthouse when Gunby was pinned beneath his horse. The 2nd Virginians were under the direct command of Colonel Samuel Hawes with the 1st under Colonel Richard Campbell. Two hundred fifty North Carolina militia were in back of the Continentals. William Washington's 3rd Continental Dragoons—only about fifty mounted due to the difficulty of procuring horses—were held in reserve.

To protect them from surprise, pickets were stationed 300 yards in front of their lines supported by Maryland, Virginia, and Delaware Continentals. Nathanael's men were enjoying the quiet morning buoyed by his orders that every man would receive two days' worth of food and a gill of spirits as soon as quartermaster Edward Carrington arrived with the stores. Their arms were stacked. Coats and shoes lay scattered. William's dragoon horses grazed peacefully at their loose tethers.

At 10:00 a.m., a group of young Virginians sat around a cooking fire and watched the oily blue smoke rise into the air. "I thought we were about to starve to death again," Private John Cassidy griped. He flipped his hoe cakes cooking in a small skillet. "We are indeed treated to two days of full rations."

"You always think you are starving even if you are not," a drummer boy known only as Jacob argued. He examined the ounce of pork dangling at the end of his fork. "It looks done."

"Well, I am going down to the rivulet that runs along the hill and wash my kettle," Private Christopher Madison said as he rose. "That was some fine victuals, and mine are all cooked for tomorrow, too."

"You eat like a pig," Jacob scoffed.

"If you boys intend on gripin', then I suggest you give me your extra gill of rum when it arrives," Jackson Killam from Virginia jested with the youngsters.

"Christopher will hand his over," John volunteered with a belly laugh.

Christopher ignored him and walked toward the little creek. He avoided the spot where some of the soldiers were washing clothes or soaking their tired feet. General Isaac Huger was among the men relaxing by the rivulet. The general stopped him. "Have you seen the rum wagon yet?" Isaac asked.

"No sir, but I will alert you as soon as I see—" Christopher's words were blown away by the sound of sharp musketry at the base of the hill. Christopher dropped his kettle and ran toward his Virginia regiment to fall in line.

The American drums beat as the pickets clashed with Lord Rawdon's vanguard. The surprised Americans, many still barefoot and half-dressed, rushed to form their lines. Christopher, John, Jacob, and Jackson listened to the approaching battle with pounding hearts and taut nerves and watched gun smoke curl up and through the towering pine trees.

Otho tried to keep his surprise concealed when he mounted his horse and galloped from the front lines to Nathanael's headquarters. When he arrived, Nathanael, who had been enjoying the rare luxury of a cup of coffee, was on his feet. "I heard the firing," Nathanael assured his adjutant.

"Aye, then. I am going back to the lines before the fighting becomes widespread," Otho said.

Nathanael abandoned his breakfast and jumped into the saddle, followed by Lewis and Ichabod. He saw North Carolina militia officer Guilford Dudley marching up the back side of the hill with the artillery and heard Otho order him, "March to the right and support Colonel Campbell."

Nathanael rode forward with a good view of the hill. Captain Robert Kirkwood's Delaware pickets were slowly being pushed back by Rawdon's vanguard. The British commander had arranged his men in a single line with his Corps of Observation in the rear, the right wing supported by 675 provincial regulars and the Volunteers of Ireland on the left.

Rawdon's line is narrow, Nathanael thought. *We can strike their flanks, rear, and front.* He quickly issued orders and sent his aides to disseminate them. "General Greene wishes you to wheel left upon the enemy's right flank," Lewis informed Richard Campbell while Ichabod communicated to Benjamin Ford that he was to wheel his men to the right.

As Rawdon advanced, Nathanael sent orders to unmask the artillery. The American gunners shredded the tightly packed British columns with volleys of whistling grapeshot. Through the clearing blue smoke, Nathanael saw the destruction and was beside himself with satisfaction. "Victory is in reach!" he exclaimed to his aide, Captain William Pierce. "Draw forth and send instructions to Colonels Gunby and Hawes to conduct a bayonet charge in the center. Then send Colonel Washington and his dragoons to turn the enemy's right flank and charge them in the rear."

Lord Rawdon's homely face turned red with rage as he saw his men fall and the Continentals charging with bayonets. He took his aggressive anger out on one of his aides, "I was told that Greene had no artillery!" He shouted orders to the Volunteers of Ireland who came up and added their fire against the Maryland ranks.

Rawdon continued to disseminate orders to his aides, "Rally, my boys, and bring up all from the rear. Lengthen our lines and avoid the flanking maneuver the American general intends on executing."

Aside from the 63rd foot, all of Rawdon's troops were American Tories fighting against American Whigs, and they were quick to take advantage of the thick woods on the hill. The firing was so intense that musket barrels became too hot to hold in their hands.

As Nathanael's infantry rolled forward so too did William and his dragoons. They swept down around the hill to avoid felled trees and heavy undergrowth, and then rode hard for Major John Coffin's dragoons on the British right flank. They clashed and swung their short blades from the saddles of their wheeling horses. Coffin's men scattered. Although deterred by the thick undergrowth, William gathered his dragoons under the direct command of captains William Parsons and Walker Baylor and fell upon the rear of the British infantry. They became bogged down in taking prisoners who were, in fact, Lord Rawdon's desperate attempt to arm as many as he could. The musicians, surgeons, and teamsters had no stomach to stand up against a force of hard galloping dragoons, and they quickly surrendered.

The American infantry continued to push forward. Many of the Marylanders under Colonel Benjamin Ford were new recruits, and some began firing without orders. Nathanael watched as Benjamin was shot off his horse and suffered a mortal wound. None of the skittish 2nd Marylanders came to their colonel's aide. Gunby's and Hawes' men continued a steady advance. Some forgot to use their bayonets and fired instead. The trusted captain of the right company, William Beatty, was shot through the heart and dropped dead.

His company, the 1st Marylanders, became deranged and fell out of line. The other companies under Colonel John Eager Howard were still advancing, and instead of pushing them all forward Colonel John Gunby saw they were marching in the form of a bow and ordered them to fall back to the foot of the hill and reform. The consequences were fatal. General Greene had told them not to fire. Now, they were being told to halt in the face of a charging British force. They broke and ran. This left the 2nd Marylanders isolated, and they too fell back followed by the 1st Virginians.

Otho saw the panic and rode toward them, but neither he nor Colonels Howard or Gunby could stop it. Nathanael was up on the ridge where he had spent most of the battle with Samuel Hawes' 2nd Virginians. He exposed himself like a captain of grenadiers and attempted to restore order. It became obvious that Lord Rawdon understood that Hawes' men were alone, and, seeing his advantage, pressed the hill to flank them and silence the American artillery.

Swept up in the tide of retreating troops, the American gunners mis-handled their frightened teams and snagged the limbers in heavy brush. The horses panicked and had to be cut from the limbers. Bitterly disappointed, Nathanael issued the order for his surviving regiments to withdraw, and they formed with the now-rallied Gunby's men at the foot of the hill.

The troubles the gunners were encountering came to Nathanael's attention as they tried to pull the cannon out of the reach of the enemy with drag ropes. Thoughts of Guilford Courthouse where his cannon were lost flashed through his head. He jumped from his saddle, and with the horse's bridle in one hand and a drag rope in the other, he encouraged the dismayed gunners, "There is not a man here who does not have the courage to take the cannon off." Seeing that their general was with the artillery, others came to help. Nathanael wasted no time, and he rode on to see what could be done about bringing the rout to a halt.

Major John Coffin's British dragoons charged toward the cannon with swords aloft and began to put some of the men dragging the cannon to the sword. The assault gave the others time to get the guns hitched to horses and safely away backed up by William's charging dragoons, each with prisoners in tow. It was a wasted effort. Bogged down by captives and the wooded lay of the land, William's cavalry could not act with effect.

Nathanael called a retreat. William caught up with the main army and delivered the prisoners he probably should not have taken. Nathanael ordered the prisoners processed. He knew Rawdon was in pursuit. He did not know that Rawdon had left Major John Coffin with his cavalry on Hobkirk's Hill to claim the ground as a British victory.

Nathanael snapped orders at William, "Go back and screen our retreat. Take Captain Kirkwood's Delaware unit with you. Take up our stragglers and wounded, and bring them back. If circumstances and time permit, bury our dead."

Nathanael led his little army three miles north of Hobkirk's Hill and stopped to camp at Saunders' Creek in the same sandy Pine Barrens where Horatio Gates had lost an army. Lord Rawdon broke off his pursuit and returned to the walls of Camden. Both commanders lost 200 men—dead, wounded, captured, and missing. Nathanael was in a vexatious mood after the loss he was certain could have been a victory. He changed his password and countersign to "Persevere" and "Fortitude" and then took out his anger on Colonel John Gunby. After Nathanael marched his army to find food near Rugeley's Mill, thirteen miles to the north of Camden, he summoned Gunby to stand before him and explain himself.

"You are aware that I do not blame the troops for the loss of our recent affair?" Nathanael asked John.

"I am aware, and I bitterly dispute that I alone was at fault for the sudden retreat of the 1st Marylanders," John argued without addressing Nathanael by his rank.

"We should have had Lord Rawdon and his whole command prisoners in three minutes if you had not ordered your regiment to retire, the greater part who were advancing rapidly at the time they were ordered off," Nathanael countered, trying to contain his rage and disappointment. But his words revealed his fear that he would be criticized for yet another loss, and John knew it, for his general had demonstrated the propensity before.

"Your general orders congratulating everyone but my corps was an insult to the Marylanders," John said.

"I will correct that and lay the blame entirely upon your shoulders," Nathanael fumed.

John, mortified by the horrible accusations General Greene piled upon him after he had fought bravely at the Battle of Guilford Courthouse, took umbrage, "I demand a court of inquiry."

For a moment Nathanael wondered, *Am I being too harsh?* But the moment passed. Nathanael could not come to terms with his disappointment and frustration.

☙

On April 28, he issued orders in the camp at Rugeley's Mill, "General Huger, Colonel Harrison, and Colonel Washington are to compose a court to inquire into the conduct of Colonel Gunby in the action of the 25th instant."

The testimony found that Gunby was exerting himself in rallying and forming his troops, only committing an error in judgment. Nathanael could not let it pass. He castigated Gunby publicly in written orders:

> *Col. Gunby's Spirit and activity were unexceptional. But his order for the regiment to retire, which broke the line, was*

extremely improper and unmilitary; and in all probability
the only cause why we did not obtain a complete victory.

For all of Nathanael's bold appearance, he desperately needed to hear the voice of friendship and an ear to listen and understand the deprivation and anxiety of his situation—one that only those gallant men by his side could appreciate. But most could not understand the daunting task that was his to achieve and the number of demands that were laid at his feet. In the quiet of the night of May 4, in an abandoned house near a creek, he took up his quill. He continued a letter he had started to his friend, politician Joseph Reed, describing the circumstances of the battle.

The words that flowed from his pen were the words of a man who in his heart feared disapproval and needed confirmation. "I have been in this department near six months, and have written you several letters, without receiving a line of remembrance. Formerly, I used to flatter myself that I had a place in your friendship, and my being sent to this unfortunate country I hope has not lessened it; for I am sure I have never had more need of it in my life, either for consolation or support."

Nathanael paused and closed his eyes. He fingered the heart locket that Caty sent him with her picture in it. What he wanted to write—what he needed to write—he had tried to convey to General Washington and all those to the north; a diatribe that came to no good end. He dipped quill into ink and continued. "The strength and resources of these states to support the war have been greatly magnified and overrated. Unless the northern states can give more sufficient support, these states must fall. Nothing but a superior army to the enemy's collective force can give relief to this distressed country—the miseries of which exceed all belief."

As the waxing gibbous moon began to set, he wrote to the Marquis de Lafayette in Virginia, "We fight, get beat, rise and fight again. We have a bloody field; but little glory."

The next morning, Colonel William Davie found Nathanael asleep at his writing desk. His aides had gone to the officers' mess in search of breakfast. William hesitated to wake up his depressed general, for sleep did not always come easy to the condition. He sat down and balanced the cup of tea he brought for Nathanael on his knee.

Nathanael groaned, and his blue eyes fluttered open. He raised his head. Ink stained one cheek. "You have something there," William indicated by brushing a finger over his own cheek. He set the cup of tea on the desk.

Nathanael rubbed his eyes and looked down at the letter he had been writing. It all came flooding back. Francis Marion was infuriated with him for accusations that he was taking horses from Tories and then had turned around and asked Francis to send him sixty or eighty good dragoon horses. Francis threatened to resign and go to the Continental Congress for satisfaction. Nathanael's response was somewhat messy where his cheek had blurred the ink:

> *It is true your task has been disagreeable, but not more so than others. Your state is invaded, your all is at stake. I left a family in distress and everything dear and valuable to come & afford you all the assistance in my power, and if you leave us in the midst of our difficulties it must throw a damp upon the spirits of the army.*

"William," Nathanael acknowledged. He rose and stretched his stiff knee. "Is this for me?" he asked indicating the cup.

"Yes. I am worried about you."

"I want to show you something." He sipped the tea and then went to a small table where he spread a crude map and slid his finger over the state of South Carolina. "You see that we must resume the partisan war. Rawdon has a decided superiority in force. He has pushed us to sufficient distance to leave him free to act on any object he wishes. He will strike at Lee and Marion, reinforce himself by all the troops that can be spared, and push me back to the mountains. The regular troops are now reduced to a handful, and I am without militia and without prospect of receiving any reinforcements. Sumter refuses to obey my orders."

"How can you be certain Rawdon will go after Lee and Marion?" William asked.

"We must calculate on the maxim that your enemy will do what he ought to do. Lord Cornwallis will establish a chain of posts along the James River in Virginia, and the Southern states, thus cut off, will die like the tail of a snake."

William studied the familiar map. "What do you want me to do?" he asked.

Nathanael pointed to the map where the Wateree River flowed near Camden and said, "You acted in this quarter in the last campaign. I wish you to point out the military positions on both sides of the river, ascending to the mountains, and give me the necessary information."

The commissary general rubbed his chin in thought.

Nathanael noticed, but he went on, the cup of tea forgotten. "I have been led to consider leaving the Carolinas not with the army but by myself to take over the American forces in Virginia. Perhaps Baron von Steuben, who I have begged to join the main Southern Army here, would arrange matters very well."

He is despaired to say such a thing, William thought.

"I know your exertions as our commissariat cause you anxiety, for it is necessary to provide food for retreat as well as for advance. I am sympathetic to the care it takes," Nathanael said. "I am asking you to write your friends in Philadelphia who are members of Congress, and inform them of the imminent danger of the army and our pressing needs. They do not hear my pleas. Your legal rhetoric must have some bearing."

William's usual self-absorbed personality crumbled under his general's lonely observations. "I will do my best, sir." He knew that the service of many of the Maryland troops had expired, and as many as a dozen were leaving daily. The long promised Continental troops from Virginia had not arrived, and now it looked as if they never would.

Despite Nathanael's moments of self-pity, which he shared privately, he was quick to try to squelch reports that the American Army had suffered a significant defeat. He wrote to several colleagues, "By mistake we got a slight repulse. The injury was not great. The Enemy suffered much more than we did."

☙

On May 11, Colonel Guilford Dudley arrived at Nathanael's headquarters for a previous breakfast invitation. The general and Otho were standing at the gate. Nathanael's broad shoulders cast a shadow across the little dirt yard. William Davie rode up and dismounted. The two new arrivals perceived Nathanael's change in demeanor. His countenance was open, and the shadow of pessimism had disappeared.

"I have sent for you," Nathanael said with gleaming eyes, "to inform you that Lord Rawdon evacuated Camden. That place was the key to the enemy's line of posts. They will now all fall or soon be evacuated. All will now go well. I shall march immediately to the Congaree. Arrange your convoys to follow us, and let me know what expresses and detachments you will want."

The news was accurate. After the fall of Fort Watson, Rawdon's communication with Charleston was cut off, and he had no hope of aid from Cornwallis. He was determined to turn and attack Greene's army again, but Nathanael moved his camp several times, and Rawdon ended up clashing with strong American pickets instead of the main army.

He informed Cornwallis of the last thing he wanted to hear:

> *Having driven in his pickets, I examined every point of his situation. I found it everywhere so strong that I could not hope to force it without suffering such loss as must have crippled my force for further enterprise.*

Rawdon withdrew back to Camden and proclaimed that he could no longer maintain the garrison. The town was evacuated and burned along with a great amount of his army's baggage. Tories, who were no longer protected within the walls, followed the British commander. Men, women, and children who once lived happily on their farms suffered the march in shame. Amid all this, Nathanael received word that Lord Cornwallis had turned back toward South Carolina.

He wrote to Francis Marion, "I beg you to take measures to discover his route and approach. Look out for Colonel Tarleton. If he should get into Camden, Colonel Lee is to return at once to the main army."

Even before Rawdon abandoned Camden, Nathanael sent Harry Lee and Francis Marion to assault Fort Motte, a supply depot and home to more than 150 troops on the Congaree River. In the meantime, Thomas Sumter attacked a garrison of Loyalist militia in Orangeburg south of Nathanael's new position on the Congaree. Fort Motte fell on May 12 after a six-day siege. Harry and Francis clashed over who was in command, and Harry's men executed some of the captives, much to Francis' disgust. Harry complained to Nathanael that Marion was, "inadequate and very discontented—this discontent arises from his nature."

The news of Fort Motte was joyous enough for Nathanael, watching the movements of Lord Rawdon, to turn his attention to Marion who he knew needed soothing. Rebecca Motte, the owner of the plantation the British had commandeered as a supply depot and banished her and her children to the small log cabin outbuilding, welcomed General Greene and his small body of cavalry with open arms.

Nathanael limped to greet Francis Marion. Francis' deformed ankles and knees caused him to limp as badly as the commander. Nathanael stood a full head above the small forty-nine-year-old Patriot from South Carolina. "General Marion," Nathanael said, extending his hand to the man he had never met.

Francis cordially returned the gesture with a firm handshake. "General Greene, I cannot express my pleasure."

The Southern accent he heard had become familiar to the general from Rhode Island even if sometimes he found it hard to understand. Francis' accent was laced with a vague French accent passed from his Huguenot father.

"Shall we enjoy a meal?" Rebecca Motte suggested and indicated the table she had prepared, knowing that General Greene was on his way to her humble home.

"I heard that you assisted General Marion and Colonel Lee in burning down your own plantation," Nathanael said to his hostess. The officers sat down to a sumptuous table—all animosity put aside.

"I am a Patriot, sir," Rebecca said. She produced a vintage bottle of wine and uncorked it.

"I wrote to you that she had the finest table!" Harry spewed to Nathanael.

Nathanael laughed, and the tension drained from his spirit. Rebecca poured glasses for all. She raised a toast and glanced at Francis, who did not drink. "To the success of our army and our cooperative Patriot militia commanders who protect our interests and provide succor."

The officers seated around the table raised a glass. "Hear! Hear!"

Despite what Nathanael had written to Francis and others that the defeat at Hobkirk's Hill was just "a mistake," for the first time Francis heard in his voice grieving determination. Francis offered, "Last fall Banastre Tarleton and his cavalry chased me and my men for seven hours through twenty-six miles of swamp. I heard that Tarleton proclaimed, 'But as for this damn old fox, the devil himself could not catch him.' Most recently, I was pursued by Colonel John Watson. He accused that I would not fight like a gentleman or a Christian. Accusations are harmful if one has not looked into the eyes of his pursuer—or the men who ask for aid."

Harry's proclamations of superiority crumbled for the moment.

Nathanael looked Francis in the eye and raised his right hand to his lips, a subconscious act of thinking. *I am commander-in-chief of this army, and my wishes should be heeded. Yet this is the way of it in this country where there are so many more men who know the situation.* He said, "I cannot operate without your knowledge, cooperation, and fortitude."

❧

Two days after Fort Motte fell, Nathanael wrote to South Carolina Governor John Rutledge, who was in Philadelphia. With the belief that the tide was turning in that state, Nathanael's concerns for citizens and the primacy of civil authority were a matter close to his heart. If Britain tried to claim undisputed authority over the Southern states a functioning patriot government could dispute that claim.

"From the state in which I find things and the confusion and persecution which I foresee, I could wish that civil government might be set up immediately, as it is of importance to have the minds of the people formed to the habits of civil rather than military authority. This is under the presumption that we are able to hold our ground, which is uncertain."

According to Nathanael's plan to hold his ground, the string of forts in South Carolina began to fall and increased panic among Loyalists and the British. Francis Marion was not the only militia general who Nathanael was obliged to soothe. On May 2, the irascible Thomas Sumter set his sights on Fort Granby on the Congaree River and laid siege to it. Behind its trenches were 300 men commanded by Maryland Loyalist Andrew Maxwell. Maxwell had a notorious appetite for plunder, and Thomas Sumter's appetite was as voracious.

Nathanael took Harry aside and confided, "General Sumter has informed me that his state troops are growing, and his mounted troops will soon be equal to any in this state. He says nearly three hundred. He wants a field piece, which I have sent him."

"Do you believe General Sumter cannot force a surrender?" Harry asked.

"I believe he can—eventually, but he has taken most of his men and gone toward Orangeburg and Monck's Corner. He thinks he can slow Rawdon's advance toward Charleston, which is to be desired. But he has admittedly turned his eyes toward preventing the British colonel from carrying off great quantities of stock and horses."

"That is often his aim is it not?" Harry asked. A sly smile emerged. "You do not wish to wait for his whims."

"I do not wish to curtail his valuable vast intelligence network and the information he returns. I am resigned to his independent operations as he will not be pushed. Nor do I wish for Lord Rawdon to come to the defense of the fort."

Harry, always happy to be seen as invaluable to his commanding officer, whether it be in action or advice, waited for his orders with zeal.

"You will proceed immediately with the van of the army," Nathanael ordered, aware of his cavalryman's enthusiasm. It was something, with all the broken promises of support, he needed to sense. "You will demand an immediate surrender of the fort. I depend upon you pushing matters vigorously."

As with Fort Motte, Harry did just that. After Sumter successfully took the Orangeburg outpost to the southwest, he returned to find that Harry had not only forced a surrender on May 15, but had allowed the commander to take his plunder as a term of surrender.

Thomas was enraged. "You come to this place where I have left a sufficient number of troops to prevent the escape of Major Maxwell until I returned," the much older militia general fumed.

Harry saw trouble coming, and he let Thomas continue his rant without comment.

"If I had known you were going to these posts, I could have employed my troops to a very great advantage," Thomas seethed. "I want General Greene to recall you. Your services are not wanted at this place. I cannot believe he put you in command of the assault on Fort Motte!"

Harry realized that this was becoming more than he had the authority to quell. "General, perhaps this should be taken up with—"

Thomas noted the mortification in Harry's eyes. "I have the utmost respect for you, yet I wish you had not gone to that place. I had it in my power to reduce Motte, and I think it for the good of the public to do without regular army."

Sumter's last statement was a direct attack on the Southern Army Continentals, and Harry had no intention of continuing to stand witness to the Gamecock's castigation. General Greene was moving toward Fort Granby, and the fall of the fort was part of his critical plans to move on to the outpost at Ninety-Six, the last British depot in South Carolina outside of Charleston.

Thomas' rant was interrupted by a post rider with orders from Nathanael for Harry. Harry leaped at the welcome distraction as the last of Thomas' men arrived. He carefully read Nathanael's instructions.

You are to join General Andrew Pickens in assaulting Augusta, Georgia. Great care should be taken to preserve the stores for the use of the public if success is realized. I have disseminated this request to General Pickens.

Harry shouted orders to his legion. "Turnabout men! We are to join General Pickens near the South Carolina-Georgia border to assault Augusta. There will be no rest for us this day."

Harry and his legion left Thomas with his frustrations and rode the seventy-five miles to Augusta in three days. Thomas was left with nothing but to turn on Nathanael.

I am convinced your reasons are cogent & your observations exceedingly just; but with the deepest regret I find the discontent and disorder among the militia so great as to leave no hope of their subsiding soon. My indisposition and want of capacity to be of service to this country, and induces me as a friend to it, to beg leave to resign my command and have taken the liberty to enclose my commission.

"This letter does not surprise me in the least," Nathanael said to Otho who, with his aide, Major Elias Brown, and Nathanael's aides, Nat Pendleton and Lewis Morris, were bent over a map trying to determine the best route to march to the last remaining British outpost outside of Charleston—Ninety-Six on the Saluda River.

"And how do you plan to respond?" Otho asked, keeping his eyes on the map.

Nathanael rubbed his forehead. "It seems I am soothing militia generals at every turn. Only Andrew Pickens has gone on to Georgia without complaint."

"You do not have authority to accept Sumter's resignation," Nat pointed out. The lawyer in him was speaking, although he knew Nathanael was aware. "He is obligated to send it to the man who gave him his commission with broad authority over South Carolina militia, Governor John Rutledge. His commission has no standing in the Continental Army."

Otho looked up from the map. Everyone knew Governor Rutledge was in Philadelphia, so there was no need to issue a reminder.

"Sumter and his soldiers are a wild, lawless band who see nothing but the spoils of what they can capture, but he is a bold partisan," Lewis commented.

"I need him to watch the motions of the enemy," Nathanael admitted. "He claims his men are disgruntled, yet he has seen to the fall of the British depot at Orangeburg." Nathanael's only choice was to write a letter of conciliation that flattered Sumter with sentiments of how important his services were to the interest and happiness of the country. To appease his disgruntled men, he agreed to share with them the goods captured at Fort Granby.

Nathanael wrote his letter and then informed his army in orders of the day on May 11, of the planned march to the fortified town of Ninety-Six in northwestern South Carolina. On that day, he received a letter from Steuben in Virginia. The Prussian had managed to drive a wedge between himself and the Virginia Assembly with his autocratic actions. He complained to Nathanael that no man was more disgusted than he at their conduct and proceedings and lack of support for the army General Greene commanded, which hinged on saving their state.

The coincidence did not go unnoticed by either man. The same day Steuben wrote those words, Nathanael sent him a letter with orders to join the Southern Army. "I find myself so beset with difficulties that I need the counsel and assistance of an officer educated in the Prussian school, and I persuade myself I shall find in you both the friend and the General I want." The letter was intercepted by a British patrol.

twenty-seven
Ninety-Six

With the fall of the British outposts, Patriot light corps patrolled the roads and blocked messages from Lord Francis Rawdon and Colonel Nisbet Balfour to the British outposts at Augusta and Ninety-Six. Balfour wrote to Cornwallis in Virginia that the enemy's parties were everywhere, and the communication by land from Savannah no longer existed. The commander at Ninety-Six never received his orders to abandon the post.

Since the fall of Charleston, Ninety-Six had served the British. Named because it was ninety-six miles from a trading post in the foothills of the Blue Ridge Mountains, it was in a flourishing part of the country, supplied with good water and open air. With Colonel William Washington and Captain Robert Kirkwood leading on the Island Ford Road to screen them from Loyalist parties along the way, Nathanael's rain-soaked force of 900 Continentals from Maryland, Virginia, Delaware, and sixty-six North Carolina militia and three brass cannon approached the stockade walls of Ninety-Six on May 22.

Nathanael, Nat Pendleton, and Thaddeus Kosciuszko halted. Otho issued orders for the army to halt as well. Nathanael contemplated the works. "I do not think we can storm the palisades of the garrison. The walls appear to be near twelve feet in height. There are 550 veteran Loyalists inside, part of General Oliver De Lancey's militia brigade from New York, under the command of Colonel John Cruger."

The freshening wind ruffled their queues under gathering gray clouds. Thunder rumbled in the distance. Nathanael surveyed the darkening sky and calmly sent Lewis to disseminate information to the troops, "It will be sundown soon. I believe a close reconnoiter is in order before we make decisions about how to proceed."

"Yes, sir," Lewis said. He spurred his horse to inform colonels and captains to let their troops know and that they were to be ready at General Greene's orders. He told Colonel John Eager Howard, "Take advantage sir and let your troops eat and take of that liquid courage rum, if there is any."

John nodded his approval. Two young privates, Noah Clark and Tristan Caryl, exchanged glances as if to say, *Are we ready for this*?

Accompanied by two guards, Nathanael, Thaddeus, and Nat made an entire circuit of the wooden palisade surrounding the town, which was linked to an earthwork in the shape of a multi-pointed star called the Star Fort. Darkness fell and with it the rain.

"The fort has a system of pointed parapets and what looks like a gun platform in the northern most salient," Nat observed as he wiped rainwater from his face.

Thaddeus drew closer to the wall. "I see a ditch surrounding the fort covered with abatis. There appears to be a communication trench." His eyes moved eastward. "There also appears to be a fortified jail, a courthouse, and a few dwellings. Do we have intelligence on their water source?"

"Yes," Nathanael said, "the main source of water is a spring west of the town, which I am certain is protected, possibly by the jail you are seeing."

Thunder clapped and lightning jagged the sky. The rain stopped. There was another closer flash and then a sharp sound. "They are shooting at us," Nat warned. He pointed to the gun platform as bullets whizzed by the three like angry hornets. The guards immediately readied arms and rode to shelter Nathanael from the gunfire.

"I think that is enough for the night," Nathanael said. His party spurred their horses out of firing range.

They rode back to the anxious troops, who saw and heard the shots. They remained silent as their general dismounted, removed his gloves, and disappeared inside his tent to speak to his engineer, aides, and adjutant. "We are going to have to lay siege. Our 900 men are not enough to storm the walls," Nathanael concluded. "We will station our army at four different points to keep the town invested. The Star Fort should be our chief target, which I can only assume has its own water supply. Colonel Kosciuszko, I defer to you to lay out a plan that will begin immediately. Know that the Star Fort's commander is aware of our presence and will react accordingly."

The tall, sophisticated engineer looked pale for a moment. *I have only studied siege warfare and am not an expert,* he thought, *but I cannot make excuses to General Greene under any circumstances.* "We shall begin immediately," he said.

Nathanael appreciated Thaddeus' prompt, optimistic response. He turned to his aide, William Pierce. "Disseminate these orders to the men who have experience as sappers, and keep those in reserve who are fit to the exertion of digging trenches. I also want fleches in which to mount artillery."

It was carried out in the dark of night. Thaddeus tried to judge where to dig the first trench based on the distance from the British fortification. All the trees were cut down for a mile around the perimeter of the town. Therefore, he had to devise a way to mark the trench without the use of planks, which would be easier to see in the dark. The troops gathered while Thaddeus marked the initial lines with a pickaxe.

Nathanael, Otho, and Edward Carrington kept shifting their eyes toward the Star Fort walls. William Washington came up and said in a low voice, "Cruger is watching us."

Nathanael nodded. "As well as some of the town's inhabitants."

"Should my dragoons set a patrol to watch for any approaching enemy reinforcements?" William asked.

"Yes," Nathanael said. "But I leave it to you to decide the particulars as some of our men will need sleep."

William nodded and went off toward the smell of dragoon horses and the sound of their restlessness. Thaddeus issued instructions to the men who were to dig that night. The boys from Maryland, Tristan Caryl and Noah Clark, stepped up to volunteer along with a hundred other men. Others were assigned to stand watch. Digging began. The exhausting and intense labor went on all night. Those not involved slept on their arms.

The sun rose and promised another scorching day. The tall, muscular Noah Clark removed his hat and wiped sweat from his forehead with his tunic sleeve. The head of his pickaxe broke off. He started to climb out of the trench for repairs when artillery opened up from the gun platform in the fort and blasted through the trench, killing some of the men and raising clouds of dust so thick that the sappers had to blink and wipe their eyes to scramble away.

"Tristan, where are you?" Noah shouted among the chaotic rush of men running for their lives. He turned, bumped into his friend, and dragged him away from the trench.

The Virginia troops who were supposed to relieve the night diggers tried to cover the fleeing men, but another cannon blast nearly deafened them. Nathanael, Thaddeus, Otho, and John Eager Howard came running. John shouted orders in an effort to protect his vulnerable Marylanders, but it was hardly necessary. The survivors cleared the trench and sprinted for the protection of camp.

A detachment of Loyalists poured into the trench from the Star Fort to the sound of bullets whistling from the parapet. The few men who remained were bayonetted and their entrenching tools were stolen. Then, the attackers retired with their booty.

"Call Colonel Basil Cameron to arrange a party to get our dead out of the trenches," Nathanael instructed Lewis. He looked up at the gun platform and then tried to discern from where in the fort walls the Loyalist detachment had sallied forth. He called his officers to attend him in his tent.

Captain William Pierce made coffee and brought salted pork to the officers for breakfast. Thaddeus sat down with a plop. "The first parallel was dug too close," Nathanael said as he accepted a cup from William. "I suggest we let our men rest and begin anew tonight at a more respectful distance and out of artillery range. Thaddeus, you remain in charge of the works. We shall see to it that our artillery is set up."

That night, a new trench was laid some 300 yards away from the fort walls. "I ain't never seen soil like this," Jackson Killam of the 1st Virginia regiment groaned as he struggled with a pickaxe to make a dent in the nearly impenetrable clay soil. He straightened up, removed his hat, and wiped sweat from his forehead with the palm of his hand.

"It is backbreaking work to be sure," Tristan Caryl agreed. He threw his prize of shoveled dirt to the side.

Noah Clark swung his pickaxe with fierce might, loosened a huge chunk of clay, and said, "I am dying of thirst. I am going to fetch a bucket of water for us." He threw his pickaxe down and climbed out of the trench. He flinched when he heard a musket discharge from the direction of the fort and then realized what the shooter was aiming at.

Colonel Basil Cameron arrived with a group of naked slaves. Jackson stopped his work and frowned when the colonel handed the slaves tools, barked orders, and pointed to the trenches.

"I ain't digging with them," Jackson protested when he saw the resignation and fear in their eyes. "It ain't right making them work like that for us when they don't belong to the army. They don't even have the dignity of a pair of breeches."

Basil squatted at the edge of the trench. "It does not matter what you think. I know you fought with people who not only own slaves, like His Excellency, General George Washington himself, and officers that bring them to battles so they may be served. I wager you have even fought side by side with them."

Jackson sprung out of the trench with his pickaxe in hand. "You ain't my commanding officer, so don't talk to me that way, Cameron, or you will not be talking out of that shithole you call a mouth no more."

"Is that so, Private Killam? I suggest you get back to work or you will find yourself dangling from the gallows."

There was a shout, and men spilled over the fort's walls armed with muskets and bayonets, rifles, and swords. Tristan was repeatedly bayoneted in the chest. His eyes widened, and he collapsed face first into the clay dirt. The slaves scattered, but like Tristan, many of them were unmercifully bayonetted. Among the noise and carnage, Jackson's voice screaming for him to get up penetrated the last of Tristan's consciousness.

Over the next few days, the men toiled night and day swinging their picks and digging into the hard baked clay. At night, they were subject to Loyalist fire and struggled in the dark, sometimes hand-to-hand to keep the enemy from killing them and stealing their tools. During the day, they labored beneath the relentless sun. Mosquitoes and flies swarmed their sweaty skin.

On June 2, with the second parallel completed, Nathanael and Otho conferred over a meager dinner in their tent. The sound of pickaxes and the troops acting as miners, those who removed the loosened dirt from the trenches, played in the background like an orchestra.

"I think we are in the dominant position at this stage," Nathanael said. He tried not to rub his right eye. The dust raised from digging trenches and smoke from constant gunfire had irritated it to the point he was afraid he was getting an infection.

Otho was aware of Nathanael's affliction, and although he wanted to tell him to summon Dr. Read, he said nothing in that regard. "We have labored for two weeks now. I agree it is time to demand a surrender. Our men are exhausted, and surely Cruger's men must be as well. They have nowhere to go."

"That is our hope. I am sending you in with a flag of truce to demand Cruger's surrender. I leave it to you as my adjutant to word the terms."

Otho's handsome face brightened. "A reminder of the reduction of all the British posts seems appropriate to begin," he said.

As the sun began to set over western South Carolina, and the waxing gibbous moon hung in the eastern sky, Otho wrote the terms of surrender in his elegant handwriting. On the morning of June 3, he and Elias, with drums beating and a small contingent of guard under a flag of truce, approached the stockade wall. The Americans toiling in the trenches were ordered to leave for the day.

"Colonel John Cruger," Otho demanded. "I am Colonel Otho Williams, General Greene's adjutant. I am here on his behalf to demand your surrender."

John Cruger's aide, Captain Thomas Sullivan, appeared at a parapet. He considered Elias for a moment with disdain and then disappeared. The fort gate swung open, and Thomas stepped out. Without a word, he motioned for Elias to come forward and then held out his hand.

Riflemen appeared at the parapet and trained their guns on the Americans. Elias consulted his colonel with a glance. Otho nodded and Elias delivered the terms to Thomas.

"Can Cruger not appear himself or does he feel that he is unable to face the American army's representative?" Elias asked Thomas with contempt.

Thomas snorted, "General Greene has not presented himself, either." He snatched the paper, returned through the gate, and slammed it shut. He delivered the terms to the colonel.

Colonel John Cruger sat at his desk beside the smoldering fireplace in his tiny office and poured a glass of rum. The forty-four-year-old well-educated, rich colonel was not to be rushed. He read the terms of surrender.

The reduction of all the British posts upon Wateree, Congaree and Santee Rivers; and your present circumstances Leave you no hope but in the generosity of the American Army. The Honourable Major General Greene has therefore commanded me to demand an immediate Surrender of your Garrison.

*The General expects a compliance with this Summons, which
I am authorized to assure you, will not be repeated. Your most
humble servant, O.H. Williams.*

Cruger chuckled and considered throwing the document in the fire
but changed his mind. He scratched out a rebuttal.

*I am honored with your Letter of this Day, intimating Major
General Greene's immediate Demand of the surrender of His
Majesty's garrison at Ninety-Six, a Compliance with which
my Duty to my Sovereign renders inadmissible at present.*

"Captain Sullivan, deliver this to the rebels," John instructed with a
sneer, "and do not tarry to wait for General Greene to show his face."

"Yes, sir," Thomas replied. He returned to the gate and swung it
open. He was startled when a sweating rider appeared instead of Colonel
Williams or Major Brown. "A message for Colonel Cruger from Lord
Francis Rawdon in response to his letter dated the 31st of May."

Thomas took the message from the rider's outstretched hand. "How
did you get through—"

The man set spurs and wheeled his horse.

Thomas shrugged and then walked toward the American picket carrying a white flag. "Colonel Cruger's response to Colonel Williams' delivered terms of surrender," he told one of the young guards. The guard left
Thomas standing there under the watchful eyes of the garrison and the
town's people, and returned with Otho.

"Colonel Cruger denies your request," Thomas said as he offered
the message. Without waiting for a response, he disappeared through
the gate.

Otho was unsurprised and went to report the denial to Nathanael.

Inside the fort, John summoned some of his officers and explained, "I
wrote to his lordship explaining that enemy fire has thus far had no effect

and that we can amply defend this and the town. My only concern is that relief might not arrive before our provisions are expended."

"And his lordship's response?" Thomas asked.

"Ships carrying three British regiments have arrived off Charleston," John said, pleased. "Lord Rawdon is now free to march to our aid without worry that Charleston might be lost. The question put is how long will it take Rawdon to organize troops and provisions and with what size force?"

Attended by William Pierce and Lewis Morris, Nathanael stood in the glaring sun outside his tent and read Cruger's rebuttal. He blinked and slapped at a mosquito that insisted on buzzing near his watering eyes.

His commissary general, Colonel William Davie, approached Otho, who was standing on the peripheral of the group. "From the dour faces, I assume Cruger rebuffed the surrender," William said. For a moment, he was distracted by soldiers hauling buckets of water into camp, dipped from the same rivulet that ran through the stockade town.

Otho considered William. William's pen frequently found criticism for his actions including those at Guilford Courthouse and Hobkirk's Hill.

Nathanael rubbed his right eye and stared at the roof of British soldiers' quarters. *Fort Motte*, he thought. *Harry and Francis set the roof on fire to drive out the British and then fired at them so they could not put out the fire.*

The next day, the excited Virginia boys, John Cassidy and Christopher Madison, were among the men who shot flaming arrows soaked in pitch from their muskets to ignite all the shingled roofs in the town. Each time one caught fire, they would whoop with laughter. But Cruger had the last laugh. That night, he ordered troops to remove the roofs. At the same time, some sallied and tore down a shelter used to protect Colonel Kosciuszko's sappers. Exasperated, Nathanael ordered an artillery barrage on the fort, but it did not have the affect he hoped.

That was not the only thing that exasperated Nathanael. He was aware of the arrival of British reinforcements at Charleston and reports that they were advancing toward Ninety-Six. It had been brought to his attention after a messenger delivered a Charleston newspaper that printed news of the advent. He was becoming impatient with the length of the siege. He wrote to the Marquis de Lafayette under his command in Virginia, "If the enemy arrives, it will be mortifying after the incredible fatigue we have gone through in carrying on our approaches and the losses we have sustained in the siege."

On June 7, the day Rawdon set out for Ninety-Six with a powerful force of 2,000, Harry Lee with his cavalry legion and Andrew Pickens and his South Carolina militia arrived fresh from their victories in reducing the British outpost of Fort Galphin in Augusta, Georgia. Harry rode in well-dressed in his short green jacket and black boots and arrived with spectacle. One of his officers, Captain Michael Rudolph, skirted the town with prisoners collected in Augusta. Cruger saw this as an insult and opened fire on the legion.

Nathanael summoned Harry to his tent. "What are you doing parading prisoners like that?"

"Do you believe I sanctioned this? Captain Rudolph has been reprimanded."

"Release them to Major Edward Hyrne, our commissioner of prisoners."

"I will do so," Harry said. An opinion danced on the end of his tongue as it always did before rushing out of his mouth, "I am appalled at the little effort that has been made to cut the enemy's water supply. Was this Colonel Kosciuszko's plan? From your letters, I gathered it is on the western end of town near a stockade fort and jail."

"The project of cutting off the water has been well weighed, considered, and rejected on mature consideration. The Star Fort dominates all the other works and therefore must be dealt with first."

"Kosciuszko is extremely amiable, and I believe a truly good man, but his blunders may lose us Ninety-Six," Harry continued boldly.

Nathanael met his challenge. "Then you are to lay siege to the stockade fort effective immediately. But you must be warned that Colonel Cruger sends detachments out nightly to attack our sappers. The attacks are fierce and frequent."

As ordered, Harry and his men began digging approaches. Colonel Cruger doubled his nocturnal attacks, sometimes on the sappers near the Star Fort and others on Harry's men digging trenches near the stockade fort. Exhaustion set in as sleep became increasingly elusive for both the Patriots and the British, which was augmented by the nightly horrible hand-to-hand combat.

On June 9, Nathanael wrote to the president of the Continental Congress, Samuel Huntington, and described Ninety-Six and explained that the siege was going exceedingly slow, and about his poor, fatigued fellows. With his family always on his mind no matter the embroilment, he dashed off a quick letter to General Washington. "My family are so unwell that I have begged Congress to transmit your Excellency's copies of my letters to them. As soon as I can get a leisure moment, I will give you a more full and particular account of matters in this quarter."

Their desperation increased. Nathanael assigned some of Andrew Pickens' men to build a Maham Tower to house sharpshooters who could fire from its top into the fort while sheltered behind protective logs. Cruger responded by ordering his men to raise the parapets on the Star Fort three feet with sandbags.

Nathanael needed to quell the desperation with eyes on the advancing forces from Charleston, for without that, he was blind and unable to gauge how much time they had to operate without an impending attack. With the knowledge that horsemen belonging to the 3rd Brigade of South Carolina Troops under Andrew Pickens were among the troops, he called for the militia general.

"I understand that Major Thomas Farrar's brigade is here," Nathanael said to Andrew when he answered the call. "I know that many of his men were at the conflict at Blackstock's Plantation last November where Thomas Sumter was wounded. Therefore, they are familiar with Sumter and can work with him if necessary to track Lord Rawdon."

"Yes, sir, they can," Andrew confirmed. "If you are asking for scouts, they are perfectly acquainted with the countryside, although many of them hail from the Spartan District near the North Carolina border."

"This is what I desire," Nathanael said. He turned to Lewis, "Summon Major Farrar, and tell him to bring the men to me who he will choose for this mission."

"Yes, sir." Lewis took the order and returned in a short time with Major Thomas Farrar and two men, one of whom Nathanael recognized— Captain Charles Chitty. "I am grateful to have your merit and fidelity under this trying and disagreeable situation," Nathanael said.

Chitty bowed deeply. "I am always at your disposal, sir."

Nathanael indicated the other man in the tent. "Your name, please."

The twenty-seven-year-old man stepped forward and bowed. "I'm Private Bailey Anderson, sir."

"Were you at Blackstock's?" Nathanael asked.

"Yes, sir. We defeated that rascal Banastre Tarleton's British regulars."

"Do you have experience scouting?"

"Yes, sir. In Roebuck's Battalion under Captain James Parson. We were out on several occasions against Indians and out laying Tories who threatened our family and friends near the Watauga Settlements on North Carolina's western border."

"I understand," Nathanael said as he thought about what he would do to defend his own family.

"Sir, if I may," Bailey said. "I was also at the Siege of Augusta in September 1780. I have some experience with Colonel John Cruger. He was sent to rescue the forces we were besieging. We were forced to retreat, and he pursued us to no avail."

The stress in Nathanael's eyes softened for a moment when he said, "We are glad to have your services, Private Anderson."

He explained the mission to the men in the tent and then dismissed them.

❧

Thaddeus' sappers began digging a tunnel meant to end at the rampart of the fort where a mine would be detonated to blast an opening for assault troops. The Polish colonel was bayonetted along with his sappers when Cruger's men found the opening to the tunnel.

Harry prevailed on Nathanael to allow him to set the stockade fort on fire and deprive Cruger of his water supply on that side. He sent out a detachment during a dark, violent, rainless storm. A sergeant and nine privates conducted the daring enterprise. During the feat, the sergeant and five privates were shot to death.

On June 12, a local man rode into camp and chatted with some of the rebels. No one gave it much thought. Locals often came into camp—mostly out of curiosity. The man suddenly held a piece of paper above his head and flapped it like a flag of truce. The Star Fort's door swung open, and the man galloped inside with a letter for the fort's commander.

"The bastards inside are cheering!" one of the Marylanders exclaimed to his commander, John Eager Howard. John, with his soft-spoken ways, made no comment. He was as exhausted as the other officers. The siege did nothing to relieve the usual tasks of issuing supplies, serving as officer of the day, and assigning men to dig trenches and provide protection for the sappers in a rotation so men would not become enervated.

During the siege, Nathanael still administered his command in the South. He sent orders to artificers to make cartridge boxes for his army and sent the governor of North Carolina a letter regarding a matter of great importance—dragoon horses. He received word from Thomas Sumter that Lord Francis Rawdon was on his way to Ninety-Six. Captain Chitty and his scout Bailey Anderson returned and confirmed Sumter's report.

In response to Nathanael's request, William Washington arrived with spurs jingling on his boots. "You sent for me, sir?" the chubby young colonel asked.

He does not look as fatigued as the rest of us, Nathanael thought with relief. He said, "I have written to General Sumter that I wish him to gall Rawdon as much as possible to delay him and deprive him of sustenance the country may provide his army. He is to collect all the force he can and give positive orders to Marion's forces to join him. I want you to link up with Sumter to support him."

"And where is General Sumter?" William asked in a quiet voice, a reflection of his youthful studies of the ministry that he abandoned when the first shots of the Revolutionary War were fired.

"The last he mentioned was that he was at Fort Granby on the Congaree River but that he was marching to fall in ahead of the enemy."

William was not a scholar, but he knew a deception when he heard one. Yet, he said nothing as it was an assumption, and he knew General Greene was beginning to feel the hopelessness of the siege. "I request a number of Colonel Lee's infantry to accompany me," William said.

"You have it at your disposal if Colonel Lee is agreeable, which he will be," Nathanael said with a slight smile. He rose from his chair, an indication that William was dismissed. As William exited his general's marquee tent, Nathanael said, "I wish you Godspeed."

William's brown eyes stung with tears that he dare not shed. *General Greene has given me his blessing, and that means more to me than all the orders and compliments in the world.*

As Nathanael waited for word from his militia generals, Rawdon and his army marched through Orangeburg unopposed and drew closer to Ninety-Six. If Sumter and Marion did not stop him, he would arrive at the fortified town in a few days. William rode into Fort Granby with his contingent of cavalry that afternoon. Sumter greeted the sweating dragoons and horses with little enthusiasm when they entered the stockade.

"So General Greene has sent you to support me, but you have wasted your time," he grumped. "I sent a detachment of my men to hang on Rawdon's rear. They were attacked and then deserted."

William dismounted and pulled off his riding gloves. "And General Marion? Where is he?"

"I ordered him to march to Ninety-Six to support General Greene but then halted him because I am uncertain of the enemy's movements nor am I aware of Marion's actual strength."

William motioned for his dragoons to dismount. The horses needed to be watered and fed as well as the men. He hesitated to bark orders at the older general. Instead, he said, "I suggest we do our best to follow through with General Greene's request."

With Sumter's refusal to budge and Francis Marion's hesitation to become part of a protracted siege, William was left with nothing. Lord Rawdon was probably beyond his reach, and he did not have the numbers to distract an army of 2,000 men.

Indeed, Rawdon was moving unobstructed. He wrote to Cornwallis in Virginia of his plans to march, but his army was suffering. They were marching in 100-degree temperatures and high humidity wearing heavy woolen uniforms. Many of them were fresh recruits from Ireland unaccustomed to the brutal weather and swarms of mosquitos and gnats. Rawdon was suffering from the effects of malaria. Men dropped dead along the march, and still he kept coming.

❧

Nathanael was in a race to complete the siege before Rawdon arrived. With artillery, Harry managed to force the British to evacuate the stockade fort that protected the rivulet and spring. Cruger was forced to dig a well inside the Star Fort that yielded nothing, but it made no difference. Nathanael tried to mask his discouragement and anger when he went to speak to Otho.

"I am calling off the assault," he said as he sat down in Otho's hot, stuffy tent. "William returned with news of generals Sumter and Marion. Neither made a real effort to hinder Rawdon's advance. We have no hope of reinforcements."

Otho poured two glasses of rum and handed one to Nathanael. He noted the look in his general's blue eyes, which normally shined with lambency, but were now dull with disappointment. "Are you certain?" Otho asked. "Is this to be the order of the day?"

Silence stretched out between them for a moment. Nathanael sighed, drank his rum, and said, "We have three choices. Retreat, stand and face Rawdon, or storm the fortifications. We do not have enough men or the strength to perform the last two. Issue orders for a retreat."

As the sun peeked over the eastern horizon on the morning of June 18, Otho's aide, Elias, stood in front of their little army, depleted further from exhaustion, disease, or death in the trenches. "The general orders this day are that we will abandon this siege and retreat eastward. The General has taken every measure in his power to stop the British advance."

Private Noah Clark asked, "Retreat? After such toil? We beg to make amends for our mistake at Hobkirk's Hill," he pleaded, referring to his Maryland line's confusion at the battle.

Even Thaddeus scowled, although one buttock was still sore from taking a bayonet to it.

"We ain't going, General Greene," Jackson Killam protested. "We broke our backs and lost men. We got pride."

The exhausted sappers agreed in unison.

Nathanael's eyes moved through the ranks. This was why he sacrificed his health—constantly fighting asthma and eye infections that depleted his energy. These men were his world, his hope, and his strength. *Am I to deny them?* Yet he knew the answer was *no.* "I will not risk our whole army. Therefore, I ask for volunteers to storm the stockade fort and the Star Fort simultaneously while riflemen in our tower keep down the heads of the British defenders with incessant firing."

Colonel Richard Campbell of Virginia stepped forward. "My regiment will storm the Star Fort backed by the 1st Maryland."

"We will lead that assault," Lieutenant Isaac Duval of the Maryland Line volunteered.

Lieutenant Samuel Seldon of the 1st Virginia came forward. "Aye, we will join them."

"Captain Kirkwood's Delaware regiment and my legion will cut the water supply at the stockade fort on the right and will continue there," Harry said.

Robert Kirkwood and his Delaware men murmured their support.

The men who would lead the assault were Nathanael's forlorn hope. They were not expected to survive the battle, yet they stood bravely.

Therefore, under the scorching South Carolina sun, Hezekiah Carr, a drummer boy for the 3rd Maryland, beat to arms, and the signal to storm the forts fired at noon. The entire American line began to fire—the artillery from their emplacements, riflemen from the Maham tower, and infantry from every available American position.

The assaulting troops wasted not a minute and plunged into the trenches; they carried muskets with fixed bayonets, rifles, axes, and pikes. The forlorn hope chopped down the abatis—sharpened tree trunks—on the fort's sloping walls and pulled down the sandbags from the parapets to make the walls easier to scale.

John Cruger launched a counterstrike with a pair of sorties to strike at the flanks of the attackers. In what was the equivalent of a dry moat, in the hellish heat of mid-afternoon, men screamed and grunted as they thrust bayonets and clubbed one another, dying in a bloody pit of horror. Ripped by crossfire from the apertures in the ramparts, the forlorn hope desperately tried to hold its ground. Lieutenants Duval and Seldon were badly wounded. One hundred fifty Patriots fell before Nathanael ordered the rest to remove from the trenches.

That night, with Rawdon bearing down on Ninety-Six, the rebels encamped outside the walls under a clear starry sky illuminated by the dim light of the waning crescent moon. The mournful groans of the wounded haunted the night. Thirty-one Americans lay dead in the trenches and on the spikey walls of the Star Fort. Their voices, which proclaimed that they had earned the right to fight Colonel John Cruger and his Loyalists, echoed in the Patriots' ears.

The next day, Nathanael and Cruger reached a humanitarian agreement to allow the Patriots to bury their dead. After digging graves in the hard clay, Nathanael's men retreated up the Saluda River. Forty hours later, Lord Rawdon's reinforcements marched into the garrison.

❧

The assault failed, but on the afternoon of June 19, Nathanael praised his troops who had attacked the forts in his general orders:

The judicious and alert behavior of the light infantry of the legion and those commanded by Captain Kirkwood, directed by Colonel Lee, met with deserved success. And there is great reason to believe that the attack on the star battery directed by Colonel Campbell would have been equally fortunate if the brave Lieutenants Duval and Seldon, who most valiantly led on the advanced parties, had not been unluckily wounded.

The siege was over, but for Nathanael and others it lingered miserably. Lieutenant Samuel Seldon, frantically trying to pull down sandbags, was hit by a musket ball in his right wrist that shattered the arm bone to the shoulder. The wound meant amputation. Men held him down as the surgeon prepared to begin his grisly work. Samuel held his right hand with his left, kept his eyes fixed on the work, and remained silent until the doctor reached the marrow. He said calmly, "I pray you, Doctor, be quick."

That afternoon Andrew Pickens sat down with the commander-in-chief over a cup of coffee. "I beg your pardon for interrupting your correspondence," Andrew said when he opened the tent flap and poked his head inside.

"Come in," Nathanael invited. "Coffee is on the fire outside if you wish to indulge."

"I have some, sir," Andrew said as he lifted the cup. He sat on the camp stool near Nathanael's writing desk. "I came out of curiosity, being a militia general from South Carolina myself. I wondered the cause of my fellow officers' failure to harass the enemy or their not joining the army."

Nathanael's forehead wrinkled as he scowled. "I assume you are referring to Sumter and Marion? I cannot believe they used every damned excuse they could possibly muster. After all their exertions in this state, and yet they let that haughty young English colonel march through as if he owned the damned place! I swear that if I did not need them when they do cooperate, I should have accepted both their resignations when they offered them to me." He pounded his fist on the desk and sent the ink pot and quill tumbling off.

Andrew flinched; his eyes widened. *General Greene never uses language like that*, he thought.

Nathanael took a deep breath. "After our unfortunate failure, someone suggested to me that I save myself and the army by retiring and abandoning the Carolinas to the occupation of their enemies and fall back to Virginia."

"And your answer?"

"I will recover South Carolina or die in the attempt."

Andrew smiled. *This is the conviction I admire in General Greene.*

Lewis entered the tent and said, "I apologize for my interruption."

"You are never an interruption," Nathanael assured him. *I must calm myself in regard to the distress Sumter and Marion has left me in.*

Lewis' eyes fell on the spilled ink pot. "I will clean that up for you, sir," he said as he began to squat before the mess.

"No, I will tend to it," Nathanael assured. He returned his attention to Andrew. "I have written to the Marquis de Lafayette in Virginia that I am endeavoring to oblige the British Army to evacuate Ninety-Six and to maneuver them down into the lower country of South Carolina."

Andrew rose and bowed. "I beg leave to gather my scattered forces. I am at your disposal in all cases, General Greene."

Nathanael would indeed soon need his services.

The Saluda River, where the American Army was camped, snaked quietly southward as the general orders of the day on the morning of June 23 were announced. "The troops are to clean their arms and accoutrements, to wash their clothes, and cook their provisions," William Pierce read. "No passes are to be—"

"General Greene, a message for you from Colonel Lee." Nathanael stopped his inspection of his horse's tack, something he preferred to do himself instead of giving the responsibility to someone else. He stroked the mare's nose and took the message. "Thank you, corporal." William's voice faded into the background as he read the note:

Lord Rawdon arrived at Ninety-Six on June 21 and repaired that evening in pursuit of us. His lordship had no provisions nor has he taken any measures to get any.

Nathanael replied:

If the British Army is in the distress you represent they cannot, they will not follow us far this morning nor am I of the opinion they will pursue us further. Our army will be on the march for the Sandy River towards the crossroad on the route to the Catawba nation.

The following day, Nathanael led his army to Timm's Tavern between the Broad and Catawba Rivers and hoped for the arrival of more militia while he waited for the enemy to show his hand. It hurt Nathanael's heart to see dismayed Patriot families trudge the roads to escape the threat of the British Army, which further fueled the civilian war in the South.

Francis Rawdon retraced his footsteps back to Ninety-Six under the realization that it was a vain effort to hold the town after Nathanael Greene had swept through South Carolina and destroyed the primary British outposts. Greene was on the loose, and Rawdon had orders to meet Colonel Alexander Stewart at Fort Granby with supplies and reinforcements.

Rawdon's distressed army suffered in the short few days they had attempted to go after Greene. As they rested, he called a meeting with Colonel John Cruger and the town leaders who gathered in the Star Fort. "Gentlemen," Rawdon began, "I must withdraw my protecting army, but we will not forget the good service you have rendered."

There were murmurs among the assembled.

"And if we choose to defend the works?" Henry Larkin, a principal figure in the town, asked.

Rawdon's homely countenance softened. "I will leave a party to aid you in defending them and send you from time to time such succor as you might need. If you had rather submit to a temporary exile, I will provide a sufficient escort for your families and goods and send you safely into British lines."

"Then my family and I will go," Henry said, "but we will choose to return if necessary."

"With Greene's army roving the countryside clamoring with Patriots, my family is better off here," Richard Templeton announced.

There were shouts of, "Hear, hear!" and exclamations of, "We will not go!"

"Very well," Rawdon said. "Colonel Cruger, you are to remain with the garrison and prepare to evacuate. If you determine it necessary to burn the works, then do so. All who wish to go, we shall leave forthwith."

He divided his troops, and with 800 infantry and sixty cavalry, the melancholy train of exiles began their weary march with Harry Lee and his legion on their heels. Dust clouded the road as they trudged under the excruciating heat of early July, followed by relentless mosquitos, gnats, and flies that would bring disease to the people who had lived in the purity of the country around Ninety-Six.

❧

Nathanael received word from a spy that Rawdon was marching toward Fort Granby. He conferred with Edward Carrington, Isaac Huger, and Otho Holland Williams.

"I plan to prevent him from establishing a post on Friday's Ferry and march by way of Winnsboro," Nathanael told his officers. "I am leaving the army with you Isaac and plan to go ahead with the cavalry under William and Harry. I hope that I might better direct the army on how to slow down Rawdon's forces sufficiently so we can collect for battle before he and Stewart rendezvous."

"I recommend leaving our baggage, stores, and invalids as we march through Winnsboro," Edward advised.

"What of the militia?" Otho asked.

"I have asked Sumter and Marion to collect all the forces they can and meet us at that place. I know you will all do your best," Nathanael said with a light in his blue eyes that his officers were familiar with when he was optimistic. "With Captain Pendleton gone, I must gather my aides to accompany me. You are dismissed."

Isaac and Edward rose and left Nathanael's headquarters, but Otho lingered. "Nathanael, I pray you are careful out there with only the cavalry to protect you," he said.

Nathanael nodded at his tall, wise adjutant and then asked, "Have you heard from your sister, Mercy?"

Otho felt tears sting the back of his eyes. "Thank you for asking after my family when we are in great distress."

"Our families lie at the heart of everything we do. I shall stay safe, my dear friend."

～

On the morning of July 6, Isaac reached Friday's Ferry on the Congaree River. A cool breeze sighed as the sun rose to burn it away. Isaac stared across the river then scanned the shore to his left and right. Not a boat was to be seen. The young South Carolina general griped to his aide, Captain Samuel Earle, "It appears his lordship has beaten us to it."

"It does, but there is a little-known crossing down the river at Howell's Ferry," Samuel said. "The conveyances may be lacking, but here we have nothing."

Otho came up. He considered the slow moving waters of the Congaree.

"Howell's Ferry," Isaac said, noting Otho's perplexed countenance.

Two days later, the army was across and joined Nathanael and the cavalry waiting at Beaver Creek. Andrew Pickens trailed in with his militia. Otho offered Andrew a handshake. "The occasion of your arrival is much needed."

"Thomas Sumter has finally decided to cooperate with us and is on his way from Waxhaws," Nathanael interjected with relief. "Francis Marion is coming from the Santee."

"Good news indeed," Isaac agreed. He, too, gave a sigh of relief.

Otho took Nathanael aside. "Did you meet with success in preventing Rawdon and Stewart from linking up?"

"Unfortunately, we were too late," Nathanael replied. "Rawdon was at Fort Granby when we arrived, but he retired with precipitation toward Orangeburg. I think we surprised him. We made a rapid march with the whole of our cavalry to intercept them before they could rendezvous but to no avail. Harry's legion hung on their rear, and one of his captains successfully killed many of Rawdon's dragoons who were off the main column."

Jingling tack and men shouting distracted Nathanael and Otho. A few of the soldiers cheered. Nathanael grinned and said, "It appears that General Sumter has kept his word."

The newcomers pulled up and dismounted. Thomas Sumter strolled toward Nathanael and Otho as if he had not a care in the world. He swept off his cap and bowed. "I am at your service, General Greene." He directed his bow at Otho. "Colonel Williams."

Otho and Nathanael exchanged humorous glances as if to say, *I suppose this means we have been honored.* Isaac came up to see for himself that Sumter was actually there.

As if not to be outdone, trotting horses and marching men appeared near the edge of the woods and then slowly entered camp. Man and beast alike looked as if they were about to melt from the heat, and a cloud of mosquitos swarmed around the sweating horses.

"Francis Marion!" Isaac exclaimed when the perspiring, slight militia general rode up. "I'll be damned. It is good to have you with us!"

"Isaac," Francis acknowledged. When he dismounted, he shot Thomas a bristly look.

Thomas pretended not to notice.

"What is our plan?" Francis asked Nathanael as he handed the reins of his horse to his personal valet, Oscar.

"We shall discuss it this afternoon. Our commissary general, Colonel William Davie, has ensured we have food and rum."

"I do not drink, General Greene."

Nathanael suppressed a chuckle. "I am aware. Well then, you can provide your own beverage. And if you are averse to eating frog legs, you can provide your own food."

Over dinner that evening, Nathanael explained, "The plan is simple. Andrew Pickens is going west to watch the enemy movements from Ninety-Six from which I have intelligence that Colonel Cruger is on his way and has vowed to burn every building from that place to Orangeburg."

"He will not do it," Thomas snorted. He did not cringe from drinking rum as his counterpart Francis did. "It is too hot. He will be lucky if his horses do not die before he reaches Orangeburg."

A snicker of approval prevailed in the tent before Nathanael continued, "We march for Orangeburg tomorrow morning." He paused to pour another glass of rum. He looked down at the frog legs on his plate, grimaced a little, and then went on, "We are 2,000 strong between militia and regulars and can cut them down if we can force them into battle."

When they set out for Orangeburg on July 11, the officers who had gathered in Nathanael's tent had no way of knowing that the meal they enjoyed together would be their last for several days. Nathanael later wondered if he should have finished those frog legs. The following day, they encamped on strong ground four miles from Orangeburg. With a few dragoons from William's 3rd Continentals, Nathanael took Lewis Morris and William Pierce with him to reconnoiter the enemy position.

What he found while looking through his pocket spyglass displeased him. "They are advantageously posted." He squinted and then continued, "They occupy several strong buildings. One appears to be a brick jail." He lowered the spyglass. "I do not think our cannon will blast them out. I have seen this before during the battle we fought at Germantown, Pennsylvania, in October 1777. General Knox's cannon failed to dislodge the enemy screened in a brick house."

"The Edisto River is at his back," Lewis noted. "There is no other passage for miles."

Nathanael rubbed his upper lip in thought. "If we can lure him out to do battle, it might be possible to achieve a victory. As it stands, our cavalry will be useless. Let us return to camp."

The little group turned their horses toward the encampment where the army was suffering for lack of meat. Nathanael relayed his observations.

"Is there a chance that we can draw them out?" Otho wondered.

"I think we can," Harry chimed in. "We can attack the British posts to the southward at Monck's Corner and Dorchester and try to draw Rawdon out to defend them. What say you, General Marion and Sumter? Are you and your men up to the task?"

"They are nothing but churches," Thomas observed. "We are certainly up to it."

"If you are offering to act in conjunction with us, then me and my men are also up to the game," Francis assured.

Nathanael's eyes moved through his footsore, hungry, saddle weary men whose tattered uniforms hung on thin sunburned bodies. Some shivered with the effects of fever. Their horses were as gaunt and spent as their riders, and their saddles were falling apart. The core of his command was the Delaware and Maryland infantry and the 3rd Light Dragoons, as well as the 1st and 2nd Virginia regiments. He focused on the young men from Maryland: Noah Clark, Basil Cameron, and James McCurdy, who had endured devastating losses. *I am certain they do not care one way or another,* he thought. *They need rest and resupply.*

Harry and William rode toward the low country with cavalry, militia, and Captain Robert Kirkwood's Delaware line for support. Nathanael turned his army northward toward a desperately needed camp of repose in the breezy High Hills of Santee in central South Carolina twenty miles south of Camden. General Steuben and the Marquis de Lafayette, who were under Nathanael's overall command, would have to reckon with Cornwallis in Virginia.

He gave up hope that the new governor of Virginia, Thomas Nelson, was listening to his pleas for militia reinforcements and warned Lafayette to avoid a general action. To Steuben he wrote that his army anxiously awaited news of a French fleet. If Steuben's gout prevented him from joining him in South Carolina, then despite what he told Lafayette, if he had the numbers, he should turn upon a general action if he found it advisable.

twenty-eight

At Eutaw Springs the Valiant Died

When Nathanael turned his back on Orangeburg, Francis Rawdon left a covering force and did the same. He marched to Charleston unmolested. The expedition Nathanael sent the militia on with Harry Lee did not meet his expectations. Yet, they did manage to throw the enemy into a panic and capture some prisoners and stores. Marion and Sumter wasted time rivaling with one another, but there was nothing Nathanael could do except cast a positive light on it to his troops and Congress with extra praise for Harry and William.

The army settled at Richardson's plantation on the High Hills of Santee, a ridge of sand, clay, and gravel that rose 200 feet above the Wateree River for twenty-four miles and was fruitful with grain that provided forage for man and beast. Spring waters and giant oak trees shaded the strongly situated encampment that was close enough to the Santee River to pose a threat to the enemy.

On July 16, Nathanael stood on the hill and inhaled the fresh air, hoping that his asthma would calm and his men could heal. He heard someone approach from behind.

"General Greene," Robert Kirkwood said as he joined his general. "I spent time calculating that it's been 100 days since we left Cornwallis and plunged into South Carolina. Our light troops have marched 771 miles through the heat of this unhealthy place."

Nathanael regarded Robert. "Why did you compile that information?"

"Numbers is a hobby I enjoy."

"It is an honorable hobby," Nathanael agreed. "It *has* been toilsome days and nights since I arrived here eight months ago. Every dawn has recalled us to labor and care, and not a night has brought the promise of rest. We have crossed hundreds of miles together through the Carolinas, and still it is not over." He exhaled a sigh. "Excuse me, Robert. Dr. Read has the hospital tent set up. I should visit some of our sick."

Robert watched Nathanael limp through the tall shady grass. He looked as thin and malnourished as his troops.

Otho issued the orders of the day. They stressed discipline, cleanliness, exercise, and all the general regulations established by Congress. He knew the greatest expectations were the expectations General Greene put upon himself, and there would be no rest for him or his pen.

When Nathanael entered the hospital tent, the smell of putrid wounds, blood, and vomit turned his stomach. The sick were laid out on ragged blankets, some occupied by three men. Dr. William Read was treating a man he recognized from the 1st Virginia regiment.

"Private Jackson Killam?" Nathanael asked as he kneeled beside him.

"Aye, sir," Jackson said.

Nathanael's eyes slipped toward Dr. Read, and he watched for a moment as the doctor washed and bandaged Jackson's bloody and ravaged feet.

"Are you without shoes?" Nathanael asked Jackson.

"Aye, sir. Since Ninety-Six."

"Did you tell someone?"

"Aye, sir. Lieutenant Samuel Seldon, but he got his arm amputated, and I reckon he ain't up to helping anyone."

Nathanael's face clouded with concern. "There are too many like you. I will inform our quartermaster, but I doubt there is much Colonel Carrington can do without pleading for them from shoemakers in the countryside. Our clothing coffers are empty." His knee protested painfully when he got to his feet. "Be well. I will inquire after your new commanding officer and let him know you are on bedrest."

Nathanael heard the distress and relief in his voice when Jackson said, "Much obliged, General."

☙

From his marquee tent, Nathanael took care of the most important business on his mind: Caty. He knew he had left her in distress, but she was the one person who he could pour his heart out to without suffering judgement on his tired yet determined soul. He wrote, "I suppose you are in Westerly. I wish I was there with you, free from the bustle of the World and the miseries of war. My very nature recoils at the horrid scenes which this country affords, and longs for a peaceful retirement where love and softer pleasures are to be found. Here, turn which way you will, you hear nothing but the mournful widow, and the plaints of fatherless child. Ruin is in every form, misery in every shape. The heart you sent me is in my watch, and picture in my bosom."

The destitution of whole districts in South Carolina was the result of a war carried on by plunder and murder between Patriots and Loyalists. Families were reduced to beggary. Nathanael aired his distress in a letter to Andrew Pickens. "I beg you to take every step in your power to bring offenders to justice. If any are caught, I want them sent to me for trial. If you can find a way to take from those who have plenty and give to the poor you have my permission to issue government receipts."

The dangers of martial law since South Carolina Governor John Rutledge went into exile ate at Nathanael, and he longed for the calm life of civil authority. When the governor rode into camp one early morning, there was much excitement among the troops and officers.

William Pierce delivered the news and resumed his responsibility to carefully label every letter Nathanael wrote or received and put them on file. Nathanael left his tent and approached John with an outstretched hand.

"Nathanael," John said with a wide smile and a firm handshake. "I had the pleasure of meeting your aide, Major Ichabod Burnet, who you sent to Philadelphia to report on the state of your army."

"What is the news from Philadelphia?"

John hesitated for a moment, knowing that what he was about to say would fill the general with anxiety. "You are being hailed as the conquering hero and idol of America, but there is talk that you are unpopular with your officers. There is even a story circulating that you abused an officer with strong language. Colonel John Trumbull, recently released from his imprisonment in London on charges of treason, has loudly criticized your deficiency in the art of retreating."

Nathanael winced.

"There are many members of Congress who know your temperament and find that story incredible, despite the harsh letters you tend to write when you are agitated," John assured. "Now that I am here, it seems we have work to do."

"Perhaps you can take some of the burden of controlling the wrongs in this state. The pillaging and plundering among Loyalists and Patriots for one." He turned to William Pierce and said, "Get the governor's things and settle him into a suitable place."

Nathanael and John walked through camp. Women bent over steaming camp kettles while their children splashed in the cool rivulets. Gray smoke from fires rose like ghosts in the hot air. Men performed drills, cared for horses, and worked to fix broken wagons. The miasma of latrines and the sick reminded John of the first time he met Nathanael in Charlotte, North Carolina, when the general had come to take over the ruined Southern Army.

John removed his hat and wiped perspiration from his brow. He reached into his bag. "I have a letter from Robert Morris, the new superintendent of Congress' Finance Department. I know you are acquainted with him. He suggests I try to sell stock in the New Bank he is organizing that will benefit you and the army. I know you are authorized to draw on the superintendent's office up to a certain amount."

"As if there is ever any money in the military chest," Nathanael scoffed. He slapped a buzzing mosquito away. "I suppose I will have to write him and debase myself again for want of funds. No one in the north understands the difficulties we are in here. I am literally sinking like a ship's crew in a storm with the vessel taking on water faster than every exertion to prevent it."

John extracted a clay pipe and pouch from his pocket. He loaded the bowl with tobacco.

"I have been inundated with letters from all quarters," Nathanael explained.

"Are some of good tidings?"

"Yes, some. The French minister wrote that notwithstanding Ninety-Six, he considers my expeditions very fortunate for the thirteen states. Daniel Morgan inquired after the old heroes, William Washington, Harry Lee, and John Eager Howard."

"But I detect not all of them were pleasant," John said.

"There are many who have grievances or deliver promises for re-inforcements, but we have not seen a man or a horse. Our cavalry are desperate for fresh horses. I have strived to get Governor Nelson of Virginia and Governor Nash of North Carolina to listen to my pleas for reinforcements, if only militia, but they do not heed me. Through General Steuben, Lafayette, Thomas Jefferson, and others, I have been kept abreast of the news from Virginia and what Cornwallis is up to now that he commands the enemy in that state."

John lit his pipe and puffed it until smoke rings appeared. Satisfied, he asked, "Do you have designs on going after him?"

"No, that is why Steuben and Lafayette are there. General Anthony Wayne has recently arrived there with Pennsylvania troops," Nathanael said thoughtfully. "Cornwallis has let Colonels Banastre Tarleton and John Graves Simcoe loose to harass Steuben and Thomas Jefferson. I have heard that Cornwallis' commander in New York, Sir Henry Clinton, is unhappy with his lordship's decision to abandon the Carolinas. I received a weeks-old letter from Lafayette saying that propositions of peace have been made and that if it comes to pass, the enemy will maintain any ground they possess at the time."

"Thus the urgency to establish civil government. Like you, I am familiar with the doctrine of *uti possidetis,* an international law that recognizes a peace treaty between parties as vesting each with the territory and property under its control unless otherwise stipulated. Charleston is still in British hands, and you obviously do not have the numbers to chase them out."

Nathanael exhaled a long sigh. "We have them trapped in Charleston for now. Sumter and Marion with the cavalry are operating south in Monck's Corner and Dorchester around the British outposts near that town. I am sanguine about their operations."

"I assume you have heard what is happening to the north with Washington? That he is planning to lay siege to New York with our French ally General Rochambeau? If it is the word in Philadelphia, then certainly Clinton is aware."

"Yes, but communication with Washington has been difficult. We believe that our letters are being intercepted, therefore caution must be used, and it keeps me ignorant of affairs there."

"What are your thoughts on that course of action?" John asked.

"I wrote to General James Varnum in Congress that I think the greatest stroke may be struck in Virginia," Nathanael said. "If the French fleet was to run up immediately into Chesapeake Bay and land a sufficient stroke to cut off Lord Cornwallis from a retreat and possess British shipping and garrisons, it will pave the way to a greater success."

John's attention was drawn to a guard standing on each side of a man whose countenance was the epitome of defiance. A soldier was reading charges against the prisoner. "Sergeant John Radley has expressed himself in a disaffected manner. He has made disrespectful comments about his commanding officer Colonel Howard. He has…"

"Colonel John Eager Howard of Maryland?" John asked Nathanael. "Howard is one of the bravest officers I know."

"Radley was found guilty by a tribunal on accounts read. I signed his death warrant." John perceived a slight tremor in his voice. "He is to be shot to death at six o'clock this afternoon. The troops are to be under arms and attend the execution."

"I am sorry, Nathanael. I know how much you loathe sentencing men to death, but discipline must be maintained at all costs."

Nathanael's eyes settled on the man whose life he had signed away. "Do not be certain of that, John. Another officer was found not guilty of disrespect to a superior officer. I disapproved of the court's decision and would have had him shot otherwise."

❧

John Trumbull's criticism of his art of retreating followed Nathanael back to his shadowy tent. He needed to reach out to someone who knew him well, an old friend who listened to his past remorse with an earnest ear. That old friend was General Henry Knox. They were last together on October 21, 1780, the day before Nathanael left for the Southern Army.

Nathanael opened the tinder box, struck the flint, and lit a spill to ignite a flame on the wick of what little was left of his candle. Shoes, clothes, and horse furniture were not the only provisions lacking in camp. Supplies of paper, ink, candles, and cartridges for firearms were growing dangerously low. His commissary officer, William Davie, was scouring the countryside for merchants and civilians who were willing to provide the necessary items.

Nevertheless, instead of focusing on an uplifting letter he had received from Lafayette assuring him that his popularity was at its highest pitch and that everyone prided in his maneuvers, Nathanael answered Trumbull's stinging accusation through a letter to Henry. "There are few generals that has run oftener, or more lustily than I have done, but I have taken care not to run too far, and commonly have run as fast forward as backward, to convince our Enemy that we were like a Crab, that could run either way."

With his sensitivity to criticism soothed a bit, he felt the necessity to remind Thomas Sumter of his duties. He wrote, "No time is to be lost, therefore push your operations night and day. Keep Col. Lee and General Marion advised of all matters from above and tell Col. Lee to thunder even at the gates of Charleston."

Nathanael's reminder was hardly necessary. Thomas and Francis attacked Biggin's Church in Monck's Corner. Thomas replied:

> *I arrived here this morning at four o'clock & found this post evacuated. Have not been able as yet to ascertain, or even gain the least knowledge of the British route.*

Disappointed that the enemy manning the church escaped, he later learned that the mission on Shubrick's Plantation was blundered. Francis felt it needlessly exposed his men, eight of whom died in the attack. However, Nathanael was pleased with the news that Colonel Wade Hampton, leading Sumter's cavalry of state troops, raided the outskirts of Charleston and created a state of alarm and fear inside Charleston, the first time the city had been threatened militarily since the British captured it in May 1780.

Angry voices rose outside. Nathanael checked his pocket watch. It was 6:00 o'clock. Otho's firm, calm voice rose above the din, and the men quieted. Nathanael rose from his writing desk, but before he could take a step a shot rang out. Thunder rolled in the distance. *Or is that the sound of another shot?* Nathanael wondered.

Lewis entered the tent, followed by Otho. Otho's countenance was strained and pale. He had spent the day with his Maryland troops in anticipation of the execution of Maryland Sergeant John Radley. He coughed, shivered, and then sat on his cot.

"I know you are not expended because of the execution," Nathanael said gently. "You know discipline must be maintained as well as I do. You are sick again."

Otho hesitated to show weakness. Since his imprisonment in 1776 and 1777, he constantly fought off fatigue, night sweats, and chills. The current campaign had been brutal on his health as it had for so many who found respite in their camp in the High Hills.

"You are not answering me," Nathanael pressed.

"Yes, I am ailing again."

"Are you going to see Dr. Read?"

Otho wiped his brow with his sleeve and said, "I have seen him. He has prescribed purging, but here in the middle of nowhere, there are few herbs to aid in the cure."

"Perhaps I can cheer you up," Nathanael said.

"I am not melancholy."

"You forget that I am frequently afflicted with asthma. It can be very taxing to the soul."

Otho exhaled a laugh. "Then what is there to cheer me?"

Nathanael smiled and his blue eyes lit up. "A letter from Caty."

Otho accepted the folded sheet in Nathanael's hand. He said, "I wrote to tell her that I please myself with the expectation of retaining and renewing an intimacy with those spirits which used to render society in the Northern Army so charming, and she is one of those spirits."

Otho opened her letter. Caty's teasing words flowed across the paper. She encouraged him to find a wife while he was still young and handsome, knowing her sentiments made him feel better. What Otho did not say was that when he had last seen Dr. Read, the doctor was certain he had consumption.

Otho was not the only sick officer in South Carolina whose illness had been exacerbated by the August heat, heavy rains, fatigue, and swarming mosquitos. Lord Francis Rawdon was suffering from recurring bouts of malaria mixed with exhaustion. He wrote to Charles Cornwallis and admitted that he was afraid he would not outlive the summer, but "as my knowledge of the country and my acquaintance with the inhabitants make me think that I can effect it better than any person here, I am determined to attempt it." Despite his brave words, Rawdon could no longer endure another day in the American South. He boarded a ship bound for England.

Nathanael received the news from Harry Lee by way of a message.

I warn you that the British might be stronger as they are making a drive to force the Loyalists into the army. But Rawdon has gone home and Colonel Alexander Stewart has taken his command. Be aware that he is moving toward McCord's Ferry near the junction of the Wateree and Congaree in an attempt to attack you. I beg of you to be alert as a Negro spy has offered to lead Stewart over the Santee River and through the swamps.

Colonel Alexander Stewart, age forty, was only a year older than Nathanael, but he had more years of experience, having joined the British Army at fourteen. However, this was his first tour in the American Revolutionary War, and some were of the opinion that he was too fond of the bottle. Stewart was forced to march his 1,500 men toward Orangeburg, South Carolina, to search for provisions. Provisions were scarce there, so they continued farther north up the Congaree River.

On August 17, Harry's cavalry galloped into camp in the pouring rain. After tending to his tired horse, the soaked colonel sought out his general. Rain pelted Nathanael's tent, which served to make the already stifling heat into a steam bath. "General Greene," Harry said as he entered. He bowed and nodded to William Pierce, Lewis Morris, Otho, and Elias, who were dining with Nathanael. "I apologize for interrupting your dinner."

"Is it news of Stewart's movements?" Nathanael asked as he laid his fork aside.

"Colonel Lee, please join us," William invited. He brought Harry a glass of wine from the cask in the corner of the tent.

Harry waved it away. "Stewart is only sixteen miles from here as the crow flies. I am encouraging you to attack him, General Greene. We may be able to force him back into Charleston."

"Our army is sick and lacks even the most essential supplies to force a march," Nathanael replied. He took up his fork and stirred the rice on his plate.

"Not if we receive reinforcements," Harry argued. "If Lord Cornwallis decides to leave Virginia to join forces with Stewart, we will be in a most distressing situation."

"We have waited in vain for reinforcements, Harry," Otho said.

Nathanael drank his wine in thought and then pointed out the obvious, "It has been raining for days, the rivers are swollen, and swamps lie between here and McCord's Ferry. But if we can get the militia up to it and some state troops, we may be able to grow our army of 1,250 men to a suitable number."

Thunder shook the sky, and the tent shivered in the wind as if it were an omen of the march to come. With his men anxiously waiting for his answer, Nathanael felt a surge of hope. They wanted to fight. He wanted to fight. If they defeated Stewart, South Carolina would be free of any British force in the field outside of Charleston. It was an opportunity that they could ill-afford to let slip away.

He said, "Lewis, call in William's cavalry and the state troops under Colonel William Henderson, who has replaced General Sumter. I will send a message to Francis Marion and Andrew Pickens relaying our intentions and route of march."

"Yes, sir," Lewis said enthusiastically.

"Captain Pierce, dictate my orders of the day that will be announced on August 22," Nathanael said with a smile. "Now would be a good time to write home to family and sweethearts." He regarded Harry's smug face. It was a familiar look that said his cavalry legion officer was basking in the fact that his offered advice was taken seriously by his commander-in-chief. "Harry," Nathanael said, "you might want to indulge in that glass of wine and enjoy this meal with us."

❧

The twenty-eight-year-old, well-educated William Pierce took Nathanael's advice and sat down that night to write to his family in Virginia. Thunder cracked, and sheets of lightning illuminated the tent he shared with Lewis,

Otho, and Nathanael. Water dripped from the worn seams and blew in through the flap. He squinted under the light of a single candle and wrote:

> *We are gathering a respectable force together, and perhaps before many weeks shall pass away, we shall again be struggling in some bloody conflict. Mischief is a-brewing by the general, who keeps us in constant hot water, and never fails to make us fight.*

Elias and Lewis issued long snores from time to time. Otho lay on his cot, resting.

Nathanael struggled with the urge to rub his strained eyes. He was afraid an eye infection would blind him at the worst possible time. He shook it off and bent over his own tiny stub of a candle. His pen scratched across the damp page as he wrote a letter to General Washington that he hoped would get through. If only His Excellency would bend some of his forces in the north their way, Charleston could be easily reduced. It was a desperate plea that Nathanael knew would go unanswered, but he refused to stop trying no matter how remote the chances.

He snuffed out his candle and lay down. When sleep finally came, Caty's face and her gentle arms caressed his fitful dreams.

The morning of August 22 dawned under clear skies. Lewis read the orders of the day. Every man listened—some with apprehension, others with enthusiastic grins. "The army will march tomorrow morning in the following order. The North Carolina brigade and two pieces of artillery. The Virginia brigade and two pieces of artillery. The baggage in the usual order according to the line of march. Assembly at four o'clock. March at five o'clock."

"I see you got you some shoes," Christopher Madison of Virginia said to Jackson Killam as the two of them, wearing ragged but clean clothes, walked back to their tent to prepare their arms and provisions.

"I hope they don't fall apart," Jackson said. "General Greene is gonna have us marchin' the long way around north through Camden then back south, so we ain't tryin' to cross the Congaree River."

The army moved out in the cool morning under a sliver of the waxing crescent moon and to the snap of drums led by the twelve-year-old drummer from Virginia known only as Jacob. Ragged regimental flags drooped in the sultry air. Horse tack jingled, wagon wheels creaked, artillery groaned on its gallopers, bare and shod feet marched to a rhythm that fell into place as they left the respite of the High Hills of Santee. Nathanael sat regally on his horse at the head of his army with his adjutant, Otho, by his side. Harry's cavalry scouted ahead for threats the enemy may have sent to stop the Southern Continental Army movement.

At Camden, where the army ferried across the Wateree on August 26, the women and children with the army were left behind. Along the way, they picked up a group of 200 newly raised militia from North Carolina under French Army officer Francois de Malmedy. On August 28, Andrew Pickens with 300 South Carolina militiamen fell in. Colonel William Washington reunited with the army as well. Under a canopy of towering pine trees and oaks bearded with moss, Nathanael's army marched for fourteen days in rain that filled the cane-infested swamps, making them impassable. His army had to skirt them.

"No one is there," Harry announced when he galloped back from McCord's Ferry.

Nathanael raised a hand and called a halt to his marching army that was dispersed down the lines. "Did you gather intelligence about his movement?"

"Yes, we heard that Stewart has fallen back to a place about forty miles south called Eutaw Springs on the Santee River below Nelson's Ferry. I believe he knows we are approaching."

"And word of Francis Marion? He went south to stop a foraging party from shipping provisions to Charleston," Nathanael pressed.

"None, sir," Harry replied.

Nathanael turned in his saddle. "Lewis, send a message to General Marion to inform him of our movement. Colonel Cameron, disseminate the word that we are stopping at Fort Motte for a few days until we hear from General Marion."

☙

While they waited, Francis answered Nathanael's message: *My men and horses are exhausted, but I have ordered a night march in your direction.*

Satisfied, the Southern Army continued their stealthy march. On the night of September 7, they linked up with Francis and encamped at Burdell's Plantation seven miles above Eutaw Springs. Nathanael ordered his troops to cook one day's provisions and allowed them a gill of rum.

The tired but restless troops prepared. Night bugs chirped in a deafening chorus of summer song. Some of the Marylanders hunched over a campfire. Noah Clark slapped at the cloud of mosquitos near his face. "I swear, they are worse than the enemy," he complained to James McCurdy.

Thomas Kahoo looked up from the frog legs he was roasting over the fire. His face was covered in red bites. "Looks like you have been to battle," Noah remarked.

"Get some sleep, boys," Colonel Basil Cameron ordered. "The morning signal will be early."

Just before dawn, on the morning of September 8, 1781, they marched slowly toward the enemy. Many of them would never see the sun set. At 7:00 a.m., they saw white tents standing in neat rows near a three-story brick mansion nestled among the oak and cypress trees with eight acres in front cleared for crops. Behind the mansion, springs bubbled and drained into Eutaw Creek, which flowed through a crevice into the Santee River. A British foraging party was rooting for sweet potatoes when the American vanguard spotted them.

After hearing rumors that the Americans were closing in from the east, Colonel Stewart sent forward Major John Coffin with a detachment. Minor skirmishing occurred before the British retreated with the Americans driving them back.

Otho gave orders, "Move in the order of battle and halt. Take a little of that liquid, which is not unnecessary to exhilarate the spirits, and then advance."

Anxious to meet the enemy, they fell into the familiar order of battle—militia up front, with orders to fire and fall back, with the more reliable Continentals behind them. This placed the militiamen from both North and South Carolina in front along with Harry's cavalry and reinforcements from Francis Marion and Andrew Pickens. Behind the militia, Continentals from Maryland and Virginia and a new North Carolina division formed the line under the overall command of Otho. Nathanael held William's cavalry and Captain Robert Kirkwood's company of Delaware Continentals in reserve.

Stewart's men were British regulars and Loyalist provincials. Stewart posted a single main line of defense to the west of the cleared field. His 63rd and 64th Regiments of Foot looked directly across at Francis Marion, many of whom had faced him down before. Stewart's own 3rd Regiment of Foot, mostly new arrivals from Ireland, held the right of his line. His center was anchored formidably with brigades from New York and New Jersey under Colonel John Cruger, Nathanael's adversary at Ninety-Six.

At 9:00 a.m., Nathanael gave the order to attack. The armies clashed on wooded grounds with intermittent clearings where the British tents were pitched—bounded to the north by Eutaw Creek, its high banks lined with thick stands of scrub oak. Musket fire exploded from both sides of the line. With Francis on the right and Andrew on the left, the Carolina militia stood fast and fired disciplined volleys.

Colonel Stewart realized that there was nothing but militia before him. He shouted, "Hold firm, my men, and drive them without leaving your ground."

The 64th regiment and the British center fired upon the militia. Two British regiments charged forward and commenced a bayonet attack. The North Carolina militia began to buckle. Jackson Killam saw that young Noah Clark was about to be bayonetted from behind. He tried to pull the boy out of the way, but the blade pierced Noah's back and slid through his abdomen. Noah looked at Jackson with terrified eyes and muttered, "Run."

Jackson fell back with some of his fellow Virginians, but the slaughter had begun, and there was hardly anywhere to take cover. The North

Carolina militia in the center broke first. Nathanael rushed to fill in the gap with North Carolina's Continentals. The Continental line's small 2-pound grasshoppers boomed. The British answered the volley. The air was choked with powder smoke and the smell of sulfur. Forbes Calhoun, a middle-aged man Jackson's age, began screaming. Jackson almost stepped on him as he tried to grope for his downed comrade.

Forbes' legs had been hit with grape shot. Ligaments, muscles and flesh hung on the shattered bones like bloody tattered rags. "Oh, Lord," Jackson muttered as Forbes reached for him with bloody hands.

"Don't let 'em trample me to death," Forbes begged.

Jackson dragged him away from the open field to a slim oak. He heard who he assumed was Colonel Stewart shouting to his British major, John Marjoribanks, to hold the right flank. He ran to join the Virginia regiment, who with the Marylanders drove toward the brick mansion in a race to get inside before British troops did. The British won the race, shouldering the door closed against the tide of Americans pushing from the other side.

Hungry, thirsty Patriot troops surged through the neat British camp. They tripped over ropes and stakes supporting the white tents. They had seen the backs of British soldiers—not a familiar sight, but living in deprivation they could not resist the temptation the British encampment provided. British marksmen opened fire from the mansion's windows, annihilating their own camp.

The American left pushed hard against Major Marjoribanks' resistance. Nathanael's horse collapsed from a shot to the head. He tumbled off and got to his feet just as William arrived to take his general's orders. "William, take your cavalry, circle around our left, and finish off Marjoribanks. His men are gathered in a thicket of trees."

"Yes, sir." William rallied his men, "Get General Greene a horse, then let us get up to it and charge!"

"We have no infantry support," one of William's captains pointed out.

William's cavalry charged anyway. They got tangled up in the scrub oaks on the river side of the mansion. The British sharpshooters inside the mansion fired at them. John Coffin's cavalry advanced to counter the American cavalry. The sharpshooters raked William and his men. His horse was shot out from underneath him and killed. William hit the ground hard, was bayonetted and taken prisoner.

"Get Colonel Lee to effect a cavalry charge in William's place," Nathanael shouted to his aide, Nat Pendleton.

Pendleton rode off through the blinding smoke and confusion.

When he returned, he said, "Colonel Lee is not to be found, sir, but Captain Joseph Eggleston, his second, has come to effect the charge."

Nathanael's face reflected discountenance for a moment. He reined in his disapproval and issued the order to Eggleston.

The Americans brought forth artillery to dislodge the British from the mansion. Marjoribanks' men launched a counteroffensive and surprised the Patriots in their camp. Colonel Wade Hampton charged in with his South Carolina dragoons and chased off Major Coffin's cavalry, but Hampton's men were raked by British fire that emptied saddles.

John Marjoribanks captured some of the American cannon. In doing so, he suffered a mortal musket ball wound to his abdomen. Colonel Richard Campbell of the Virginia Continentals was shot in the chest. Jackson Killam and John Cassidy watched him fall and disappear under the fog of cannon smoke.

John Cassidy began to run toward Colonel Campbell, but Jackson held him back. "Stay out of the line of fire. You can't help him now." Then, strangely, they heard dogs barking.

At the same time, John Eager Howard and his Marylanders assaulted the brick mansion. The British blasted them from the windows. A snapping noise popped in John's ear, and he realized he could not control his right arm. One of his lieutenants lost his head to a cannon ball, and another's body twisted and he fell. Despite John's pain and Dr. Read's insistence that he treat his wound on the field, John stayed with his men.

Nathanael's army was falling apart before his eyes. They were suffering debilitating losses, and his men were scattered across the field. Many of his commanders were dead or wounded. He sent one of his newly acquired aides, twenty-five-year-old South Carolina native Captain Thomas Shubrick, to issue a retreat.

Otho came up to offer support as the American troops extricated from the British camp and joined the units that had been attacking the brick house in a slow, steady retreat. What was left of the artillery pulled out. The four hour battle was over.

Nathanael's face was covered with black powder smoke, and sweat rolled down his cheeks, exposing little rivulets of sunburned skin. He rallied his bloodied, exhausted forces in the woods, all whose countenances were stained in the same manner. The militia cheered, "We have made our stand!" The Continentals proclaimed, "We conducted a brilliant charge."

Their general rode among them. "I thank you all for your courage and tenacity. I believe we have good hope of driving the enemy from the field. We have crippled them and accomplished much in stopping them from reaping the rich harvests of the Congaree and Santee."

Colonel Stewart reformed his men and neared the edge of the woods. The shouts of "Huzzah!" and brave jubilation deterred him from further action. The pitiful cries of the wounded and dying pierced the fading sounds of battle. Some lay under the punishing sun while others were shrouded under the shade of oak and cypress trees.

Nathanael's repulsed but not broken cavalry gathered and covered their march through the worst heat of the day. His bruised and battered men's canteens were dry, and the only place they could find drinkable water was at Burdell's Plantation from whence they had begun that day.

James McCurdy had a twisted ankle, and he leaned heavily on his comrade Thomas Kahoo. Colonel John Eager Howard struggled to put one foot in front of the other. His broken collarbone throbbed with each step. Jackson glanced back at the place he knew Noah Clark and Forbes Calhoun lay dead in the lingering smoke and acrid smell of battle.

Nathanael's heart ached from the loss of so many of his men and Stewart's men as well. Already many were suffering from fly blow; their cries were the song of want and despair that hurt those who could hear it. The dogs Jackson heard barking earlier lay among the British as bloodied and ruined as their masters.

Harry came up with a smattering of his dragoons. Nathanael neglected to reprimand Harry for his absence. "I want you to dispatch to the British commander a proposal that both armies should unite in paying the last offices of our dead."

Harry did so, relieved that no explanation for the foray he took upon himself during the battle was questioned.

Nathanael left a picket guard under Colonel Wade Hampton on the battlefield. He sent Nat Pendleton to ride through the woods to gather stragglers. Nat came upon little groups bearing men on crude litters. The dying Colonel Richard Campbell of Virginia was among them, gently supported by some of his men. Nat dismounted and went to him.

"Who won the battle?" Richard asked in coherent agony.

"We took the field and defeated the enemy," Nat soothed.

"Then I die content." Richard's voice faded. Nat would never hear it again.

Both sides had sustained horrendous casualties. Because the British remained on the field, they claimed victory. The following day, Sunday, September 9, in the pouring rain, they broke their muskets and threw them in Eutaw Creek, stoved-in rum casks, and limped back to Charleston, leaving behind seventy wounded. Major John Marjoribanks was taken to Wantoot Plantation. Harry Lee and Francis Marion, who had lost five of his own men, hung on Stewart's rear. If Stewart turned around, the American Army would return to finish him off.

Nathanael's army marched back toward the High Hills of Santee with prisoners in tow. On the way, they stopped on the field to reflect on the appalling losses. Many of his men were sick with fever and literally had nothing to cover them but a breech cloth because they had not received a rag of clothing all summer. When they reached camp, ten men were forced to share one tent.

Issuing the necessary orders and writing the most urgent letters were Nathanael's first priorities. He wrote letters to Congress that praised the gallantry of his men and the impact of the battle on his troops—who he much respected. Otho and John beamed with pride when they were singled out for their uncommon bravery. There were glowing words for the militia who fought with a degree of firmness that reflected the highest honor upon that class of soldiers. He directed Congress to present thanks to his aides Captains Thomas Shubrick, William Pierce, and Nat Pendleton in testimony of their good conduct during the whole of the action. His thanks extended to Major Edward Hyrne, commissioner of prisoners who bore the task of detaining and securing British prisoners and seeing to their care.

But there were dark letters to write. A veteran of ten battles, Nathanael wrote, "Eutaw Springs was by far the most bloody and obstinate I ever saw. Our sick and wounded are in a most deplorable situation, and numbers of brave fellows who have bled in the Cause of their Country."

The melancholy letter urged him to perform his sacred duty and visit the wounded, nearly 350 of his own men and 300 British prisoners. In addition, there were at least 100 who were suffering from the seasonal fever and other debilitating ailments. When he entered the hospital tent, he was accosted by miasma so strong he fought back the urge to gag. But these were his men, and nothing would turn him away.

He walked slowly among the groaning wounded to acknowledge and ask after each one who was coherent enough to respond. Dr. Read saw him and offered a nod of approval. He came upon John Eager Howard, whose right arm was in a sling.

Sweat rolled down John's face and he tasted salt on his lips when he said, "I am honored that you acknowledged me to Congress so graciously, and I regret that I am useless to the army. My deeper regret, however, is those who lay dead on the field."

"No man who has behaved as you have is ever useless," Nathanael assured. "Has Otho been by to see you?"

"Yes. He is certain I shall be going home and offered to write a letter to my brother in Maryland."

"I suppose you will," Nathanael said. "Rest and heal, John."

A teenaged North Carolina militiaman reached for Nathanael with a bloody hand missing three fingers. "General Greene," the boy pleaded.

Nathanael squatted, unmindful of the sharp pain in his knee. "What is your name, son?"

"Luke Murphy, sir. I was on the front line when the battle started, but I could do no good when I lost my fingers. General Jethro Sumner, my commander, don't know I'm here."

"I assure you he does, but if that is not the case, I will see to it that he gets you home somehow."

Luke bit his lip and then said, "I thank you for your kindness."

Nathanael got to his feet. He thought about his cavalry colonel William Washington, who had been bayoneted and captured. His actions were a blur in Nathanael's mind as William had assaulted Major John Majoribanks and sent his men flying. Perhaps he had mixed up the white-coated cavalry officers of the 3rd Light Dragoons as they engaged in other parts of the field when their commander fell.

"Where are William Washington's wounded?" Nathanael asked Dr. Read.

"In the hut next door," the doctor said.

Faces young and full of promise—husbands, sons, fathers, and brothers. Nathanael thought that if it were he who lay among these men, his fear of dying and leaving his family in distress would overcome his fear of losing his own life. He recognized some of their faces: Major Matthew Perry, a trumpeter named Lorentz Miller, and Lieutenant James Simmons. It was then he felt tears sting his blue eyes, already irritated from the smoke of the battle.

Nathanael fought to compose himself, but it was of no use. He said to them, "It was a trying duty imposed upon you, but it was unavoidable. I could not help it."

What hurt him the most was the number of unanswered responses to roll call the next morning as 450 men did not answer to their names. Of those missing, 114 would never reply. A letter arrived from William Washington that night.

With a stiff, ambling gait, Nathanael walked outside, sat on a log, and gazed up at the stars and the waning crescent moon. Mosquitoes buzzed incessantly. Frogs peeped. Crickets chirped. He thought of Nancy Ward, the blue-eyed, fair-haired girl he had been in love with and to whom he had proposed marriage in 1772. Nancy had rejected his amorous attempts and broke his heart. That was before he married Caty. The letter from William was unsealed. It read:

Sir,

I have the Misfortune to be a Prisoner of war, I am wounded with a Bayonet in my Breast, which together with the Contusion from the fall of my Horse which was killed makes me extremely sore. I should be extremely obliged if Capt. Watts would send my clothing to me as soon as possible. I am informed by Col. Stewart that I am not to be indulged with Parole on any Latitude. I have been treated politely by many of the British officers. I have the Honor to be your Very Humble. Servant. W. Washington.

The tears Nathanael had managed to control flooded his emotions. If he had looked in a mirror, he would have been shocked by his own countenance that at age thirty-nine was becoming haggard and lined with worry and exhaustion.

On September 16, 1781, he read a weeks' old letter from the Marquis de Lafayette. Washington and the French allied forces under General Rochambeau were marching from New York to Virginia where Lord Cornwallis had settled his army. They were entrenched in the village of Yorktown that lay against the York River and emptied into the Chesapeake Bay. A French fleet under Admiral de Grasse sailed into the Chesapeake and subsequently defeated a British fleet, giving the allied forces control of the Virginia coastline.

It buoyed Nathanael's spirits enough to write a letter to Henry Knox who he believed was in Yorktown. "My Dear Friend, Where you are I know not, but if you are where I wish you, it is with General Washington in Virginia; the prospect is so bright and the glory so great, that I want you to be there to share in them."

There was another matter that needed attended regarding Yorktown. Harry Lee swaggered into Nathanael's tent. His smart uniform with white breeches and a short green coat looked worn and stained. He swept off his hat.

Nathanael came right to the point, "Captain Rudolph is off to Virginia searching for men and supplies to fortify your legion. Have you heard from him?"

"No, sir, I have not."

"Choose a second to command in your stead here. I am sending you to Virginia. Your mission is two-fold. I want you to report on the state of the Southern Army to General Washington. We believe our letters are getting intercepted. There are rumors that some were printed in Rivington's Gazette in New York."

"May I inquire as to why you see me fit to do this?"

"You and His Excellency are both Virginians and are friendly. Furthermore, our Virginia regiments are going home at the end of the year, and we need reinforcements. I have written to His Excellency asking for troops as I am told he has 15,000. But I have heard that several hundred new Maryland and Delaware recruits who were on their way here have been retained at Yorktown. We will be sorely lacking when the Virginians leave us at the end of the year."

"It will be my honor to do so," Harry said as he tried to suppress his excitement at the prospect of seeing Washington again.

Nathanael suppressed his pleasure at seeing Harry enthusiastic and the knowledge that he would do his best under the circumstances. "I will write a letter to Marquis de Lafayette explaining the assignment. You will leave immediately."

twenty-nine

You Have My Utmost Respect

September 18 was the hottest day Caty could remember. Even the breeze off Block Island Sound did little to cool the farmhouse in Westerly. She waited until the sun disappeared far below the horizon to feed her little menagerie of four their dinner and then tuck them into bed. Sleep eluded her. Her mind conjured moments when she and Nathanael were in the throes of conjugal felicity regardless of the fear of another pregnancy. Now, she would give anything to feel his strong body next to hers—to consummate their love and future with another child, for if he died, that is all she would have left of him.

"I cannot think this way," she scolded herself as she rose from her bed. She avoided lighting a precious candle, poured a glass of wine, and drank the glass quickly, hoping it would make her sleepy. The last letter she had received from Nathanael lay on the small side table in the living room. His words beckoned her to read them although she had done so many times. They were always written in the same mournful tone warning her of the horrors taking place in the South and forbidding her to join him.

She lit a spill from the smoldering embers in the fireplace, and the candle wick flamed. Before settling down to read, she looked in on the children. Four-year-old Patty cuddled with her three-year-old sister Cornelia. Caty ran a finger through Patty's blonde curls, her hair like that of her father's. She kissed the sleeping little girls' cheeks.

Five-year-old George lay splayed on his narrow bed. Twenty-month-old Nat had his brother trapped beneath his feet. Caty sat beside the boys. Nat's resemblance to his father was remarkable. *Will he look like Nathanael when he grows?*

She closed the bedroom door and settled in an old wingback chair that had seen better days before the farm in Westerly fell into neglect. A tear rolled down her cheek. If she had known that her husband had cried for his horribly wounded soldiers, perhaps her tears would have flooded the letter. She wiped the tear away with one delicate finger and reread:

> *If you take it in your mind to come to this place it would require a guard to secure you from the insults and villainy of the Tories. South Carolina and Georgia have been the seat, and are still, of a hot bloody war. Therefore, you would have no resting place in this county. Besides, the hot season of the year would have made sad havoc with your slender constitution. It is true our separation has been long and my wishes are equally strong with yours for a happy meeting.*

She was startled by pounding on the door. "Caty, it is me, Jeremiah," the caller announced. In almost bitter contemplation she thought, *Why is he here at this time of night, especially when I am improperly dressed? But he knows that does he not?*

"A moment," she said. She rushed to don her dressing robe.

She took a deep breath and opened the door. There he stood, handsome and desirable, a temptation that she despised and longed for at the same moment.

"Are you going to invite me in?" he asked.

"Yes, of course. Why are you here?"

"I have brought flour, wine, pork, pins, and a bolt of material as Nathanael has asked me to do when I could."

"I thought you were sending your assistant, Mr. Wiles."

"I am still standing out here," Jeremiah pointed out. "Sundries and supplies are not the only thing I have brought."

"The children are asleep," she warned as he crossed the threshold. *My children with Nathanael,* she thought, hoping to remind him that he was entering her husband's home. But her tongue felt tied even as he hauled in the provisions and sat down without invitation.

He reached to pour a glass of wine. "Why are you here alone?"

"I am not here alone. I have my paid man, Hercules, for outside chores. My cousin, Sammy, and his wife, Phebe, come by to see me and make sure all is well."

He took a sip of wine. "And is it?"

"What is the news, Jeremiah?" Caty insisted with a bit of fear in her voice. *Surely, if Nathanael is dead, he would have told me immediately instead of dallying with my feelings.*

"General Lord Cornwallis is entrenched in the village of Yorktown, Virginia. They say he has no way to escape unless the British fleet comes to his aid. The Marquis de Lafayette with General Anthony Wayne are keeping him confined. Washington is on his way."

Caty put a hand to her mouth. "Then why is Nathanael not in Virginia? Should he not be there?"

Jeremiah smiled at her question and the innocent look in her flashing dark eyes. "Do you not understand what your brilliant husband has done? The news of his last battle at a place called Eutaw Springs in South Carolina has sealed the fate of the British Army in that state. Despite his losses, there is nothing left there for the British to hold on to except Charleston. How long they can maintain that position is now in question. Nathanael has cut them off from their land supply line. Cornwallis has been pushed out."

Caty wrinkled her brow. "How far is Charleston and Virginia from where Nathanael is now?"

Jeremiah sat his glass aside. Her innocent question endeared him to explain. He rose and went into the kitchen in the back of the farmhouse. She followed. He cleared away the bowls and utensils that cluttered the top of the preparation table and pinched a cooling piece of coal from the tamped-down fireplace. He drew a long line that represented the east coast from Boston to Savannah. She leaned in and set the candle on the table. He drew a rough sketch of Virginia, North Carolina, South Carolina, and Georgia.

"This is Virginia where Lord Cornwallis is entrenched," he said, marking a spot near Yorktown. He drew a line that extended through North Carolina and then into South Carolina. He drew an "X" near Camden. "This is where Nathanael is now. You remember. He wrote you from the High Hills of Santee last July. The very letter you clutch in your hand."

Caty glanced at the wrinkled letter, dampened from her sweaty palms.

"Charleston is here," Jeremiah said as he swept the piece of coal southward to the coast. Savannah is here on the coast of Georgia. Cornwallis is a 300-mile march from Nathanael's position. He must hold the Carolinas and Georgia. As long as Charleston, Savannah, and Wilmington, North Carolina are in British hands, there is still work to do in the South."

"He refuses to let me join him. I feel as if I am a widow. I feel..." she swallowed hard. "But I *do* understand his fears for me, and I *do* understand that if he tried to march his army 300 miles in the oppressive heat of the South, many—including him—would never reach Virginia."

Jeremiah dropped the tiny piece of coal on the table and closed his eyes. He wanted to comfort her, but she was forbidden fruit. Betraying Nathanael would be worse than Eve tempting Adam with the apple as the serpent looked on. Thoughts of his wife, May, were not enough to deter desire, so he focused on his son, Daniel.

"I should go. The ride home to Hartford will take much of the night, but it will give me time to think." He paused, expecting Caty to ask him what he needed to think about, but she said nothing.

"This may be the last time we see one another again for a long time," Jeremiah said. "At the request of French General Rochambeau, I am serving as commissary to his troops in America. If there is to be a joint Franco-American siege on Cornwallis under the command of Washington, I will be there."

He kissed her on the cheek. "I will send a servant to help you with domestic duties. I know how much you hate them, and, with honesty, this place needs cleaned and spruced. I can see that even in the darkness that shrouds this house."

Caty laughed although her throat was swollen with unspoken words and threatening tears. She escorted him to the door. As his wagon disappeared into the dark under the dim light of a waning crescent moon, she sighed. His handsome countenance and educated manner were a distraction that she could not give in to despite her loneliness.

"Momma?"

She closed the door and picked up little Nat, who stood there with a finger in his mouth. She pressed her nose into his soft baby hair. He smelled like her family—the vague fragrance of jasmine she infused in her clumsy attempt to make lye soap, the remnants of wine and honey she had given the boys for a cough, and the scent of mint, her favorite wildflower that she often kept in a vase on the dresser in her bedroom.

With the wind off Block Island Sound whistling through the eaves, she vowed, despite Nathanael's stern warnings, to stay in Rhode Island, that she would find a way to feel his arms around her and his sensuous lips upon hers.

❧

While his wife was racked with longing for the touch of his hands and the sound of his voice, Nathanael offered just that to his sick and wounded as he traveled the line of hospitals that extended 100 miles north as far as Charlotte, North Carolina, to make certain of their condition. When British Colonels Banastre Tarleton and John Graves Simcoe invaded Virginia, the Southern Army's hospital stores were intercepted and destroyed on their way to camp.

Nathanael's doctors, James Browne, William Read, and Richard Pindell, pleaded with their general to write Congress and beg for supplies.

In October, he wrote to the new president of the Continental Congress, Thomas McKean, "Our sick and wounded have suffered greatly. The extent of our hospitals, the malignity of disorders, and increasing sick since the battle at Eutaw, together with the numerous wounded and the great number of our physicians who have fallen sick in service, have left us in a deplorable condition. Hospital stores and medicine have been extremely scarce. We have no bark, coffee, or sugar."

He turned to his commissary general Colonel William Davie. With the knowledge that hard money was impossible to come by to make purchases for his little army, he admonished Davie in the sternest manner to procure salt. "I shall only observe that an army that has received no pay for two years, distressed for the want of clothes, subsisted with no spirits, and often short in the usual allowances of meat and bread, will mutiny if we fail in the article of salt."

Davie, who often took offense but was not heartless and always about his duty, wrote back, "I will do all in my scanty power to procure that which will alleviate their sufferings."

As Nathanael made demands and begged for basics that no man should have to suffer without, and his commander-in-chief was besieging Cornwallis, he was lifted as a great hero and general. The months of sacrifice and perseverance led to the acknowledgment and laurels he so desperately needed and wanted but had not expected—certainly not from Congress, who had threatened to remove him from the Continental Army after his stinging resignation letter as quartermaster general in July 1780.

Before going to inspect his hospitals, he sent his aide, Captain William Pierce, to Philadelphia to report on the battle to Congress. Pierce wrote an excited letter to his general that read:

> *Not a man in the army stands as high with them as you, General Greene, save General Washington. Some are comparing you to Julius Caesar.*

The admiration poured in as he made his way back to the High Hills of Santee with his small contingent of guard and Lewis Morris by his side. He learned that Henry Knox wrote to John Adams in Holland that *The exalted talents of General Greene have been amply displayed in North and South Carolina—without an army, without Means, without anything he has performed Wonders.* His former aide, Thomas Paine, had not forgotten his general. He gloated that Nathanael had judiciously done what needed to be done to save and serve the country.

Nathanael and Lewis stopped for the night at a farm ten miles north of the High Hills of Santee to find shelter from a brewing storm. Lewis dismounted and rapped on the door. An old woman answered and shoved a candle through the door with one hand and a pistol in the other. "I will shoot you," she warned. "Rascally Loyalists. They killed my husband and then tried to run me off my own farm. I ain't doing it!"

Lewis glanced at Nathanael to keep from bursting out in laughter. "Madam, General Greene is seeking a place to lodge for the night. We are asking for accommodations and victuals. Of course, we will reimburse you for your trouble."

"With what?" she snapped. "Everyone knows the American Army is destitute."

Nathanael dismounted. He handed his pistols and his sword to one of his dragoon guards and stepped on the stoop. He bowed. His smile lit up his lambent eyes and accentuated his handsome face in the dim light. He said, "My name is Nathanael Greene. Tell me, have the Loyalists been about lately?"

The old lady scowled. "Is this a trick?" White lightning streaked across the sky. Fat raindrops peppered the windows. She looked up and then looked into Nathanael's eyes. "The Loyalists have not been about lately, and I know why. We all know why. If you are who you say you are, then it is my pleasure to accommodate you."

The small guard of dragoons, survivors from William Washington's 3rd Continentals, dismounted. "They stay in the barn," she croaked as she let

Nathanael and Lewis pass the threshold. After a meager dinner of rice and fresh beef, Nathanael spent a few hours writing letters. One to Washington to explain the condition of his army. Another to Virginia militia colonels John Sevier and Isaac Shelby, who had led the attack on Kings Mountain, South Carolina on October 7, 1780, and annihilated British Major Patrick Ferguson and his Loyalist soldiers. A third to the Philadelphia financier Robert Morris to whom he had to appeal for funds and who often left him struggling and embarrassed before he attempted to come through.

Exhausted, he dropped onto the bed beside Lewis. He rubbed his eyes, winced, and then sneezed. The bed was dusty, a sure formula for an asthma attack he could little afford. Lewis coughed, reddening his already ruddy face. He had seemed unsteady as he stood on the old lady's stoop. There was a limit to what either of them could endure, and now it had caught up to them like a harbinger of what they would find when they returned to camp.

It was a cool, breezy morning on October 15 when Nathanael rode into camp. It held the promise of better days when the sickly season would dissipate for winter. Otho, who Nathanael had left in charge of the army in his absence, greeted him when he entered his tent dirty and tired from the road.

"I received your letter of the 10th," Nathanael said as he removed his hat, riding gloves, and coat. "Please tell me there is better news than you relayed about those suffering from dysentery and fever."

"I cannot," Otho said. "Our physicians and surgeons are sick, and the three who are well enough to work are treating as many wounded officers as possible. Several of our soldiers are dead, and others dying. The number of sick does not decrease."

"And you?" Nathanael asked. "Are you among those who are not healing?"

"Have you seen yourself?" Otho asked. "You and Lewis both look as if you need to sleep for a few days."

Lewis took up a pitcher and announced, "I will fetch you some water from the spring, General Greene."

"You are not my servant, Lewis," Nathanael said.

"No matter, I am going to the river to wash even if it means I have to sit there under the watchful eyes of every man in camp until my toes wrinkle."

Nathanael chuckled, unbuttoned his waist coat, and pulled it off. "I do need an hour to clean up." He sat down and pulled off his boots and then rummaged through his sparse baggage. "I thought I had a clean shirt and a pair of stockings," he murmured. "I suppose like so many in this army who have not received a rag of clothing all summer, I will become entirely naked with nothing but a breech cloth to cover me."

"Perhaps not. With Colonels Carrington and Davie both in Virginia, there may be a chance to remedy that," Otho said. "Colonel Davie has procured the salt you asked for. Carrington is attempting to collect and forward the requested clothing, but I suppose without Mr. Morris' generous pockets or support from that state, it will be futile." Otho pointed to Nathanael's desk that was covered in correspondence, some wrapped in red tape. "All this arrived while you were gone. Nat Pendleton compiled it for you."

Nathanael's eyes moved through the piles. A letter from George Washington lay atop one of them. One of his letters had gotten through. He broke the seal and unfolded the letter.

Camp before York 6th Oct. 1781

> *How happy am I, my dear Sir, in at length having it in my power to congratulate you upon a victory as splendid as I hope it will prove important. Fortune must have been coy indeed had she not yielded at last to so persevering a pursuer as you have been—I hope she is yours, she will change her appellation of fickle to that of constant. I shall always take pleasure in giving Mrs. Greene's letters a conveyance and should she persist in the resolution of undertaking so long a journey as that from New England to Carolina. With much truth and sincere affection, I am Dr Sir Yr obedt*

> *Geo: Washington*

Nathanael read the words again and thought, *This short letter means more to me than any others I have received after all the years I spent under Washington's guiding hand and the trust I have earned in his eyes.*

He laid the letter on the desk and took up another from Colonel Harry Lee. The letter from Harry was discouraging and terse:

No troops coming on to you, but a perfect monopoly has taken place of men and supplies to fight a decreased small army.

Lewis returned with the pitcher full of water and poured it in a bowl on a side stand in the marquee tent. Nathanael pulled off his torn sweat-stained shirt and washed his face and neck. "Perhaps I need to go down to the river with Lewis," he said as the water in the bowl turned a dusty brown.

Otho struggled to curb his impatience, "There are other serious matters we need to discuss. We have not a cartridge or an ounce of powder in store. I was unable to fill Francis Marion's request for ammunition. Governor Rutledge has tasked Marion to perform in the effort to restore civil government to this state."

"Otho, as my adjutant, and from our long standing association, you have my utmost respect. But if I do not tend to myself for a few minutes, I am afraid you may be leading this army without me."

"My apologies. I will find Private Peters, the steward who normally washes your clothes, and a contingent to ensure your modesty while you bathe. Perhaps that is the most I can do to help besides allow you the quiet to sleep."

&

Otho waited as anxiously as Nathanael did for militia colonels John Sevier and Isaac Shelby to arrive from Virginia. When they marched into camp a few days apart, Otho assigned them to serve under Francis Marion. It was with an air of concern that he watched what was left of his Maryland brigade gather in little groups, talking of the conditions in camp and lack of pay.

Otho's tall shadow draped a group of privates hunched around a campfire. "Why did you not come to me?" he asked. The men got to their feet and saluted.

"We figured you could not do anything to ease this, Colonel," Thomas Kahoo admitted. "Shall we direct our memorials to General Greene?"

"I told them to come to you, Colonel Williams," Colonel Basil Cameron barked. His eyes met the eye of each man around the fire. "But instead, they have spread discontent."

"We know General Greene will lend a sympathetic ear," James McCurdy admitted. "We believe our commissary officer will as well, but we can no longer endure such conditions as these. I have not been able to send a pence to my wife in Baltimore."

"It is not going to do no good," an older soldier slurred as he stumbled toward the group of Marylanders. "Maybe you cannot see it, but we here in South Carolina have been seeing it all along. We all may as well desert, so stand by it, boys. Damn my blood, if I would give an inch."

"Who the hell are you?" Basil demanded of the man.

"Who the hell are you?" the man retorted. "A Yankee who ain't got no sense to—"

Basil seized the man by the scruff of his neckerchief. "I will pound some sense into your drunken head."

"That is enough," Otho ordered. "Both of you stand down." He approached the intoxicated man. "I know you. Timothy Griffin of South Carolina. Why are you here? Should you not be with General Pickens who has gone west to suppress raids by the Cherokees and Loyalist bands in the Ninety-Six district?"

Timothy spit on Otho's boots. "I ain't going there to fight them heathens."

Otho's rare temper flared. Before he had a chance to call a guard, three of Nathanael's dragoon guards were on Timothy. He twisted and screamed, "Get your filthy hands off me!"

The dragoons tied his hands behind his back, and one said, "We will see to it your mouth is shut for good."

As they dragged Timothy off, he saw General Greene standing with his arms crossed on the edge of the neat rows of tattered tents. At that moment, the belligerent soldier from South Carolina sobered. He knew it was the last day of his life.

რ

Neither Congress nor the states had money to buy the supplies Nathanael needed, therefore, he was forced to barter for goods and services. Baron von Steuben in Virginia was faced with the same situation because paper money was useless. The Baron had to pawn a gold watch and his silverware to buy a new horse and medical care for his aide.

Yet Nathanael never gave up pleading for help from Congress. "We are in great distress this moment for want of tents, canteens and axes. Nothing has been more distressing for us than the want of artificers. In this part of the country, there are so few manufacturing towns and artisans generally so scare and hard to be got." It was with much relief that reinforcements and supplies arrived at the High Hills of Santee from North Carolina in late October.

The distressing news that North Carolina Governor Thomas Burke had been kidnapped and carried off to the British outpost at Wilmington, North Carolina, filtered to camp. Burke was sent to Sullivan's Island near Charleston and imprisoned. Nathanael made General Jethro Sumner commanding officer of Continental Army forces in North Carolina and sent him as far as Halifax to promote the public good. His constant fear that Cornwallis would somehow evade Yorktown and escape through North Carolina led him to order Sumner to keep him constantly advised.

Governor Burke violated his parole that stipulated he would not cross into American lines. He escaped after the British commander in Charleston ignored his pleas for a choice. He entered camp, looking thin and harried.

"You should not be here," Nathanael said sternly, "I cannot condone violation of parole. If I did that, the camp would be filled with men who believe this is a safe haven. I have not a blind eye to the devastating raids the British are conducting out of Wilmington, but my force is too small and too sick to move more than whom I have already sent under General Jethro Sumner."

"I do not need your approbation, Nathanael, only your protection. But if that is not being offered, then I shall go back to North Carolina and resume my governorship and secure my home and my family."

"I cannot allow it now that you have come here," Nathanael said.

Thomas raised an eyebrow. "We are friends, Nathanael, or I assume we are."

"This is a matter of personal honor among gentlemen. If you leave, I will hold a court of inquiry to investigate your conduct. Do not force me to do so. You are needed to take the reins of the political evolution here in the South, but not this way."

"Then I bid you adieu, Nathanael. If I am a fugitive and a prisoner among this army, then like all fugitives, I must flee." Burke left camp with impetuous flair. He jumped into the saddle and spurred his horse through the ranks, causing men to dodge his path and stare after his retreating figure that soon disappeared among the trees.

Otho witnessed the confrontation. "Do you intend to carry out your threat?" he asked Nathanael, although he was certain of the answer.

"Immediately. Make the arrangements."

Two days later, the court found that as the enemy had legal claim upon Governor Thomas Burke as a prisoner of war, that leaving headquarters before the matter could be settled or adjusted, and taking the government under those circumstances was considered highly reprehensible and dishonorable to the state of North Carolina.

Otho delivered the court's decision to Burke through a courier. In return, he received a belligerent letter from the governor accusing him of overwhelming ignorance. There were more disagreements and wrongs committed that Nathanael was forced to address. Francis Marion and Colonel Peter Horry began a long-running argument over destroyed property, horses, and rank. It was a previous contention that flared when Nathanael dispatched Francis to cut off Alexander Stewart's retreat toward Charleston.

Francis' forces were unable to get behind Stewart's force as 300 fresh British troops came up to Monck's Corner from Charleston to cover the retreat.

Horry complained to Nathanael, "I used to submit to General Marion's orders with pleasure, but at present, I assure you it is disagreeable lately. I shall receive orders from no other person but yourself."

"Did we not lay down clear lines of authority?" Nathanael asked Governor John Rutledge, who had come to camp to discuss the sale of indigo that might see profits to benefit Nathanael's troops as well as Francis Marion.

"Apparently we did not," John said noncommittedly. "They look to you to solve their differences."

"General Marion is a good man. Few of us are without faults. I suppose I must facilitate their reconciliation," Nathanael said.

Captain Thomas Shubrick interrupted the conversation. "General Greene, there is a civilian here to see you. He says he was assaulted by Captain Eggleston."

"Send him in," Nathanael said and gathered his patience.

The man entered with his hat in his hand and nervously bowed. Nathanael's guard surrounded him, but refrained intimidation. "My name is Garrett Barron, your Excellency. One of your cavalrymen threatened to slice my ear off if I did not give him my horse."

Nathanael motioned to Thomas to take notes. The aide did as he was told and took up quill and paper. "Mr. Barron, where do you reside?" Nathanael asked.

"Near Fort Motte, sir."

"Are you injured?"

"No, sir, but I feel ill at ease. And, well…I thought in the beginning I was being accosted by that Tarleton fellow who used to ride through here with that British general…the one who…went to Virginia."

"Did he take your horse?" Nathanael asked.

"No, sir." Garrett tossed a nervous glance at one of the dragoons.

"Be assured that Captain Eggleston will no longer be a threat," Nathanael soothed.

"Yes, sir, but what if I encounter—"

"Captain Shubrick, ensure Mr. Barron is escorted out of camp without harm," Nathanael ordered. "And find Captain Eggleston and send him to me."

Mr. Barron bowed profusely. "Thank you, your Excellency." He followed Thomas out of the marquee tent.

Governor Rutledge looked amused. "Since when are you being addressed as 'Your Excellency'?"

"I have no notion to explain why he did so," Nathanael said. "I suppose it is a compliment."

The tent flap rustled. "Captain Joseph Eggleston," one of Nathanael's guards announced.

"I am *your* captain," Joseph corrected the dragoon.

Nathanael sat at his desk. Joseph came to attention. "A Mr. Garrett Barron was here. He said you threatened him when he refused to give you his horse. My first question is why were you threatening to take his horse?"

"General Greene, our cavalry horses are much spent as you know, and I thought—"

"I did not authorize seizing civilian horses in that manner. Promissory notes must be issued, and you know this," Nathanael scolded.

"Yes, sir, but the man insulted me before I had a chance to follow procedure," Joseph protested.

"You cannot treat the inhabitants with too much delicacy, nor should the least encouragement be given to the soldiers, either to invade the property of the people or offer them any insults. This conduct is what has made the British so very odious. Mr. Barrett assumed you were Colonel Banastre Tarleton."

Joseph's green eyes widened. "Why would he think that with Cornwallis in Virginia?"

"Civilians are uncertain of those still garrisoned in Charleston," Nathanael said. "I issue a warning this time, but next time, there shall be a harsher consequence. You are dismissed."

Joseph turned to leave. As he stepped out of the tent, there was a loud whoop followed by shouts of "Huzzah!" and a musket discharge.

Nathanael got to his feet, and despite his limp, rushed outside with John Rutledge on his heels. A post rider Nathanael recognized had entered camp. The rider leapt from his saddle and ran toward Nathanael waving a letter. "General Greene! Colonel Williams! Governor Rutledge! News from Yorktown. Lord Cornwallis has surrendered!"

Otho jogged toward Nathanael and John Rutledge. John Eager Howard, unmindful of his healing collarbone, led a wave of the ragged, sickly, and thin men who made up the Southern Army. The rider handed Nathanael a single sheet that bore the familiar seal of Colonel Harry Lee. "I did not read it," the rider said. "The word is spreading like wildfire."

William Pierce, Lewis Morris, Nat Pendleton, and Thomas Shubrick gathered near their general as if he needed support. Nathanael's eyes fell on his little army. It was to these men he owed everything. It was these men who had chased Cornwallis from the Carolinas into his own trap on the shores of the York River. He believed they deserved to hear the words delivered in his voice. He broke the seal, and on that glorious, warm autumn day, with the leaves on the trees beginning to turn, the words he read painted a vivid picture. The camp silenced.

Yorktown, 21 October 1781

My dear General,

At noon on Friday, the 19th instant of this month, the British and Hessians marched out of their works onto Hampton Roads where the allied armies were lined up two ranks deep in a line that stretched for more than a mile with the French on the left and the Americans on the right and General Washington and Rochambeau at their respective heads. Our troops, many of them ragged and barefoot were to a man beaming. The French and American regimental bands played music. Colonel John Laurens and the Comte de Noailles penned the articles of surrender. They denied Cornwallis the honors of war, just as Sir Henry Clinton had denied General Benjamin Lincoln when he surrendered the American garrison at Charleston, South Carolina. Claiming illness, Lord Cornwallis sent his second, General Charles O'Hara in his stead to offer the surrender sword. O'Hara offered it to General Rochambeau who indicated General Washington who indicated his second-in-command General Lincoln. Lincoln accepted the sword and indicated where the British army was to ground their arms. The enemy's eyes brimmed with tears. The humiliation is repaid. Further, Colonel Banastre Tarleton surrendered the British troops across the York from Yorktown to the French. It was the proudest day of our lives. I am as always, your most Humbled and Obed't servant.

Col Lee

Those with hats tossed them in the air. Some sang made up tunes to praise Washington and Rochambeau. "I wonder what old King George will say now?" they declared.

Nathanael leaned in toward Lewis and said, "Send word to the regimental officers to open the commissary and casks of rum. Today, we celebrate."

All that day, the men, and the women and children who had returned from Camden to resume following the army, indulged in the celebratory firing of cannon in a *feu de joie*. Muskets discharged, music played, and dancing commenced. Nathanael, Otho, and John Rutledge were sitting outside on a log, basking in the revelry.

Otho elbowed Nathanael, "We have company."

"Indeed we do," Nathanael said and rose.

Otho and John got to their feet. Several ladies approached with baskets on their arms and dressed in lace finery as if for a party. "We are looking for General Greene," a young blonde girl with bright blue eyes drawled.

"I am General Greene," Nathanael said. "This is Colonel Otho Williams and Governor John Rutledge. To what do we owe this pleasure?"

"We live on the plantation yon near the river. We heard the news of the British surrender and the sounds of gaiety coming from camp," an older woman who resembled the blonde young lady said. "I am Mrs. Andrew Lazier, and these are my daughters, Miss Charlotte and Sarah Lazier. We have bottles of fine wine, brandy, and sweets to celebrate this great victory with the general who made it all possible."

Nathanael's thoughts rushed to his beloved Caty, and he wondered, *Does she know about the victory?* He supposed he should write to her and to congratulate General Washington. But this day was for resting and comradery. There would be time for that tomorrow.

⁂

British and Hessian soldiers, totaling 7,000, surrendered at Yorktown. King George III responded to the news with a speech in November that called loudly for, "…a firm concurrence and assistance to frustrate the designs of our enemies, equally prejudicial to the real interests of America and to those of Great Britain."

The English Prime Minister, Lord North, paced his apartment on Downing Street in London and exclaimed, "O God! It is all over!"

News of the King's speech would not come to Nathanael's attention until some months later when it was printed in the *Charleston Royal Gazette*. Lord North's proclamation that it was all over was far from the truth. As long as the British held Savannah, Charleston, and Wilmington, North Carolina, Nathanael's army could not rest nor the militia under Francis Marion and Andrew Pickens, partisans he counted on to do their duty. His army was far from ready or able to take on those British strongholds. He pleaded with Washington to convince the French fleet and, along with the bulk of Washington's army, to aid him in reducing the British held garrisons now that they were disposed of the siege in Yorktown.

While he waited for Washington's response, he received a flurry of letters—some uplifting, others distressing, and two that changed his world at that moment.

He received one from Henry Knox. Henry wrote that Yorktown was a happy fight for America and that Nathanael would soon receive reinforcements that would relieve him from many perplexities. He wanted to join his old friend in South Carolina.

> *I would fly to you with more rapidity than most fat men. I am so linked in with the cursed cannon that I know not how to tear myself from them. Mrs. Knox is at Mount Vernon in Lady Washington's stead. We are expecting another child. I sigh for domestic felicity, and I know you do the same.*

The next letter distressed Nathanael and the words reminded him of what he had sacrificed during the long arduous campaign in the South that seemed to have no end. General von Steuben had managed to alienate the Virginia Assembly and others with his rigid military doctrines. He would not be able to fulfill his dream of joining Nathanael in South Carolina. Instead, he was forced to travel to Philadelphia and beg for pay like a pauper. He wrote:

> *I sacrifice my time, my interest & my health and what is more than all these, I risk a reputation gained by twenty-seven years' service in Europe. Can you blame me for quitting when all my Zeal and my military experience is attended with so little success & procures me so little satisfaction?*

I do not blame him, Nathanael thought. *It is a terrible picture of the rewards of long service.*

Nathanael poured a glass of rum before opening the next letter. It was from Thomas McKean, the president of the Continental Congress. Nathanael walked outside and looked up at the November 1 full moon, which cast bright spots and long shadows that illuminated the night.

Campfires crackled, and orange sparks popped little fireworks into the air. The picket guards who moved about their duty whispered. A baby cried. A mother murmured soothing words. A puppy that had not gone to bed with its master bounded toward Nathanael and insisted on a pet with its pink tongue dripping in excitement.

Nathanael obliged the puppy, which barked sharply as he turned to step inside his tent to face the letter from Congress. Nathanael raised a finger to his lips and whispered to the dog, "Be quiet." He sat at his writing desk and broke the letter's seal while his aides and officers slumbered. It read:

> *The American Congress to Nathaniel Greene, a distinguished general for victory at Eutaw Springs on September 8, 1781, resolved on October 29, 1781: That the thanks of the United States in Congress assembled, be presented to Major-General Greene, for his wise, decisive and magnanimous conduct in the action of the 8th of September last, near the Eutaw Springs, in South Carolina, in which, with a force inferior in number to that of the enemy, he obtained a most signal victory over the British army commanded by Colonel Stewart. That a British standard be presented to Major General Greene, as an honorable testimony of his merit, and a golden medal emblematical of the battle and victory aforesaid.*

As he read, his breath caught. Not until he began to feel faint did he inhale. His vision blurred, and his blue eyes stung with tears. He tasted salt from the stream that stained his cheeks and wet his lips. All of the months of sacrifice and perseverance had led to the recognition and laurels he so desperately needed and wanted. It was reparation for each criticism of his strategy, for each plea that went ignored, and for each mistake he had made and borne.

Yet, he was not alone in the glory and hardship. He contained his elation and let his tent mates sleep. In the morning, he would stand before his troops once again and deliver the thanks of the United States in Congress.

❧

Orange and pink streaks swept across the wispy sky like the careful strokes of an artist's brush certain of his choice of colors and the freedom to express his joy. The aroma of distant rain wafted on the breeze. Surrounded by his guard, Nathanael stepped into the back of a wagon so he could be heard. Soldiers who had roused early for orders of the day rubbed their eyes and stood at attention with combed hair and clean faces. Attending muster disheveled, especially if the general was issuing orders himself, was unacceptable.

"I received a letter from Mr. Thomas McKean, the honorable president of the Continental Congress in recognition of the late action at Eutaw Springs," Nathanael began. "That the thanks of the United States in Congress be presented to the officers and men of the Maryland and Virginia brigades, and Delaware battalion of Continental troops. The officers and men of the legionary corps and artillery. The brigade of North Carolina. The officers and men of the state corps of South Carolina. To the officers and men of the militia."

Nathanael glanced at his adjutant. Otho never shirked his duties, even on days he coughed up blood or shivered uncontrollably. The general's voice strengthened, "That a Sword be presented to Colonel Williams of the Maryland line for his great military skill and uncommon exertions on this occasion." He paused to swallow the lump in his throat and continued, "That Major General Greene be desired to present the thanks of Congress, to Captains Pierce and Pendleton, Major Hyrne and Morris and Captain Shubrick, his aides-de-camp. To Brigadier General Marion of the South Carolina militia."

The moment arrived to announce his personal merit—a Congressional gold medal. He studied the attentive, delighted countenances before him— some standing in wagons to meet their general's gaze, legs dangling from trees, small children draped over shoulders, men astride saddles, anywhere they could settle to hear his voice.

He bowed to his army and said, "The General thanks you. Orders of the day are suspended this morning." He stepped out of the wagon. The smell of pork cooking induced him to walk toward the officers' mess to eat breakfast.

"I know what you did," Otho said as he fell in beside Nathanael. "Why did you not tell them?"

"You know I am waiting to hear word of General Washington's success in convincing the French fleet to support us seaward with land reinforcements from His Excellency's army."

"You are evading my question," Otho said.

"It is my job to make our troops and the militia successful. I have cajoled, shamed, praised, and ordered them about just as I have been by civilian authorities and my superiors these many years. In your confidence, I can admit that I *do* deserve that gold medal. Yet our work is not done, and without help, it may never be completed." Nathanael stopped walking. "The truth is that I am so tired of this war. Tired of seeing the inhabitants here suffer. Tired of the deprivation we endure for a cause we believe in. My friend, Henry Knox, feels the same and without shame."

Otho thought of his oldest sister, Mercy, and his brother, Elie, his fond correspondents at home in Maryland and how he longed to see them again. It was the fate of a dedicated soldier that had to be endured unless, like Maryland Colonel Benjamin Ford, who died of the wounds he received at Hobkirk's Hill, God took your soul first.

The day Harry Lee rode into camp from Virginia with some of his legion, those who had been wounded at Eutaw Springs prepared to go home. The Maryland regiments gathered around Colonel John Eager Howard, whose still-healing broken collarbone limited his ability to fight or fire his musket.

"Colonel Howard, will you take this letter to my wife?" James McCurdy asked.

"Of course," he responded and slipped the letter into his baggage.

"We shall think of you with bravery and fondness, sir," Thomas Kahoo said to John.

"You have been one of the good ones," John assured his young private.

Otho offered his hand and said, "It has been my pleasure to serve with you."

"And mine with you," John returned as he grasped Otho's hand and shook it.

Nathanael joined the group of well-wishers. John said to him, "I will do my best to raise recruits for the new 5th Maryland Regiment. When its ranks are filled, I hope I will be convalesced enough to lead them."

"Take this with you," Nathanael said as he offered a letter. "It is to be used when you are in need of a recommendation."

John took the letter. The words meant more to him than any he had read.

> *This will be handed to you by Colonel Howard, as good an officer as the world affords. He has great ability and the best disposition to promote the service. My obligations to him are great.*

John Eager Howard, accompanied by his brother, rode out of the encampment in the High Hills of Santee toward his future. He never entirely recovered from his wound. He would find a wife, whom he adored, and she would soothe the aches of the past.

When Nathanael received a response dated October 31 to his plea for help from his commander-in-chief, it stung. Washington wrote:

> *Every Argument & Persuasive had been used with the French Admiral to induce him to aid the Combined Army, in an operation against Charleston, but the advanced Season, The orders of His Court, and his own Engagements to be punctual to a certain Time Fixed on for his ulterior operations, all forbid his Compliance, & I am obliged to submit. Nothing therefore remains, but to give you a respectable Reinforcement; & to return myself to the Northward with the remainder of the Troops.*

There was an encouraging note. Washington was sending reinforcements from Pennsylvania, Maryland, and Delaware under the command of Generals Arthur St. Clair and Anthony Wayne.

Nathanael shared the news with his officers, "The prospect of 1,200 additional troops is promising, but I have heard through my spies that General Alexander Leslie has replaced Colonel Nisbet Balfour as commander of Charleston and is expecting 5,000 reinforcements. If this is true, we will be hopelessly outnumbered and possibly driven out of South Carolina. We will be more distressed when our Virginia troops leave at the end of the year. I have written to Colonel Davie in Virginia asking him to give no sleep to his eyes until he gets troops on the march."

"There are times when our inferior numbers are a determent, but we have never conceded to yield," Otho reminded with a twinkle in his merry blue eyes.

Nathanael relaxed a little and afforded a smile. "It is true," he agreed. "As small as our reinforcements are, we have never let it blind us to our purpose of driving the enemy from the bounty in the countryside. Leslie is responsible for feeding 15,000 civilians and soldiers in Charleston. I hear he is ill and has ordered the evacuation of Wilmington, North Carolina, which has relieved us from having to reduce that garrison."

Nathanael paused and considered the tireless dedication the men around him never failed to provide. He supposed he must be forthcoming with letters he received from some of his old friends, such as generals James Varnum, John Sullivan, and Philip Schuyler who sat in Congress. "I have been asked to take a newly formed position as Minister of War."

"This, coming from Congress—a body of men who denounced you and threatened to oust you from the army for failing to show due deference to civilian leaders when you submitted your resignation as quartermaster general?" Captain Nat Pendleton asked in disbelief.

"Do you believe I would abandon you and our cause? I have no desire to be a politician after what I have seen. I have turned it down. The more I am in an army, the more I am acquainted with human nature and the less fond I am of political life," Nathanael assured.

But there were other reasons Nathanael turned it down. He told Congress that he was poor and that he did not wish to climb to stations where he had neither fortune nor friends to support him. "Eminence always begets envy, and it is much more difficult to support ourselves in high places than to arrive at them," he wrote.

Dusk fell early on that mid-November day that cast a chill over the High Hills of Santee. The camp quieted when supper was done. The chores, drills, and daily routine of the day summoned sleep to those who had labored whether with their hands or their minds.

Thomas Shubrick and Nat Pendleton wrote letters to loved ones, quickly scratching out their words before the candle sputtered and flamed. Otho coughed on occasion, but he slept peacefully. Nathanael rubbed his aching eyes and tried to ignore the wheezing in his chest. He reached for the leather express pouch that contained the endless letters he received. He emptied the contents onto his desk and checked the pouch. There was one lingering inside.

He recognized the delicate handwriting. It was from Caty.

My dearest husband, I have heard the news of the victory at Yorktown. Now, there is nothing that can deter me from seeing you. By the time you receive this, I hope to be on my way to South Carolina with our son George.

He fingered the locket in his waistcoat with Caty's picture in it. It was the first night he had slept blissfully in months.

thirty

We Shall Have the Devil to Pay

Caty heard her hired man, Hercules, add wood to the fire in the living room in her farmhouse in Westerly. She glanced out the kitchen window. Leafless branches clattered like bones in the wind. Thick low hanging clouds threatened snow.

Little George bounded into the kitchen with a log and dumped it on the cooking fire. "Do not do that," Caty scolded. "Do you want to see your dinner ruined?"

George shrugged. "What are you cooking?"

"Do you not have eyes?" his nearly four-year-old sister, Patty, asked with a titter. She displayed a turnip from the preparation table for his inspection.

"That is women's work," George announced with the authority of a boy who would soon be six.

"Who says?" Patty challenged. She ran after him on little legs deformed with rickets and the turnip tight in her grasp.

Cornelia paused playing with her doll to stare at her siblings. Nat toddled after Patty. He tripped over his own feet and fell. He emitted a screech of pain and frustration.

Caty stopped chopping onions and laid the knife aside. She put Nat on her hip and kissed his wet cheeks. "Patty, put the turnip back on the table. George, ask Hercules to light the candles. Uncle Sammy and Aunt Phebe will be here soon, and dinner is not ready yet."

The children minded their mother. Cornelia got up and ran into the living room shouting, "Uncle Sammy is coming!"

Caty smiled and put Nat on his feet. Sammy Ward, Jr. was her cousin, and although he was fifteen years younger than Nathanael, they had always been close. She turned to her cooking, a necessary chore in which she did not excel, but tonight she had turnips, onions, cod, and winter squash and dried garden herbs. Her fingers brushed the vague outline of the Atlantic Coast of the United States that Jeremiah Wadsworth had drawn for her last summer when he explained where Nathanael was and what he was doing.

Where is Nathanael at this moment? she wondered.

"Momma, Uncle Sammy is here!" George shouted, shattering her thoughts. "He brought books for me and Patty."

Caty wiped her hands with her apron and prepared to meet her guests, but Sammy and Phebe swept into the kitchen before she had the chance. "You look radiant!" Caty exclaimed when she saw Phebe, whose child, due in January, slept in her round belly.

Excitement radiated off Sammy as if he were aglow.

"What is it?" Caty asked. She shifted her gaze from one cousin to the other.

Sammy's dark eyes brightened further. "The schooner, *Adventure*, arrived in Newport a few days ago. It came directly from Virginia by way of Yorktown. Lord Cornwallis has surrendered to the allied forces under Washington!"

Caty drew in a deep breath and then said, "Are you certain?"

"Yes, there is no doubt." He handed her a copy of the *Providence Gazette*. "On the second page."

Caty thumbed open the paper. A squeal escaped her throat. The children and Hercules came running. She threw her arms around Sammy's neck.

He had done his duty in the war. He was held prisoner in Quebec, Canada after Colonel Benedict Arnold's small army attacked the British garrison there on New Year's Eve 1775. Sammy's health was never the same after his release.

Phebe helped Caty finish dinner preparations over which they excitedly discussed the possibility that the British threat in the South was diminished or the notion that the war was at an end. That night, Caty put her children to bed and kissed their sweet faces, innocent of the dangers their father faced in the South. She decided that nothing could stop her from going to Nathanael no matter the length and hazards of the journey.

George sighed in his sleep. *Should I bring him to a place I have no vision of so he can see his father? He has been the strength I have clung to this last year as he has grown into the boisterous curious child I once was and the practical person his father is.*

The answer was yes.

~

"It looks lovely," Caty exclaimed when Major William Blodget, Nathanael's former aide, brought her two-horse phaeton to Westerly freshly painted with the Greene coat-of-arms on the doors.

The merry, fat major chuckled and said, "I am honored to escort you as far as Philadelphia, Mrs. Greene."

Jacob and Peggy arrived to take Patty, Cornelia, and Nat to Coventry where they would care for them while Caty was away.

"Are you certain this is the wisest course?" Jacob asked. His propensity to look on the bleak side of things sometimes caused Caty to doubt her decisions, but not this time. She was so elated to be on her way that she hugged Jacob. The Quaker frowned, but it was merely a gesture that he did not mean.

"The children will be safe," Peggy promised. "Your father has asked that they spend time with your family on Block Island. I will see to it."

"Thank you, Peggy," Caty said. She gazed at the children she was leaving behind and told herself it was for their own good. She climbed into the phaeton and settled in beside George. The road to Philadelphia was familiar. What lay beyond was an enigma.

~

The last time Caty was in Philadelphia in the spring of 1780, Nathanael was Quartermaster General and fighting with Congress over money, supplies, policy, and commissions. Loyalists had stared, sometimes spitting insults when she walked the streets with an escort while Nathanael was in meetings. Her phaeton rolled through the streets of a contrasted city with welcoming celebratory illuminations of lanterns and candles placed on windowsills. Large transparent paintings lit from behind covered many windows like glowing shades. Patriotic and allegoric themes were everywhere.

The celebrations, however, were not for her. General George Washington and his wife, Martha, were in Philadelphia. Despite the still powerful British presence in America, the victory at Yorktown left a feeling that the Revolution was as good as won. Nathanael's recent success at Eutaw Springs reinforced that perception. Both he and Washington were hailed as national heroes.

Caty and little George were welcomed into the household of the bachelor Colonel Clement Biddle, who was one of Nathanael's deputies during his days as quartermaster and a fellow soldier during the early years of the war.

"Mrs. Greene," Clement greeted and offered his hand as she alit from her phaeton. "My house has been prepared for your comfort."

"Colonel Clement, this is my son, George Washington Greene," Caty said with pride.

"I am pleased to meet you, young man," Clement said gallantly.

George glanced at his mother and recalled her lessons on how to greet adults. *You are a general's son. You must always be polite*, she had coached. "Thank you, sir."

Clement ordered their baggage unloaded. "I have sent a message to General Washington. He and Lady Washington have been looking forward to your arrival and expect you for dinner. General Washington is here to discuss the state of the army with Congress."

Caty was aware of His Excellency's reasons for coming to Philadelphia during the brilliant social season, which he now found dull but she adored. He was facing the same financial difficulties with Congress that Nathanael faced in the South—no available money to give bounties or support and pay the existing army. It was symptom of larger problems, one of which was that Congress was unable to levy a federal tax to pay for the war.

That evening, dressed in finery she had not worn during the dark days she spent in Westerly, Caty arrived like a beacon of light at the handsome three-story townhouse on South Third Street. George was smitten in her company, as many officers and aides were when she came to the army's winter cantonments for a personal visit or exchanged teasing letters.

"My dearest Mrs. Greene," he said with a sweeping bow and delight in his blue-gray eyes. He kissed the back of her hand. "It is with much pleasure that we are able to have you with us."

"I am pleased to have a companion with whom I can talk and who I have known for so many years," Martha said as she clasped Caty's hands and kissed her cheek. "How long are you staying in Philadelphia?"

"Only a few days." *She looks wan, even frail,* Caty noted of her fifty-year-old friend.

"Do you recall the night we danced for three hours without sitting down?" George asked Caty over their meal of potatoes, baked ham, meat pie, bread and butter, wine, coffee, and fruit pie. "It was at a party in the Middlebrook, New Jersey encampment."

"How could I forget?" Caty asked. "Nathanael called it a 'pretty little frisk.'"

Martha offered a small smile in response. She, too, had been at that "little frisk," and the joy of the night seemed colorless.

"May I inquire as to the success of your business here in Philadelphia?" Caty asked George. A servant appeared to refill her glass of wine, which she drank with relish. "I only ask because I assume it will affect Nathanael's army in the South."

"It is no secret, the troubles we still endure politically. In fact, I have written to Nathanael telling him that I shall endeavor to stimulate Congress to the best improvement of our late success at Yorktown by taking the most vigorous and effectual measures to be ready for an early and decisive campaign next year."

"Do you believe Congress is languid?"

"Yes. My greatest fear is that they may think our work too nearly closed. I shall employ every means in my power to keep this fatal mistake from happening. If it does, no part of the blame shall be mine." George's eyes drifted to his reticent wife. With his meal finished, he rose and said, "I have correspondence to attend to. Please excuse me for tonight."

"Of course, General Washington," Caty said.

"At this point, there is no need for formality. Call me George." He turned to leave and then paused. "I am not the boy's father, but I wonder if it is wise that you take your son to an unhealthy part of the country and deny him a formal education here in Philadelphia?"

Caty thought of the lonely nights she had spent with little George as her companion. He laughed when she read the novel *Tristram Shandy* that belonged to Nathanael. When he was a boy, Nathanael made his brothers laugh by mimicking the squat, uncourtly character, Dr. Slop. When the other children were asleep, she taught him the alphabet and how to read in the quiet living room. *How can I leave him behind?* she thought.

There was something in Martha's eyes that said she had left a child behind.

Over glasses of claret, Martha poured her heart out to Caty. "My son, Jacky, has died," she sobbed. "I came here to escape Mount Vernon, which has become a house of mourning. George feels little grief over his stepson's loss. He attached himself to George as an aide, but he succumbed to camp fever at Yorktown and died on November 5 at age twenty-six." Martha wiped tears from her cheeks, and her chest heaved in agony. "I admit Jacky did not do well at his studies or farming, and his Abingdon Plantation has fallen into ruins. His wife, Nelly, and their four children have gone to

Mount Vernon for a while. It would be a joy if you would visit them on your journey south. Lucy Knox is there soon to give birth."

Caty remembered Martha telling her that her two youngest children died as toddlers before she met General Washington and the third, Patsy, died in 1773 at age seventeen. Her last child was gone. Caty could not imagine the pain.

"What can I do to comfort you?" Caty asked.

"Just your cheerful presence is a comfort," Martha sniffed. "In fact, my husband is not the only hero they are honoring in Philadelphia. General Greene's name is on everyone's lips. While you are here, I am certain you will receive invitations to the parties of the social season. I think you should attend if you have the time."

Caty's dark eyes brightened. It seemed like a lifetime since she had had fun, and she intended on making the most of it. As always, she would be the belle of the ball, but this time, she would also be the wife of a knighted warrior.

Despite a growing peace movement brought on by the surrender at York-town, neither King George III nor many of his ministers were willing to give up the fight to maintain their rule over America. And Nathanael was unwilling to give up his fight.

On November 18, the day Caty left Rhode Island on her journey south, Nathanael's army struck their tents for the last time in the High Hills of Santee. As small and weak as his army was, he intended to push the British out of the South Carolina low country and as far into Charleston as possible until they had nowhere to go but out to sea.

It took three days to get the troops, artillery, and supply wagons across the Wateree River. Then, the army marched down the west side of the river and crossed the Congaree at McCord's Ferry. Their left flank was protect-ed by Francis Marion, who reported that Colonel Alexander Stewart was again loose in the low country and stationed at Monck's Corners thirty-two miles north of Charleston. Thomas Sumter cooperated with Nathanael and searched for Loyalists who might be hiding in the swamps near Orangeburg.

On November 24, they camped at Buckhead. Nathanael sent a letter to Francis Marion in response to two of his recent letters. He was relieved to hear that Thomas Sumter had written Francis to share news. He was uncertain about the state of the enemy, so he sent a major to exchange thoughts on operations with the militia generals.

Francis wrote:

> *Stewart made the move only in bravado with a view to regain a hold on public opinion which had been forfeited by their recent retreat.*

On the other hand, Nathanael scolded him about complaints he received from the enemy concerning one of Francis' men dragging off convalescents and burning hospitals. "The act is inhumane. However, if burning the hospitals was to destroy stores, then I wish to have materials to contradict their charges."

The worst news from Francis was that militia colonels John Sevier and Isaac Shelby and their riflemen were going home to Virginia. Nathanael wrote, "If they leave us before reinforcements arrive, it will both embarrass and expose us. Reinforcements are on the march, and they will be here before many days. Tell them therefore that I beg them to continue with you before they arrive."

Nathanael was left to consider what he could do until Generals St. Clair and Wayne arrived from Yorktown. He shared his thoughts and concerns about Francis' news with Otho, including Stewart's decision to abandon Monck's Corners and drop down to Goose Creek near Charleston.

Nathanael pointed at a spot on the map. "This is Monck's Corner," he said as he tapped the map. He slid his finger due south for approximately ten miles. "Colonel Stewart has moved here to Goose Creek, leaving the British fortified post in Dorchester on the Ashley River exposed."

Otho's handsome face creased in a grin. "Therefore, we can cut off his communication and push the enemy still further into Charleston."

"That is my thought. I am going to form a flying party with elements of Harry's legion and William's cavalry and a detachment of Maryland and Delaware troops. I will take some of General Sumter's men as well. We shall launch a surprise attack—hit and run. I want you to take the rest of army to Four Holes."

Otho thought of everything he had done to hold the remnants of Horatio Gates' decimated army together when Gates abandoned them, and General Johann De Kalb died of his wounds after the devastating loss at Camden the year before. Those had been days clouded with poverty and despair not so unlike the desperation the army suffered now—yet it was different. There was hope, and he was one of its shepherds.

"Otho?" Nathanael asked, which snapped his adjutant back to the issue at hand.

He shook his head to clear it and said, "I will get the Continental troops prepared for the mission. Harry is finally recovering from the fever he was suffering. Are you going to speak to him?"

"Yes."

Otho turned to leave. "Wait," Nathanael said. "If something should happen to me, write to Caty and tell her what happened, and look out for her."

"Of course, but what do you mean?"

"I received a letter this morning from Henry Knox who is in Philadelphia. She is there and is on her way here." He excitedly handed the letter to Otho and went on. "I told Henry that I heard rumors but did not give much credit to them as the undertaking is so arduous. I painted a picture for her of the dangers and difficulties. Perhaps her wishes have got the better of her prudence."

"So it seems, but could you have expected less?" Otho asked. He read the letter from Henry:

Mrs. Greene is in this City and in charming health, and intends with young George to wing her way to the High Hills of Santee. Mrs. Knox presented me with another son two days

ago, whom I should name after you were not for the con-
founded name given by your Quaker Father - as it is I shall
call him after some Roman whose Character I think you may
like – give my love to Colonels Williams and Laurens. Adieu
My dear friend, H Knox

"Colonel Laurens?" Otho asked, noting Henry's last sentence. "Is he coming to camp?"

"He should be here any day," Nathanael said of the twenty-six-year-old aide to Washington who had composed the articles of capitulation when Cornwallis surrendered at Yorktown. "He wanted to come home to South Carolina. His family owns a plantation at Monck's Corner on the Cooper River. They call it Mepkin."

❧

"Lewis told me that you were feeling better," Nathanael said when he found Harry brushing his horse.

Harry put aside his task. The young colonel smiled and bowed. "I am perfectly recovered from my indisposition."

"Colonel Laurens wrote to me last night that by good intelligence from Charleston, he has great reason to believe that the rumors of Leslie's reinforcements are within a day or two sail of Charleston. If that is true, then we shall have the devil to pay."

"And perhaps it is a high price," Harry agreed.

"I am leaving today for Dorchester. Colonel Williams is in command of the army in my absence, but I am putting you in charge of all the army's cavalry. With William Washington taken prisoner, his light dragoon regiment needs a capable leader. Your legion will scout between the Ashley and the Edisto Rivers. Yet, if any military object invites our attention in any other quarter, you are not confined to this particular district."

Harry expected this show of confidence although Nathanael was taking a part of his legion with him to Dorchester. Nathanael was aware of his cavalry colonel's mental peacock feathers. They served to augment

Nathanael's decision. "I want you to protect the inhabitants from British plundering and especially the Negroes from whom the enemy get all their best intelligence. I cannot stress the importance of this."

Thomas Shubrick interrupted the conversation, "General Greene, your detachment is ready to deploy," he announced.

"Thank you, Thomas," Nathanael said. To Harry he said, "Colonel Laurens will be here soon. I want you to cooperate with him. No squabbling over rank. When he arrives, the two of you will observe John's Island south of Charleston. The British have cattle and horses pastured there. We will want to prevent raids launched from that location."

Harry's ego suffered a bit with the news of Lauren's impending ride into camp. The young aide was rich, educated, and dashing—cut from the same cloth as Harry. The desire for glory was another characteristic they shared. Harry sensed that General Greene knew this and was issuing a clandestine warning to follow his orders without question.

Nathanael swung into the saddle, and his detachment mounted up. With drums muffled to avoid alerting the enemy or spies, Nathanael led the way surrounded by cavalry, his aides, Lewis and William, and the infantry following. He turned in the saddle and saluted Captain Nat Pendleton, Otho, and Otho's aide, Major Elias Brown. Harry shielded his eyes from the sun. *It is strange to have my legion off like this,* he thought.

The cavalry spread out in a broad front to cut off the enemy's attempt to communicate. They slowly moved through the wildest and less-traveled paths. Swamps filled with water delivered swarms of mosquitoes. The horseman splashed into the swamps looking for Loyalists that lurked behind the smooth trunks of cypress trees.

"They know we are coming," Nathanael said to Colonel Wade Hampton, who commanded Thomas Sumter's cavalry. "It is too quiet."

"Let us hope they are anxious," Wade replied with a smirk. "My boys are liable to give them something they do not expect."

As they approached the fortifications at Dorchester on the night of November 30, British Major Thomas Fraser received a report from two

Loyalists who had indeed been hiding in the swamps. The rebels were coming from the north. "We have seen General Greene, and we suppose he is throwing his whole army against us!" one of them exclaimed. Fraser ordered his garrison to sleep on their arms. Every man listened anxiously for the sound of Greene's advance.

On the morning of December 1, after a sleepless night, Fraser sent fifty cavalrymen to reconnoiter the American position. Nathanael and Wade heard the thunder of horses and saw them coming through the thick stands of pine trees. With the element of surprise gone, Nathanael ordered the bugler to sound the attack.

Wade shouted to his cavalry men, "Charge!"

His men put spurs to horse. The infantry followed with Nathanael leading the way. Wade's men, characteristic of the bravado of Sumter's militia cavalry, attacked the small detachment of the enemy with short swords slashing, and soon they had killed at least ten and taken several prisoners. The enemy's whole horse of 150 came out immediately, but with no infantry to support them, Nathanael's detachment of 400 drove them back into their garrison with precipitation.

That night, Nathanael's men encamped at Vandomeres plantation. He wrote to Otho to inform him of his successful operation. "The enemy evacuated it the same night and burnt their works, stores and forage and retired to the Quarter House at Charleston Neck. They appear to have been much alarmed and have disgraced themselves not a little by their precipitate retreat. You are to take the army to Round O across the Edisto River. Send Colonel Kosciuszko to find a good camp."

Otho praised Nathanael for achieving his objective and added that he hoped he could keep what he had gotten. Nathanael felt that he *could* keep what he had gotten. With each bold stroke that caused the enemy to cringe and fall back, Nathanael believed that the threat of his presence caused panic. It was a good feeling, something he strived for, and he settled for nothing less than the constant harassment he could deliver because his little army was incapable of meeting the enemy in a general action. Therefore, he planned to take measures to continue the momentum. First, he and his detachment needed to reunite with his main army.

☙

Round O laid to the west between Savannah and Charleston, a place from which the Southern Army could cut off communications between the two British-held cities. Unlike Four Holes, where feeding the army was difficult due to lack of forage and provisions, Round O laid in the midst of a rich rice district. Wild game and waterfowl were plentiful.

With a company of Pioneers, black soldiers employed to perform engineering and construction tasks and some of the best guides in the country, Otho led the army through the dark swamps of the low country sheeted with tannin-stained, slow-flowing water. Bald cypress trees and tupelo gum trees dominated the deepest areas of the swamp that teemed with alligators, mosquitoes, and snakes. Spanish moss bearded the occasional oak tree where warblers sung unseen from the boughs. Frogs croaked incessantly. Great egrets and white ibis waded in the shallows. The bogs, where scrub palmetto bushes with bayonet leaves so sharp that they scratched the horses' fetlocks and cut the men's legs, slowed the army's progress.

Thomas Kahoo cringed at every razor sting that tattered his already torn and soaked stockings.

"You are bleeding," James McCurdy pointed out to his comrade.

"I'm aware. Have you seen yourself?" Thomas asked. "You have leeches on your arms."

James bent his arms, and his eyes widened in horror. His forearms below his rolled up sleeves were covered in the black parasites. He shook his arms as if the leeches would come loose. "For God's sake, how do I get them off me?"

Jackson Killam came up when he realized that Thomas and James had stopped walking. "Pinch 'em off," he advised, "but don't leave the mouth on your skin."

James shook his head vehemently. "I am not doing that. I am going to find Dr. Read." He ran off, oblivious to the punishing palmetto bushes.

The army continued its slow march until it reached Ferguson's Mills above the waters of the swamps and bogs. Otho called a halt. He issued orders to Colonel Thaddeus Kosciuszko, "You are to scout ahead and find a suitable campsite at Round O. When that is accomplished, the army will leave for that place. Take a contingent of guard and some of the Pioneers as a precaution."

Thaddeus, his alert engineer's mind always churning, said, "I have heard the land is fertile with clean running water. This mission should prove a pleasure." He went to gather his small force.

With his engineer off and the ragged army settled in for the night, Otho wrote to Nathanael informing him of their whereabouts and that they would remain there until Kosciuszko returned. It was a sleepless night for many men who dreamed of water filled with snakes.

By December 7, the Southern Army was encamped at Roger Saunders' plantation on the Pon Pon River at Round O. Otho immediately established stern military discipline. This was his brand of command before Nathanael took over the Southern Army. It was something he and his general had in common—the propensity for detail and discipline that paired them like hand in glove.

❧

While Otho was keeping the army busy with routine orders and Nathanael was making his way through the swamps toward Round O, General Alexander Leslie in Charleston was bemoaning his situation in letters to General Henry Clinton in New York and Lord George Germain, the former Secretary of State to the Colonies, in London. With Nathanael's cavalry and the militia's cavalry buzzing the countryside, Alexander felt as if he were being surrounded by gnats he could not swat.

> *My being entirely destitute of real cavalry creates infinite difficulties and obliges me to supply their place with mounted infantry, who from inexperience in that line must fight under every disadvantage. The great superiority of the enemy horse renders it impossible to procure any certain intelligence.*

Alexander was quartered in John Rutledge's mansion overlooking Charleston harbor. He put a hand to his stomach and grimaced. He had had a good and long career in the battles and occupation of America. It seemed easier when he was a colonel in February 1775, and General Thomas Gage, the military governor of Massachusetts, ordered him to march on Salem where he was to seize cannon and powder from rebel militia. His mission failed when he encountered a large, abusive crowd of residents and militia who had raised the drawbridge over the North River.

The event that came to be known as Leslie's Retreat did not stain his reputation. He was promoted to lieutenant general, a rank he shared with Cornwallis and Clinton. To Clinton in New York, he wrote that Greene's army was reported to be in his rear. Greene was strangling him, and it was with much sorrow that he was obliged to inform Lord Germain of the almost total revolt of the province of South Carolina since the misfortune in Virginia. He grieved for the Loyalist families deprived of their possessions and means of support. They were a burden upon him that he could not humanely avoid.

From his window, Alexander watched his meager reinforcements disembark at the docks. There were only sixty artillerymen and 500 New York troops—not nearly the number the enemy believed was en route. He was tired of the war, like his adversary Nathanael Greene. He wanted to go home to Scotland and see his grown daughter, Mary Anne. His wife, Rebecca, died a year after her birth. He wondered how many times he would have to beg Clinton for permission to go home before he became so ill that he would be unable to travel.

❧

Nathanael arrived at Round O on December 9 to a well-organized camp. He made the plantation house his headquarters. Many fine plantations had been burned in the civil war that raged between Americans in the South, their residents driven from their homes with nowhere to go. His success at Dorchester brought him no respite, and he promptly began writing letters of instruction.

In an unexpected turn of events, he found Thomas Sumter cooperative when he asked him to monitor activity in the largely Loyalist Orangeburg district and to relinquish Colonel Wade Hampton's whole force of 110 men for his own use. Nathanael wrote, "The enemy no longer has command of the countryside, and it is in our best interest to change the plan of the war."

Thomas replied:

> *My men have informed me that there are no fewer than some 1,500 Loyalists hiding in the swamps along the Edisto River. I will do my best to induce them to surrender and withdraw from the British if you promise their protection. Many are women and children, but I will do all I can.*

Thomas was right. They came out at night looking for food and necessities, and he feared that if he sent them home, many would be privately injured.

Nathanael encouraged, "Keep up the good work of trying to bring them in. It will save the lives of so many people. The measure is consistent with the principles of human nature."

Gathering his screening force, he wrote to Francis Marion to tell him where Sumter was and assigned him to patrol the army's left a little south near Monck's Corner and the Cooper River. Colonel Wade Hampton was patrolling the region below Four Holes. Harry Lee and his legion guarded the front between the Edisto and Ashley Rivers, concealing the dangerous fact that the army could only muster 800 men from headquarters. The British were confined to Charleston Neck, the city, and the outer islands.

Nathanael tried to keep his anxieties at bay. With the threat of British reinforcements, he turned to governors and military officials to beg for help but was met with every excuse imaginable. His consolation was that the enemy dared not venture into the countryside, and if they did, his patrols chased them away.

As threatening as the enemy was, his own army was still without essential supplies and provisions. He asked South Carolina Colonel Peter Horry for assistance. "Our horses have neither cloaks nor blankets. All kinds of cloth we are in want of and in the greatest distress on the same account; nearly one half our soldiers have not a shoe on their feet and not a blanket to ten men on the line. I hope if the officers stand by me as they always have, we shall get through our difficulties."

He placed his quill in its holder and exercised his cramped fingers stained with ink. The floorboards creaked under his boots as he limped out onto the porch in the dim light of a crisp day. Otho was authorizing huntsmen to kill game for the commissary. Nathanael recognized some of the men gathered around—Jackson Killam and Christopher Madison from Virginia, Thomas Kahoo and James McCurdy of Maryland, Patrick Cullen of Delaware. Thomas and James had no shirts. Jackson had no shoes. Yet they cheerfully waited with rifles in hand to do their duty for the commissary. Thomas Young of South Carolina sneaked something from his hand and gave it to the eager puppy that bounced among them, his ears flopping.

For a moment, Nathanael wondered what he would do without his adjutant's careful instruction. He remembered Caty teasing Otho about getting married as soon as possible before his alluring handsome face faded.

"General Greene, am I late?"

Nathanael's reverie shattered. Twenty-seven-year-old Colonel John Laurens was standing before him. "Colonel," Nathanael said as he offered his ink-stained hand. "You are not late. Colonels Williams, Kosciuszko, and Cameron are coming up just now."

John returned the handshake. The two officers had known each other for four years, both present at the battles of Brandywine, Monmouth, and Rhode Island. As Washington's aide, John had constant contact with all of Washington's major generals. When Charleston fell to the British in May 1780, John was there with General Lincoln's imprisoned troops until he was exchanged six months later.

"Have you heard from your father?" Nathanael asked as they walked into the house. He knew that Henry Laurens, a former president of the Continental Congress, had gone to the Netherlands in 1779 as an ambassador and was captured by the British, charged with treason, and imprisoned in the Tower of London.

"Have you not heard?" John asked, surprised. "He is going to be exchanged for Lord Charles Cornwallis who will be paroled to England."

Nathanael hesitated. *Surely I would remember that important piece of news if it was forthcoming.*

John read the uncertainty on the general's countenance. He wondered how much he knew about the wife and child he had abandoned in England. It was a marriage John opposed but had consummated to preserve his honor.

"I hope your father remains safe," Nathanael said. "He was always cooperative and fair."

Nathanael's aides, Nat, Lewis, and Thomas, rose when their general and the colonel entered the office. When the other colonels arrived, Nathanael announced, "I purposed to ask Governor Rutledge that we arm and train slaves in Georgia and South Carolina. In exchange, they would be paid and clothed like regular troops and win their freedom. That they would make good soldiers, I have not the least doubt. We are in desperate need of reinforcements, and I see no reason not to recruit them."

Lewis said with a frown, "I see the poor, unhappy blacks who, to the disgrace of human nature, are subject to every species of oppression while we are contending for the rights and liberties of mankind."

"It may prove a great means of preventing the enemy from further attempts upon this country when they find they have not only the whites, but the blacks to contend with," Nathanael replied. "I spoke to Colonel Lee about this before he left on patrol. He and I were of the mind that if they were welcomed into the American Army, they might be less inclined to do the king's bidding and spy for the British."

"This will not go over well," John warned. "Political leaders in the South are fearful of putting weapons in the hands of blacks."

"Yours is very much a northerner's point of view, if you will excuse me, General Greene. It was tried in 1779," Basil said. "Congress authorized the recruitment of 3,000 black slaves with compensation to their owners. South Carolina and Georgia vetoed it."

"Governor Rutledge has not replied to me, but I hope that he will present my request when the legislature convenes next month," Nathanael said, undeterred. "Or perhaps sooner if he can convene a council."

"I shall be happy to introduce a bill for this proposal. In my father's absence, I am a representative to the state," John offered. "We are admittedly slave owners, but I find myself adverse to the practice. I asked father that he free the forty I stand to inherit, but he is not in a place where he can act upon it."

On Christmas Eve, Nathanael received a letter from John Rutledge from the High Hills of Santee informing him that he would indeed have to wait for the legislature to convene. "Your proposal is alarming," Rutledge wrote.

However, good news arrived that the 5,000 reinforcements General Leslie was expecting never materialized and that he had no transports for regular troops. As encouraging as it was, Nathanael was apprehensive over what the enemy would do next. More importantly, he was impatient for Caty's safe arrival.

On Christmas day, he delivered a message to his army:

> *The General wishes the army a Merry Christmas; and that it may be so, he directs that the usual proportion of spirits be issued to the officers and men.*

Most were far from their families, and all they had was one another.

thirty-one

You Cannot Cease to Be a Soldier

Caty stared through a living room window in the house of Colonel Clement Biddle, her host in Philadelphia. Lights from the other homes were obliterated in the blizzard that punished the city and isolated the residents. The crackling fireplace emitted a cheerful warm glow on her son George, who was absorbed in the book his Uncle Sammy had given him before they left Rhode Island. Caty closed the curtains and sat beside him.

"Would you like to go to school?" she asked.

"Will there be a teacher and other children?" the six-year-old asked.

"Yes, of course. You will be expected to behave and do your lessons just as you do for me at home."

George nodded and returned his attention to his book. She slipped a hand under his chin and tilted it up to meet her eyes. "Mr. Charles Petit, a friend of your father's, has offered to see to your schooling here in Philadelphia," she said gently. "That means you will not be traveling south with me."

"Will Papa not miss me?"

"I am certain he will, but of more importance, he will be proud of your schooling."

Colonel Biddle entered the parlor with several guests. Caty rose to receive them. Another Christmas Eve, and her family was not together.

꩜

As Martha Washington had predicted, after the blizzard passed, invitations to parties of the social season poured in, and Caty was persuaded to stay. She went shopping. Her gowns were old, and it would not do for the wife of a national hero and major general to look out of fashion. The invitations often designated her as the guest of honor.

Henry Knox was in attendance at one of the parties. The two greeted one another as the band played a minuet in the background and champagne flowed. "My dear Mrs. Greene," Henry said in his booming voice, "I have written your husband to tell him that you look as charming and as healthy as ever."

"That is quite the compliment coming from you," Caty said.

Henry patted his girth and laughed. "I would ask you to dance, but I am not nimble on the dance floor."

"I have seen you dance, sir, and I disagree," Caty giggled. She slid his champagne glass out of his hand and set it on a table heaped with a variety of delicious delicacies. "Shall we?"

"I should feel guilty," Henry began as they performed the steps of the minuet, "Lucy is at Mount Vernon where she has been since the beginning of the Yorktown siege. She has given me a new son we have named Marcus Aurelius after a Roman emperor."

"Martha told me the good news even as she grieves for her own son. I hope he brings much joy to your family after having lost your precious baby girl the year before."

"I think it would bring Lucy much joy to see you on your journey south. Perhaps you could stop and see my son and cheer her with your company."

"Now, who is being charming?" Caty laughed.

The music stopped, and Caty was surrounded by anxious partners who wished to dance. Her eye caught the sour face of Ichabod Burnet, an aide to Nathanael and her escort on the remainder of her journey. He complained to William Blodget of the delay. No matter, Caty intended to stay for a few weeks. She sent a message to Nathanael that she would resume her travels soon and relayed verbal messages through friends on their way to camp from Philadelphia.

The whirlwind days in Philadelphia came to a close. To Ichabod Burnet's relief, Caty packed her phaeton for the journey to Mount Vernon. The Washingtons arrived at Colonel Biddle's home to see her off.

"I have written to Nathanael that you are in perfect health and good spirits and thinking no difficulties too great not to be surmounted in the performance of your visit to South Carolina. It shall be my endeavor to strew the way with flowers," George said to Caty with gracious admiration. "Your fortitude is to be admired."

Caty kissed Martha on both cheeks and said, "Farewell, my dearest friend. My heart and thoughts are always with you." To Colonel Biddle, she said, "Thank you for your hospitality."

The moment she dreaded was upon her. Little George stood beside Colonel Charles Petit. He seemed so small yet so grown. *I will not cry*, she told herself. "Be a good boy and tend to your schooling. I hope you make many new friends. I will write to you, and you must promise to do the same. Remember, make your father proud. He is fighting for our freedom."

"I promise, Momma."

~

Nathanael was never so happy to see anyone as he was to see General Anthony Wayne march into camp with his Pennsylvania line in early January.

"That was quite the march," Anthony said as he removed his riding gloves and tromped into the plantation house living room with muddy boots. "Disagreeable country the closer we got to this place. I hear the mosquitoes are as big as birds."

Nathanael laughed at his old comrade's assessment. Anthony was as dashing and well-loved by the ladies as any man he knew. He was aware that Caty saw that in Anthony as well, but it never sparked his jealousy. Anthony was a married man. Unlike many generals' wives, his wife, Polly, refused to leave their home in Pennsylvania to be with him at camp.

"What are we doing with the devils in this state?" Anthony asked as he searched the living room for rum. "You do have spirits?" he asked when his hunt turned up nothing.

"We do but go easy. We have to wait for weeks to get resupplied. My quartermaster, Edward Carrington, is still in Virginia and sending what he can as we cannot get any here in this place. Have you word from General St. Clair?" Nathanael asked.

Anthony found the rum and poured a glass. He peeled off his coat, tossed off his hat, and sat down. "He will arrive soon. The Virginians refused to come because they have not been paid." He leaned forward and said, "Do not expect much. St. Clair has marched the Maryland and Delaware regiments so fast that half of them fell sick and had to be left behind."

The sound of drum and fife floated across the fields of Saunders plantation. Anthony peered out a window. "Speaking of which, I believe General St. Clair has arrived."

Nathanael and Anthony walked out to welcome Arthur. His ragged, filthy regiments looked as if they had marched 1,000 miles through the dust of the Sahara Desert. The Maryland and Delaware regiments already in camp gathered around and offered food and drink to their home state fellows. Otho arrived to help.

"Arthur," Nathanael said gallantly, "we are very glad to have you here."

Arthur's long face looked strained. He had been court-martialed for abandoning his command at Fort Ticonderoga when British General Simon Fraser marched on it in July 1777 as part of General John Burgoyne's campaign to take Albany. Burgoyne surrendered to General Horatio Gates at Saratoga three months later. Nevertheless, Arthur was humiliated.

The tension between Anthony and Arthur vibrated through camp. Nathanael was forced to separate them. On January 9, he sent a corps of dragoons, some artillery, and militia to Georgia with Anthony. "The British are still up along the Savannah River, and the Loyalists and Indians are active. The Patriots are in desperate need of help," Nathanael told Anthony. "You are to drive the British into Savannah and force them to surrender. Protect the patriots of that neighborhood. Many have no avenue of recourse, and they are afraid as many Natives, aligned with the British, threaten their lives."

Anthony gallantly gathered his force. He was proud of his nickname, "Mad Anthony," and he intended to live up to it. It did not imply madness, it implied determination.

⁊

On January 18, 1782, the South Carolina General Assembly met at Jacksonborough about ten miles south of Round O. Nathanael had persuaded Governor Rutledge to hold the meeting there to humiliate the British in Charleston and show citizens that his army was watching. In support, he moved the army to Skirring's Plantation a few miles east of Jacksonborough.

While his army benefited from the beautiful, prosperous region with an abundance of fruits, vegetables, and lovely gardens, the assembly gathered. The spectators watched the council members file in to take their seats on long benches. Some members had been on British prison ships. Others were weary, mutilated victims of Loyalist vengeance. There were soldiers seamed with scars and plantation owners who had lost everything.

The onlookers whispered behind cupped hands, "That is Henry Laurens' son, John." When the short, slender figure of indomitable endurance entered, their eyes fixed upon him and pointed out, "There is Francis Marion." Thomas Sumter arrived burdened with the lingering effects of the wounds to his chest and shoulder that he received at Blackstock's in 1780. Nathanael and Lewis slid into the back of the meetinghouse while the delegates finished seating.

Governor Rutledge rose and addressed the assembly, "We have seen our darkest days, and now let us do the duty that stands before us in this present hour."

He gave a nod to John Mathews who they voted as his successor. Progress was made in reestablishing the government and supplying for widows and orphans in the state. Means to calm the raging civil war among civilians was discussed. After a controversial battle, Nathanael's slave enlistment bill was voted down. Many were fearful of what would become of their farms with no labor source, more so than the fear of slaves taking up arms against them.

Murmuring commenced. Nathanael and John Laurens exchanged disappointed glances. Governor Rutledge called everyone to attention, and the room silenced. He said, "The wisdom, prudence, address, and bravery of the great and gallant General Greene and the intrepidity of the officers and men under his command—a general who is justly entitled, from his many signal services, to honorable and singular remarks of your approbation and gratitude."

John Laurens stood and as head of the appropriation committee announced, "We pass a bill, vesting in General Nathanael Greene, in consideration of his important services, the sum of ten thousand guineas. This sum will go to the purchase of a plantation among those confiscated from Loyalists by the state."

The spectators and the assembly rose and applauded the measure. Nathanael was surprised and honored. He stood and bowed. "I thank you for your generosity and high opinion of my services."

The assembly dispersed. Men filed by to offer congratulations.

When the room was empty, John Rutledge approached Nathanael and said, "You are pleased, but I see a distant disapproval in your eyes."

"The hostilities are not over," Nathanael said. "And you know how I feel about pressing a plan to return confiscated property to the Loyalists when the war is over. It is a subject that deserves attention."

John raised an eyebrow, "We have given it much attention. Are you saying that you will not accept this gift from South Carolina?"

Nathanael raised a smile. His eyes shifted to Lewis before he said, "I graciously accept it. My finances are tenuous, and this will help me make a new start when the war is over."

"We all need a new start," John agreed. "I believe the plantation the council has in mind is called Boone's Barony on the Edisto River. There are some 6,600 acres. The value lay in the crops it produces; therefore, you will need additional slaves to work the land. Your northern values may need to be tossed out the window."

I am fighting for the rights of men, and nothing can be said in the defense of slavery, Nathanael thought. *What can I say in my own defense when my business affairs are beginning to fall apart in the north, as my brother Jacob has informed me?*

Nathanael did not have time to dwell on the morality of the subject. His army needed attention, his wife was on her way, and some of his officers had asked for permission to go home.

❧

On February 9, as the sun peeked over the eastern horizon, Nathanael dashed off a letter to his friend and business partner Jeremiah Wadsworth. "Colonel Williams is in a hurry to be gone, and I have got up a little earlier than common to finish this before breakfast. He has been relieved of his duties as adjutant general to be replaced by Colonel Josiah Harmar. It was not my choice. The choice was left to Congress."

Nathanael was not going to let his sagacious friend set out for Philadelphia empty-handed. He continued his correspondence in a letter to George Washington recommending Otho's promotion to brigadier general. "I am under many and singular obligations to him for his zeal and long service and for his uncommon exertions to promote the operations in this department. I recommend a promotion for which his standing and justice authorize his claim."

Otho arrived for breakfast as Nathanael finished his letters. He entered the office carrying his tall, erect figure with grace, but beneath it, he ached with rheumatism. A servant brought coffee and cornmeal cakes as he lowered into a chair.

"I plan on moving the army to Bacon's Bridge after you leave. I wish you were coming with us on the march," Nathanael said.

Otho stirred his coffee. There was a moment of awkward silence. "I will not completely abandon you. I will go home to Maryland and do what I can for the army from there. Perhaps I can assist John Eager Howard now that he has gone back to our home state to recruit a new regiment."

"I am sending letters with you," Nathanael said. He palmed one from the pile he intended to pack in an express case. "This is my recommendation to General Washington for your promotion to brigadier. Deliver it with care, my friend."

Otho put his coffee cup aside. He was not used to struggling for words, but at the moment the struggle seemed insurmountable. After nearly seven years, he was leaving the army. He had endured a year and a half as a British prisoner in conditions that ruined his health. His service in the South, where everything was difficult to obtain and achieve, was not so different, yet they had persevered. The friendships he formed, especially after Nathanael's arrival, added value to his life like his dearly missed brothers and sister. But he could not say those words. And he knew he did not have to. Nathanael understood.

When the Southern Army said goodbye to their fair and wise colonel, Nathanael reminded him, "Mrs. Greene says you must get married, that you owe it to society, and that your own happiness depends on it."

Although the war was at a stalemate, the depravity and effects of illness caused yet another friend and valuable officer to slip from Nathanael's grasp. Harry Lee requested leave from the army. Unlike Otho, Harry had a flare for the dramatic, and he made it known, "My friends and foes persecute me and see me as unworthy with indifference to my efforts to advance the cause of my country. However, as disgusted as I am with human nature, I wish from motives of self, to make my way easy and comfortable."

Nathanael experienced another sting to the heart. It was true. Many of Lee's men did not like him, and he had foreseen this melancholy reason to seek the comforts of home. "You say your friends are not disposed to do justice to your exertions. If you mean me, and anything appears in my conduct to confirm it, it has been owing to error in judgement or accident and not to disinclination. Whatever may be the source of your wounds, I wish it was in my power to heal them," Nathanael commiserated. "You know I love you as a friend."

What Nathanael did not admit was that like so many men in his army, he, too, was feeling unwell. Dr. Read had warned him to rest, or his fever would worsen. Rest was not something Nathanael could afford unless the fever drove him to his bed. Harry's complaints were his responsibility.

"I will go about my duty as you have asked me to scout near Charleston," Harry said. "Perhaps it will give me time to see this in a different light."

Harry returned a few days later bemoaning that Nathanael had given luster to some officers and corps and others he had not. "You know of my devotion to you. My attachment to you will end only with my life." Harry went on, "But I cannot brush off the imbecility of my mind and your slights regarding your reports on the battle at Eutaw Springs."

"Do you believe that I have not felt this ache when so many of my triumphs in the North were overlooked by the public, and General Washington failed to give me due praise for my exertions no matter the reason?" Nathanael asked, exasperated.

"I am sorry my stupid conduct has caused so much trouble."

"Go home, Harry. You are yet a young man. You will get married, but you cannot cease to be a soldier."

"And what of my legion? Who will command them? My second, Captain Joseph Eggleston, has gone to Virginia."

"Colonel John Laurens will take your legion," Nathanael said.

Harry's anger returned. "He is an irresponsible officer—an experimenter who will waste the troops very fast."

Despite Harry's gloomy musings of disapproval, his legion gathered around to see him off as he climbed into a carriage with fifteen guineas in his pocket. John Laurens was among them. He had commanded troops for a brief time when he stormed Redoubt 10 with Colonel Alexander Hamilton during the siege of Yorktown. His bravado was not satisfied by aiding other men, even Washington.

Harry afforded one last glance at Nathanael, who stood on the porch of the Shirring Plantation with his arms crossed over his torn coat, a sign that he was suffering for want of clothing along with his troops. Harry's extreme admiration for his general, and the expectation of the same, led him to a dismal end he could not reconcile.

Caty spent a month in the house that George Washington spent years renovating and improving on the Potomac River—his beloved Mount Vernon. Lucy Knox was a gracious hostess in Martha Washington's absence. They often sat on the piazza on the back of the house that overlooked the Potomac River, drank wine, and talked.

"I cannot stay here forever," Lucy said as they enjoyed a cool mid-March evening. "But Henry and I have no home of our own. Our two oldest children are off at school. Our new son is here with me. I have been a wanderer this whole war."

Caty exhaled a sigh and said, "Aside from the farm Nathanael owns in Westerly, we have no home of our own, either. Spell Hall, the house in Coventry, is occupied by his brother Jacob and his family. It was never really ours. It was Greene family property."

Lucy heaved to her feet with a suddenness that startled Caty. "Enough of this gloom," she announced. "Do you remember the parties we held at the Middlebrook encampment in 1779? We shall have another as grand before we see you off."

Three days later, Mount Vernon was lit with hundreds of candles. Festoons made of flowers adorned the walls, and bowls of local cuisine— dried fruit, stews, pies, dumplings, cabbage, potatoes, and gravies—were prepared by enslaved people who worked the kitchens in Mount Vernon and set an excellent table.

Caty danced as she had never danced before, and when she thought her heart content, a message arrived for her from Jeremiah Wadsworth. She hurried to the privacy of her above stairs bedroom. The note read:

> *I arrived in Philadelphia and was much disappointed to find that you had departed the day before. I had hoped to see you. If only you had let me know.*

Her head swam, not because of the music that filtered up the stairs or the copious amount of wine she had indulged in, but because his disappointment and desire exuded from the stroke of each letter. She sat at the writing desk and stared out the window at the dark, winding ribbon of the Potomac. *How do I reply?* she wondered as she tried to calm her fluttering heart.

With quill, ink, and paper at her disposal, she let her emotions guide her hand. "I am trembling for fear I shall not have the pleasure of seeing you before I go to the South, but I know your time is entirely taken up. Be assured if I cannot see you, I shall go mourning all the way. I hope you will excuse me, my dear friend."

She sprinkled pounce on the paper to dry the ink and sealed the letter. The weather was improving, and she supposed it was time to go. The ill-humored Major Ichabod Burnet was anxious to leave, and she did not want to have to appease him anymore than needed.

Two days later, she climbed into her phaeton. Before she resumed her journey, she sent a note to John Mathews, the governor-elect of South Carolina, instructing him to, "Tell General Greene that I claim the privilege of being met by him personally at least five miles from headquarters."

Virginia provided pleasant taverns in which to stay and enthusiastic inhabitants who greeted her as if she were a queen en route to see her king. They followed the Great Wagon Road, the same road Nathanael had traveled when he went in search of the remnants of the Southern Army in December 1780. In late March, they crossed the Dan River and into North Carolina. Her carriage bumped along the rough red clay roads and through vast stretches of pine and oak where pine needles blanketed the ground and green grasses reached for the sun.

Here she witnessed the destruction Nathanael had warned her about: miles of burned homes and ruined fields. On occasion, they passed dead horses or cows, their carcasses rotting in the sun and picked clean by vultures. With the onset of spring, flies and mosquitoes sometimes swarmed the carriage. Inhabitants, wary of strangers, stared at her phaeton.

She whispered to Major Burnet, "Maybe we should not have gotten the Greene family crest painted on the carriage doors."

"It matters not. Either way, you are a stranger in this hostile land. General Greene told you not to come, and yet you would not listen," he growled.

Caty leaned back in her seat and stared out the window. There was no point in pursuing an argument. They stopped for the night at the only tavern in Salisbury, North Carolina.

Ichabod wrote to Nathanael:

> We arrived at this place after the most disagreeable ride indeed. Mrs. Greene has endured it with fortitude and appears to be much less affected than expected.

By the time Ichabod Burnet's letter reached him, Nathanael had moved the army to Bacon's Bridge on the Ashley River two miles north of Charleston Neck.

☙

On April 5, 1782, more than three months after Caty left Rhode Island, she approached Nathanael's camp. On the road ahead, a group of horsemen appeared. One of them spurred his horse and rushed on in front of his companions. Her driver brought the phaeton to a halt. Without regard for lady-like conduct, Caty threw open the carriage door. Nathanael jumped from his saddle. For the first time in nearly two years, she was in his strong arms.

Nathanael kissed her with abandoned passion. Ichabod took the reins of Nathanael's horse as his general climbed into his wife's phaeton. On the ride to camp, Caty's joy was tempered by his appearance. He was bronzed by long exposure to the Southern sun and thinner than she had ever seen him. His uniform was in shoddy condition. He was thirty-nine years old, and he looked as if he held the worries of the world on his broad shoulders and on his lined countenance. His lambent blue eyes reflected a look of strained worry.

She stroked his cheek and murmured, "Until now, I did not realize what you have given to the Patriot cause."

"And why is that my angel?" he asked. He kissed the top of her dark head.

"Your letters did not draw the picture. Your handsome face sketches it all." She ran a finger across his right cheekbone. "Your eye is becoming infected, is it not?"

He grasped her finger and placed it on her lap. The last thing he wanted to do was talk about his eye that indeed felt as if infection was setting in.

The phaeton rolled into camp anchored by the abandoned plantation house of John Waring that served as Nathanael's headquarters and officers' quarters, although many had gone home. Hundreds of his enlisted men were literally as naked as they day they were born except a clout about their middle because the army had received no clothes all winter. Naked or not, they were busy digging latrines, exercising with their companies, cleaning firearms, repairing wagon wheels, caring for horses, and cooking food with their messmates. The few women and children who followed the army performed many of the chores beside their husbands. Smoke from campfires twisted into the air, a smell Caty associated with camp life since the siege of Boston in 1775.

Lewis Morris, Nat Pendleton, William Pierce, and Thomas Shubrick appeared on the plantation house lawn when the phaeton parked. Of the four, Caty recognized Lewis. Nathanael ordered them to bring her baggage in the house and jealously whisked her away before her charms seduced his aides.

In his above stairs bedroom, Caty removed her hat, gloves, and cloak. She peered out the window where rice fields stretched as far as the eye could see. Nathanael gently turned her to face him. "I am dusty from the road," she protested when he removed the pins from her hair. It flowed down her back like a dark waterfall that allured him as much as the thought of her stepping into a bathtub.

She looked up at him and saw more than lust in his blue eyes. Everything he was—his fierce devotion, his rugged hardships and competency, his sacrificial perseverance—served to entice her need for his touch. She invited him to take whatever he wanted; a gift reserved for her husband who had never had a day's leave and never had a moment when he could let his guard down.

Nathanael fumbled with the strings on her bodice and kissed her neck. She drew his hand away. As she untied each string she whispered in his ear, "If I am to be undressed, then I expect you to do the same."

He heeded her expectation without argument or words. As they luxuriated in one another's touch, the sounds of the busy camp outside the open window faded into oblivion. Although he had lost weight and suffered from malnutrition, the muscles in his broad chest and shoulders, still strong from the days he had pounded smelt into anchors, rippled with strength as he laid her on the bed.

After their connubial felicity was gratified, Caty laid her head on his chest and listened to his heartbeat calm. He heaved a sigh. "My angel, I cannot tell you how many nights I imagined you by my side in my bed."

She reached to finger the locket around his neck; the one she had sent to him last spring with her picture in it.

"I love you now as I loved you the day we were married," Nathanael said. He propped up on his elbow. "You have changed. You are so much more beautiful than I remembered."

Caty put a finger to his lips. "For just this day, we will not leave this room and bask in the silence of our adoration."

Nathanael laughed. "I should think you will starve in doing so."

Her hands traveled down his chest to his thighs. "I think I shall not."

⮞

Caty did not starve, and after a bath and dinner, she found Nathanael at his desk. "Who are you writing?"

"Henry Knox. My joy at having you here has spilled over into my pen. I am conveying the news and that you are in better health and spirits than I could have expected after such a disagreeable journey." He kissed her pert nose. "You are kinder to me than I am just to you."

"And this letter to Colonel Biddle?" she asked teasingly as she snatched the unsealed letter from the top of a pile.

"Give me that," Nathanael teased in return.

She stepped back gripping the letter. "And what did you tell my gracious host in Philadelphia?"

"Caty," Nathanael warned. But a smile softened his face as she read:

> *Can you believe it that Mrs. Greene is at Camp in South Carolina! I feel myself under great obligations for her for persevering under such a variety of difficulties to come and see me. You know I am one of the old-fashioned sort of people fond of my sweetheart, and therefore must be supremely happy at meeting.*

She placed the letter in his outstretched hand and kissed his lips. "I love you, and I am glad that you are happy and content with me. Now, I promised Captain Pendleton that I would play a game of backgammon with him. I brought the game along, hoping someone would match wits." She slipped a hand under his chin and examined his right eye. The smallpox scar on his eyeball looked inflamed. "Do not strain your eyes too much tonight," she warned and turned to leave.

"Caty, there are matters we need to discuss."

"Oh? About the children?"

His smile dissipated. "No, about our finances—a matter of great importance that affects them, too. I received a letter from Jeremiah Wadsworth."

Caty eased into a chair across from Nathanael's desk. She stopped breathing for moment before she realized that Jeremiah would never write an inappropriate letter to her husband regarding their flirtations, which amounted to little.

"The business venture we embarked on in 1779 had come to its conclusion, and I have only garnered ten percent of my original 10,000 pound investment." Nathanael continued, "I assume our farm in Westerly is worthless at this point. I told you about the plantation the state of South Carolina gifted me for my services. It will take money to hire Negroes and see a profit. But there is more."

He got up and paced for a moment before he said, "North Carolina has given me 25,000 acres of land along the Cumberland River, some of which runs up into Tennessee. Georgia has gifted me a plantation called Mulberry Grove on the Savannah River near Savannah. It, too, will need investments for improvements. We are land rich but cash poor."

"I see."

"I do not think you do." He rubbed his upper lip with his forefinger to calm himself before he said, "My troops are starving and bored. Some are even deserting. Part of the Pennsylvania line that General Wayne left here are restless. I do not trust the British lying quietly in Charleston. Silence often means reinforcing."

"What does that have to do with our finances?" she asked.

Nathanael continued the course of his conversation, "Virginia and Maryland sent me money, but their currency is worthless in South Carolina. Robert Morris, the financier in Philadelphia, and General Benjamin Lincoln, our Minister of War, have given me permission to do what I see fit to buy clothes and provisions for my troops."

"What of the provisions they have sent you from the North?"

"They tend not to make it to us if they send any at all. I suspect they are being stolen along the way."

"Nathanael, I still do not understand what you are saying."

He rubbed his forehead and ran his hands through his hair. "You are right. I am letting my anxiety rule my mind. Mr. Morris has put out contracts for supplying my army, and only one merchant from Charleston, John Banks, has responded." Guilt accosted him. "I hope I have not spoiled your evening with Captain Pendleton. I believe Colonel Kosciuszko has an amusing story to tell about pretty ladies and drawing pictures."

Caty rose to leave.

"There is one more thing," Nathanael said. "I have written to Dr. Witherspoon, who is seeing to George's schooling. Our son is gentle, and I have asked that severity be withheld as, sometimes, mildness is essential. He will be in good hands."

Nathanael received an unusual letter from General Washington in Philadelphia that exuded the same melancholy that pervaded the Southern Army:

> *To participate and divide our feelings, hopes, fears, and expectations with a friend is almost the only source of pleasure and consolation left us in the present languid and unpromising state of our affairs.*

With the letter came the news that General Sir Guy Carleton, the military Governor of Quebec from 1768 to 1778, had been recalled from England to take Sir Henry Clinton's place as commander-in-chief of the British Army in America. The French Admiral de Grasse, who had valiantly defended the Chesapeake Bay from the British Navy, which forced Cornwallis' entrapment in Yorktown, had been defeated in the West Indies by British Admiral George Rodney, dashing any hope for further assistance from the French by sea.

Nathanael replied to Washington, "You know me too well to suppose I will shrink from small difficulties, but how feeble are the best intentions, and how vain an obstinate perseverance against an unequal force."

The distressful news was followed by what he feared—the Pennsylvania troops staged a mutiny. Lewis came to Nathanael after delivering the orders of the day. "I have been told by your steward's wife, Becky Peters, that rascal George Gornell is inciting the men from Pennsylvania. What is worse is that Mrs. Peters said that they are going to use it as a distraction to have British cavalry storm into camp and seize you and your staff and drag you to Charleston. Thomas and I tried to put a stop to it, but they insulted us."

Nathanael, who was having breakfast with Caty, remained calm. He put his coffee cup aside, rose, and said, "No need to worry, my angel."

"I am not worried," she said. "If you recall, I have witnessed this type of alarm many times before." *I know how this will end*, she thought.

"I will have my guards seize Gornell and bring him here. I shall speak to the men," Nathanael told Lewis. He snatched his sword and scabbard from the peg on the wall and buckled it around his waist. His guards followed him outside to the edge of a clearing where the Pennsylvanians were responding to Gornell's speech as if he were a preacher. Some of the Maryland line watched.

"We can no longer go on without pay!" Gornell preached.

"No work with no pay!" the men chanted.

"What are you filling your empty stomachs with? Tree bark? Shoe leather? Oh! We have no shoes," Gornell went on. His incitement was met with silence. He turned around. Nathanael was standing behind him with his hand on the hilt of his sword. "General Greene. Have you come to fix our problems and fears?"

"I have come to fix yours," Nathanael replied with a sneer. His guards seized Gornell by the arms and dragged him away, unmindful of Gornell's threats that he would see them dead.

The Pennsylvania men stepped back as Nathanael walked toward them. "Your complaints are justified," he said. "We all suffer for want of necessities."

"I can wager that you do not, general," Terrence Elder said and spat on the ground. "What do you dine on this morning for breakfast when the rest of us have rice and barely an ounce of beef?"

"We have no rum," John Speer contended.

"I understand that you are miserable," Nathanael said, "but I will not tolerate rebellion in the ranks. I warn you, you had better be quiet. I act with decision, and George Gornell will suffer for his action as well as any of you who speak."

Murmuring commenced.

"I said to be quiet," Nathanael warned. "If you believe that I have not spent sleepless nights and anxious days over the lack of food and clothing in this camp, then you have no business here as I cannot trust you. At sundown, you will see what this has fraught."

As the sun cast pink and orange rays over the Ashley River, drums beat the dead march. Dragoon guards accompanied George Gornell to the gallows. He walked with resolution and tossed his hat and coat to a fellow threadbare soldier. Nathanael and his officers observed in silence among the troops on the grand parade ground as Gornell hung from his neck until dead. Caty let the curtain drop from her hand and turned away from the living room window.

Anthony Wayne returned from Georgia in July 1782 after successfully achieving the goals of his tough assignment—to win over local Loyalists, pacify Indian allies of the British, and support the state government. Parties of Indians trying to reinforce the British were captured, lectured, and released rather than killed. Pardons were offered to anyone who deserted the British forces. The waning war and Anthony's hit-and-run tactics trapped the British in Savannah, Georgia, and then suddenly, they were ordered to evacuate the city. He returned to the Southern Army camp to find that Georgia had awarded him a plantation near Mulberry Grove. He and Nathanael had neighboring plantations.

He entered the Waring plantation in time to hear an argument coming from Nathanael's office. Captain Michael Rudolph's voice filtered through the open door, "We object to Colonel John Laurens' succession to Colonel Lee. Laurens is an outsider."

"We will resign if you do this," Captain Jacob Carey threatened.

"I have suggested that Colonel Laurens command the infantry and Colonel George Baylor command the cavalry with General Mordecai Gist of Maryland in overall authority," Nathanael said, his patience growing thin. "You protested that suggestion."

"We have no objection to Colonel Baylor," Michael Rudolph said. "As Captain Carey said, we will resign if you split the legion."

"Aye, Captain Rudolph is senior officer among us," Michael's brother John argued. "He deserves to be elevated to commander. General Gist has only just arrived in this place." He stomped his foot and pointed his finger at Nathanael. "If not, I give my resignation at this moment."

Nathanael saw Anthony out of the corner of his eye. He said, "I accept your resignations rather than relinquish my right as commander-in-chief to use any unit as I wish."

Anthony suppressed a chuckle and disappeared from the doorway. The cavalrymen dispersed with grumbling and head shaking. They knew that General Greene would place the dispute before Congress and that the members would agree with their Southern general.

"Perhaps it is prudent to consider our objections," Captain Patrick Carnes suggested to his fellow horseman. He bowed to Nathanael and then left the room as the others filed out.

When they were gone, Nathanael poured a glass of rum that had arrived by shipment from Virginia. He rubbed his forehead and leaned back in his chair. "Are you coming in?" he asked.

Anthony strode into the room dressed in his dashing special made uniform and tossed off his hat. "How long did the argument go on?" he asked as he helped himself to a glass of rum.

"Two hours," Nathanael said. "There is a constant fever of discontent in camp. That aside, I wish to congratulate you on your success in Georgia and the gift of your plantation. You have acquitted yourself with great honor. There is much to celebrate with the British withdrawal from Savannah."

"Every ounce of food we procured was either at the price of blood or the hazard of life," Anthony said. "Is General St. Clair still here?"

"No, he has gone home to Pennsylvania. General Leslie proposed a truce while you were gone. He also asked for permission to collect provisions and forage along the lower Santee River. I refused both. Francis Marion's eyes and ears have been open to British forays since they sent a detachment out while the legislature was in session. Colonel Peter Horry was in charge of Francis' troops, and they were defeated in the engagement."

"You are worried that with peace on the horizon, the British will turn and bite us in a grand scale," Anthony said.

"Yes, and I do not have the authority to agree to a truce without Congress' consent, but I have reported my reasons. A cease-fire will make it more difficult to negotiate peace with honor." He told Anthony about the change in the British high command and the news of Admiral de Grasse's defeat. "General Rochambeau has refused to harken to my pleas of help. General Washington said they are going home soon."

Anthony refilled his glass of rum and yawned. "I have not had a good night's sleep since January, but I believe I can stay awake long enough to dine with Mrs. Greene if you will have me."

"She has asked after you many times since the days we used to spend in camp in the North," Nathanael said. He took on a serious tone, "I advise that you change out of those clothes. She may not find you as charming with the smell of a five month campaign lingering on you."

The sickly season arrived with the onset of summer and reached its peak in August 1782. Seeking a healthier location, Nathanael moved the army to Ashley Hill Plantation where the ground was higher and dry. The "fever" plagued the camp like rats scurrying through medieval towns. But it was not rats that brought the plague, it was deprivation. Men and women were not able to fend off illness or swarms of mosquitoes that made no distinction among enlisted soldiers, officers, servants, or slaves. Death was so prevalent that Nathanael issued an order to cease playing the dead march at soldiers'

funerals because it had a tendency to depress the spirits of the sick in camp.

With several of his aides and officers horribly ill and Caty showing signs of succumbing, Nathanael sent a request under a flag of truce to General Alexander Leslie that he allow his sick to recuperate on Kiawah Island and provide passes for them. Although he had been denied a cease-fire, Leslie agreed to the humanitarian calling. His note read: *I see no reason to deny you now that Savannah has been evacuated.*

To Nathanael's consternation and delight, his cavalry officer Colonel William Washington had been paroled as a prisoner of war. He rode into camp with his new young wife, Jane Elliot, both showing signs of illness. Nathanael and William exchanged introductions between their wives and themselves.

"Thomas Shubrick has sent along cooks and servants and Dr. Johnson, one of our camp surgeons, to Kiawah Island in advance of my convalescents' arrival," Nathanael explained. "Captain Pendleton and Major Lewis are both ill. There are quite a few others who are going. I am concerned about Mrs. Greene, and she, too, will be sent away from this fetid low country."

"We cannot go without something to entertain us," Caty insisted. "I have packed a backgammon table and playing cards. I am certain we will find other sources to delight us."

"Mr. Washington loves to gamble at the backgammon table," Jane teased her husband. "Give him a chance, and he will race horses through the surf." Jane kissed his sunburned cheeks.

"It is true," William said cheerfully. "I will need a partner to challenge."

With horses and carriages packed, the little party of convalescents embarked on their fifty mile journey to the southwest of Charleston, where cooling ocean breezes awaited to blow away their ailments. Caty leaned out the window of her phaeton and blew a kiss to Nathanael. He smiled and waved. *She is in good hands, although more likely, they are in her good hands.*

Nathanael's decision to deny General Alexander Leslie a truce compelled the British general to send out large foraging expeditions in boats despite the knowledge that Continental and militia forces would attack. Nathanael heard the rumors and sent Francis Marion toward the Pee Dee River to investigate, but the British raided abandoned rice plantations south of Marion's position. Then, Leslie sent a foraging expedition along the Combahee River. Nathanael ordered out the Light Corps under General Mordecai Gist of Maryland, who had arrived months earlier from Yorktown. Gist marched that day, and on August 25, arrived on the north side of the river at Combahee Ferry.

Nathanael had temporarily detached John Laurens from the Light Corps to gather intelligence. John was at Stock's plantation hospital ill with fever when he heard of the British expedition. He dashed off a note to Nathanael: *Will you be so good to inform me whether anything is to be done?*

The answer was yes, and it was enough for John to abandon his intelligence mission and rejoin his unit. John Laurens was not Harry Lee. Lee was careful of his men's lives and had often indulged them. Laurens was careless in his ceaseless quest for personal glory. The rumors that swirled about the relationship he had with Colonel Alexander Hamilton, one of George Washington's top aides, left John unconcerned. His exertions for the American cause earned him the darling of many hearts, including Nathanael.

When John arrived with his small unit, General Mordecai Gist already had a redoubt thrown up twelve miles downriver at Tar Bluff on Chehaw Neck.

"What is happening?" John asked Mordecai.

"We have thrown up a work to annoy the enemy's shipping."

"I wish to take command of the post," John said.

Mordecai hesitated and then said, "You may go downriver with fifty infantry and a howitzer." Mordecai had no idea that John was riding into a trap. The British had already come ashore. Mordecai learned of this and conducted a forced march to aid John.

When John arrived, he ordered, "Charge!" Then he set spurs to his horse and confronted the British. The sting of a musket ball pierced his abdomen as he was shot from his saddle. He fell into a rice paddy. Water soaked his uniform and stung his flayed wound. The last thing he saw were the green blades surrounding him like an aquatic grave. The twenty-seven-year-old promising flower of South Carolina died seventy miles from his home at Mepkin while his father was in Amsterdam negotiating preliminary articles of peace.

General Gist rode into camp with the lamentable news. The calamity did not surprise Nathanael or anyone in camp, but it was their general's responsibility to relay the regrettable action to George Washington, the Marquis de Lafayette, and worse, to Alexander Hamilton to whom Laurens was exceedingly close.

thirty-two

Don't Sacrifice to Make What They Can Never Restore You

The balmy breezes off the Atlantic Ocean ruffled Caty's hair as she stood in the surf, boldly barefoot and stripped to her shift. Caty tasted wet salt on her lips as she splashed into the waves to catch up with her new companion, Lilly Fenwick, the wife of a Maryland captain. Sunlight flickered like diamond points of light that glittered with each swell.

Horses pounded the beach and threw sand and sprays of water from their hooves. Caty and Lilly laughed and waded out of the water. They threw blankets around their shoulders. William Washington and Nat Pendleton were racing again; their competitive streak had not been satisfied with mere games of backgammon. They brought their steeds to a halt.

Caty shielded her eyes from the sun. Her ringing laughter blew away with the wind. "How wonderful! You are both looking much better. I suppose the quinine we consumed is working."

The men dismounted. "The cook sent us to tell you that dinner is ready," William said cheerfully. "But be assured there will be more competitions to come."

"I suppose I will have to arbitrate," she said in mock horror.

"Mrs. Washington will see to that," Nat said. "Aside from making cigars for William, I believe her other task is to shower him with kisses, which he hungrily returns, interrupting our game."

With their horses' reins in hand, the gentlemen escorted the ladies.

Caty and Lilly made themselves presentable before dinner. The table was laid out with fish, crab, oranges, and figs; fare taken from the island's bounty. Caty helped herself to a generous glass of wine. Her complexion shined with sun and health.

"Mrs. Greene, a message for you from Captain Shubrick," Lewis said. He handed her the note and sat at the table.

My dear Mrs. Greene. Major Morris informed me that everyone is feeling better and that you will soon be coming back to camp. I beg you to hasten your arrival. General Greene is very sick with the fever. I am certain your tender care will assist in his recovery.

❧

Escorted by Nat Pendleton, Caty arrived at the Ashley Hill Plantation in a state of panic. When Dr. Read greeted her at the door, she demanded, "Where is he?"

"He is upstairs. I have had the devil of time keeping him abed."

She bounded up the stairs and burst into the bedroom. Much to her relief, he was sitting up, but when he looked at her, she saw that his eyes were badly infected. His skin was yellow, a reminder of the jaundice he once suffered.

"Nathanael," Caty breathed. She sat beside him and pulled him into her arms. His body trembled beneath her touch, but it was born from illness and not want. He laid his head on her chest. "Are you taking your quinine?" she asked gently.

He nodded into her breast. She lifted his head so she could see into his eyes. Their usual lambency was blurred by the infection that ravaged his eyesight with pain, swelling, and redness. There was little she could offer in the way of nursing except to lay down beside him and bring him whatever he desired to help ease his suffering.

On that late September night with the full moon peering into their bedroom window, the Greenes slept fitfully while many of the men in camp were buried. The miasma of death and disease lingered like an unwelcomed guest. Nathanael's little army was dying in droves, and it would not help the cause nor give them honor to have their general die with them.

Anthony Wayne also succumbed to the fever, which he declared he dreaded more than the devil or British bullets. Like Nathanael, he was not up to an engagement if the British renewed the conflict. Caty nursed them both. She and Anthony had a chance to renew their old friendship. His wife, Polly, refused to have anything to do with Anthony's military career, and the swaggering ladies' man did not care. Instead, he resumed his flirtations with Caty from the days they had been at Valley Forge and told her stories about his exploits in Virginia and Georgia.

Two days after her return, Caty found Nathanael at his desk after she had gone to make a pot of tea for the two of them. Rays of bright sunshine filtered through the window as he struggled to read a letter. "What are you doing?" she scolded as she set the teapot aside.

"I have business that cannot wait," Nathanael said. "If I lie about for days, all that is falling apart will fall further."

Caty's stomach lurched. "What is…falling…apart?"

"My army is dissolving before my eyes, and I can no longer leave the matter to other hands. Do you remember that I told you about the clothing contracts Mr. Robert Morris bid on? I agreed to do business with the Charleston merchant John Banks who won the bid?"

"Yes."

"I gave my officers two months' advanced pay so they could buy clothing. The money was in the form of drafts against the United States with Morris as their agent. Banks has had difficulty getting anyone to accept these drafts, so he used them to buy tobacco in Virginia. He found a roundabout way to sell the tobacco to the British in the West Indies and then use the cash to pay merchants for the clothing they sell to him. This illegal scheme has been found out, and my name has been associated with it. Congress has gotten wind of it. They have delayed paying Banks' creditors."

"Surely no one believes you are involved in such a scheme?" Caty asked. "That is a blatant accusation of dishonorable intentions."

"They must, or they would not have delayed the payments. Now Banks has refused to deliver the provisions and clothing without a guarantee. Major Ichabod Burnet is a partner of Banks'." Nathanael paused to wipe his irritated eyes and then said, "His creditors agreed to assign the guarantee to me in the amount of 30,000 pounds."

"With what have you backed that signature?"

"It amounts to a personal loan that Congress will reimburse me for once the war is over."

Caty pursed her lips and tossed him a suspicious glance. Congress was want for money, a problem that had thus far crippled the Continental Army. Her husband felt its destitution profoundly.

Nathanael sensed her dubiety and said, "What choice do I have? I conferred with Banks, asking why he had associated my name with his merchant house as if I were agreeable to his scheme. He said that was not his intention and would testify to it. I also conferred with Edward Carrington and Anthony."

"When will the provisions arrive?" Caty asked.

"Some have arrived, otherwise we would not have candles, soap, or writing paper. It is still not enough. Among all this, I am being criticized for accepting the states' gifts of plantations and my need to procure enslaved people to work the fields and tend to livestock and equipment. This time from Mr. Warner Mifflin, a pious Quaker from Philadelphia who has announced my shortcomings to that city."

He handed Caty the letter he had been reading.

You took thy commission from Congress who had in their Declaration of Independence set forth in such clear terms its being the Natural right of all men. Should thy after all countenance slavery it would be a stigma to thy character and you a Quaker.

Her family had a few slaves when she was a little girl on Block Island. Caty did not remember if they were treated with kindness or if the treatment made no difference in the quality of their lives.

"You did defend yourself?" she asked, her voice rising in distress.

His voice quivered in response, "It felt like an excuse more than a defense. I cannot pretend to know how attached slaves are to their work and a plantation as a man is to his family. What am I to do? I have already begun the process of procuring slaves for Boone's Barony."

"We shall do this together, no matter the cost or criticism. Are we not partners? Are we not to face our future together?"

Nathanael got up and took the letter from Caty's hand. He held her in a tight embrace. "The freedom of our country has driven me to this," he said, "but the future of our little family is always first on my mind. Without my sacrifices, there will be no future. Peace seems probable. News that the British are evacuating Charleston cannot lull us into a false sense of security. I believe nothing until it is signed, sealed, and delivered."

Rumors of the evacuation swirled for weeks. In October, General Guy Carleton wrote to Alexander Leslie telling him the evacuation was not a matter of choice but of deplorable necessity in consequence of an unsuccessful war. It would end any and all offensive actions in the United States.

There was a delay in the evacuation due to lack of proper planning and transports, of which Leslie had no control. Then in early November, Francis Marion's vigilant informers told the militia general that British frigates had weighed anchor in Charleston Harbor, brought there to conduct the evacuation. Francis relayed the observation to Nathanael. In turn,

Nathanael asked Francis to keep his militia intact until the British were out of the city in case the withdrawal was delayed.

Over the next month, some 4,000 Loyalists and 5,000 slaves set sail for Florida, New York, Nova Scotia, and England. Some whites along with black slaves were taken to Jamaica where they would be hired out or sold again in the West Indies, an environment even more brutal than South Carolina.

Nathanael made preliminary plans with the civil authorities and told Governor John Mathews, "Respecting the mode of taking possession of Charleston, I have to inform you that should the enemy evacuate the place, your wishes shall be carried into execution as far as possible."

Mathews replied that the security of the city was of paramount concern to his council.

The long awaited negotiation came. With some 130 sail awaiting Leslie's troops, he asked Nathanael for a peaceful transfer of power.

I propose that upon the firing of the morning gun an American advance march to the outermost British redoubt. If it has been evacuated, they should continue their march until they sight the British rear guard, where upon the Americans will maintain a distance of 200 yards until we are embarked.

Nathanael received the proposal through Anthony Wayne. "Send word that I approve with the stipulation that they agree not to set fire to the town after boarding. I want you to lead our vanguard that will follow the British as they have requested. Governor Mathews and I intended on arriving in the city on that day."

"Yes, sir," Anthony said with a grin. He could not turn down a flamboyant show of victory.

On the morning of December 14, one British regiment after another marched to Gadsden's dock and filed into waiting transports. At 11:00 a.m., Leslie's rear guard started marching down King Street to the music of fife and drum. Behind them, marching slowly, Anthony's force of 300 light infantry, eighty cavalry, and two 6-pound cannon advanced with music playing and colors flying through a street devoid of spectators as the last of the British transports moved away from the dock.

At 3:00 p.m., Nathanael and Governor Mathews fell in behind thirty dragoons and rode into the city. They were followed by a small group of dignitaries: General Mordecai Gist, South Carolina native General William Moultrie, who was in charge of the American prisoners in Charleston, and other officers. Caty rolled behind in her phaeton with prominent ladies. A guard of 180 cavalry brought up the rear. A throng of citizens followed.

The streets, balconies, doors, and windows that were deserted when the British marched to the docks were now alive with elated inhabitants cheering, "God bless you, gentlemen! You are welcome home!" Nathanael heard his name on every tongue proclaiming, "Our conquering hero! You are the maestro!" Flowers, lace, and every glimmer of patriotic fare showered the triumphal entourage he led to the Charleston County Courthouse on Broad Street.

Among all the celebration and revelry, the militia was conspicuously absent. Before marching into the city, Governor Mathews met with Nathanael over the matter. "I do not want anyone to enter Charleston for the evacuation without my specific permission. I believe the militia's presence might lead to violence with the Loyalists."

Nathanael shot Mathews a look of disapproval. "These men bled for our cause. Without them, the day we have waited for would not be possible."

"Soothe them in any way you see fit," Mathews said. "You have handed civil authority to those of us who can conduct that business, and therefore it is your responsibility to oblige me."

The governor was right. Nathanael did as he asked. He told Francis Marion he could enter the city with a few friends, but Francis maintained his dignity and begged off, claiming he had not been inoculated for smallpox.

As the conquering hero entered the bastion of the Rice Kings of South Carolina, he dismissed the dragoons and let everyone go on to do as they pleased. He escorted Caty's phaeton to John Rutledge's mansion near the courthouse and dismounted. "My angel," he said gallantly. He swept off his hat and opened the carriage door. "This will be army headquarters and our residence. A celebratory dinner will be held tonight once Anthony procures the beef and poultry I have requested."

Caty stepped out of the carriage. Behind her, she heard cheers and shouts of, "It is Lady Greene!" Nathanael's triumph was hers as well. She took Nathanael's offered arm and asked, "What do you think of the city?"

"It is not so large or elegant as I expected," Nathanael said as the two approached the house. "Yet there are many spacious and noble houses and buildings."

John Rutledge, his wife, Elizabeth, and their seven children welcomed the Greenes and Nathanael's staff into their home. John's brother, Edward, lived across the street. William Washington and his bride, Jane, bought a stylish house on the corner of Church and South Battery. Many nights were spent around the fireplace in one home or another, where the men swapped tales of their experiences in camp. Caty's ringing laughter and enthusiasm for each story brought happiness to a situation that improved daily as families began to return to Charleston and establish their lives again.

"We should hold a ball in honor of our victorious army," Caty suggested one night over wine and a game of Whist with the wives at headquarters.

"I think that is a splendid idea!" Elizabeth Rutledge exclaimed.

Jane's face paled.

"Are you ill my dear?" Elizabeth asked.

Jane brightened a bit and leaned in toward Caty and Elizabeth. "I am expecting a baby," she chortled. The girls squealed with delight, but Jane's face took on a serious look. "Do you not need to confer with General Greene on hosting a ball?" she asked Caty.

Caty laughed. "I will confer with him, and I am certain he will not deny me."

Lewis Morris, Thomas Shubrick, William Washington, Nat Pendleton, and Thaddeus Kosciuszko were hunched over a game of Loo. Cigar and pipe smoke snaked through the room and up the chimney. Everyone looked up in response to Jane's question except William, who kept his eyes on the table. If he did not win a trick, he would be forced to pay the agreed stake to the pool.

Caty's skirts rustled when she crossed the room. "Colonel Kosciuszko, I am recruiting your help to decorate whatever venue is decided. I know you have artistic skills beyond drawing redoubts and maps. I have seen your sketches."

Thaddeus rose. "I am flattered, Mrs. Greene, and if permission is given, I am at your service."

As the others played cards, Nathanael spent the evening alone, scratching pen across paper in reports to authorities regarding the evacuation of Charleston. After two years of bloody war, he was exultant to attain his goal, but his letters were restrained. The criticisms he had endured as far back as the fall of Forts Washington and Lee in November 1776 were still painful. The fear that the people would become complacent before peace was officially signed drove the content of his letters to friends.

He wrote to Jeremiah Wadsworth, "Now let malice swell, and envy snarl, the work is complete; and adds a finishing lustre to all our operations."

To Dr. John Witherspoon, who was seeing to little George's education, he confided, "I wish private repose may not seduce the minds of the people from their public obligations. Pleasure is too apt to steal upon us after a long series of hardships and sufferings."

Nathanael snuffed out the candle. He heard the conversation in the other room and considered joining the Loo game, but his chest was tight, and the wheezing in his lungs roared in his ears. He climbed the stairs with a glass of whiskey and prepared for bed. He was washing his face and hands and neck in the bowl on the dresser when Caty slipped into the room.

She immediately heard his labored breathing. All thoughts of a planned party drained from her mind. She kissed away droplets of water that rolled down his bare back. Without toweling off, he turned to face her. "You may have your party," he said with a smile that lit up his blue eyes. "How can I deny your esteem with the people as much as they esteem me? You know I am not much for parties, but I know you have your heart set on it." He drew in a breath and said, "And I know your absent children are a great deduction that you must keep from burdening your heart too much."

Caty thought she had succeeded in hiding her longing for her little ones. The years she and Nathanael were separated did nothing to change what he saw in her soul. She ran a delicate hand down his cheek. He would not be up to domestic pleasures tonight, nor would he be able to sleep. If there was no sleep for him, there would be no sleep for her, either.

❧

The victory ball was held on January 2, 1783 at Dillon's Long Hall. The hall was decorated in grand style to the credit of Thaddeus and his staff. Caty made paper flowers and hung them on the walls, and Thaddeus draped festoons of magnolia leaves around the ballroom. The army band struck up music, and the officers escorted the ladies to the dance floor. Nathanael remained standing at the edge like a wallflower.

Caty took his hand and said, "Come, my darling. I need a dance partner."

"This is all very elegant and pleasing, but you know I do not relish these types of amusements," he reminded.

"As if you did not sneak out of the house as a teenager to go dancing," she teased and tugged at his hand.

"You will have one dance, and that is all," Nathanael said decorously. He limped to the floor. Once the dance began his limp evaporated. He was as graceful as any who clasped hands and whirled around the floor.

Anthony appeared when the minuet was over and a new tune struck up. With gallantry, he asked Caty, "May I have this dance?" He was aware that Nathanael did not care for the party, but he was more than willing to see to it that Nathanael's wife enjoyed every minute. The evening spun out into glorious revelry, and with wine flowing, Caty danced the night away with General Anthony Wayne.

No party or celebration could ease the problems Nathanael still faced. The war was not over, and his army was still his responsibility. They were clothed due to deliveries from the merchants who had accepted John Banks' credit, but food remained an issue.

On New Year's Eve 1782, he wrote to General Mordecai Gist, "I wish you a happy new year. If the year continues as badly as it has begun, we shall end badly as we have nothing to eat for man or beast."

After the victory ball, Nathanael and Caty took a trip to Savannah, Georgia, accompanied by his staff and guards. Their wagons and carriages traveled the swampy coastal roads. The city was in the throes of their own celebrations. Nathanael met with Governor Lyman Hall. He was driven by the need to raise funds Congress could use to reimburse his 30,000 pound output for his soldiers' clothing.

Congress had passed a national five percent tax on imports—a part of a plan to pay for the war. Georgia and Rhode Island refused to pay the tax. Yet again, Nathanael was forced to press upon those who had the power to help. At a meeting of the assembly, he told Governor Hall, "Each state, no matter how poor, must bear its share of the burden if our nation is to survive."

Governor Hall was sympathetic, but Georgia's treasury was bankrupt. He attempted to pacify Nathanael. "I will have someone escort you to the Mulberry Grove plantation that the State of Georgia gifted you. Perhaps, fruitful possibilities abound in that place, which will help you find a solution."

Nathanael's entourage bumped along the west shore of the Savannah River to Mulberry Grove. Caty alit from her carriage. The elegant house was in ruins. The landscape was dotted with huge oak trees draped in Spanish moss and palm trees; their fronds rustled and fluttered in the wind. Gardens, although run down, promised abundance in the spring. "It is lovely!" she exclaimed. "The possibilities *are* endless."

Nathanael took in every detail as far as his eye could see of the 1,300 acre rice plantation. "I suppose if we ever decide to live in the South, this would be a fine place."

Caty heard the hesitation in his voice. Any improvements would take money. She was aware of his struggle with the state of South Carolina over Boone's Barony and the right to keep the slaves who were there when he was given the property. Yet, she could not comprehend the magnitude.

On the ride back to Charleston, she confessed, "I do not understand why your enormous land holdings cannot be converted into money."

"There is no market to sell plantations in this impoverished, war-torn country," Nathanael explained. "I have neither the time nor the capital to get them in profitable working order. There are already judgements against me in the courts to satisfy my debt to pay for John Banks' bad investments, which in turn have prevented payment to merchants for their goods."

"The personal guarantee you signed?" Caty asked.

"Yes, they are coming after me for that reason." He sighed and looked out the carriage window at the swampy landscape. "I did not want to tell you this, but I have had to borrow money from Mr. Robert Morris, the Marquis de Lafayette, and Jeremiah Wadsworth just to support you and the children until I am free to attended to my business."

Caty remained as stubborn as a child and refused to believe that things had gone that awry. "Surely, you have another plan," she protested.

It was of no use. When they returned to Charleston, Nathanael found himself in a war with the state he had so valiantly defended. Benjamin Guerard was elected to succeed Mathews as governor. With John Rutledge and John Mathews no longer in political power, Nathanael lost the support of their relationship. Guerard clashed with him. General Thomas Sumter sat on the assembly and harbored bitter feelings toward Nathanael for harsh words he had uttered to the militia general.

The clash was over the five percent import tax. South Carolina had rescinded payment. Nathanael saw the danger in losing the impost. *Surely, the civil government in which I have had a hand in restoring will see my argument as valid,* he thought.

As he did with anything that presented danger to the army, he aired his opinions. On March 8, 1783, he addressed the South Carolina legislature, hoping to persuade that body not to rescind its ratification of the proposed federal impost. "It is known Congress has no money, and the measures of the states will determine the conduct of the army. You are infringing on the sole power in all matters relating to war and peace the sovereign authority of the United States."

Governor Guerard replied, "There is no enemy within the borders of South Carolina. We find your arguments and the impost unacceptable and without utility."

Those in legislature fumed that Nathanael was behaving like a military dictator.

Nathanael, deeply surprised, struck back, "I did not conceive I was invading parliamentary freedom of debate and decision. I thought I was in the way of my duty in making the representation. I think so still; and if my expressions were less guarded, it was from a persuasion I merited the confidence of the people."

His exertions were not heeded.

On April 16, around 11:00 a.m., a post rider galloped up to the John Rutledge mansion. The man sprung from the saddle and told the guard outside, "I have an important message from Philadelphia for Major General Greene."

Nathanael and Caty were having a late breakfast with his staff, the Rutledges, and Anthony Wayne and his staff. Nathanael accepted the message from the guard. Those around the table silenced. Nathanael afforded a moment to control his voice before he said, "Negotiators from the United States have signed preliminary articles of peace with Great Britain. The war is over."

Apparently, the news had reached others and shouts erupted in the streets. The diners at the Rutledge house pounded one another on the back and hugged their women. John Rutledge filled glasses with ale and proposed a toast to the valiant cause and its success. Nathanael exchanged eye contact with Caty, who Anthony was smothering in his arms. It was nearly eight years to the day since he had left her pregnant, standing at the door of Spell Hall in Coventry as he rode off to war.

As they digested the news, copies of King George III's December 1782 speech to Parliament arrived. He proclaimed that he did not hesitate to call them free and independent states, and thus admitting their separation from the Crown of his kingdoms, he had sacrificed every consideration of his own wishes.

Peace between nations was at hand. It was not for Nathanael. His restless soldiers clamored to go home. "I sympathize with your desire, but any who leave before they are discharged or furloughed will be treated as deserters," he warned. "Ships will arrive to take you to Philadelphia where you can muster out of the service properly." There were many men who cared little for their general's warning. They set foot for home along the dusty trails and the Great Wagon Road northward.

The unrest led to men and officers appropriating army property. Captain James Gunn, a Continental Army dragoon, purloined a horse. Nathanael ordered a court of inquiry, where Gunn claimed he had lost a horse in the army and had a right to take one in its place. The court found in favor of Gunn. Nathanael strongly disagreed and reprimanded Gunn in general orders. Nathanael was stung with bitter criticism for depriving his officers of the only indemnity they had been able to get for their losses.

It stirred suspicion of his dealings with John Banks and Company when it became known that Nathanael had signed notes guaranteeing Banks payment to his creditors. Accusations that Nathanael was partnered with Banks and his speculations and investments haunted him. Nat Pendleton, Edward Carrington, and Anthony Wayne rallied to his side.

He was summoned to appear before a justice. His records and papers related to his transactions with Banks were brought under examination. He was forced to swear an oath that he had no connection to Banks of a private nature.

"I am not conscious of having done anything in my whole life that should render a measure of this sort necessary," he pleaded in his defense.

"If I had not signed the notes for Banks, the army would have mutinied and disbanded for lack of clothing and provisions."

Still, suspicion clung to him like chains that he would never be able to break. Sensitivity to criticism was his weakness, and like any torment, it was not easy to endure. He received a letter from George Washington that helped ease his tribulation.

> *It is with pleasure that I congratulate you on the glorious end you have put to the hostilities in the Southern States. The honor and advantages of it, I hope you will live long to enjoy. If histographers should be hearty enough to fill the pages of history, it will not be believed that such a great country as Great Britain has employed for eight years in this country. I let no opportunity slip to inquire after your son, George. I hear he is a fine, promising boy.*

From the beginning of the war, Washington demonstrated faith and friendship in Nathanael. Washington did not see his limp as an embarrassment. He had not been judged unfit for command because of his lack of experience or education. Forts fell under his command in 1776, yet Washington's confidence in him never wavered. Nathanael had served his mentor in every way expected and to the best of his ability.

Yet the judgmental and vicious voices I hear from others cut like a knife and threaten my reputation, Nathanael thought.

On the eve of the last days of the war, he decided the best way to comfort himself was in comforting those who *did* believe in him despite his shortcomings and mistakes. He wrote to Washington, "I beg leave to congratulate your Excellency upon the return in smiles of peace, and the happy establishment of our Independence. This important event must be doubly welcome to you, who has so successfully conducted the War through such a variety of difficulties to so happy a close. I feel a singular satisfaction in having preserved your confidence and esteem through the whole progress of war."

No matter the crescendo of his critics, there remained countless soldiers, officers, and militiamen who fought beside him, planned with him, believed in him, idolized him, and would do it all over again under his firm hand and compassion to achieve liberty and stand together on the line of splendor.

To honor them he wrote to the president of the Continental Congress, Elias Boudinot, "I should be wanting in gratitude to the Army was I to omit expressing my warmest acknowledgements for the zeal and activity with which they attempted and preserved in every enterprise, and for the patience and dignity with which they bore their sufferings. Perhaps no army ever exhibited greater proofs of patriotism and public virtue."

At the end of May, transport ships began to arrive in Charleston Harbor.

෨

On the warm day June 1, Caty drifted into Nathanael's office and poured a glass of wine. He was reading poems by the Roman poet Horace. It was a tattered book, one of many he had kept with him since the beginning of the war that provided inspiration when he felt the need. He set the book aside. "What is it?" he asked.

She gazed out the window. With distant feelings, she watched the troops embark near the battery on the waterfront. "I feel as if this place has stripped us of our hopes and dreams. It all seemed so bright, and now it is a dull picture that I can no longer endure looking at." She turned away, sighed, and sipped her wine. "It is time to go home to our children. Do you realize that it has been over a year since I have seen them? They need their father as well."

Nathanael rose and grasped her shoulders. "I cannot leave yet. Not until all the troops are gone. My aide, Major William Pierce, and Colonel Kosciuszko are leaving on the first transport for Philadelphia. I am certain the colonel will be more than happy to have you as a traveling companion."

A smile fluttered across her lips. "The women of Charleston will be devastated when he goes. I am certain I have never met a man so adored by so many women."

"I will make the arrangements. Procure a female traveling companion. Pack right away. The transport will leave in a few days."

"How am I to endure this voyage without you? You know I have been terrified of the ocean since I was a little girl."

"You will be fine."

Feeling as if he was belittling her fears, she pulled away from his grasp and swept up the stairs. The following morning, he watched her board the ship, a small dark figure that, unknown to them both, was carrying another child.

❧

The heartbeat of Philadelphia erased the memory of each groan of the ship and torture of a rolling sea. The Continental Congress had retired to Princeton, New Jersey, but the celebrations of independence and victory were the voice of the city. Colonel Charles Petit was waiting for Caty when she arrived at his home.

George bounded down the stairs. "Mother! Mother!" he cried. He ran into her arms, nearly knocking her down.

Caty squatted and pulled him close to her breast and then held him at arms' length. "I cannot believe how much you have grown. And listen to you, calling me Mother instead of Momma."

His merry dark eyes widened. "You know, I am big now. I am seven and a half."

"Come help me with my things. I want to hear all about school and your friends."

Caty spent two evenings with George and Colonel Petit. Her presence in the city spread, and party invitations and visitors began to arrive, much to her delight. Anthony was one of those visitors, looking dapper in his impeccably designed uniform. He wasted not a moment inviting Caty to accompany him to occasions.

"I cannot go without proper outfits," Caty giggled. "Would you care to escort me on a shopping spree?"

"That, my dear Mrs. Greene, is ladies' business. I hope it will not delay our attendance at the social held at the state house this weekend," Anthony said provocatively.

"I suppose this means that your wife, Polly, is not in the city to revel the honors conveyed upon you as Pennsylvania's own war hero."

"Polly cares nothing about it, but Mary Vining may be suspicious of my attention to you."

"Oh? Who is this woman who stands as my rival among the many who vie for your affections?" she teased.

"Buy your clothes and baubles, Caty. I will have you on my arm on Saturday night and many nights to come. Therefore, your *rivals* will have to wait their turn."

Suspecting she was pregnant, she went on a wild spending spree, buying fashionable clothing. Gowns layered with petticoats and garnished with garters, gold tassels, and hoops. Anthony whirled her around the dance floor for hours, stopping to take refreshment from glasses of champagne and extravagant food.

The adoration and attention she had received in Charleston before things began to decay were lavished upon her, and she basked in it. "She is General Greene's wife, our hero of the South," many whispered behind cupped hands or in bold-faced admiration of the twenty-eight-year-old Mrs. Greene. Officers and their wives threw endless parties. Caty danced all night as if she were a girl again, popular and sought after as ever.

"I cannot arrive to the balls in rented carriages," she told Charles Petit. "I wish to have a new phaeton built with a new pair of horses grandly furnitured." Pending her journey home to Rhode Island, she then asked that he order a four-wheel chariot.

Charles frowned but said nothing and did as she asked. As Nathanael's previous quartermaster deputy and friend, he was privy to Nathanael's financial situation. It was not his place to meddle in private affairs or inform Caty of them despite the knowledge that he could end up footing the bill.

After a night spent at a gala party in the countryside, she returned to Philadelphia. With her new phaeton and chariot finished, she made plans to go home. To her surprise, a letter awaited from Nathanael. Exasperated and worn out from the summer heat and endless paperwork, he reprimanded her for her purchases that amounted to 1,400 dollars.

> *Charles Petit has paid the sum but he wants the money as soon as I arrive. Of the 1,000 pounds I invested with Jeremiah Wadsworth in 1779, I have not fifty left. You have placed me under great perplexity.*

Not only was she angry with Nathanael, Charles Petit felt the sting of her indignation. "How could you go to my husband without telling me?" she accused.

"Caty, you could not expect me to fulfill your wishes when you yourself have no way to pay for them."

She ripped the letter to shreds. The pieces floated to the rug. "I no longer belong here. My children need me."

"Or perhaps you need them," Charles said gently.

It took a week to make arrangements for her driver and her lady escort. During that time, another letter arrived from Nathanael. He had no way to pay Petit, who he already owed for George's education. He went on to say:

> *I have not heard from you. Notwithstanding all I wrote you the other day, I love you most affectionately. I have not been pleased with myself since I wrote that letter and you know self-reproach is a painful companion. You naturally have a generous disposition, and perhaps a little vanity which renders you a prey to the artful and designing.*

❧

In the last week of June under the brutal summer sun, Caty and her son climbed into her new chariot. "I must apologize for my prior outburst," she said to Charles. "I had no right to treat you as such after everything you have done for us. After all the years you supported Nathanael and believed in him, like that nasty Banks affair."

"I am not unmindful of your challenges. I accept your apology. Safe travels."

He nodded at the driver. The chariot lurched forward. His affairs with the Greenes were not at an end. He worried how much longer Nathanael could bear his crushing burdens. However, he knew no other man with the physical constitution and mental balance to overcome vicissitudes of the Southern Campaign and conquer the British in the South. In his heart, he knew Caty had those same qualities.

She and George stopped for a few nights in New York City. From there, the roads changed into the familiar roads she traveled in Rhode Island. The house in Coventry came into view. The waters of the Pawtuxet River bubbled merrily over rocks beyond the steep bank of the front yard.

Jacob and Peggy and their seven children lavished her and George with uncharacteristic hugs and kisses. In previous years, Caty would have resented what she would have considered a false display, but after all this time she knew it was not. The first words that passed her lips were, "I can never thank you enough for what you have done for my children."

She entered the familiar house and wandered into Nathanael's extensive library. She trailed her fingers across the book spines. His eager and curious mind had devoured them like a fine meal. The familiar heavy sound of hammers and the whir of the furnace in the family iron forge filtered through the windows.

"The house no longer belongs to Nathanael," Jacob said, startling her. "We had to arrange a business settlement that removed the house from the Greene family's hands and solely into mine. I am not unaware of the pain this will cause you."

The pain stabbed like knife. *Nathanael and I have no home, no chance of having one, and without that, is there hope that we can have a future?* she wondered. She could not comprehend the effort it would take to transform the property that they held in the South into a home.

"I am going to Block Island to gather the other children. I will not be coming back. I shall stay there until I find a home to rent in Newport," she said. Caty was not religious, but she thought, *God help us.*

Most of Nathanael's aides and officers, the men who comprised his military family, had gone home to make new lives or return to their old lives. He fought a mild fever that passed. The plantations he owned were becoming a financial burden that taxed his resources and his credit to the limit. He received a letter from his overseer, Roger Saunders, at Boone's Barony in South Carolina:

> *There are a number of slaves who have been forced off the plantation who want to return, but there are not enough hands to plant the rice and corn fields. There are also livestock, seed, tools, and provisions to buy.*

Nathanael struggled with his opposition to slavery. The man he admired most, George Washington, was a slave owner as were many men he fought with during the war. The Rice Kings of the South were slave owners. If he was to make something of himself and provide for his family, he felt he had no choice. Therefore, he took Saunders' advice. The overseer expected a crop that would yield 250 barrels of rice and 1,500 bushels of corn.

It was with great relief that he received a message that there were enough ships to take his soldiers home. On June 21, although William Washington had left the army, he and his wife, Jane, and many civilians gathered on the parade ground to hear General Nathanael Greene give final orders to his troops.

Nathanael's eyes moved through the men who had stayed until the end. The vestiges of those who were furloughed, deserted, perished, or reassigned stood among them like ghosts. He recognized them and knew their names—privates Jackson Killam, James McCurdy, John Cassidy, Thomas Kahoo, and a drummer boy known only as Jacob. There were the men of the Maryland, Delaware, Virginia, and Pennsylvania lines who had withstood the terror of an advancing sea of redcoats.

Without benefit of an aide or adjutant, Nathanael drew his soldiers to attention and began, "The general joined this army when it was in affliction, when its spirits were low, its prospects gloomy. He now parts with it crowned in success, and in full triumph. We have trod the paths of adversity together, and have felt the sunshine of better fortune. We found a people in distress, and a country groaning under oppression. It has been our happiness to relieve them. Your generous confidence, amidst surrounding difficulties; your persevering tempers, against the tide of misfortune; paved the way to success."

His army disbanded with words of well wishes on every tongue, promises to write, and put all to memory. When they were gone, Nathanael ached with loneliness, and his mind turned to his beloved Rhode Island. His pen was his only comfort as he waited for the last ships to embark. Their sailing was the signal for personal freedom.

To his distant relative, William Greene, now governor of Rhode Island and in whose house Caty had grown up, he wrote, "I feel for Rhode Island what I cannot for any other spot on Earth. What is it that recalls this attachment; and how is it that neither time nor change of place can alter it?"

To Charles Petit he lamented, "I am left like Sampson after Delilah cut his locks."

It was his former adjutant and old friend, Otho Holland Williams, to whom he poured his heart out with the distress of a man who suffered more than physical loneliness.

*My Dearest Friend. I think you have acted wisely in resign-
ing and leaving the army. All the gentlemen of my family
are going into civilian life. I am left alone. If there is peace,
I expect to be to the Northward soon also. Now you have
become a citizen, you ought to perform all the duties, and
engage in all. Get married, and live happily in domestic character. Get as large a fortune as you can, but don't sacrifice to
make what they can never restore you.*

Colonel Edward Carrington wiped the back of his neck with his handkerchief. "What were we thinking, setting off in the heat of mid-August?"

Major Edmund Hyrne swatted a fly that continually buzzed around
his sweaty face. "You wanted to go home to Virginia and agreed to this
conveyance."

Nathanael ignored the two. He was driving the carriage, absorbed in
watching the city of Charleston diminish from sight. The baggage wagon,
driven by a servant named Jack, creaked behind the carriage. Another
servant on horseback, Matthew, followed. Every landmark was a passage in
time that brought Nathanael closer to home. They crossed the Santee River
that ran north to the mountains. Rice, indigo, hemp, and Indian corn were
its great staples, yet poverty abounded.

Friends and acquaintances threw open their doors and provided
welcome lodging, rest, and company. South Carolina melted into North
Carolina and on into Virginia, where Colonel Carrington parted ways.
General George Weedon received his longtime comrade and kept Nathanael
and Major Hyrne in Fredericksburg for two days, holding a reception to
celebrate the hero of the South.

On September 12, as they approached George Washington's home at
Mount Vernon, the carriage jolted and then suddenly overturned. Nathanael
was thrown to the ground. The carriage fell on him. The top collapsed and
the harness broke. Edmund climbed out unhurt. The servants halted the

wagon and ran to help. Disoriented, Nathanael lifted the carriage and closed his eyes in anticipation of being killed. As he did, the horse started running and drew the carriage after him until the harness gave way.

"My God, General Greene, are you alright?" Edmund gasped. He squatted and began to slip his arms underneath Nathanael's back.

"Do not touch him, sir," Jack advised. "You could do more harm than good."

Nathanael lay there for a few minutes; he looked up at the blue cloud-streaked sky until he caught his breath. With the help of the servants, he gingerly got to his feet. Bruised and battered, he said, "I am fine, but it appears our carriage is not."

"You could have been killed!" Edmund exclaimed.

"As well as you," Nathanael said. His leg was sore, and his limp was pronounced as he examined the broken carriage.

Matthew went to fetch the horse and returned, holding it by the bridle. "Dumfries is just a few miles. Colonel Grayson lives there. I expect we can get a repair there."

With the carriage repaired and Nathanael feeling sore and shaken, they arrived at Mount Vernon. It was the first time any of them except Nathanael had seen the beautiful house. George and Martha Washington were in Princeton, New Jersey, but George's cousin, Lund, was there and acted the gracious host.

At the end of September, they passed out of Virginia and into Maryland. In Baltimore, the close feelings of friendship and brothers-in-arms were rekindled when Nathanael was reunited with Colonels Otho Holland Williams and John Eager Howard. They detained him for four days, during which they had a great celebration.

Baltimore faded into the distance. The road ahead was familiar—some of which he had reconnoitered in 1777. The band of four crossed Brandywine Creek that drained into the Delaware River. Three times, he had passed over that road, once in advance, once in retreat, and once to take command of the Southern Army; with doubt and anxiety as companions each time. He still carried those companions, but this time he saw the villages and towns in a different light as if civilization had transformed into the peaceful place he remembered from when he was a boy.

On October 1, they entered Philadelphia. The whole city was waiting for him. Officers, soldiers, dignitaries, and civilians thronged the streets and windows. The vast crowds were silent as his carriage rolled toward his lodgings. Nathanael gazed at the faces that lined the streets. The last time he was in Philadelphia was with Baron von Steuben on their way to the South. The inhabitants had paid little attention to his presence.

"Is this for us?" Nathanael wondered aloud.

Edmund smiled and said, "They know a hero when they see one."

Girls tossed flowers. Boys waved small American flags. Then, harmonious voices rose. "Honor to the victor of the South! Long life to Greene!"

"I think now your triumph is complete," Edmund said.

In true Philadelphia style, the celebrations were elaborate. Nathanael took the most pleasure in seeing old friends—Joseph Reed, Clement Biddle, Charles Petit, and Robert Morris among them. It seemed that when he thought he found moments of happiness, something happened to stop the clock. At a grand gala held at the State House, Charles Petit confided, "Some of our old quartermaster accounts remain unsettled with Congress. You and I and John Cox will be fortunate if we do not find some claims upon us."

Nathanael let the music in the background wash over his thoughts before he said, "I am aware, but I can do nothing if they find it necessary. Congress has no means to pay me for the years of my service."

Charles regarded Nathanael with sorrowful eyes. "That is not all. John Banks speculated with the bills you gave him for the army contract, and his company Hunter, Banks & Company is bankrupt. His creditors will be howling at your door."

"Some were already howling before I left Charleston."

"It will be much louder, I wager. I am sorry."

Nathanael rubbed his forehead, walked to the bar, and ordered Madeira.

Charles' gaze followed and he thought, *I know what he has sacrificed for this country. I spent years as a quartermaster deputy under his command. I read his desperate letters to Congress from the south. He and his family deserve better.*

Nathanael disappeared from sight when a group of adoring ladies pressed him for his attentions. A man stood on the periphery. Charles Willson Peale—a patriot and artist from Maryland—was already acquainted with Nathanael. He had painted the general's portrait in 1778. Peale waited until the ladies dispersed. His offer topped off the gala evening, "I would be honored to paint your portrait again, General Greene, this time as the conquering hero."

Nathanael longed to move on alone where the shores of Rhode Island waited to embrace him and the cool winds off Narragansett Bay sang familiar songs. Where seagulls and puffins sailed the blue skies. Regardless of his desires, business kept him in Philadelphia.

From his desk, he wrote to Caty, "I tremble at my situation when I think of the enormous sums I owe. I seem to be doomed to a life of slavery."

If he were to become rich and influential or at the least earn enough money to care for his family, he had to clear himself of debt. Again, the Quaker in him was convinced that he had no choice and that his slaves would be not be worse off but better under his ownership. He replied to a letter from his broker and took care of plantation business, which included the purchase of enslaved people.

&

In the first week of October, his journey took him to Trenton, New Jersey. He was welcomed into the home of his former quartermaster general deputy, John Cox. To his surprise, General Washington was there preparing to leave for Princeton.

The tall commander-in-chief pulled Nathanael into his strong arms as if he were a long lost son. They gazed at one another while tears seeped down their cheeks. "Over the course of the war, there has not been a moment I lost faith in you, not a moment of distrust through the perils and trials we have suffered," George assured.

Nathanael swiped away his salty tears. "You have been my guiding light. You have been my ablest mentor, and I have missed you."

George sniffed and his mood changed. "We have done it, my friend! We have seen it to the end. Of all my generals, you and Henry Knox are the only two who have been by my side or fighting for the cause since the day we met at the siege of Boston."

Over dinner with John Cox, his wife, and six daughters, they talked of family, business, and the future. "I know you are burdened with crushing debt," George confided as they sat by the fire over claret as they had done in the early years when pressing matters concerning strategy, logistics, and political considerations were the order of the day. "This is your albatross to bear, which I cannot help you with."

"I am aware of the shortcomings of Congress as we strive to build a new nation," Nathanael acknowledged. "Disagreements and lack of money have plagued it and us from the onset. It besets our foreign allies and enemies."

"I am trying to cope with the problems and factions that contend the army's officers do not deserve half-pay for life, among other considerations. Some of our comrades such as General Gates have interfered to the contrary."

"So I have heard. There are political grumblings and whispers regarding the fear that you will grasp the reins of a new monarchy that we fought so hard to sever."

"That is ludicrous and is in no way my plan," George said. "But you must have plans for your own future? Do you plan to move to the South?"

"Caty and I have not talked about it."

"I can offer advice on the mechanics of becoming a planter."

"I can ill-afford to ignore any advice from those with experience," Nathanael said gravely.

"Tell me of Caty and the children," George said in an attempt to navigate Nathanael away from his burdens. "Martha is in Princeton visiting friends."

They talked of their families until George said, "I leave in the morning to join Martha and establish my headquarters at Rocky Hill. I am to issue a farewell address to the army from there. I imagine you will want to request permission to go home and be relieved of your duties."

Under guard, the two friends set out for Princeton. "Have you heard from Henry Knox?" Nathanael asked George. "I have not had the pleasure of a letter from my old friend for some time now."

"I left Henry in charge of the army while I am away. General Benjamin Lincoln submitted his resignation as secretary of war. Benjamin recommended Henry as his successor, a position Henry desires. I pledged to lobby Congress on his behalf. We all must find our paths back to civilian life. His wife, Lucy, gave birth to another son on July 6, a happy occasion."

When they arrived at Nassau Hall, where the Continental Congress was in session, they were greeted by a messenger bearing an invitation to an informal dinner hosted by its president, Elias Boudinot. The dusty travelers were grateful for the relaxing evening. As pleasing as it was, Nathanael was restless.

On Tuesday, October 7, 1783, he stood before Congress as they read his request to go home.

> *I beg leave to inform Congress that I have just arrived from my southern command, the business of which I hope, has been closed agreeable to their intention in furloughing all the soldiers and putting a stop to every Continental expense. It is now going on nine years since I have had an opportunity to visit my family or friends, or pay the least attention to my private fortune. I wish, therefore, for permission from Congress to go to Rhode Island, having already obtained the consent of the Commander-in-chief.*

A committee was formed, and after some deliberation, they decided to award Nathanael two cannon captured in the South as a public testament of his wisdom, fortitude, and military skill. It was resolved that the commander-in-chief be informed that, "Major General Greene has the permission of Congress to visit his family at Rhode Island."

thirty-three
Elusive Peace

The ship carrying the man who saved the South arrived in Newport Harbor under darkness of night. Save for the passengers, sailors, and workers, the docks were deserted. He tightened his cloak against the damp chill. With his baggage in hand, he walked the short distance to the house Caty had rented. A single candle flickered in the window of an above stairs bedroom.

The front door was locked. He stood there as if he were a stranger who had been barred from his private life. Then, Caty was there, her hair flowing down her back and her dark eyes exuding every reason he had come home. They fell into one another's arms, caressed by the harbor breeze that ruffled his cloak and fluttered her locks.

Nathanael removed her arms from around his neck. "Are you going to let me in, or shall I find somewhere else to sleep tonight?" he teased.

He carried his baggage over the threshold. The house was cold, but the love he desired was not. She lit candles. He kindled a fire in the hearth. Flames jumped to life. Now, he could see her clearly. Her nightdress clung to her slim body and the small round mound of her pregnant belly.

"It is all over now. Do not worry anymore," he assured with kisses on her cheeks and neck.

Tears stung her eyes. She exhaled a laugh and touched his face as if she were blind and needed to feel every curve, blemish, and line.

"Where are the children?" Nathanael asked.

"Sleeping. Nat just returned from a visit with my father on Block Island. They are great companions. Father joked that he wandered about as ragged as a Continental. He and Patty look so much like you." Caty pressed a hand to her heart. "Oh, you must be hungry, tired, and in need of a washbowl."

"I am all those things, but most of all I am in need of being a part of my family. Caty, I do not know my children. How can a man not know his own children?"

"It will come, my love. Tomorrow, we reunite as a family."

That night, he lay next to Caty and listened to her soft breathing. Through the open curtains, he stared at the weak light of the waxing crescent moon in the western sky. Over nine years had passed since they were married, and now he was forty-one years old. He wondered, *Can I ever be the same man who marched off to war?*

At dawn, the sound of little feet pattering, high-pitched laughter, and clattering jerked Nathanael awake. He lunged out of bed. His sword was not in reach. The enemy was approaching, and he was not dressed. A little girl's voice said, "Momma did *so* say that Papa was home."

Nathanael pressed a hand to his forehead. *Who would bring a child to a battle? No one. She is my child.* He saw that the blankets on the other side of the bed were tossed, and Caty was gone. With the apprehension of a person who was about to be thrust into a social situation burdened with anxiety, he dressed and limped downstairs to meet his children. He prayed they would not judge him harshly for his imperfection.

They were eating breakfast, a messy affair that Caty orchestrated to perfection. All four little faces turned to stare at their father. "Is there a plate for me?" Nathanael asked his oldest child, George, who was nearly eight and the only child he assumed remembered him.

Six-year-old Patty shifted her blue eyes to her five-year-old sister, Cornelia. They giggled and then looked down at their plates. Nat, who would be four in January, squiggled in his seat.

George patted the empty chair beside him. "Here, Papa. Your seat is here."

Nathanael took his seat.

Cornelia nibbled her bread and asked, "What is your name?"

Nathanael was taken aback, but her dark eyes held the genuine question.

"It is Nathanael. You, however, will address me as father."

Cornelia stared.

"Would you like to take a walk with me after breakfast?" he asked, realizing that he should not be issuing commands like a major general to his children.

"Can George come with us?" she asked.

"Of course."

Caty laid a plate before Nathanael. "Eat your breakfast first," she insisted and sat down with her own meal before her.

"You walk like I do," Patty observed to her father. She slid out of her chair and demonstrated the difficulties rickets had inflicted on her legs. Little Nat laughed at his big sister.

Caty and Nathanael exchanged sorrowful, amused glances. He recalled the day when the Kentish Guards had denied him a lieutenancy because his limp was unbecoming of an officer. "You will become a fine lady someday," Nathanael assured his daughter. "Do not let anyone tell you otherwise."

Patty smiled. Her blonde curls bounced when she nodded and shot a triumphant look at Nat.

It was late morning when Nathanael walked hand-in-hand with George and Cornelia through the streets of Newport that revealed the destruction the British left behind after three years of occupation. Barely a tree was standing on the whole of Aquidneck Island. Planking on the wharves and houses on the waterfront had been pulled down and used for firewood. Burned-out shells of buildings blackened a landscape already devoid of greenery.

Yet it did not curtail his contentment. He wrote to William Greene in East Greenwich:

> *I arrived at this place night before last and am happy to set my foot once more on the land of my nativity.*

William replied:

> *We have planned celebrations and reunions in your honor. We shall be awaiting your arrival as soon as you find it convenient and are hoping that is sooner than later.*

Caty felt unwell and balked over going to East Greenwich. "Aunt Catharine has never forgiven me for behaving in a manner she disapproved of when I used to visit you at winter cantonments," she complained.

"I am going to Coventry and Potowomut to see my family first," Nathanael said. "I would appreciate your company, my angel, if your health will allow it. If crossing the bay will make you ill—"

She put a finger to his lips. "I will bear that trip. The words of thanks and congratulations have been pouring in from friends and politicians. It is your family from whom you need to hear the same, and we shall hear them together."

Nathanael's heart skipped a beat as they pulled up to Spell Hall, the house in which he had lived alone for four years before marriage and the war changed everything. The smoky, acrid smell of the iron forge brought back memories of the days he pumped the trip hammer and pounded smelt into anchors beside the men he supervised.

His family poured out with exhilarated pride and joy. Jacob and Peggy with their brood of seven led the way with his younger brothers—Kitt,

William, Elihu, Perry—and their spouses and children. His cousin, Griffin, brought up the rear, sporting that rogue look that often got him and Nathanael in trouble as youths. To his delight, Sammy Ward, Jr. and his wife, Phebe, arrived from Westerly with their new baby girl.

Everyone talked at once. Their questions flew. They shared the news of their lives, and laughter echoed through the large house that overlooked the Pawtuxet River. Some of the men from the iron forge arrived. They pounded Nathanael on the back with arms so strong they nearly knocked him over. Nathanael returned the punishing greeting with equal verve.

He forgot about his crushing burdens until that evening when everyone but Jacob and Griffin went home. Jacob brought out tankards of beer, and the three settled in front of the fireplace in the library. Firelight danced across Nathanael's face.

I am the elder brother, and he looks older than I, Jacob thought. He said, "Your farm in Westerly is run down."

"I am aware," Nathanael said. "Caty rented it out after she lived there for a time. I suppose I need to have it repaired, but I am not certain that is feasible at this time. I have tried to extend my fortune in the South and have acquired 7,000 acres on Cumberland Island off the coast of Georgia. The land is fertile and covered with magnificent live oaks and pine. If I can have the timber cut and sold on the main land it will prosper."

"We three are still business partners," Jacob said. "With the difficulties you have been facing, what do you think about opening a trade with Charleston or Savannah? That certainly would benefit the transactions for timber."

"We could purchase a ship, like the old days when we used to run the *Fortune* down the coast loaded with hogsheads of rum and dodging port levies," Griffin added with enthusiasm.

Nathanael laughed and rubbed a finger over his upper lip. "I suppose it would be bad business now, but I am interested in the proposal. However, I must say, all the good words and congratulations do not put money in my hands, and without that, I am destitute."

❧

The winter of 1784 brought no relief to the pressures Nathanael faced. He received news that a hurricane had wiped out his rice crop on his Boone's Barony plantation in South Carolina, and what the hurricane had not destroyed, the bobolinks had. Further, some of his best horses died, and the carriage he left was ruined by exposure to the weather. His overseer, Roger Saunders, saddled Nathanael with more debt to pay for the losses and more enslaved people to work the land.

There was some brightness in the dark. He was elected president of the Rhode Island Society of the Cincinnati, a nationwide organization conceived by Henry Knox with George Washington at its head and Alexander Hamilton as secretary. It was made up of officers of the Continental Army who served together in the war and held the promise of proliferating ideas, achievements, and friendships of the Revolution. Membership was passed down to eldest sons.

The uplifting news compelled him to follow the source of laughter filtering through the windows. He pulled back the curtain. Winter sun warmed the pane, and what he saw warmed his heart. He threw on a coat and went outside. In the chill of an early February afternoon the day before Caty's twenty-ninth birthday, she and the children were playing Puss in the Corner, a child's game where the player known as "Puss" stood in the middle and the other four stood at corners.

A very pregnant Caty was Puss. The children giggled and attempted to exchange places with each other. Puss attempted to gain a corner during the exchange. She succeeded, and Cornelia became Puss. Cornelia pouted and stomped to her place in the center of the arena.

Nat deserted his corner and ran with upraised hands to his father. "Play with us!" he shouted with glee.

Nathanael lifted Nat and swung him around before putting him back on his feet. He narrowed his eyes at Caty and asked, "Should you be playing this game with the babe due in a little over a month?"

Caty laughed and said, "Then you shall take my place."

The children clapped and jumped up and down and cheered, "Papa should be Puss."

Friends and neighbors stopped to stare. *Was this General Greene playing like a boy with his children? Was this the destitute fatherless family who had struggled so long with only a mother to guide them?* Indeed it was.

They played until sunset. Nathanael lost his corner and then regained it as if he were still commanding in the South where he fought, got beat, and rose again to fight another day. He wrapped his arm around Caty's shoulders and rested his hand on her protruding belly as they went into the house for dinner and a quiet evening.

Their evenings did not remain quiet. Nathanael worried about Caty giving birth in the drafty old house near the wharves. He moved his family to a stately house away from the dank air near the city's wharves that cost eighty-five dollars more a year. Old friends from the army stopped at the Greene home during their various visits to the state. Colonel Thaddeus Kosciuszko charmed everyone in Newport who came to pay their respects. General Baron von Steuben visited with his dog Azor. The older Prussian's rough demeanor put the children off, but they had never had a dog. They romped and played with him until they wore the poor thing out.

When twenty-seven-year-old Marquis de Lafayette returned to the United States on his first tour since the war, he came to Newport to visit his old comrade and commander. The Frenchman swept through the threshold and with gentleness proclaimed, "My dear Mrs. Greene. It has been too long since we last met."

He charmed his longtime acquaintance without effort. "Since when do you call me Mrs. Greene?" she breathed. "It is Caty."

He felt four pair of eyes upon him—two blue and two brown. He benevolently bowed to the little ones and said in his French accent, "I am a good friend of your father's. We have met, but so many years have passed that you have all grown into lovely flowers."

Cornelia tittered at her first crush. "What is your name?"

"You, little miss, and your siblings may call me 'our dear marquis.'"

Patty elbowed her little sister, but she too looked smitten.

They spent evenings discussing the war, Lafayette's wife, Adrienne, and their children in France. "I would very much like to see more of Rhode Island than this devastated place where we tried to dislodge the British in 1778 and found ourselves at odds with the French Admiral d'Estaing. I hear Rhode Island is a fertile paradise," Lafayette said. He considered Caty. "I do not want to interfere if—"

"Please, you will not be interfering if my husband deems a tour of our little state necessary to your wishes," Caty said without looking to Nathanael for his approval. "The babe is not due for another month."

Nathanael's blue eyes lit up in appreciation of Caty's allure and maturing generosity. "It would be my honor. Caty's brother, Billy, is coming to take little Nat to Block Island to visit his grandfather until the child arrives so she has more time to rest."

"Oh, I have a gift," Lafayette said. He rose and extracted a pair of white silk gloves from his bag. He presented them to Nathanael. "I did not wish to forget before I leave."

Nathanael fingered the smooth fabric. "It is my honor to accept this handsome gift."

The two left the following morning. Nathanael escorted Lafayette to Coventry, Potowomut, East Greenwich, and Providence. At every stop, Lafayette was hailed with excitement and honored by Nathanael's family, politicians, and common folk who had heard tales of the great Frenchman who came to America using his own funds to fight for independence.

As those whirlwind days passed and February turned to March, Caty still had not given birth. Her health declined. Nathanael wrote to Henry Knox, "Mrs. Greene's situation has prevented me from visiting Boston. I expect her to put to bed every hour."

What he did not tell Henry was that on a trip to Providence, he slipped on ice and wrenched his stomach muscles. The pain spread into his chest, and he was unable to ride a horse. It was another reason that his planned trip to take care of business in South Carolina and Georgia had to wait.

He received a letter from Washington in the first week of April concerning the Society of the Cincinnati. A clamor ignited from people like Benjamin Franklin, Samuel Adams, and John Adams who proclaimed the society reeked of Old World traditions and anti-republican privilege. As president of the society, Washington was particularly worried about it. He wrote from Mount Vernon:

> *I wish that you could make it convenient to be at the general meeting of the Society of Cincinnati, before you take your departure for South Carolina. To me it should seem indispensable that the Meeting May next should be composed of the best abilities of the representation.*

Although he was president of the Rhode Island State chapter, Nathanael's situation prevented his attendance of the first general meeting in Philadelphia. Absorbed by his own difficulties and unaware of the clamor, he did his best and wrote to Joseph Reed in Philadelphia to warn him of the current of public prejudice directed against the Cincinnati.

George, Patty, and Cornelia spent the night at a neighbor's home. The Greene house would have been quiet on that cool morning of April 17 if Caty's cries had ceased. Nathanael watched the sun rise and then paced the downstairs rooms as her struggle to give birth reached a crescendo. Her doctor was there with two midwives and a wet nurse. *Surely nothing can go awry,* Nathanael told himself although he knew everything could go awry.

A baby cried. Caty silenced. Nathanael fought the urge to bound up the stairs and burst into the room. He waited for what seemed like an eternity before a door creaked open. "General Greene, you may come up now," a woman's voice said with authority.

He grasped the rail and took a breath. The familiar odor of blood that exuded from battlefields and hospitals wafted down the stairs. He shook his head to clear the horrifying thought. When he reached the landing, a midwife, who he remembered as Nancy, smiled and stepped aside when he entered the room. Caty was sitting up in bed with a tiny bundle in her arms.

"It is a girl," she said with a weak smile.

Four years had passed since Nat was born in the Morristown, New Jersey encampment. At that time, Nathanael was distracted with quartermaster duties and anxiety. This time, his wife and child had his full attention. "May I hold her?" he asked.

Caty passed the bundle to him. He grimaced at the lingering pain in his chest from the accident on the ice. He looked down at the tiny sleeping babe with a scruff of black hair. Nathanael stroked her cheek with the back of his right index finger. *Her skin is so soft I cannot feel it.* Then a thought struck him. *How am I going to feed her when I can barely afford to feed the rest of my family?*

"Louisa Catharine," Caty interrupted his thoughts.

"What?"

"I want to name her Louisa Catharine," Caty said.

The social season in Newport regained the social eminence it had pre-war. Caty rapidly recovered from Louisa's birth. She was anxious to answer the many invitations to attend socials. Nathanael balked; still he basked in the joy of seeing his wife rejuvenated. On a late May afternoon, Caty primped in her dressing room for the evening ahead.

Cornelia and Patty were "helping" their mother with her adornments. Nathanael stood in the doorway and watched the arraying of his beautiful wife. Her dark hair drifted from her poised head over ivory shoulders, her dainty shoes glinted with diamond buckles, and delicate laces enmeshed her in filmy glory. Caty turned to look at her husband.

"You are a vision which will center all eyes upon you," he said.

"You are not dressed," Caty scolded as she slipped on an earring. "Did you see your new suit?"

No matter how elegant his wife looked, the dark cloak of bad news veiled him as if it were a shroud. He decided to keep it to himself for that night, but Caty would have to be told of his affairs that beckoned from afar.

"I shall dress right away, my angel," he conceded and turned to leave. He paused and said, "You always look beautiful, but tonight you look breathtaking."

The evening was dominated by music, dancing, food, and spirits. Laughing friends and neighbors behaved as if they did not have to consider the cost of their extravagant attire, including Nathanael's wife. He, like so many other Continental Army officers, had gone into debt to clothe and feed their soldiers. Unlike the others, Nathanael had no way to extricate himself. It was the high price of freedom that he swore nine years before he would pay, without realizing the true cost.

Governor William Greene brought glasses of champagne and sat beside Nathanael. "You appear pensive," he said.

Nathanael accepted the offered glass and sipped it. "I was thinking. These happy faces are what we fought for, although political talk of discontent is unsurprising. I have heard it everywhere."

"Your mind is not on faces or politics."

"No," Nathanael agreed. He hesitated. The last thing he wanted to talk about was his embarrassing financial situation. He had borne enough criticism and accusations.

William sensed his relative's mental struggle, and he waited for Nathanael to come to terms with what he had to say.

Nathanael finally offered, "I have to leave for Philadelphia and then South Carolina to tend to my property. I do not know how to tell Caty that the shadows that drape us are growing ever longer."

"I hear your farm in Westerly is attached for debt," William said.

"Yes. I am going to Philadelphia to meet with Congress about settling my army accounts. Further, a committee of Congress headed by Thomas Jefferson has informed me that I overdrew my six thousand dollar allowance for personal expenses when Caty was in South Carolina."

"Congress has no money, Nathanael. Their national debt amounts to almost thirty million dollars, and they cannot tax the states to pay for it. You know this."

Caty's laughter rang out. "Why are you sitting here like unbecoming girls who cannot attract a suitor?" She extended her delicate hand to Nathanael. "Finish your champagne and flatter me with a dance."

"I think I will look for my own wife," William said. He disappeared among the sea of party goers.

Caty sat down. She snapped open her elegant fan and cooled herself. "I will not force you to dance. I will, however, beg of you to tell me what you told my uncle and what you did not tell him."

"What I did not tell him?"

"Yes. I saw the letter, Nathanael. I am not blind. I know John Banks is bankrupt. That letter you received from the London firm which holds the bills you guaranteed, Newcome and Collett, states that you are responsible for the money Banks owes them for the army clothing you purchased."

"I have replied and told them to hound Banks." He glanced at the whirling dancers and two gentlemen coming toward them. "We will talk at home," he said to Caty.

That night, with the bright face of the full moon looking in on him, Nathanael wrote a letter to John Banks, who he assumed was still in Charleston. "You know what you have done in the affair of my signature. Free me from my embarrassment, and you are safe, but if you neglect to do me this justice, you must abide the consequences."

On July 7, 1784, Nathanael boarded a sloop he owned with his brother and cousin, the *Charleston Packet,* to exact his promise. He arrived in the humidity and heat of South Carolina on August 1 and rode to his Boone's Barony plantation. His overseer, Roger Saunders, informed him with docility, "That rascal Banks was here. He claimed he was acting as your lawyer and asked for money, which I gave him."

Nathanael felt his asthma flare as he tried to contain his temper. In the worst of times, it betrayed him like an enemy who compelled him to wheeze in an act of revenge. "I assure you, Mr. Saunders, it is not your fault that he has deceived you. I am not the only person who has been taken by this man."

"Well, I hear Banks has left Charleston and gone to North Carolina to dodge his circumstances."

The news did not surprise Nathanael. One of Banks' business partners, Robert Forsyth, was a lawyer in Charleston and represented Banks. Forsyth could offer no relief. By September 1, a frustrated Nathanael wrote Caty to tell her he was going to North Carolina. "Providence has designed Banks for a scourge for some of my evil deeds. I verily believe if I was to meet him I should put him to death. He is the greatest monster and most finished villain that this age has produced."

God's divine care through Providence that he believed was working against him proved to be as harsh as he imagined. On October 1, he arrived in Washington, a small town in eastern North Carolina on the Pamlico River. The modicum of hope that he could settle things with Banks evaporated. He wrote to Forsyth, "John Banks is dead and buried. My prospects are now worse than ever. I leave this place with the business that brought me here hanging over my head like a threatening cloud which embitters every moment of my life."

There was nothing left to do but go to Virginia to see the firm of Hunter and Banks himself and to confer with his former quartermaster, Colonel Edward Carrington, who had a law firm in the war-torn city of Richmond.

"Nathanael, I am delighted to see you, even under the harsh circumstances. Please, have a seat," Edward said. "I have arranged for a late dinner in my office if that is suitable."

Clacking carriage wheels and jingling horse tack, the chortle of drunken men, and the laughter of ladies floated unfiltered through the open windows. The noise distracted Nathanael as if the bedlam surrounding him never quieted. He managed to suppress it and explain what had happened to Banks.

Edward nodded thoughtfully and then said, "I will write a letter to Mr. Forsyth and ask for a statement of how much Banks has paid his creditors. A court of Chancery may relieve you of whatever amount Banks has paid them."

"Can we not sue the administration of the Banks estate?" Nathanael asked.

"Oh, here is out meal," Edward interrupted. Servants set plates of ham, cabbage, and dumplings before the two men. Ale was poured from pitchers then left on the table. The servants slipped out quietly.

"Yes, we can try, but I doubt little will come out of it," Edward said as he cut a piece of ham. He chewed thoughtfully and then said, "I will look into some of Banks' partners and see if there is an avenue there. I would not be hopeful. You are not the only man who is feeling the thorn of Banks' bankruptcy, and there may be many judgements already filed."

Nathanael pushed the food on his plate around with his fork.

"Have you filed a claim in Congress for your debt on behalf of the army?" Edward asked.

"Yes. I have begged for their consideration. My family will be financially ruined if I am put in debtor's prison or worse if I die."

"I shall try to exercise vigilance concerning your case. I owe you that as a fellow soldier and more importantly as a friend. Is there no one who you were close friends with before or during the war who is willing to step up to help?"

"I have borrowed vast amounts of money."

Edward pointed his fork at Nathanael. "Eat. It will not do to starve yourself to death. Irony can be cruel."

❧

Caty sailed to Block Island to see her family and fetch little Nat. When she returned home, a letter Nathanael wrote from Charleston before leaving for North Carolina was waiting along with a cask of rum. Through the problems he faced with Banks, his mind was ever on his family.

I begin to feel anxious about the little girls. Desire your brother Billy to write to Doctor Stiles at Yale University to recommend a good young man and get his terms. Me thinks this mode will be a little more expensive than boarding the

girls abroad or sending them to school, and they may be better
taught at home and their morals and manners much more
attended to. What do you think my dear?

The news she clung to was that he was coming home. She and the children met him at the docks in Newport. The children dodged the disembarking passengers and ran to greet their papa.

Patty's eyes glittered when she asked, "Did you bring us gifts?"

Nathanael squatted and tweaked her on the nose. "Where did you get an idea like that?"

"My friend, Betsey, said her father brings her gifts when he comes home from his travels."

"Is that a rule?" Nathanael feigned with amusement.

Patty nodded vigorously. Cornelia giggled.

"Then I shall remember it for next time." He took his sons by the hand and kissed his wife. "I have missed you all more than you can know," he told her. "I think it is time for us to discuss our finances and our future."

"I realize that," she assured. "We cannot go on like this."

The couple sat before the fire on a cold November night and watched snow fall in ghostly silence outside the windows. Caty's senses numbed as she listened to her husband's glum words. "I never owned so much property as I do now, and yet never felt so poor..." As he talked, she hoped at some point they would achieve the lucidity to see the road their lives must take.

"Are you listening, my angel?" Nathanael asked.

"Yes, and what I hear is that this situation, the constant need to go to the South to develop and oversee our plantations, is futile unless we are there to supervise and manage business affairs. As things are now, our family will be torn asunder."

"I do not wish to be rich as I did before the war ended. I just wish to be independent. We are condemned to a life of slavery," he said. The irony of using enslaved people to reach their dream weighed on both of them, but not enough to consider doing otherwise.

"I had envisioned a life of wealth and leisure," Caty confessed. "It has been shattered. Now it seems we can only hope to survive, and I will do whatever we need to do to achieve that. How much development is there ahead of us?"

"Mulberry Grove and its rice fields have not been developed at all, and the house needs repairs," Nathanael admitted. "If it is agreed that we see that place as our future—and it has a future—then I will endeavor to hasten it."

"That requires you to leave us again, does it not?"

Nathanael looked at her with sorrowful blue eyes.

Caty wiped at a tear that rolled down her beautiful cheek. "I suppose I can learn to be a farmer's wife."

Nathanael got up and pulled her into his arms. "I will make one final attempt in recovering our fortune lost in the Banks affair. If that fails, then we will make our lives in Georgia."

On January 7, 1785, Caty drove Nathanael to the docks and watched as he boarded the *Union*, a ship bound for Charleston. She felt as if her heart would burst as its sails disappeared over the horizon. Her greatest fear was that he would never come back. *I have no choice. There are five little ones waiting for me at home. What I did not tell him was that I am experiencing signs of pregnancy.*

❧

A few days out from port, the *Union* was caught in a winter storm. Waves pounded the deck. Sails whipped in the wind and spars snapped. Her captain dislocated his leg, and the first mate, in an attempt to aid, was greatly injured. Nathanael had long ago owned the ship *Fortune* with his brothers and was not easily shaken. He thought of Caty, who was frightened of every rolling movement of a ship. He resolved not to tell her of the perils of the *Union*.

On January 28, the ship limped into Charleston. When he came ashore, he was immediately accosted by a waiting impatient messenger. "Are you General Greene?"

This cannot be a good sign, Nathanael thought as he acknowledged the messenger. The message was from his overseer at Boone's Barony. Heavy rains had flooded Nathanael's ripened rice crop, leaving him with a fraction of what he intended to sell. Alone and frustrated, he found his way to William Washington's house.

William was surprised to find his general standing at the door like a forlorn puppy. "You look exhausted," he observed as Nathanael stepped over the threshold. "But that does not deter my happiness at seeing you."

"I am on my way to my plantation in Georgia. I beg of you a night's lodging and a horse."

"You may stay as long as you need," William said.

As tempting as the invitation was to sit in front of a fire and discuss the old days, Nathanael was off the next morning. He rode the swampy coastal roads through cold wind and rain. When he saw the plantation house rise in the distance, relief overcame him. He wished nothing more than to rest a few days, but rest was not what he had come to do. After meeting with his overseer, William Gibbons, to discuss some improvements on the house, Nathanael was surprised to see a familiar figure riding across the fields.

"Praise God. It is Anthony Wayne," Nathanael said to his overseer. He started out to meet him. The two old friends shook hands. "When did you arrive from Pennsylvania?" Nathanael asked.

"Last November. Do you not remember? Georgia saw fit to award me a plantation for chasing the British out of their state, the very mission you tasked me to complete," Anthony said cheerfully. "I have been mired in learning about planting and all the expenses it brings about." He pointed to the northward. "My plantation, Richmond, is adjacent to Mulberry Grove."

They walked the fields of their plantations together, like two old war heroes, yet they were both young men. Anthony was thirty-nine. Nathanael was forty-two. They shared stories of their hopes and dreams that both men had fought to maintain.

"My wife, Polly, will have nothing to do with moving to Georgia," Anthony explained. "You know she refuses to leave Pennsylvania. I believe I will be a lonely planter."

Nathanael chuckled to himself. *Anthony is far from lonely under any circumstances.* "We are moving here. Caty and I have discussed the matter at length. I will be here for quite some time getting the house livable and seeing to matters concerning my land on Cumberland Island."

They parted when the sun went down. Through the trying times ahead, they often dined and discussed the fine art of planting, harvesting, and selling rice. One evening as they were finishing dinner, the weekly post arrived late. Nathanael brought the leather express pouch into the living room and tossed it on a table. He poured a tankard of rum and stared at the pouch.

Anthony wandered in from the dining room. His eyes fell on the pouch. He was not blind to the reason Nathanael had not opened it. With each message or inquiry, Nathanael was wary of the content. "I suppose it is time for me to go home," Anthony said as he reached for his coat and hat. "You know, there may be a letter in there from Caty."

"No, stay," Nathanael said. "I have been getting threatening letters from a former cavalry officer under my command, Captain James Gunn. I had a court of inquiry look into his reasons for taking a horse that belonged to the army and claiming it as personal property."

"A grudge?"

"He insists that I abused him in a way a gentleman could not ignore and is demanding a duel. I answered that no man while I was in the army ever heard me use language indelicate or that would disgrace a gentleman. He lives across the Savannah River on a South Carolina plantation."

"Do you believe he will attempt to carry out his threats?"

"Yes, and no matter what I say, he will not stand down." Nathanael indicated the pouch with a nod. "He has probably refuted me again."

"Open it," Anthony insisted.

Nathanael did as Anthony asked. Indeed, there was another letter from Gunn. "This time he has set a time and place for the duel. The letter reads that I am to meet him at four o'clock tomorrow on neutral ground near his plantation and to bring a second and the arms necessary on those occasions."

"The man is trying to get attention by behaving deranged. Remember that you are the superior officer. He cannot hold you to his standard. If you need me, you know where I shall be. Good night."

On March 2, the day Gunn proposed the duel, Nathanael wrote a terse response. "I will never establish a precedent for subjecting superior officers to the call of inferior officers for what the former have done in the execution of their public duty."

Gunn replied that if that was the case, he would shoot Nathanael on sight.

From that day on, Nathanael carried a pistol in his pocket, but the unmet challenge gnawed at him. He wrote to Washington that if he thought his honor would not suffer, he would not hesitate to answer the contest.

Washington agreed. He wrote:

> *Your honor and reputation will not only stand perfectly acquitted for the non-acceptance of his challenge, but that your prudence and judgment would have been condemnable for accepting of it, in the eyes of the world, because if a commanding officer is amenable to private calls he has a dagger always at his breast.*

With the Gunn affair still ringing in his ears, Nathanael and a friend, Colonel Robert Hawkins, visited his vast holdings on Cumberland Island. They rode the twenty-mile-long island where a large part of it was excellent for growing indigo. On the Atlantic side, there was a beach eighteen miles long, as level as a floor. Everything about the island felt healthy and delightful. Nathanael's mind moved rapidly toward how to raise funds to improve it for commercial success.

He and Hawkins sailed to St. Augustine, Florida in late March. He was determined to find people who were willing to colonize and develop the property on Cumberland Island and engage in logging so he could get his lumber business started. The voyage took them down the inter-coastal river in a canoe and to the door of the Spanish governor, Don Vincent de Zespedes. Zespedes was cordial and helpful as much as possible.

Nathanael reported the whole visit to Caty. "We were introduced to his Lady and daughters, and compliments flew from side to side like a shuttlecock in the hand of good players. You know I am not very excellent at fine speeches. My Spanish was soon exhausted; but what I lacked in conversation I made up in bowing."

He went on to describe the daughters. "They are not handsome, and their complexions are rather tawny, but they have sweet languishing eyes. They look as if they could love with great violence. They did everything to please if not to inspire softer emotions. Hawkins professed himself smitten."

As enchanting as the daughters were, the voyage to Florida was unsuccessful. Before he made plans to go back to Newport, he conferred with his lawyers and engaged in long sessions and conferences regarding the Banks affair. He decided instead of writing to Caty about the outcome, he would bring her the bad news in person. There was no need to upset her further. She was awaiting the birth of their sixth child.

In mid-August 1785, Nathanael arrived at the docks of Newport. He had traveled with a group of South Carolinians seeking to escape the heat and sickly season that had plagued his Southern Army. Caty was not waiting in her carriage. He trudged the steep hill to the rented house on Mill Street. The front door was locked, forcing him to knock.

He was surprised when a woman he vaguely recognized answered with baby Louisa on her hip. She stepped aside to let him pass. He kissed Louisa's cheek. She plopped a thumb into her mouth.

"You do not remember me do you, General Greene?" the woman asked. "My name is Nancy Wright. I midwifed your last little girl. Mrs. Greene is—"

The four older children came running. "Papa! Papa!"

Nathanael dropped his baggage and squatted to encompass them all in his arms.

"Momma has a baby," Nat announced. "She will be our new playmate."

Nathanael rose and took the stairs two at a time. He entered the bedroom where Caty slept with a new baby girl curled in her arms. He gently sat on the edge of the bed and gazed at mother and daughter. Boys were considered preferable, but daughters held him captive from which there was no way to escape.

Caty's eyes fluttered open. She smiled up into his face. "Is she not beautiful?"

He kissed her forehead. "You are both beautiful."

Caty placed the baby in his arms. "Have you named her?" he asked as he cradled her.

"Not yet."

"I think she should be named Catharine after her mother," he said as he stroked her soft cheek as he had done when Louisa was born.

Caty beamed with love and approval. "Tell me of your trip to the South. I received your letters, but I sensed you were leaving something out."

Nathanael returned the baby to Caty's arms. "Rest, my angel."

"No, you must tell me what happened with Banks."

"There is no hope of relief from my indebtedness. There is nothing left to do but move to Mulberry Grove. We can sell off our other land when the market is better and cultivate our plantation. I cannot expect you to agree to such a move without recovery and consideration."

"We talked about this before you left. We are agreed as one."

That night, Nathanael slept in the bedroom with his sons so he would not disturb Caty. In the middle of the night, he heard the door creak open. "Papa?" a voice coughed. He threw on his banyan and stepped into the hallway. "What is it, Patty?" She coughed and issued a small cry. "I am afraid to wake Momma."

"What is wrong?"

"Cornelia is coughing, and I cannot sleep."

Nathanael put a hand to his daughter's forehead. To his relief, she was not feverish. "I will tuck you in bed, my sweet, and look in on Cornelia."

"I want Momma," Patty cried.

"I know you do. You must suffice with me tonight unless you want me to wake Mrs. Wright."

Patty shook her head. "Will you stay with us until we fall asleep?"

"Of course."

In the morning, Nathanael jerked awake. He had fallen asleep in the tiny chair in his daughters' room. Their bed was empty. He heard coughing downstairs. He looked in on Caty. She was awake and nursing Catharine. "I hear them," she said. "Call the doctor and keep them away from the baby."

The doctor confirmed what Caty feared. "The older girls have whooping cough. George and Nat are showing signs of the disease. It will progress. Keep them in bed and separated from the baby. I will give you instructions on what to give them before bed to restore the balance of the bodily humors and calm the cough."

As the doctor warned, the children became sicker. Their cries for "Momma" anguished Caty. Nathanael, with the nurse, frantically tried to care for them and keep them comfortable. Days later, as the older children began to recover, baby Catharine began to cough. Nathanael and Caty tended to her night and day.

On the evening of August 28, Nathanael, exhausted from caring for the children, dozed off on the living room couch. Caty's hysterical voice snapped him awake. "Nathanael! She stopped breathing! Nathanael! Nathanael!" He stumbled up the stairs and rushed into the bedroom. Caty's beautiful face contorted. "She is not breathing. Help her! Make her breathe!" Nathanael took the infant from his wife's arms. Her little face was red, and her tiny eyes were closed. Nathanael pressed a hand to her still chest. "I have no idea how to help her!" he cried.

Caty collapsed on the bed in a grief-stricken sea of tears.

I have never felt so helpless, he thought. He looked up. Five scared faces stood at the doorway. Fifteen-month-old Louisa began to cry. "Caty, the children," Nathanael said with gentleness.

She sat up and took her dead baby in her arms. "Talk to them," she begged.

The horrors and deprivations of war and his crushing debt paled in comparison to telling his children their adored baby sister had died. Then, he bought a baby-sized coffin.

"I will lose my mind if you put her in that dark place," Caty sobbed.

"She has to be buried, my angel."

"Where? We have no affiliation to a church in Newport."

"I will take care of it," Nathanael said softly.

For weeks, Caty lay in bed and stared at the walls. Her arms ached for the baby she would never hold again. The children peeked into her room frightened and confused. Struggling with his own grief, Nathanael did all he could to comfort them and Caty. He provided Caty with meals cooked by others who had come to pay their respects.

"You must eat, my angel," he prodded.

"I cannot," she moaned.

He set the tray aside and pulled her into his arms. He kissed the top of her dark head and said, "Our future has not been shattered. The beautiful place where we can begin anew awaits us. Mulberry Grove has fruit trees and gardens that are run down but can be revived with tender care. Cumberland Island is a flourishing expanse of the loveliest beaches I have ever seen. Our children will grow up in the healthy air of an unspoiled place."

Caty sniffed and nodded into his chest.

"I cannot promise that there will be parties to your liking, but I am certain you can remedy that." He lifted her chin so he could see her eyes. "I know this melancholy will not pass quickly. However, we must move on with our plans. Do you agree?"

"Yes, I agree," she said weakly.

"I am worried about the children's education. You have been unable to instruct them these past weeks, and furthermore, I know of no schools near Mulberry Grove. Do you remember I asked you to inquire about a tutor through Dr. Ezra Stiles at Yale? Did your brother send the inquiry?"

"Yes. He received an answer. The letter is unopened."

"I will see to it."

Caty exhaled a sigh of relief. *A tutor will be a godsend*, she thought.

Dr. Stiles, a friend of Nathanael's from before the war, recommended Phineas Miller, a twenty-one-year-old graduate of Yale. *He has gentle manners and a fine intellect,* Stiles wrote. Nathanael offered the teaching job to Miller, who agreed to accompany the family to Georgia and to the terms of three pounds a month plus board.

Nathanael prepared to move his family to Georgia. He wrote to Jeremiah Wadsworth in Connecticut about baby Catharine's death and to let him know they were leaving as soon as Caty felt well enough to travel. With Caty in the care of Mrs. Wright, he rode to the house in Coventry. He packed up his books and spent a few days with his brothers and their families. During the years he was gone, his family had adjusted to his absence. Yet, his brothers were distressed.

"We shall be separated forever," Kitt observed with sadness. "My children will not remember you."

Jacob was unusually quiet. He told his wife, Peggy, "I fear for him for reasons I cannot ascertain." Peggy regarded Jacob closely. He often had a melancholy outlook, but this time she could not ignore it.

His cousin Griffin arrived from Potowomut. "You know I will be visiting as soon as possible," he promised with laughing eyes. "You will need a rogue to get into to trouble with. I am selling a ship you have an interest in and will forward your share of the profits." He sobered and said, "I will miss you, cousin."

Nathanael climbed into his carriage packed with his books and other personal items he had left behind when the war broke out. He looked back at his extended family standing in the yard until they disappeared from his sight.

When he arrived home, Phineas Miller was there. "General Greene. I did not mean to intrude upon your wife," the tutor said. "I was unaware you were away, otherwise I would have waited until you came home."

"Mr. Miller, your arrival is a pleasure. Help me unloaded my books from the carriage."

"You have collected these over the years?" he asked, inspecting the spines once the crates were carried into the house. "I am impressed. John Locke's *An Essay on Human Understanding* and William Blackstone's *Commentaries on the Laws of England*. There are many respected titles here."

"Excuse me, Mr. Miller, I must look in on Caty. I suppose the two of you have met and conferred."

"Yes, sir. I have met your five children as well. They are delightful and well-mannered. And please call me Phineas."

Caty was sitting up in bed nibbling on bread and cheese. A glass of wine sat on the bedside table. "My angel, are you feeling better?" Nathanael asked.

Caty's voice quivered. "I know why I have been feeling so unwell. I have missed my monthly complaint. There is no doubt I am pregnant again."

Accosted with guilt, Nathanael's breath caught in his throat. "I should not have—"

Caty put a finger to his lips. "I want this baby. I need this baby. It is just that I am so tired."

He did not know what to say. He had made every effort to care for her and relieve her of her burdens, but there had been that moment when he was rapt with his needs.

She attempted to soothe his inner struggle, "I am very happy with Mr. Miller. He is kind and has taken a great interest in the children. He is an avid conversationalist. We have had many good chats. For that, I am grateful." She slid her slim hand into his. "I am ready to meet our future."

Although Caty was still feeling unwell, she and Nathanael packed up their house. Caty's father, John Littlefield, and her brother, Billy, arrived from Block Island to wish them well.

The news that the Greenes were leaving brought people to his door demanding payment for every little debt. He wondered how much worse it would get once he was in Georgia. It prompted him to attend to one last task. He wrote his will.

> *In the name of God Amen. I Nathanael Greene late Major General in the Army of the United States of America do make and declare this to be my last and only will and Testament. Witness my hand and Seal at Newport this eleventh day of October 1785.*

He assigned Caty his Executrix and bequeathed everything to her and the children, with the condition if they all passed before coming into the property, it would be divided equally among his five brothers. He gave special care to his children's education.

> *As I am convinced that the happiness of my Children will depend in an eminent degree on their education; I hope my Sons will come forward and take an Active part in the Affairs of their Country; their education should be liberal. My Daughters should not be less suitable to their Station, and Circumstances. But above all things let their Morals be well attended to. This advice is properly attended to will prove the best Legacy of a fond father.*

On October 14, 1785, the Greenes, along with the widowed nurse, Nancy Wright, and Phineas Miller, boarded a ship bound for Savannah, Georgia. The seas heaved and the ship creaked. Caty, confined to her cabin with her nurse, was terrified of every rolling wave. The pitching made her violently ill. She thought she would lose her mind when the ship weathered a gale.

Nathanael assumed charge of the children. They were a little sick at first, but then they were happy the rest of the voyage and less trouble than he thought they would be. During a calm day, he took them up on the quarterdeck.

"Look there," he said as the waters separated, and a large right whale breached.

"There is another one," George exclaimed. "See it?"

His children's joy could not erase the terror their mother suffered. He wrote to Jeremiah Wadsworth how grievous it was to see Caty's distress. The bright spot was that Phineas Miller endured it well, and he was able to carry on lessons with the children when the weather permitted.

On October 30, the ship slipped up the Savannah River to the bustling docks near Bay Street. Nathanael's former aide and lawyer, Nat Pendleton, met them as they disembarked. While Nathanael stayed to supervise unloading their personal belongings and carriages, Nat's new wife, Susan, took pity on Caty and saw her, the nurse, and the children to the Pendleton house at the corner of Bay and Barnard Street on a bluff overlooking the harbor.

"You are welcome to stay as long as you like," Susan told Caty when they were settled into the big house. "Was your passage tolerable? You look pale."

Caty did not know this woman and regarded her with distance. But it was discourteous to avoid the question, and she candidly answered, "Our passage was torment made all the more so that I am with child."

Nathanael, Phineas, and Nat arrived after making arrangements for most of the Greenes' personal belongings to be shipped upriver fourteen miles to Mulberry Grove. The arrangements included hired servants to prepare the plantation house for his family.

On sunny days, Caty and Nathanael explored their new hometown, sometimes with the children, other times alone. They strolled down Bay Street to the Coffee House, taking care not to venture beyond where taverns and whorehouses were frequented by sailors. Nathanael was gratified when they walked down Broughton Street with its assortment of shops. Despite his empty pockets, he indulged Caty in wares from an importer who specialized in items such as petticoats, lute strings, linen, diapers, silk hose, and fancy fans.

One night, they attended a play called *The Tragedy of the Orphan* for four shillings. Caty turned to Nathanael and said, "I am feeling much better. Do you agree it is time to move on to our new home?"

Nathanael passionately kissed Caty in the dark theater. "I agree, my angel."

thirty-four

Mulberry Grove

I n the last week of November, the Greenes traveled the Augusta Road up-river to Mulberry Grove. Their carriages rolled through a gate and down the shadowy lane lined with a vast forest of oak trees bearded with Spanish moss and thick with vines and shrubs. Before ownership was transferred to Nathanael and Caty, the plantation was owned by Loyalist Dr. Patrick Graham. Graham had planted mulberry saplings to cultivate a silkworm industry and then developed the land for growing rice.

The silkworm industry was gone, but beyond the river and forest, acres of newly cultivated rice fields stretched out as far as the eye could see. A two-story brick building with chimneys on both ends loomed before them as the Greenes' carriages came to a stop. The house, unoccupied for years, was magnificent, but it would need more work to make it livable.

No matter, Caty was delighted. She alit from the carriage like an excited young girl about to meet her first suitor. The beauty she had seen in the plantation when they visited in 1783 had not faded. With some of the improvements Nathanael had commissioned, it shined brighter.

"It is beautiful," she exclaimed as the children tumbled out of their carriage and ran toward the front door. Louisa toddled after her big brothers and sisters and fell. She wailed. Nathanael lifted her and set her on his hip. He quieted her tears while Caty gazed at the Georgian structure.

"Our prospects and dreams are here, my darling," Caty cooed. "Will you show me around as soon as we are unpacked?"

"Let us do it now," he said with excitement and escorted her into the house.

Two wide glass windows flanked the double front door. "The Savannah River flows just beyond the lane. I can see the islands in the river and South Carolina on the other shore," Caty pointed out. She called the children. "Come, walk with your father and me over our new property."

The Greenes toured their outbuildings—a coach house and stables, a kitchen, a smokehouse, and a fifty-foot-long poultry house. "What is that on top of the poultry house?" George asked.

Nathanael set Louisa on her feet and shaded his eyes from the sun. "It is a pigeon house. It will hold quite a flock."

"Why do we need pigeons?" Patty asked.

"They are good for pigeon pie," Nathanael said.

"Did we eat pigeons in Rhode Island?" she asked.

Nathanael grinned and asked, "Momma, do you care to explain?"

Caty laughed. "I have no explanation. I suppose I will have to learn how to make this pigeon pie."

Phineas Miller joined the Greenes on their tour, for it was his new home as well.

Cornelia reached for his hand. "Would you like to see the gardens?"

"I will be pleased to do so, Miss Greene," he teased. They clasped hands and started away. Nat ran after them and snatched Phineas' fingers. Caty and Nathanael exchanged gratified smiles. There was no doubt they had chosen wisely when they hired Phineas.

"Can we get a dog?" George asked. "General Steuben had a dog, so I think we should have one, too."

"Wait until we settle in," Caty said. "Then we may talk about it."

"Whose little houses are those?" Cornelia wondered at the rows of cabins made of tabby edging the property. Dark faces appeared as the Greenes approached.

Caty's and Nathanael's eyes met as if to say, *How do we tell our children that we have enslaved people and that is where they live?* They would have to be told the truth.

≈

By New Year 1786, the Greenes, their tutor, and Caty's nurse were delightfully situated in their new home. Nathanael's beloved books lined the shelves of their new library. Fear of isolation at Mulberry Grove, unlike the busy town of Newport, dissolved with a constant flow of visitors. Nat Pendleton and his wife, Susan, often traveled from Savannah to spend the night with Nathanael and Caty.

Anthony Wayne tossed off his fiery nickname "Mad Anthony" when he was at the Greenes' table. "I have decided to participate in politics," he announced one night over after-dinner brandy. "I have joined the Federalist Party as their doctrines of centralization, federalism, and protectionism are attractive."

"Federalists favor a strong national government versus the anti-Federalist doctrine of small localized governments at the state level with limited national authority," Caty quipped. "Fear of standing armies is another pivotal point between the two."

"Why, my dear Caty, when did you become inclined to study political maxims?" Anthony asked. His eyes lingered on Caty's beautiful countenance.

"You have not been paying attention, sir."

Nathanael stifled a chuckle. Both Caty and Anthony were predisposed to flirtations that he refused to take seriously despite the gossip. He glanced at Phineas, who was outright staring. He was still learning the conviviality and intelligence his mistress possessed that brought men like Alexander Hamilton, Jeremiah Wadsworth, and the Marquis de Lafayette to their smitten knees.

"I agree with your view of politics," Nathanael said to Anthony. "However, I do not see myself an active participant in politics. But I see

Nationalism gaining ground and the forces of political disintegration weakening."

"Do you have an interest in politics, Mr. Miller?" Anthony inquired.

"Yes, sir, I do. I enjoy a good debate between the virtues of Federalism and Anti-federalism. However, my views tend toward yours."

Anthony refilled his glass of brandy and held it high as if to offer a toast. "Very good. However, this spring, General Greene and I will be immersed in the fine art of rice planting."

"Perhaps our discussions will have to wait until this summer," Nathanael said. "I am immersed in finding a force of laborers for logging on Cumberland Island. There are twenty men there now, but the operation is going slowly. That cannot wait until spring."

The mild winters in Southern Georgia when the mosquitoes were less relentless called the family outside. On a late March afternoon, Nathanael raced six-year-old Nat to the banks of the river with George and several black boys he had taken to playing with running ahead. The boys spent the day making little rafts, some complete with paper sails. They skidded to the shore and carefully launched their vessels that bobbed on the tiny waves.

"Fetch the fishing poles, and do not poke out your eye," Nathanael told Nat. The boy gathered the poles they kept by the river. Father and son scooped up minnows that edged the shore and baited their hooks while George and his playmates poled their rafts along the water's edge.

Caty observed from the living room window, always in fear that one of them would drown. The baby moved. She put a hand to her swollen belly; she felt as protective of her unborn child as those she watched with concern. Phineas' gentle voice floated from the library, where he was teaching Patty and Cornelia geography of the United States. The girls loved to draw a finger up the map northward toward Rhode Island.

Caty turned away from the window and went out back to the kitchen. Two scullery maids were cleaning vegetables and plucking chickens for dinner. The weight of feeding a household and often the enslaved families was a difficult burden in her advanced state of pregnancy. She had not envisioned her days filled with the endless domestic skills she lacked.

As darkness fell, Nathanael and the boys bounded into the house, wet and dirty from their afternoon adventures. Nat brandished a string of large-mouth bass. "Look what we caught, Mother. Can we eat them tonight?"

Nathanael shrugged at Caty. He had no say in what was for dinner.

"Of course, otherwise they will spoil," Caty indulged. "It will delay dinner if you are hungry. Now, go clean up, all of you."

With their stomachs full, the Greenes and Phineas relaxed in the living room. Nathanael patted his lap in an invitation for his children to gather around. He sat Nat and Louisa on his lap and burst into a chorus of "Yankee Doodle Dandy." For a moment the children were stunned. *Was this Papa singing a funny song?*

"Come on, children, sing with me," he encouraged. That evening they sang "Yankee Doodle Dandy" and "The Old Man in the Woods" repeatedly, often interrupted with gales of laughter.

By spring, 200 acres of Mulberry Grove were planted with rice and corn. After his lessons, George walked the fields with his father. Nathanael explained how rice grew and how it was to be harvested. "Someday, this will be yours," he said to his ten-year-old son. "You must understand the vast responsibility you will have to the land, and those who toil upon it, for you will toil as well. It will be your future if you choose. Keep the bobolinks away. They will eat all the rice before the crop can be recovered."

Despite the happy days, Nathanael was still crushed under his debt. He received a letter from John Collett, who represented the London house of Newcomen and Collett, one of the two businesses that supplied his Southern Army with clothes late in the war and to whom Nathanael had guaranteed funds. He feared for his family if his lands were attached for debt, or worse, he would be jailed in debtors' prison leaving them helpless.

In his despair he wrote to Henry Knox. "I have been so embarrassed and perplexed in my private affairs for a long time past, which originated in the progress of the war, that I have but little spirit or pleasure on such subjects. My family is in distress, and I am overwhelmed with difficulties; and God knows when or where they will end. I work hard and live poor, but I fear all this will not extricate me."

He went on to say that Caty would soon give birth and that the children had been inoculated for smallpox. He asked Henry for his honest opinion about sending George to school in France under the care of the Marquis de Lafayette. Then, he responded to Collett's letter, giving him the myriad of reasons he could not repay the firm.

Nathanael was not only responsible for his family, but also the health and well-being of his enslaved people. One morning, he heard the housekeeper's son, Plato, one of the little boys who played with George, squalling as if he had seen the devil. His harried mother ran outside. To her relief, Nathanael dashed toward the stables where Plato stood sobbing.

"What happened, Abigail?" Nathanael asked Plato's mother.

"He say a horse kicked 'im in the face."

"Come here, son," Nathanael instructed. He handed the boy his handkerchief. "Dry your tears, and let me look at you." Plato did as he was told. Nathanael grimaced. Plato's upper lip was cut from his nose downward and the end of his nose was split open.

"You need stitches," Nathanael observed. "Can you stitch a wound?" he asked Abigail.

"No, sir."

"Mrs. Greene is resting. If you will provide me with needle and thread, I will make an attempt."

He encouraged Plato to follow him into the house. Abigail arrived with needle and thread. Nathanael set to work. Although the suturing hurt the boy, he held still. When it was done, Nathanael said, "I am in hopes it will not disfigure you greatly but cannot pronounce positively; it bled so freely as to render the operation difficult."

While Nathanael was washing blood off his hands, Phineas called for him. "Mrs. Greene! General Greene! Patty has taken a sort of fit."

Nathanael ran into the library where Patty lay lifelessly on the couch. Caty waddled down the stairs. "What has happened?" she gasped, mindless of Patty's frightened siblings.

Phineas' young face was flushed with worry. "We were doing math lessons and she suddenly stopped talking and collapsed."

"Take the other children outside," Nathanael told Phineas.

The children resisted. "You must come with me so your momma and papa can help her," Phineas coaxed.

Caty cupped her daughter's face in her hand and shook her. "Patty! Patty, wake up." She laid an ear to her chest. "She is breathing." She looked up at Nathanael. "What should we do? We do not know what is wrong!"

Nathanael searched his memory. *What did I see my army surgeons do when men collapsed like this? They operated a purge. But with what?*

Caty shouted at her husband. "We must do something now!"

He blurted out, "An upward purge, but I am not certain—" Then, he raced to the kitchen. In a moment, he returned with a cup of tea mixed with tobacco. "Get this down her. It will make her vomit."

Caty snatched the cup, nearly spilling the liquid. She lifted Patty's head and poured a bit of the tea down her throat. Patty coughed. Caty poured more. Patty gagged, and her eyes fluttered open. The word "Momma" and vomit ejected from her mouth simultaneously. Caty issued a small cry and hugged her oldest daughter to her breast. Patty began to sob. Her parents exchanged tearful relieved sighs.

When Anthony arrived that night for supper, with Patty safely tucked in bed under the watchful eye of Mrs. Wright, Nathanael explained their eventful day. "We had a serious call for all our medical knowledge. I hardly know which is the greatest quack, Caty or me. Patty fell unconscious, but we got her to puke, which restored her. The accidents made me think of Job's messengers."

"It sounds as if the medical practice was successful," Anthony quipped. "Perhaps I will come to you for your services if needed."

"I received good news that I forgot to convey in all the rush today," Nathanael said. His eyes moved to Caty. "If I may indulge it here, my angel, since it is unknown to you as well?"

She gave him a tired smile and nodded.

"There has been a settlement with John Banks' estate. We now own all of Cumberland Island. I plan to improve the house at Dungeness to escape the lowland summer heat as it approaches."

Caty's dark eyes brightened in gratitude. She dreaded the thought of giving birth during the sultry summer.

Later on, with the family asleep, Nathanael took advantage of this favorite time to write in the peace of the late evening. He stood at his library window and looked at the twinkling night sky that the new moon phase proudly displayed. He paused to gather the pleasant thoughts that had so often eluded him the past few years.

The worn writing desk he had purchased in 1770 when he built the house in Coventry was nestled against another window where he could contemplate his next words as his pen scratched them out. The old furniture was comfortable, and he hoped to replace it when he was again financially independent.

He set aside his pecuniary woes to write an uplifting letter to his brother. "My dear Jacob. This is a busy time with us. We are planting. The garden is delightful. The fruit trees and flowering shrubs form a pleasing variety. We have green peas almost fit to eat and as fine a lettuce you have ever saw. The mockingbirds surround us evening and morning. The weather is mild and the vegetable kingdom progressing to perfection, and the orchards are full of a variety of fruits. Some of the strawberries are three inches around. We will be obliged to leave it before we can taste of them as we plan to spend the summer on Cumberland Island."

᷼

On April 29, John Collett of the firm Newcomen and Collett responded to Nathanael's letter that told him he had no way to repay his debt to them.

*I am very Sensible Sir of the disagreeable Situation in which
you are placed, & I assure you it is by no means my intention
to add to your difficulties. I am in Savannah, where I shall
await our answer.*

Nathanael supposed an answer was warranted. He poured a glass of
wine and nearly spilled it when he heard Caty's panicked voice. He ran
through the downstairs rooms and collided with a red-faced scullery maid.
"Mrs. Greene has fallen. Come quick!"

Dread attacked Nathanael like a succubus. He found Caty on the
kitchen floor attended by another scullery maid. "Caty, my God!"

Feared marred Caty's face. "I slipped on the floor and turned my
ankle. My hip is painful as if I have broken it."

All the amateur medical care in the world had not prepared
Nathanael for the horror of seeing his pregnant wife lying helpless. He
slid his arms under her arms. "Caty, you must try to get up at my instruction." He turned to the maids, "Help me. When she tries to get to her
feet, steady her."

As she was lifted from the floor, Caty instinctively put a hand to her
belly. She tested her weight against the pain in her hip. "I do not think it
is broken."

"Can you climb the stairs?" Nathanael asked.

"I do not think I can." She looked into her husband's blue eyes that
reflected her apprehension. "Take me to Mrs. Wright's room on the first
floor. I will need her attendance anyway."

Mrs. Wright fussed over Caty and brought her clean linens and whatever she wished to eat.

In the early morning hours of April 30, Caty's dread was realized.
Abigail took the children for a walk and then busied them with lessons on
how to plant seedlings. George, Patty, and Cornelia were not fooled by the
distraction, and fear for their mother kept them clinging to the housekeeper.
Nathanael tried to keep his mind focused by writing to his old friend and

Caty's cousin, Sammy Ward, Jr. in Rhode Island, but his fingers produced a scrawl that was unreadable.

Caty's moans quieted. A door groaned open. Nathanael replaced his quill in its holder. Footsteps creaked in the hall. He rose and awaited the news. When Mrs. Wright appeared in the library door, he realized he was holding his breath.

"General Greene, your son was born alive," she said gently.

He stood there for a minute until she coaxed him along.

Caty was lying in the narrow bed with a tiny baby in her arms. Sweat clung to her hair and her tears wet her new son's downy hair. Nathanael pulled up a chair and gazed at the child. "May I hold him?" he asked.

Caty laid the babe in Nathanael's arms. His small face was ashen, and his eyes were closed. Tears slid down Nathanael's cheeks and blurred his lambent blue eyes. The little bundle in his arms was growing cold.

Several days later, on May 10, while the Greene family mourned the loss of the baby and Caty lay weak and exhausted from her nearly full-term miscarriage, Nathanael received a letter from John Collett. He wanted to know when Nathanael could meet him face-to-face. There was no use putting it off. He responded that he would meet Collett in Savannah.

Laughter rang out from above stairs. Nathanael glanced up at the floor. Phineas was spending much time in Caty's room, more than Nathanael approved. He had written to Jeremiah Wadsworth that the tutor was a smart young man who did his job well. But he felt pangs of jealousy he did not harbor in response to public gossip about Caty and Anthony.

He climbed the stairs, dismissed a perplexed Phineas, and explained to Caty that he had to face Collett. "I will ride with you," she volunteered. "I need to get out of the house."

Nathanael packed up his carriage, and with Caty by his side, he turned it down the Augusta Road toward Savannah. The meeting was a failure, and the two men agreed to meet again in a month. It was unlike him to brood, but his silence propelled Caty to search for something uplifting. "Perhaps supper with Anthony will brighten your evening." His lack of response worried her.

Caty's vigor began to return, but she often had to stop what she was doing and rest. Rural Southern social customs called for constant visits back and forth among the neighbors. It was a strain on Caty's breeding that required her to always return the first call. The foreign demands of plantation life often drained her spirits.

On a particularly fatiguing day, she went to seek the comfort of Nathanael's arms. After searching the house, she peered out the living room window. He was sitting alone on the bank of the Savannah River with his head in his hands. She walked down to the river. Careful not to startle him, she stood there for a minute.

She whispered, "Nathanael?"

He looked up at her with red wet eyes. She was shocked to see the haggard face of a man and ex-soldier who had sworn to give everything, including his life and his future, to the cause of freedom, and in doing so, had done just that. She sat beside him on the grass and tucked an arm around his waist. There was no need to ask him what was wrong. Her heart ached, and her resolve strengthened. She, too, had sacrificed. Only as one could they survive and thrive.

Caty laid her head on his broad shoulders that had carried the weight of an American Revolution and a steadfast courage that had never wavered, even when the debts he incurred to clothe and feed an army broke his back. The dreaded voices of criticism failed to quiet his resoluteness.

He stared at the wide, flowing waters and listened to Caty's reassuring voice, "We will learn all there is to know about the rice business and perhaps become one of the Rice Kings of the South. Think of the days we shall spend on Cumberland Island with the fruits of the ocean at our fingertips while our children run along the miles of long sandy beach you told me about."

He nodded but remained silent.

She slid a finger under his chin and forced him to look at her. "I have seen my thirty-first birthday and you have not yet seen your forty-fourth. We can have more children."

She smiled and kissed his sensuous lips.

He returned the kiss.

They remained by the shore for an hour locked in the embrace of a husband and wife who had endured. Indeed, they had a future, wherever it took them, as long as they were together.

Nathanael had an appointment with John Collett on Monday, June 11 in Savannah at the home of Nat Pendleton. The children saw their parents off and ran after the carriage as it rumbled down the long shady lane. In Savannah, the meeting was long and tedious, and little was achieved. The Greenes spent the night with the Pendletons. The following morning, they started home. As they rolled up the Augusta Road, their carriage top shaded them from the intense June sun.

Caty said, "Do not forget that we have an invitation to have a mid-day meal with Mr. William Gibbons who owns a plantation not far from ours."

"I have not forgotten, my angel."

William Gibbons and his wife, Betsy, greeted the Greenes as they alit from their carriage. They relaxed over a pleasant meal on the veranda overlooking the river.

"General Greene, you expressed interest in seeing my rice fields. Do you care to take a walk?" William asked.

"I would enjoy that," Nathanael replied.

Nathanael and William excused themselves. William placed a hat on his head. His guest walked beside him without an umbrella or a hat. They walked through the calf-deep fields of crops that required arduous cultivation. The two inspected William's system of irrigation works—levees, ditches, culverts, floodgates, and drains.

"These have to be maintained to control and regulate the flow of water onto and off the fields," William explained. "But I suppose you already know that from growing the crop in South Carolina."

Nathanael wiped his brow with a handkerchief. "I am here to learn. This business is much more complicated than I imagined, and it requires every exertion I am capable of applying."

The two returned to the plantation house, their faces pink with sunburn.

Nathanael extended his hand to William, "Thank you for a pleasant and informative afternoon."

He and Caty climbed into their carriage. Nathanael mopped his neck and face. "Are you feeling all right?" Caty asked. "You keep wiping your face, but you are not sweating."

"I have a headache," he admitted.

A knot formed in Caty's stomach. He rarely complained of headaches.

It was early evening when they arrived home. The children tumbled out of the house in a cacophony of joy. The noise worsened Nathanael's pounding head. He helped Caty step out of the carriage and then said, "I think I will lie down for a bit." He walked past his little brood without a word.

"Is Papa sick?" Louisa asked with wide blue eyes.

Caty took Louisa's hand to reassure the little girl. She watched Nathanael disappear into the house. The knot in her stomach grew tighter. That night, she slipped into bed and scrutinized his sleeping face. There were no signs of fever, and his breathing came easily.

The next morning, the sun awakened him, and the bright rays draped across the bed hurt his eyes. Dressed only in his nightshirt, he rose and closed the curtain. He grimaced and issued a little grunt that woke Caty. His habit of rubbing his forehead did not alarm her; it was the intensity with which he was doing it.

"You still have a headache," she observed as she donned her dressing robe. "Go back to bed. I will bring you breakfast."

He did so in silence. When, she returned he was lying down with a cloth over his eyes. The smell of bacon provoked him to say, "I am not hungry."

"Drink some coffee and eat. It may help your headache," she coaxed. "I will eat with you, my darling. All I ask is that you try."

Wednesday, June 14, passed slowly for Caty and the children as their worries were focused on the father and husband who rarely took to his bed.

Phineas sat with the family and kept the children busy with lessons. Unable to concentrate on anything that kept her hands occupied, Caty tried not to fidget. She constantly went upstairs to peek in on Nathanael. When he was awake, she brought him wine and rubbed his pounding forehead.

I have too much to do. I cannot lie in bed, he thought. *One more day of rest, and then surely this will pass.* Caty's gentle touch unintentionally aggravated the pain. A moan escaped him, and for a moment he wondered, *Did that sound come from my throat?*

Afraid she was doing more harm than good, Caty removed her hand.

"Do not worry…my angel. I will…be…better tomorrow."

Every vein in Caty's body froze. His words had come out in a slurred mumble. Now, she realized that the forehead she had been caressing was swollen. "I think it is time we call a doctor. I am sending word to Nat Pendleton to bring Dr. John Brickell from Savannah right away. I will also send a note to Anthony."

Nathanael tried to tell her how bad the pain was above his eyes and that the itching signs of an infection worsened it, but he could not invoke the right words. Caty rushed into the library. She took Phineas aside and explained Nathanael's condition and that she was sending for a doctor.

"Please do not tell the children. Have Mrs. Wright feed them and look after them."

Phineas' countenance reflected her fear. "What should I tell them?"

"I do not know. They may need to leave. Perhaps go to the Gibbons' home. They have children the same age. It could…be a…party," Caty stuttered. "Help me, Phineas. I am frightened."

He took her by the shoulders. "Look at me. I will do whatever is necessary. Now, write your messages and I will see they are delivered."

Nat Pendleton arrived late the next afternoon. "Where is he?" Nat insisted. Nat's bravado crumbled when he saw Nathanael. His whole forehead was red and swollen, and there was bruising around his eyes. "Nathanael," Nat coaxed. "Can you hear me? Answer me."

His answer was so weak, it was barely perceptible. "I can hear you."

The housekeeper escorted Dr. Brickell into the room. "My God, what has happened?" he asked.

Caty explained the progression of his condition.

"Very well. I will have to bleed him," the doctor said.

Nat led Caty out of the room. In the hallway, he said, "I think you should send your children away. Tell me where to take them."

Caty swallowed hard. Her mouth felt as if fear had stuffed cotton in it, but she managed to spit it out. She gathered the children while Mrs. Wright packed their things. "Mr. Pendleton is going to take you to Mr. Gibbons' house where you are going to stay for a few days. You remember his children. You can spend time playing with them and not worry about your lessons."

"Why?" Cornelia asked.

"I want you to have some fun, my sweet."

Caty shifted her attention to George. Her son's stricken face told her everything—he knew—but he was wise enough not to tell his siblings. "Look after the others," she whispered and wiped a tear from his cheek. His lip quivered, and he nodded mutely.

Her eyes lingered on the children. Her gaze remained on Patty and Nat the longest. They looked so much like their father with their blue eyes and blond hair. She kissed them and encouraged them to go. Nat Pendleton carried their bags downstairs, and, with Mrs. Wright, left through the back door and loaded them in his carriage.

The front door opened and then banged shut. Anthony's voice echoed in the entryway. Caty ran downstairs and collapsed in his arms. He held her close and listened to her sobbing explanation.

Nathanael heard the commotion. It sounded far away as if in another universe. Dr. Brickell opened a vein in his arm and then performed the scarification to produce a series of small cuts.

Nathanael registered the pain, but it flitted from his mind. He managed to ask, "What is happening?"

"I am bleeding you, General Greene. I am certain you will feel better in the morning."

"Morning?" Nathanael mumbled. "Did we...attack last night?"

He never heard the answer. His world went dark.

Dr. Brickell found Caty, Anthony, and Phineas in the living room. The housekeeper, Abigail, was pouring glasses of wine to calm nerves. "He is resting comfortably," the doctor said. "Stay with him. When he wakes up, he may be confused for a short time." He offered a sympathetic smile to Caty. "Providence will look after him, and I believe it will smile upon him."

Caty wanted to scream that she did not believe, but it seemed like a useless gesture. "Thank you, Dr. Brickell. Was he able to speak?"

Dr. Brickell's eyes moved to each anxious face. "He has fallen into a stupor."

Caty woke with a start. She massaged a crick in her neck and rose from the bedside chair. To her horror, Nathanael's whole head was swollen and inflamed. She stifled a scream, and without decorum or concern for her disarrayed appearance, she burst into the room where Anthony was sleeping. "Anthony! Come quickly!"

She ran back to Nathanael's bedside. Her hands shook horribly as she reached to touch his face. "Talk to me," she pleaded. "Open your eyes and talk to me, my darling. You cannot go! You cannot leave us! Please!"

Anthony gasped when he entered the room. He roused Phineas and told him, "Go fetch Dr. Edward McCloud. He lives three miles north on the Craven plantation."

Phineas scrambled to his feet and pulled on his shirt. "What has happened? Is he dead?"

"No, but he will be if you do not get going."

Phineas fumbled with his boots. He did not bother to put on his waistcoat or a hat before he was out the door and on his way.

Anthony returned to find Caty sobbing uncontrollably. She shrugged off his attempts to calm her but said, "He cannot die like this. Not after everything he has done for his country and for us. He harbored not a selfish moment even when the tasks he faced were abhorrent to his nature. He rarely said an unkind word about anyone. He is my hero and my best friend. We have so much left to do. Oh, God, I will have to tell his brothers."

Anthony let her rant until she finally realized that everything she was saying, he already knew. She inhaled a quivering breath, fingered the tears that stung her eyes, and wiped her nose with the back of her hand. She sniffed, and her chest heaved with little hiccups.

Phineas returned with Dr. McCloud. He examined Nathanael and pronounced, "He appears to be suffering from sunstroke. I will perform the usual remedies." Caty stayed while Nathanael was bled again and then blistered with a hot poultice that contained irritants that produced a water blister, which was then drained for toxins. Nathanael was unresponsive to the painful procedures. The doctor finished his work. Before he left, he said, "I am sorry, Mrs. Greene. Your husband was much admired and a hero we shall never forget."

The death sentence was passed. Her mind rushed back to their wedding day twelve years before when she was a girl of nineteen and he was a handsome man of thirty-three. She had had many suitors, but none possessed the lambent blue eyes in which she could see love and admiration. There had been times when she was jealous of his absences and other women and he of her, but it was born out of the passion of the young. From the day the Rhode Island Assembly chose him for generalship of the Army of Observation, her pride in him burst at the seams. The long, lonely, sometimes poverty-stricken days she resented crumbled with the past.

All through Saturday and Sunday, Caty and Anthony never left his bedside. Anthony tried to remain stoic to steady Caty, but she found her own strength. Nat Pendleton arrived on Sunday night and joined the quiet vigil.

On June 19, 1786, as the sun peeked over the horizon, the mockingbirds and blue jays chirped a chorus to welcome the new day. Nathanael never saw it. At 6:00 a.m., he stopped breathing. He was forty-three.

thirty-five

I Have Seen a Great and Good Man Die

Anthony and Nat left Caty alone with her dead husband. The limp the Kentish Guards had once publicly criticized and the asthma that kept him awake at night were gone. The smallpox scar on his right eye ceased to cause discomfort.

She filled a basin with water and fragrant yellow jasmine petals and dabbed his inflamed head, ears, and infected eyes. She cut off his night shirt so she could see his familiar strong body one last time and smell his scent. With dry eyes, she gently washed his muscular shoulders and arms that had once pounded smelt into anchors and had not diminished with time. When she finished bathing his body, her delicate finger traced his sensuous lips that always enticed her to let him kiss her neck. She brushed her lips over the small patch of hair on his broad chest and laid her head on it.

Her fingers moved down to his belly button and then to the curve of his hip. The tears she tried to contain burst like water from a broken levee. He was growing cold, and with him the seeds of their happiness and future. "My love," she whispered. "I will carry on and see to the future we promised one another we would live. I will use every resource and every ounce of determination I possess to relieve you of the burdens you carry to your final rest. I promise—" She dozed in a pool of tears with her arm draped across his chest.

While Caty slept and the clock struck midnight, Anthony sat at his old friend's desk and penned a letter to Colonel James Jackson in Savannah. As he wrote, the years of war and the campaigns he and Nathanael had participated in washed through his memories. There were the battles at Brandywine and Germantown when the Continental Army tried and failed to keep British General William Howe from taking Philadelphia. And the winter cantonments and the great forage of 1778 launched from Valley Forge that Nathanael commanded. He entrusted Anthony to lead a foraging army of his own. Nathanael's confidence in Anthony was so great that he sent him to Georgia in early 1782 to put a stop to the British invasion in that state.

Anthony's pen scratched across the paper:

> *I have often wrote you but never on so distressing occasion. My dear friend General Greene is no more. He departed this morning a six o'clock a.m. He was great as a soldier, greater as a citizen, immaculate as a friend. His corpse will be at Major Pendleton's this night the funeral from thence this evening. The honors, the great honors of war are due his remains. You, as a soldier, will take the proper order on this melancholy affair. Pardon this scrawl; my feelings are too much affected, because I have seen a great and good man die.*

With Anthony's letter, the shocking news of Nathanael's death spread throughout Savannah and the nation. Only the week before, he was walking the streets of Savannah with the firm tread of young health.

On the morning of June 20, Caty carefully laid out the uniform he wore on formal occasions as a major general of the Continental Army that had transformed itself into an army of the United States. Mrs. Wright and Abigail ensured his uniform was neatly pressed and he was carefully dressed. White silk gloves, a gift from the Marquis de Lafayette, were slipped on his hands, and his gold epaulets were buttoned onto his shoulders. Caty combed his hair, braided his queue, and shaved the stubble from his swollen face.

A carriage rolled up to the house. She peered out the window. Mr. Gibbons had brought the children home. She closed her eyes and pressed a hand to her mouth.

"Give yourself a moment before you tell them," Mrs. Wright encouraged.

Caty nodded. She met the children at the front door. Five faces stared up at her. *How do I tell them their father is dead and that we are preparing to bury him this very day?* She found the tender courage required of a mother to cushion and soothe the heartbreak.

When she and the children were dressed, Caty sat with Phineas and members of the household and waited. Anthony broke the silence, "The bargemen are here, Caty. It is time."

"Do you want me to take the children to the kitchen?" Mrs. Wright asked.

"No, I want them to remember everything about this dolorous day."

Some of the Negroes who lived on the plantation came inside and under Caty's supervision carried Nathanael's body out to the barge that waited on the shore of the Savannah River. The barge was prepared with a bed of fragrant pine boughs, magnolia and mulberry leaves, and vines of yellow jasmine. Nathanael was laid in a coffin that rested on the greenery. Torches were lit on each side of the barge.

Phineas brought the children outside. The sight of their dead father broke the dam their mother had tried to shelter them behind. The bargemen poled the barge away from the plantation landing and guided it down the Savannah River. When the barge was out of sight, Caty walked to the house to prepare for the ride to Savannah where she and the children would meet the barge at Nat Pendleton's dock.

In the yard surrounding the house, the Negroes who toiled on the plantation stood in solemn silence. George's playmates stepped forward with wildflowers in their hands. They offered the flowers to the Greene children and bowed. As Caty's carriage started down the shady lane to Augusta Road, she heard them singing low and mournful.

A scattering of people from the rural countryside gathered in respect as the barge moved down the river. As the vessel approached the harbor, ships anchored there lowered their flags to half-mast.

When Caty, Phineas, and the children arrived in Savannah, the town was shrouded in deep silence and sorrow. The streets were deserted. Shops and businesses closed for the day. The Chatham County militia and a large crowd were gathered at the dock in front of the Pendleton house. This was the place from which Nathanael had started nine days before on his fatal ride home. Anthony was there. He chivalrously helped the family from the carriage and cleared the way for them.

"Are you alright?" he asked Caty as they reached the dock.

She looked into his eyes and saw his own crushing grief, yet he was concerned with her state of mind. "I am keeping a picture of his eyes in my thoughts. They are where I looked for strength."

The barge arrived. A light infantry corps brought the coffin ashore and then carried it to the Pendleton home. For five hours, Nathanael's body laid in state in the living room while mourners filed past to pay their respects and say their last goodbyes.

Caty numbly accepted offers of condolences and empathic words. At five o'clock, the pallbearers placed the coffin in the waiting hearse. Caty and Phineas stepped out where a sea of people had gathered. It seemed the whole town had turned out for the mournful occasion. An artillery corps followed by the light infantry with their guns reversed and militia led the funeral procession. Next in the procession came state officials and men of prominence, many who knew the heroic general. Dragoons flanked the hearse. As the march began, the guns from Fort Wayne fired once a minute. A band played the woeful "Dead March of Saul" with muffled drums.

Caty's carriage rolled up with Phineas in the driver's seat. She nudged the children inside, and they took their place in the long line of mourners. Behind them, members of the Society of the Cincinnati and throngs of citizens ended the procession. They thudded under the hot June sun through the sandy streets of Savannah to Colonial Cemetery where a vault had been hastily opened. The infantry regiment filed off to the left and right and rested on their arms until the coffin and pallbearers and long train of mourners passed through.

There were no clergymen in Savannah, so a judge took his stand at the head of the coffin and read the funeral service of the Church of England. Caty wanted to take her children and run where she could wake from the nightmare, but Anthony's and Phineas' presence kept her from indulging in her dream. Nathanael would not have been upset if she had stayed home and wept alone.

As Nathanael's coffin was placed in the vault, the artillery boomed a thirteen-gun salute. The mourners melted away. Caty stared as they bricked up the vault. *How has it come to this so quickly? How has his life ended in such a manner?* She turned away from the lonely vault. In their sudden grief, no one thought to erect a marker.

"I found it [the South] in confusion and distress and restored it to freedom and tranquility."

— Major General Nathanael Greene

Afterword
Nathanael

When Nathanael Greene died, a national hero was lost who deserved to live a long and happy life. The tidings of his death spread fast and far throughout the nation and overseas. They reached George Washington at Mount Vernon through a letter from Colonel Harry Lee, then a member of Congress in Philadelphia.

> *Your friend and second, the patriot and noble Greene is no more—on the 19th June after 3 days fever he left this world. Universal grief reigns here. How hard the fate of the U[nited] States, to lose such a son in the middle of life—irreparable loss. But he is gone, I am incapable to say more. May health attend you my dear General.*

It was a severe blow to Washington. He wrote to the Marquis de Lafayette:

General Greene's death is an event which has given such general concern, and is so much regretted by his numerous friends that I can scarce persuade myself to touch upon it, even so far as to say that in him you have lost a man who was affectionately regarded and was a sincere admirer of you.

Two weeks after Nathanael's death, Congress passed a resolution to erect a monument to him at the seat of the national government. The statue by Henry Kirke Brown, a gift from Rhode Island, was erected in 1877 in Stanton Park, Washington D.C., in the Capitol Hill Neighborhood. The inscription at the base reads:

Sacred To The Memory of Nathanael Greene, Esquire
A Native Of The State Of Rhode Island
Who Died On The 19th Of June 1786
Late Major General In The Service Of The U.S.
And Commander Of Their Army In The Southern
Department
The United States Congress Assembled
In Honor Of His Patriotism,
Valor, And Ability Have Erected This Monument

*Equestrian Statue of General Nathanael Greene in
Washington D.C., Author image rights ©Alamy Ltd.

The Society of Cincinnati moved to allow Nathanael's son, George Washington Greene, membership upon his eighteenth birthday. On July 4, 1789, Alexander Hamilton delivered a eulogy for Nathanael at a national meeting of the Society in New York City:

> *But where alas is now this consummate General, this brave soldier, this discerning statesman, this steady patriot, this virtuous citizen, this amiable man? Why was he not longer spared to a country which he so dearly loved, which he was so well able to serve, which still seems so much to stand in need*

of his services? Why was he only allowed to assist in laying the foundation and not permitted to aid in rearing the super- structure of American greatness?

In 1901, the Rhode Island Society of the Cincinnati decreed to find Nathanael's remains in Colonial Cemetery where his bones had rested in the unmarked brick vault since his death. City workers searched four vaults. The fourth revealed a rotted coffin that contained the intact skeleton of a man. A corroded silver coffin plate was sunk into the breastbone, but the numbers "1786" were visible. Metal buttons embossed with an eagle and silk gloves filled with finger bones indicated an officer. The femur bones revealed that the man was about 5'10". When the coffin plate was cleaned it read: Nathanael Greene Obit. June 19, 1786 Aetat 44 years

On November 14, 1902, and with full military honors, Nathanael's remains and those of his eighteen-year-old son George, who was also buried in the vault, were reinterred in Johnson Square in Savannah under an existing monument to the heroic major general.

*1902 Military Funeral Procession for General Nathanael Greene. Author image rights ©Alamy Ltd.

Caty

After Nathanael's death, Caty maintained a close relationship with George and Martha Washington. Their son George went to France to receive an education under the care of the Marquis de Lafayette. She also maintained close ties to the men who were a part of her and Nathanael's life. Her power of fascination remained strong. She was a widow who feared for the security of her family. She had a stormy affair with Jeremiah Wadsworth and intense relationships with Nat Pendleton and Anthony Wayne.

In 1791, she stood before Congress with an indemnity claim to settle Nathanael's estate and debts. Alexander Hamilton helped her prepare, and she was supported by old friends such as Henry Knox, Benjamin Lincoln, Governor John Mathews, and William Washington. Anthony Wayne held a seat in Congress and fought furiously for her settlement. Thomas Sumter, who harbored ill feelings for Nathanael, tried to block Caty's claim. On April 27, 1792, she was awarded $47,000, and for the first time since the war, her family was solvent. Soon after, Anthony disappeared from her life. He went west to join the military. He died of complications from gout on December 15, 1796, during a trip to Fort Presque Isle, a military post near Pittsburgh, Pennsylvania.

By this time, Caty and her children's tutor ten years her junior,

Phineas Miller, had drawn up a legal agreement concerning their relationship and prospective marriage. All five children were living at Mulberry Grove. Her oldest child, George, drowned in the Savannah River in 1793 soon after coming home from France. He was eighteen years old. His body was floated down the river to Colonial Cemetery in Savannah and placed in the vault beside that of his father's.

Enter Eli Whitney, a graduate of Yale who went to Georgia to accept a teaching position. Caty invited Eli to live in her home so he could read law and work on his new cotton gin invention. Phineas and Eli formed a business partnership with Caty as a silent backer to finance Whitney's cotton gin invention. The venture needed more capital than Caty could provide. Caty and Phineas invested in a land scheme—the Yazoo Company. The company collapsed, and Caty once again faced poverty. She married Phineas on May 31, 1796 in Philadelphia, much to Eli's chagrin, for he was in love with her.

In 1800, Mulberry Grove was sold, and the family moved to Cumberland Island at Dungeness where fourteen years before, Nathanael began construction of his family's future summer home. The island yielded everything the family needed to survive. Three years later, at age thirty-nine, the gentle and faithful Phineas died of blood poisoning after pricking his finger on a thorn.

Caty was faced with selling Phineas' part of the Miller estate, which was tied up in his company with Whitney. There were also the settlements against her estate for legal fees, loans, etc. For a time, she sold live oaks to a lumber company in an effort to salvage the cotton gin company.

Eli Whitney returned to his home in New Haven, Connecticut, yet he was tormented by his love for Caty. She was now past childbearing age, and he wanted a family. She wrote him letters, cajoling him to come to her side, offering her sentiments on his health and his aloofness. On a trip to New York to endeavor to settle her final legal affairs with Nathanael's and Phineas' estates, she begged him to visit her. When he came at last, she recognized the final hopelessness of her dream of marriage with Eli. She often asked him to come back to Georgia, but he never returned.

*Catharine Littlefield Greene Miller in her mid-fifties circa
1809 attributed to James Frothingham.
Image courtesy of General Nathanael Greene Homestead

*We have a party of eighteen to eat Turtle with us tomorrow.
I wish you were the nineteenth. Our fruit begins to flow in
upon us—to partake of which I long for you...*

She grew and found, as Nathanael once suggested, that self-pity made a sad companion. In the last week of August 1814, Caty was struck with a fever. She died on September 2, 1814, under the care of her daughter, Louisa. Regardless of the whispered gossip about her behavior during her marriage to Nathanael, Caty loved Nathanael unconditionally. Her strengths and weaknesses allowed her to face the consequences of war and meet them with courage the rest of her life.

Author's Note

I am the author of a four-book multiple award-winning adult historical fantasy series about the American Revolution titled *Angels and Patriots,* which spans the revolution from December 1774 through October 1781. Nathanael Greene plays an important part in the series. From the first words I wrote about him in book two subtitled, *The Cause of 1776,* my interest in him blossomed.

Like the military leaders of his day, Nathanael Greene believed in family and the moral strength of a just cause; the values of his society and principles of their cause; prudence for the cost of human life; civil control over military; and the formation of a strong republican/nationalist government. He possessed an unwavering determination to tackle even the most egregious tasks with enthusiasm, compassion, loyalty, and love for family. He had innate human flaws and character. Sometimes, those flaws were endearing, other times not, but flaws are what make us human.

I wonder if these were the same characteristics that General George Washington saw in him and which elevated Nathanael in his commander-in-chief's eyes. He became one of his most capable generals and heir apparent if something were to happen to Washington during the war. I researched this book through primary and secondary resources, including the hundreds of letters between Nathanael and others, and letters between those who had a stake in his life. I read and used biographies of not only Nathanael, but also the biographies of men and women who knew him, fought with him, and respected him—and some who did not—for without their points of view, we would have an incomplete picture.

His wife, Caty, also won a place in my heart. I researched her part in this story with the same detail and vigor.

Nathanael Greene deserves to be recognized for his exertions that made a new nation possible. His name should be as familiar to the average American as George Washington, Alexander Hamilton, Thomas Jefferson, or John Adams. I hope you have enjoyed reading *The Line of Splendor* and have learned something about a true hero of the Revolutionary War who is often referred to as "The Savior of the South." I know I did.

July 2023
Salina B Baker

Bibliography

Barnwell, Joseph W. "The Evacuation of Charleston by the British in 1782." The South Carolina Historical and Genealogical Magazine 11, no. 1 (1910): 1–26. http://www.jstor.org/stable/27575255.

Beakes, John H. Jr. *Otho Holland Williams in The American Revolution*. Charleston, South Carolina: The Nautical and Aviation Publishing Co. of American, 2015.

Brady, Patricia. *Martha Washington An American Life*. New York: Penguin Group, 2005.

Buchannan, John. *The Road to Charleston*. Charlottesville: University of Virginia Press, 2019.

Buchannan, John. *The Road to Guilford Courthouse*. Toronto: John Wiley & Sons, Inc., 1997.

Carbone, Gerald M. *Nathanael Greene A Biography of the American Revolution*, 2008.

Cole, Ryan. *Light-Horse Harry Lee The Rise and Fall of A Revolutionary Hero*. Washington, DC: Regnery History, 2019.

Fischer, David Hackett. *Washington's Crossing*. Oxford University Press, 2004.

Flexner, James Thomas. *Washington The Indispensable Man*. New York: Back Bay Books, 1974.

Gardiner, Asa Bird. *The Discovery of the Remains of Major-General Nathanael Greene, First President of the Rhode Island Cincinnati*. New York: The Blumberg Press, 1901 (Kessinger Publishing, LLC (September 10, 2010).

Gibbes, R.W., M.D. *Documentary History of the American Revolution, Considering of Letters and Papers Relating to the Contest for Liberty Chiefly in South Carolina*. Columbia, South Carolina: Banner Steam-Power Press, 1853.

Golway, Terry. *Washington's General Nathanael Greene and the Triumph of the American Revolution*. New York: Henry Holt and Company, 2004.

Greene, George Washington. *The Life of Nathanael Greene, Major General in the Army of the Revolution*. 3 Volumes. New York: Hurd and Houghton. Cambridge: Riverside Press, 1871.

Greene, Nathanael. "Letter of General Nath'l. Greene to Gen'l. Washington, 1781." The Pennsylvania Magazine of History and Biography 30, no. 3 (1906): 359–65. http://www.jstor.org/stable/20085346.

Harris, Michael C. *Brandywine*. California: Savas Beatie LLC, 2017.

Higginbotham, John. *Daniel Morgan Revolutionary Rifleman*. Chapel Hill, North Carolina: The University of North Carolina Press, 1961.

Johnson, William. *Sketches of the Life and Correspondence of Nathanael Greene Volume 1 and II*. Charleston, South Carolina: A. E. Miller, 1822.

Lender, Mark Edward and Stone, Gary Wheeler. *Fatal Sunday*. Norman: University of Oklahoma Press, 2016.

Bibliography

Lockhart, Paul. *The Drillmaster of Valley Forge*. New York: Harper Collins, 2008.

Martin, Joseph Plumb. *Memoir of a Revolutionary Soldier*. New York: Dover Publications, 2006 (Originally published as *Some of the Adventures, dangers, and Sufferings of Joseph Plumb Martin*, Glazier, Masters & Co., Hallowell, Maine, 1830).

Murphy, Daniel. *William Washington American Light Dragoon*. Pennsylvania: Westholme Publishing, LLC, 2014.

Oller, John. *The Swamp Fox*. New York: Da Capo Press, 2016.

Piecusch, Jim, and John H. Beakes, Jr. *Cool Deliberate Courage John Eager Howard in the American Revolution*. Berwyn Heights, Maryland: Heritage Books, Inc., 2009.

Puls, Mark. *Henry Knox Visionary General of the American Revolution*. New York: Palgrave Macmillan, 2008.

Reed, William B. *Life and Correspondence of Joseph Reed*. Philadelphia: Lindsay and Blakiston, 1847.

Schecter, Barnet. *The Battle for New York*. New York: Walker and Company, 2002.

Showman, Richard K., ed. *The Papers of Nathanael Greene: Volume I, V and VII*. Chapel Hill and London: University of North Carolina Press, 1989.

Stegeman, John F. and Janet A. *Caty A Biography of Catharine Littlefield Greene*. Athens, Georgia: University of Georgia Press, 1977.

Tarleton, Banastre. *A History of the Campaigns of 1780 and 1781, in the Southern Province of North America.* Ann Arbor: University of Michigan Library, 2009.

Thayer, Theodore. *Nathanael Greene Strategist Of The American Revolution.* New York: Twayne Publishers, 1960.

Upham, Charles Wentworth. *The Life of General Washington: First President of the United States, Volume I.* London: Officer of the National Illustrated Library, 1852.

Waters, Andrew. *The Quaker and the Gamecock.* Havertown, PA: Casemate Publishers, 2019.

Waters, Andrew. *To The End of World.* Yardley, Yardley, PA: Westholme Publishing, LLC, 2020.

Founders Archives Resources

"Eulogy on Nathanael Greene, [4 July 1789]," *Founders Online,* National Archives, https://founders.archives.gov/documents/Hamilton/01-05-02-0141. [Original source: *The Papers of Alexander Hamilton,* vol. 5, *June 1788–November 1789,* ed. Harold C. Syrett. New York: Columbia University Press, 1962, pp. 345–359.]
https://founders.archives.gov/documents/Hamilton/01-05-02-0141

"To George Washington from Major General Nathanael Greene, 15 August 1776," *Founders Online,* National Archives, https://founders.archives.gov/documents/Washington/03-06-02-0024. [Original source: *The Papers of George Washington,* Revolutionary War Series, vol. 6, *13 August 1776–20 October 1776,* ed. Philander D. Chase and Frank E. Grizzard, Jr. Charlottesville: University Press of Virginia, 1994, pp. 29–31.]

https://founders.archives.gov/documents/Washington/03-06-02-0024

"To George Washington from Major General Nathanael Greene, 18 November 1776," *Founders Online,* National Archives, https://founders.archives.gov/documents/Washington/03-07-02-0125. [Original source: *The Papers of George Washington*, Revolutionary War Series, vol. 7, *21 October 1776–5 January 1777*, ed. Philander D. Chase. Charlottesville: University Press of Virginia, 1997, pp. 175–176.]
https://founders.archives.gov/documents/Washington/03-07-02-0125

"To George Washington from Major General Nathanael Greene, 24 November 1777," *Founders Online,* National Archives, https://founders.archives.gov/documents/Washington/03-12-02-0373. [Original source: *The Papers of George Washington*, Revolutionary War Series, vol. 12, *26 October 1777–25 December 1777*, ed. Frank E. Grizzard, Jr. and David R. Hoth. Charlottesville: University Press of Virginia, 2002, pp. 376–379.]
https://founders.archives.gov/documents/Washington/03-12-02-0373

"To George Washington from Major General Nathanael Greene, 27 July 1780," *Founders Online,* National Archives, https://founders.archives.gov/documents/Washington/03-27-02-0267. [Original source: *The Papers of George Washington*, Revolutionary War Series, vol. 27, *5 July–27 August 1780*, ed. Benjamin L. Huggins. Charlottesville: University of Virginia Press, 2019, pp. 319–322.] https://founders.archives.gov/documents/Washington/03-27-02-0267

"To Thomas Jefferson from Nathanael Greene, 6 December 1780," Founders Online, National Archives, https://founders.archives.gov/documents/Jefferson/01-04-02-0222. [Original source: The Papers of Thomas Jefferson, vol. 4, 1 October 1780–24 February 1781, ed. Julian P. Boyd. Princeton: Princeton University Press, 1951, pp. 183–185.]
https://founders.archives.gov/documents/Jefferson/01-04-02-0222

"To George Washington from Major General Nathanael Greene, 5 August 1780," Founders Online, National Archives, https://founders.archives.gov/documents/Washington/03-27-02-0390. [Original source: The Papers of George Washington, Revolutionary War Series, vol. 27, 5 July–27 August 1780, ed. Benjamin L. Huggins. Charlottesville: University of Virginia Press, 2019, pp. 433–434.]
https://founders.archives.gov/documents/Washington/03-27-02-0390

"From George Washington to Major General Nathanael Greene, 15 August 1780," *Founders Online,* National Archives, https://founders.archives.gov/documents/Washington/03-27-02-0490. [Original source: *The Papers of George Washington*, Revolutionary War Series, vol. 27, *5 July–27 August 1780*, ed. Benjamin L. Huggins. Charlottesville: University of Virginia Press, 2019, p. 533.]
https://founders.archives.gov/documents/Washington/03-27-02-0490

Also by Salina B Baker

Angels and Patriots: Book One
Sons of Liberty, Lexington & Concord, Bunker Hill

Angels and Patriots: Book Two
The Cause of 1776

Angels and Patriots: Book Three
The Year of the Hangman

Angels and Patriots: Book Four
The Hand of Providence and The Brotherhood's Sword

The Shipbuilder

The Transcendent

Printed in the USA
CPSIA information can be obtained
at www.ICGtesting.com
JSHW020510101123
51638JS00016B/187/J